Murder at the Manor

A Mystery Guild Lost Classics Omnibus

Murder at the Manor

The Seven Dials Mystery
Crooked House
Ordeal by Innocence

by
Agatha Christie

Mystery Guild
Garden City, New York

This edition published by arrangement with Wacey International, U.K.

ISBN: 0-7394-3828-X

Manufactured in the United States of America.

Contents

The Seven Dials Mystery

Introduction

BY VAL McDERMID

Things that everybody knows about Agatha Christie: she produced a lot of books that still outsell the competition; she was the greatest plotter of the classic detective story; she did a vanishing act and turned up amnesiac in Harrogate, identified by the banjo player in the hotel band; she wrote the longest-running play in theatrical history, *The Mousetrap*; and she couldn't write thrillers.

So why am I suggesting that anyone would want to read *The Seven Dials Mystery*? After all, it has all the ingredients of the classic 1920s thriller, as exemplified by A.E.W. Mason, Sapper and John Buchan. Secret plans, evil foreigners, marvellous cars with running boards and powerful engines, the joint threats of Germany and Communist Russia, house parties, young men wandering round with loaded revolvers and plucky young women—they're all there by the bucketload.

Oh, and let's not forget the secret society that meets behind closed doors, whose members are masked so not even they know who the other members are. Bulldog Drummond and Richard Hannay territory, surely? Which we know that Christie can't do. Right?

Wrong. Because *The Seven Dials Mystery* isn't a thriller. It's a pastiche of a thriller, an antidote to the gung-ho chest-beating of the boys. It's wry, it's got its tongue planted firmly in its cheek and it subverts the whole genre it appears to be part of, not least because as well as all of this, it also delivers cleverly dovetailed plotting with a typical Christie flourish at the end. "Ah yes," we sigh. "Fooled again." If one of our Young Turks did something similar with the thriller now, we'd all nod sagely and go, "how very post-modern, how very self-referential and knowing, how very metafictional."

But that was then and this is now. So Christie gets no credit for poking her tongue out at the big boys who set the agenda for what a thriller should be. I mean, how can a nice middle-class wife and mother be considered a subversive? How embarrassing would that be for the leather-jacketed iconoclasts?

But the fact remains that *The Seven Dials Mystery* really doesn't perform as expected.

As well as showing that when it came to sleight of hand, Agatha Christie just couldn't help herself, what *The Seven Dials Mystery* reveals is the side of its author that everybody seems to forget. (Not surprisingly, when you look at those stern jacket photographs . . .) She had a sense of humour. It was sly and shrewd, and never far from the surface.

It's there in the very first Jane Marple mystery in the character of Griselda, the hopelessly inappropriate wife of the very conservative vicar. And it continues in the Marple novels with, for example, a series of sly digs at Miss Marple's nephew, the literary novelist Raymond West, whose pretensions are a constant source of bubble-bursting on Christie's part.

And it's there in the Poirot mysteries too. Perhaps Christie's funniest as well as her most self-referential character appears regularly there—the crime writer Ariadne Oliver. Mrs. Oliver, with her perpetually bursting bags of apples and her disregard for convention, is clearly a thinly disguised version of Christie herself.

Where Christie has her Belgian detective whom she came to dislike intensely, Mrs. Oliver has a Finn. She is constantly to be heard complaining bitterly about her folly in creating a depressive detective from a country about which she knew nothing and has had to learn far too much. She moans that her publisher and her readers won't let her kill him off because they like him too much. All of this is delivered in such a way that it's impossible to avoid a wry smile at the character's expense and at Christie's too.

From the very first paragraph of *The Seven Dials Mystery*, we should be in no doubt that we're in a world of Wodehousian insouciance. No one could have written such an opening, not even in 1929, without being conscious of its parodic quality.

> *That amiable youth, Jimmy Thesiger, came racing down the big staircase at Chimneys two steps at a time. So precipitate was his descent that he collided with Tredwell, the stately butler, just as the latter was crossing the hall bearing a fresh supply of hot coffee. Owing to the marvellous presence of mind and masterly agility of Tredwell, no casualty occurred. "Sorry," apologized Jimmy. "I say, Tredwell, am I the last down?"*

Substitute Bertie Wooster for Jimmy Thesiger and Jeeves for Tredwell, and it wouldn't feel at all out of place. I think it's safe to say that Christie wasn't setting up in competition with Buchan and Sapper when she wrote this novel.

When critics consider Christie now, they often point to the apparent intolerance and lack of political correctness revealed by her attitudes to class and to other races. It's true that she patronises the lower classes and is extraordinarily offensive about Jews, Germans and Russians, among others. But in this she reflected the attitudes of a woman of her class and generation. It would have been remarkable if she had displayed different attitudes. Even a feminist icon like Virginia Woolf, writing at around the same time, displays an unnerving lack of insight into the lives and dreams of the "servant classes."

But that hasn't stopped people leaping on Christie as an example of all that is worst about the English. She's accused of snobbery, of insensitivity, of racial and class stereotyping.

But how valid are these criticisms? For myself, I've always thought that the true test of people's beliefs lies in their sense of humour. What they find funny will tell you far more about someone than their serious professions of belief. It's often seemed to me that those we make the butts of our jokes are those for whom we nurse our deepest and most secret contempt.

So what does Christie make fun of in this novel?

Well, first there is the aristocracy. The egotistical, indolent and almost indigent Lord Caterham (a title absurd in itself, Caterham being the epitome of stifling Home Counties suburbia) is drawn with affection, but where Buchan or Sapper would have shown him as a figure of status, worthy of respect and trust, Christie shows him as a figure of fun who is indulged by his feisty daughter. He's a not-too distant relative of Wodehouse's Lord Emsworth.

Christie teases the nouveau riche just as wickedly. Sir Oswald and Lady Coote are perceptively lampooned, the one for his over-reaching ambition, the other for her failure to escape her lower middle-class sensibilities. We see her treated with disdain by the servants, while her husband fails to see how little acceptance his wealth, his title and his material success have brought him.

But the upper middle classes are given no more leeway than the arrivistes. *The Seven Dials Mystery* is peppered with ineffectual Oxbridge Foreign Office young men being rescued by their women. The men are silly asses, who avoid disaster more by luck and having the right people behind them than by finely honed judgement.

But most importantly, prejudice comes under the cosh. There are several characters in *The Seven Dials Mystery* about whom we are invited to make knee-jerk judgements, from the mysterious East European countess to the apparently reliable but unimaginative Scotland Yard detective. All of these snap decisions would fall into line with the received bigotry of the time.

Yet by the end of the novel, Christie has forced a reversal of almost all of these positions.

I'm not suggesting that she was actually a secret radical who was aiming to subvert the narrow-minded intolerance of her time and class. That would be patently absurd, for Agatha Christie was no revolutionary.

But she was far less of a hidebound conservative than is generally assumed. There is clearly more to *The Seven Dials Mystery* than a facile attempt to turn everything on its head in order to make the "least likely person" hypothesis work. There is, I believe, clear evidence that Christie saw her world with a far clearer and colder eye than those who disparage her understand.

The Seven Dials Mystery is the perfect antidote to anyone who has overdosed on the classic English thriller from between the wars. But it's also worth reading for the sheer skill with which Christie plays with her readers' expectations and uses them to play the cleverest of narrative tricks with us.

It's all sleight of hand. And the quickness of Christie's hand still continues to deceive our eyes, all those years later.

I

On Early Rising

That amiable youth, Jimmy Thesiger, came racing down the big staircase at Chimneys two steps at a time. So precipitate was his descent that he collided with Tredwell, the stately butler, just as the latter was crossing the hall bearing a fresh supply of hot coffee. Owing to the marvellous presence of mind and masterly agility of Tredwell, no casualty occurred.

"Sorry," apologized Jimmy. "I say, Tredwell, am I the last down?"

"No, sir, Mr. Wade has not come down yet."

"Good," said Jimmy, and entered the breakfast room.

The room was empty save for his hostess, and her reproachful gaze gave Jimmy the same feeling of discomfort he always experienced on catching the eye of a defunct codfish exposed on a fishmonger's slab. Yet, hang it all, why should the woman look at him like that? To come down at a punctual nine-thirty when staying in a country house simply wasn't done. To be sure, it was now a quarter past eleven which was, perhaps, the outside limit, but even then—

"Afraid I'm a bit late, Lady Coote. What?"

"Oh! it doesn't matter," said Lady Coote in a melancholy voice.

As a matter of fact, people being late for breakfast worried her very much. For the first ten years of her married life, Sir Oswald Coote (then plain Mr.) had, to put it baldly, raised hell if his morning meal were even a half minute later than eight o'clock. Lady Coote had been disciplined to regard unpunctuality as a deadly sin of the most unpardonable nature. And habit dies hard. Also, she was an earnest woman, and she could not help asking herself what possible good these young people would ever do in the world without early rising. As Sir Oswald so often said, to reporters and others: "I attribute my success entirely to my habits of early rising, frugal living, and methodical habits."

Lady Coote was a big, handsome woman in a tragic sort of fashion. She had large, dark, mournful eyes and a deep voice. An artist looking for a model for "Rachel mourning for her children" would have hailed Lady Coote with delight. She would have done well, too, in melodrama, staggering through the falling snow as the deeply wronged wife of the villain.

She looked as though she had some terrible secret sorrow in her life, and yet if the truth be told, Lady Coote had had no trouble in her life whatever, except the meteoric rise to prosperity of Sir Oswald. As a young girl she had been a jolly flamboyant creature, very much in love with Oswald Coote, the aspiring young man in the bicycle shop next to her father's hardware store. They had lived very happily, first in a couple of rooms, and then in a tiny house, and then in a larger house, and then in successive houses of increasing magnitude, but always within a reasonable distance of "the Works" until now Sir Oswald had reached such an eminence that he and "the Works" were no longer interdependent, and it was his pleasure to rent the very largest and most magnificent mansions available all over England. Chimneys was a historic place, and in renting it from the Marquis of Caterham for two years, Sir Oswald felt that he had attained the top notch of his ambition.

Lady Coote was not nearly so happy about it. She was a lonely woman. The principal relaxation of her early married life had been talking to "the girl"—and even when "the girl" had been multiplied by three, conversation with her domestic staff had still been the principal distraction of Lady Coote's day. Now, with a pack of housemaids, a butler like an archbishop, several footmen of imposing proportions, a bevy of scuttling kitchen and scullery maids, a terrifying foreign chef with a "temperament" and a housekeeper of immense proportions who alternately creaked and rustled when she moved, Lady Coote was as one marooned on a desert island.

She sighed now, heavily, and drifted out through the open window, much to the relief of Jimmy Thesiger who at once helped himself to more kidneys and bacon on the strength of it.

Lady Coote stood for a few moments tragically on the terrace and then nerved herself to speak to MacDonald, the head gardener, who was surveying the domain over which he ruled with an autocratic eye. MacDonald was a very chief and prince among head gardeners. He knew his place—which was to rule. And he ruled—despotically.

Lady Coote approached him nervously.

"Good-morning, MacDonald."

"Good-morning, m'lady."

He spoke as head gardeners should speak—mournfully, but with dignity—like an emperor at a funeral.

"I was wondering—could we have some of those late grapes for dessert to-night?"

"They're no fit for picking yet," said MacDonald.

He spoke kindly but firmly.

"Oh," said Lady Coote.

She plucked up courage.

"Oh! but I was in the end house yesterday, and I tasted one and they seemed very good."

MacDonald looked at her, and she blushed. She was made to feel that she had taken an unpardonable liberty. Evidently the late Marchioness of Caterham had never committed such a solecism as to enter one of her own hothouses and help herself to grapes.

"If you had given orders, m'lady, a bunch should have been cut and sent in to you," said MacDonald severely.

"Oh, thank you," said Lady Coote. "Yes, I will do that another time."

"But they're no properly fit for picking yet."

"No," murmured Lady Coote. "No, I suppose not. We'd better leave it then."

MacDonald maintained a masterly silence. Lady Coote nerved herself once more.

"I was going to speak to you about the piece of lawn at the back of the rose garden. I wondered if it could be used as a bowling green. Sir Oswald is very fond of a game of bowls."

"And why not?" thought Lady Coote to herself. She had been instructed in her history of England. Had not Sir Francis Drake and his knightly companions been playing a game of bowls when the Armada was sighted?

Surely a gentlemanly pursuit and one to which MacDonald could not reasonably object. But she had reckoned without the predominant trait of a good head gardener, which is to oppose any and every suggestion made to him.

"Nae doot it could be used for that purpose," said MacDonald noncommittally.

He threw a discouraging flavour into the remark, but its real object was to lure Lady Coote on to her destruction.

"If it was cleared up and—er—cut—and—er—all that sort of thing," she went on hopefully.

"Aye," said MacDonald slowly. "It could be done. But it would mean taking William from the lower border."

"Oh!" said Lady Coote doubtfully. The words "lower border" conveyed absolutely nothing to her mind—except a vague suggestion of a Scottish song—but it was clear that to MacDonald they constituted an insuperable objection.

"And that would be a pity," said MacDonald.

"Oh! of course," said Lady Coote. "It *would*."

And wondered why she agreed so fervently.

MacDonald looked at her very hard.

"Of course," he said, "if it's your *order*, m'lady—"

He left it like that. But his menacing tone was too much for Lady Coote. She capitulated at once.

"Oh! no," she said. "I see what you mean, MacDonald. N-no—William had better get on with the lower border."

"That's what I thocht meself, m'lady."

"Yes," said Lady Coote. "Yes. Certainly."

"I thocht you'd gree, m'lady," said MacDonald.

"Oh! certainly," said Lady Coote again.

MacDonald touched his hat and moved away.

Lady Coote sighed unhappily and looked after him. Jimmy Thesiger, replete with kidneys and bacon, stepped out on to the terrace beside her, and sighed in quite a different manner.

"Topping morning, eh?" he remarked.

"Is it?" said Lady Coote, absently. "Oh! yes, I suppose it is. I hadn't noticed."

"Where are the others? Punting on the lake?"

"I expect so. I mean, I shouldn't wonder if they were."

Lady Coote turned and plunged abruptly into the house again. Tredwell was just examining the coffee pot.

"Oh, dear," said Lady Coote. "Isn't Mr.—Mr.—"

"Wade, m'lady?"

"Yes, Mr. Wade. Isn't he down *yet*?"

"No, m'lady."

"It's very late."

"Yes, m'lady."

"Oh! dear. I suppose he will come down *sometime*, Tredwell?"

"Oh, undoubtedly, m'lady. It was eleven thirty yesterday morning when Mr. Wade came down, m'lady."

Lady Coote glanced at the clock. It was now twenty minutes to twelve. A wave of human sympathy rushed over her.

"It's very hard luck on you, Tredwell. Having to clear and then get lunch on the table by one o'clock."

"I am accustomed to the ways of young gentlemen, m'lady."

The reproof was dignified, but unmistakable. So might a prince of the Church reprove a Turk or an infidel who had unwittingly committed a solecism in all good faith.

Lady Coote blushed for the second time that morning. But a welcome interruption occurred. The door opened and a serious, spectacled young man put his head in.

"Oh! there you are, Lady Coote. Sir Oswald was asking for you."

"Oh, I'll go to him at once, Mr. Bateman."

Lady Coote hurried out.

Rupert Bateman, who was Sir Oswald's private secretary, went out the other way, through the window where Jimmy Thesiger was still lounging amiably.

"Morning, Pongo," said Jimmy. "I suppose I shall have to go and make myself agreeable to those blasted girls. You coming?"

Bateman shook his head and hurried along the terrace and in at the library window. Jimmy grinned pleasantly at his retreating back. He and Bateman had been at school together, when Bateman had been a serious, spectacled boy, and had been nicknamed Pongo for no earthly reason whatever.

Pongo, Jimmy reflected, was very much the same sort of ass now that he had been then. The words "Life is real, life is earnest" might have been written specially for him.

Jimmy yawned and strolled slowly down to the lake. The girls were there, three of them—just the usual sort of girls, two with dark, shingled heads and one with a fair, shingled head. The one that giggled most was (he thought) called Helen—and there was another called Nancy—and the third one was, for some reason, addressed as Socks. With them were his two friends, Bill Eversleigh and Ronny Devereux, who were employed in a purely ornamental capacity at the Foreign Office.

"Hallo," said Nancy (or possibly Helen). "It's Jimmy. Where's what's his name?"

"You don't mean to say," said Bill Eversleigh, "that Gerry Wade's not up *yet*? Something ought to be done about it."

"If he's not careful," said Ronny Devereux, "he'll miss his breakfast altogether one day—find it's lunch or tea instead when he rolls down."

"It's a shame," said the girl called Socks. "Because it worries Lady Coote so. She gets more and more like a hen that wants to lay an egg and can't. It's too bad."

"Let's pull him out of bed," suggested Bill. "Come on, Jimmy."

"Oh! let's be more subtle than that," said the girl called Socks. Subtle was a word of which she was rather fond. She used it a great deal.

"I'm not subtle," said Jimmy. "I don't know how."

"Let's get together and do something about it tomorrow morning," suggested Ronny vaguely. "You know, get him up at seven. Stagger the household. Tredwell loses his false whiskers and drops the tea urn. Lady Coote has hysterics and faints in Bill's arms—Bill being the weight carrier. Sir Oswald says 'Ha!' and steel goes up a point and five eighths. Pongo registers emotion by throwing down his spectacles and stamping on them."

"You don't know Gerry," said Jimmy. "I daresay enough cold water *might* wake him—judiciously applied, that is. But he'd only turn over and go to sleep again."

"Oh! we must think of something more subtle than cold water," said Socks.

"Well, what?" asked Ronny bluntly. And nobody had any answer ready.

"We ought to be able to think of something," said Bill. "Who's got any brains?"

"Pongo," said Jimmy. "And here he is, rushing along in a harried manner as usual. Pongo was always the one for brains. It'd been his misfortune from his youth upwards. Let's turn Pongo on to it."

Mr. Bateman listened patiently to a somewhat incoherent statement. His attitude was that of one poised for flight. He delivered his solution without loss of time.

"I should suggest an alarum clock," he said briskly. "I always use one myself for fear of oversleeping. I find that early tea brought in in a noiseless manner is sometimes powerless to awaken one."

He hurried away.

"An alarum clock." Ronny shook his head. "*One* alarum clock. It would take about a dozen to disturb Gerry Wade."

"Well, why not?" Bill was flushed and earnest. "I've got it. Let's all go into Market Basing and buy an alarum clock each."

There was laughter and discussion. Bill and Ronny went off to get hold of cars. Jimmy was deputed to spy upon the dining-room. He returned rapidly.

"He's there right enough. Making up for lost time and wolfing down toast and marmalade. How are we going to prevent him coming along with us?"

It was decided that Lady Coote must be approached and instructed to hold him in play. Jimmy and Nancy and Helen fulfilled this duty. Lady Coote was bewildered and apprehensive.

"A rag? You will be careful, won't you, my dears? I mean, you won't smash the furniture and wreck things or use too much water. We've got to hand this house over next week, you know. I shouldn't like Lord Caterham to think—"

Bill, who had returned from the garage, broke in reassuringly.

"That's all right, Lady Coote. Bundle Brent—Lord Caterham's daughter—is a great friend of mine. And there's nothing she'd stick at—absolutely nothing! You can take it from me. And anyway there's not going to be any damage done. This is quite a quiet affair."

"Subtle," said the girl called Socks.

Lady Coote went sadly along the terrace just as Gerald Wade emerged from the breakfast-room. Jimmy Thesiger was a fair, cherubic, young man, and all that could be said of Gerald Wade was that he was fairer and more cherubic, and that his vacuous expression made Jimmy's face quite intelligent by contrast.

"Morning, Lady Coote," said Gerald Wade. "Where are all the others?"

"They've all gone to Market Basing," said Lady Coote.

"What for?"

"Some joke," said Lady Coote in her deep, melancholy voice.

"Rather early in the morning for jokes," said Mr. Wade.

"It's not so very early in the morning," said Lady Coote pointedly.

"I'm afraid I was a bit late coming down," said Mr. Wade with engaging frankness. "It's an extraordinary thing, but wherever I happen to be staying, I'm always last to be down."

"Very extraordinary," said Lady Coote.

"I don't know why it is," said Mr. Wade, meditating. "I can't think, I'm sure."

"Why don't you just get up?" suggested Lady Coote.

"Oh!" said Mr. Wade. The simplicity of the solution rather took him aback.

Lady Coote went on earnestly.

"I've heard Sir Oswald say so many times that there's nothing for getting a young man on in the world like punctual habits."

"Oh! I know," said Mr. Wade. "And I have to when I'm in town. I mean, I have to be round at the jolly old Foreign Office by eleven o'clock. You mustn't think I'm always a slacker, Lady Coote. I say, what awfully jolly flowers you've got down in that lower border. I can't remember the names of them, but we've got some at home—those mauve thingummybobs. My sister's tremendously keen on gardening."

Lady Coote was immediately diverted. Her wrongs rankled within her.

"What kind of gardeners do you have?"

"Oh! just one. Rather an old fool, I believe. Doesn't know much, but he does what he's told. And that's a great thing, isn't it?"

Lady Coote agreed that it was with a depth of feeling in her voice that would have been invaluable to her as an emotional actress. They began to discourse on the iniquities of gardeners.

Meanwhile the expedition was doing well. The principal emporium of Market Basing had been invaded and the sudden demand for alarum clocks was considerably puzzling the proprietor.

"I wish we'd got Bundle here," murmured Bill. "You know her, don't you, Jimmy? Oh, you'd like her. She's a splendid girl—a real good sport—and mark you, she's got brains too. You know her, Ronny?"

Ronny shook his head.

"Don't know Bundle? Where have you been vegetating? She's simply it."

"Be a bit more subtle, Bill," said Socks. "Stop blethering about your lady friends and get on with the business."

Mr. Murgatroyd, owner of Murgatroyd's Stores, burst into eloquence.

"If you'll allow me to advise you, Miss, I should say—*not* the 7/11 one. It's a good clock—I'm not running it down, mark you, but I should strongly advise this kind at 10/6. Well worth the extra money. Reliability, you understand. I shouldn't like you to say afterwards—"

It was evident to everybody that Mr. Murgatroyd must be turned off like a tap.

"We don't want a reliable clock," said Nancy.

"It's got to go for one day, that's all," said Helen.

"We don't want a subtle one," said Socks. "We want one with a good loud ring."

"We want—" began Bill, but was unable to finish, because Jimmy, who was of a mechanical turn of mind, had at last grasped the mechanism. For the next five minutes the shop was hideous with the loud raucous ringing of many alarum clocks.

In the end six excellent starters were selected.

"And I'll tell you what," said Ronny handsomely, "I'll get one for Pongo. It was his idea, and it's a shame that he should be out of it. He shall be represented among those present."

"That's right," said Bill. "And I'll take an extra one for Lady Coote. The more the merrier. And she's doing some of the spade work. Probably gassing away to old Gerry now."

Indeed at this precise moment Lady Coote was detailing a long story about MacDonald and a prize peach and enjoying herself very much.

The clocks were wrapped up and paid for. Mr. Murgatroyd watched the cars drive away with a puzzled air. Very spirited the young people of the upper classes nowadays, very spirited indeed, but not at all easy to understand. He turned with relief to attend to the vicar's wife, who wanted a new kind of dripless teapot.

2

Concerning Alarum Clocks

"Now where shall we put them?"

Dinner was over. Lady Coote had been once more detailed for duty. Sir Oswald had unexpectedly come to the rescue by suggesting bridge—not that suggesting is the right word. Sir Oswald as became one of "Our Captains of Industry" (No. 7 of Series I), merely expressed a preference and those around him hastened to accommodate themselves to the great man's wishes.

Rupert Bateman and Sir Oswald were partners against Lady Coote and Gerald Wade, which was a very happy arrangement. Sir Oswald played bridge, like he did everything else, extremely well, and liked a partner to correspond. Bateman was as efficient a bridge player as he was a secretary. Both of them confined themselves strictly to the matter in hand, merely uttering in curt short barks, "Two no trumps," "Double," "Three spades." Lady Coote and Gerald Wade were amiable and discursive and the young man never failed to say at the conclusion of each hand, "I say, partner, you played that simply splendidly," in tones of simple admiration which Lady Coote found both novel and extremely soothing. They also held very good cards.

The others were supposed to be dancing to the wireless in the big ballroom. In reality they were grouped around the door of Gerald Wade's bedroom, and the air was full of subdued giggles and the loud ticking of clocks.

"Under the bed in a row," suggested Jimmy in answer to Bill's question.

"And what shall we set them at? What time, I mean? All together so that there's one glorious what not, or at intervals?"

The point was hotly disputed. One party argued that for a champion sleeper like Gerry Wade the combined ringing of eight alarum clocks was necessary. The other party argued in favour of steady and sustained effort.

In the end the latter won the day. The clocks were set to go off one after the other, starting at 6:30 A.M.

"And I hope," said Bill virtuously, "that this will be a lesson to him."

"Hear, hear," said Socks.

The business of hiding the clocks was just being begun when there was a sudden alarm.

"Hist," cried Jimmy. "Somebody's coming up the stairs."

There was a panic.

"It's all right," said Jimmy. "It's only Pongo."

Taking advantage of being dummy, Mr. Bateman was going to his room for a handkerchief. He paused on his way and took in the situation at a glance. He then made a comment, a simple and practical one.

"He will hear them ticking when he goes to bed."

The conspirators looked at each other.

"What did I tell you?" said Jimmy in a reverent voice. "Pongo always *did* have brains!"

The brainy one passed on.

"It's true," admitted Ronny Devereux, his head on one side. "Eight clocks all ticking at once do make a devil of a row. Even old Gerry, ass as he is, couldn't miss it. He'll guess something's up."

"I wonder if he is," said Jimmy Thesiger.

"Is what?"

"Such an ass as we all think."

Ronny stared at him.

"We all know old Gerald."

"Do we?" said Jimmy. "I've sometimes thought that—well, that it isn't possible for anyone to be quite the ass old Gerry makes himself out to be."

They all stared at him. There was a serious look on Ronny's face.

"Jimmy," he said, "you've got brains."

"A second Pongo," said Bill encouragingly.

"Well, it just occurred to me, that's all," said Jimmy, defending himself.

"Oh! don't let's all be subtle," cried Socks. "What are we to do about these clocks?"

"Here's Pongo coming back again. Let's ask him," suggested Jimmy.

Pongo, urged to bring his great brain to bear upon the matter, gave his decision.

"Wait till he's gone to bed and got to sleep. Then enter the room very quietly and put the clocks down on the floor."

"Little Pongo's right again," said Jimmy. "On the word one all park clocks, and then we'll go downstairs and disarm suspicion."

Bridge was still proceeding—with a slight difference. Sir Oswald was now playing with his wife and was conscientiously pointing out to her the mistakes she had made during the play of each hand. Lady Coote accepted reproof good-humouredly, and with a complete lack of any real interest. She reiterated, not once but many times:

"I see, dear. It's so kind of you to tell me."

And she continued to make exactly the same errors.

At intervals, Gerald Wade said to Pongo:

"Well played, partner, jolly well played."

Bill Eversleigh was making calculations with Ronny Devereux.

"Say he goes to bed about twelve—what do you think we ought to give him—about an hour?"

He yawned.

"Curious thing—three in the morning is my usual time for bye-bye, but to-night, just because I know we've got to sit up a bit, I'd give anything to be a mother's boy and turn in right away."

Every one agreed that he felt the same.

"My dear Maria," rose the voice of Sir Oswald in mild irritation, "I have told you over and over again not to hesitate when you are wondering whether to finesse or not. You give the whole table information."

Lady Coote had a very good answer to this—namely that as Sir Oswald was dummy, he had no right to comment on the play of the hand. But she did not make it. Instead she smiled kindly, leaned her ample chest well forward over the table, and gazed firmly into Gerald Wade's hand where he sat on her right.

Her anxieties lulled to rest by perceiving the queen, she played the knave and took the trick and proceeded to lay down her cards.

"Four tricks and the rubber," she announced. "I think I was very lucky to get four tricks there."

"Lucky," murmured Gerald Wade, as he pushed back his chair and came over to the fireplace to join the others. "Lucky, she calls it. That woman wants watching."

Lady Coote was gathering up notes and silver.

"I know I'm not a good player," she announced in a mournful tone which nevertheless held an undercurrent of pleasure in it. "But I'm really very lucky at the game."

"You'll never be a bridge player, Maria," said Sir Oswald.

"No dear," said Lady Coote, "I know I shan't. You're always telling me so. And I do try so hard."

"She does," said Gerald Wade *sotto voce*. "There's no subterfuge about it. She'd put her head right down on your shoulder if she couldn't see into your hand any other way."

"I know you try," said Sir Oswald. "It's just that you haven't any card sense."

"I know, dear," said Lady Coote. "That's what you're always telling me. And you owe me another ten shillings, Oswald."

"Do I?" Sir Oswald looked surprised.

"Yes. Seventeen hundred—eight pounds ten. You've only given me eight pounds."

"Dear me," said Sir Oswald. "My mistake."

Lady Coote smiled at him sadly and took up the extra ten-shilling note. She was very fond of her husband, but she had no intention of allowing him to cheat her out of ten shillings.

Sir Oswald moved over to a side table and became hospitable with whisky and soda. It was half past twelve when general good-nights were said.

Ronny Devereux, who had the room next door to Gerald Wade's, was told off to report progress. At a quarter to two he crept round tapping at doors. The party, pyjamaed and dressing-gowned, assembled with various scuffles and giggles and low whispers.

"His light went out about twenty minutes ago," reported Ronny in a hoarse whisper. "I thought he'd never put it out. I opened the door just now and peeped in, and he seems sound off. What about it?"

Once more the clocks were solemnly assembled. Then another difficulty arose.

"We can't all go barging in. Make no end of a row. One person's got to do it and the others can hand him the what-nots from the door."

Hot discussion then arose as to the proper person to be selected.

The three girls were rejected on the grounds that they would giggle. Bill Eversleigh was rejected on the grounds of his height, weight and heavy tread, also for his general clumsiness, which latter clause he fiercely denied. Jimmy Thesiger and Ronny Devereux were considered possibles, but in the end an overwhelming majority decided in favour of Rupert Bateman.

"Pongo's the lad," agreed Jimmy. "Anyway, he walks like a cat—always did. And then, if Gerry should waken up, Pongo will be able to think of some rotten silly thing to say to him. You know, something plausible that'll calm him down and not rouse his suspicions."

"Something subtle," suggested the girl Socks thoughtfully.

"Exactly," said Jimmy.

Pongo performed his job neatly and efficiently. Cautiously opening the bedroom door, he disappeared into the darkness inside bearing the two largest clocks. In a minute or two he reappeared on the threshold and two more were handed to him and then again twice more. Finally he emerged. Every one held his breath and listened. The rhythmical breathing of Gerald Wade could still be heard, but drowned, smothered and buried beneath the triumphant, impassioned ticking of Mr. Murgatroyd's eight alarum clocks.

3

The Joke That Failed

"Twelve o'clock," said Socks despairingly.

The joke—as a joke—had not gone off any too well. The alarum clocks, on the other hand, had performed their part. They had gone off—with a vigour and *élan* that could hardly have been surpassed and which had sent Ronny Devereux leaping out of bed with a confused idea that the day of judgment had come. If such had been the effect in the room next door, what must it have been at close quarters? Ronny hurried out in the passage and applied his ear to the crack of the door.

He expected profanity—expected it confidently and with intelligent anticipation. But he heard nothing at all. That is to say, he heard nothing of what he expected. The clocks were ticking all right—ticking in a loud, arrogant, exasperating manner. And presently another went off, ringing with a crude, deafening note that would have aroused acute irritation in a deaf man.

There was no doubt about it; the clocks had performed their part faithfully. They did all and more than Mr. Murgatroyd had claimed for them. But apparently they had met their match in Gerald Wade.

The syndicate was inclined to be despondent about it.

"The lad isn't human," grumbled Jimmy Thesiger.

"Probably thought he heard the telephone in the distance and rolled over and went to sleep again," suggested Helen (or possibly Nancy).

"It seems to me very remarkable," said Rupert Bateman seriously. "I think he ought to see a doctor about it."

"Some disease of the ear-drums," suggested Bill hopefully.

"Well, if you ask me," said Socks, "I think he's just spoofing us. Of course they woke him up. But he's just going to do us down by pretending that he didn't hear anything."

Every one looked at Socks with respect and admiration.

"It's an idea," said Bill.

"He's subtle, that's what it is," said Socks. "You'll see, he'll be extra late for breakfast this morning—just to show us."

And since the clock now pointed to some minutes past twelve the general opinion was that Socks' theory was a correct one. Only Ronny Devereux demurred.

"You forget, I was outside the door when the first one went off. Whatever old Gerry decided to do later, the first one must have surprised him. He'd have let out something about it. Where did you put it, Pongo?"

"On a little table close to his ear," said Mr. Bateman.

"That was thoughtful of you, Pongo," said Ronny. "Now, tell me." He turned to Bill. "If a whacking great bell started ringing within a few inches of your ear at half past six in the morning, what would you say about it?"

"Oh! Lord," said Bill. "I should say—" He came to a stop.

"Of course you would," said Ronny. "So should I. So would anyone. What they call the natural man would emerge. Well, it didn't. So I say that Pongo is right—as usual—and that Gerry has got an obscure disease of the ear-drums."

"It's now twenty past twelve," said one of the other girls sadly.

"I say," said Jimmy slowly, "that's a bit beyond anything, isn't it? I mean a joke's a joke. But this is carrying it a bit far. It's a shade hard on the Cootes."

Bill stared at him.

"What are you getting at?"

"Well," said Jimmy, "somehow or other—it's not like old Gerry."

He found it hard to put into words just what he meant to say. He didn't want to say too much, and yet—He saw Ronny looking at him. Ronny was suddenly alert.

It was at that moment Tredwell came into the room and looked round him hesitatingly.

"I thought Mr. Bateman was here," he explained apologetically.

"Just gone out this minute through the window," said Ronny. "Can I do anything?"

Tredwell's eyes wandered from him to Jimmy Thesiger and then back again. As though singled out, the two young men left the room with him. Tredwell closed the dining-room door carefully behind him.

"Well," said Ronny. "What's up?"

"Mr. Wade not having yet come down, sir, I took the liberty of sending Williams up to his room."

"Yes."

"Williams has just come running down in a great state of agitation, sir." Tredwell paused—a pause of preparation. "I am afraid, sir, the poor young gentleman must have died in his sleep."

Jimmy and Ronny stared at him.

"Nonsense," cried Ronny at last. "It's—it's impossible. Gerry—" His face worked suddenly. "I'll—I'll run up and see. That fool Williams may have made a mistake."

Tredwell stretched out a detaining hand. With a queer, unnatural feeling of detachment, Jimmy realized that the butler had the whole situation in hand.

"No, sir, Williams has made no mistake. I have already sent for Dr. Cartwright, and in the meantime I have taken the liberty of locking the door, preparatory to informing Sir Oswald of what has occurred. I must now find Mr. Bateman."

Tredwell hurried away. Ronny stood like a man dazed.

"Gerry," he muttered to himself.

Jimmy took his friend by the arm and steered him out through a side door on to a secluded portion of the terrace. He pushed him down on to a seat.

"Take it easy, old son," he said kindly. "You'll get your wind in a minute."

But he looked at him rather curiously. He had had no idea that Ronny was such a friend of Gerry Wade's.

"Poor old Gerry," he said thoughtfully. "If ever a man looked fit, he did."

Ronny nodded.

"All that clock business seems so rotten now," went on Jimmy. "It's odd, isn't it, why farce so often seems to get mixed up with tragedy?"

He was talking more or less at random, to give Ronny time to recover himself. The other moved restlessly.

"I wish that doctor would come. I want to know—"

"Know what?"

"What he—died of."

Jimmy pursed up his lips.

"Heart?" he hazarded.

Ronny gave a short, scornful laugh.

"I say, Ronny," said Jimmy.

"Well?"

Jimmy found a difficulty in going on.

"You don't mean—you aren't thinking—I mean, you haven't got it into your head that—that, well, I mean he wasn't biffed on the head or anything? Tredwell's locking the door and all that."

It seemed to Jimmy that his words deserved an answer, but Ronny continued to stare straight out in front of him.

Jimmy shook his head and relapsed into silence. He didn't see that there was anything to do except just wait. So he waited.

It was Tredwell who disturbed them.

"The doctor would like to see you two gentlemen in the library, if you please, sir."

Ronny sprang up. Jimmy followed him.

Dr. Cartwright was a thin, energetic young man with a clever face. He greeted them with a brief nod. Pongo, looking more serious and spectacled than ever, performed introductions.

"I understand you were a great friend of Mr. Wade's," the doctor said to Ronny.

"His greatest friend."

"H'm. Well, this business seems straightforward enough. Sad, though. He looked a healthy young chap. Do you know if he was in the habit of taking stuff to make him sleep?"

"Make him *sleep*?" Ronny stared. "He always slept like a top."

"You never heard him complain of sleeplessness."

"Never."

"Well, the facts are simple enough. There'll have to be an inquest, I'm afraid, nevertheless."

"How did he die?"

"There's not much doubt; I should say an overdose of chloral. The stuff was by his bed. And a bottle and glass. Very sad, these things are."

It was Jimmy who asked the question which he felt was trembling on his friend's lips, and yet which the other could somehow or other not get out.

"There's no question of—foul play?"

The doctor looked at him sharply.

"Why do you say that? Any cause to suspect it, eh?"

Jimmy looked at Ronny. If Ronny knew anything now was the time to speak. But to his astonishment Ronny shook his head.

"No cause whatever," he said clearly.

"And suicide—eh?"

"Certainly not."

Ronny was emphatic. The doctor was not so clearly convinced.

"No troubles that you know of? Money troubles? A woman?"

Again Ronny shook his head.

"Now about his relations. They must be notified."

"He's got a sister—a half-sister rather. Lives at Deane Priory. About twenty miles from here. When he wasn't in town Gerry lived with her."

"H'm," said the doctor. "Well, she must be told."

"I'll go," said Ronny. "It's a rotten job, but somebody's got to do it." He looked at Jimmy. "You know her, don't you?"

"Slightly. I've danced with her once or twice."

"Then we'll go in your car. You don't mind, do you? I can't face it alone."

"That's all right," said Jimmy reassuringly. "I was going to suggest it myself. I'll go and get the old bus cranked up."

He was glad to have something to do. Ronny's manner puzzled him. What did he know or suspect? And why had he not voiced his suspicions, if he had them, to the doctor?

Presently the two friends were skimming along in Jimmy's car with a cheerful disregard for such things as speed limits.

"Jimmy," said Ronny at last, "I suppose you're about the best pal I have—now."

"Well," said Jimmy, "what about it?"

He spoke gruffly.

"There's something I'd like to tell you. Something you ought to know."

"About Gerry Wade?"

"Yes, about Gerry Wade."

Jimmy waited.

"Well?" he inquired at last.

"I don't know that I ought to," said Ronny.

"Why?"

"I'm bound by a kind of promise."

"Oh! Well then, perhaps you'd better not."

There was a silence.

"And yet, I'd like—You see, Jimmy, your brains are better than mine."

"They could easily be that," said Jimmy unkindly.

"No, I can't," said Ronny suddenly.

"All right," said Jimmy. "Just as you like."

After a long silence, Ronny said:

"What's she like?"

"Who?"

"This girl. Gerry's sister."

Jimmy was silent for some minutes, then he said in a voice that had somehow or other altered:

"She's all right. In fact—well, she's a corker."

"Gerry was very devoted to her, I knew. He often spoke of her."

"She was very devoted to Gerry. It—it's going to hit her hard."

"Yes, a nasty job."

They were silent till they reached Deane Priory.

Miss Loraine, the maid told them, was in the garden. Unless they wanted to see Mrs. Coker—

Jimmy was eloquent that they did not want to see Mrs. Coker.

"Who's Mrs. Coker?" asked Ronny as they went round into the somewhat neglected garden.

"The old trout who lives with Loraine."

They had stepped out into a paved walk. At the end of it was a girl with two black spaniels. A small girl, very fair, dressed in shabby old tweeds. Not at all the girl that Ronny had expected to see. Not, in fact, Jimmy's usual type.

Holding one dog by the collar, she came down the pathway to meet them.

"How do you do," she said. "You mustn't mind Elizabeth. She's just had some puppies and she's very suspicious."

She had a supremely natural manner and, as she looked up smiling, the faint wild rose flush deepened in her cheeks. Her eyes were a very dark blue—like cornflowers.

Suddenly they widened—was it with alarm? As though, already, she guessed.

Jimmy hastened to speak.

"This is Ronny Devereux, Miss Wade. You must often have heard Gerry speak of him."

"Oh! yes." She turned a lovely, warm, welcoming smile on him. "You've both been staying at Chimneys, haven't you? Why didn't you bring Gerry over with you?"

"We—er—couldn't," said Ronny, and then stopped.

Again Jimmy saw the look of fear flash into her eyes.

"Miss Wade," he said, "I'm afraid—I mean, we've got bad news for you."

She was on the alert in a moment.

"Gerry?"

"Yes—Gerry. He's—"

She stamped her foot with sudden passion.

"Oh! tell me—tell me—" She turned suddenly on Ronny. "*You'll* tell me."

Jimmy felt a pang of jealousy, and in that moment he knew what up to now he had hesitated to admit to himself. He knew why Helen and Nancy and Socks were just "girls" to him and nothing more.

He only *half* heard Ronny's voice saying gravely:

"Yes, Miss Wade, I'll tell you. Gerry is dead."

She had plenty of pluck. She gasped and drew back, but in a minute or two she was asking eager, searching questions. How? When?

Ronny answered her as gently as he could.

"*Sleeping* draught? Gerry?"

The incredulity in her voice was plain. Jimmy gave her a glance. It was almost a glance of warning. He had a sudden feeling that Loraine in her innocence might say too much.

In his turn he explained as gently as possible the need for an inquest. She shuddered. She declined their offer of taking her back to Chimneys with them, but explained she would come over later. She had a two-seater of her own.

"But I want to be—be alone a little first," she said piteously.

"I know," said Ronny.

"That's all right," said Jimmy.

They looked at her, feeling awkward and helpless.

"Thank you both ever so much for coming."

They drove back in silence and there was something like constraint between them.

"My God! that girl's plucky," said Ronny once.

Jimmy agreed.

"Gerry was my friend," said Ronny. "It's up to me to keep an eye on her."

"Oh! rather. Of course."

They said no more.

On returning to Chimneys Jimmy was waylaid by a tearful Lady Coote.

"That poor boy," she kept repeating. "That poor boy."

Jimmy made all the suitable remarks he could think of.

Lady Coote told him at great length various details about the decease of various dear friends of hers. Jimmy listened with a show of sympathy and at last managed to detach himself without actual rudeness.

He ran lightly up the stairs. Ronny was just emerging from Gerald Wade's room. He seemed taken aback at the sight of Jimmy.

"I've been in to see him," he said. "Are you going in?"

"I don't think so," said Jimmy, who was a healthy young man with a natural dislike to being reminded of death.

"I think all his friends ought to."

"Oh! do you?" said Jimmy, and registered to himself an impression that Ronny Devereux was damned odd about it all.

"Yes. It's a sign of respect."

Jimmy sighed, but gave in.

"Oh! very well," he said, and passed in, setting his teeth a little.

There were white flowers arranged on the coverlet, and the room had been tidied and set to rights.

Jimmy gave one quick, nervous glance at the still, white face. Could that be cherubic, pink Gerry Wade? That still peaceful figure. He shivered.

As he turned to leave the room, his glance swept the mantelshelf and he stopped in astonishment. The alarum clocks had been ranged along it neatly in a row.

He went out sharply. Ronny was waiting for him.

"Looks very peaceful and all that. Rotten luck on him," mumbled Jimmy.

Then he said:

"I say, Ronny, who arranged all those clocks like that in a row?"

"How should I know? One of the servants, I suppose."

"The funny thing is," said Jimmy, "that there are seven of them, not eight. One of them's missing. Did you notice that?"

Ronny made an inaudible sound.

"Seven instead of eight," said Jimmy, frowning. "I wonder why."

4

A Letter

"Inconsiderate, that's what I call it," said Lord Caterham.

He spoke in a gentle, plaintive voice and seemed pleased with the adjective he had found.

"Yes, distinctly inconsiderate. I often find these self-made men *are* inconsiderate. Very possibly that is why they amass such large fortunes."

He looked mournfully out over his ancestral acres, of which he had today regained possession.

His daughter, Lady Eileen Brent, known to her friends and society in general as "Bundle," laughed.

"You'll certainly never amass a large fortune," she observed dryly, "though you didn't do so badly out of old Coote, sticking him for this place. What was he like? Presentable?"

"One of those large men," said Lord Caterham, shuddering slightly, "with a red square face and iron-grey hair. Powerful, you know. What they call a forceful personality. The kind of man you'd get if a steam-roller were turned into a human being."

"Rather tiring?" suggested Bundle sympathetically.

"Frightfully tiring, full of all the most depressing virtues like sobriety and punctuality. I don't know which are the worst, powerful personalities or earnest politicians. I do so prefer the cheerful inefficient."

"A cheerful inefficient wouldn't have been able to pay you the price you asked for this old mausoleum," Bundle reminded him.

Lord Caterham winced.

"I wish you wouldn't use that word, Bundle. We were just getting away from the subject."

"I don't see why you're so frightfully sensitive about it," said Bundle. "After all, people must die somewhere."

"They needn't die in my house," said Lord Caterham.

"I don't see why not. Lots of people have. Masses of stuffy old great grandfathers and grandmothers."

"That's different," said Lord Caterham. "Naturally I expect Brents to die here—they don't count. But I do object to strangers. And I especially object to inquests. The thing will become a habit soon. This is the second.

You remember all that fuss we had four years ago? For which, by the way, I hold George Lomax entirely to blame."

"And now you're blaming poor old steam-roller Coote. I'm sure he was quite as annoyed about it as anyone."

"Very inconsiderate," said Lord Caterham obstinately. "People who are likely to do that sort of thing oughtn't to be asked to stay. And you may say what you like, Bundle, I don't like inquests. I never have and I never shall."

"Well, this wasn't the same sort of thing as the last one," said Bundle soothingly. "I mean, it wasn't a murder."

"It might have been—from the fuss that thick-head of an inspector made. He's never got over that business four years ago. He thinks every death that takes place here must necessarily be a case of foul play fraught with grave political significance. You've no idea the fuss he made. I've been hearing about it from Tredwell. Tested everything imaginable for fingerprints. And of course they only found the dead man's own. The clearest case imaginable—though whether it was suicide or accident is another matter."

"I met Gerry Wade once," said Bundle. "He was a friend of Bill's. You'd have liked him, Father. I never saw anyone more cheerfully inefficient than he was."

"I don't like anyone who comes and dies in my house on purpose to annoy me," said Lord Caterham obstinately.

"But I certainly can't imagine anyone murdering him," continued Bundle. "The idea's absurd."

"Of course it is," said Lord Caterham. "Or would be to anyone but an ass like Inspector Raglan."

"I daresay looking for fingerprints made him feel important," said Bundle soothingly. "Anyway, they brought it in 'Death by misadventure,' didn't they?"

Lord Caterham acquiesced.

"They had to show some consideration for the sister's feelings."

"Was there a sister? I didn't know."

"Half-sister, I believe. She was much younger. Old Wade ran away with her mother—he was always doing that sort of thing. No woman appealed to him unless she belonged to another man."

"I'm glad there's one bad habit you haven't got," said Bundle.

"I've always led a very respectable God-fearing life," said Lord Caterham. "It seems extraordinary, considering how little harm I do to anybody, that I can't be let alone. If only—"

He stopped as Bundle made a sudden excursion through the window.

"MacDonald," called Bundle in a clear, autocratic voice.

The emperor approached. Something that might possibly have been taken for a smile of welcome tried to express itself on his countenance, but the natural gloom of gardeners dispelled it.

"Your ladyship?" said MacDonald.

"How are you?" said Bundle.

"I'm no verra grand," said MacDonald.

"I wanted to speak to you about the bowling green. It's shockingly overgrown. Put someone on to it, will you?"

MacDonald shook his head dubiously.

"It would mean taking William from the lower border, m'lady."

"Damn the lower border," said Bundle. "Let him start at once. And, MacDonald—"

"Yes, m'lady?"

"Let's have some of those grapes in from the far house. I know it's the wrong time to cut them because it always is, but I want them all the same. See?"

Bundle re-entered the library.

"Sorry, Father," she said, "I wanted to catch MacDonald. Were you speaking?"

"As a matter of fact I was," said Lord Caterham. "But it doesn't matter. What were you saying to MacDonald?"

"Trying to cure him of thinking he's God Almighty. But that's an impossible task. I expect the Cootes have been bad for him. MacDonald wouldn't care one hoot, or even two hoots for the largest steam-roller that ever was. What's Lady Coote like?"

Lord Caterham considered the question.

"Very like my idea of Mrs. Siddons," he said at last. "I should think she went in a lot for amateur theatricals. I gather she was very upset about the clock business."

"What clock business?"

"Tredwell has just been telling me. It seems the house-party had some joke on. They bought a lot of alarum clocks and hid them about this young Wade's room. And then, of course, the poor chap was dead. Which made the whole thing rather beastly."

Bundle nodded.

"Tredwell told me something else rather odd about the clocks," continued Lord Caterham, who was now quite enjoying himself. "It seems that somebody collected them all and put them in a row on the mantelpiece after the poor fellow was dead."

"Well, why not?" said Bundle.

"I don't see why not myself," said Lord Caterham. "But apparently there was some fuss about it. No one would own up to having done it, you see. All the servants were questioned and swore they hadn't touched the beastly things. In fact, it was rather a mystery. And then the coroner asked questions at the inquest, and you know how difficult it is to explain things to people of that class."

"Perfectly foul," agreed Bundle.

"Of course," said Lord Caterham, "it's very difficult to get the hang of things afterwards. I didn't quite see the point of half the things Tredwell told me. By the way, Bundle, the fellow died in your room."

Bundle made a grimace.

"Why need people die in my room?" she asked with some indignation.

"That's just what I've been saying," said Lord Caterham, in triumph. "Inconsiderate. Everybody's damned inconsiderate nowadays."

"Not that I mind," said Bundle valiantly. "Why should I?"

"I should," said her father. "I should mind very much. I should dream things, you know—spectral hands and clanking chains."

"Well," said Bundle, "Great Aunt Louisa died in *your* bed. I wonder you don't see her spook hovering over you."

"I do sometimes," said Lord Caterham, shuddering. "Especially after lobster."

"Well, thank heavens I'm not superstitious," declared Bundle.

Yet that evening, as she sat in front of her bedroom fire, a slim, pyjamaed figure, she found her thoughts reverting to that cheery, vacuous young man, Gerry Wade. Impossible to believe that anyone so full of the joy of living could deliberately have committed suicide. No, the other solution must be the right one. He had taken a sleeping draught and by a pure mistake had swallowed an overdose. That *was* possible. She did not fancy that Gerry Wade had been overburdened in an intellectual capacity.

Her gaze shifted to the mantelpiece and she began thinking about the story of the clocks. Her maid had been full of that, having just been primed by the second housemaid. She had added a detail which apparently Tredwell had not thought worth while retailing to Lord Caterham, but which had piqued Bundle's curiosity.

Seven clocks had been neatly ranged on the mantelpiece; the last and remaining one had been found on the lawn outside, where it had obviously been thrown from the window.

Bundle puzzled over that point now. It seemed such an extraordinarily purposeless thing to do. She could imagine that one of the maids might have tidied the clocks and then, frightened by the inquisition into the matter, have denied doing so. But surely no maid would have thrown a clock into the garden.

Had Gerry Wade done so when its first sharp summons woke him? But no; that again was impossible. Bundle remembered hearing that his death must have taken place in the early hours of the morning, and he would have been in a comatose condition for some time before that.

Bundle frowned. This business of the clocks *was* curious. She must get hold of Bill Eversleigh. He had been there, she knew.

To think was to act with Bundle. She got up and went over to the writing desk. It was an inlaid affair with a lid that rolled back. Bundle sat down at it, pulled a sheet of notepaper towards her and wrote.

DEAR BILL,—

She paused to pull out the lower part of the desk. It had stuck half-way, as she remembered it often did. Bundle tugged at it impatiently but it did not move. She recalled that on a former occasion an envelope had been pushed back with it and had jammed it for the time being. She took a thin paper-knife and slipped it into the narrow crack. She was so far successful that a corner of white paper showed. Bundle caught hold of it and drew it out. It was the first sheet of a letter, somewhat crumpled.

It was the date that first caught Bundle's eye. A big flourishing date that leaped out from the paper. Sept. 21st.

"September 21st," said Bundle slowly. "Why, surely that was—"

She broke off. Yes, she was sure of it. The 22nd was the day Gerry Wade was found dead. This, then, was a letter he must have been writing on the very evening of the tragedy.

Bundle smoothed it out and read it. It was unfinished.

MY DARLING LORAINE,—I will be down on Wednesday. Am feeling awfully fit and rather pleased with myself all round. It will be heavenly to see you. Look here, do forget what I said about that Seven Dials business. I thought it was going to be more or less of a joke, but it isn't—anything but. I'm sorry I ever said anything about it—it's not the kind of business kids like you ought to be mixed up in. So forget about it, see?

Something else I wanted to tell you—but I'm so sleepy I can't keep my eyes open.

Oh, about Lurcher; I think—

Here the letter broke off.

Bundle sat frowning. Seven Dials. Where was that? Some rather slummy district of London, she fancied. The words Seven Dials reminded her of something else, but for the moment she couldn't think of what. Instead her attention fastened on two phrases. "Am feeling awfully fit . . ." and "I'm so sleepy I can't keep my eyes open."

That didn't fit in. That didn't fit in at all. For it was that very night that Gerry Wade had taken such a heavy dose of chloral that he never woke again. And if what he had written in that letter was true, why should he have taken it?

Bundle shook her head. She looked round the room and gave a slight shiver. Supposing Gerry Wade were watching her now. In this room he had died . . .

She sat very still. The silence was unbroken save for the ticking of her little gold clock. That sounded unnaturally loud and important.

Bundle glanced towards the mantelpiece. A vivid picture rose before her mind's eye. The dead man lying on the bed, and seven clocks ticking on the mantelpiece—ticking loudly, ominously . . . ticking . . . ticking . . .

5

The Man in the Road

"Father," said Bundle, opening the door of Lord Caterham's special sanctum and putting her head in, "I'm going up to town in the Hispano. I can't stand the monotony down here any longer."

"We only got home yesterday," complained Lord Caterham.

"I know. It seems like a hundred years. I'd forgotten how dull the country could be."

"I don't agree with you," said Lord Caterham. "It's peaceful, that's what it is—peaceful. And extremely comfortable. I appreciate getting back to Tredwell more than I can tell you. That man studies my comfort in the most marvellous manner. Somebody came round only this morning to know if they could hold a tally for girl guides here—"

"A rally," interrupted Bundle.

"Rally or tally—it's all the same. Some silly word meaning nothing whatever. But it would have put me in a very awkward position—having to refuse—in fact, I probably shouldn't have refused. But Tredwell got me out of it. I've forgotten what he said—something damned ingenious which couldn't hurt anybody's feelings and which knocked the idea on the head absolutely."

"Being comfortable isn't enough for me," said Bundle. "I want excitement."

Lord Caterham shuddered.

"Didn't we have enough excitement four years ago?" he demanded plaintively.

"I'm about ready for some more," said Bundle. "Not that I expect I shall find any in town. But at any rate I shan't dislocate my jaw with yawning."

"In my experience," said Lord Caterham, "people who go about looking for trouble usually find it." He yawned. "All the same," he added, "I wouldn't mind running up to town myself."

"Well, come on," said Bundle. "But be quick, because I'm in a hurry."

Lord Caterham, who had begun to rise from his chair, paused.

"Did you say you were in a hurry?" he asked suspiciously.

"In the devil of a hurry," said Bundle.

"That settles it," said Lord Caterham. "I'm not coming. To be driven by you in the Hispano when you're in a hurry—no, it's not fair on any elderly man. I shall stay here."

"Please yourself," said Bundle, and withdrew.

Tredwell took her place.

"The vicar, my lord, is most anxious to see you, some unfortunate controversy having arisen about the status of the Boys' Brigade."

Lord Caterham groaned.

"I rather fancied, my lord, that I had heard you mention at breakfast that you were strolling down to the village this morning to converse with the vicar on the subject."

"Did you tell him so?" asked Lord Caterham eagerly.

"I did, my lord. He departed, if I may say so, hotfoot. I hope I did right, my lord?"

"Of course you did, Tredwell. You are always right. You couldn't go wrong if you tried."

Tredwell smiled benignly and withdrew.

Bundle, meanwhile, was sounding the Klaxon impatiently before the lodge gates, while a small child came hastening out with all speed from the lodge, admonishment from her mother following her.

"Make haste, Katie. That be her ladyship in a mortal hurry as always."

It was indeed characteristic of Bundle to be in a hurry, especially when driving a car. She had skill and nerve and was a good driver; had it been otherwise her reckless pace would have ended in disaster more than once.

It was a crisp October day, with a blue sky and a dazzling sun. The sharp tang of the air brought the blood to Bundle's cheeks and filled her with the zest of living.

She had that morning sent Gerald Wade's unfinished letter to Loraine Wade at Deane Priory, enclosing a few explanatory lines. The curious impression it had made upon her was somewhat dimmed in the daylight, yet it still struck her as needing explanation. She intended to get hold of Bill Eversleigh sometime and extract from him fuller details of the house-party which had ended so tragically. In the meantime, it was a lovely morning and she felt particularly well and the Hispano was running like a dream.

Bundle pressed her foot down on the accelerator and the Hispano responded at once. Mile after mile vanished, traffic stops were few and far between and Bundle had a clear stretch of road in front of her.

And then, without any warning whatever, a man reeled out of the hedge and on to the road right in front of the car. To stop in time was out of the question. With all her might Bundle wrenched at the steering wheel and swerved out to the right. The car was nearly in the ditch—nearly, but not quite. It was a dangerous manoeuvre, but it succeeded. Bundle was almost certain that she had missed the man.

She looked back and felt a sickening sensation in the middle of her anatomy. The car had not passed over the man, but nevertheless it must have struck him in passing. He was lying face downwards on the road, and he lay ominously still.

Bundle jumped out and ran back. She had never yet run over anything more important than a stray hen. The fact that the accident was hardly her fault did not weigh with her at the minute. The man had seemed drunk, but drunk or not, she had killed him. She was quite sure she had killed him. Her heart beat sickeningly in great pounding thumps, sounding right up in her ears.

She knelt down by the prone figure and turned him very gingerly over. He neither groaned nor moaned. He was young, she saw, rather a pleasant-faced young man, well dressed and wearing a small toothbrush moustache.

There was no external mark of injury that she could see, but she was quite positive that he was either dead or dying. His eyelids flickered and the eyes half opened. Piteous eyes, brown and suffering, like a dog's. He seemed to be struggling to speak. Bundle bent right over.

"Yes," she said. "Yes?"

There was something he wanted to say, she could see that. Wanted to say badly. And she couldn't help him, couldn't do anything.

At last the words came, a mere sighing breath:

"*Seven Dials . . . tell . . .*"

"Yes," said Bundle again. It was a name he was trying to get out—trying with all his failing strength. "Yes. Who am I to tell?"

"*Tell . . . Jimmy Thesiger . . .*" He got it out at last, and then suddenly, his head fell back and his body went limp.

Bundle sat back on her heels, shivering from head to foot. She could never have imagined that anything so awful could have happened to her. He was dead—and she had killed him.

She tried to pull herself together. What must she do now? A doctor—that was her first thought. It was possible—just possible—that the man might only be unconscious, not dead. Her instinct cried out against the possibility, but she forced herself to act upon it. Somehow or other she must get him into the car and take him to the nearest doctor's. It was a deserted stretch of country road and there was no one to help her.

Bundle, for all her slimness, was strong. She had muscles of whipcord. She brought the Hispano as close as possible, and then, exerting all her strength, she dragged and pulled the inanimate figure into it. It was a horrid business, and one that made her set her teeth, but at last she managed it.

Then she jumped into the driver's seat and started off. A couple of miles brought her into a small town and on inquiry she was quickly directed to the doctor's house.

Dr. Cassell, a kindly, middle-aged man, was startled to come into his surgery and find a girl there who was evidently on the verge of collapse.

Bundle spoke abruptly.

"I—I think I've killed a man. I ran over him. I brought him along in the car. He's outside now. I—I was driving too fast, I suppose. I've always driven too fast."

The doctor cast a practised glance over her. He stepped over to a shelf and poured something into a glass. He brought it over to her.

"Drink this down," he said, "and you'll feel better. You've had a shock."

Bundle drank obediently and a tinge of colour came into her pallid face. The doctor nodded approvingly.

"That's right. Now I want you to sit quietly here. I'll go out and attend to things. After I've made sure there's nothing to be done for the poor fellow, I'll come back and we'll talk about it."

He was away some time. Bundle watched the clock on the mantelpiece. Five minutes, ten minutes, a quarter of an hour, twenty minutes—would he never come?

Then the door opened and Dr. Cassell reappeared. He looked different—Bundle noticed that at once—grimmer and at the same time more alert. There was something else in his manner that she did not quite understand, a suggestion of repressed excitement.

"Now then, young lady," he said, "let's have this out. You ran over this man, you say. Tell me just how the accident happened?"

Bundle explained to the best of her ability. The doctor followed her narrative with keen attention.

"Just so; the car didn't pass over his body?"

"No. In fact, I thought I'd missed him altogether."

"He was reeling, you say?"

"Yes, I thought he was drunk."

"And he came from the hedge?"

"There was a gate just there, I think. He must have come through the gate."

The doctor nodded, then he leaned back in his chair and removed his pince-nez.

"I've no doubt at all," he said, "that you're a very reckless driver, and that you'll probably run over some poor fellow and do for him one of these days—but you haven't done it this time."

"But—"

"The car never touched him. *This man was shot.*"

6

Seven Dials Again

Bundle stared at him. And very slowly the world, which for the last three quarters of an hour had been upside down, shifted till it stood once more the right way up. It was quite two minutes before Bundle spoke, but when she did it was no longer the panic-stricken girl but the real Bundle, cool, efficient, and logical.

"How could he be shot?" she said.

"I don't know how he could," said the doctor dryly. "But he was. He's got a rifle bullet in him all right. He bled internally, that's why you didn't notice anything."

Bundle nodded.

"The question is," the doctor continued, "who shot him? You saw nobody about?"

Bundle shook her head.

"It's odd," said the doctor. "If it was an accident, you'd expect the fellow who did it would come running to the rescue—unless just possibly he didn't know what he'd done."

"There was no one about," said Bundle. "On the road, that is."

"It seems to me," said the doctor, "that the poor lad must have been running—the bullet got him just as he passed through the gate and he came reeling on to the road in consequence. You didn't hear a shot?"

Bundle shook her head.

"But I probably shouldn't anyway," she said, "with the noise of the car."

"Just so. He didn't say anything before he died?"

"He muttered a few words."

"Nothing to throw light on the tragedy?"

"No. He wanted something—I don't know what—told to a friend of his. Oh! yes, and he mentioned Seven Dials."

"H'm," said Doctor Cassell. "Not a likely neighborhood for one of his class. Perhaps his assailant came from there. Well, we needn't worry about that now. You can leave it in my hands. I'll notify the police. You must, of course, leave your name and address, as the police are sure to want to question you. In fact, perhaps you'd better come round to the police station with me now. They might say I ought to have detained you."

They went together in Bundle's car. The police inspector was a slow-speaking man. He was somewhat overawed by Bundle's name and address when she gave it to him, and he took down her statement with great care.

"Lads!" he said. "That's what it is. Lads practising! Cruel stupid, them young varmints are. Always loosing off at birds with no consideration for anyone as may be the other side of a hedge."

The doctor thought it a most unlikely solution, but he realized that the case would soon be in abler hands and it did not seem worth while to make objections.

"Name of deceased?" asked the sergeant, moistening his pencil.

"He had a cardcase on him. He appears to have been a Mr. Ronald Devereux, with an address in the Albany."

Bundle frowned. The name Ronald Devereux awoke some chord of remembrance. She was sure she had heard it before.

It was not until she was half-way back to Chimneys in the car that it came to her. Of course! Ronny Devereux. Bill's friend in the Foreign Office. He and Bill and—yes—Gerald Wade.

As this last realization came to her, Bundle nearly went into the hedge. First Gerald Wade—then Ronny Devereux. Gerry Wade's death might have been natural—the result of carelessness—but Ronny Devereux's surely bore a more sinister interpretation.

And then Bundle remembered something else. Seven Dials! When the dying man had said it, it had seemed vaguely familiar. Now she knew why. Gerald Wade had mentioned Seven Dials in that last letter of his written to his sister on the night before his death. And that again connected up with something else that escaped her.

Thinking all these things over, Bundle had slowed down to such a sober pace that nobody would have recognized her. She drove the car round to the garage and went in search of her father.

Lord Caterham was happily reading a catalogue of a forthcoming sale of rare editions and was immeasurably astonished to see Bundle.

"Even you," he said, "can't have been to London and back in this time."

"I haven't been to London," said Bundle. "I ran over a man."

"What?"

"Only I didn't really. He was shot."

"How could he have been?"

"I don't know how he could have been, but he was."

"But why did you shoot him?"

"I didn't shoot him."

"You shouldn't shoot people," said Lord Caterham in a tone of mild remonstrance. "You shouldn't really. I daresay some of them richly deserve it—but all the same it will lead to trouble."

"I tell you I didn't shoot him."

"Well, who did?"

"Nobody knows," said Bundle.

"Nonsense," said Lord Caterham. "A man can't be shot and run over without anyone having done it."

"He wasn't run over," said Bundle.

"I thought you said he was."

"I said I thought I had."

"A tyre burst, I suppose," said Lord Caterham. "That does sound like a shot. It says so in detective stories."

"You really are perfectly impossible, Father. You don't seem to have the brains of a rabbit."

"Not at all," said Lord Caterham. "You come in with a wildly impossible tale about men being run over and shot and I don't know what, and then you expect me to know all about it by magic."

Bundle sighed wearily.

"Just attend," she said. "I'll tell you all about it in words of one syllable."

"There," she said when she had concluded. "Now have you got it?"

"Of course. I understand perfectly now. I can make allowances for your being a little upset, my dear. I was not far wrong when I remarked to you before starting out that people looking for trouble usually found it. I am thankful," finished Lord Caterham with a slight shiver, "that I stayed quietly here."

He picked up the catalogue again.

"Father, where is Seven Dials?"

"In the East End somewhere, I fancy. I have frequently observed buses going there—or do I mean Seven Sisters? I have never been there myself, I am thankful to say. Just as well, because I don't fancy it is the sort of spot I should like. And yet, curiously enough, I seem to have heard of it in some connection just lately."

"You don't know a Jimmy Thesiger, do you?"

Lord Caterham was now engrossed in his catalogue once more. He had made an effort to be intelligent on the subject of Seven Dials. This time he made hardly any effort at all.

"Thesiger," he murmured vaguely. "Thesiger. One of the Yorkshire Thesigers?"

"That's what I'm asking you. Do attend, Father. This is important."

Lord Caterham made a desperate effort to look intelligent without really having to give his mind to the matter.

"There *are* some Yorkshire Thesigers," he said earnestly. "And unless I am mistaken some Devonshire Thesigers also. Your Great Aunt Selina married a Thesiger."

"What good is that to me?" cried Bundle.

Lord Caterham chuckled.

"It was very little good to her, if I remember rightly."

"You're impossible," said Bundle, rising. "I shall have to get hold of Bill."

"Do, dear," said her father absently as he turned a page. "Certainly. By all means. Quite so."

Bundle rose to her feet with an impatient sigh.

"I wish I could remember what that letter said," she murmured more to herself than aloud. "I didn't read it very carefully. Something about a joke—that the Seven Dials business wasn't a joke."

Lord Caterham emerged suddenly from his catalogue.

"Seven Dials?" he said. "Of course. I've got it now."

"Got what?"

"I know why it sounded so familiar. George Lomax has been over. Tredwell failed for once and let him in. He was on his way up to town. It seems he's having some political party at the Abbey next week and he got a warning letter."

"What do you mean by a warning letter?"

"Well, I don't really know. He didn't go into details. I gather it said, 'Beware' and 'Trouble is at hand,' and all those sort of things. But anyway it was written from Seven Dials, I distinctly remember his saying so. He was going up to town to consult Scotland Yard about it. You know George?"

Bundle nodded. She was well acquainted with that public-spirited Cabinet Minister, George Lomax, His Majesty's permanent Under Secretary of State for Foreign Affairs, who was shunned by many because of his inveterate habit of quoting from his public speeches in private. In allusion to his bulging eyeballs, he was known to many—Bill Eversleigh among others—as Codders.

"Tell me," she said, "was Codders interested at all in Gerald Wade's death?"

"Not that I ever heard of. He may have been, of course."

Bundle said nothing for some minutes. She was busily engaged in trying to remember the exact wording of the letter she had sent on to Loraine Wade, and at the same time she was trying to picture the girl to whom it had been written. What sort of a girl was this to whom, apparently, Gerald Wade was so devoted? The more she thought over it, the more it seemed to her that it was an unusual letter for a brother to write.

"Did you say the Wade girl was Gerry's half-sister?" she asked suddenly.

"Well, of course, strictly speaking, I suppose she isn't—wasn't, I mean—his sister at all."

"But her name's Wade?"

"Not really. She wasn't old Wade's child. As I was saying, he ran away with his second wife, who was married to a perfect blackguard. I suppose the Courts gave the rascally husband the custody of the child, but he certainly didn't avail himself of the privilege. Old Wade got very fond of the child and insisted that she should be called by his name."

"I see," said Bundle. "That explains it."

"Explains what?"

"Something that puzzled me about that letter."

"She's rather a pretty girl, I believe," said Lord Caterham. "Or so I've heard."

Bundle went upstairs thoughtfully. She had several objects in view. First she must find this Jimmy Thesiger. Bill, perhaps, would be helpful there. Ronny Devereux had been a friend of Bill's. If Jimmy Thesiger was a friend of Ronny's, the chances were that Bill would know him too. Then there was the girl, Loraine Wade. It was possible that she could throw some light on the problem of Seven Dials. Evidently Gerry Wade had said something to her about it. His anxiety that she should forget the fact had a sinister suggestion.

7

Bundle Pays a Call

Getting hold of Bill presented few difficulties. Bundle mot
town on the following morning—this time without advent
way—and rang him up. Bill responded with alacrity, and m
suggestions as to lunch, tea, dinner and dancing. All of whic
Bundle turned down as made.

"But in a day or two, I'll come and frivol with you, Bill.
ment I'm up on business."

"Oh," said Bill. "What a beastly bore."

"It's not that kind," said Bundle. "It's anything but bo
know anyone called Jimmy Thesiger?"

"Of course. So do you."

"No, I don't," said Bundle.

"Yes, you do. You must. Everyone knows old Jimm

"Sorry," said Bundle. "Just for once I don't seem

"Oh! but you must know Jimmy—pink-faced c
ass. But really he's got as many brains as I have."

"You don't say so," said Bundle. "He must feel
walks about."

"Was that meant for sarcasm?"

"It was a feeble effort at it. What does Jimmy

"How do you mean, what does he do?"

"Does being at the Foreign Office prevent you from und
your native language?"

"Oh! I see, you mean, has he got a job? No, he just tools around. Why should he do anything?"

"In fact, more money than brains?"

"Oh! I wouldn't say that. I told you just now that he had more brains than you'd think."

Bundle was silent. She was feeling more and more doubtful. This gilded youth did not sound a very promising ally. And yet it was his name that had come first to the dying man's lips. Bill's voice chimed in suddenly with singular appropriateness.

Jermy
was a pause.
there still?"
ys there."
never knows with these dashed teleph
you, Bill."

have to be disposed of and got rid of before she could broach her own business. It was not a topic she could introduce before a stranger.

Now, as she looked more closely, an extraordinary idea rose in her brain. Could it be? Yes, the girl was in deep mourning; her black, silk-clad ankles showed that. It was a long shot, but Bundle was convinced that her idea was right. She drew a long breath.

"Look here," she said. "Are you by any chance Loraine Wade?"

Loraine's eyes opened wide.

"Yes, I am. How clever of you to know. We've never met, have we?"

Bundle shook her head.

"I wrote to you yesterday, though. I'm Bundle Brent."

"It was so very kind of you to send me Gerry's letter," said Loraine. "I've written to thank you. I never expected to see you here."

"I'll tell you why I'm here," said Bundle. "Did you know Ronny Devereux?"

Loraine nodded.

"He came over the day that Gerry—you know. And he's been to see me two or three times since. He was one of Gerry's greatest friends."

"I know. Well—he's dead."

Loraine's lips parted in surprise.

"Dead! But he always seemed so fit."

Bundle narrated the events of the preceding day as briefly as possible. A look of fear and horror came into Loraine's face.

"Then it is true. It is true."

"What's true?"

"What I've thought—what I've been thinking all these weeks. Gerald didn't die a natural death. He was killed."

"You've thought that, have you?"

"Yes. Gerry would never have taken things to make him sleep." She gave the little ghost of a laugh. "He slept much too well to need them. I always thought it queer. And he thought so too—I know he did."

"Who?"

"Ronny. And now this happens. Now he's killed too." She paused and then went on: "That's what I came for to-day. That letter of Gerry's you sent me—as soon as I read it, I tried to get hold of Ronny, but they said he was away. So I thought I'd come and see Jimmy—he was Ronny's other great friend. I thought perhaps he'd tell me what I ought to do."

"You mean—" Bundle paused. "About—Seven Dials."

Loraine nodded.

"You see—" she began.

But at that moment Jimmy Thesiger entered the room.

8

Visitors for Jimmy

We must at this point go back to some twenty minutes earlier. To a moment when Jimmy Thesiger, emerging from the mists of sleep, was conscious of a familiar voice speaking unfamiliar words.

His sleep-ridden brain tried for a moment to cope with the situation, but failed. He yawned and rolled over again.

"A young lady, sir, has called to see you."

The voice was implacable. So prepared was it to go on repeating the statement indefinitely that Jimmy resigned himself to the inevitable. He opened his eyes and blinked.

"Eh, Stevens?" he said. "Say that again."

"A young lady, sir, has called to see you."

"Oh!" Jimmy strove to grasp the situation. "Why?"

"I couldn't say, sir."

"No, I suppose not. No," he thought it over. "I suppose you couldn't."

Stevens swooped down upon a tray by the bedside.

"I will bring you some fresh tea, sir. This is cold."

"You think that I ought to get up and—er—see the lady?"

Stevens made no reply, but he held his back very stiff and Jimmy read the signs correctly.

"Oh! very well," he said. "I suppose I'd better. She didn't give her name?"

"No, sir."

"H'm. She couldn't be by any possible chance my Aunt Jemima, could she? Because if so, I'm damned if I'm going to get up."

"The lady, sir, could not possibly be anyone's aunt, I should say, unless the youngest of a large family."

"Aha," said Jimmy. "Young and lovely. Is she—what kind is she?"

"The young lady, sir, is most undoubtedly strictly *comme il faut*, if I may use the expression."

"You may use it," said Jimmy graciously. "Your French pronunciation, Stevens, if I may say so, is very good. Much better than mine."

"I am gratified to hear it, sir. I have lately been taking a correspondence course in French."

"Have you really? You're a wonderful chap, Stevens."

Stevens smiled in a superior fashion and left the room. Jimmy lay trying to recall the names of any young and lovely girls strictly *comme il faut* who might be likely to come and call upon him.

Stevens re-entered with fresh tea, and as Jimmy sipped it he felt a pleasurable curiosity.

"You've given her the paper and all that, I hope, Stevens," he said.

"I supplied her with the *Morning Post* and *Punch*, sir."

A ring at the bell took him away. In a few minutes he returned.

"Another young lady, sir."

"What?"

Jimmy clutched his head.

"Another young lady; she declines to give her name, sir, but says her business is important."

Jimmy stared at him.

"This is damned odd, Stevens. Damned odd. Look here, what time did I come home last night?"

"Just upon five o'clock, sir."

"And was I—er—how was I?"

"Just a little cheerful, sir—nothing more. Inclined to sing 'Rule Britannia.'"

"What an extraordinary thing," said Jimmy. "'Rule Britannia,' eh? I cannot imagine myself in a sober state ever singing 'Rule Britannia.' Some latent patriotism must have emerged under the stimulus of—er—just a couple too many. I was celebrating at the 'Mustard and Cress,' I remember. Not nearly such an innocent spot as it sounds, Stevens." He paused. "I was wondering—"

"Yes, sir?"

"I was wondering whether under the aforementioned stimulus I had put an advertisement in a newspaper asking for a nursery governess or something of that sort."

Stevens coughed.

"*Two* girls turning up. It looks odd. I shall eschew the 'Mustard and Cress' in future. That's a good word, Stevens—*eschew*—I met it in a cross word the other day and took a fancy to it."

Whilst he was talking Jimmy was rapidly apparelling himself. At the end of ten minutes he was ready to face his unknown guests. As he opened the door of his sitting-room the first person he saw was a dark, slim girl who was totally unknown to him. She was standing by the mantelpiece, leaning against it. Then his glance went on to the big leather covered armchair, and his heart missed a beat. Loraine!

It was she who rose and spoke first a little nervously.

"You must be very surprised to see me. But I had to come. I'll explain in a minute. This is Lady Eileen Brent."

"Bundle—that's what I'm usually known as. You've probably heard of me from Bill Eversleigh."

"Oh! rather, of course I have," said Jimmy, endeavouring to cope with the situation. "I say, do sit down and let's have a cocktail or something."

But both girls declined.

"As a matter of fact," continued Jimmy, "I'm only just out of bed."

"That's what Bill said," remarked Bundle. "I told him I was coming round to see you, and he said you wouldn't be up."

"Well, I'm up now," said Jimmy encouragingly.

"It's about Gerry," said Loraine. "And now about Ronny—"

"What do you mean by 'and now about Ronny'?"

"He was shot yesterday."

"What?" cried Jimmy.

Bundle told her story for the second time. Jimmy listened like a man in a dream.

"Old Ronny—shot," he murmured. "What *is* this damned business?"

He sat down on the edge of a chair, thinking for a minute or two, and then spoke in a quiet, level voice.

"There's something I think I ought to tell you."

"Yes," said Bundle encouragingly.

"It was on the day Gerry Wade died. On the way over to break the news to *you*"—he nodded at Loraine—"in the car Ronny said something to me. That is to say, he started to tell me something. There was something he wanted to tell me, and he began about it, and then he said he was bound by a promise and couldn't go on."

"Bound by a promise," said Loraine thoughtfully.

"That's what he said. Naturally I didn't press him after that. But he was odd—darned odd—all through. I got the impression then that he suspected—well, foul play. I thought he'd tell the doctor so. But no, not even a hint. So I thought I'd been mistaken. And afterwards, with the evidence and all—well, it seemed such a very clear case. I thought my suspicions had been all bosh."

"But you think Ronny still suspected?" asked Bundle.

Jimmy nodded.

"That's what I think now. Why, none of us have seen anything of him since. I believe he was playing a lone hand—trying to find out the truth about Gerry's death, and what's more, I believe he *did* find out. That's why the devils shot him. And then he tried to send word to me, but could only get out those two words."

"Seven Dials," said Bundle, and shivered a little.

"Seven Dials," said Jimmy gravely. "At any rate we've got that to go on with."

Bundle turned to Loraine.

"You were just going to tell me—"

"Oh! yes. First, about the letter." She spoke to Jimmy.

"Gerry left a letter. Lady Eileen—"

"Bundle."

"Bundle found it." She explained the circumstances in a few words.

Jimmy listened, keenly interested. This was the first he had heard of the letter. Loraine took it from her bag and handed it to him. He read it, then looked across at her.

"This is where you can help us. What was it Gerry wanted you to forget?"

Loraine's brows wrinkled a little in perplexity.

"It's so hard to remember exactly now. I opened a letter of Gerry's by mistake. It was written on cheap sort of paper, I remember, and very illiterate handwriting. It had some address in Seven Dials at the head of it. I realized it wasn't for me, so I put it back in the envelope without reading it."

"Sure?" asked Jimmy very gently.

Loraine laughed for the first time.

"I know what you think, and I admit that women *are* curious. But, you see, this didn't even look interesting. It was a kind of list of names and dates."

"Names and dates," said Jimmy thoughtfully.

"Gerry didn't seem to mind much," continued Loraine. "He laughed. He asked me if I had ever heard of the Mafia, and then said it would be queer if a society like the Mafia started in England—but that that kind of secret society didn't take on much with English people. 'Our criminals,' he said, 'haven't got a picturesque imagination.'"

Jimmy pursed up his lips into a whistle.

"I'm beginning to see," he said. "Seven Dials must be the headquarters of some secret society. As he says in his letter to you, he thought it rather a joke to start with. But evidently it wasn't a joke—he says as much. And there's something else; his anxiety that you should forget what he'd told you. There can be only one reason for that—if that society suspected that you had any knowledge of its activity, you too would be in danger. Gerald realized the peril, and he was terribly anxious—for you."

He stopped, then he went on quietly:

"I rather fancy that we're all going to be in danger—if we go on with this."

"If—?" cried Bundle indignantly.

"I'm talking to you two. It's different for me. I was poor old Ronny's pal." He looked at Bundle. "You've done your bit. You've delivered the message he sent me. No; for God's sake keep out of it, you and Loraine."

Bundle looked questioningly at the other girl. Her own mind was definitely made up, but she gave no indication of it just then. She had no wish to push Loraine Wade into a dangerous undertaking. But Loraine's small face was alight at once with indignation.

"You say that! Do you think for one minute I'd be contented to keep out of it—when they killed Gerry—my own dear Gerry, the best and dearest and kindest brother any girl ever had. The only person belonging to me I had in the whole world!"

Jimmy cleared his throat uncomfortably. Loraine, he thought, was wonderful; simply wonderful.

"Look here," he said awkwardly, "you mustn't say that. About being alone in the world—all that rot. You've got lots of friends—only too glad to do what they can. See what I mean?"

It is possible that Loraine did, for she suddenly blushed, and to cover her confusion began to talk nervously.

"That's settled," she said. "I'm going to help. Nobody's going to stop me."

"And so am I, of course," said Bundle.

They both looked at Jimmy.

"Yes," he said slowly. "Yes, quite so."

They looked at him inquiringly.

"I was just wondering," said Jimmy, "how we were going to begin."

9

Plans

Jimmy's words lifted the discussion at once into a more practical sphere.

"All things considered," he said, "we haven't got much to go on. In fact, just the words Seven Dials. As a matter of fact I don't even know exactly where Seven Dials is. But, anyway, we can't very well comb out the whole of that district, house by house."

"We could," said Bundle.

"Well, perhaps we could eventually—though I'm not so sure. I imagine it's a well-populated area. But it wouldn't be very subtle."

The word reminded him of the girl Socks and he smiled.

"Then, of course, there's the part of the country where Ronny was shot. We could nose around there. But the police are probably doing everything we could do, and doing it much better."

"What I like about you," said Bundle sarcastically, "is your cheerful and optimistic disposition."

"Never mind her, Jimmy," said Loraine softly. "Go on."

"Don't be so impatient," said Jimmy to Bundle. "All the best sleuths approach a case this way, by eliminating unnecessary and unprofitable investigation. I'm coming now to the third alternative—Gerald's death. Now that we know it was murder—by the way, you do both believe that, don't you?"

"Yes," said Loraine.

"Yes," said Bundle.

"Good. So do I. Well, it seems to me that there we do stand some faint chance. After all, if Gerry didn't take the chloral himself, someone must have got into his room and put it there—dissolved it in the glass of water, so that when he woke up he drank it off. And of course left the empty box or bottle or whatever it was. You agree with that?"

"Ye-es," said Bundle slowly. "But—"

"Wait. And that someone must have been in the house at the time. It couldn't very well have been someone from outside."

"No," agreed Bundle, more readily this time.

"Very well. Now, that narrows down things considerably. To begin with, I suppose a good many of the servants are family ones—they're your lot, I mean."

"Yes," said Bundle. "Practically all the staff stayed when we let it. All the principal ones are there still—of course there have been changes among the under servants."

"Exactly—that's what I am getting at. *You*,"—he addressed Bundle—"must go into all that. Find out when new servants were engaged—what about footmen, for instance?"

"One of the footmen is new. John, his name is."

"Well, make inquiries about John. And about any others who have only come recently."

"I suppose," said Bundle slowly, "it must have been a servant. It couldn't have been one of the guests?"

"I don't see how that's possible."

"Who were there exactly?"

"Well, there were three girls—Nancy and Helen and Socks—"

"Socks Daventry? I know her."

"May have been. Girl who was always saying things were subtle."

"That's Socks all right. Subtle is one of her words."

"And then there were Gerry Wade and me and Bill Eversleigh and Ronny. And, of course, Sir Oswald and Lady Coote. Oh! and Pongo."

"Who's Pongo?"

"Chap called Bateman—secretary to old Coote. Solemn sort of cove but very conscientious. I was at school with him."

"There doesn't seem anything very suspicious there," remarked Loraine.

"No, there doesn't," said Bundle. "As you say, we'll have to look amongst the servants. By the way, you don't suppose that clock being thrown out of the window had anything to do with it."

"A clock thrown out of the window," said Jimmy, staring. It was the first he had heard of it.

"I can't see how it can have anything to do with it," said Bundle. "But it's odd somehow. There seems no sense in it."

"I remember," said Jimmy slowly. "I went in to—to see poor old Gerry, and there were the clocks ranged along the mantelpiece. I remember noticing there were only seven—not eight."

He gave a sudden shiver and explained himself apologetically.

"Sorry. But somehow those clocks have always given me the shivers. I dream of them sometimes. I'd hate to go into that room in the dark and see them there in a row."

"You wouldn't be able to see them if it was dark," said Bundle practically. "Not unless they had luminous dials—Oh!" She gave a sudden gasp and the colour rushed into her cheeks. "Don't you see? *Seven Dials*!"

The others looked at her doubtfully, but she insisted with increasing vehemence.

"It must be. It can't be a coincidence."

There was a pause.

"You may be right," said Jimmy Thesiger at last. "It's—it's dashed odd."

Bundle started questioning him eagerly.

"Who bought the clocks?"

"All of us."

"Who thought of them?"

"All of us."

"Nonsense, somebody must have thought of them first."

"It didn't happen that way. We were discussing what we could do to get Gerry up, and Pongo said an alarum clock, and somebody said one would be no good, and somebody else—Bill Eversleigh, I think—said why not get a dozen. And we all said good egg and hoofed off to get them. We got one each and an extra one for Pongo and one for Lady Coote—just out of the generosity of our hearts. There was nothing premeditated about it—it just happened."

Bundle was silenced, but not convinced.

Jimmy proceeded to sum up methodically.

"I think we can say we're sure of certain facts. There's a secret society, with points of resemblance to the Mafia, in existence. Gerry Wade came to know about it. At first he treated it as rather a joke—as an absurdity, shall we say. He couldn't believe in its being really dangerous. But later something happened to convince him, and then he got the wind up in earnest. I rather fancy he must have said something to Ronny Devereux about it. Anyway, when he was put out of the way, Ronny suspected, and he must have known enough to get on the same track himself. The unfortunate thing is that we've got to start quite from the outer darkness. We haven't got the knowledge the other two had."

"Perhaps that's an advantage," said Loraine coolly. "They won't suspect us and therefore they won't be trying to put us out of the way."

"I wish I felt sure about that," said Jimmy in a worried voice. "You know, Loraine, old Gerry himself wanted you to keep out of it. Don't you think you could—"

"No, I couldn't," said Loraine. "Don't let's start discussing that again. It's only a waste of time."

At the mention of the word time, Jimmy's eyes rose to the clock and he uttered an exclamation of astonishment. He rose and opened the door.

"Stevens."

"Yes, sir?"

"What about a spot of lunch, Stevens? Could it be managed?"

"I anticipated that it would be required, sir. Mrs. Stevens has made preparations accordingly."

"That's a wonderful man," said Jimmy, as he returned, heaving a sigh of relief. "Brain, you know. Sheer brain. He takes correspondence courses. I sometimes wonder if they'd do any good to me."

"Don't be silly," said Loraine.

Stevens opened the door and proceeded to bring in a most recherché meal. An omelette was followed by quails and the very lightest things in soufflés.

"Why are men so happy when they're single?" said Loraine tragically. "Why are they so much better looked after by other people than by us?"

"Oh! but that's rot, you know," said Jimmy. "I mean, they're not. How could they be? I often think—"

He stammered and stopped. Loraine blushed again.

Suddenly Bundle let out a whoop and both the others started violently.

"Idiot," said Bundle. "Imbecile. Me, I mean. I knew there was something I'd forgotten."

"What?"

"You know Codders—George Lomax, I mean?"

"I've heard of him a good deal," said Jimmy. "From Bill and Ronny, you know."

"Well, Codders is giving some sort of a dry party next week—and he's had a warning letter from Seven Dials."

"What?" cried Jimmy excitedly, leaning forward. "You can't mean it?"

"Yes, I do. He told Father about it. Now what do you think that points to?"

Jimmy leant back in his chair. He thought rapidly and carefully. At last he spoke. His speech was brief and to the point.

"Something's going to happen at that party," he said.

"That's what I think," said Bundle.

"It all fits in," said Jimmy almost dreamily.

He turned to Loraine.

"How old were you when the war was on?" he asked unexpectedly.

"Nine—no, eight."

"And Gerry, I suppose, was about twenty. Most lads of twenty fought in the war. Gerry didn't."

"No," said Loraine, after thinking a minute or two. "No, Gerry wasn't a soldier. I don't know why."

"I can tell you why," said Jimmy. "Or at least I can make a very shrewd guess. He was out of England from 1915 to 1918. I've taken the trouble to find that out. And nobody seems to know exactly where he was. I think he was in Germany."

The colour rose in Loraine's cheeks. She looked at Jimmy with admiration.

"How clever of you."

"He spoke German well, didn't he?"

"Oh! yes, like a native."

"I'm sure I'm right. Listen, you two. Gerry Wade was at the Foreign Office. He appeared to be the same sort of amiable idiot—excuse the term, but you know what I mean—as Bill Eversleigh and Ronny Devereux. A purely ornamental excrescence. But in reality he was something quite different. I think Gerry Wade was the real thing. Our secret service is supposed to be the best in the world. I think Gerry Wade was pretty high up in that service. And that explains everything! I remember saying idly that last evening at Chimneys that Gerry couldn't be quite such an ass as he made himself out to be."

"And if you're right?" said Bundle, practical as ever.

"Then the thing's bigger than we thought. This Seven Dials business isn't merely criminal—it's international. One thing's certain, somebody has got to be at this house-party of Lomax's."

Bundle made a slight grimace.

"I know George well—but he doesn't like me. He'd never think of asking me to a serious gathering. All the same, I might—"

She remained a moment lost in thought.

"Do you think *I* could work it through Bill?" asked Jimmy. "He's bound to be there as Codders's right hand man. He might bring me along somehow or other."

"I don't see why not," said Bundle. "You'll have to prime Bill and make him say the right things. He's incapable of thinking of them for himself."

"What do you suggest?" asked Jimmy humbly.

"Oh! it's quite easy. Bill describes you as a rich young man—interested in politics, anxious to stand for Parliament. George will fall at once. You know what these political parties are: always looking for new, rich young men. The richer Bill says you are, the easier it will be to manage."

"Short of being described as Rothschild, I don't mind," said Jimmy.

"Then I think that's practically settled. I'm dining with Bill tomorrow night, and I'll get a list of who is to be there. That will be useful."

"I'm sorry you can't be there," said Jimmy. "But on the whole I think it's all for the best."

"I'm not so sure I shan't be there," said Bundle. "Codders hates me like poison—but there are other ways."

She became meditative.

"And what about me?" asked Loraine in a small, meek voice.

"You're not on in this act," said Jimmy instantly. "See? After all, we've got to have someone outside to—er—"

"To what?" said Loraine.

Jimmy decided not to pursue this tack. He appealed to Bundle.

"Look here," he said. "Loraine must keep out of this, mustn't she?"

"I certainly think she'd better."

"Next time," said Jimmy kindly.

"And suppose there isn't a next time," said Loraine.

"Oh! there probably will be. Not a doubt of it."

"I see. I'm just to go home and—wait."

"That's it," said Jimmy, with every appearance of relief. "I thought you'd understand."

"You see," explained Bundle, "three of us forcing our way in might look rather suspicious. And you would be particularly difficult. You do see that, don't you?"

"Oh! yes," said Loraine.

"Then it's settled—you do nothing," said Jimmy.

"I do nothing," said Loraine meekly.

Bundle looked at her in sudden suspicion. The tameness with which Loraine was taking it seemed hardly natural. Loraine looked at her. Her eyes were blue and guileless. They met Bundle's without a quiver even of the lashes. Bundle was only partly satisfied. She found the meekness of Loraine Wade's highly suspicious.

10

Bundle Visits Scotland Yard

Now it may be said at once that in the foregoing conversation each one of the three participants had, as it were, held something in reserve. That "Nobody tells everything" is a very true motto.

It may be questioned, for instance, if Loraine Wade was perfectly sincere in her account of the motives which had led her to seek out Jimmy Thesiger.

In the same way, Jimmy Thesiger himself had various ideas and plans connected with the forthcoming party at George Lomax's which he had no intention of revealing to—say, Bundle.

And Bundle herself had a fully-fledged plan which she proposed to put into immediate execution and which she had said nothing whatever about.

On leaving Jimmy Thesiger's rooms, she drove to Scotland Yard, where she asked to see Superintendent Battle.

Superintendent Battle was rather a big man. He worked almost entirely on cases of a delicate political nature. On such a case he had come to Chimneys four years ago, and Bundle was frankly trading on his remembering this fact.

After a short delay, she was taken along several corridors and into the Superintendent's private room. Battle was a stolid-looking man with a wooden face. He looked supremely unintelligent and more like a commissionaire than a detective.

He was standing by the window when she entered, gazing in an expressionless manner at some sparrows.

"Good afternoon, Lady Eileen," he said. "Sit down, won't you?"

"Thank you," said Bundle. "I was afraid you mightn't remember me."

"Always remember people," said Battle. He added: "Got to in my job."

"Oh!" said Bundle, rather damped.

"And what can I do for you?" inquired the Superintendent.

Bundle came straight to the point.

"I've always heard that you people at Scotland Yard have lists of all secret societies and things like that that are formed in London."

"We try to keep up to date," said Superintendent Battle cautiously.

"I suppose a great many of them aren't really dangerous."

"We've got a very good rule to go by," said Battle. "The more they talk, the less they'll do. You'd be surprised how well that works out."

"And I've heard that very often you let them go on?"

Battle nodded.

"That's so. Why shouldn't a man call himself a Brother of Liberty and meet twice a week in a cellar and talk about rivers of blood—it won't hurt either him or us. And if there is trouble any time, we know where to lay our hands on him."

"But sometimes, I suppose," said Bundle slowly, "a society may be more dangerous than anyone imagines?"

"Very unlikely," said Battle.

"But it *might* happen," persisted Bundle.

"Oh! it *might*," admitted the Superintendent.

There was a moment or two's silence. Then Bundle said quietly:

"Superintendent Battle, could you give me a list of secret societies that have their headquarters in Seven Dials?"

It was Superintendent Battle's boast that he had never been seen to display emotion. But Bundle could have sworn that just for a moment his eyelids flickered and he looked taken aback. Only for a moment, however. He was his usual wooden self as he said:

"Strictly speaking, Lady Eileen, there's no such place as Seven Dials nowadays."

"No?"

"No. Most of it is pulled down and rebuilt. It was rather a low quarter once, but it's very respectable and high class nowadays. Not at all a romantic spot to poke about in for mysterious secret societies."

"Oh!" said Bundle, rather nonplussed.

"But all the same I should very much like to know what put that neighborhood into your head, Lady Eileen?"

"Have I got to tell you?"

"Well, it saves trouble, doesn't it? We know where we are, so to speak?"

Bundle hesitated for a minute.

"There was a man shot yesterday," she said slowly. "I thought I had run over him—"

"Mr. Ronald Devereux?"

"You know about it, of course. Why has there been nothing in the papers?"

"Do you really want to know that, Lady Eileen?"

"Yes, please."

"Well, we just thought we should like to have a clear twenty-four hours—see? It will be in the papers tomorrow."

"Oh!" Bundle studied him, puzzled.

What was hidden behind that immovable face? Did he regard the shooting of Ronald Devereux as an ordinary crime or as an extraordinary one?

"He mentioned Seven Dials when he was dying," said Bundle slowly.

"Thank you," said Battle. "I'll make a note of that."

He wrote a few words on the blotting pad in front of him.

Bundle started on another tack.

"Mr. Lomax, I understand, came to see you yesterday about a threatening letter he had had."

"He did."

"And that was written from Seven Dials?"

"It had Seven Dials written at the top of it, I believe."

Bundle felt as though she was battering hopelessly on a locked door.

"If you'll let me advise you, Lady Eileen—"

"I know what you're going to say."

"I should go home and—well, think no more about these matters."

"Leave it to you, in fact?"

"Well," said Superintendent Battle, "after all, we *are* the professionals."

"And I'm only an amateur? Yes, but you forget one thing—I mayn't have your knowledge and skill—but I have one advantage over you. I can work in the dark."

She thought that the Superintendent seemed a little taken aback, as though the force of her words struck home.

"Of course," said Bundle, "if you won't give me a list of secret societies—"

"Oh! I never said that. You shall have a list of the whole lot."

He went to the door, put his head through and called out something, then came back to his chair. Bundle, rather unreasonably, felt baffled. The ease with which he acceded to her request seemed to her suspicious. He was looking at her now in a placid fashion.

"Do you remember the death of Mr. Gerald Wade?" she asked abruptly.

"Down at your place, wasn't it? Took an overdraught of sleeping mixture."

"His sister says he never took things to make him sleep."

"Ah!" said the Superintendent. "You'd be surprised what a lot of things there are that sisters don't know."

Bundle again felt baffled. She sat in silence till a man came in with a typewritten sheet of paper, which he handed to the Superintendent.

"Here you are," said the latter when the other had left the room. "The Blood Brothers of St. Sebastian. The Wolf Hounds. The Comrades of

Peace. The Comrades Club. The Friends of Oppression. The Children of Moscow. The Red Standard Bearers. The Herrings. The Comrades of the Fallen—and half a dozen more."

He handed it to her with a distinct twinkle in his eye.

"You give it to me," said Bundle, "because you know it's not going to be the slightest use to me. Do you want me to leave the whole thing alone?"

"I should prefer it," said Battle. "You see—if you go messing round all these places—well, it's going to give us a lot of trouble."

"Looking after me, you mean?"

"Looking after you, Lady Eileen."

Bundle had risen to her feet. Now she stood undecided. So far the honours lay with Superintendent Battle. Then she remembered one slight incident, and she based a last appeal upon it.

"I said just now that an amateur could do some things which a professional couldn't. You didn't contradict me. That's because you're an honest man, Superintendent Battle. You knew I was right."

"Go on," said Battle quietly.

"At Chimneys you let me help. Won't you let me help now?"

Battle seemed to be turning the thing over in his mind. Emboldened by his silence, Bundle continued.

"You know pretty well what I'm like, Superintendent Battle. I butt into things. I'm a Nosey Parker. I don't want to get in your way or to try and do things that you're doing and can do a great deal better. But if there's a chance for an amateur, let me have it."

Again there was a pause, and then Superintendent Battle said quietly:

"You couldn't have spoken fairer than you have done, Lady Eileen. But I'm just going to say this to you. What you propose is dangerous. And when I say dangerous, I *mean* dangerous."

"I've grasped that," said Bundle. "I'm not a fool."

"No," said Superintendent Battle. "Never knew a young lady who was less so. What I'll do for you, Lady Eileen, is this. I'll just give you one little hint. And I'm doing it because I never have thought much of the motto 'Safety First.' In my opinion half the people who spend their lives avoiding being run over by buses had much better be run over and put safely out of the way. They're no good."

This remarkable utterance issuing from the conventional lips of Superintendent Battle quite took Bundle's breath away.

"What was the hint you were going to give me?" she asked at last.

"You know Mr. Eversleigh, don't you?"

"Know Bill? Why, of course. But what—"

"I think Mr. Bill Eversleigh will be able to tell you all you want to know about Seven Dials."

"Bill knows about it? *Bill*?"

"I didn't say that. Not at all. But I think, being a quick-witted young lady, you'll get what you want from him.

"And now," said Superintendent Battle firmly, "I'm not going to say another word."

11

Dinner with Bill

Bundle set out to keep her appointment with Bill on the following evening full of expectation.

Bill greeted her with every sign of elation.

"Bill really *is* rather nice," thought Bundle to herself. "Just like a large, clumsy dog that wags its tail when it's pleased to see you."

The large dog was uttering short staccato yelps of comment and information.

"You look tremendously fit, Bundle. I can't tell you how pleased I am to see you. I've ordered oysters—you do like oysters, don't you? And how's everything? What did you want to go mouldering about abroad so long? Were you having a very gay time?"

"No, deadly," said Bundle. "Perfectly foul. Old diseased colonels creeping about in the sun, and active, wizened spinsters running libraries and churches."

"Give me England," said Bill. "I bar this foreign business—except Switzerland. Switzerland's all right. I'm thinking of going this Christmas. Why don't you come along?"

"I'll think of it," said Bundle. "What have you been doing with yourself lately, Bill?"

It was an incautious query. Bundle had merely made it out of politeness and as a preliminary to introducing her own topics of conversation. It was, however, the opening for which Bill had been waiting.

"That's just what I've been wanting to tell you about. You're brainy, Bundle, and I want your advice. You know that musical show, 'Damn Your Eyes'?"

"Yes."

"Well, I'm going to tell you about one of the dirtiest pieces of work imaginable. My God! the theatrical crowd. There's a girl—a Yankee girl—a perfect stunner—"

Bundle's heart sank. The grievances of Bill's lady friends were always interminable—they went on and on and there was no stemming them.

"This girl, Babe St. Maur her name is—"

"I wonder how she got that name?" said Bundle sarcastically.

Bill replied literally.

"She got it out of *Who's Who*. Opened it and jabbed her finger down on a page without looking. Pretty nifty, eh? Her real name's Goldschmidt or Abrameier—something quite impossible."

"Oh! quite," agreed Bundle.

"Well, Babe St. Maur is pretty smart. And she's got muscles. She was one of the eight girls who made the living bridge—"

"Bill," said Bundle desperately, "I went to see Jimmy Thesiger yesterday morning."

"Good old Jimmy," said Bill. "Well, as I was telling you, Babe's pretty smart. You've got to be nowadays. She can put it over on most theatrical people. If you want to live, be high-handed, that's what Babe says. And mind you, she's the goods all right. She can act—it's marvellous how that girl can act. She'd not much chance in 'Damn Your Eyes'—just swamped in a pack of good-looking girls. I said why not try the legitimate stage—you know, Mrs. Tanqueray—that sort of stuff—but Babe just laughed—"

"Have you seen Jimmy at all?"

"Saw him this morning. Let me see, where was I? Oh, yes, I hadn't got to the rumpus yet. And mind you it was jealousy—sheer, spiteful jealousy. The other girl wasn't a patch on Babe for looks and she knew it. So she went behind her back—"

Bundle resigned herself to the inevitable and heard the whole story of the unfortunate circumstances which had led up to Babe St. Maur's summary disappearance from the cast of "Damn Your Eyes." It took a long time. When Bill finally paused for breath and sympathy, Bundle said:

"You're quite right, Bill, it's a rotten shame. There must be a lot of jealousy about—"

"The whole theatrical world's rotten with it."

"It must be. Did Jimmy say anything to you about coming down to the Abbey next week?"

For the first time, Bill gave his attention to what Bundle was saying.

"He was full of a long rigmarole he wanted me to stuff Codders with. About wanting to stand in the Conservative interest. But you know, Bundle, it's too damned risky."

"Stuff," said Bundle. "If George *does* find him out, he won't blame you. You'll just have been taken in, that's all."

"That's not it at all," said Bill. "I mean it's too damned risky for Jimmy. Before he knows where he is, he'll be parked down somewhere like Tooting West, pledged to kiss babies and make speeches. You don't know how thorough Codders is and how frightfully energetic."

"Well, we'll have to risk that," said Bundle. "Jimmy can take care of himself all right."

"You don't know Codders," repeated Bill.

"Who's coming to this party, Bill? Is it anything very special?"

"Only the usual sort of muck. Mrs. Macatta for one."

"The M.P.?"

"Yes, you know, always going off the deep end about Welfare and Pure Milk and Save the Children. Think of poor Jimmy being talked to by her."

"Never mind Jimmy. Go on telling me."

"Then there's a Hungarian, what they call a Young Hungarian. Countess something unpronounceable. She's all right."

He swallowed as though embarrassed and Bundle observed that he was crumbling his bread nervously.

"Young and beautiful?" she inquired delicately.

"Oh! rather."

"I didn't know George went in for female beauty much."

"Oh! he doesn't. She runs baby feeding in Buda Pesth—something like that. Naturally she and Mrs. Macatta want to get together."

"Who else?"

"Sir Stanley Digby—"

"The Air Minister?"

"Yes. And his secretary, Terence O'Rourke. He's rather a lad, by the way—or used to be in his flying days. Then there's a perfectly poisonous German chap called Herr Eberhard. I don't know who he is, but we're all making the hell of a fuss about him. I've been twice told off to take him out to lunch, and I can tell you, Bundle, it was no joke. He's not like the Embassy chaps, who are all very decent. This man sucks in soup and eats peas with a knife. Not only that, but the brute is always biting his fingernails—positively gnaws at them."

"Pretty foul."

"Isn't it? I believe he invents things—something of the kind. Well, that's all. Oh! yes, Sir Oswald Coote."

"And Lady Coote?"

"Yes, I believe she's coming too."

Bundle sat lost in thought for some minutes. Bill's list was suggestive, but she hadn't time to think out various possibilities just now. She must get on to the next point.

"Bill?" she said. "What's all this about Seven Dials?"

Bill at once looked horribly embarrassed. He blinked and avoided her glance.

"I don't know what you mean," he said.

"Nonsense," said Bundle. "I was told you know all about it."

"About what?"

This was rather a poser. Bundle shifted her ground.

"I don't see what you want to be so secretive for," she complained.

"Nothing to be secretive about. Nobody goes there much now. It was only a craze."

This sounded puzzling.

"One gets so out of things when one is away," said Bundle in a sad voice.

"Oh! you haven't missed much," said Bill. "Everyone went there just to say they had been. It was boring really, and, my God, you *can* get tired of fried fish."

"Where did everyone go?"

"To the Seven Dials Club, of course," said Bill, staring. "Wasn't that what you were asking about?"

"I didn't know it by that name," said Bundle.

"Used to be a slummy sort of district round about Tottenham Court Road way. It's all pulled down and cleaned up now. But the Seven Dials Club keeps to the old atmosphere. Fried fish and chips. General squalor. Kind of East End stunt, but awfully handy to get at after a show."

"It's a night club, I suppose," said Bundle. "Dancing and all that?"

"That's it. Awfully mixed crowd. Not a posh affair. Artists, you know, and all sorts of odd women and a sprinkling of our lot. They say quite a lot of things, but I think that that's all bunkum myself, just said to make the place go."

"Good," said Bundle. "We'll go there to-night."

"Oh! I shouldn't do that," said Bill. His embarrassment had returned. "I tell you it's played out. Nobody goes there now."

"Well, we're going."

"You wouldn't care for it, Bundle. You wouldn't really."

"You're going to take me to the Seven Dials Club and nowhere else, Bill. And I should like to know why you are so unwilling?"

"I? Unwilling?"

"Painfully so. What's the guilty secret?"

"Guilty secret?"

"Don't keep repeating what I say. You do it to give yourself time."

"I don't," said Bill indignantly. "It's only—"

"Well? I know there's something. You never can conceal anything."

"I've got nothing to conceal. It's only—"

"Well?"

"It's a long story—You see, I took Babe St. Maur there one night—"

"Oh! Babe St. Maur again."

"Why not?"

"I didn't know it was about her—" said Bundle, stifling a yawn.

"As I say, I took Babe there. She rather fancied a lobster. I had a lobster under my arm—"

The story went on—When the lobster had been finally dismembered in a struggle between Bill and a fellow who was a rank outsider, Bundle brought her attention back to him.

"I see," she said. "And there was a row?"

"Yes, but it was *my* lobster. I'd bought it and paid for it. I had a perfect right—"

"Oh! you had, you had," said Bundle hastily. "But I'm sure that's all forgotten now. And I don't care for lobsters anyway. So let's go."

"We may be raided by the police. There's a room upstairs where they play baccarat."

"Father will have to come out and bail me out, that's all. Come on, Bill."

Bill still seemed rather reluctant, but Bundle was adamant, and they were soon speeding to their destination in a taxi.

The place, when they got to it, was much as she imagined it would be. It was a tall house in a narrow street, 14 Hunstanton Street; she noted the number.

A man whose face was strangely familiar opened the door. She thought he started slightly when he saw her, but he greeted Bill with respectful recognition. He was a tall man, with fair hair, a rather weak, anaemic face and slightly shifty eyes. Bundle puzzled to herself where she could have seen him before.

Bill had recovered his equilibrium now and quite enjoyed doing showman. They danced in the cellar, which was very full of smoke—so much so that you saw everyone through a blue haze. The smell of fried fish was almost overpowering.

On the wall were rough charcoal sketches, some of them executed with real talent. The company was extremely mixed. There were portly foreigners, opulent Jewesses, a sprinkling of the really smart, and several ladies belonging to the oldest profession in the world.

Soon Bill led Bundle upstairs. There the weak-faced man was on guard, watching all those admitted to the gambling room with a lynx eye. Suddenly recognition came to Bundle.

"Of course," she said. "How stupid of me. It's Alfred, who used to be second footman at Chimneys. How are you, Alfred?"

"Nicely, thank you, your ladyship."

"When did you leave Chimneys, Alfred? Was it long before we got back?"

"It was about a month ago, m'lady. I got a chance of bettering myself, and it seemed a pity not to take it."

"I suppose they pay you very well here," remarked Bundle.

"Very fair, m'lady."

Bundle passed in. It seemed to her that in this room the real life of the club was exposed. The stakes were high, she saw that at once, and the people gathered round the two tables were of the true type—hawk-eyed, haggard, with the gambling fever in their blood.

She and Bill stayed there for about half an hour. Then Bill grew restive.

"Let's get out of this place, Bundle, and go on dancing."

Bundle agreed. There was nothing to be seen here. They went down again. They danced for another half hour, had fish and chips, and then Bundle declared herself ready to go home.

"But it's so early," Bill protested.

"No, it isn't. Not really. And, anyway, I've got a long day in front of me to-morrow."

"What are you going to do?"

"That depends," said Bundle mysteriously. "But I can tell you this, Bill, the grass is not going to grow under my feet."

"It never does," said Mr. Eversleigh.

12

Inquiries at Chimneys

Bundle's temperament was certainly not inherited from her father, whose prevailing characteristic was a wholly amiable inertia. As Bill Eversleigh had very justly remarked, the grass never did grow under Bundle's feet.

On the morning following her dinner with Bill, Bundle woke full of energy. She had three distinct plans which she meant to put into operation that day, and she realized that she was going to be slightly hampered by the limits of time and space.

Fortunately she did not suffer from the affliction of Gerry Wade, Ronny Devereux and Jimmy Thesiger—that of not being able to get up in the morning. Sir Oswald Coote himself would have had no fault to find with her on the score of early rising. At half-past eight Bundle had breakfasted and was on her way to Chimneys in the Hispano.

Her father seemed mildly pleased to see her.

"I never know when you're going to turn up," he said. "But this will save me ringing up, which I hate. Colonel Melrose was here yesterday about the inquest."

Colonel Melrose was Chief Constable of the county, and an old friend of Lord Caterham.

"You mean the inquest on Ronny Devereux? When is it to be?"

"To-morrow. Twelve o'clock. Melrose will call for you. Having found the body, you'll have to give evidence, but he said you needn't be at all alarmed."

"Why on earth should I be alarmed?"

"Well, you know," said Lord Caterham apologetically, "Melrose is a bit old-fashioned."

"Twelve o'clock," said Bundle. "Good. I shall be here, if I'm still alive."

"Have you any reason to anticipate not being alive?"

"One never knows," said Bundle. "The strain of modern life—as the newspapers say."

"Which reminds me that George Lomax asked me to come over to the Abbey next week. I refused, of course."

"Quite right," said Bundle. "We don't want you mixed up in any funny business."

"Is there going to be any funny business?" asked Lord Caterham with a sudden awakening of interest.

"Well—warning letters and all that, you know," said Bundle.

"Perhaps George is going to be assassinated," said Lord Caterham hopefully. "What do you think, Bundle—perhaps I'd better go after all."

"You curb your bloodthirsty instincts and stay quietly at home," said Bundle. "I'm going to talk to Mrs. Howell."

Mrs. Howell was the housekeeper, that dignified, creaking lady who had struck such terror to the heart of Lady Coote. She had no terrors for Bundle, whom, indeed, she always called Miss Bundle, a relic of the days when Bundle had stayed at Chimneys, a long-legged, impish child, before her father had succeeded to the title.

"Now, Howelly," said Bundle, "let's have a cup of rich cocoa together, and let me hear all the household news."

She gleaned what she wanted without much difficulty, making mental notes as follows:

"Two new scullery maids—village girls—doesn't seem much there. New third housemaid—head housemaid's niece. That sounds all right. Howelly seems to have bullied poor Lady Coote a good deal. She would."

"I never thought the day would come when I should see Chimneys inhabited by strangers, Miss Bundle."

"Oh! one must go with the times," said Bundle. "You'll be lucky, Howelly, if you never see it converted into desirable flats with use of superb pleasure grounds."

Mrs. Howell shivered all down her reactionary aristocratic spine.

"I've never seen Sir Oswald Coote," remarked Bundle.

"Sir Oswald is no doubt a very clever gentleman," said Mrs. Howell distantly.

Bundle gathered that Sir Oswald had not been liked by his staff.

"Of course, it was Mr. Bateman who saw to everything," continued the housekeeper. "A very efficient gentleman. A very efficient gentleman indeed, and one who knew the way things ought to be done."

Bundle led the talk on to the topic of Gerald Wade's death. Mrs. Howell was only too willing to talk about it, and was full of pitying ejaculations about the poor young gentleman, but Bundle gleaned nothing new. Presently she took leave of Mrs. Howell and came downstairs again, where she promptly rang for Tredwell.

"Tredwell, when did Alfred leave?"

"It would be about a month ago now, my lady."

"Why did he leave?"

"It was by his own wish, my lady. I believe he has gone to London. I was not dissatisfied with him in any way. I think you will find the new footman, John, very satisfactory. He seems to know his work and to be most anxious to give satisfaction."

"Where did he come from?"

"He had excellent references, my lady. He had lived last with Lord Mount Vernon."

"I see," said Bundle thoughtfully.

She was remembering that Lord Mount Vernon was at present on a shooting trip in East Africa.

"What's his last name, Tredwell?"

"Bower, my lady."

Tredwell paused for a minute or two and then, seeing that Bundle had finished, he quietly left the room. Bundle remained lost in thought.

John had opened the door to her on her arrival that day, and she had taken particular notice of him without seeming to do so. Apparently, he was the perfect servant, well trained, with an expressionless face. He had, perhaps, a more soldierly bearing than most footmen and there was something a little odd about the shape of the back of his head.

But these details, as Bundle realized, were hardly relevant to the situation. She sat frowning down at the blotting paper in front of her. She had a pencil in her hand and was idly tracing the name Bower over and over again.

Suddenly an idea struck her and she stopped dead, staring at the word. Then she summoned Tredwell once more.

"Tredwell, how is the name Bower spelt?"

"B-A-U-E-R, my lady."

"That's not an English name."

"I believe he is of Swiss extraction, my lady."

"Oh! That's all, Tredwell, thank you."

Swiss extraction? No. German! That martial carriage, that flat back to the head. And he had come to Chimneys a fortnight before Gerry Wade's death.

Bundle rose to her feet. She had done all she could here. Now to get on with things! She went in search of her father.

"I'm off again," she said. "I've got to go and see Aunt Marcia."

"Got to see Marcia?" Lord Caterham's voice was full of astonishment. "Poor child, how did you get let in for that?"

"Just for once," said Bundle, "I happen to be going of my own free will."

Lord Caterham looked at her in amazement. That anyone could have a genuine desire to face his redoubtable sister-in-law was quite incomprehensible to him. Marcia, Marchioness of Caterham, the widow of his late brother Henry, was a very prominent personality. Lord Caterham admitted that she had made Henry an admirable wife and that but for her in all probability he would never have held the office of Secretary of State for Foreign Affairs. On the other hand, he had always looked upon Henry's early death as a merciful release.

It seemed to him that Bundle was foolishly putting her head into the lion's mouth.

"Oh! I say," he said. "You know, I shouldn't do that. You don't know what it may lead to."

"I know what I hope it's going to lead to," said Bundle. "I'm all right, Father, don't you worry about me."

Lord Caterham sighed and settled himself more comfortably in his chair. He went back to his perusal of the *Field*. But in a minute or two Bundle suddenly put her head in again.

"Sorry," she said. "But there's one other thing I wanted to ask you. What is Sir Oswald Coote?"

"I told you—a steam-roller."

"I don't mean your personal impression of him. How did he make his money—trouser buttons or brass beds or what?"

"Oh! I see. He's steel. Steel and iron. He's got the biggest steel works, or whatever you call it, in England. He doesn't, of course, run the show personally now. It's a company or companies. He got me in as a director of something or other. Very good business for me—nothing to do except go down to the city once or twice a year to one of those hotel places—Cannon Street or Liverpool Street—and sit round a table where they have very nice new blotting paper. Then Coote or some clever Johnny makes a speech simply bristling with figures, but fortunately you needn't listen to it—and I can tell you, you often get a jolly good lunch out of it."

Uninterested in Lord Caterham's lunches, Bundle had departed again before he had finished speaking. On the way back to London, she tried to piece together things to her satisfaction.

As far as she could see, steel and infant welfare did not go together. One of the two, then, was just padding—presumably the latter. Mrs. Macatta and the Hungarian countess could be ruled out of court. They were camouflage. No, the pivot of the whole thing seemed to be the unattractive Herr Eberhard. He did not seem to be the type of man whom George Lomax would normally invite. Bill had said vaguely that he invented. Then there was the Air Minister and Sir Oswald Coote, who was steel. Somehow that seemed to hang together.

Since it was useless speculating further, Bundle abandoned the attempt and concentrated on her forthcoming interview with Lady Caterham.

The lady lived in a large gloomy house in one of London's higher class squares. Inside it smelt of sealing wax, bird seed and slightly decayed flowers. Lady Caterham was a large woman—large in every way. Her proportions were majestic, rather than ample. She had a large beaked nose, wore gold rimmed pince-nez and her upper lip bore just the faintest suspicion of a moustache.

She was somewhat surprised to see her niece, but accorded her a frigid cheek, which Bundle duly kissed.

"This is quite an unexpected pleasure, Eileen," she observed coldly.

"We've only just got back, Aunt Marcia."

"I know. How is your father? Much as usual?"

Her tone conveyed disparagement. She had a poor opinion of Alastair Edward Brent, ninth Marquis of Caterham. She would have called him, had she known the term, a "poor fish."

"Father is very well. He's down at Chimneys."

"Indeed. You know, Eileen, I never approved of the letting of Chimneys. The place is, in many ways, a historical monument. It should not be cheapened."

"It must have been wonderful in Uncle Henry's day," said Bundle with a slight sigh.

"Henry realized his responsibilities," said Henry's widow.

"Think of the people who stayed there," went on Bundle ecstatically. "All the principal statesmen of Europe."

Lady Caterham sighed.

"I can truly say that history has been made there more than once," she observed. "If only your father—"

She shook her head sadly.

"Politics bore Father," said Bundle, "and yet they are about the most fascinating study there is, I should say. Especially if one knew about them from the inside."

She made this extravagantly untruthful statement of her feelings without even a blush. Her aunt looked at her with some surprise.

"I am pleased to hear you say so," she said. "I always imagined, Eileen, that you cared for nothing but this modern pursuit of pleasure."

"I used to," said Bundle.

"It is true that you are still very young," said Lady Caterham thoughtfully. "But with your advantages, and if you were to marry suitably, you might be one of the leading political hostesses of the day."

Bundle felt slightly alarmed. For a moment she feared that her aunt might produce a suitable husband straight away.

"But I feel such a fool," said Bundle. "I mean I know so little."

"That can easily be remedied," said Lady Caterham briskly. "I have any amount of literature I can lend you."

"Thank you, Aunt Marcia," said Bundle, and proceeded hastily to her second line of attack.

"I wondered if you knew Mrs. Macatta, Aunt Marcia?"

"Certainly I know her. A most estimable woman with a brilliant brain. I may say that as a general rule I do not hold with women standing for Parliament. They can make their influence felt in a more womanly fashion." She paused, doubtless to recall the womanly way in which she had forced a reluctant husband into the political arena and the marvellous success which had crowned his and her efforts. "But still, times change. And the work Mrs. Macatta is doing is of truly national importance, and of the utmost value to all women. It is, I think I may say, true womanly work. You must certainly meet Mrs. Macatta."

Bundle gave a rather dismal sigh.

"She's going to be at a house-party at George Lomax's next week. He asked Father, who, of course, won't go, but he never thought of asking me. Thinks I'm too much of an idiot, I suppose."

It occurred to Lady Caterham that her niece was really wonderfully improved. Had she, perhaps, had an unfortunate love affair? An unfortunate love affair, in Lady Caterham's opinion, was often highly beneficial to young girls. It made them take life seriously.

"I don't suppose George Lomax realizes for a moment that you have—shall we say, grown up? Eileen, dear," she said, "I must have a few words with him."

"He doesn't like me," said Bundle. "I know he won't ask me."

"Nonsense," said Lady Caterham. "I shall make a point of it. I knew George Lomax when he was so high." She indicated a quite impossible height. "He will be only too pleased to do me a favour. And he will be sure to see for himself that it is vitally important that the present day young girls of our own class should take an intelligent interest in the welfare of their country."

Bundle nearly said: "Hear, hear," but checked herself.

"I will find you some literature now," said Lady Caterham, rising.

She called in a piercing voice, "Miss Connor."

A very neat secretary with a frightened expression came running. Lady Caterham gave her various directions. Presently Bundle was driving back to Brook Street with an armful of the driest looking literature imaginable.

Her next proceeding was to ring up Jimmy Thesiger. His first words were full of triumph.

"I've managed it," he said. "Had a lot of trouble with Bill, though. He'd got it into his thick head that I should be a lamb among the wolves. But I made him see sense at last. I've got a lot of thingummybobs now and I'm studying them. You know, blue books and white papers. Deadly dull—but one must do the thing properly. Have you ever heard of the Santa Fé boundary dispute?"

"Never," said Bundle.

"Well, I'm taking special pains with that. It went on for years and was very complicated. I'm making it my subject. Nowadays one has to specialize."

"I've got a lot of the same sort of things," said Bundle. "Aunt Marcia gave them to me."

"Aunt who?"

"Aunt Marcia—Father's sister-in-law. She's very political. In fact, she's going to get me invited to George's party."

"No? Oh, I say, that will be splendid." There was a pause and then Jimmy said:

"I say, I don't think we'd better tell Loraine that—eh?"

"Perhaps not."

"You see, she mayn't like being out of it. And she really must be kept out of it."

"Yes."

"I mean you can't let a girl like that run into danger!"

Bundle reflected that Mr. Thesiger was slightly deficient in tact. The prospect of *her* running into danger did not seem to give him any qualms whatever.

"Have you gone away?" asked Jimmy.

"No, I was only thinking."

"I see. I say, are you going to the inquest to-morrow?"

"Yes; are you?"

"Yes. By the way, it's in the evening papers. But tucked away in a corner. Funny—I should have thought they'd have made rather a splash about it."

"Yes—so should I."

"Well," said Jimmy, "I must be getting on with my task. I've just got to where Bolivia sent us a Note."

"I suppose I must get on with my little lot," said Bundle. "Are you going to swot at it all the evening?"

"I think so. Are you?"

"Oh, probably. Good-night."

They were both liars of the most unblushing order. Jimmy Thesiger knew perfectly well that he was taking Loraine Wade out to dinner.

As for Bundle, no sooner had she rung off than she attired herself in various nondescript garments belonging, as a matter of fact, to her maid. And having donned them, she sallied out on foot deliberating whether bus or tube would be the best route by which to reach the Seven Dials Club.

13

The Seven Dials Club

Bundle reached 14 Hunstanton Street about 6 P.M. At that hour, as she rightly judged, the Seven Dials Club was a dead spot. Bundle's aim was a simple one. She intended to get hold of the ex-footman Alfred. She was convinced that once she had got hold of him the rest would be easy. Bundle had a simple autocratic method of dealing with retainers. It seldom failed, and she saw no reason why it should fail now.

The only thing of which she was not certain was how many people inhabited the club premises. Naturally she wished to disclose her presence to as few people as possible.

Whilst she was hesitating as to her best line of attack, the problem was solved for her in a singularly easy fashion. The door of No. 14 opened and Alfred himself came out.

"Good afternoon, Alfred," said Bundle pleasantly.

Alfred jumped.

"Oh! good afternoon, your ladyship. I—I didn't recognize your ladyship just for a moment."

Paying a tribute in her own mind to her maid's clothing, Bundle proceeded to business.

"I want a few words with you, Alfred. Where shall we go?"

"Well—really, my lady—I don't know—it's not what you might call a nice part round here—I don't know, I'm sure—"

Bundle cut him short.

"Who's in the club?"

"No one at present, my lady."

"Then we'll go in there."

Alfred produced a key and opened the door. Bundle passed in. Alfred, troubled and sheepish, followed her. Bundle sat down and looked straight at the uncomfortable Alfred.

"I suppose you know," she said crisply, "that what you're doing here is dead against the law?"

Alfred shifted uncomfortably from one foot to the other.

"It's true as we've been raided twice," he admitted. "But nothing compromising was found, owing to the neatness of Mr. Mosgorovsky's arrangements."

"I'm not talking of the gambling only," said Bundle. "There's more than that—probably a great deal more than you know. I'm going to ask you a direct question, Alfred, and I should like the truth, please. *How much were you paid for leaving Chimneys?*"

Alfred looked twice round the cornice as though seeking for inspirations, swallowed three or four times, and then took the inevitable course of a weak will opposed to a strong one.

"It was this way, your ladyship. Mr. Mosgorovsky, he come with a party to visit Chimneys on one of the show days. Mr. Tredwell, he was indisposed like—an ingrowing toe-nail as a matter of fact—so it fell to me to show the parties over. At the end of the tour, Mr. Mosgorovsky, he stays behind the rest, and after giving me something handsome, he falls into conversation."

"Yes," said Bundle encouragingly.

"And the long and the short of it was," said Alfred, with a sudden acceleration of his narrative, "that he offers me a hundred pound down to leave that instant minute and to look after this here club. He wanted someone as was used to the best families—to give the place a tone, as he put it. And, well, it seemed flying in the face of providence to refuse—let alone that the wages I get here are just three times what they were as second footman."

"A hundred pounds," said Bundle. "That's a very large sum, Alfred. Did they say anything about who was to fill your place at Chimneys?"

"I demurred a bit, my lady, about leaving at once. As I pointed out, it wasn't usual and might cause inconvenience. But Mr. Mosgorovsky, he knew of a young chap—been in good service and ready to come any minute. So I mentioned his name to Mr. Tredwell and everything was settled pleasant like."

Bundle nodded. Her own suspicions had been correct and the *modus operandi* was much as she had thought it to be. She essayed a further inquiry.

"Who is Mr. Mosgorovsky?"

"Gentleman as runs this club. Russian gentleman. A very clever gentleman too."

Bundle abandoned the getting of information for the moment and proceeded to other matters.

"A hundred pounds is a very large sum of money, Alfred."

"Larger than I ever handled, my lady," said Alfred with simple candour.

"Did you never suspect that there was something wrong?"

"Wrong, my lady?"

"Yes. I'm not talking about the gambling. I mean something far more serious. You don't want to be sent to penal servitude, do you, Alfred?"

"Oh, Lord, my lady, you don't mean it?"

"I was at Scotland Yard the day before yesterday," said Bundle impressively. "I heard some very curious things. I want you to help me, Alfred, and if you do, well—if things go wrong, I'll put in a good word for you."

"Anything I can do, I shall be only too pleased, my lady. I mean, I would anyway."

"Well, first," said Bundle, "I want to go all over this place—from top to bottom."

Accompanied by a mystified and scared Alfred, she made a very thorough tour of inspection. Nothing struck her eye till she came to the gaming room. There she noticed an inconspicuous door in a corner, and the door was locked.

Alfred explained readily.

"That's used as a getaway, your ladyship. There's a room and a door on to a staircase what comes out in the next street. That's the way the gentry goes when there's a raid."

"But don't the police know about it?"

"It's a cunning door, you see, my lady. Looks like a cupboard, that's all."

Bundle felt a rising excitement.

"I must get in here," she said.

Alfred shook his head.

"You can't, my lady; Mr. Mosgorovsky, he has the key."

"Well," said Bundle, "there are other keys."

She perceived that the lock was a perfectly ordinary one which probably could be easily unlocked by the key of one of the other doors. Alfred, rather troubled, was sent to collect likely specimens. The fourth that Bundle tried fitted. She turned it, opened the door and passed through.

She found herself in a small, dingy apartment. A long table occupied the centre of the room with chairs ranged round it. There was no other furniture in the room. Two built-in cupboards stood on either side of the fireplace. Alfred indicated the nearer one with a nod.

"That's it," he explained.

Bundle tried the cupboard door, but it was locked, and she saw at once that this lock was a very different affair. It was of the patent kind that would only yield to its own key.

" 'Ighly ingenious, it is," explained Alfred. "It looks all right when opened. Shelves, you know, with a few ledgers and that on 'em. Nobody'd ever suspect, but you touch the right spot and the whole thing swings open."

Bundle had turned round and was surveying the room thoughtfully. The first thing she noticed was that the door by which they had entered was carefully fitted round with baize. It must be completely soundproof. Then her eyes wandered to the chairs. There were seven of them, three each side and one rather more imposing in design at the head of the table.

Bundle's eyes brightened. She had found what she was looking for. This, she felt sure, was the meeting place of the secret organization. The place was almost perfectly planned. It looked so innocent—you could reach it just by stepping through from the gaming room, or you could arrive there by the secret entrance—and any secrecy, any precautions were easily explained by the gaming going on in the next room.

Idly, as these thoughts passed through her mind, she drew a finger across the marble of the mantelpiece. Alfred saw and misinterpreted the action.

"You won't find no dirt, not to speak of," he said. "Mr. Mosgorovsky, he ordered the place to be swept out this morning, and I did it while he waited."

"Oh!" said Bundle, thinking very hard. "This morning, eh?"

"Has to be done sometimes," said Alfred. "Though the room's never what you might call used."

Next minute he received a shock.

"Alfred," said Bundle, "you've got to find me a place in this room where I can hide."

Alfred looked at her in dismay.

"But it's impossible, my lady. You'll get me into trouble and I'll lose my job."

"You'll lose it anyway when you go to prison," said Bundle unkindly. "But as a matter of fact, you needn't worry, nobody will know anything about it."

"And there ain't no place," wailed Alfred. "Look round for yourself, your ladyship, if you don't believe me."

Bundle was forced to admit that there was something in this argument. But she had the true spirit of one undertaking adventures.

"Nonsense," she said with determination. "There has *got* to be a place."

"But there ain't one," wailed Alfred.

Never had a room shown itself more unpropitious for concealment. Dingy blinds were drawn down over the dirty window panes, and there were no curtains. The window sill outside, which Bundle examined, was about four inches wide! Inside the room there were the table, the chairs and the cupboards.

The second cupboard had a key in the lock. Bundle went across and pulled it open. Inside were shelves covered with an odd assortment of glasses and crockery.

"Surplus stuff as we don't use," explained Alfred. "You can see for yourself, my lady, there's no place here as a cat could hide."

But Bundle was examining the shelves.

"Flimsy work," she said. "Now then, Alfred, have you got a cupboard downstairs where you could shove all this glass? You have? Good. Then get a tray and start to carry it down at once. Hurry—there's no time to lose."

"You can't, my lady. And it's getting late, too. The cooks will be here any minute now."

"Mr. Mosgo-what-not doesn't come till later, I suppose?"

"He's never here much before midnight. But, oh, my lady—"

"Don't talk so much, Alfred," said Bundle. "Get that tray. If you stay here arguing, you *will* get into trouble."

Doing what is familiarly known as "wringing his hands," Alfred departed. Presently he returned with a tray, and having by now realized that his protests were useless, he worked with a nervous energy quite surprising.

As Bundle had seen, the shelves were easily detachable. She took them down, ranged them upright against the wall, and then stepped in.

"H'm," she remarked. "Pretty narrow. It's going to be a tight fit. Shut the door on me carefully, Alfred—that's right. Yes, it can be done. Now I want a gimlet."

"A gimlet, my lady?"

"That's what I said."

"I don't know—"

"Nonsense, you must have a gimlet—perhaps you've got an auger as well. If you haven't got what I want, you'll have to go out and buy it, so you'd better try hard to find the right thing."

Alfred departed and returned presently with quite a creditable assortment of tools. Bundle seized what she wanted and proceeded swiftly and efficiently to bore a small hole at the level of her right eye. She did this from the outside so that it should be less noticeable, and she dared not make it too large lest it should attract attention.

"There, that'll do," she remarked at last.

"Oh! but, my lady, my lady—"

"Yes?"

"But they'll find you—if they should open the door."

"They won't open the door," said Bundle, "because you are going to lock it and take the key away."

"And if by chance Mr. Mosgorovsky should ask for the key?"

"Tell him it's lost," said Bundle briskly. "But nobody's going to worry about this cupboard—it's only here to attract attention from the other one and make a pair. Go on, Alfred, someone might come at any time. Lock me in and take the key and come and let me out when everyone's gone."

"You'll be taken bad, my lady. You'll faint—"

"I never faint," said Bundle. "But you might as well get me a cocktail. I shall certainly need it. Then lock the door of the room again—don't forget—and take all the door keys back to their proper doors. And, Alfred—don't be too much of a rabbit. Remember, if anything goes wrong, I'll see you through."

"And that's that," said Bundle to herself when, having served the cocktail, Alfred had finally departed.

She was not nervous lest Alfred's nerve should fail and he should give her away. She knew that his sense of self-preservation was far too strong for that. His training alone helped him to conceal private emotions beneath the mask of the well trained servant.

Only one thing worried Bundle. The interpretation she had chosen to put upon the cleaning of the room that morning might be all wrong. And if so—Bundle sighed in the narrow confines of the cupboard. The prospect of spending long hours in it for nothing was not attractive.

14

The Meeting of the Seven Dials

It would be as well to pass over the sufferings of the next four hours as quickly as possible. Bundle found her position extremely cramped. She had judged that the meeting, if meeting there was to be, would take place at a time when the club was in full swing—somewhere probably between the hours of midnight and 2 A.M.

She was just deciding that it must be at least six o'clock in the morning when a welcome sound came to her ears, the sound of the unlocking of a door.

In another minute the electric light was switched on. The hum of voices, which had come to her for a minute or two rather like the far-off roar of sea waves, ceased as suddenly as it had begun, and Bundle heard the sound of a bolt being shot. Clearly someone had come in from the gaming room next door, and she paid tribute to the thoroughness with which the communicating door had been rendered sound proof.

In another minute the intruder came into her line of vision—a line of vision that was necessarily somewhat incomplete but which yet answered its purpose. A tall man, broad shouldered and powerful looking, with a long black beard. Bundle remembered having seen him sitting at one of the baccarat tables on the preceding night.

This, then, was Alfred's mysterious Russian gentleman, the proprietor of the club, the sinister Mr. Mosgorovsky. Bundle's heart beat faster with excitement. So little did she resemble her father that at this minute she fairly gloried in the extreme discomfort of her position.

The Russian remained for some minutes standing by the table, stroking his beard. Then he drew a watch from his pocket and glanced at the time. Nodding his head as though satisfied, he again thrust his hand into his pocket, and, pulling out something that Bundle could not see, he moved out of her line of vision.

When he reappeared again, she could hardly help giving a gasp of surprise.

His face was now covered by a mask—but hardly a mask in the conventional sense. It was not shaped to the face. It was a mere piece of material hanging in front of the features like a curtain in which two slits were pierced for the eyes. In shape it was round and on it was the representation of a clock face, with the hands pointing to six o'clock.

"The Seven Dials!" said Bundle to herself.

And at that minute there came a new sound—seven muffled taps.

Mosgorovsky strode across to where Bundle knew was the other cupboard door. She heard a sharp click, and then the sound of greetings in a foreign tongue.

Presently she had a view of the newcomers.

They also wore clock masks, but in their case the hands were in a different position—four o'clock and five o'clock respectively. Both men were in evening dress—but with a difference. One was an elegant, slender young man wearing evening clothes of exquisite cut. The grace with which he moved was foreign rather than English. The other man could be better described as wiry and lean. His clothes fitted him sufficiently well, but no more, and Bundle guessed at his nationality even before she heard his voice.

"I reckon we're the first to arrive at this little meeting."

A full pleasant voice with a slight American drawl, and an inflection of Irish behind it.

The elegant young man said in good, but slightly stilted, English:

"I had much difficulty in getting away to-night. These things do not always arrange themselves fortunately. I am not, like No. 4 here, my own master."

Bundle tried to guess at his nationality. Until he spoke, she had thought he might be French, but the accent was not a French one. He might possibly, she thought, be an Australian, or a Hungarian, or even a Russian.

The American moved to the other side of the table, and Bundle heard a chair being pulled out.

"One o'clock's being a great success," he said. "I congratulate you on taking the risk."

Five o'clock shrugged his shoulders.

"Unless one takes risks—" He left the sentence unfinished.

Again seven taps sounded, and Mosgorovsky moved across to the secret door.

She failed to catch anything definite for some moments since the whole company were out of sight, but presently she heard the bearded Russian's voice upraised.

"Shall we begin proceedings?"

He himself came round the table and took the seat next to the armchair at the top. Sitting thus, he was directly facing Bundle's cupboard. The elegant five o'clock took the place next to him. The third chair that side was out of Bundle's sight, but the American, No. 4, moved into her line of vision for a moment or two before he sat down.

On the near side of the table also, only two chairs were visible, and as she watched a hand turned the second—really the middle chair—down. And then with a swift movement, one of the newcomers brushed past the cupboard and took the chair opposite Mosgorovsky. Whoever sat there had, of course, their back directly turned to Bundle—and it was at that back that Bundle was staring with a good deal of interest, for it was the back of a singularly beautiful woman very much *décolleté*.

It was she who spoke first. Her voice was musical, foreign—with a deep seductive note in it. She was glancing towards the empty chair at the head of the table.

"So we are not to see No. 7 to-night?" she said. "Tell me, my friends, shall we ever see him?"

"That's darned good," said the American. "Darned good! As for seven o'clock—*I'm* beginning to believe there is no such person."

"I should not advise you to think that, my friend," said the Russian pleasantly.

There was a silence—rather an uncomfortable silence, Bundle felt.

She was still staring as though fascinated at the beautiful back in front of her. There was a tiny black mole just below the right shoulder blade that enhanced the whiteness of the skin. Bundle felt that at last the term "beautiful adventuress," so often read, had a real meaning for her. She was quite certain that this woman had a beautiful face—a dark Slavonic face with passionate eyes.

She was recalled from her imaginings by the voice of the Russian, who seemed to act as master of ceremonies.

"Shall we get on with our business? First to our absent comrade! No. 2!"

He made a curious gesture with his hand towards the turned down chair next to the woman, which every one present imitated, turning to the chair as they did so.

"I wish No. 2 were with us to-night," he continued. "There are many things to be done. Unsuspected difficulties have arisen."

"Have you had his report?" It was the American who spoke.

"As yet—I have nothing from him." There was a pause. "I cannot understand it."

"You think it may have—gone astray?"

"That is—a possibility."

"In other words," said five o'clock softly, "there is—danger."

He spoke the word delicately—and yet with relish.

The Russian nodded emphatically.

"Yes—there's danger. Too much is getting known about us—about this place. I know of several people who suspect." He added coldly: "They must be silenced."

Bundle felt a little cold shiver pass down her spine. If she were to be found, would she be silenced? She was recalled suddenly to attention by a word.

"So nothing has come to light about Chimneys?"

Mosgorovsky shook his head.

"Nothing."

Suddenly No. 5 leant forward.

"I agree with Anna; where is our president—No. 7? He who called us into being. Why do we never see him?"

"No. 7," said the Russian, "has his own ways of working."

"So you always say."

"I will say more," said Mosgorovsky. "I pity the man—or woman—who comes up against him."

There was an awkward silence.

"We must get on with our business," said Mosgorovsky quietly. "No. 3, you have the plans of Wyvern Abbey?"

Bundle strained her ears. So far she had neither caught a glimpse of No. 3, nor had she heard his voice. She heard it now and recognized it as unmistakable. Low, pleasant, indistinct—the voice of a well-bred Englishman.

"I've got them here, sir."

Some papers were shoved across the table. Everyone bent forward. Presently Mosgorovsky raised his head again.

"And the list of guests?"

"Here."

The Russian read them.

"Sir Stanley Digby. Mr. Terence O'Rourke. Sir Oswald and Lady Coote. Mr. Bateman. Countess Anna Radzky. Mrs. Macatta. Mr. James Thesiger—" he paused and then asked sharply:

"Who is Mr. James Thesiger?"

The American laughed.

"I guess you needn't worry any about him. The usual complete young ass."

The Russian continued reading.

"Herr Eberhard and Mr. Eversleigh. That completes the list."

"Does it?" said Bundle silently. "What about that sweet girl, Lady Eileen Brent?"

"Yes, there seems nothing to worry about there," said Mosgorovsky. He looked across the table. "I suppose there's no doubt whatever about the value of Eberhard's invention?"

Three o'clock made a laconic British reply.

"None whatever."

"Commercially it should be worth millions," said the Russian. "And internationally—well, one knows only too well the greed of nations."

Bundle had an idea that behind his mask he was smiling unpleasantly.

"Yes," he went on, "a gold mine."

"Well worth a few lives," said No. 5, cynically, and laughed.

"But you know what inventions are," said the American. "Sometimes these darned things won't work."

"A man like Sir Oswald Coote will have made no mistake," said Mosgorovsky.

"Speaking as an aviator myself," said No. 5, "the thing is perfectly feasible. It has been discussed for years—but it needed the genius of Eberhard to bring it to fruition."

"Well," said Mosgorovsky, "I don't think we need discuss matters any further. You have all seen the plans. I do not think our original scheme can be bettered. By the way, I hear something about a letter of Gerald Wade's that has been found—a letter that mentions this organization. Who found it?"

"Lord Caterham's daughter—Lady Eileen Brent."

"Bauer should have been on to that," said Mosgorovsky. "It was careless of him. Who was the letter written to?"

"His sister, I believe," said No. 3.

"Unfortunate," said Mosgorovsky. "But it cannot be helped. The inquest on Ronald Devereux is to-morrow. I suppose that has been arranged for?"

"Reports as to local lads having been practising with rifles have been spread everywhere," said the American.

"That should be all right then. I think there is nothing further to be said. I think we must all congratulate our dear one o'clock and wish her luck in the part she has to play."

"Hurrah!" cried No. 5. "To Anna!"

All hands flew out in the same gesture which Bundle had noticed before.

"To Anna!"

One o'clock acknowledged the salutation with a typically foreign gesture. Then she rose to her feet and the others followed suit. For the first time, Bundle caught a glimpse of No. 3 as he came to put Anna's cloak round her—a tall, heavily built man.

Then the party filed out through the secret door. Mosgorovsky secured it after them. He waited a few moments and then Bundle heard him unbolt the other door and pass through, after extinguishing the electric light.

It was not until two hours later that a white and anxious Alfred came to release Bundle. She almost fell into his arms and he had to hold her up.

"Nothing," said Bundle. "Just stiff, that's all. Here, let me sit down."

"Oh, Gord, my lady, it's been awful."

"Nonsense," said Bundle. "It all went off splendidly. Don't get the wind up now it's all over. It might have gone wrong, but thank goodness it didn't."

"Thank goodness, as you say, my lady. I've been in a twitter all the evening. They're a funny crowd, you know."

"A damned funny crowd," said Bundle, vigorously massaging her arms and legs. "As a matter of fact, they're the sort of crowd I always imagined until tonight only existed in books. In this life, Alfred, one never stops learning."

15

The Inquest

Bundle reached home about 6 A.M. She was up and dressed by half-past nine, and rang up Jimmy Thesiger on the telephone.

The promptitude of his reply somewhat surprised her, till he explained that he was going down to attend the inquest.

"So am I," said Bundle. "And I've got a lot to tell you."

"Well, suppose you let me drive you down and we can talk on the way. How about that?"

"All right. But allow a bit extra because you'll have to take me to Chimneys. The Chief Constable's picking me up there."

"Why?"

"Because he's a kind man," said Bundle.

"So am I," said Jimmy. "Very kind."

"Oh! you—you're an ass," said Bundle. "I heard somebody say so last night."

"Who?"

"To be strictly accurate—a Russian Jew. No, it wasn't. It was—"

But an indignant protest drowned her words.

"I may be an ass," said Jimmy. "I daresay I am—but I won't have Russian Jews saying so. What were you doing last night, Bundle?"

"That's what I'm going to talk about," said Bundle. "Good-bye for the moment."

She rang off in a tantalizing manner which left Jimmy pleasantly puzzled. He had the highest respect for Bundle's capabilities, though there was not the slightest trace of sentiment in his feelings towards her.

"She's been up to something," he opined, as he took a last hasty drink of coffee. "Depend upon it, she's been up to something."

Twenty minutes later, his little two-seater drew up before the Brook Street house and Bundle, who had been waiting, came tripping down the steps. Jimmy was not ordinarily an observant young man, but he noticed that there were black rings around Bundle's eyes and that she had all the appearance of having had a late night the night before.

"Now then," he said, as the car began to nose her way through the suburbs, "what dark deeds have you been up to?"

"I'll tell you," said Bundle. "But don't interrupt until I've finished."

It was a somewhat long story, and Jimmy had all he could do to keep sufficient attention on the car to prevent an accident. When Bundle had finished he sighed—then looked at her searchingly.

"Bundle?"

"Yes?"

"Look here, you're not pulling my leg?"

"What do you mean?"

"I'm sorry," apologized Jimmy, "but it seems to me as though I'd heard it all before—in a dream, you know."

"I know," said Bundle sympathetically.

"It's impossible," said Jimmy, following out his own train of thought. "The beautiful foreign adventuress, the international gang, the mysterious No. 7, whose identity nobody knows—I've read it all a hundred times in books."

"Of course you have. So have I. But it's no reason why it shouldn't really happen."

"I suppose not," admitted Jimmy.

"After all—I suppose fiction is founded on the truth. I mean unless things did happen, people couldn't think of them."

"There is something in what you say," agreed Jimmy. "But all the same I can't help pinching myself to see if I'm awake."

"That's how I felt."

Jimmy gave a deep sigh.

"Well, I suppose we are awake. Let me see, a Russian, an American, an Englishman—a possible Austrian or Hungarian—and the lady who may be any nationality—for choice Russian or Polish—that's a pretty representative gathering."

"And a German," said Bundle. "You've forgotten the German."

"Oh!" said Jimmy slowly. "You think—"

"The absent No. 2 is Bauer—our footman. That seems to me quite clear from what they said about expecting a report which hadn't come in—though what there can be to report about Chimneys, I can't think."

"It must be something to do with Gerry Wade's death," said Jimmy. "There's something there we haven't fathomed yet. You say they actually mentioned Bauer by name?"

Bundle nodded.

"They blamed him for not having found that letter."

"Well, I don't see what you could have clearer than that. There's no going against it. You'll have to forgive my first incredulity, Bundle—but you know, it was rather a tall story. You say they knew about my going down to Wyvern Abbey next week?"

"Yes, that's when the American—it was him, not the Russian—said they needn't worry—you were only the usual kind of ass."

"Ah!" said Jimmy. He pressed his foot down on the accelerator viciously and the car shot forward. "I'm very glad you told me that. It gives me what you might call a personal interest in the case."

He was silent for a minute or two and then he said:

"Did you say that German inventor's name was Eberhard?"

"Yes. Why?"

"Wait a minute. Something's coming back to me. Eberhard, Eberhard—yes, I'm sure that was the name."

"Tell me."

"Eberhard was a Johnny who'd got some patent process he applied to steel. I can't put the thing properly because I haven't got the scientific knowledge—but I know the result was that it became so toughened that a wire was as strong as a steel bar had previously been. Eberhard had to do with aeroplanes and his idea was that the weight would be so enormously reduced that flying would be practically revolutionized—the cost of it, I mean. I believe he offered his invention to the German Government, and they turned it down, pointed out some undeniable flaw in it—but they did it rather nastily. He set to work and circumvented the difficulty, whatever it was, but he'd been offended by their attitude and swore they shouldn't have his ewe lamb. I always thought the whole thing was probably bunkum, but now—it looks differently."

"That's it," said Bundle eagerly. "You must be right, Jimmy. Eberhard must have offered his invention to our Government. They've been taking, or are going to take, Sir Oswald Coote's expert opinion on it. There's going to be an unofficial conference at the Abbey. Sir Oswald, George, the Air Minister and Eberhard. Eberhard will have the plans or the process or whatever you call it—"

"Formula," suggested Jimmy. "I think 'formula' is a good word myself."

"He'll have the formula with him, and the Seven Dials are out to steal the formula. I remember the Russian saying it was worth millions."

"I suppose it would be," said Jimmy.

"And well worth a few lives—that's what the other man said."

"Well, it seems to have been," said Jimmy, his face clouding over. "Look at this damned inquest to-day. Bundle, are you sure Ronny said nothing else?"

"No," said Bundle. "Just that. *Seven Dials. Tell Jimmy Thesiger*. That's all he could get out, poor lad."

"I wish we knew what he knew," said Jimmy. "But we've found out one thing. I take it that the footman, Bauer, must almost certainly have been responsible for Gerry's death. You know, Bundle—"

"Yes?"

"Well, I'm a bit worried sometimes. Who's going to be the next one! It really isn't the sort of business for a girl to be mixed up in."

Bundle smiled in spite of herself. It occurred to her that it had taken Jimmy a long time to put her in the same category as Loraine Wade.

"It's far more likely to be you than me," she remarked cheerfully.

"Hear, hear," said Jimmy. "But what about a few casualties on the other side for a change? I'm feeling rather bloodthirsty this morning. Tell me, Bundle, would you recognize any of these people if you saw them?"

Bundle hesitated.

"I think I should recognize No. 5," she said at last. "He's got a queer way of speaking—a kind of venomous, lisping way—that I think I'd know again."

"What about the Englishman?"

Bundle shook her head.

"I saw him least—only a glimpse—and he's got a very ordinary voice. Except that he's a big man, there's nothing much to go by."

"There's the woman, of course," continued Jimmy. "She ought to be easier. But then, you're not likely to run across her. She's probably putting in the dirty work being taken out to dinner by amorous Cabinet Ministers and getting State secrets out of them when they've had a couple. At least, that's how it's done in books. As a matter of fact, the only Cabinet Minister I know drinks hot water with a dash of lemon in it."

"Take George Lomax, for instance, can you imagine him being amorous with beautiful foreign women?" said Bundle with a laugh.

Jimmy agreed with her criticism.

"And now about the man of mystery—No. 7," went on Jimmy. "You've no idea who he could be?"

"None whatever."

"Again—by book standard, that is—he ought to be someone we all know. What about George Lomax himself?"

Bundle reluctantly shook her head.

"In a book, it would be perfect," she agreed. "But knowing Codders—" And she gave herself up to a sudden uncontrollable mirth. "Codders, the great criminal organizer," she gasped. "Wouldn't it be marvellous?"

Jimmy agreed that it would. Their discussion had taken some time and his driving had slowed down involuntarily once or twice. They arrived at Chimneys, to find Colonel Melrose already there waiting. Jimmy was introduced to him and they all three proceeded to the inquest together.

As Colonel Melrose had predicted, the whole affair was very simple.

Bundle gave her evidence. The doctor gave his. Evidence was given of rifle practice in the neighbourhood. A verdict of death by misadventure was brought in.

After the proceedings were over, Colonel Melrose volunteered to drive Bundle back to Chimneys, and Jimmy Thesiger returned to London. For all his light-hearted manner, Bundle's story had impressed him profoundly. He set his lips closely together.

"Ronny, old boy," he murmured, "I'm going to be up against it. And you're not here to join in the game."

Another thought flashed into his mind. Loraine! Was she in danger?

After a minute or two's hesitation, he went over to the telephone and rang her up.

"It's me—Jimmy. I thought you'd like to know the result of the inquest. Death by misadventure."

"Oh, but—"

"Yes, but I think there's something behind that. The coroner had had a hint. Someone's at work to hush it up. I say, Loraine—"

"Yes?"

"Look here. There's—there's some funny business going about. You'll be very careful, won't you? For my sake."

He heard the quick note of alarm that sprang into her voice.

"Jimmy—but then it's dangerous—for *you*."

He laughed.

"Oh, *that's* all right. I'm the cat that had nine lives. Bye-bye, old thing."

He rang off and remained a minute or two lost in thought. Then he summoned Stevens.

"Do you think you could go out and buy me a pistol, Stevens?"

"A pistol, sir?"

True to his training, Stevens betrayed no hint of surprise.

"What kind of a pistol would you be requiring?"

"The kind where you put your finger on the trigger and the thing goes on shooting until you take it off again."

"An automatic, sir."

"That's it," said Jimmy. "An automatic. And I should like it to be a blue-nosed one—if you and the shopman know what that is. In American stories, the hero always takes his blue-nosed automatic from his hip pocket."

Stevens permitted himself a faint, discreet smile.

"Most American gentlemen that I have known, sir, carry something very different in their hip pockets," he observed.

Jimmy Thesiger laughed.

16

The House Party at the Abbey

Bundle drove over to Wyvern Abbey just in time for tea on Friday afternoon. George Lomax came forward to welcome her with considerable *empressement*.

"My dear Eileen," he said, "I can't tell you how pleased I am to see you here. You must forgive my not having invited you when I asked your father, but to tell the truth I never dreamed that a party of this kind would appeal to you. I was both—er—surprised and—er—delighted when Lady Caterham told me of your—er—interest in—er—politics."

"I wanted to come so much," said Bundle in a simple, ingenuous manner.

"Mrs. Macatta will not arrive till the later train," explained George. "She was speaking at a meeting in Manchester last night. Do you know Thesiger? Quite a young fellow, but a remarkable grasp of foreign politics. One would hardly suspect it from his appearance."

"I know Mr. Thesiger," said Bundle, and she shook hands solemnly with Jimmy, whom she observed had parted his hair in the middle in the endeavour to add earnestness to his expression.

"Look here," said Jimmy in a low hurried voice, as George temporarily withdrew. "You mustn't be angry, but I've told Bill about our little stunt."

"Bill?" said Bundle, annoyed.

"Well, after all," said Jimmy, "Bill is one of the lads, you know. Ronny was a pal of his and so was Gerry."

"Oh! I know," said Bundle.

"But you think it's a pity? Sorry."

"Bill's all right, of course. It isn't that," said Bundle. "But he's—well, Bill's a born blunderer."

"Not mentally very agile?" suggested Jimmy. "But you forget one thing—Bill's got a very hefty fist. And I've an idea that a hefty fist is going to come in handy."

"Well, perhaps you're right. How did he take it?"

"Well, he clutched his head a good bit, but—I mean the facts took some driving home. But by repeating the thing patiently in words of one syllable I at last got it into his thick head. And, naturally, he's with us to the death, as you might say."

George reappeared suddenly.

"I must make some introductions, Eileen. This is Sir Stanley Digby—Lady Eileen Brent. Mr. O'Rourke." The Air Minister was a little round man with a cheerful smile. Mr. O'Rourke, a tall young man with laughing blue eyes and a typical Irish face, greeted Bundle with enthusiasm.

"And I thinking it was going to be a dull political party entirely," he murmured in an adroit whisper.

"Hush," said Bundle. "I'm political—very political."

"Sir Oswald and Lady Coote you know," continued George.

"We've never actually met," said Bundle, smiling.

She was mentally applauding her father's descriptive powers.

Sir Oswald took her hand in an iron grip and she winced slightly.

Lady Coote, after a somewhat mournful greeting, had turned to Jimmy Thesiger, and appeared to be registering something closely akin to pleasure. Despite his reprehensible habit of being late for breakfast, Lady Coote had a fondness for this amiable, pink-faced young man. His air of irrepressible good nature fascinated her. She had a motherly wish to cure him of his bad habits and form him into one of the world's workers. Whether, once formed, he would be as attractive was a question she had never asked herself. She began now to tell him of a very painful motor accident which had happened to one of her friends.

"Mr. Bateman," said George briefly, as one who would pass on to better things.

A serious, pale-faced young man bowed.

"And now," continued George, "I must introduce you to Countess Radzky."

Countess Radzky had been conversing with Mr. Bateman. Leaning very far back on a sofa, with her legs crossed in a daring manner, she was smoking a cigarette in an incredibly long turquoise studded holder.

Bundle thought she was one of the most beautiful women she had ever seen. Her eyes were very large and blue, her hair was coal black, she had a matte skin, the slightly flattened nose of the Slav, and a sinuous, slender body. Her lips were reddened to a degree with which Bundle was sure Wyvern Abbey was totally unacquainted.

She said eagerly: "This is Mrs. Macatta—yes?"

On George's replying in the negative and introducing Bundle, the Countess gave her a careless nod, and at once resumed her conversation with the serious Mr. Bateman.

Bundle heard Jimmy's voice in her ear:

"Pongo is absolutely fascinated by the lovely Slav," he said. "Pathetic, isn't it? Come and have some tea."

They drifted once more into the neighbourhood of Sir Oswald Coote.

"That's a fine place of yours, Chimneys," remarked the great man.

"I'm glad you liked it," said Bundle meekly.

"Wants new plumbing," said Sir Oswald. "Bring it up to date, you know."

He ruminated for a minute or two.

"I'm taking the Duke of Alton's place. Three years. Just while I'm looking round for a place of my own. Your father couldn't sell if he wanted to, I suppose."

Bundle felt her breath taken away. She had a nightmare vision of England with innumerable Cootes in innumerable counterparts of Chimneys—all, be it understood, with an entirely new system of plumbing installed.

She felt a sudden violent resentment which, she told herself, was absurd. After all, contrasting Lord Caterham with Sir Oswald Coote, there was no doubt as to who would go to the wall. Sir Oswald had one of those powerful personalities which make all those with whom they come in contact appear faded. He was, as Lord Caterham had said, a human steam-roller. And yet, undoubtedly, in many ways, Sir Oswald was a stupid man. Apart from his special line of knowledge and his terrific driving force, he was probably intensely ignorant. A hundred delicate appreciations of life which Lord Caterham could and did enjoy were a sealed book to Sir Oswald.

Whilst indulging in these reflections Bundle continued to chat pleasantly. Herr Eberhard, she heard, had arrived, but was lying down with a nervous headache. This was told her by Mr. O'Rourke, who managed to find a place by her side and keep it.

Altogether, Bundle went up to dress in a pleasant mood of expectation, with a slight nervous dread hovering in the background whenever she thought of the imminent arrival of Mrs. Macatta. Bundle felt that dalliance with Mrs. Macatta was going to prove no primrose path.

Her first shock was when she came down, demurely attired in a black lace frock, and passed along the hall. A footman was standing there—at least a man dressed as a footman. But that square, burly figure lent itself badly to the deception. Bundle stopped and stared.

"Superintendent Battle," she breathed.

"That's right, Lady Eileen."

"Oh!" said Bundle uncertainly. "Are you here to—to—"

"Keep an eye on things."

"I see."

"That warning letter, you know," said the Superintendent, "fairly put the wind up Mr. Lomax. Nothing would do for him but that I should come down myself."

"But don't you think—" began Bundle, and stopped. She hardly liked to suggest to the Superintendent that his disguise was not a particularly efficient one. He seemed to have "police officer" written all over him, and Bundle could hardly imagine the most unsuspecting criminal failing to be put on his guard.

"You think," said the Superintendent stolidly, "that I might be recognized?"

He gave the final word a distinct capital letter.

"I did think so—yes—" admitted Bundle.

Something that might conceivably have been intended for a smile crossed the woodenness of Superintendent Battle's features.

"Put them on their guard, eh? Well, Lady Eileen, why not?"

"Why not?" echoed Bundle, rather stupidly, she felt.

Superintendent Battle was nodding his head slowly.

"We don't want any unpleasantness, do we?" he said. "Don't want to be too clever—just show any light-fingered gentry that may be about—well, just show them that there's somebody on the spot, so to speak."

Bundle gazed at him in some admiration. She could imagine that the sudden appearance of so renowned a personage as Superintendent Battle might have a depressing effect on any scheme and the hatchers of it.

"It's a great mistake to be too clever," Superintendent Battle was repeating. "The great thing is not to have any unpleasantness this weekend."

Bundle passed on, wondering how many of her fellow guests had recognized or would recognize the Scotland Yard detective. In the drawing-room George was standing with a puckered brow and an orange envelope in his hand.

"Most vexatious," he said. "A telegram from Mrs. Macatta to say she will be unable to be with us. Her children are suffering from mumps."

Bundle's heart gave a throb of relief.

"I especially feel this on your account, Eileen," said George kindly. "I know how anxious you were to meet her. The Countess too will be sadly disappointed."

"Oh, never mind," said Bundle. "I should hate it if she'd come and given me mumps."

"A very distressing complaint," agreed George. "But I do not think that infection could be carried that way. Indeed, I am sure that Mrs. Macatta would have run no risk of that kind. She is a most highly principled woman, with a very real sense of her responsibilities to the community. In these days of national stress, we must all take into account—"

On the brink of embarking on a speech, George pulled himself up short.

"But it must be for another time," he said. "Fortunately there is no hurry in your case. But the Countess, alas, is only a visitor to our shores."

"She's a Hungarian, isn't she?" said Bundle, who was curious about the Countess.

"Yes. You have heard, no doubt, of the Young Hungarian party? The Countess is a leader in that party. A woman of great wealth, left a widow at an early age, she has devoted her money and her talents to the public service. She has especially devoted herself to the problem of infant mortality—a terrible one under present conditions in Hungary. I—Ah! here is Herr Eberhard."

The German inventor was younger than Bundle had imagined him. He was probably not more than thirty-three or four. He was boorish and ill at ease, and yet his personality was not an unpleasing one. His blue eyes were more shy than furtive, and his more unpleasant mannerisms, such as the one that Bill had described of gnawing his finger nails, arose, she thought, more from nervousness than from any other cause. He was thin and weedy in appearance and looked anaemic and delicate.

He conversed rather awkwardly with Bundle in stilted English and they both welcomed the interruption of the joyous Mr. O'Rourke. Presently Bill bustled in—there is no other word for it. In the same such way does a favoured Newfoundland make his entrance, and at once came over to Bundle. He was looking perplexed and harassed.

"Hullo, Bundle. Heard you'd got here. Been kept with my nose to the grindstone all the blessed afternoon or I'd have seen you before."

"Cares of State heavy to-night?" suggested O'Rourke sympathetically.

Bill groaned.

"I don't know what your fellow's like," he complained. "Looks a good-natured, tubby little chap. But Codders is absolutely impossible. Drive, drive, drive, from morning to night. Everything you do is wrong, and everything you haven't done you ought to have done."

"Quite like a quotation from the prayer book," remarked Jimmy, who had just strolled up.

Bill glanced at them reproachfully.

"Nobody knows," he said pathetically, "what I have to put up with."

"Entertaining the Countess, eh?" suggested Jimmy. "Poor Bill, that must have been a sad strain—to a woman hater like yourself."

"What's this?" asked Bundle.

"After tea," said Jimmy with a grin, "the Countess asked Bill to show her round the interesting old place."

"Well, I couldn't refuse, could I?" said Bill, his countenance assuming a brick-red tint.

Bundle felt faintly uneasy. She knew, only too well, the susceptibility of Mr. William Eversleigh to female charms. In the hands of a woman like the Countess, Bill would be as wax. She wondered once more whether Jimmy Thesiger had been wise to take Bill into their confidence.

"The Countess," said Bill, "is a very charming woman. And no end intelligent. You should have seen her going round the house. All sorts of questions she asked."

"What kind of questions?" asked Bundle suddenly.

Bill was vague.

"Oh! I don't know. About the history of it. And old furniture. And—oh! all sorts of things."

At that moment the Countess swept into the room. She seemed a shade breathless. She was looking magnificent in a close-fitting black velvet gown. Bundle noticed how Bill gravitated at once into her immediate neighbourhood. The serious, spectacled young man joined him.

"Bill and Pongo have both got it badly," observed Jimmy Thesiger with a laugh.

Bundle was by no means so sure that it was a laughing matter.

17

After Dinner

George was not a believer in modern innovations. The Abbey was innocent of anything so up to date as central heating. Consequently, when the ladies entered the drawing-room after dinner, the temperature of the room was woefully inadequate to the needs of modern evening clothes. The fire that burnt in the well burnished steel grate became as a magnet. The three women huddled round it.

"Brrrrrrrrrrr!" said the Countess, a fine, exotic, foreign sound.

"The days are drawing in," said Lady Coote, and drew a flowered atrocity of a scarf closer about her ample shoulders.

"Why on earth doesn't George have the house properly heated?" said Bundle.

"You English, you never heat your houses," said the Countess.

She took out her long cigarette holder and began to smoke.

"That grate is old-fashioned," said Lady Coote. "The heat goes up the chimney instead of into the room."

"Oh!" said the Countess.

There was a pause. The Countess was so plainly bored by her company that conversation became difficult.

"It's funny," said Lady Coote, breaking the silence, "that Mrs. Macatta's children should have mumps. At least, I don't mean exactly funny—"

"What," said the Countess, "are mumps?"

Bundle and Lady Coote started simultaneously to explain. Finally, between them, they managed it.

"I suppose Hungarian children have it?" asked Lady Coote.

"Eh?" said the Countess.

"Hungarian children. They suffer from it?"

"I do not know," said the Countess. "How should I?"

Lady Coote looked at her in some surprise.

"But I understood that you worked—"

"Oh, that!" The Countess uncrossed her legs, took her cigarette holder from her mouth and began to talk rapidly.

"I will tell you some horrors," she said. "Horrors that I have seen. Incredible! You would not believe!"

And she was as good as her word. She talked fluently and with a graphic power of description. Incredible scenes of starvation and misery were painted by her for the benefit of her audience. She spoke of Buda Pesth shortly after the war and traced its vicissitudes to the present day. She was dramatic, but she was also, to Bundle's mind, a little like a gramophone record. You turned her on, and there you were. Presently, just as suddenly, she would stop.

Lady Coote was thrilled to the marrow—that much was clear. She sat with her mouth slightly open and her large, sad, dark eyes fixed on the Countess. Occasionally, she interpolated a comment of her own.

"One of my cousins had three children burned to death. Awful, wasn't it?"

The Countess paid no attention. She went on and on. And she finally stopped as suddenly as she had begun.

"There!" she said. "I have told you! We have money—but no organization. It is organization we need."

Lady Coote sighed.

"I've heard my husband say that nothing can be done without regular methods. He attributes his own success entirely to that. He declares he would have never got on without them."

She sighed again. A sudden fleeting vision passed before her eyes of a Sir Oswald who had not got on in the world. A Sir Oswald who retained, in all essentials, the attributes of that cheery young man in the bicycle shop. Just for a second it occurred to her how much pleasanter life might have been for her if Sir Oswald had *not* had regular methods.

By a quite understandable association of ideas she turned to Bundle.

"Tell me, Lady Eileen," she said, "do you like that head gardener of yours?"

"MacDonald? Well—" Bundle hesitated. "One couldn't exactly *like* MacDonald," she explained apologetically. "But he's a first class gardener."

"Oh! I know he is," said Lady Coote.

"He's all right if he's kept in his place," said Bundle.

"I suppose so," said Lady Coote.

She looked enviously at Bundle, who appeared to approach the task of keeping MacDonald in his place so light heartedly.

"I'd just adore a high-toned garden," said the Countess dreamily.

Bundle stared, but at that moment a diversion occurred. Jimmy Thesiger entered the room and spoke directly to her in a strange, hurried voice.

"I say, will you come and see those etchings now? They're waiting for you."

Bundle left the room hurriedly, Jimmy close behind her.

"What etchings?" she asked, as the drawing-room door closed behind her.

"No etchings," said Jimmy. "I'd got to say something to get hold of you. Come on, Bill is waiting for us in the library. There's nobody there."

Bill was striding up and down the library, clearly in a very perturbed state of mind.

"Look here," he burst out, "I don't like this."

"Don't like what?"

"You being mixed up in this. Ten to one there's going to be a rough house and then—"

He looked at her with a kind of pathetic dismay that gave Bundle a warm and comfortable feeling.

"She ought to be kept out of it, oughtn't she, Jimmy?"

He appealed to the other.

"I've told her so," said Jimmy.

"Dash it all, Bundle, I mean—someone might get hurt."

Bundle turned round to Jimmy.

"How much have you told him?"

"Oh! everything."

"I haven't got the hang of it all yet," confessed Bill. "You in that place in Seven Dials and all that." He looked at her unhappily. "I say, Bundle, I wish you wouldn't."

"Wouldn't what?"

"Get mixed up in these sorts of things."

"Why not?" said Bundle. "They're exciting."

"Oh, yes—exciting. But they may be damnably dangerous. Look at poor old Ronny."

"Yes," said Bundle. "If it hadn't been for your friend Ronny, I don't suppose I should ever have got what you call 'mixed up' in this thing. But I am. And it's no earthly use your bleating about it."

"I know you're the most frightful sport, Bundle, but—"

"Cut out the compliments. Let's make plans."

To her relief, Bill reacted favourably to the suggestion.

"You're right about the formula," he said. "Eberhard's got some sort of formula with him, or rather Sir Oswald has. The stuff has been tested out at his works—very secretly and all that. Eberhard has been down there with him. They're all in the study now—what you might call coming down to brass tacks."

"How long is Sir Stanley Digby staying?" asked Jimmy.

"Going back to town to-morrow."

"H'm," said Jimmy. "Then one thing's quite clear. If, as I suppose, Sir Stanley will be taking the formula with him, any funny business there's going to be will be tonight."

"I suppose it will."

"Not a doubt of it. That narrows the thing down very comfortably. But the bright lads will have to be their very brightest. We must come down to details. First of all, where will the sacred formula be to-night? Will Eberhard have it, or Sir Oswald Coote?"

"Neither. I understand it's to be handed over to the Air Minister this evening, for him to take to town to-morrow. In that case O'Rourke will have it. Sure to."

"Well, there's only one thing for it. If we believe someone's going to have a shot at pinching that paper, we've got to keep watch to-night, Bill, my boy."

Bundle opened her mouth as though to protest, but shut it again without speaking.

"By the way," continued Jimmy, "did I recognize the commissionaire from Harrods in the hall this evening, or was it our old friend Lestrade from Scotland Yard?"

"Scintillating, Watson," said Bill.

"I suppose," said Jimmy, "that we are rather butting in on his preserves."

"Can't be helped," said Bill. "Not if we mean to see this thing through."

"Then it's agreed," said Jimmy. "We divide the night into two watches?"

Again Bundle opened her mouth, and again shut it without speaking.

"Right you are," agreed Bill. "Who'll take first duty?"

"Shall we spin for it?"

"Might as well."

"All right. Here goes. Heads you first and I second. Tails, vice versa."

Bill nodded. The coin spun in the air. Jimmy bent to look at it.

"Tails," he said.

"Damn," said Bill. "You get first half and probably any fun that's going."

"Oh, you never know," said Jimmy. "Criminals are very uncertain. What time shall I wake you? Three thirty?"

"That's about fair, I think."

And now, at last, Bundle spoke:

"What about *me*?" she asked.

"Nothing doing. You go to bed and sleep."

"Oh!" said Bundle. "That's not very exciting."

"You never know," said Jimmy kindly. "You may be murdered in your sleep whilst Bill and I escape scot-free."

"Well, there's always that possibility. Do you know, Jimmy, I don't half like the look of that Countess. I suspect her."

"Nonsense," cried Bill hotly. "She's absolutely above suspicion."

"How do you know?" retorted Bundle.

"Because I do. Why, one of the fellows at the Hungarian Embassy vouched for her."

"Oh!" said Bundle, momentarily taken aback by his fervour.

"You girls are all the same," grumbled Bill. "Just because she's a jolly good-looking woman—"

Bundle was only too well acquainted with this unfair masculine line of argument.

"Well, don't you go and pour confidences into her shell-pink ear," she remarked. "I'm going to bed. I was bored stiff in that drawing-room and I'm not going back."

She left the room. Bill looked at Jimmy.

"Good old Bundle," he said. "I was afraid we might have trouble with her. You know how keen she is to be in everything. I think the way she took it was just wonderful."

"So did I," said Jimmy. "It staggered me."

"She's got some sense, Bundle has. She knows when a thing's plumb impossible. I say, oughtn't we to have some lethal weapons? Chaps usually do when they're going on this sort of stunt."

"I have a blue-nosed automatic," said Jimmy with gentle pride. "It weighs several pounds and looks most murderous. I'll lend it to you when the time comes."

Bill looked at him with respect and envy.

"What made you think of getting that?" he said.

"I don't know," said Jimmy carelessly. "It just came to me."

"I hope we shan't go and shoot the wrong person," said Bill with some anxiety.

"That would be unfortunate," said Mr. Thesiger gravely.

18

Jimmy's Adventures

Our Chronicle must here split into three separate and distinct portions. The night was to prove an eventful one and each of the three persons involved saw it from his or her own individual angle.

We will begin with that pleasant and engaging youth, Mr. Jimmy Thesiger, at a moment when he has at last exchanged final good-nights with his fellow conspirator, Bill Eversleigh.

"Don't forget," said Bill, "3 A.M. If you're still alive, that is," he added kindly.

"I may be an ass," said Jimmy, with rancorous remembrance of the remark Bundle had repeated to him, "but I'm not nearly so much of an ass as I look."

"That's what you said about Gerry Wade," said Bill slowly. "Do you remember? And that very night he—"

"Shut up, you damned fool," said Jimmy. "Haven't you got *any* tact?"

"Of course I've got tact," said Bill. "I'm a budding diplomatist. All diplomatists have tact."

"Ah!" said Jimmy. "You must be still in what they call the larval stage."

"I can't get over Bundle," said Bill, reverting abruptly to a former topic. "I should certainly have said that she'd be—well, difficult. Bundle's improved. She's improved very much."

"That's what your Chief was saying," said Jimmy. "He said he was agreeably surprised."

"I thought Bundle was laying it on a bit thick myself," said Bill. "But Codders is such an ass he'd swallow anything. Well, night-night. I expect you'll have a bit of a job waking me when the time comes—but stick to it."

"It won't be much good if you've taken a leaf out of Gerry Wade's book," said Jimmy maliciously.

Bill looked at him reproachfully.

"What the hell do you want to go and make a chap uncomfortable for?" he demanded.

"You're only getting your own back," said Jimmy. "Toddle along."

But Bill lingered. He stood uncomfortably, first on one foot and then on the other.

"Look here," he said.

"Yes?"

"What I mean to say is—well, I mean you'll be all right and all that, won't you? It's all very well ragging, but when I think of poor old Gerry—and then poor old Ronny—"

Jimmy gazed at him in exasperation. Bill was one of those who undoubtedly meant well, but the result of his efforts would not be described as heartening.

"I see," he remarked, "that I shall have to show you Leopold."

He slipped his hand into the pocket of the dark blue suit into which he had just changed and held out something for Bill's inspection.

"A real, genuine, blue-nosed automatic," he said with modest pride.

"No, I say," Bill said. "Is it really?"

He was undoubtedly impressed.

"Stevens, my man, got him for me. Warranted clean and methodical in his habits. You press the button and Leopold does the rest."

"Oh!" said Bill. "I say, Jimmy?"

"Yes?"

"Be careful, won't you? I mean, don't go loosing that thing off at anybody. Pretty awkward if you shot old Digby walking in his sleep."

"That's all right," said Jimmy. "Naturally, I want to get value out of Leopold now I've bought him, but I'll curb my bloodthirsty instincts as far as possible."

"Well, night-night," said Bill for the fourteenth time, and this time really did depart.

Jimmy was left alone to take up his vigil.

Sir Stanley Digby occupied a room at the extremity of the west wing. A bathroom adjoined it on one side, and on the other a communicating door led into a smaller room, which was tenanted by Mr. Terence O'Rourke. The doors of these three rooms gave on to a short corridor. The watcher had a simple task. A chair placed inconspicuously in the shadow of an oak press just where the corridor ran into the main gallery formed a perfect vantage ground. There was no other way into the west wing, and anyone going to or from it could not fail to be seen. One electric light was still on.

Jimmy ensconced himself comfortably, crossed his legs and waited. Leopold lay in readiness across his knee.

He glanced at his watch. It was twenty minutes to one—just an hour since the household had retired to rest. Not a sound broke the stillness, except for the far-off ticking of a clock somewhere.

Somehow or other, Jimmy did not much care for that sound. It recalled things. Gerald Wade—and those seven ticking clocks on the mantelpiece . . . .Whose hand had placed them there, and why? He shivered.

It was a creepy business, this waiting. He didn't wonder that things happened at spiritualistic séances. Sitting in the gloom, one got all worked up—ready to start at the least sound. And unpleasant thoughts came crowding in on a fellow.

Ronny Devereux! Ronny Devereux and Gerry Wade! Both young, both full of life and energy; ordinary, jolly, healthy young men. And now, where were they? Dank earth . . . worms getting them . . . Ugh! why couldn't he put these horrible thoughts out of his mind?

He looked again at his watch. Twenty minutes past one only. How the time crawled.

Extraordinary girl, Bundle! Fancy having the nerve and the daring actually to get into the midst of that Seven Dials place. Why hadn't he had the nerve and the initiative to think of that? He supposed because the thing *was* so fantastic.

No. 7. Who the hell could No. 7 be? Was he, perhaps, in the house at this minute? Disguised as a servant. He couldn't, surely, be one of the guests. No, that was impossible. But then, the whole thing was impossible. If he hadn't believed Bundle to be essentially truthful—well, he would have thought she had invented the whole thing.

He yawned. Queer, to feel sleepy, and yet at the same time strung up. He looked again at his watch. Ten minutes to two. Time was getting on.

And then, suddenly, he held his breath and leaned forward, listening. He had heard something.

The minutes went past. . . . There it was again. The creak of a board. . . . But it came from downstairs somewhere. There it was again! A slight, ominous creak. Somebody was moving stealthily about the house.

Jimmy sprang noiselessly to his feet. He crept silently to the head of the staircase. Everything seemed perfectly quiet. Yet he was quite certain he had really heard that stealthy sound. It was not imagination.

Very quietly and cautiously he crept down the staircase, Leopold clasped tightly in his right hand. Not a sound in the big hall. If he had been correct in assuming that the muffled sound came from directly beneath him, then it must have come from the library.

Jimmy stole to the door of it, listened, but heard nothing; then, suddenly flinging open the door, he switched on the lights.

Nothing! The big room was flooded with light. But it was empty.

Jimmy frowned.

"I could have sworn—" he murmured to himself.

The library was a large room with three windows which opened on to the terrace. Jimmy strode across the room. The middle window was unlatched.

He opened it and stepped out on the terrace, looking from end to end of it. Nothing!

"Looks all right," he murmured to himself. "And yet—"

He remained for a minute lost in thought. Then he stepped back into the library. Crossing to the door, he locked it and put the key in his pocket. Then he switched off the light. He stood for a minute listening, then crossed softly to the open window and stood there, Leopold ready in his hand.

Was there, or was there not, a soft patter of feet along the terrace? No—his imagination. He grasped Leopold tightly and stood listening. . . .

In the distance a stable clock chimed two.

19

Bundle's Adventures

Bundle Brent was a resourceful girl—she was also a girl of imagination. She had foreseen that Bill, if not Jimmy, would make objections to her participation in the possible dangers of the night. It was not Bundle's idea to waste time in argument. She had laid her own plans and made her own arrangements. A glance from her bedroom window shortly before dinner had been highly satisfactory. She had known that the gray walls of the Abbey were plentifully adorned with ivy, but the ivy outside her window was particularly solid looking and would present no difficulties to one of her athletic propensities.

She had no fault to find with Bill's and Jimmy's arrangements as far as they went. But in her opinion they did not go far enough. She offered no criticism, because she intended to see to that side of things herself. Briefly, while Jimmy and Bill were devoting themselves to the inside of the Abbey, Bundle intended to devote her attentions to the outside.

Her own meek acquiescence in the tame rôle assigned to her gave her an infinity of pleasure, though she wondered scornfully how either of the two men could be so easily deceived. Bill, of course, had never been famous for scintillating brain power. On the other hand, he knew, or should know, his Bundle. And she considered that Jimmy Thesiger, though only slightly acquainted with her, ought to have known better than to imagine that she could be so easily and summarily disposed of.

Once in the privacy of her own room, Bundle set rapidly to work. First she discarded her evening dress and the negligible trifle which she wore beneath it, and started again, so to speak, from the foundations. Bundle had not brought her maid with her, and she herself had packed. Otherwise, the puzzled Frenchwoman might have wondered why her lady took a pair of riding breeches and no further equine equipment.

Arrayed in riding breeches, rubber-soled shoes, and a dark-coloured pullover, Bundle was ready for the fray. She glanced at the time. As yet, it was only half-past twelve. Too early by far. Whatever was going to happen would not happen for some time yet. The occupants of the house must all be given time to get off to sleep. Half past one was the time fixed by Bundle for the start of operations.

She switched off her light and sat down by the window to wait. Punctually at the appointed moment, she rose, pushed up the sash and swung her leg over the sill. The night was a fine one, cold and still. There was starlight but no moon.

She found the descent very easy. Bundle and her two sisters had run wild in the park at Chimneys as small children, and they could all climb like cats. Bundle arrived on a flower-bed, rather breathless, but quite unscathed.

She paused a minute to take stock of her plans. She knew that the rooms occupied by the Air Minister and his secretary were in the west wing; that was the opposite side of the house from where Bundle was now standing. A terrace ran along the south and west side of the house, ending abruptly against a walled fruit garden.

Bundle stepped out of her flower-bed and turned the corner of the house to where the terrace began on the south side. She crept very quietly along it, keeping close to the shadow of the house. But, as she reached the second corner, she got a shock, for a man was standing there, with the clear intention of barring her way.

The next instant she had recognized him.

"Superintendent Battle! You did give me a fright!"

"That's what I'm here for," said the Superintendent pleasantly.

Bundle looked at him. It struck her now, as so often before, how remarkably little camouflage there was about him. He was large and solid and noticeable. He was, somehow, very English. But of one thing Bundle was quite sure. Superintendent Battle was no fool.

"What are you really doing here?" she asked, still in a whisper.

"Just seeing," said Battle, "that nobody's about who shouldn't be."

"Oh!" said Bundle, rather taken aback.

"You, for instance, Lady Eileen. I don't suppose you usually take a walk at this time of night."

"Do you mean," said Bundle slowly, "that you want me to go back?"

Superintendent Battle nodded approvingly.

"You're very quick, Lady Eileen. That's just what I do mean. Did you—er—come out of a door, or the window?"

"The window. It's easy as anything climbing down this ivy."

Superintendent Battle looked up at it thoughtfully.

"Yes," he said. "I should say it would be."

"And you want me to go back?" said Bundle. "I'm rather sick about that. I wanted to go round on to the west terrace."

"Perhaps you won't be the only one who'll want to do that," said Battle.

"Nobody could miss seeing you," said Bundle rather spitefully.

The Superintendent seemed rather pleased than otherwise.

"I hope they won't," he said. "No *unpleasantness*. That's my motto. And if you'll excuse me, Lady Eileen, I think it's time you were going back to bed."

The firmness of his tone admitted of no parley. Rather crestfallen, Bundle retraced her steps. She was halfway up the ivy when a sudden idea occurred to her, and she nearly relaxed her grip and fell.

Supposing Superintendent Battle suspected *her*.

There had been something—yes, surely there had been something in his manner that vaguely suggested the idea. She couldn't help laughing as she crawled over the sill into her bedroom. Fancy the solid Superintendent suspecting *her!*

Though she had so far obeyed Battle's orders as to return to her room, Bundle had no intention of going to bed and sleeping. Nor did she think that Battle had really intended her to do so. He was not a man to expect impossibilities. And to remain quiescent when something daring and exciting might be going on was a sheer impossibility to Bundle.

She glanced at her watch. It was ten minutes to two. After a moment or two of irresolution, she cautiously opened her door. Not a sound. Everything was still and peaceful. She stole cautiously along the passage.

Once she halted, thinking she heard a board creak somewhere, but then convinced that she was mistaken, she went on again. She was now in the main corridor, making her way to the west wing. She reached the angle of intersection and peered cautiously round—then she stared in blank surprise.

The watcher's post was empty. Jimmy Thesiger was not there.

Bundle stared in complete amazement. What had happened? Why had Jimmy left his post? What did it mean?

And at that moment she heard a clock strike two.

She was still standing there, debating what to do next, when suddenly her heart gave a leap and then seemed to stand still.

The door handle of Terence O'Rourke's room was slowly turning.

Bundle watched, fascinated. But the door did not open. Instead the knob returned slowly to its original position. What did it mean?

Suddenly Bundle came to a resolution. Jimmy, for some unknown reason, had deserted his post. She must get hold of Bill.

Quickly and noiselessly, Bundle fled along the way she had come. She burst unceremoniously into Bill's room.

"Bill, wake up! Oh, do wake up!"

It was an urgent whisper she sent forth, but there came no response to it.

"Bill," breathed Bundle.

Impatiently she switched on the lights, and then stood dumbfounded.

The room was empty, and the bed had not even been slept in.

Where then was Bill?

Suddenly she caught her breath. *This was not Bill's room.* The dainty négligé thrown over a chair, the feminine knick-knacks on the dressing-table, the black velvet evening dress thrown carelessly over a chair—Of course, in her haste she had mistaken the doors. This was the Countess Radzky's room.

But where, oh, where, was the Countess?

And just as Bundle was asking herself this question, the silence of the night was suddenly broken, and in no uncertain manner.

The clamour came from below. In an instant Bundle had sped out of the Countess's room and downstairs. The sounds came from the library—a violent crashing of chairs being overturned.

Bundle rattled vainly at the library door. It was locked. But she could clearly hear the struggle that was going on within—the panting and scuffling, curses in manly tones, the occasional crash as some light piece of furniture came into the line of battle.

And then, sinister and distinct, breaking the peace of the night for good and all, two shots in rapid succession.

20

Loraine's Adventures

Loraine Wade sat up in bed and switched on the light. It was exactly ten minutes to one. She had gone to bed early—at half-past nine. She possessed the useful art of being able to wake herself up at the required time, so she had been able to enjoy some hours of refreshing sleep.

Two dogs slept in the room with her, and one of these now raised his head and looked at her inquiringly.

"Quiet, Lurcher," said Loraine, and the big animal put his head down again obediently, watching her from between his shaggy eyelashes.

It is true that Bundle had once doubted the meekness of Loraine Wade, but that brief moment of suspicion had passed. Loraine had seemed so entirely reasonable, so willing to be kept out of everything.

And yet, if you studied the girl's face, you saw that there was strength of purpose in the small, resolute jaw and the lips that closed together so firmly.

Loraine rose and dressed herself in a tweed coat and skirt. Into one pocket of the coat she dropped an electric torch. Then she opened the drawer of her dressing table and took out a small ivory-handled pistol—almost a toy in appearance. She had bought it the day before at Harrods and she was very pleased with it.

She gave a final glance round the room to see if she had forgotten anything, and at that moment the big dog rose and came over to her, looking up at her with pleading eyes and wagging his tail.

Loraine shook her head.

"No, Lurcher. Can't go. Missus can't take you. Got to stay here and be a good boy."

She dropped a kiss on the dog's head, made him lie down on his rug again, and then slipped noiselessly out of the room, closing the door behind her.

She let herself out of the house by a side door and made her way round to the garage, where her little two-seater car was in readiness. There was a gentle slope, and she let the car run silently down it, not starting the engine till she was some way from the house. Then she glanced at the watch on her arm and pressed her foot down on the accelerator.

She left the car at a spot she had previously marked down. There was a gap there in the fencing that she could easily get through. A few minutes later, slightly muddy, Loraine stood inside the grounds of Wyvern Abbey.

As noiselessly as possible, she made her way towards the venerable ivy-covered building. In the distance a stable clock chimed two.

Loraine's heart beat faster as she drew near to the terrace. There was no one about—no sign of life anywhere. Everything seemed peaceful and undisturbed. She reached the terrace and stood there, looking about her.

Suddenly, without the least warning, something from above fell with a flop almost at her feet. Loraine stooped to pick it up. It was a brown paper packet, loosely wrapped. Holding it, Loraine looked up.

There was an open window just above her head, and even as she looked a leg swung over it and a man began to climb down the ivy.

Loraine waited for no more. She took to her heels and ran, still clasping the brown paper packet.

Behind her, the noise of a struggle suddenly broke out. A hoarse voice: "Lemme go"; another that she knew well: "Not if I know it—ah, you would, would you?"

Still Loraine ran—blindly, as though panic stricken—right round the corner of the terrace—and slap into the arms of a large, solidly built man.

"There, there," said Superintendent Battle kindly.

Loraine was struggling to speak.

"Oh, quick—oh, quick! They're killing each other. Oh, do be quick!"

There was a sharp crack of a revolver shot—and then another.

Superintendent Battle started to run. Loraine followed. Back round the corner of the terrace and along to the library window. The window was open.

Battle stooped and switched on an electric torch. Loraine was close beside him, peering over his shoulder. She gave a little sobbing gasp.

On the threshold of the window lay Jimmy Thesiger in what looked like a pool of blood. His right arm lay dangling in a curious position.

Loraine gave a sharp cry.

"He's dead," she wailed. "Oh, Jimmy—Jimmy—he's dead!"

"Now, now," said Superintendent Battle soothingly, "don't you take on so. The young gentleman isn't dead, I'll be bound. See if you can find the lights and turn them on."

Loraine obeyed. She stumbled across the room, found the switch by the door and pressed it down. The room was flooded with light. Superintendent Battle uttered a sigh of relief.

"It's all right—he's only shot in the right arm. He's fainted through loss of blood. Come and give me a hand with him."

There was a pounding on the library door. Voices were heard, asking, expostulating, demanding.

Loraine looked doubtfully at it.

"Shall I—"

"No hurry," said Battle. "We'll let them in presently. You come and give me a hand."

Loraine came obediently. The Superintendent had produced a large, clean pocket-handkerchief and was neatly bandaging the wounded man's arm. Loraine helped him.

"He'll be all right," said the Superintendent. "Don't you worry. As many lives as cats, these young fellows. It wasn't the loss of blood knocked him out either. He must have caught his head a crack on the floor as he fell."

Outside the knocking on the door had become tremendous. The voice of George Lomax, furiously upraised, came loud and distinct:

"Who is in there? Open the door at once."

Superintendent Battle sighed.

"I suppose we shall have to," he said. "A pity."

His eyes darted round, taking in the scene. An automatic lay by Jimmy's side. The Superintendent picked it up gingerly, holding it very delicately and examined it. He grunted and laid it on the table. Then he stepped across and unlocked the door.

Several people almost fell into the room. Nearly everybody said something at the same minute. George Lomax, spluttering with obdurate words which refused to come with sufficient fluency, exclaimed:

"The—the—the meaning of this? Ah! It's you, Superintendent. What's happened? I say—what has—happened?"

Bill Eversleigh said: "My God! Old Jimmy!" and stared at the limp figure on the ground.

Lady Coote, clad in a resplendent purple dressing gown, cried out: "The poor boy!" and swept past Superintendent Battle to bend over the prostrate Jimmy in a motherly fashion.

Bundle said: "Loraine!"

Herr Eberhard said: "Gott im Himmel!" and other words of that nature.

Sir Stanley Digby said: "My God, what's all this?"

A housemaid said: "Look at the blood," and screamed with pleasurable excitement.

A footman said: "Lor!"

The butler said, with a good deal more bravery in his manner than had been noticeable a few minutes earlier: "Now then, this won't do!" and waved away underservants.

The efficient Mr. Rupert Bateman said to George: "Shall we get rid of some of these people, sir?"

Then they all took fresh breath.

"Incredible!" said George Lomax. "Battle, what has *happened*?"

Battle gave him a look, and George's discreet habits assumed their usual sway.

"Now then," he said, moving to the door, "everyone go back to bed, please. There's been a—er—"

"A little accident," said Superintendent Battle easily.

"A—er—an accident. I shall be much obliged if everyone will go back to bed."

Everyone was clearly reluctant to do so.

"Lady Coote—please—"

"The poor boy," said Lady Coote in a motherly fashion.

She rose from a kneeling position with great reluctance. And as she did so, Jimmy stirred and sat up.

"Hallo!" he said thickly. "What's the matter?"

He looked round him vacantly for a minute or two and then intelligence returned to his eye.

"Have you got him?" he demanded eagerly.

"Got who?"

"The man. Climbed down the ivy. I was by the window there. Grabbed him and we had no end of a set to—"

"One of those nasty, murderous cat burglars," said Lady Coote. "Poor boy."

Jimmy was looking round him.

"I say—I'm afraid we—er—have made rather a mess of things. Fellow was as strong as an ox and we went fairly waltzing around."

The condition of the room was clear proof of this statement. Everything light and breakable within a range of twelve feet that could be broken *had* been broken.

"And what happened then?"

But Jimmy was looking round for something.

"Where's Leopold? The pride of the blue-nosed automatics."

Battle indicated the pistol on the table.

"Is this yours, Mr. Thesiger?"

"That's right. That's little Leopold. How many shots have been fired?"

"One shot."

Jimmy looked chagrined.

"I'm disappointed in Leopold," he murmured. "I can't have pressed the button properly, or he'd have gone on shooting."

"Who shot first?"

"I did, I'm afraid," said Jimmy. "You see, the man twisted himself out of my grasp suddenly. I saw him making for the window and I closed my finger down on Leopold and let him have it. He turned in the window and fired at me and—well, I suppose after that I took the count."

He rubbed his head rather ruefully.

But Sir Stanley Digby was suddenly alert.

"Climbing down the ivy, you said? My God, Lomax, you don't think they've got away with it?"

He rushed from the room. For some curious reason nobody spoke during his absence. In a few minutes Sir Stanley returned. His round, chubby face was white as death.

"My God, Battle," he said, "they've got it. O'Rourke's fast asleep—drugged, I think. I can't wake him. And the papers have vanished."

21

The Recovery of the Formula

"Der liebe Gott!" said Herr Eberhard in a whisper.

His face had gone chalky white.

George turned a face of dignified reproach on Battle.

"Is this true, Battle? I left all arrangements in your hands."

The rock-like quality of the Superintendent showed out well. Not a muscle of his face moved.

"The best of us are defeated sometimes, sir," he said quietly.

"Then you mean—you really mean—that the document is gone?"

But to everyone's intense surprise Superintendent Battle shook his head.

"No, no, Mr. Lomax, it's not so bad as you think. Everything's all right. But you can't lay the credit for it at my door. You've got to thank this young lady."

He indicated Loraine, who stared at him in surprise. Battle stepped across to her and gently took the brown paper parcel which she was still clutching mechanically.

"I think, Mr. Lomax," he said, "that you will find what you want here."

Sir Stanley Digby, quicker in action than George, snatched at the package and tore it open, investigating its contents eagerly. A sigh of relief escaped him and he mopped his brow. Herr Eberhard fell upon the child of his brain and clasped it to his heart, whilst a torrent of German burst from him.

Sir Stanley turned to Loraine, shaking her warmly by the hand.

"My dear young lady," he said, "we are infinitely obliged to you, I am sure."

"Yes, indeed," said George. "Though I—er—"

He paused in some perplexity, staring at a young lady who was a total stranger to him. Loraine looked appealingly at Jimmy, who came to the rescue.

"Er—this is Miss Wade," said Jimmy. "Gerald Wade's sister."

"Indeed," said George, shaking her warmly by the hand. "My dear Miss Wade, I must express my deep gratitude to you for what you have done. I must confess that I do not quite see—"

He paused delicately and four of the persons present felt that explanations were going to be fraught with much difficulty. Superintendent Battle came to the rescue.

"Perhaps we'd better not go into that just now, sir," he suggested tactfully.

The efficient Mr. Bateman created a further diversion.

"Wouldn't it be wise for someone to see to O'Rourke? Don't you think, sir, that a doctor had better be sent for?"

"Of course," said George. "Of course. Most remiss of us not to have thought of it before." He looked towards Bill. "Get Dr. Cartwright on the telephone. Ask him to come. Just hint, if you can, that—er—discretion should be observed."

Bill went off on his errand.

"I will come up with you, Digby," said George. "Something, possibly, could be done—measures should, perhaps, be taken—whilst awaiting the arrival of the doctor."

He looked rather helplessly at Rupert Bateman. Efficiency always makes itself felt. It was Pongo who was really in charge of the situation.

"Shall I come up with you, sir?"

George accepted the offer with relief. Here, he felt, was someone on whom he could lean. He experienced that sense of complete trust in Mr. Bateman's efficiency which came to all those who encountered that excellent young man.

The three men left the room together. Lady Coote, murmuring in deep rich tones: "The poor young fellow. Perhaps I could do something—" hurried after them.

"That's a very motherly woman," observed the Superintendent thoughtfully. "A very motherly woman. I wonder—"

Three pairs of eyes looked at him inquiringly.

"I was wondering," said Superintendent Battle slowly, "where Sir Oswald Coote may be."

"Oh!" gasped Loraine. "Do you think he's been murdered?"

Battle shook his head at her reproachfully.

"No need for anything so melodramatic," he said. "No—I rather think—"

He paused, his head on one side, listening—one large hand raised to enjoin silence.

In another minute they all heard what his sharper ears had been the first to notice—footsteps coming along the terrace outside. They rang out clearly with no kind of subterfuge about them. In another minute the window was blocked by a bulky figure which stood there regarding them and who conveyed, in an odd way, a sense of dominating the situation.

Sir Oswald, for it was he, looked slowly from one face to another. His keen eyes took in the details of the situation. Jimmy, with his roughly bandaged arm; Bundle, in her somewhat anomalous attire; Loraine, a perfect stranger to him. His eyes came last to Superintendent Battle. He spoke sharply and crisply:

"What's been happening here, officer?"

"Attempted robbery, sir."

"*Attempted*—eh?"

"Thanks to this young lady, Miss Wade, the thieves failed to get away with it."

"Ah!" he said again, his scrutiny ended. "And now, officer, what about *this?*"

He held out a small Mauser pistol which he carried delicately by the butt.

"Where did you find that, Sir Oswald?"

"On the lawn outside. I presume it must have been thrown down by one of the thieves as he took to his heels. I've held it carefully, as I thought you might wish to examine it for finger-prints."

"You think of everything, Sir Oswald," said Battle.

He took the pistol from the other, handling it with equal care, and laid it down on the table beside Jimmy's Colt.

"And now, if you please," said Sir Oswald, "I should like to hear exactly what occurred."

Superintendent Battle gave a brief résumé of the events of the night. Sir Oswald frowned thoughtfully.

"I understand," he said sharply. "After wounding and disabling Mr. Thesiger, the man took to his heels and ran, throwing away the pistol as he did so. What I cannot understand is why no one pursued him."

"It wasn't till we heard Mr. Thesiger's story that we knew there was anyone to pursue," remarked Superintendent Battle dryly.

"You didn't—er—catch sight of him making off as you turned the corner of the terrace?"

"No, I missed him by just about forty seconds, I should say. There's no moon and he'd be invisible as soon as he'd left the terrace. He must have leapt for it as soon as he'd fired the shot."

"H'm," said Sir Oswald. "I still think that a search should have been organized. Someone else should have been posted—"

"There are three of my men in the grounds," said the Superintendent quietly.

"Oh!" Sir Oswald seemed rather taken aback.

"They were to hold and detain anyone attempting to leave the grounds."

"And yet—they haven't done so?"

"And yet they haven't done so," agreed Battle gravely.

Sir Oswald looked at him as though something in the words puzzled him. He said sharply:

"Are you telling me all that you know, Superintendent Battle?"

"All that I *know*—yes, Sir Oswald. What I think is a different matter. Maybe I think some rather curious things—but until thinking's got you somewhere it's no use talking about it."

"And yet," said Sir Oswald slowly, "I should like to know what you think, Superintendent Battle."

"For one thing, sir, I think there's a lot too much ivy about this place—excuse me, sir, you've got a bit on your coat—yes, a great deal too much ivy. It complicates things."

Sir Oswald stared at him, but any reply he might have contemplated making was arrested by the entrance of Rupert Bateman.

"Oh, there you are, Sir Oswald. I'm so glad. Lady Coote has just discovered that you were missing—and she has been insisting upon it that you had been murdered by the thieves. I really think, Sir Oswald, that you had better come to her at once. She is terribly upset."

"Maria is an incredibly foolish woman," said Sir Oswald. "Why should I be murdered? I'll come with you, Bateman."

He left the room with his secretary.

"That's a very efficient young man," said Battle, looking after them. "What's his name—Bateman?"

Jimmy nodded.

"Bateman—Rupert," he said. "Commonly known as Pongo. I was at school with him."

"Were you? Now, that's interesting, Mr. Thesiger. What was your opinion of him in those days?"

"Oh, he was always the same sort of ass."

"I shouldn't have thought," said Battle mildly, "that he was an ass."

"Oh, you know what I mean. Of course he wasn't really an ass. Tons of brains and always swotting at things. But deadly serious. No sense of humour."

"Ah!" said Superintendent Battle. "That's a pity. Gentlemen who have no sense of humour get to taking themselves too seriously—and that leads to mischief."

"I can't imagine Pongo getting into mischief," said Jimmy. "He's done extremely well for himself so far—dug himself in with old Coote and looks like being a permanency in the job."

"Superintendent Battle," said Bundle.

"Yes, Lady Eileen?"

"Don't you think it very odd that Sir Oswald didn't say what he was doing wandering about in the garden in the middle of the night?"

"Ah!" said Battle. "Sir Oswald's a great man—and a great man always knows better than to explain unless an explanation is demanded. To rush into explanations and excuses is always a sign of weakness. Sir Oswald knows that as well as I do. He's not going to come in explaining and apologizing—not he. He just stalks in and hauls *me* over the coals. He's a big man, Sir Oswald."

Such a warm admiration sounded in the Superintendent's tones that Bundle pursued the subject no further.

"And now," said Superintendent Battle, looking round with a slight twinkle in his eye, "now that we're together and friendly like—I *should* like to hear just how Miss Wade happened to arrive on the scene so pat."

"She ought to be ashamed of herself," said Jimmy. "Hoodwinking us all as she did."

"Why should I be kept out of it all?" cried Loraine passionately. "I never meant to be—no, not the very first day in your rooms when you both explained how the best thing for me to do was to stay quietly at home and keep out of danger. I didn't say anything, but I made up my mind then."

"I half suspected it," said Bundle. "You were so surprisingly meek about it. I might have known you were up to something."

"I thought you were remarkably sensible," said Jimmy Thesiger.

"You would, Jimmy dear," said Loraine. "It was easy enough to deceive you."

"Thank you for these kind words," said Jimmy. "Go on, and don't mind me."

"When you rang up and said there might be danger, I was more determined than ever," went on Loraine. "I went to Harrods and I bought a pistol. Here it is."

She produced the dainty weapon, and Superintendent Battle took it from her and examined it.

"Quite a deadly little toy, Miss Wade," he said. "Have you had much—er—practice with it?"

"None at all," said Loraine. "But I thought if I took it with me—well, that it would give me a comforting feeling."

"Quite so," said Battle gravely.

"My idea was to come over here and see what was going on. I left the car in the road and climbed through the hedge and came up to the terrace. I was just looking about me when—plop—something fell right at my feet. I picked it up and then looked to see where it could have come from. And then I saw the man climbing down the ivy and I ran."

"Just so," said Battle. "Now, Miss Wade, can you describe that man at all?"

The girl shook her head.

"It was too dark to see much. I think he was a big man—but that's about all."

"And now you, Mr. Thesiger." Battle turned to him. "You struggled with the man—can you tell me anything about him?"

"He was a pretty hefty individual—that's all I can say. He gave a few hoarse whispers—that's when I had him by the throat. He said, 'Lemme go, guvnor,' something like that."

"An uneducated man, then?"

"Yes, I suppose he was. He spoke like one."

"I still don't quite understand about the packet," said Loraine. "Why should he throw it down as he did? Was it because it hampered him climbing?"

"No," said Battle. "I've got an entirely different theory about that. That packet, Miss Wade, was deliberately thrown down to you—or so I believe."

"To *me?*"

"Shall we say—to the person the thief thought you were."

"This is getting very involved," said Jimmy.

"Mr. Thesiger, when you came into this room, did you switch on the light at all?"

"Yes."

"And there was no one in the room?"

"No one at all."

"But previously you thought you heard someone moving about down here?"

"Yes."

"And then, after trying the window, you switched off the light again and locked the door?"

Jimmy nodded.

Superintendent Battle looked slowly round him. His glance was arrested by a big screen of Spanish leather which stood near one of the bookcases.

Brusquely he strode across the room and looked behind it.

He uttered a sharp ejaculation, which brought the three young people quickly to his side.

Huddled on the floor, in a dead faint, lay the Countess Radzky.

22

The Countess Radzky's Story

The Countess's return to consciousness was very different from that of Jimmy Thesiger. It was more prolonged and infinitely more artistic.

Artistic was Bundle's word. She had been zealous in her ministrations—largely consisting of the application of cold water—and the Countess had instantly responded, passing a white, bewildered hand across her brow and murmuring faintly.

It was at this point that Bill, at last relieved from his duties with telephone and doctors, had come bustling into the room and had instantly proceeded to make (in Bundle's opinion) a most regrettable idiot of himself.

He had hung over the Countess with a concerned and anxious face and had addressed a series of singularly idiotic remarks to her:

"I say, Countess. It's all right. It's really all right. Don't try to talk. It's bad for you. Just lie still. You'll be all right in a minute. It'll all come back to you. Don't say anything till you're quite all right. Take your time. Just lie still and close your eyes. You'll remember everything in a minute. Have another sip of water. Have some brandy. That's the stuff. Don't you think, Bundle, that some brandy . . . ?"

"For God's sake, Bill, leave her alone," said Bundle crossly. "She'll be all right."

And with an expert hand she flipped a good deal of cold water on to the exquisite make-up of the Countess's face.

The Countess flinched and sat up. She looked considerably more wide awake.

"Ah!" she murmured. "I am here. Yes, I am here."

"Take your time," said Bill. "Don't talk till you feel quite all right again."

The Countess drew the folds of a very transparent négligé closer around her.

"It is coming back to me," she murmured. "Yes, it is coming back."

She looked at the little crowd grouped around her. Perhaps something in the attentive faces struck her as unsympathetic. In any case she smiled deliberately up at the one face which clearly displayed a very opposite emotion.

"Ah, my big Englishman," she said very softly, "do not distress yourself. All is well with me."

"Oh! I say, but are you sure?" demanded Bill anxiously.

"Quite sure." She smiled at him reassuringly. "We Hungarians, we have nerves of steel."

A look of intense relief passed over Bill's face. A fatuous look settled down there instead—a look which made Bundle earnestly long to kick him.

"Have some water," she said coldly.

The Countess refused water. Jimmy, kindlier to beauty in distress, suggested a cocktail. The Countess reacted favourably to this suggestion. When she had swallowed it, she looked round once more, this time with a livelier eye.

"Tell me, what has happened?" she demanded briskly.

"We were hoping you might be able to tell us that," said Superintendent Battle.

The Countess looked at him sharply. She seemed to become aware of the big, quiet man for the first time.

"I went to your room," said Bundle. "The bed hadn't been slept in and you weren't there."

She paused—looking accusingly at the Countess. The latter closed her eyes and nodded her head slowly.

"Yes, yes, I remember it all now. Oh, it was horrible!" She shuddered. "Do you want me to tell you?"

Superintendent Battle said, "If you please" at the same moment that Bill said, "Not if you don't feel up to it."

The Countess looked from one to the other, but the quiet, masterful eye of Superintendent Battle won the game.

"I could not sleep," began the Countess. "The house—it oppressed me. I was all, as you say, on wires, the cat on the hot bricks. I knew that in the state I was in it was useless to think of going to bed. I walked about my room. I read. But the books placed there did not interest me greatly. I thought I would come down here and find something more absorbing."

"Very natural," said Bill.

"Very often done, I believe," said Battle.

"So as soon as the idea occurred to me, I left my room and came down. The house was very still—"

"Excuse me," interrupted the Superintendent, "but can you give me an idea of the time when this occurred?"

"I never know the time," said the Countess superbly, and swept on with her story.

"The house was very quiet. One could even hear the little mouse run, if there had been one. I come down the stairs—very quietly—"

"Very quietly?"

"Naturally, I do not want to disturb the household," said the Countess reproachfully. "I come in here. I go into this corner and I search the shelves for a suitable book."

"Having, of course, switched on the light?"

"No, I did not switch on the light. I had, you see, my little electric torch with me. With that, I scanned the shelves."

"Ah!" said the Superintendent.

"Suddenly," continued the Countess dramatically, "I hear something. A stealthy sound. A muffled footstep. I switch out my torch and listen. The footsteps draw nearer—stealthy, horrible footsteps. I shrink behind the screen. In another minute the door opens and the light is switched on. The man—the burglar is in the room."

"Yes, but I say—" began Mr. Thesiger.

A large-sized foot pressed his, and realizing that Superintendent Battle was giving him a hint, Jimmy shut up.

"I nearly died of fear," continued the Countess. "I tried not to breathe. The man waited for a minute, listening. Then, still with that horrible, stealthy tread—"

Again Jimmy opened his mouth in protest, and again shut it.

"—he crossed to the window and peered out. He remained there for a minute or two, then he recrossed the room and turned out the lights again, locking the door. I am terrified. He is in the room, moving stealthily about in the dark. Ah, it is horrible. Suppose he should come upon me in the dark! In another minute I hear him again by the window. Then silence. I hope that perhaps he may have gone out that way. As the minutes pass and I hear no further sound, I am almost sure that he has done so. Indeed I am in the very act of switching on my torch and investigating when—*prestissimo!*—it all begins."

"Yes?"

"Ah! But it was terrible—never—never shall I forget it! Two men trying to murder each other. Oh, it was horrible! They reeled about the room, and furniture crashed in every direction. I thought, too, that I heard a woman scream—but that was not in the room. It was outside somewhere. The criminal had a hoarse voice. He croaked rather than spoke. He kept saying, 'Lemme go—lemme go.' The other man was a gentleman. He had a cultured, English voice."

Jimmy looked gratified.

"He swore—mostly," continued the Countess.

"Clearly a gentleman," said Superintendent Battle.

"And then," continued the Countess, "a flash and a shot. The bullet hit the bookcase beside me. I—I suppose I must have fainted."

She looked up at Bill. He took her hand and patted it.

"You poor dear," he said. "How rotten for you."

"Silly idiot," thought Bundle.

Superintendent Battle had moved on swift, noiseless feet over to the bookcase a little to the right of the screen. He bent down, searching. Presently he stooped and picked something up.

"It wasn't a bullet, Countess," he said. "It's the shell of the cartridge. Where were you standing when you fired, Mr. Thesiger?"

Jimmy took up a position by the window.

"As nearly as I can say, about here."

Superintendent Battle placed himself in the same spot.

"That's right," he agreed. "The empty shell would throw right rear. It's a .455. I don't wonder the Countess thought it was a bullet in the dark. It hit the bookcase about a foot from her. The bullet itself grazed the window frame and we'll find it outside to-morrow—unless your assailant happens to be carrying it about in him."

Jimmy shook his head regretfully.

"Leopold, I fear, did not cover himself with glory," he remarked sadly.

The Countess was looking at him with most flattering attention.

"Your arm!" she exclaimed. "It is all tied up! Was it you then—"

Jimmy made her a mock bow.

"I'm so glad I've got a cultured English voice," he said. "And I can assure you that I wouldn't have dreamed of using the language I did if I had had any suspicion that a lady was present."

"I did not understand all of it," the Countess hastened to explain. "Although I had an English governess when I was young—"

"It isn't the sort of thing she'd be likely to teach you," agreed Jimmy. "Kept you busy with your uncle's pen, and the umbrella of the gardener's niece. I know the sort of stuff."

"But what has happened?" asked the Countess. "That is what I want to know. I demand to know what has happened."

There was a moment's silence whilst everybody looked at Superintendent Battle.

"It's very simple," said Battle mildly. "Attempted robbery. Some political papers stolen from Sir Stanley Digby. The thieves nearly got away with them, but thanks to this young lady"—he indicated Loraine—"they didn't."

The Countess flashed a glance at the girl—rather an odd glance.

"Indeed," she said coldly.

"A very fortunate coincidence that she happened to be there," said Superintendent Battle, smiling.

The Countess gave a little sigh and half closed her eyes again.

"It is absurd, but I still feel extremely faint," she murmured.

"Of course you do," cried Bill. "Let me help you up to your room. Bundle will come with you."

"It is very kind of Lady Eileen," said the Countess, "but I should prefer to be alone. I am really quite all right. Perhaps you will just help me up the stairs?"

She rose to her feet, accepted Bill's arm and, leaning heavily on it, went out of the room. Bundle followed as far as the hall but, the Countess reiterating her assurance—with some tartness—that she was quite all right, she did not accompany them upstairs.

But as she stood watching the Countess's graceful form, supported by Bill, slowly mounting the stairway, she stiffened suddenly to acute attention. The Countess's négligé, as previously mentioned, was thin—a mere veil of orange chiffon. Through it Bundle saw distinctly below the right shoulder blade *a small black mole*.

With a gasp, Bundle swung impetuously round to where Superintendent Battle was just emerging from the library. Jimmy and Loraine had preceded him.

"There," said Battle. "I've fastened the window and there will be a man on duty outside. And I'll lock this door and take the key. In the morning we'll do what the French call reconstruct the crime—Yes, Lady Eileen, what is it?"

"Superintendent Battle, I must speak to you—at once."

"Why, certainly, I—"

George Lomax suddenly appeared, Dr. Cartwright by his side.

"Ah, there you are, Battle. You'll be relieved to hear that there's nothing seriously wrong with O'Rourke."

"I never thought there would be much wrong with Mr. O'Rourke," said Battle.

"He's had a strong hypnotic administered to him," said the doctor. "He'll wake perfectly all right in the morning. Perhaps a bit of a head, perhaps not. Now then, young man, let's look at this bullet wound of yours."

"Come on, nurse," said Jimmy to Loraine. "Come and hold the basin or my hand. Witness a strong man's agony. You know the stunt."

Jimmy, Loraine and the doctor went off together. Bundle continued to throw agonized glances in the direction of Superintendent Battle, who had been buttonholed by George.

The Superintendent waited patiently till a pause occurred in George's loquacity. He then swiftly took advantage of it.

"I wonder, sir, if I might have a word privately with Sir Stanley? In the little study at the end there."

"Certainly," said George. "Certainly. I'll go and fetch him at once."

He hurried off upstairs again. Battle drew Bundle swiftly into the drawing-room and shut the door.

"Now, Lady Eileen, what is it?"

"I'll tell you as quickly as I can—but it's rather long and complicated."

As concisely as she could, Bundle related her introduction to the Seven Dials Club and her subsequent adventures there. When she had finished, Superintendent Battle drew a long breath. For once, his facial woodenness was laid aside.

"Remarkable," he said. "Remarkable. I wouldn't have believed it possible—even for you, Lady Eileen. I ought to have known better."

"But you did give me a hint, Superintendent Battle. You told me to ask Bill Eversleigh."

"It's dangerous to give people like you a hint, Lady Eileen. I never dreamt of your going to the lengths you have."

"Well, it's all right, Superintendent Battle. My death doesn't lie at your door."

"Not yet, it doesn't," said Battle grimly.

He stood as though in thought, turning things over in his mind.

"What Mr. Thesiger was about, letting you run into danger like that, I can't think," he said presently.

"He didn't know till afterwards," said Bundle. "I'm not a complete mug, Superintendent Battle. And anyway, he's got his hands full looking after Miss Wade."

"Is that so?" said the Superintendent. "Ah!"

He twinkled a little.

"I shall have to detail Mr. Eversleigh to look after you, Lady Eileen."

"Bill!" said Bundle contemptuously. "But Superintendent Battle, you haven't heard the end of my story. The woman I saw there—Anna—No. 1. Yes, No. 1 is the Countess Radzky."

And rapidly she went on to describe her recognition of the mole.

To her surprise the Superintendent hemmed and hawed.

"A mole isn't much to go upon, Lady Eileen. Two women might have an identical mole very easily. You must remember that the Countess Radzky is a very well-known figure in Hungary."

"Then this isn't the real Countess Radzky. I tell you I'm sure this is the same woman I saw there. And look at her to-night—the way we found her. I don't believe she ever fainted at all."

"Oh, I shouldn't say that, Lady Eileen. That empty shell striking the bookcase beside her might have frightened any woman half out of her wits."

"But what was she doing there anyway? One doesn't come down to look for a book with an electric torch."

Battle scratched his cheek. He seemed unwilling to speak. He began to pace up and down the room, as though making up his mind. At last he turned to the girl.

"See here, Lady Eileen, I'm going to trust you. The Countess's conduct *is* suspicious. I know that as well as you do. It's very suspicious—but we've got to go carefully. There mustn't be any unpleasantness with the Embassies. One has got to be *sure*."

"I see. If you were *sure* . . ."

"There's something else. During the war, Lady Eileen, there was a great outcry about German spies being left at large. Busybodies wrote letters to the papers about it. We paid no attention. Hard words didn't hurt us. The small fry were left alone. Why? Because through them, sooner or later, *we got the big fellow—the man at the top*."

"You mean?"

"Don't bother about what I mean, Lady Eileen. But remember this. *I know all about the Countess*. And I want her let alone.

"And now," added Superintendent Battle ruefully, "I've got to think of something to say to Sir Stanley Digby!"

23

Superintendent Battle in Charge

It was ten o'clock on the following morning. The sun poured in through the windows of the library, where Superintendent Battle had been at work since six. On a summons from him, George Lomax, Sir Oswald Coote and Jimmy Thesiger had just joined him, having repaired the fatigues of the night with a substantial breakfast. Jimmy's arm was in a sling, but he bore little other trace of the night's affray.

The Superintendent eyed all three of them benevolently, somewhat with the air of a kindly curator explaining a museum to little boys. On the table beside him were various objects, neatly labelled. Amongst them Jimmy recognized Leopold.

"Ah, Superintendent," said George, "I have been anxious to know how you have progressed. Have you caught the man?"

"He'll take a lot of catching, he will," said the Superintendent easily.

His failure in that respect did not appear to rankle with him.

George Lomax did not look particularly well pleased. He detested levity of any kind.

"I've got everything taped out pretty clearly," went on the detective.

He took up two objects from the table.

"Here we've got the two bullets. The largest is a .455, fired from Mr. Thesiger's Colt automatic. Grazed the window sash and I found it embedded in the trunk of that cedar tree. This little fellow was fired from the Mauser .25. After passing through Mr. Thesiger's arm, it embedded itself in this arm chair here. As for the pistol itself—"

"Well?" said Sir Oswald eagerly. "Any fingerprints?"

Battle shook his head.

"The man who handled it wore gloves," he said slowly.

"A pity," said Sir Oswald.

"A man who knew his business would wear gloves. Am I right in thinking, Sir Oswald, that you found this pistol just about twenty yards from the bottom of the steps leading up to the terrace?"

Sir Oswald stepped to the window.

"Yes, almost exactly, I should say."

"I don't want to find fault, but it would have been wiser on your part, sir, to leave it exactly as you found it."

"I am sorry," said Sir Oswald stiffly.

"Oh, it doesn't matter. I've been able to reconstruct things. There were your footprints, you see, leading up from the bottom of the garden, and a place where you had obviously stopped and stooped down, and a kind of dent in the grass which was highly suggestive. By the way, what was your theory of the pistol being there?"

"I presumed that it had been dropped by the man in his flight."

Battle shook his head.

"Not dropped, Sir Oswald. There are two points against that. To begin with, there is only one set of footprints crossing the lawn just there—your own."

"I see," said Sir Oswald thoughtfully.

"Can you be sure of that, Battle?" put in George.

"Quite sure, sir. There is one other set of tracks crossing the lawn, Miss Wade's, but they are a good deal farther to the left."

He paused, and then went on: "And there's the dent in the ground. The pistol must have struck the ground with some force. It all points to its having been thrown."

"Well, why not?" said Sir Oswald. "Say the man fled down the path to the left. He'd leave no footprints on the path and he'd hurl the pistol away from him into the middle of the lawn, eh, Lomax?"

George agreed by a nod of the head.

"It's true that he'd leave no footprints on the path," said Battle, "but from the shape of the dent and the way the turf was cut, I don't think the pistol was thrown from that direction. I think it was thrown from the terrace here."

"Very likely," said Sir Oswald. "Does it matter, Superintendent?"

"Ah, yes, Battle," broke in George. "Is it—er—strictly relevant?"

"Perhaps not, Mr. Lomax. But we like to get things just so, you know. I wonder now if one of you gentlemen would take this pistol and throw it. Will you, Sir Oswald? That's very kind. Stand just here in the window. Now fling it into the middle of the lawn."

Sir Oswald complied, sending the pistol flying through the air with a powerful sweep of his arm. Jimmy Thesiger drew near with breathless interest. The Superintendent lumbered off after it like a well-trained retriever. He reappeared with a beaming face.

"That's it, sir. Just the same kind of mark. Although, by the way, you sent it a good ten yards farther. But then, you're a very powerfully built man, aren't you, Sir Oswald? Excuse me, I thought I heard someone at the door."

The Superintendent's ears must have been very much sharper than anyone else's. Nobody else had heard a sound, but Battle was proved right, for Lady Coote stood outside, a medicine glass in her hand.

"Your medicine, Oswald," she said, advancing into the room. "You forgot it after breakfast."

"I'm very busy, Maria," said Sir Oswald. "I don't want my medicine."

"You would never take it if it wasn't for me," said his wife serenely, advancing upon him. "You're just like a naughty little boy. Drink it up now."

And meekly, obediently, the great steel magnate drank it up!

Lady Coote smiled sadly and sweetly at everyone.

"Am I interrupting you? Are you very busy? Oh, look at those revolvers. Nasty, noisy, murdering things. To think, Oswald, that you might have been shot by the burglar last night."

"You must have been alarmed when you found he was missing, Lady Coote," said Battle.

"I didn't think of it at first," confessed Lady Coote. "This poor boy here"—she indicated Jimmy—"being shot—and everything so dreadful, but so exciting. It wasn't till Mr. Bateman asked me where Sir Oswald was that I remembered he'd gone out half an hour before for a stroll."

"Sleepless, eh, Sir Oswald?" asked Battle.

"I am usually an excellent sleeper," said Sir Oswald. "But I must confess that last night I felt unusually restless. I thought the night air would do me good."

"You came out through this window, I suppose?"

Was it his fancy, or did Sir Oswald hesitate for a moment before replying?

"Yes."

"In your pumps too," said Lady Coote, "instead of putting thick shoes on. What would you do without me to look after you?"

She shook her head sadly.

"I think, Maria, if you don't mind leaving us—we have still a lot to discuss."

"I know, dear, I'm just going."

Lady Coote withdrew, carrying the empty medicine glass as though it were a goblet out of which she had just administered a death potion.

"Well, Battle," said George Lomax, "it all seems clear enough. Yes, perfectly clear. The man fires a shot, disabling Mr. Thesiger, flings away the weapon, runs along the terrace and down the gravel path."

"Where he ought to have been caught by my men," put in Battle.

"Your men, if I may say so, Battle, seem to have been singularly remiss. They didn't see Miss Wade come in. If they could miss her coming in, they could easily miss the thief going out."

Superintendent Battle opened his mouth to speak, then seemed to think better of it. Jimmy Thesiger looked at him curiously. He would have given a lot to know just what was in Superintendent Battle's mind.

"Must have been a champion runner," was all the Scotland Yard man contented himself with saying.

"How do you mean, Battle?"

"Just what I say, Mr. Lomax. I was round the corner of the terrace myself not fifty seconds after the shot was fired. And for a man to run all that distance towards me and get round the corner of the path before I appeared round the side of the house—well, as I say, he must have been a champion runner."

"I am at a loss to understand you, Battle. You have some idea of your own which I have not yet—er—grasped. You say the man did not go across the lawn and now you hint—What exactly do you hint? That the man did not go down the path? Then in your opinion—er—where *did* he go?"

For answer, Superintendent Battle jerked an eloquent thumb upwards.

"Eh?" said George.

The Superintendent jerked harder than ever. George raised his head and looked at the ceiling.

"Up there," said Battle. "Up the ivy again."

"Nonsense, Superintendent. What you are suggesting is impossible."

"Not at all impossible, sir. He'd done it once. He could do it twice."

"I don't mean impossible in that sense. But if the man wanted to escape, he'd never bolt back into the house."

"Safest place for him, Mr. Lomax."

"But Mr. O'Rourke's door was still locked on the inside when we came to him."

"And how did you get to him? Through Sir Stanley's room. That's the way our man went. Lady Eileen tells me she saw the door knob of Mr. O'Rourke's door move. That was when our friend was up there the first time. I suspect the key was under Mr. O'Rourke's pillow. But his exit is clear enough the second time—through the communicating door and through Sir Stanley's room, which, of course, was empty. Like everyone else, Sir Stanley is rushing downstairs to the library. Our man's got a clear course."

"And where did he go then?"

Superintendent Battle shrugged his burly shoulders and became evasive.

"Plenty of ways open. Into an empty room on the other side of the house and down the ivy again—out through a side door—or, just possibly, if it was an inside job, he—well, stayed in the house."

George looked at him in shocked surprise.

"Really, Battle, I should—I should feel it very deeply if one of my servants—er—I have the most perfect reliance on them—it would distress me very much to have to suspect—"

"Nobody's asking you to suspect anyone, Mr. Lomax. I'm just putting all the possibilities before you. The servants may be all right—probably are."

"You have disturbed me," said George. "You have disturbed me greatly."

His eyes appeared more protuberant than ever.

To distract him, Jimmy poked delicately at a curious blackened object on the table.

"What's this?" he asked.

"That's exhibit Z," said Battle. "The last of our little lot. It is, or rather it has been, a glove."

He picked it up, the charred relic, and manipulated it with pride.

"Where did you find it?" asked Sir Oswald.

Battle jerked his head over his shoulder.

"In the grate—nearly burnt, but not quite. Queer; looks as though it had been chewed by a dog."

"It might possibly be Miss Wade's," suggested Jimmy. "She has several dogs."

The Superintendent shook his head.

"This isn't a lady's glove—no, not even the large kind of loose glove ladies wear nowadays. Fit it on, sir, a moment."

He adjusted the blackened object over Jimmy's hand.

"You see—it's large even for you."

"Do you attach importance to this discovery?" inquired Sir Oswald coldly.

"You never know, Sir Oswald, what's going to be important or what isn't."

There was a sharp tap at the door and Bundle entered.

"I'm so sorry," she said apologetically, "but Father has just rung up. He says I must come home because everybody is worrying him."

She paused.

"Yes, my dear Eileen?" said George encouragingly, perceiving that there was more to come.

"I wouldn't have interrupted you—only that I thought it might perhaps have something to do with all this. You see, what has upset Father is that one of our footmen is missing. He went out last night and hasn't come back."

"What is the man's name?" It was Sir Oswald who took up the cross-examination.

"John Bauer."

"An Englishman?"

"I believe he calls himself a Swiss—but I think he's a German. He speaks English perfectly, though."

"Ah!" Sir Oswald drew in his breath with a long, satisfied hiss. "And he has been at Chimneys—how long?"

"Just under a month."

Sir Oswald turned to the other two.

"Here is our missing man. You know, Lomax, as well as I do, that several foreign Governments are after the thing. I remember the man now perfectly—tall, well-drilled fellow. Came about a fortnight before we left. A clever move. Any new servants here would be closely scrutinized, but at Chimneys, five miles away—" He did not finish the sentence.

"You think the plan was laid so long beforehand?"

"Why not? There are millions in that formula, Lomax. Doubtless Bauer hoped to get access to my private papers at Chimneys, and to learn something of forthcoming arrangements from them. It seems likely that he may have had an accomplice in this house—someone who put him wise to the lie of the land and who saw to the doping of O'Rourke. But Bauer was the man Miss Wade saw climbing down the ivy—the big, powerful man."

He turned to Superintendent Battle.

"Bauer was your man, Superintendent. And, somehow or other, you let him slip through your fingers."

24

Bundle Wonders

There was no doubt that Superintendent Battle was taken aback. He fingered his chin thoughtfully.

"Sir Oswald is right, Battle," said George. "This is the man. Any hope of catching him?"

"There may be, sir. It certainly looks—well, suspicious. Of course the man may turn up again—at Chimneys, I mean."

"Do you think it likely?"

"No, it isn't," confessed Battle. "Yes, it certainly looks as though Bauer were the man. But I can't quite see how he got in and out of these grounds unobserved."

"I have already told you my opinion of the men you posted," said George. "Hopelessly inefficient—I don't want to blame you, Superintendent, but—" His pause was eloquent.

"Ah, well," said Battle lightly, "my shoulders are broad."

He shook his head and sighed.

"I must get to the telephone at once. Excuse me, gentlemen. I'm sorry, Mr. Lomax—I feel I've rather bungled this business. But it's been puzzling, more puzzling than you know."

He strode hurriedly from the room.

"Come into the garden," said Bundle to Jimmy. "I want to talk to you."

They went out together through the window. Jimmy stared down at the lawn, frowning.

"What's the matter?" asked Bundle.

Jimmy explained the circumstances of the pistol throwing.

"I'm wondering," he ended, "what was in old Battle's mind when he got Coote to throw the pistol. Something, I'll swear. Anyhow, it landed up about ten yards farther than it should have done. You know, Bundle, Battle's a deep one."

"He's an extraordinary man," said Bundle. "I want to tell you about last night."

She retailed her conversation with the Superintendent. Jimmy listened attentively.

"So the Countess is No. 1," he said thoughtfully. "It all hangs together very well. No. 2—Bauer—comes over from Chimneys. He climbs up into O'Rourke's room, knowing that O'Rourke has had a sleeping draught administered to him—by the Countess somehow or other. The arrangement is that he is to throw down the papers to the Countess, who will be waiting below. Then she'll nip back through the library and up to her room. If Bauer's caught leaving the grounds, they'll find nothing on him. Yes, it was a good plan—but it went wrong. No sooner is the Countess in the library than she hears me coming and has to jump behind the screen. Jolly awkward for her, because she can't warn her accomplice. No. 2 pinches the papers, looks out of the window, sees, as he thinks, the Countess waiting, pitches the papers down to her and proceeds to climb down the ivy, where he finds a nasty surprise in the shape of me waiting for him. Pretty nervy work for the Countess waiting behind her screen. All things considered, she told a pretty good story. Yes, it all hangs together very well."

"Too well," said Bundle decidedly.

"Eh?" said Jimmy, surprised.

"What about No. 7—No. 7, who never appears, but lives in the background. The Countess and Bauer? No, it's not so simple as that. Bauer was here last night, yes. But he was only here in case things went wrong—as they have done. His part is the part of scapegoat; to draw all attention from No. 7—the boss."

"I say, Bundle," said Jimmy anxiously, "you haven't been reading too much sensational literature, have you?"

Bundle threw him a glance of dignified reproach.

"Well," said Jimmy, "I'm not yet like the Red Queen. I can't believe six impossible things before breakfast."

"It's after breakfast," said Bundle.

"Or even after breakfast. We've got a perfectly good hypothesis which fits the facts—and you won't have it at any price, simply because like the old riddle, you want to make things more difficult."

"I'm sorry," said Bundle, "but I cling passionately to a mysterious No. 7 being a member of the house-party."

"What does Bill think?"

"Bill," said Bundle coldly, "is impossible."

"Oh!" said Jimmy. "I suppose you've told him about the Countess? He ought to be warned. Heaven knows what he'll go blabbing about otherwise."

"He won't hear a word against her," said Bundle. "He's—oh, simply idiotic. I wish you'd drive it home to him about that mole."

"You forget I wasn't in the cupboard," said Jimmy. "And anyway I'd rather not argue with Bill about his lady friend's mole. But surely he can't be such an ass as not to see that everything fits in?"

"He's every kind of ass," said Bundle bitterly. "You made the greatest mistake, Jimmy, in ever telling him at all."

"I'm sorry," said Jimmy. "I didn't see it at the time—but I do now. I was a fool, but dash it all, old Bill—"

"You know what foreign adventuresses are," said Bundle. "How they get hold of one."

"As a matter of fact, I don't," said Jimmy. "One has never tried to get hold of me." And he sighed.

For a moment or two there was silence. Jimmy was turning things over in his mind. The more he thought about them, the more unsatisfactory they seemed.

"You say that Battle wants the Countess let alone," he said at last.

"Yes."

"The idea being that through her he will get at someone else?"

Bundle nodded.

Jimmy frowned deeply as he tried to see where this led. Clearly Battle had some very definite idea in his mind.

"Sir Stanley Digby went up to town early this morning, didn't he?" he said.

"Yes."

"O'Rourke with him?"

"Yes, I think so."

"You don't think—no, that's impossible!"

"What?"

"That O'Rourke can be mixed up in this in any way?"

"It's possible," said Bundle thoughtfully. "He's got what one calls a very vivid personality. No, it wouldn't surprise me if—oh, to tell the truth, nothing would surprise me! In fact, there's only one person I'm really sure isn't No. 7."

"Who's that?"

"Superintendent Battle."

"Oh! I thought you were going to say George Lomax."

"Ssh, here he comes."

George was, indeed, bearing down upon them in an unmistakable manner. Jimmy made an excuse and slipped away. George sat down by Bundle.

"My dear Eileen, must you really leave us?"

"Well, Father seems to have got the wind up rather badly. I think I'd better go home and hold his hand."

"This little hand will indeed be comforting," said George, taking it and pressing it playfully. "My dear Eileen, I understand your reasons and I honour you for them. In these days of changed and unsettled conditions—"

"He's off," thought Bundle desperately.

"—when family life is at a premium—all the old standards falling!—it becomes our class to set an example—to show that we, at least, are unaffected by modern conditions. They call us the Die Hards—I am proud of the term—I repeat I am proud of the term! There are things that *should* die hard—dignity, beauty, modesty, the sanctity of family life, filial respect—who dies if these shall live? As I was saying, my dear Eileen, I envy you the privileges of your youth. Youth! What a wonderful thing! What a wonderful word! And we do not appreciate it until we grow to—er—maturer years. I confess, my dear child, that I have in the past been disappointed by your levity. I see now it was but the careless and charming levity of a child. I perceive now the serious and earnest beauty of your mind. You will allow me, I hope, to help you with your reading?"

"Oh, thank you," said Bundle faintly.

"And you must never be afraid of me again. I was shocked when Lady Caterham told me that you stood in awe of me. I can assure you that I am a very humdrum sort of person."

The spectacle of George being modest struck Bundle spellbound. George continued.

"Never be shy with me, dear child. And do not be afraid of boring me. It will be a great delight to me to—if I may say so—form your budding mind. I will be your political mentor. We have never needed young women of talent and charm in the Party more than we need them to-day. You may well be destined to follow in the footsteps of your aunt, Lady Caterham."

This awful prospect knocked Bundle out completely. She could only stare helplessly at George. This did not discourage him—on the contrary. His main objection to women was that they talked too much. It was seldom that he found what he considered a really good listener. He smiled benignantly at Bundle.

"The butterfly emerging from the chrysalis. A wonderful picture. I have a very interesting work on political economy. I will look it out now, and you can take it to Chimneys with you. When you have finished it, I will discuss it with you. Do not hesitate to write to me if any point puzzles you. I have many public duties, but by unsparing work I can always make time for the affairs of my friends. I will look for the book."

He strode away. Bundle gazed after him with a dazed expression. She was roused by the unexpected advent of Bill.

"Look here," said Bill, "what the hell was Codders holding your hand for?"

"It wasn't my hand," said Bundle wildly. "It was my budding mind."

"Don't be an ass, Bundle."

"Sorry, Bill, but I'm a little worried. Do you remember saying that Jimmy ran a grave risk coming down here?"

"So he does," said Bill. "It's frightfully hard to escape from Codders once he's got interested in you. Jimmy will be caught in the toils before he knows where he is."

"It's not Jimmy who's got caught—it's me," said Bundle wildly. "I shall have to meet endless Mrs. Macattas, and read political economy and discuss it with George, and Heavens knows where it will end!"

Bill whistled.

"Poor old Bundle. Been laying it on a bit thick, haven't you?"

"I must have done. Bill, I feel horribly entangled."

"Never mind," said Bill consolingly. "George doesn't really believe in women standing for Parliament, so you won't have to stand up on platforms and talk a lot of junk, or kiss dirty babies in Bermondsey. Come and have a cocktail. It's nearly lunch time."

Bundle got up and walked by his side obediently.

"And I do so hate politics," she murmured piteously.

"Of course you do. So do all sensible people. It's only people like Codders and Pongo who take them seriously and revel in them. But all the same," said Bill, reverting suddenly to a former point, "you oughtn't to let Codders hold your hand."

"Why on earth not?" said Bundle. "He's known me all my life."

"Well, I don't like it."

"Virtuous William—Oh, I say, look at Superintendent Battle."

They were just passing in through a side door. A cupboard-like room opened out of the little hallway. In it were kept golf clubs, tennis racquets, bowls and other features of country house life. Superintendent Battle was conducting a minute examination of various golf clubs. He looked up a little sheepishly at Bundle's exclamation.

"Going to take up golf, Superintendent Battle?"

"I might do worse, Lady Eileen. They say it's never too late to start. And I've got one good quality that will tell at any game."

"What's that?" asked Bill.

"I don't know when I'm beaten. If everything goes wrong, I turn to and start again!"

And with a determined look on his face, Superintendent Battle came out and joined them, shutting the door behind him.

25

Jimmy Lays His Plans

Jimmy Thesiger was feeling depressed. Avoiding George, whom he suspected of being ready to tackle him on serious subjects, he stole quietly away after lunch. Proficient as he was in details of the Santa Fé boundary dispute, he had no wish to stand an examination on it this minute.

Presently what he hoped would happen came to pass. Loraine Wade, also unaccompanied, strolled down one of the shady garden paths. In a moment Jimmy was by her side. They walked for some minutes in silence and then Jimmy said tentatively:

"Loraine?"

"Yes?"

"Look here, I'm a bad chap at putting things—but what about it? What's wrong with getting a special license and being married and living together happy ever afterwards?"

Loraine displayed no embarrassment at this surprising proposal. Instead she threw back her head and laughed frankly.

"Don't laugh at a chap," said Jimmy reproachfully.

"I can't help it. You were so funny."

"Loraine—you are a little devil."

"I'm not. I'm what's called a thoroughly nice girl."

"Only to those who don't know you—who are taken in by your delusive appearance of meekness and decorum."

"I like your long words."

"All out of cross-word puzzles."

"So educative."

"Loraine dear, don't beat about the bush. Will you or won't you?"

Loraine's face sobered. It took on its characteristic appearance of determination. Her small mouth hardened and her little chin shot out aggressively.

"No, Jimmy. Not while things are as they are at present—all unfinished."

"I know we haven't done what we set out to do," agreed Jimmy. "But all the same—well, it's the end of a chapter. The papers are safe at the Air Ministry. Virtue triumphant. And—for the moment—nothing doing."

"So—let's get married?" said Loraine with a slight smile.

"You've said it. Precisely the idea."

But again Loraine shook her head.

"No, Jimmy. Until this thing's rounded up—until we're safe—"

"You think we're in danger?"

"Don't you?"

Jimmy's cherubic pink face clouded over.

"You're right," he said at last. "If that extraordinary rigmarole of Bundle's is true—and I suppose, incredible as it sounds, it must be true—then we're not safe till we've settled with—No. 7!"

"And the others?"

"No—the others don't count. It's No. 7 with his own ways of working that frightens me. Because I don't know who he is or where to look for him."

Loraine shivered.

"I've been frightened," she said in a low voice. "Ever since Gerry's death. . . ."

"You needn't be frightened. There's nothing for you to be frightened about. You leave everything to me. I tell you, Loraine—*I'll get No. 7 yet.* Once we get him—well, I don't think there'll be much trouble with the rest of the gang, whoever they are."

"If you get him—and suppose he gets you?"

"Impossible," said Jimmy cheerfully. "I'm much too clever. Always have a good opinion of yourself—that's my motto."

"When I think of the things that might have happened last night—" Loraine shivered.

"Well, they didn't," said Jimmy. "We're both here, safe and sound—though I must admit my arm is confoundedly painful."

"Poor boy."

"Oh, one must expect to suffer in a good cause. And what with my wounds and my cheerful conversation, I've made a complete conquest of Lady Coote."

"Oh! Do you think that important?"

"I've an idea it may come in useful."

"You've got some plan in your mind, Jimmy. What is it?"

"The young hero never tells his plans," said Jimmy firmly. "They mature in the dark."

"You are an idiot, Jimmy."

"I know. I know. That's what everyone says. But I can assure you, Loraine, there's a lot of brain-work going on underneath. Now what about your plans? Got any?"

"Bundle has suggested that I should go to Chimneys with her for a bit."

"Excellent," said Jimmy approvingly. "Nothing could be better. I'd like an eye kept on Bundle anyway. You never know what mad thing she won't be up to next. She's so frightfully unexpected. And the worst of it is, she's so astonishingly successful. I tell you, keeping Bundle out of mischief is a whole-time job."

"Bill ought to look after her," suggested Loraine.

"Bill's pretty busy elsewhere."

"Don't you believe it," said Loraine.

"What? Not the Countess? But the lad's potty about her."

Loraine continued to shake her head.

"There's something there I don't quite understand. But it's not the Countess with Bill—it's Bundle. Why, this morning Bill was talking to me when Mr. Lomax came out and sat down by Bundle. He took her hand or something, and Bill was off like—like a rocket."

"What a curious taste some people have," observed Mr. Thesiger. "Fancy anyone who was talking to you wanting to do anything else. But you surprise me very much, Loraine. I thought our simple Bill was enmeshed in the toils of the beautiful foreign adventuress. Bundle thinks so, I know."

"Bundle may," said Loraine, "but I tell you, Jimmy, it isn't so."

"Then what's the big idea?"

"Don't you think it possible that Bill is doing a bit of sleuthing on his own?"

"Bill? He hasn't got the brains."

"I'm not so sure. When a simple, muscular person like Bill does set out to be subtle, no one ever gives him credit for it."

"And in consequence he can put in some good work. Yes, there's something in that. But all the same I'd never have thought it of Bill. He's doing the Countess's little woolly lamb to perfection. I think you're wrong, you know, Loraine. The Countess is an extraordinarily beautiful woman—not my type, of course," put in Mr. Thesiger hastily—"and old Bill has always had a heart like an hotel."

Loraine shook her head, unconvinced.

"Well," said Jimmy, "have it your own way. We seem to have more or less settled things. You go back with Bundle to Chimneys, and for heaven's sake keep her from poking about in that Seven Dials place again. Heaven knows what will happen if she does."

Loraine nodded.

"And now," said Jimmy, "I think a few words with Lady Coote would be advisable."

Lady Coote was sitting on a garden seat doing wool-work. The subject was a disconsolate and somewhat misshapen young woman weeping over an urn.

Lady Coote made room for Jimmy by her side, and he promptly, being a tactful young man, admired her work.

"Do you like it?" said Lady Coote, pleased. "It was begun by my Aunt Selina the week before she died. Cancer of the liver, poor thing."

"How beastly," said Jimmy.

"And how is the arm?"

"Oh, it's feeling quite all right. Bit of a nuisance and all that, you know."

"You'll have to be careful," said Lady Coote in a warning voice. "I've known blood-poisoning set in—and in that case you might lose your arm altogether."

"Oh! I say, I hope not."

"I'm only warning you," said Lady Coote.

"Where are you hanging out now?" inquired Mr. Thesiger. "Town—or where?"

Considering that he knew the answer to his query perfectly well, he put the question with a praiseworthy amount of ingenuousness.

Lady Coote sighed heavily.

"Sir Oswald has taken the Duke of Alton's place. Letherbury. You know it, perhaps?"

"Oh, rather. Topping place, isn't it?"

"Oh, I don't know," said Lady Coote. "It's a very large place, and gloomy, you know. Rows of picture galleries with such forbidding looking people. What they call Old Masters are very depressing, I think. You should have seen a little house we had in Yorkshire, Mr. Thesiger. When Sir Oswald was plain Mr. Coote. Such a nice lounge hall and a cheerful drawing-room with an inglenook—a white striped paper with a frieze of wistaria I chose for it, I remember. Satin stripe, you know, not moiré. Much better taste, I always think. The dining-room faced northeast, so we didn't get much sun in it, but with a good bright scarlet paper and a set of those comic hunting prints—why, it was as cheerful as Christmas."

In the excitement of these reminiscences, Lady Coote dropped several little balls of wool, which Jimmy dutifully retrieved.

"Thank you, my dear," said Lady Coote. "Now, what was I saying? Oh!—about houses—yes, I do like a cheerful house. And choosing things for it gives you an interest."

"I suppose Sir Oswald will be buying a place of his own one of these days," suggested Jimmy. "And then you can have it just as you like."

Lady Coote shook her head sadly.

"Sir Oswald talks of a firm doing it—and you know what that means."

"Oh! But they'd consult you!"

"It would be one of those grand places—all for the antique. They'd look down on the things I call comfortable and homey. Not but that Sir Oswald wasn't very comfortable and satisfied in his home always, and I daresay his tastes are just the same underneath. But nothing will suit him now but the best! He's got on wonderfully, and naturally he wants something to show for it, but many's the time I wonder where it will end."

Jimmy looked sympathetic.

"It's like a runaway horse," said Lady Coote. "Got the bit between its teeth and away it goes. It's the same with Sir Oswald. He's got on, and he's got on, till he can't stop getting on. He's one of the richest men in England now—but does that satisfy him? No, he wants still more. He wants to be—I don't know what he wants to be! I can tell you, it frightens me sometimes!"

"Like the Persian Johnny," said Jimmy, "who went about wailing for fresh worlds to conquer."

Lady Coote nodded acquiescence without much knowing what Jimmy was talking about.

"What I wonder is—will his stomach stand it?" she went on tearfully. "To have him an invalid—with his ideas—oh, it won't bear thinking of."

"He looks very hearty," said Jimmy, consolingly.

"He's got something on his mind," said Lady Coote. "Worried, that's what he is. *I* know."

"What's he worried about?"

"I don't know. Perhaps something at the works. It's a great comfort for him having Mr. Bateman. Such an earnest young man—and so conscientious."

"Marvellously conscientious," agreed Jimmy.

"Oswald thinks a lot of Mr. Bateman's judgment. He says that Mr. Bateman is always right."

"That was one of his worst characteristics years ago," said Jimmy feelingly.

Lady Coote looked slightly puzzled.

"That was an awfully jolly week-end I had with you at Chimneys," said Jimmy. "I mean it would have been awfully jolly if it hadn't been for poor old Gerry kicking the bucket. Jolly nice girls."

"I find girls very perplexing," said Lady Coote. "Not romantic, you know. Why, I embroidered some handkerchiefs for Sir Oswald with my own hair when we were engaged."

"Did you?" said Jimmy. "How marvellous. But I suppose girls haven't got long enough hair to do that nowadays."

"That's true," admitted Lady Coote. "But, oh, it shows in lots of other ways. I remember when I was a girl, one of my—well, my young men—picked up a handful of gravel, and a girl who was with me said at once that he was treasuring it because my feet had trodden on it. Such a pretty idea, I thought. Though it turned out afterwards that he was taking a course of mineralogy—or do I mean geology?—at a technical school. But I liked the idea—and stealing a girl's handkerchief and treasuring it—all those sort of things."

"Awkward if the girl wanted to blow her nose," said the practical Mr. Thesiger.

Lady Coote laid down her wool-work and looked searchingly but kindly at him.

"Come now," she said, "isn't there some nice girl that you fancy? That you'd like to work and make a little home for?"

Jimmy blushed and mumbled.

"I thought you got on very well with one of those girls at Chimneys that time—Vera Daventry."

"Socks?"

"They do call her that," admitted Lady Coote. "I can't think why. It isn't pretty."

"Oh, she's a topper," said Jimmy. "I'd like to meet her again."

"She's coming down to stay with us next week-end."

"Is she?" said Jimmy, trying to infuse a large amount of wistful longing into the two words.

"Yes. Would—would you like to come?"

"I *would*," said Jimmy heartily. "Thanks ever so much, Lady Coote."

And reiterating fervent thanks, he left her.

Sir Oswald presently joined his wife.

"What has that young jackanapes been boring you about?" he demanded. "I can't stand that young fellow."

"He's a dear boy," said Lady Coote. "And so brave. Look how he got wounded last night."

"Yes, messing around where he'd no business to be."

"I think you're very unfair, Oswald."

"Never done an honest day's work in his life. A real waster if there ever was one. He'd never get on if he had his way to make in the world."

"You must have got your feet damp last night," said Lady Coote. "I hope you won't get pneumonia. Freddie Richards died of it the other day. Dear me, Oswald, it makes my blood run cold to think of you wandering about with a dangerous burglar loose in the grounds. He might have shot you. I've asked Mr. Thesiger down for next week-end, by the way."

"Nonsense," said Sir Oswald. "I won't have that young man in my house, do you hear, Maria?"

"Why not?"

"That's my business."

"I'm so sorry, dear," said Lady Coote placidly. "I've asked him now, so it can't be helped. Pick up that ball of pink wool, will you, Oswald?"

Sir Oswald complied, his face black as thunder. He looked at his wife and hesitated. Lady Coote was placidly threading her wool needle.

"I particularly don't want Thesiger down next week-end," he said at last. "I've heard a good deal about him from Bateman. He was at school with him."

"What did Mr. Bateman say?"

"He'd no good to say of him. In fact, he warned me very seriously against him."

"He did, did he?" said Lady Coote thoughtfully.

"And I have the highest respect for Bateman's judgment. I've never known him wrong."

"Dear me," said Lady Coote. "What a mess I seem to have made of things. Of course, I should never have asked him if I had known. You should have told me all this before, Oswald. It's too late now."

She began to roll up her work very carefully. Sir Oswald looked at her, made as if to speak, then shrugged his shoulders. He followed her into the house. Lady Coote, walking ahead, wore a very faint smile on her face. She was fond of her husband, but she was also fond—in a quiet, unobtrusive, wholly womanly manner—of getting her own way.

26

Mainly About Golf

"That friend of yours is a nice girl, Bundle," said Lord Caterham.

Loraine had been at Chimneys for nearly a week, and had earned the high opinion of her host—mainly because of the charming readiness she had shown to be instructed in the science of the mashie shot.

Bored by his winter abroad, Lord Caterham had taken up golf. He was an execrable player and in consequence was profoundly enthusiastic over the game. He spent most of his mornings lofting mashie shots over various shrubs and bushes—or, rather, essaying to loft them, hacking large bits out of the velvety turf and generally reducing MacDonald to despair.

"We must lay out a little course," said Lord Caterham, addressing a daisy. "A sporting little course. Now then, just watch this one, Bundle. Off the right knee, slow back, keep the head still and use the wrists."

The ball, heavily topped, scudded across the lawn and disappeared into the unfathomed depths of a great bank of rhododendrons.

"Curious," said Lord Caterham. "What did I do then, I wonder? As I was saying. Bundle, that friend of yours is a very nice girl. I really think I am inducing her to take quite an interest in the game. She hit some excellent shots this morning—really quite as good as I could do myself."

Lord Caterham took another careless swing and removed an immense chunk of turf. MacDonald, who was passing, retrieved it and stamped it firmly back. The look he gave Lord Caterham would have caused anyone but an ardent golfer to sink through the earth.

"If MacDonald has been guilty of cruelty to Cootes, which I strongly suspect," said Bundle, "he's being punished now."

"Why shouldn't I do as I like in my own garden?" demanded her father. "MacDonald ought to be interested in the way my game is coming on—the Scotch are a great golfing nation."

"You poor old man," said Bundle. "You'll never be a golfer—but at any rate it keeps you out of mischief."

"Not at all," said Lord Caterham. "I did the long sixth in five the other day. The pro was very surprised when I told him about it."

"He would be," said Bundle.

"Talking of Cootes, Sir Oswald plays a fair game—a very fair game.

Not a pretty style—too stiff. But straight down the middle every time. But curious how the cloven hoof shows—won't give you a six-inch putt! Makes you put it in every time. Now I don't like that."

"I suppose he's a man who likes to be sure," said Bundle.

"It's contrary to the spirit of the game," said her father. "And he's not interested in the theory of the thing either. Says he just plays for exercise and doesn't bother about style. Now, that secretary chap, Bateman, is quite different. It's the theory interests him. I was slicing badly with my spoon; and he said it all came from too much right arm; and he evolved a very interesting theory. It's all left arm in golf—the left arm is the arm that counts. He says he plays tennis left handed but golf with ordinary clubs because there his superiority with the left arm tells."

"And did he play very marvellously?" inquired Bundle.

"No, he didn't," confessed Lord Caterham. "But then he may have been off his game. I see the theory all right and I think there's a lot in it. Ah! Did you see that one, Bundle? Right over the rhododendrons. A perfect shot. Ah! If one could be sure of doing that every time—Yes, Tredwell, what is it?"

Tredwell addressed Bundle.

"Mr. Thesiger would like to speak to you on the telephone, my lady."

Bundle set off at full speed for the house, yelling "Loraine, Loraine," as she did so. Loraine joined her just as she was lifting the receiver.

"Hallo, is that you, Jimmy?"

"Hallo. How are you?"

"Very fit, but a bit bored."

"How's Loraine?"

"She's all right. She's here. Do you want to speak to her?"

"In a minute. I've got a lot to say. To begin with, I'm going down to the Cootes' for the week-end," he said significantly. "Now, look here, Bundle, you don't know how one gets hold of skeleton keys, do you?"

"Haven't the foggiest. Is it really necessary to take skeleton keys to the Cootes'?"

"Well, I had a sort of idea they'd come in handy. You don't know the sort of shop one gets them at?"

"What you want is a kindly burglar friend to show you the ropes."

"I do, Bundle, I do. And unfortunately, I haven't got one. I thought perhaps your bright brain might grapple successfully with the problem. But I suppose I shall have to fall back upon Stevens as usual. He'll be getting some funny ideas in his head soon about me—first a blue-nosed automatic—and now skeleton keys. He'll think I've joined the criminal classes."

"Jimmy?" said Bundle.

"Yes?"

"Look here—be careful, won't you? I mean if Sir Oswald finds you nosing around with skeleton keys—well, I should think he could be very unpleasant when he likes."

"Young man of pleasing appearance in the dock! All right, I'll be careful. Pongo's the fellow I'm really frightened of. He sneaks around so on those flat feet of his. You never hear him coming. And he always did have a genius for poking his nose in where he wasn't wanted. But trust to the boy hero."

"Well, I wish Loraine and I were going to be there to look after you."

"Thank you, nurse. As a matter of fact, though, I have a scheme—"

"Yes?"

"Do you think you and Loraine might have a convenient car breakdown near Letherbury to-morrow morning? It's not so very far from you, is it?"

"Forty miles. That's nothing."

"I thought it wouldn't be—to you! Don't kill Loraine though. I'm rather fond of Loraine. All right, then—somewhere round about quarter to half past twelve."

"So that they invite us to lunch?"

"That's the idea. I say, Bundle, I ran into that girl Socks yesterday and what do you think—Terence O'Rourke is going to be down there this week-end!"

"Jimmy, do you think he—"

"Well—suspect everyone, you know. That's what they say. He's a wild lad, and daring as they make them. I wouldn't put it past him to run a secret society. He and the Countess might be in this together. He was out in Hungary last year."

"But he could pinch the formula any time."

"That's just what he couldn't. He'd have to do it under circumstances where he couldn't be suspected. But the retreat up the ivy and into his own bed—well, that would be rather neat. Now for instructions. After a few polite nothings to Lady Coote, you and Loraine are to get hold of Pongo and O'Rourke by hook or by crook and keep them occupied till lunch time. See? It oughtn't to be difficult for a couple of beautiful girls like you."

"You're using the best butter, I see."

"A plain statement of fact."

"Well, at any rate, your instructions are duly noted. Do you want to talk to Loraine now?"

Bundle passed over the receiver and tactfully left the room.

27

Nocturnal Adventure

Jimmy Thesiger arrived at Letherbury on a sunny autumn afternoon and was greeted affectionately by Lady Coote and with cold dislike by Sir Oswald. Aware of the keen match-making eye of Lady Coote upon him, Jimmy took pains to make himself extremely agreeable to Socks Daventry.

O'Rourke was there in excellent spirits. He was inclined to be official and secretive about the mysterious events at the Abbey, about which Socks catechized him freely, but his official reticence took a novel form—namely that of embroidering the tale of events in such a fantastic manner that nobody could possibly guess what the truth might have been.

"Four masked men with revolvers? Is that really so?" demanded Socks severely.

"Ah! I'm remembering how that there was the round half dozen of them to hold me down and force the stuff down my throat. Sure, and I thought it was poison, and I done for entirely."

"And what was stolen, or what did they try and steal?"

"What else but the crown jewels of Russia that were brought to Mr. Lomax secretly to deposit in the Bank of England."

"What a bloody liar you are," said Socks without emotion.

"A liar? I? And the jewels brought over by aeroplane with my best friend as pilot. This is secret history I'm telling you, Socks. Will you ask Jimmy Thesiger there if you don't believe me. Not that I'd be putting any trust in what he'd say."

"Is it true," said Socks, "that George Lomax came down without his false teeth? That's what I want to know."

"There were two revolvers," said Lady Coote. "Nasty things. I saw them myself. It's a wonder this poor boy wasn't killed."

"Oh, I was born to be hanged," said Jimmy.

"I hear that there was a Russian countess there of subtle beauty," said Socks. "And that she vamped Bill."

"Some of the things she said about Buda Pesth were too dreadful," said Lady Coote. "I shall never forget them. Oswald, we must send a subscription."

Sir Oswald grunted.

"I'll make a note of it, Lady Coote," said Rupert Bateman.

"Thank you, Mr. Bateman. I feel one ought to do something as a thank offering. I can't imagine how Sir Oswald escaped being shot—letting alone die of pneumonia."

"Don't be foolish, Maria," said Sir Oswald.

"I've always had a horror of cat burglars," said Lady Coote.

"Think of having the luck to meet one face to face. How thrilling!" murmured Socks.

"Don't you believe it," said Jimmy. "It's damned painful." And he patted his right arm gingerly.

"How is the poor arm?" inquired Lady Coote.

"Oh, pretty well all right now. But it's been the most confounded nuisance having to do everything with the left hand. I'm no good whatever with it."

"Every child should be brought up to be ambidextrous," said Sir Oswald.

"Oh!" said Socks, somewhat out of her depth. "Is that like seals?"

"Not amphibious," said Mr. Bateman. "Ambidextrous means using either hand equally well."

"Oh!" said Socks, looking at Sir Oswald with respect. "Can you?"

"Certainly; I can write with either hand."

"But not with both at once?"

"That would not be practical," said Sir Oswald shortly.

"No," said Socks thoughtfully. "I suppose that would be a bit too subtle."

"It would be a grand thing now in a Government department," observed Mr. O'Rourke, "if one could keep the right hand from knowing what the left hand was doing."

"Can you use both hands?"

"No, indeed. I'm the most right-handed person that ever was."

"But you deal cards with your left hand," said the observant Bateman. "I noticed the other night."

"Oh, but that's different entirely," said Mr. O'Rourke easily.

A gong with a sombre note pealed out and everyone went upstairs to dress for dinner.

After dinner Sir Oswald and Lady Coote, Mr. Bateman and Mr. O'Rourke played bridge and Jimmy passed a flirtatious evening with Socks. The last words Jimmy heard as he retreated up the staircase that night were Sir Oswald saying to his wife:

"You'll never make a bridge player, Maria."

And her reply:

"I know, dear. So you always say. You owe Mr. O'Rourke another pound, Oswald. That's right."

It was some two hours later that Jimmy crept noiselessly (or so he hoped) down the stairs. He made one brief visit to the dining-room and then found his way to Sir Oswald's study. There, after listening intently for a minute or two, he set to work. Most of the drawers of the desk were locked, but a curiously shaped bit of wire in Jimmy's hand soon saw to that. One by one the drawers yielded to his manipulations.

Drawer by drawer he sorted through methodically, being careful to replace everything in the same order. Once or twice he stopped to listen, fancying he heard some distant sound. But he remained undisturbed.

The last drawer was looked through. Jimmy now knew—or could have known had he been paying attention—many interesting details relating to steel; but he had found nothing of what he wanted—a reference to Herr Eberhard's invention or anything that could give him a clue to the identity of the mysterious No. 7. He had, perhaps, hardly hoped that he would. It was an off-chance and he had taken it—but he had not expected much result—except by sheer luck.

He tested the drawers to make sure that he had relocked them securely. He knew Rupert Bateman's powers of minute observation and glanced round the room to make sure that he had left no incriminating trace of his presence.

"That's that," he muttered to himself softly. "Nothing there. Well, perhaps I'll have better luck to-morrow morning—if the girls only play up."

He came out of the study, closing the door behind him and locking it. For a moment he thought he heard a sound quite near him, but decided he had been mistaken. He felt his way noiselessly along the great hall. Just enough light came from the high vaulted windows to enable him to pick his way without stumbling into anything.

Again he heard a soft sound—he heard it quite certainly this time and without the possibility of making a mistake. He was not alone in the hall. Somebody else was there, moving as stealthily as he was. His heart beat suddenly very fast.

With a sudden spring he jumped to the electric switch and turned on the lights. The sudden glare made him blink—but he saw plainly enough. Not four feet away stood Rupert Bateman.

"My goodness, Pongo," cried Jimmy, "you did give me a start. Slinking about like that in the dark."

"I heard a noise," explained Mr. Bateman severely. "I thought burglars had got in and I came down to see."

Jimmy looked thoughtfully at Mr. Bateman's rubber-soled feet.

"You think of everything, Pongo," he said genially. "Even a lethal weapon."

His eye rested on the bulge in the other's pocket.

"It's as well to be armed. One never knows whom one may meet."

"I am glad you didn't shoot," said Jimmy. "I'm a bit tired of being shot at."

"I might easily have done so," said Mr. Bateman.

"It would be dead against the law if you did," said Jimmy. "You've got to make quite sure the beggar's house-breaking, you know, before you pot at him. You mustn't jump to conclusions. Otherwise you'd have to explain why you shot a guest on a perfectly innocent errand like mine."

"By the way, what did you come down for?"

"I was hungry," said Jimmy. "I rather fancied a dry biscuit."

"There are some biscuits in a tin by your bed," said Rupert Bateman.

He was staring at Jimmy very intently through his horn-rimmed spectacles.

"Ah! That's where the staff work has gone wrong, old boy. There's a tin there with 'Biscuits for Starving Visitors' on it. But when the starving visitor opened it—nothing inside. So I just toddled down to the dining-room."

And with a sweet, ingenuous smile, Jimmy produced from his dressing-gown pocket a handful of biscuits.

There was a moment's pause.

"And now I think I'll toddle back to bed," said Jimmy. "Night-night, Pongo."

With an affectation of nonchalance, he mounted the staircase. Rupert Bateman followed him. At the doorway of his room, Jimmy paused as if to say good-night once more.

"It's an extraordinary thing about these biscuits," said Mr. Bateman. "Do you mind if I just—"

"Certainly, laddie, look for yourself."

Mr. Bateman strode across the room, opened the biscuit box and stared at its emptiness.

"Very remiss," he murmured. "Well, good-night."

He withdrew. Jimmy sat on the edge of his bed listening for a minute.

"That was a narrow shave," he murmured to himself. "Suspicious sort of chap, Pongo. Never seems to sleep. Nasty habit of his prowling around with a revolver."

He got up and opened one of the drawers of the dressing-table. Beneath an assortment of ties lay a pile of biscuits.

"There's nothing for it," said Jimmy. "I shall have to eat all the damned things. Ten to one, Pongo will come prowling round in the morning."

With a sigh, he settled down to a meal of biscuits for which he had no inclination whatever.

28

Suspicions

It was just on the appointed hour of twelve o'clock that Bundle and Loraine entered the park gates, having left the Hispano at an adjacent garage.

Lady Coote greeted the two girls with surprise, but distinct pleasure, and immediately pressed them to stay to lunch.

O'Rourke, who had been reclining in an immense arm chair, began at once to talk with great animation to Loraine, who was listening with half an ear to Bundle's highly technical explanation of the mechanical troubles which had affected the Hispano.

"And we said," ended Bundle, "how marvellous that the brute should have broken down just here! Last time it happened was on a Sunday at a place called Little Spedlington under the Hill. And it lived up to its name, I can tell you."

"That would be a grand name on the films," remarked O'Rourke.

"Birthplace of the simple country maiden," suggested Socks.

"I wonder now," said Lady Coote, "where Mr. Thesiger is?"

"He's in the billiard-room, I think," said Socks. "I'll fetch him."

She went off, but had hardly gone a minute when Rupert Bateman appeared on the scene, with the harassed and serious air usual with him.

"Yes, Lady Coote? Thesiger said you were asking for me. How do you do, Lady Eileen—"

He broke off to greet the two girls, and Loraine immediately took the field.

"Oh, Mr. Bateman! I've been wanting to see you. Wasn't it you who was telling me what to do for a dog when he is continually getting sore paws?"

The secretary shook his head.

"It must have been someone else, Miss Wade. Though, as a matter of fact, I do happen to know—"

"What a wonderful young man you are," interrupted Loraine. "You know about everything."

"One should keep abreast of modern knowledge," said Mr. Bateman seriously. "Now about your dog's paws—"

Terence O'Rourke murmured *sotto voce* to Bundle:

"'Tis a man like that that writes all those little paragraphs in the weekly papers. 'It is not generally known that to keep a brass fender uniformly bright,' etc.; 'The dorper beetle is one of the most interesting characters in the insect world'; 'The marriage customs of the Fingalese Indians,' and so on."

"General information, in fact."

"And what more horrible two words could you have?" said Mr. O'Rourke, and added piously: "Thank the heavens above I'm an educated man and know nothing whatever upon any subject at all."

"I see you've got clock golf here," said Bundle to Lady Coote.

"I'll take you on at it, Lady Eileen," said O'Rourke.

"Let's challenge those two," said Bundle. "Loraine, Mr. O'Rourke and I want to take you and Mr. Bateman on at clock golf."

"Do play, Mr. Bateman," said Lady Coote, as the secretary showed a momentary hesitation. "I'm sure Sir Oswald doesn't want you."

The four went out on the lawn.

"Very cleverly managed, what?" whispered Bundle to Loraine. "Congratulations on our girlish tact."

The round ended just before one o'clock, victory going to Bateman and Loraine.

"But I think you'll agree with me, partner," said Mr. O'Rourke, "that we played a more sporting game."

He lagged a little behind with Bundle.

"Old Pongo's a cautious player—he takes no risks. Now, with me it's neck or nothing. And a fine motto through life, don't you agree, Lady Eileen?"

"Hasn't it ever landed you in trouble?" asked Bundle, laughing.

"To be sure it has. Millions of times. But I'm still going strong. Sure, it'll take the hangman's noose to defeat Terence O'Rourke."

Just then Jimmy Thesiger strolled round the corner of the house.

"Bundle, by all that's wonderful!" he exclaimed.

"You've missed competing in the Autumn Meeting," said O'Rourke.

"I'd gone for a stroll," said Jimmy. "Where did these girls drop from?"

"We came on our flat feet," said Bundle. "The Hispano let us down."

And she narrated the circumstances of the breakdown.

Jimmy listened with sympathetic attention.

"Hard luck," he vouchsafed. "If it's going to take some time, I'll run you back in my car after lunch."

A gong sounded at that moment and they all went in. Bundle observed Jimmy covertly. She thought she had noticed an unusual note of exultance in his voice. She had the feeling that things had gone well.

After lunch they took a polite leave of Lady Coote, and Jimmy volunteered to run them down to the garage in his car. As soon as they had started the same word burst simultaneously from both girls' lips:

"Well?"

Jimmy chose to be provoking.

"Well?"

"Oh, pretty hearty, thanks. Slight indigestion owing to over indulgence in dry biscuits."

"But what has happened?"

"I tell you. Devotion to the cause made me eat too many dry biscuits. But did our hero flinch? No, he did not."

"Oh, Jimmy," said Loraine reproachfully, and he softened.

"What do you really want to know?"

"Oh, everything. Didn't we do it well? I mean, the way we kept Pongo and Terence O'Rourke in play."

"I congratulate you on the handling of Pongo. O'Rourke was probably a sitter—but Pongo is made of other stuff. There's only one word for that lad—it was in the *Sunday Newsbag* cross-word last week. Word of ten letters meaning everywhere at once. Ubiquitous. That describes Pongo down to the ground. You can't go anywhere without running into him—and the worst of it is you never hear him coming."

"You think he's dangerous?"

"Dangerous? Of course he's not dangerous. Fancy Pongo being dangerous. He's an ass. But, as I said just now, he's an ubiquitous ass. He doesn't even seem to need sleep like ordinary mortals. In fact, to put it bluntly, the fellow's a damned nuisance."

And, in a somewhat aggrieved manner, Jimmy described the events of the previous evening.

Bundle was not very sympathetic.

"I don't know what you think you're doing anyway, mouching round here."

"No. 7," said Jimmy crisply. "That's what I'm after. No. 7."

"And you think you'll find him in this house?"

"I thought I might find a clue."

"And you didn't?"

"Not last night—no."

"But this morning," said Loraine, breaking in suddenly. "Jimmy, you did find something this morning. I can see it by your face."

"Well, I don't know if it is anything. But during the course of my stroll—"

"Which stroll didn't take you far from the house, I imagine."

"Strangely enough, it didn't. Round trip in the interior, we might call it.

Well, as I say, I don't know whether there's anything in it or not. But I found this."

With the celerity of a conjuror he produced a small bottle and tossed it over to the girls. It was half full of a white powder.

"What do you think it is?" asked Bundle.

"A white crystalline powder, that's what it is," said Jimmy. "And to any reader of detective fiction those words are both familiar and suggestive. Of course, if it turns out to be a new kind of patent tooth-powder, I shall be chagrined and annoyed."

"Where did you find it?" asked Bundle sharply.

"Ah!" said Jimmy, "that's my secret."

And from that point he would not budge in spite of cajolery and insult.

"Here we are at the garage," he said. "Let's hope the high-mettled Hispano has not been subjected to any indignities."

The gentleman at the garage presented a bill for five shillings and made a few vague remarks about loose nuts. Bundle paid him with a sweet smile.

"It's nice to know we all get money for nothing sometimes," she murmured to Jimmy.

The three stood together in the road, silent for the moment as they each pondered the situation.

"I know," said Bundle suddenly.

"Know what?"

"Something I meant to ask you—and nearly forgot. Do you remember that glove that Superintendent Battle found—the half-burnt one?"

"Yes."

"Didn't you say that he tried it on your hand?"

"Yes—it was a shade big. That fits in with the idea of its being a big, hefty man who wore it."

"That's not at all what I'm bothering about. Never mind the size of it. George and Sir Oswald were both there too, weren't they?"

"Yes."

"He could have given it to either of them to fit on?"

"Yes, of course—"

"But he didn't. He chose you. Jimmy, don't you see what that means?"

Mr. Thesiger stared at her.

"I'm sorry, Bundle. Possibly the jolly old brain isn't functioning as well as usual, but I haven't the faintest idea what you're talking about."

"Don't you see, Loraine?"

Loraine looked at her curiously, but shook her head. "Does it mean anything in particular?"

"Of course it does. Don't you see—Jimmy had his right hand in a sling."

"By Jove, Bundle," said Jimmy slowly. "It was rather odd now I come to think of it; it's being a left hand glove, I mean. Battle never said anything."

"He wasn't going to draw attention to it. By trying it on you it might pass without notice being drawn to it, and he talked about the size just to put everybody off. But surely it must mean that the man who shot at you held the pistol in his *left* hand."

"So we've got to look for a left-handed man," said Loraine thoughtfully.

"Yes, and I'll tell you another thing. That was what Battle was doing looking through the golf clubs. He was looking for a left-handed man's."

"By Jove," said Jimmy suddenly.

"What is it?"

"Well, I don't suppose there's anything in it, but it's rather curious."

He retailed the conversation at tea the day before.

"So Sir Oswald Coote is ambidextrous?" said Bundle.

"Yes. And I remember now on that night at Chimneys—you know, the night Gerry Wade died—I was watching the bridge and thinking idly how awkwardly someone was dealing—and then realizing that it was because they were dealing with the left hand. Of course, it must have been Sir Oswald."

They all three looked at each other. Loraine shook her head.

"A man like Sir Oswald Coote! It's impossible. What could he have to gain by it?"

"It seems absurd," said Jimmy. "And yet—"

"No. 7 has his own ways of working," quoted Bundle softly. "Supposing this is the way Sir Oswald has really made his fortune?"

"But why stage all that comedy at the Abbey when he'd had the formula at his own works?"

"There might be ways of explaining that," said Loraine. "The same line of argument you used about Mr. O'Rourke. Suspicion had to be diverted from him and placed in another quarter."

Bundle nodded eagerly.

"It all fits in. Suspicion is to fall on Bauer and the Countess. Who on earth would ever dream of suspecting Sir Oswald Coote?"

"I wonder if Battle does," said Jimmy slowly.

Some chord of memory vibrated in Bundle's mind. *Superintendent Battle plucking an ivy leaf off the millionaire's coat.*

Had Battle suspected all the time?

29

Singular Behaviour of George Lomax

"Mr. Lomax is here, my lord."

Lord Caterham started violently, for, absorbed in the intricacies of what not to do with the left wrist, he had not heard the butler approach over the soft turf. He looked at Tredwell more in sorrow than in anger.

"I told you at breakfast, Tredwell, that I should be particularly engaged this morning."

"Yes, my lord, but—"

"Go and tell Mr. Lomax that you have made a mistake, that I am out in the village, that I am laid up with the gout, or, if all else fails, that I am dead."

"Mr. Lomax, my lord, has already caught sight of your lordship when driving up the drive."

Lord Caterham sighed deeply.

"He would. Very well, Tredwell, I am coming." In a manner highly characteristic, Lord Caterham was always most genial when his feelings were in reality the reverse. He greeted George now with a heartiness quite unparalleled.

"My dear fellow, my dear fellow. Delighted to see you. Absolutely delighted. Sit down. Have a drink. Well, well, this is splendid!"

And having pushed George into a large arm-chair, he sat down opposite him and blinked nervously.

"I wanted to see you very particularly," said George.

"Oh!" said Lord Caterham faintly, and his heart sank, whilst his mind raced actively over all the dread possibilities that might lie behind that simple phrase.

"*Very* particularly," said George with heavy emphasis.

Lord Caterham's heart sank lower than ever. He felt that something was coming worse than anything he had yet thought of.

"Yes?" he said, with a courageous attempt at nonchalance.

"Is Eileen at home?"

Lord Caterham felt reprieved, but slightly surprised.

"Yes, yes," he said. "Bundle's here. Got that friend of hers with her—

the little Wade girl. Very nice girl—*very* nice girl. Going to be quite a good golfer one day. Nice easy swing—"

He was chatting garrulously on when George interrupted with ruthlessness:

"I am glad Eileen is at home. Perhaps I might have an interview with her presently?"

"Certainly, my dear fellow, certainly." Lord Caterham still felt very surprised, but was still enjoying the sensation of reprieve. "If it doesn't bore you."

"Nothing could bore me less," said George. "I think, Caterham, if I may say so, that you hardly appreciate the fact that Eileen is grown up. She is no longer a child. She is a woman, and if I may say so, a very charming and talented woman. The man who succeeds in winning her love will be extremely lucky. I repeat it—extremely lucky."

"Oh, I daresay," said Lord Caterham. "But she's very restless, you know. Never content to be in one place for more than two minutes together. However, I daresay young fellows don't mind that nowadays."

"You mean that she is not content to stagnate. Eileen has brains, Caterham; she is ambitious. She interests herself in the questions of the day, and brings her fresh and vivid young intellect to bear upon them."

Lord Caterham stared at him. It occurred to him that what was so often referred to as "the strain of modern life," had begun to tell upon George. Certainly his description of Bundle seemed to Lord Caterham ludicrously unlike.

"Are you sure you are feeling quite well?" he asked anxiously.

George waved the inquiry aside impatiently.

"Perhaps, Caterham, you begin to have some inkling of my purpose in visiting you this morning. I am not a man to undertake fresh responsibilities lightly. I have a proper sense, I hope, of what is due to the position I hold. I have given this matter my deep and earnest consideration. Marriage, especially at my age, is not to be undertaken without full—er—consideration. Equality of birth, similarity of tastes, general suitability, and the same religious creed—all these things are necessary and the pros and cons have to be weighed and considered. I can, I think, offer my wife a position in society that is not to be despised. Eileen will grace that position admirably. By birth and breeding she is fitted for it, and her brains and her acute political sense cannot but further my career to our mutual advantage. I am aware, Caterham, that there is—er—some disparity in years. But I can assure you that I feel full of vigour—in my prime. The balance of years should be on the husband's side. And Eileen has serious tastes—an older man will suit her better than some young jackanapes without either experience or *savoir-faire*. I can assure you, my dear Caterham, that I will cherish her—er—exquisite youth; I will cherish it—er—it will be appreciated. To watch the exquisite flower of her mind unfolding—what a privilege! And to think that I never realized—"

He shook his head deprecatingly and Lord Caterham, finding his voice with difficulty, said blankly:

"Do I understand you to mean—ah, my dear fellow, you can't want to marry Bundle?"

"You are surprised. I suppose to you it seems sudden. I have your permission, then, to speak to her?"

"Oh, yes," said Lord Caterham. "If it's permission you want—of course you can. But you know, Lomax, I really shouldn't if I were you. Just go home and think it over like a good fellow. Count twenty. All that sort of thing. Always a pity to propose and make a fool of yourself."

"I daresay you mean your advice kindly, Caterham, though I must confess that you put it somewhat strangely. But I have made up my mind to put my fortune to the test. I may see Eileen?"

"Oh, it's nothing to do with me," said Lord Caterham hastily; "Eileen settles her own affairs. If she came to me to-morrow and said she was going to marry the chauffeur, I shouldn't make any objections. It's the only way nowadays. Your children can make life damned unpleasant if you don't give in to them in every way. I say to Bundle, 'Do as you like, but don't worry me,' and really, on the whole, she is amazingly good about it."

George stood up, intent upon his purpose.

"Where shall I find her?"

"Well, really, I don't know," said Lord Caterham vaguely. "She might be anywhere. As I told you just now, she's never in the same place for two minutes together. No repose."

"And I suppose Miss Wade will be with her? It seems to me, Caterham, that the best plan would be for you to ring the bell and ask your butler to find her, saying that I wish to speak to her for a few minutes."

Lord Caterham pressed the bell obediently.

"Oh, Tredwell," he said, when the bell was answered, "just find her ladyship, will you? Tell her Mr. Lomax is anxious to speak to her in the drawing-room."

"Yes, my lord."

Tredwell withdrew. George seized Lord Caterham's hand and wrung it warmly, much to the latter's discomfort.

"A thousand thanks," he said. "I hope soon to bring you good news."

He hastened from the room.

"Well," said Lord Caterham. "Well!"

And after a long pause:

"What *has* Bundle been up to?"

The door opened again.

"Mr. Eversleigh, my lord."

As Bill hastened in, Lord Caterham caught his hand and spoke earnestly.

"Hullo, Bill. You're looking for Lomax, I suppose? Look here, if you want to do a good turn, hurry into the drawing-room and tell him the Cabinet have called an immediate meeting, or get him away somehow. It's really not fair to let the poor devil make an ass of himself all for some silly girl's prank."

"I've not come for Codders," said Bill. "Didn't know he was here. It's Bundle I want to see. Is she anywhere about?"

"You can't see her," said Lord Caterham. "Not just now, at any rate. George is with her."

"Well—what does it matter?"

"I think it does rather," said Lord Caterham. "He's probably spluttering horribly at this minute, and we mustn't do anything to make it worse for him."

"But what is he saying?"

"Heaven knows," said Lord Caterham. "A lot of damned nonsense, anyway. Never say too much, that was always my motto. Grab the girl's hand and let events take their course."

Bill stared at him.

"But look here, sir, I'm in a hurry. I must talk to Bundle—"

"Well, I don't suppose you'll have to wait long. I must confess I'm rather glad to have you here with me—I suppose Lomax will insist on coming back and talking to me when it's all over."

"When what's all over? What is Lomax supposed to be doing?"

"Hush," said Lord Caterham. "He's proposing."

"Proposing? Proposing what?"

"Marriage. To Bundle. Don't ask me why. I suppose he's come to what they call the dangerous age. I can't explain it any other way."

"Proposing to Bundle? The dirty swine. At his age."

Bill's face grew crimson.

"He says he's in the prime of life," said Lord Caterham cautiously.

"He? Why, he's decrepit—senile! I—" Bill positively choked.

"Not at all," said Lord Caterham coldly. "He's five years younger than I am."

"Of all the damned cheek! Codders and Bundle! A girl like Bundle! You oughtn't to have allowed it."

"I never interfere," said Lord Caterham.

"You ought to have told him what you thought of him."

"Unfortunately modern civilization rules that out," said Lord Caterham regretfully. "In the Stone Age now—but, dear me, I suppose even then I shouldn't be able to do it—being a small man."

"Bundle! Bundle! Why, I've never dared to ask Bundle to marry me because I knew she'd only laugh. And George—a disgusting wind-bag, an unscrupulous, hypocritical old hot-air merchant—a foul, poisonous self advertiser—"

"Go on," said Lord Caterham. "I'm enjoying this."

"My God!" said Bill simply and with feeling. "Look here, I must be off."

"No, no, don't go. I'd much rather you stayed. Besides, you want to see Bundle."

"Not now. This has driven everything else out of my head. You don't know where Jimmy Thesiger is by any chance? I believe he was staying with the Cootes. Is he there still?"

"I think he went back to town yesterday. Bundle and Loraine were over there on Saturday. If you'll only wait—"

But Bill shook his head energetically and rushed from the room. Lord Caterham tiptoed out into the hall, seized a hat and made a hurried exit by the side door. In the distance he observed Bill streaking down the drive in his car.

"That young man will have an accident," he thought.

Bill, however, reached London without any mischance, and proceeded to park his car in St. James's Square. Then he sought out Jimmy Thesiger's rooms. Jimmy was at home.

"Hullo, Bill. I say, what's the matter? You don't look your usual bright little self."

"I'm worried," said Bill. "I was worried anyway, and then something else turned up and gave me a jolt."

"Oh!" said Jimmy. "How lucid. What's it all about? Can I do anything?"

Bill did not reply. He sat staring at the carpet and looking so puzzled and uncomfortable that Jimmy felt his curiosity aroused.

"Has anything very extraordinary occurred, William?" he asked gently.

"Something damned odd. I can't make head or tail of it."

"The Seven Dials business?"

"Yes—the Seven Dials business. I got a letter this morning."

"A letter? What sort of a letter?"

"A letter from Ronny Devereux's executors."

"Good Lord! After all this time!"

"It seems he left instructions. If he was to die suddenly, a certain sealed envelope was to be sent to me exactly a fortnight after his death."

"And they've sent it to you?"

"Yes."

"You've opened it?"

"Yes."

"Well—what did it say?"

Bill turned a glance upon him, such a strange and uncertain one that Jimmy was startled.

"Look here," he said. "Pull yourself together, old man. It seems to have knocked the wind out of you, whatever it is. Have a drink."

He poured out a stiff whisky and soda and brought it over to Bill, who took it obediently. His face still bore the same dazed expression.

"It's what's in the letter," he said. "I simply can't believe it, that's all."

"Oh, nonsense," said Jimmy. "You must get into the habit of believing six impossible things before breakfast. I do it regularly. Now then, let's hear all about it. Wait a minute."

He went outside.

"Stevens?"

"Yes, sir."

"Just go out and get me some cigarettes, will you? I've run out."

"Very good, sir."

Jimmy waited till he heard the front door close. Then he came back into the sitting-room. Bill was just in the act of setting down his empty glass. He looked better, more purposeful and more master of himself.

"Now then," said Jimmy. "I've sent Stevens out so that we can't be overheard. Are you going to tell me all about it?"

"It's so incredible."

"Then it's sure to be true. Come on, out with it."

Bill drew a deep breath.

"I will. I'll tell you everything."

30

An Urgent Summons

Loraine, playing with a small and delectable puppy, was somewhat surprised when Bundle rejoined her after an absence of twenty minutes, in a breathless state and with an indescribable expression on her face.

"Whoof," said Bundle, sinking on to a garden seat. "Whoof."

"What's the matter?" asked Loraine, looking at her curiously.

"George is the matter—George Lomax."

"What's he been doing?"

"Proposing to me. It was awful. He spluttered and he stuttered, but he would go through with it—he must have learnt it out of a book, I think. There was no stopping him. Oh, how I hate men who splutter! And, unfortunately, I didn't know the reply."

"You must have known what you wanted to do."

"Naturally I'm not going to marry an apoplectic idiot like George. What I mean is, I didn't know the correct reply from the book of etiquette. I could only just say flatly: 'No, I won't.' What I ought to have said was something about being very sensible of the honour he had done me and so on and so on. But I got so rattled that in the end I jumped out of the window and bolted."

"Really, Bundle, that's not like you."

"Well, I never dreamt of such a thing happening. George—who I always thought hated me—and he did too. What a fatal thing it is to pretend to take an interest in a man's pet subject. You should have heard the drivel George talked about my girlish mind and the pleasure it would be to form it. My mind! If George knew one quarter of what was going on in my mind, he'd faint with horror!"

Loraine laughed. She couldn't help it.

"Oh, I know it's my own fault. I let myself in for this. There's Father dodging round that rhododendron. Hallo, Father."

Lord Caterham approached with a hangdog expression.

"Lomax gone, eh?" he remarked with somewhat forced geniality.

"A nice business you let me in for," said Bundle. "George told me he had your full approval and sanction."

"Well," said Lord Caterham, "what did you expect me to say? As a matter of fact, I didn't say that at all, or anything like it."

"I didn't really think so," said Bundle. "I assumed that George had talked you into a corner and reduced you to such a state that you could only nod your head feebly."

"That's very much what happened. How did he take it? Badly?"

"I didn't wait to see," said Bundle. "I'm afraid I was rather abrupt."

"Oh, well," said Lord Caterham, "perhaps that was the best way. Thank goodness in the future Lomax won't always be running over as he has been in the habit of doing, worrying me about things. Everything is for the best they say. Have you seen my jigger anywhere?"

"A mashie shot or two would steady my nerves, I think," said Bundle. "I'll take you on for sixpence, Loraine."

An hour passed very peacefully. The three returned to the house in a harmonious spirit. A note lay on the hall table.

"Mr. Lomax left that for you, my lord," explained Tredwell. "He was much disappointed to find that you had gone out."

Lord Caterham tore it open. He uttered a pained ejaculation and turned upon his daughter. Tredwell had retired.

"Really, Bundle, you might have made yourself clear, I think."

"What do you mean?"

"Well, read this."

Bundle took it and read:

"MY DEAR CATERHAM—I am sorry not to have had a word with you. I thought I made it clear that I wanted to see you again after my interview with Eileen. She, dear child, was evidently quite unaware of the feelings I entertained towards her. She was, I am afraid, much startled. I have no wish to hurry her in any way. Her girlish confusion was very charming, and I entertain an even higher regard for her, as I much appreciate her maidenly reserve. I must give her time to become accustomed to the idea. Her very confusion shows that she is not wholly indifferent to me and I have no doubts of my ultimate success.

"Believe me, dear Caterham,
"Your sincere friend,
"GEORGE LOMAX."

"Well," said Bundle. "Well, I'm damned!"

Words failed her.

"The man must be mad," said Lord Caterham. "No one could write those things about you, Bundle, unless they were slightly touched in the head. Poor chap, poor chap. But what persistence! I don't wonder he got into the Cabinet. It would serve him right if you did marry him, Bundle."

The telephone rang and Bundle moved forward to answer it. In another minute George and his proposal were forgotten, and she was beckoning eagerly to Loraine. Lord Caterham went off to his own sanctum.

"It's Jimmy," said Bundle. "And he's tremendously excited about something."

"Thank goodness I've caught you," said Jimmy's voice. "There's no time to be lost. Loraine's there, too?"

"Yes, she's here."

"Well, look here, I haven't got time to explain everything—in fact, I can't through the telephone. But Bill has been round to see me with the most amazing story you ever heard. If it's true—well, if it's true, it's the biggest scoop of the century. Now, look here, this is what you've got to do. Come up to town at once, both of you. Garage the car somewhere and go straight to the Seven Dials Club. Do you think that when you get there you can get rid of that footman fellow?"

"Alfred? Rather. You leave that to me."

"Good. Get rid of him and watch out for me and Bill. Don't show yourselves at the windows, but when we drive up, let us in at once. See?"

"Yes."

"That's all right then. Oh, Bundle, don't let on that you're going up to town. Make some other excuse. Say you're taking Loraine home. How would that do?"

"Splendidly. I say, Jimmy, I'm thrilled to the core."

"And you might as well make your will before starting."

"Better and better. But I wish I knew what it was all about."

"You will as soon as we meet. I'll tell you this much. We're going to get ready the hell of a surprise for No. 7!"

Bundle hung up the receiver and turned to Loraine, giving her a rapid résumé of the conversation. Loraine rushed upstairs and hurriedly packed her suitcase, and Bundle put her head round her father's door.

"I'm taking Loraine home, Father."

"Why? I had no idea she was going to-day."

"They want her back," said Bundle vaguely. "Just telephoned. Bye-bye."

"Here, Bundle, wait a minute. When will you be home?"

"Don't know. Expect me when you see me."

With this unceremonious exit Bundle rushed upstairs, put a hat on, slipped into her fur coat and was ready to start. She had already ordered the Hispano to be brought round.

The journey to London was without adventure, except such as was habitually provided by Bundle's driving. They left the car at a garage and proceeded direct to the Seven Dials Club.

The door was opened to them by Alfred. Bundle pushed her way past him without ceremony and Loraine followed.

"Shut the door, Alfred," said Bundle. "Now, I've come here especially to do you a good turn. The police are after you."

"Oh, my lady!"

Alfred turned chalk white.

"I've come to warn you because you did me a good turn the other night," went on Bundle rapidly. "There's a warrant out for Mr. Mosgorovsky, and the best thing you can do is to clear out of here as quick as you can. If you're not found here, they won't bother about you. Here's ten pounds to help you get away somewhere."

In three minutes' time an incoherent and badly scared Alfred had left 14 Hunstanton Street with only one idea in his head—never to return.

"Well, I've managed that all right," said Bundle with satisfaction.

"Was it necessary to be so—well, drastic?" Loraine demurred.

"It's safer," said Bundle. "I don't know what Jimmy and Bill are up to, but we don't want Alfred coming back in the middle of it and wrecking everything. Hallo, here they are. Well, they haven't wasted much time. Probably watching round the corner to see Alfred leave. Go down and open the door to them, Loraine."

Loraine obeyed. Jimmy Thesiger alighted from the driving seat.

"You stop there for a moment, Bill," he said. "Blow the horn if you think anyone's watching the place."

He ran up the steps and banged the door behind him. He looked pink and elated.

"Hallo, Bundle, there you are. Now then, we've got to get down to it. Where's the key of the room you got into last time?"

"It was one of the downstairs keys. We'd better bring the lot up."

"Right you are, but be quick. Time's short."

The key was easily found, the baize-lined door swung back and the three entered. The room was exactly as Bundle had seen it before, with the seven chairs grouped round the table. Jimmy surveyed it for a minute or two in silence. Then his eye went to the two cupboards.

"Which is the cupboard you hid in, Bundle?"

"This one."

Jimmy went to it and flung the door open. The same collection of miscellaneous glassware covered the shelves.

"We shall have to shift all this stuff," he murmured. "Run down and get Bill, Loraine. There's no need for him to keep watch outside any longer."

Loraine ran off.

"What are you going to do?" inquired Bundle impatiently.

Jimmy was down on his knees, trying to peer through the crack of the other cupboard door.

"Wait till Bill comes and you shall hear the whole story. This is his staff work—and a jolly creditable bit of work it is. Hallo—what's Loraine flying up the stairs for as though she'd got a mad bull after her?"

Loraine was indeed racing up the stairs as fast as she could. She burst in upon them with an ashen face and terror in her eyes.

"Bill—Bill—oh, Bundle—Bill!"

"What about Bill?"

Jimmy caught her by the shoulder.

"For God's sake, Loraine, what's happened?"

Loraine was still gasping.

"Bill—I think he's dead—he's in the car still—but he doesn't move or speak. I'm sure he's dead."

Jimmy muttered an oath and sprang for the stairs, Bundle behind him, her heart pounding unevenly and an awful feeling of desolation spreading over her.

Bill—dead? Oh, no! Oh, no! Not that. Please God—not that.

Together she and Jimmy reached the car, Loraine behind them.

Jimmy peered under the hood. Bill was sitting as he had left him, leaning back. But his eyes were closed and Jimmy's pull at his arm brought no response.

"I can't understand it," muttered Jimmy. "But he's not dead. Cheer up, Bundle. Look here, we've got to get him into the house. Let's pray to goodness no policeman comes along. If anybody says anything, he's our sick friend we're helping into the house."

Between the three of them they got Bill into the house without much difficulty, and without attracting much attention, save for an unshaven gentleman, who said sympathetically:

"Genneman's 'ad a couple, I shee," and nodded his head sapiently.

"Into the little back room downstairs," said Jimmy. "There's a sofa there."

They got him safely on to the sofa and Bundle knelt down beside him and took his limp wrist in her hand.

"His pulse is beating," she said. "What is the matter with him?"

"He was all right when I left him just now," said Jimmy. "I wonder if someone's managed to inject some stuff into him. It would be easily done—just a prick. The man might have been asking him the time. There's only one thing for it. I must get a doctor at once. You stay here and look after him."

He hurried to the door, then paused.

"Look here—don't be scared, either of you. But I'd better leave you my revolver. I mean—just in case. I'll be back just as soon as I possibly can."

He laid the revolver down on the little table by the sofa, then hurried off. They heard the front door bang behind him.

The house seemed very still now. The two girls stayed motionless by Bill. Bundle still kept her finger on his pulse. It seemed to be beating very fast and irregularly.

"I wish we could do something," she whispered to Loraine. "This is awful."

Loraine nodded.

"I know. It seems ages since Jimmy went and yet it's only a minute and a half."

"I keep hearing things," said Bundle. "Footsteps and boards creaking upstairs—and yet I know it's only imagination."

"I wonder why Jimmy left us the revolver," said Loraine. "There can't really be danger."

"If they could get Bill—" said Bundle and stopped. Loraine shivered.

"I know—but we're in the house. Nobody can get in without our hearing them. And anyway we've got the revolver."

Bundle turned her attention back again to Bill.

"I wish I knew what to do. Hot coffee. You give them that sometimes."

"I've got some smelling-salts in my bag," said Loraine. "And some brandy. Where is it? Oh, I must have left it in the room upstairs."

"I'll get it," said Bundle. "They might do some good."

She sped quickly up the stairs, across the gaming room and through the open door into the meeting place. Loraine's bag was lying on the table.

As Bundle stretched out her hand to take it, she heard a noise from behind her. Hidden behind the door a man stood ready with a sand-bag in his hand. Before Bundle could turn her head, he had struck.

With a faint moan, Bundle slipped down, an unconscious heap, upon the floor.

31

The Seven Dials

Very slowly Bundle returned to consciousness. She was aware of a dark, spinning blackness, the centre of which was a violent, throbbing ache. Punctuating this were sounds. A voice that she knew very well saying the same thing over and over again.

The blackness spun less violently. The ache was now definitely located as being in Bundle's own head. And she was sufficiently herself to take an interest in what the voice was saying.

"Darling, darling Bundle. Oh, darling Bundle. She's dead; I know she's dead. Oh, my darling. Bundle, darling, darling Bundle. I do love you so. Bundle—darling—darling—"

Bundle lay quite still with her eyes shut. But she was now fully conscious. Bill's arms held her closely.

"Bundle, darling—Oh, dearest, darling Bundle. Oh, my dear love. Oh, Bundle—Bundle. What shall I do? Oh, darling one—my Bundle—my own dearest, sweetest Bundle. Oh, God, what shall I do? I've killed her. I've killed her."

Reluctantly—very reluctantly—Bundle spoke.

"No, you haven't, you silly idiot," she said.

Bill gave a gasp of utter amazement.

"Bundle—you're alive?"

"Of course I'm alive."

"How long have you been—I mean when did you come to?"

"About five minutes ago."

"Why didn't you open your eyes—or say something?"

"Didn't want to. I was enjoying myself."

"Enjoying yourself?"

"Yes. Listening to all the things you were saying. You'll never say them so well again. You'll be too beastly self-conscious."

Bill had turned a dark brick-red.

"Bundle—you really didn't mind? You know, I *do* love you so. I have for ages. But I never have dared tell you so."

"You silly juggins," said Bundle. "Why?"

"I thought you'd only laugh at me. I mean—you've got brains and all that—you'll marry some bigwig."

"Like George Lomax?" suggested Bundle.

"I don't mean a fatuous ass like Codders. But some really fine chap who'll be worthy of you—though I don't think anyone could be that," ended Bill.

"You're rather a dear, Bill."

"But, Bundle, seriously, could you ever? I mean, could you ever bring yourself to?"

"Could I ever bring myself to do what?"

"Marry me. I know I'm awfully thick-headed—but I do love you, Bundle. I'd be your dog or your slave or your anything."

"You're very like a dog," said Bundle. "I like dogs. They're so friendly and faithful and warmhearted. I think that perhaps I could just bring myself to marry you, Bill—with a great effort, you know."

Bill's response to this was to relinquish his grasp of her and recoil violently. He looked at her with amazement in his eyes.

"Bundle—you don't mean it?"

"There's nothing for it," said Bundle. "I see I shall have to relapse into unconsciousness again."

"Bundle—darling—" Bill caught her to him. He was trembling violently. "Bundle—do you really mean it—do you?—you don't know how much I love you."

"Oh, Bill," said Bundle.

There is no need to describe in detail the conversation of the next ten minutes. It consisted mostly of repetitions.

"And do you really love me?" said Bill, incredulously, for the twentieth time as he at last released her.

"Yes—yes—yes. Now do let's be sensible. I've got a racking head still, and I've been nearly squeezed to death by you. I want to get the hang of things. Where are we and what's happened?"

For the first time, Bundle began to take stock of her surroundings. They were in the secret room, she noted, and the baize door was closed and presumably locked. They were prisoners, then!

Bundle's eyes came back to Bill. Quite oblivious of her question he was watching her with adoring eyes.

"Bill, darling," said Bundle, "pull yourself together. We've got to get out of here."

"Eh?" said Bill. "What? Oh, yes. That'll be all right. No difficulty about that."

"It's being in love makes you feel like that," said Bundle. "I feel rather the same myself. As though everything's easy and possible."

"So it is," said Bill. "Now that I know you care for me—"

"Stop it," said Bundle. "Once we begin again any serious conversation will be hopeless. Unless you pull yourself together and become sensible, I shall very likely change my mind."

"I shan't let you," said Bill. "You don't think that once having got you I'd be such a fool as to let you go, do you?"

"You would not coerce me against my will, I hope," said Bundle grandiloquently.

"Wouldn't I?" said Bill. "You just watch me do it, that's all."

"You really are rather a darling, Bill. I was afraid you might be too meek, but I see there's going to be no danger of that. In another half hour you'd be ordering me about. Oh, dear, we're getting silly again. Now, look here, Bill, we've got to get out of here."

"I tell you that'll be quite all right. I shall—"

He broke off, obedient to a pressure from Bundle's hand. She was leaning forward, listening intently. Yes, she had not been mistaken. A step was crossing the outer room. The key was thrust into the lock and turned. Bundle held her breath. Was it Jimmy coming to rescue them—or was it someone else?

The door opened and the black-bearded Mr. Mosgorovsky stood on the threshold.

Immediately Bill took a step forward, standing in front of Bundle.

"Look here," he said, "I want a word with you privately."

The Russian did not reply for a minute or two. He stood stroking his long, silky, black beard and smiling quietly to himself.

"So," he said at last, "it is like that. Very well. The lady will be pleased to come with me."

"It's all right, Bundle," said Bill. "Leave it to me. You go with this chap. Nobody's going to hurt you. I know what I'm doing."

Bundle rose obediently. That note of authority in Bill's voice was new to her. He seemed absolutely sure of himself and confident of being able to deal with the situation. Bundle wondered vaguely what it was that Bill had—or thought he had—up his sleeve.

She passed out of the room in front of the Russian. He followed her, closing the door behind him and locking it.

"This way, please," he said.

He indicated the staircase and she mounted obediently to the floor above. Here she was directed to pass into a small, frowsy room, which she took to be Alfred's bedroom.

Mosgorovsky said: "You will wait here quietly, please. There must be no noise."

Then he went out, closing the door behind him and locking her in.

Bundle sat down on a chair. Her head was aching badly still and she felt incapable of sustained thought. Bill seemed to have the situation well in hand. Sooner or later, she supposed, someone would come and let her out.

The minutes passed. Bundle's watch had stopped, but she judged that over an hour had passed since the Russian had brought her here. What was happening? What, indeed, *had* happened?

At last she heard footsteps on the stairs. It was Mosgorovsky once more. He spoke very formally to her.

"Lady Eileen Brent, you are wanted at an emergency meeting of the Seven Dials Society. Please follow me."

He led the way down the stairs and Bundle followed him. He opened the door of the secret chamber and Bundle passed in, catching her breath in surprise as she did so.

She was seeing for the second time what she had only had a glimpse of the first time through her peephole. The masked figures were sitting round the table. As she stood there, taken aback by the suddenness of it, Mosgorovsky slipped into his place, adjusting his clock mask as he did so.

But this time the chair at the head of the table was occupied. No. 7 was in his place.

Bundle's heart beat violently. She was standing at the foot of the table directly facing him and she stared and stared at the mocking piece of hanging stuff, with the clock dial on it, that hid his features.

He sat quite immovable and Bundle got an odd sensation of power radiating from him. His inactivity was not the inactivity of weakness—and she wished violently, almost hysterically, that he would speak—that he would make some sign, some gesture—not just sit there like a gigantic spider in the middle of its web waiting remorselessly for its prey.

She shivered and as she did so Mosgorovsky rose. His voice, smooth, silky, persuasive, seemed curiously far away.

"Lady Eileen, you have been present unasked at the secret councils of this society. It is therefore necessary that you should identify yourself with our aims and ambitions. The place 2 o'clock, you may notice, is vacant. It is that place that is offered to you."

Bundle gasped. The thing was like a fantastic nightmare. Was it possible that she, Bundle Brent, was being asked to join a murderous secret society? Had the same proposition been made to Bill, and had he refused indignantly?

"I can't do that," she said bluntly.

"Do not answer precipitately."

She fancied that Mosgorovsky, beneath his clock mask, was smiling significantly into his beard.

"You do not as yet know, Lady Eileen, what it is you are refusing."

"I can make a pretty good guess," said Bundle.

"Can you?"

It was the voice of 7 o'clock. It awoke some vague chord of memory in Bundle's brain. Surely she knew that voice?

Very slowly No. 7 raised a hand to his head and fumbled with the fastening of the mask.

Bundle held her breath. At last—she was going to *know*.

The mask fell.

Bundle found herself looking into the expressionless, wooden face of Superintendent Battle.

32

Bundle Is Dumbfounded

"That's right," said Battle, as Mosgorovsky leapt up and came round to Bundle. "Get a chair for her. It's been a bit of a shock, I can see."

Bundle sank down on a chair. She felt limp and faint with surprise. Battle went on talking in a quiet, comfortable way wholly characteristic of him.

"You didn't expect to see me, Lady Eileen. No, and no more did some of the others sitting round this table. Mr. Mosgorovsky's been my lieutenant in a manner of speaking. He's been in the know all along. But most of the others have taken their orders blindly from him."

Still Bundle said no word. She was—a most unusual state of affairs for her—simply incapable of speech.

Battle nodded at her comprehendingly, seeming to understand the state of her feelings.

"You'll have to get rid of one or two preconceived ideas of yours, I'm afraid, Lady Eileen. About this society, for instance—I know it's common enough in books—a secret organization of criminals with a mysterious super-criminal at the head of it whom no one ever sees. That sort of thing may exist in real life, but I can only say that I've never come across anything of the sort, and I've had a good deal of experience one way or another.

"But there's a lot of romance in the world, Lady Eileen. People, especially young people, like reading about such things, and they like still better really *doing* them. I'm going to introduce you now to a very creditable band of amateurs that has done remarkably fine work for my Department, work that nobody else could have done. If they've chosen rather melodramatic trappings, well, why shouldn't they? They've been willing to face real danger—danger of the very worst kind—and they've done it for these reasons: love of danger for its own sake—which to my mind is a very healthy sign in these Safety First days—and an honest wish to serve their country.

"And now, Lady Eileen, I'm going to introduce you. First of all, there's Mr. Mosgorovsky, whom you already know in a manner of speaking. As you're aware, he runs the club and he runs a host of other things too. He's our most valuable Secret Anti-Bolshevist Agent in England. No. 5 is Count Andras of the Hungarian Embassy, a very near and dear friend of the late Mr. Gerald Wade. No. 4 is Mr. Hayward Phelps, an American journalist, whose British sympathies are very keen and whose aptitude for scenting 'news' is remarkable. No. 3—"

He stopped, smiling, and Bundle stared dumbfounded into the sheepish, grinning face of Bill Eversleigh.

"No. 2," went on Battle in a graver voice, "can only show an empty place. It is the place belonging to Mr. Ronald Devereux, a very gallant young gentleman who died for his country if any man ever did. No. 1—well, No. 1 was Mr. Gerald Wade, another very gallant gentleman who died in the same way. His place was taken—not without some grave misgivings on my part—by a lady—a lady who has proved her fitness to have it and who has been a great help to us."

The last to do so, No. 1, removed her mask, and Bundle looked without surprise into the beautiful, dark face of Countess Radzky.

"I might have known," said Bundle resentfully, "that you were too completely the beautiful foreign adventuress to be anything of the kind really."

"But you don't know the real joke," said Bill. "*Bundle, this is Babe St. Maur*—you remember my telling you about her and what a ripping actress she was—and she's about proved it."

"That's so," said Miss St. Maur in pure transatlantic nasal. "But it's not a terrible lot of credit to me, because Poppa and Momma came from the part of Yurrup—so I got the patter fairly easy. Gee, but I nearly gave myself away once at the Abbey, talking about gardens."

She paused and then said abruptly:

"It's—it's not been just fun. You see, I was kinder engaged to Ronny, and when he handed in his checks—well, I had to do something to track down the skunk who murdered him. That's all."

"I'm completely bewildered," said Bundle. "Nothing is what it seems."

"It's very simple, Lady Eileen," said Superintendent Battle. "It began with some of the young people wanting a bit of excitement. It was Mr. Wade who first got on to me. He suggested the formation of a band of what you might call amateur workers to do a bit of secret service work. I warned him that it might be dangerous—but he wasn't the kind to weigh that in the balance. I made it plain to him that any one who came in must do so on that understanding. But, bless you, that wasn't going to stop any of Mr. Wade's friends. And so the thing began."

"But what was the object of it all?" asked Bundle.

"We wanted a certain man—wanted him badly. He wasn't an ordinary crook. He worked in Mr. Wade's world, a kind of Raffles, but much more dangerous than any Raffles ever was or could be. He was out for big stuff, international stuff. Twice already valuable secret inventions had been stolen, and clearly stolen by someone who had inside knowledge. The professionals had had a try—and failed. Then the amateurs took on—and succeeded."

"Succeeded?"

"Yes—but they didn't come out of it unscathed. The man was dangerous. Two lives fell victim to him and he got away with it. But the Seven Dials stuck to it. And as I say, they succeeded. Thanks to Mr. Eversleigh, the man was caught at last red-handed."

"Who was he?" asked Bundle. "Do I know him?"

"You know him very well, Lady Eileen. His name is Mr. Jimmy Thesiger, and he was arrested this afternoon."

33

Battle Explains

Superintendent Battle settled to explain. He spoke comfortably and cozily.

"I didn't suspect him myself for a long time. The first hint of it I had was when I heard what Mr. Devereux's last words had been. Naturally, you took them to mean that Mr. Devereux was trying to send word to Mr. Thesiger that the Seven Dials had killed him. That's what the words seemed to mean on their face value. But of course I knew that that couldn't be so. It was the Seven Dials that Mr. Devereux wanted told—and what he wanted them told was something about Mr. Jimmy Thesiger.

"The thing seemed incredible, because Mr. Devereux and Mr. Thesiger were close friends. But I remembered something else—that these thefts must have been committed by someone who was absolutely in the know. Someone who, if not in the Foreign Office himself, was in the way of hearing all its chit-chat. And I found it very hard to find out where Mr. Thesiger got his money. The income his father left him was a small one, yet he was able to live at a most expensive rate. Where did the money come from?

"I knew that Mr. Wade had been very excited by something that he had found out. He was quite sure that he was on the right track. He didn't confide in anyone about what he thought that track was, but he did say something to Mr. Devereux about being on the point of making sure. That was just before they both went down to Chimneys for the week-end. As you know, Mr. Wade died there—apparently from an overdose of a sleeping draught. It seemed straight-forward enough, but Mr. Devereux did not accept that explanation for a minute. He was convinced that Mr. Wade had been very cleverly put out of the way and that someone in the house must actually be the criminal we were all after. He came, I think, very near confiding in Mr. Thesiger, for he certainly had no suspicions of him at that moment. But something held him back.

"Then he did rather a curious thing. He arranged seven clocks upon the mantelpiece, throwing away the eighth. It was meant as a symbol that the Seven Dials would revenge the death of one of their members—and he watched eagerly to see if anyone betrayed themselves or showed signs of perturbation."

"And it was Jimmy Thesiger who poisoned Gerry Wade?"

"Yes, he slipped the stuff into a whisky and soda which Mr. Wade had downstairs before retiring to bed. That's why he was already feeling sleepy when he wrote that letter to Miss Wade."

"Then the footman, Bauer, hadn't anything to do with it?" asked Bundle.

"Bauer was one of our people, Lady Eileen. It was thought likely that our crook would go for Herr Eberhard's invention and Bauer was got into the house to watch events on our behalf. But he wasn't able to do much. As I say, Mr. Thesiger administered the fatal dose easily enough. Later, when everyone was asleep, a bottle, glass and empty chloral bottle were placed by Mr. Wade's bedside by Mr. Thesiger. Mr. Wade was unconscious then, and his fingers were probably pressed round the glass and the bottle so that they should be found there if any questions should arise. I don't know what effect the seven clocks on the mantelpiece made on Mr. Thesiger. He certainly didn't let on anything to Mr. Devereux. All the same, I think he had a bad five minutes now and again thinking of them. And I think he kept a pretty wary eye on Mr. Devereux after that.

"We don't know exactly what happened next. No one saw much of Mr. Devereux after Mr. Wade's death. But it is clear that he worked along the same lines that he knew Mr. Wade had been working on and reached the same result—namely, that Mr. Thesiger was the man. I fancy, too, that he was betrayed in the same way."

"You mean?"

"Through Miss Loraine Wade; Mr. Wade was devoted to her—I believe he hoped to marry her—she wasn't really his sister, of course—and there is no doubt that he told her more than he should have done. But Miss Loraine Wade was devoted body and soul to Mr. Thesiger. She would do anything he told her. She passed on the information to him. In the same way, later, Mr. Devereux was attracted to her, and probably warned her against Mr. Thesiger. So Mr. Devereux in turn was silenced—and died trying to send word to the Seven Dials that his murderer was Mr. Thesiger."

"How ghastly," cried Bundle. "If I had only known."

"Well, it didn't seem likely. In fact, I could hardly credit it myself. But then we came to the affair at the Abbey. You will remember how awkward it was—specially awkward for Mr. Eversleigh here. You and Mr. Thesiger were hand in glove. Mr. Eversleigh had already been embarrassed by your insisting on being brought to this place, and when he found that you had actually overheard what went on at a meeting, he was dumbfounded."

The Superintendent paused and a twinkle came into his eye.

"So was I, Lady Eileen. I never dreamed of such a thing being possible. You put one over on me there all right.

"Well, Mr. Eversleigh was in a dilemma. He couldn't let you into the secret of the Seven Dials without letting Mr. Thesiger in also—and that would never do. It all suited Mr. Thesiger very well, of course, for it gave him a bona fide reason for getting himself asked to the Abbey, which made things much easier for him.

"I may say that the Seven Dials had already sent a warning letter to Mr. Lomax. That was to ensure his applying to me for assistance, so that I should be able to be on the spot in a perfectly natural manner. I made no secret of my presence, as you know."

And again the Superintendent's eyes twinkled.

"Well, ostensibly, Mr. Eversleigh and Mr. Thesiger were to divide the night into two watches. Really, Mr. Eversleigh and Miss St. Maur did so. She was on guard at the library window when she heard Mr. Thesiger coming and had to dart behind the screen.

"And now comes the cleverness of Mr. Thesiger. Up to a point he told a perfectly true story, and I must admit that with the fight and everything, I was distinctly shaken—and began to wonder whether he had had anything to do with the theft at all, or whether we were completely on the wrong track. There were one or two suspicious circumstances that pointed in an entirely different direction, and I can tell you I didn't know what to make of things, when something turned up to clinch matters.

"I found the burnt glove in the fireplace with the teeth marks on it—and then—well—I knew that I'd been right after all. But, upon my word, he was a clever one."

"What actually happened?" said Bundle. "Who was the other man?"

"There wasn't any other man. Listen, and I'll show you how in the end I reconstructed the whole story. To begin with, Mr. Thesiger and Miss Wade are in this together. And they have a rendezvous for an exact time. Miss Wade comes over in her car, climbs through the fence and comes up to the house. She's got a perfectly good story if any one stops her—the one she told eventually. But she arrived unmolested on the terrace just after the clock had struck two.

"Now, I may say to begin with that she was seen coming on in. My men saw her, but they had orders to stop nobody coming in—only going out. I wanted, you see, to find out as much as possible. Miss Wade arrives on the terrace, and at that minute a parcel falls at her feet and she picks it up. A man comes down the ivy and she starts to run. What happens next? The struggle—and presently the revolver shots. What will everyone do? Rush to the scene of the fight. And Miss Loraine Wade could have left the grounds and driven off with the formula safely in her possession.

"But things don't happen quite like that. Miss Wade runs straight into my arms. And at that moment the game changes. It's no longer attack but defence. Miss Wade tells her story. It is perfectly true and perfectly sensible.

"And now we come to Mr. Thesiger. One thing struck me at once. The bullet wound alone couldn't have caused him to faint. Either he had fallen and hit his head—or—well, he hadn't fainted at all. Later we had Miss St. Maur's story. It agreed perfectly with Mr. Thesiger's—there was only one suggestive point. Miss St. Maur said that after the lights were turned out and Mr. Thesiger went over to the window, he was so still that she thought he must have left the room and gone outside. Now, if any one is in the room, you can hardly help hearing their breathing if you are listening for it. Supposing, then, that Mr. Thesiger *had* gone outside. Where next? Up the ivy to Mr. O'Rourke's room—Mr. O'Rourke's whisky and soda having been doped the night before. He gets the papers, throws them down to the girl, climbs down the ivy again, and—starts the fight. That's easy enough when you come to think of it. Knock the tables down, stagger about, speak in your own voice and then in a hoarse half-whisper. And then, the final touch, the two revolver shots. His own Colt automatic, bought openly the day before, is fired at an imaginary assailant. Then, with his left gloved hand, he takes from his pocket the small Mauser pistol and shoots himself through the fleshy part of the right arm. He flings the pistol through the window, tears off the glove with his teeth, and throws it into the fire. When I arrive he is lying on the floor in a faint."

Bundle drew a deep breath.

"You didn't realize all this at the time, Superintendent Battle?"

"No, that I didn't. I was taken in as much as anyone could be. It wasn't till long afterwards that I pieced it all together. Finding the glove was the beginning of it. Then I made Sir Oswald throw the pistol through the window. It fell a good way farther on than it should have done. But a man who is right-handed doesn't throw nearly as far with the left hand. Even then it was only suspicion—and a very faint suspicion at that.

"But there was one point struck me. The papers were obviously thrown down for someone to pick up. If Miss Wade was there by accident, who was the real person? Of course, for those who weren't in the know, that question was answered easily enough—the Countess. But there I had the pull over you. *I knew the Countess was all right*. So what follows? Why, the idea that the papers had actually been picked up by the person they were meant for. And the more I thought of it, the more it seemed to me a very remarkable coincidence that Miss Wade should have arrived at the exact moment she did."

"It must have been very difficult for you when I came to you full of suspicion about the Countess."

"It was, Lady Eileen. I had to say something to put you off the scent. And it was very difficult for Mr. Eversleigh here, with the lady coming out of a dead faint and no knowing what she might say."

"I understand Bill's anxiety now," said Bundle. "And the way he kept urging her to take time and not talk till she felt quite all right."

"Poor old Bill," said Miss St. Maur. "That poor baby had to be vamped against his will—getting madder'n a hornet every minute."

"Well," said Superintendent Battle, "there it was. I suspected Mr. Thesiger—but I couldn't get definite proof. On the other hand, Mr. Thesiger himself was rattled. He realized more or less what he was up against in the Seven Dials—but he wanted badly to know who No. 7 was. He got himself asked to the Cootes' under the impression that Sir Oswald Coote was No. 7."

"I suspected Sir Oswald," said Bundle, "especially when he came in from the garden that night."

"I never suspected him," said Battle. "But I don't mind telling you that I *did* have my suspicions of that young chap, his secretary."

"Pongo?" said Bill. "Not old Pongo?"

"Yes, Mr. Eversleigh, old Pongo as you call him. A very efficient gentleman and one that could have put anything through if he'd a mind to. I suspected him partly because he'd been the one to take the clocks into Mr. Wade's room that night. It would have been easy for him to put the bottle and glass by the bedside then. And then, for another thing, he was left-handed. That glove pointed straight to him—if it hadn't been for one thing—"

"What?"

"The teeth marks—only a man whose right hand was incapacitated would have needed to tear off that glove with his teeth."

"So Pongo was cleared."

"So Pongo was cleared, as you say. I'm sure it would be a great surprise to Mr. Bateman to know he was ever suspected."

"It would," agreed Bill. "A solemn card—a silly ass like Pongo. How you could ever think—"

"Well, as far as that goes, Mr. Thesiger was what you might describe as an empty-headed young ass of the most brainless description. One of the two was playing a part. When I decided that it was Mr. Thesiger, I was interested to get Mr. Bateman's opinion of him. All along, Mr. Bateman had the gravest suspicions of Mr. Thesiger and frequently said as much to Sir Oswald."

"It's curious," said Bill, "but Pongo always is right. It's maddening."

"Well, as I say," went on Superintendent Battle, "we got Mr. Thesiger fairly on the run, badly rattled over this Seven Dials business and uncertain just where the danger lay. That we got him in the end was solely through Mr. Eversleigh. He knew what he was up against, and he risked his life cheerfully. But he never dreamt that you would be dragged into it, Lady Eileen."

"My God, no," said Bill with feeling.

"He went round to Mr. Thesiger's rooms with a cooked-up tale," continued Battle. "He was to pretend that certain papers of Mr. Devereux's had come into his hands. Those papers were to suggest a suspicion of Mr. Thesiger. Naturally, as the honest friend, Mr. Eversleigh rushed round, sure that Mr. Thesiger would have an explanation. We calculated that if we were right, Mr. Thesiger would try and put Mr. Eversleigh out of the way, and we were fairly certain as to the way he'd do it. Sure enough, Mr. Thesiger gave his guest a whisky and soda. During the minute or two that his host was out of the room, Mr. Eversleigh poured that into a jar on the mantelpiece, but he had to pretend, of course, that the drug was taking effect. It would be slow, he knew, not sudden. He began his story, and Mr. Thesiger at first denied it all indignantly, but as soon as he saw (or thought he saw) that the drug was taking effect, he admitted everything and told Mr. Eversleigh that he was the third victim.

"When Mr. Eversleigh was nearly unconscious, Mr. Thesiger took him down to the car and helped him in. The hood was up. He must already have telephoned to you unknown to Mr. Eversleigh. He made a clever suggestion to you. You were to say that you were taking Miss Wade home.

"You made no mention of a message from him. Later, when your body was found here, Miss Wade would swear that you had driven her home and gone up to London with the idea of penetrating into this house by yourself.

"Mr. Eversleigh continued to play his part, that of the unconscious man. I may say that as soon as the two young men had left Jermyn Street, one of my men gained admission and found the doctored whisky, which contained enough hydro-chloride of morphia to kill two men. Also the car they were in was followed. Mr. Thesiger drove out of town to a well-known golf course, where he showed himself for a few minutes, speaking of playing a round. That, of course, was for an alibi, should one be needed. He left the car with Mr. Eversleigh in it a little way down the road. Then he drove back to town and to the Seven Dials Club. As soon as he saw Alfred leave, he drove up to the door, spoke to Mr. Eversleigh as he got out in case you might be listening and came into the house and played his little comedy.

"When he pretended to go for a doctor, he really only slammed the door and then crept quietly upstairs and hid behind the door of this room, where Miss Wade would presently send you up on some excuse. Mr. Eversleigh, of course, was horrorstruck when he saw you, but he thought it best to keep up the part he was playing. He knew our people were watching the house, and he imagined that there was no immediate danger intended to you. He could always 'come to life' at any moment. When Mr. Thesiger threw his revolver on the table and apparently left the house it seemed safer than ever. As for the next bit—" He paused, looking at Bill. "Perhaps you'd like to tell that, sir."

"I was still lying on that bally sofa," said Bill, "trying to look done in and getting the fidgets worse and worse. Then I heard someone run down the stairs, and Loraine got up and went to the door. I heard Thesiger's voice, but not what he said. I heard Loraine say: 'That's all right—it's gone splendidly.' Then he said: 'Help me carry him up. It will be a bit of a job, but I want them both together there—a nice little surprise for No. 7.' I didn't quite understand what they were jawing about, but they hauled me up the stairs somehow or other. It *was* a bit of a job for them. I made myself a dead weight all right. They heaved me in here, and then I heard Loraine say: 'You're sure it's all right. She won't come round?' And Jimmy said—the damned blackguard: 'No fear. I hit with all my might.'

"They went away and locked the door, and then I opened my eyes and saw you. My God, Bundle, I shall never feel so perfectly awful again. I thought you were dead."

"I suppose my hat saved me," said Bundle.

"Partly," said Superintendent Battle. "But partly it was Mr. Thesiger's wounded arm. He didn't realize it himself—but it had only half its usual strength. Still, that's all no credit to the Department. We didn't take the care of you we ought to have done, Lady Eileen—and it's a black blot on the whole business."

"I'm very tough," said Bundle. "And also rather lucky. What I can't get over is Loraine being in it. She was such a gentle little thing."

"Ah!" said the Superintendent. "So was the Pentonville murderess that killed five children. You can't go by that. She's got bad blood in her—her father ought to have seen the inside of a prison more than once."

"You've got her too?"

Superintendent Battle nodded.

"I daresay they won't hang her—juries are softhearted. But young Thesiger will swing all right—and a good thing too—a more utterly depraved and callous criminal I never met.

"And now," he added. "If your head isn't aching too badly, Lady Eileen. What about a little celebration? There's a nice little restaurant round the corner."

Bundle heartily agreed.

"I'm starving, Superintendent Battle. Besides," she looked round, "I've got to get to know all my colleagues."

"The Seven Dials," said Bill. "Hurrah! Some fizz is what we need. Do they run to fizz at this place, Battle?"

"You won't have anything to complain of, sir. You leave it to me."

"Superintendent Battle," said Bundle, "you are a wonderful man. I'm sorry you're married already. As it is, I shall have to put up with Bill."

34

Lord Caterham Approves

"Father," said Bundle, "I've got to break a piece of news to you. You're going to lose me."

"Nonsense," said Lord Caterham. "Don't tell me that you're suffering from galloping consumption or a weak heart or anything like that, because I simply don't believe it."

"It's not death," said Bundle. "It's marriage."

"Very nearly as bad," said Lord Caterham. "I suppose I shall have to come to the wedding, all dressed up in tight, uncomfortable clothes, and give you away. And Lomax may think it necessary to kiss me in the vestry."

"Good heavens! You don't think I'm going to marry George, do you?" cried Bundle.

"Well, something like that seemed to be in the wind last time I saw you," said her father. "Yesterday morning, you know."

"I'm going to be married to some one a hundred times nicer than George," said Bundle.

"I hope so, I'm sure," said Lord Caterham. "But one never knows. I don't feel you're really a good judge of character, Bundle. You told me that young Thesiger was a cheerful inefficient, and from all I hear now it seems that he was one of the most efficient criminals of the day. The sad thing is that I never met him. I was thinking of writing my reminiscences soon—with a special chapter on murderers I have met—and by a purely technical oversight, I never met this young man."

"Don't be silly," said Bundle. "You know you haven't got the energy to write reminiscences or anything else."

"I wasn't actually going to write them myself," said Lord Caterham. "I believe that's never done. But I met a very charming girl the other day and that's her special job. She collects the material and does all the actual writing."

"And what do you do?"

"Oh, just give her a few facts for half an hour every day. Nothing more than that." After a slight pause, Lord Caterham said: "She was a nice-looking girl—very restful and sympathetic."

"Father," said Bundle, "I have a feeling that without me you will run into deadly danger."

"Different kinds of danger suit different kinds of people," said Lord Caterham.

He was moving away, when he turned back and said over his shoulder:

"By the way, Bundle, who *are* you marrying?"

"I was wondering," said Bundle, "when you were going to ask me that. I'm going to marry Bill Eversleigh."

The egoist thought it over for a minute. Then he nodded in complete satisfaction.

"Excellent," he said. "He's scratch, isn't he? He and I can play together in the foursomes in the Autumn Meeting."

Crooked House

I

I first came to know Sophia Leonides in Egypt towards the end of the war. She held a fairly high administrative post in one of the Foreign Office departments out there. I knew her first in an official capacity, and I soon appreciated the efficiency that had brought her to the position she held, in spite of her youth (she was at that time just twenty two).

Besides being extremely easy to look at, she had a clear mind and a dry sense of humour that I found very delightful. We became friends. She was a person whom it was extraordinarily easy to talk to and we enjoyed our dinners and occasional dances very much.

All this I knew; it was not until I was ordered East at the close of the European war that I knew something else—that I loved Sophia and that I wanted to marry her.

We were dining at Shepheard's when I made this discovery. It did not come to me with any shock of surprise, but more as the recognition of a fact with which I had been long familiar. I looked at her with new eyes—but I saw what I had already known for a long time. I liked everything I saw. The dark crisp hair that sprang up proudly from her forehead, the vivid blue eyes, the small square fighting chin, and the straight nose. I liked the well-cut light grey tailormade, and the crisp white shirt. She looked refreshingly English and that appealed to me strongly after three years without seeing my native land. Nobody, I thought, could be more English—and even as I was thinking exactly that, I suddenly wondered if, in fact, she was, or indeed could be, as English as she looked. Does the real thing ever have the perfection of a stage performance?

I realised that much and freely as we had talked together, discussing ideas, our likes and dislikes, the future, our immediate friends and acquaintances—Sophia had never mentioned her home or her family. She knew all about me (she was, as I have indicated, a good listener) but about her I knew nothing. She had, I supposed, the usual background, but she had never talked about it. And until this moment I had never realised the fact.

Sophia asked me what I was thinking about.

I replied truthfully: "You."

"I see," she said. And she sounded as though she did see.

"We may not meet again for a couple of years," I said. "I don't know when I shall get back to England. But as soon as I do get back, the first thing I shall do will be to come and see you and ask you to marry me."

She took it without batting an eyelash. She sat there, smoking, not looking at me.

For a moment or two I was nervous that she might not understand.

"Listen," I said. "The one thing I'm determined not to do, is to ask you to marry me now. That wouldn't work out anyway. First you might turn me down, and then I'd go off miserable and probably tie up with some ghastly woman just to restore my vanity. And if you didn't turn me down what could we do about it? Get married and part at once? Get engaged and settle down to a long waiting period? I couldn't stand your doing that. You might meet someone else and feel bound to be 'loyal' to me. We've been living in a queer hectic get-on-with-it-quickly atmosphere. Marriages and love affairs making and breaking all round us. I'd like to feel you'd gone home, free and independent, to look round you and size up the new post-war world and decide what you want out of it. What is between you and me, Sophia, has got to be permanent. I've no use for any other kind of marriage."

"No more have I," said Sophia.

"On the other hand," I said, "I think I'm entitled to let you know how I—well—how I feel."

"But without undue lyrical expression?" murmured Sophia.

"Darling—don't you understand? I've tried not to say I love you—"

She stopped me.

"I do understand, Charles. And I like your funny way of doing things. And you may come and see me when you come back—if you still want to—"

It was my turn to interrupt.

"There's no doubt about that."

"There's always a doubt about everything, Charles. There may always be some incalculable factor that upsets the apple cart. For one thing, you don't know much about me, do you?"

"I don't even know where you live in England."

"I live at Swinly Dean."

I nodded at the mention of the well-known outer suburb of London which boasts three excellent golf courses for the city financier.

She added softly in a musing voice: "In a little crooked house . . ."

I must have looked slightly startled, for she seemed amused, and explained by elaborating the quotation " *'And they all lived together in a lit-*

tle crooked house' That's us. Not really such a little house either. But definitely crooked—running to gables and halftimbering!"

"Are you one of a large family? Brothers and sisters?"

"One brother, one sister, a mother, a father, an uncle, an aunt by marriage, a grandfather, a great aunt and a step grandmother."

"Good gracious!" I exclaimed, slightly overwhelmed.

She laughed.

"Of course we don't normally all live together. The war and blitzes have brought that about—but I don't know—" she frowned reflectively—"perhaps spiritually the family has always lived together—under my grandfather's eye and protection. He's rather a Person, my grandfather. He's over eighty, about four foot ten, and everybody else looks rather dim beside him."

"He sounds interesting," I said.

"He is interesting. He's a Greek from Smyrna. Aristide Leonides." She added, with a twinkle, "He's extremely rich."

"Will anybody be rich after this is over?"

"My grandfather will," said Sophia with assurance. "No Soak-the-rich tactics would have any effect on him. He'd just soak the soakers.

"I wonder," she added, "if you'll like him?"

"Do you?" I asked.

"Better than anyone in the world," said Sophia.

2

It was over two years before I returned to England. They were not easy years. I wrote to Sophia and heard from her fairly frequently. Her letters, like mine, were not love letters. They were letters written to each other by close friends—they dealt with ideas and thoughts and with comments on the daily trend of life. Yet I know that as far as I was concerned, and I believed as far as Sophia was concerned too, our feeling for each other grew and strengthened.

I returned to England on a soft grey day in September. The leaves on the trees were golden in the evening light. There were playful gusts of wind. From the airfield I sent a telegram to Sophia.

"Just arrived back. Will you dine this evening Mario's nine o'clock Charles."

A couple of hours later I was sitting reading the Times; and scanning the Births Marriages and Death column my eye was caught by the name Leonides:

> On Sept. 19th, at Three Gables, Swinly Dean, Aristide Leonides, beloved husband of Brenda Leonides, in his eighty-fifth year. Deeply regretted.

There was another announcement immediately below:

> Leonides. Suddenly, at his residence Three Gables, Swinly Dean, Aristide Leonides. Deeply mourned by his loving children and grandchildren. Flowers to St. Eldred's Church, Swinly Dean.

I found the two announcements rather curious. There seemed to have been some faulty staff work resulting in overlapping. But my main preoccupation was Sophia. I hastily sent her a second telegram:

"Just seen news of your grandfather's death. Very sorry. Let me know when I can see you. Charles."

A telegram from Sophia reached me at six o'clock at my father's house. It said:

"Will be at Mario's nine o'clock. Sophia."

The thought of meeting Sophia again made me both nervous and excited. The time crept by with maddening slowness. I was at Mario's waiting twenty minutes too early. Sophia herself was only five minutes late.

It is always a shock to meet again someone whom you have not seen for a long time but who has been very much present in your mind during that period. When at last Sophia came through the swing doors our meeting seemed completely unreal. She was wearing black, and that, in some curious way, startled me! Most other women were wearing black, but I got it into my head that it was definitely mourning—and it surprised me that Sophia should be the kind of person who did wear black—even for a near relative.

We had cocktails—then went and found our table. We talked rather fast and feverishly—asking after old friends of the Cairo days. It was artificial conversation but it tided us over the first awkwardness. I expressed commiseration for her grandfather's death and Sophia said quietly that it had been "very sudden." Then we started off again reminiscing. I began to feel, uneasily, that something was the matter—something, I mean, other than the first natural awkwardnesses of meeting again. There was something wrong, definitely wrong, with Sophia herself. Was she, perhaps, going to tell me that she had found some other man whom she cared for more than she did for me? That her feeling for me had been "all a mistake?"

Somehow I didn't think it was that—I didn't know what it was. Meanwhile we continued our artificial talk.

Then, quite suddenly, as the waiter placed coffee on the table and retired bowing, everything swung into focus. Here were Sophia and I sitting together as so often before at a small table in a restaurant. The years of our separation might never have been.

"Sophia," I said.

And immediately she said, "Charles!"

I drew a deep breath of relief.

"Thank goodness that's over," I said. "What's been the matter with us?"

"Probably my fault. I was stupid."

"But it's all right now?"

"Yes, it's all right now."

We smiled at each other.

"Darling!" I said. And then: "How soon will you marry me?"

Her smile died. The something, whatever it was, was back.

"I don't know," she said. "I'm not sure, Charles, that I can ever marry you."

"But, Sophia! Why not? Is it because you feel I'm a stranger? Do you want time to get used to me again? Is there someone else? No—" I broke off. "I'm a fool. It's none of those things."

"No, it isn't." She shook her head. I waited. She said in a low voice:

"It's my grandfather's death."

"Your grandfather's death? But why? What earthly difference can that make? You don't mean—surely you can't imagine—is it money? Hasn't he left any? But surely, dearest—"

"It isn't money." She gave a fleeting smile. "I think you'd be quite willing to 'take me in my shift' as the old saying goes. And grandfather never lost any money in his life."

"Then what is it?"

"It's just his death—you see, I think, Charles, that he didn't just—die. I think he may have been—killed . . ."

I stared at her.

"But—what a fantastic idea. What made you think of it?"

"I didn't think of it. The doctor was queer to begin with. He wouldn't sign a certificate. They're going to have a post mortem. It's quite clear that they suspect something is wrong."

I didn't dispute that with her. Sophia had plenty of brains; any conclusions she had drawn could be relied upon.

Instead I said earnestly:

"Their suspicions may be quite unjustified. But putting that aside, supposing that they are justified, how does that affect you and me?"

"It might under certain circumstances. You're in the Diplomatic Service. They're rather particular about wives. No—please don't say all the things that you're just bursting to say. You're bound to say them—and I believe you really think them—and theoretically I quite agree with them. But I'm proud—I'm devilishly proud. I want our marriage to be a good thing for everyone—I don't want to represent one half of a sacrifice for love! And, as I say, it may be all right . . ."

"You mean the doctor—may have made a mistake?"

"Even if he hasn't made a mistake, it won't matter—so long as the right person killed him."

"What do you mean, Sophia?"

"It was a beastly thing to say. But, after all, one might as well be honest."

She forestalled my next words.

"No, Charles, I'm not going to say any more. I've probably said too much already. But I was determined to come and meet you tonight—to see you myself and make you understand. We can't settle anything until this is cleared up."

"At least tell me about it."

She shook her head.

"I don't want to."

"But—Sophia—"

"No, Charles. I don't want you to see us from my angle. I want you to see us unbiassed from the outside point of view."

"And how am I to do that?"

She looked at me, a queer light in her brilliant blue eyes.

"You'll get that from your father," she said.

I had told Sophia in Cairo that my father was Assistant Commissioner of Scotland Yard. He still held that office. At her words, I felt a cold weight settling down on me.

"It's as bad as that, then?"

"I think so. Do you see a man sitting at a table by the door all alone—rather a nice-looking stolid ex-Army type?"

"Yes."

"He was on Swinly Dean platform this evening when I got into the train."

"You mean he's followed you here?"

"Yes. I think we're all—how does one put it?—under observation. They more or less hinted that we'd all better not leave the house. But I determined to see you." Her small square chin shot out pugnaciously. "I got out of the bathroom window and shinned down the water pipe."

"Darling!"

"But the police are very efficient. And of course there was the telegram I sent you. Well—never mind—we're here—together . . . But from now on, we've both got to play a lone hand."

She paused and then added:

"Unfortunately—there's no doubt—about our loving each other."

"No doubt at all," I said. "And don't say unfortunately. You and I have survived a world war, we've had plenty of near escapes from sudden death—and I don't see why the sudden death of just one old man—how old was he, by the way?"

"Eighty five."

"Of course. It was in the Times. If you ask me, he just died of old age, and any self-respecting G.P. would accept the fact."

"If you'd known my grandfather," said Sophia, "you'd have been surprised at his dying of anything!"

3

I'd always taken a certain amount of interest in my father's police work, but nothing had prepared me for the moment when I should come to take a direct and personal interest in it.

I had not yet seen the Old Man. He had been out when I arrived, and after a bath, a shave and a change I had gone out to meet Sophia. When I returned to the house, however, Glover told me that he was in his study.

He was at his desk, frowning over a lot of papers. He jumped up when I came in.

"Charles! Well, well, it's been a long time."

Our meeting, after five years of war, would have disappointed a Frenchman. Actually all the emotion of reunion was there all right. The Old Man and I are very fond of each other, and we understand each other pretty well.

"I've got some whisky," he said. "Say when. Sorry I was out when you got here. I'm up to the ears in work. Hell of a case just unfolding."

I leaned back in my chair and lit a cigarette.

"Aristide Leonides?" I asked.

His brows came down quickly over his eyes. He shot me a quick appraising glance. His voice was polite and steely.

"Now what makes you say that, Charles?"

"I'm right then?"

"How did you know about this?"

"Information received."

The Old Man waited.

"My information," I said, "came from the stable itself."

"Come on, Charles, let's have it."

"You mayn't like it," I said. "I met Sophia Leonides out in Cairo. I fell in love with her. I'm going to marry her. I met her tonight. She dined with me."

"Dined with you? In London? I wonder just how she managed to do that? The family were asked—oh, quite politely, to stay put."

"Quite so. She shinned down a pipe from the bathroom window."

The Old Man's lips twitched for a moment into a smile.

"She seems," he said, "to be a young lady of some resource."

"But your police force is fully efficient," I said. "A nice Army type tracked her to Mario's. I shall figure in the reports you get. Five foot eleven, brown hair, brown eyes, dark blue pinstripe suit etc."

The Old Man looked at me hard.

"Is this—serious?" he asked.

"Yes," I said. "It's serious, dad."

There was a moment's silence.

"Do you mind?" I asked.

"I shouldn't have minded—a week ago. They're a well established family—the girl will have money—and I know you. You don't lose your head easily. As it is—"

"Yes, dad?"

"It may be all right, if—"

"If what?"

"If the right person did it."

It was the second time that night I had heard that phrase. I began to be interested.

"Just who is the right person?"

He threw a sharp glance at me.

"How much do you know about it all?"

"Nothing."

"Nothing?" He looked surprised. "Didn't the girl tell you?"

"No . . . She said she'd rather I saw it all—from an outside point of view."

"Now I wonder why that was?"

"Isn't it rather obvious?"

"No, Charles. I don't think it is."

He walked up and down frowning. He had lit a cigar and the cigar had gone out. That showed me just how disturbed the old boy was.

"How much do you know about the family?" he shot at me.

"Damnall! I know there was the old man and a lot of sons and grandchildren and in-laws. I haven't got the ramifications clear." I paused and then said, "You'd better put me in the picture, dad."

"Yes." He sat down. "Very well then—I'll begin at the beginning—with Aristide Leonides. He arrived in England when he was twenty four."

"A Greek from Smyrna."

"You do know that much?"

"Yes, but it's about all I do know."

The door opened and Glover came in to say that Chief Inspector Taverner was here.

"He's in charge of the case," said my father. "We'd better have him in. He's been checking up on the family. Knows more about them than I do."

I asked if the local police had called in the Yard.

"It's in our jurisdiction. Swinly Dean is Greater London."

I nodded as Chief Inspector Taverner came into the room. I knew Taverner from many years back. He greeted me warmly and congratulated me on my safe return.

"I'm putting Charles in the picture," said the Old Man. "Correct me if I go wrong, Taverner. Leonides came to London in 1884. He started up a little restaurant in Soho. It paid. He started up another. Soon he owned seven or eight of them. They all paid hand over fist."

"Never made any mistakes in anything he handled," said Chief Inspector Taverner.

"He'd got a natural flair," said my father. "In the end he was behind most of the well known restaurants in London. Then he went into the catering business in a big way."

"He was behind a lot of other business as well," said Taverner. "Second hand clothes trade, cheap jewellery stores, lots of things. Of course," he added thoughtfully. "He was always a twister."

"You mean he was a crook?" I asked.

Taverner shook his head.

"No, I don't mean that. Crooked, yes—but not a crook. Never anything outside the law. But he was the sort of chap that thought up all the ways you can get round the law. He's cleaned up a packet that way even in this last war, and old as he was. Nothing he did was ever illegal—but as soon as he'd got on to it, you had to have a law about it, if you know what I mean. But by that time he'd gone on to the next thing."

"He doesn't sound a very attractive character," I said.

"Funnily enough, he was attractive. He'd got personality, you know. You could feel it. Nothing much to look at. Just a gnome—ugly little fellow—but magnetic—women always fell for him."

"He made a rather astonishing marriage," said my father. "Married the daughter of a country squire—an M.F.H."

I raised my eyebrows. "Money?"

The Old Man shook his head.

"No, it was a love match. She met him over some catering arrangements for a friend's wedding—and she fell for him. Her parents cut up rough, but she was determined to have him. I tell you, the man had charm—there was something exotic and dynamic about him that appealed to her. She was bored stiff with her own kind."

"And the marriage was happy?"

"It was very happy, oddly enough. Of course their respective friends didn't mix (those were the days before money swept aside all class distinctions) but that didn't seem to worry them. They did without friends. He built a rather preposterous house at Swinly Dean and they lived there and had eight children."

"This is indeed a family chronicle."

"Old Leonides was rather clever to choose Swinly Dean. It was only beginning to be fashionable then. The second and third golf courses hadn't been made. There was a mixture there of Old Inhabitants who were passionately fond of their gardens and who liked Mrs. Leonides, and rich City men who wanted to be in with Leonides, so they could take their choice of acquaintances. They were perfectly happy, I believe, until she died of pneumonia in 1905."

"Leaving him with eight children?"

"One died in infancy. Two of the sons were killed in the last war. One daughter married and went to Australia and died there. An unmarried daughter was killed in a motor accident. Another died a year or two ago. There are two still living—the eldest son, Roger, who is married but has no children, and Philip who married a well known actress and has three children, your Sophia, Eustace and Josephine."

"And they are all living at—what is it?—Three Gables?"

"Yes. The Roger Leonides were bombed out early in the war. Philip and his family have lived there since 1938. And there's an elderly aunt, Miss de Haviland, sister of the first Mrs. Leonides. She always loathed her brother-in-law apparently, but when her sister died she considered it her duty to accept her brother-in-law's invitation to live with him and bring up the children."

"She's very hot on duty," said Inspector Taverner. "But she's not the kind that changes her mind about people. She always disapproved of Leonides and his methods—"

"Well," I said, "it seems a pretty good house full. Who do you think killed him?"

Taverner shook his head.

"Early days," he said, "early days to say that."

"Come on, Taverner," I said. "I bet you think you know who did it. We're not in court, man."

"No," said Taverner gloomily. "And we never may be."

"You mean he may not have been murdered?"

"Oh, he was murdered all right. Poisoned. But you know what these poisoning cases are like. It's very tricky getting the evidence. Very tricky. All the possibilities may point one way—"

"That's what I'm trying to get at. You've got it all taped out in your mind, haven't you?"

"It's a case of very strong probability. It's one of those obvious things. The perfect set-up. But I don't know, I'm sure. It's tricky."

I looked appealingly at the Old Man.

He said slowly:

"In murder cases, as you know, Charles, the obvious is usually the right solution. Old Leonides married again, ten years ago."

"When he was seventy five?"

"Yes, he married a young woman of twenty four."

I whistled.

"What sort of a young woman."

"A young woman out of a tea shop. A perfectly respectable young woman—good looking in an anaemic, apathetic sort of way."

"And she's the strong probability?"

"I ask you, sir," said Taverner. "She's only thirty four now—and that's a dangerous age. She likes living soft. And there's a young man in the house. Tutor to the grandchildren. Not been in the war—got a bad heart or something. They're as thick as thieves."

I looked at him thoughtfully. It was, certainly, an old and familiar pattern. The mixture as before. And the second Mrs. Leonides was, my father had emphasized, very respectable. In the name of respectability many murders have been committed.

"What was it?" I asked. "Arsenic?"

"No. We haven't got the analyst's report yet—but the doctor thinks it's eserine."

"That's a little unusual, isn't it? Surely easy to trace the purchaser."

"Not this thing. It was his own stuff, you see. Eyedrops."

"Leonides suffered from diabetes," said my father. "He had regular injections of insulin. Insulin is given out in small bottles with a rubber cap. A hypodermic needle is pressed down through the rubber cap and the injection drawn up."

I guessed the next bit.

"And it wasn't insulin in the bottle, but eserine?"

"Exactly."

"And who gave him the injection?" I asked.

"His wife."

I understood now what Sophia had meant by the "right person."

I asked: "Does the family get on well with the second Mrs. Leonides?"

"No. I gather they are hardly on speaking terms."

It all seemed clearer and clearer. Nevertheless, Inspector Taverner was clearly not happy about it.

"What don't you like about it?" I asked him.

"If she did it, Mr. Charles, it would have been so easy for her to substitute a bona fide bottle of insulin afterwards. In fact, if she is guilty, I can't imagine why on earth she didn't do just that."

"Yes, it does seem indicated. Plenty of insulin about?"

"Oh yes, full bottles and empty ones. And if she'd done that, ten to one the doctor wouldn't have spotted it. Very little is known of the post mortem appearances in human poisoning by eserine. But as it was he checked up on the insulin (in case it was the wrong strength or something like that) and so, of course, he soon spotted that it wasn't insulin."

"So it seems," I said thoughtfully, "that Mrs. Leonides was either very stupid—or possibly very clever."

"You mean—"

"That she may be gambling on your coming to the conclusion that nobody could have been as stupid as she appears to have been. What are the alternatives? Any other—suspects?"

The Old Man said quietly:

"Practically anyone in the house could have done it. There was always a good store of insulin—at least a fortnight's supply. One of the phials could have been tampered with, and replaced in the knowledge that it would be used in due course."

"And anybody, more or less, had access to them?"

"They weren't locked away. They were kept on a special shelf in the medicine cupboard in the bathroom of his part of the house. Everybody in the house came and went freely."

"Any strong motive?"

My father sighed.

"My dear Charles, Aristide Leonides was enormously rich! He had made over a good deal of his money to his family, it is true, but it may be that somebody wanted more."

"But the one that wanted it most would be the present widow. Has her young man any money?"

"No. Poor as a Church mouse."

Something clicked in my brain. I remembered Sophia's quotation. I suddenly remembered the whole verse of the nursery rhyme:

There was a crooked man and he went a crooked mile
He found a crooked sixpence beside a crooked stile
He had a crooked cat which caught a crooked mouse
And they all lived together in a little crooked house.

I said to Taverner:

"How does she strike you—Mrs. Leonides? What do you think of her?"

He replied slowly:

"It's hard to say—very hard to say. She's not easy. Very quiet—so you don't know what she's thinking. But she likes living soft—that I'll swear I'm right about. Puts me in mind, you know, of a cat, a big purring lazy cat . . . Not that I've anything against cats. Cats are all right . . ."

He sighed.

"What we want," he said, "is evidence."

Yes, I thought, we all wanted evidence that Mrs. Leonides had poisoned her husband. Sophia wanted it, and I wanted it, and Chief Inspector Taverner wanted it.

Then everything in the garden would be lovely!

But Sophia wasn't sure, and I wasn't sure, and I didn't think Chief Inspector Taverner was sure either. . . .

4

On the following day I went down to Three Gables with Taverner. My position was a curious one. It was, to say the least of it, quite unorthodox. But the Old Man has never been highly orthodox.

I had a certain standing. I had worked with the Special Branch at the Yard during the early days of the war.

This, of course, was entirely different—but my earlier performances had given me, so to speak, a certain official standing.

My father said:

"If we're ever going to solve this case, we've got to get some inside dope. We've got to know all about the people in that house. We've got to know them from the inside—not the outside. You're the man who can get that for us."

I didn't like it. I threw my cigarette end into the grate as I said:

"I'm a police spy? Is that it? I'm to get the inside dope from Sophia whom I love and who both loves and trusts me, or so I believe."

The Old Man became quite irritable. He said sharply:

"For Heaven's sake don't take the commonplace view. To begin with, you don't believe, do you, that your young woman murdered her grandfather?"

"Of course not. The idea's absolutely absurd."

"Very well—we don't think so either. She's been away for some years; she has always been on perfectly amicable terms with him. She has a very generous income and he would have been, I should say, delighted to hear of her engagement to you and would probably have made a handsome marriage settlement on her. We don't suspect her. Why should we? But you can make quite sure of one thing. If this thing isn't cleared up, that girl won't marry you. From what you've told me I'm fairly sure of that. And mark this, it's the kind of crime that may never be cleared up. We may be reasonably sure that the wife and her young man were in cahoots over it—but proving it will be another matter. There's not even a case to put up to the D.P.P. so far. And unless we get definite evidence against her, there'll always be a nasty doubt. You see that, don't you?"

Yes, I saw that.

The Old Man then said quietly:

"Why not put it to her?"

"You mean—ask Sophia if I—" I stopped.

The Old Man was nodding his head vigorously.

"Yes, yes . . . I'm not asking you to worm your way in without telling the girl what you're up to. See what she has to say about it."

And so it came about that the following day I drove down with Chief Inspector Taverner and Detective Sergeant Lamb to Swinly Dean.

A little way beyond the golf course, we turned in at a gateway where I imagined that before the war there had been an imposing pair of gates. Patriotism or ruthless requisitioning had swept these away. We drove up a long curving drive flanked with rhododendrons and came out on a gravelled sweep in front of the house.

It was incredible! I wondered why it had been called Three Gables. Eleven Gables would have been more apposite! The curious thing was that it had a strange air of being distorted—and I thought I knew why. It was the type, really, of a cottage, it was a cottage swollen out of all proportion. It was like looking at a country cottage through a gigantic magnifying glass. The slantwise beams, the half-timbering, the gables—it was a little crooked house that had grown like a mushroom in the night!

Yet I got the idea. It was a Greek restauranter's idea of something English. It was meant to be an Englishman's home—built the size of a castle! I wondered what the first Mrs. Leonides had thought of it. She had not, I fancied, been consulted or shown the plans. It was, most probably, her exotic husband's little surprise. I wondered if she had shuddered or smiled.

Apparently she had lived there quite happily.

"Bit overwhelming, isn't it?" said Inspector Taverner. "Of course, the old gentleman built on to it a good deal—making it into three separate houses, so to speak, with kitchens and everything. It's all tip top inside, fitted up like a luxury hotel."

Sophia came out of the front door. She was hatless and wore a green shirt and a tweed skirt.

She stopped dead when she saw me.

"You?" she exclaimed.

I said:

"Sophia, I've got to talk to you. Where can we go?"

For a moment I thought she was going to demur, then she turned and said: "This way."

We walked down across the lawn. There was a fine view across Swinly Dean's No. 1 course—away to a clump of pine trees on a hill, and beyond it, to the dimness of hazy countryside.

Sophia led me to a rockgarden, now somewhat neglected, where there was a rustic wooden seat of great discomfort, and we sat down.

"Well?" she said.

Her voice was not encouraging.

I said my piece—all of it.

She listened very attentively. Her face gave little indication of what she was thinking, but when I came at last to a full stop, she sighed. It was a deep sigh.

"Your father," she said, "is a very clever man."

"The Old Man has his points. I think it's a rotten idea myself—but—"

She interrupted me.

"Oh, no," she said. "It isn't a rotten idea at all. It's the only thing that might be any good. Your father, Charles, knows exactly what's been going on in my mind. He knows better than you do."

With sudden almost despairing vehemence, she drove one clenched hand into the palm of the other.

"I've got to have the truth. I've got to know."

"Because of us? But, dearest—"

"Not only because of us, Charles. I've got to know for my own peace of mind. You see, Charles, I didn't tell you last night—but the truth is—I'm afraid."

"Afraid?"

"Yes—afraid—afraid—afraid. The police think, your father thinks, everybody thinks—that it was Brenda."

"The probabilities—"

"Oh yes, it's quite probable. It's possible. But when I say, 'Brenda probably did it' I'm quite conscious that it's only wishful thinking. Because, you see, I don't really think so."

"You don't think so?" I said slowly.

"I don't know. You've heard about it all from the outside as I wanted you to. Now I'll show it to you from the inside. I simply don't feel that Brenda is that kind of a person—she's not the sort of person, I feel, who would ever do anything that might involve her in any danger. She's far too careful of herself."

"How about this young man? Laurence Brown."

"Laurence is a complete rabbit. He wouldn't have the guts."

"I wonder."

"Yes, we don't really know, do we? I mean, people are capable of surprising one frightfully. One gets an idea of them into one's head, and sometimes it's absolutely wrong. Not always—but sometimes. But all the same, Brenda—" she shook her head—"she's always acted so completely in character. She's what I call the harem type. Likes sitting about and eating sweets and having nice clothes and jewellery and reading cheap novels and going to the cinema. And it's a queer thing to say, when one remembers that he was eighty five, but I really think she was rather thrilled by grandfather. He had a power, you know. I should imagine he could make a woman feel—oh—rather like a queen—the Sultan's favourite! I think—I've always thought—that he made Brenda feel as though she were an exciting romantic person. He's been clever with women all his life—and that kind of thing is a sort of art—you don't lose the knack of it, however old you are."

I left the problem of Brenda for the moment and harked back to a phrase of Sophia's which had disturbed me.

"Why did you say," I asked, "that you were afraid?"

Sophia shivered a little and pressed her hands together.

"Because it's true," she said in a low voice. "It's very important, Charles, that I should make you understand this. You see, we're a very queer family . . . There's a lot of ruthlessness in us—and—different kinds of ruthlessness. That's what's so disturbing. The different kinds."

She must have seen incomprehension in my face. She went on, speaking energetically.

"I'll try and make what I mean clear. Grandfather, for instance. Once when he was telling us about his boyhood in Smyrna, he mentioned, quite casually, that he had stabbed two men. It was some kind of a brawl—there had been some unforgivable insult—I don't know—but it was just a thing that had happened quite naturally. He'd really practically forgotten about it. But it was, somehow, such a queer thing to hear about, quite casually, in England."

I nodded.

"That's one kind of ruthlessness," went on Sophia, "and then there was my grandmother. I only just remember her, but I've heard a good deal about her. I think she might have had the ruthlessness that comes from having no imagination whatever. All those foxhunting forbears—and the old Generals, the shoot 'em down type. Full of rectitude and arrogance, and not a bit afraid of taking responsibility in matters of life and death."

"Isn't that a bit far fetched?"

"Yes, I daresay—but I'm always rather afraid of that type. It's full of rectitude but it is ruthless. And then there's my own mother—she's an actress—she's a darling, but she's got absolutely no sense of proportion. She's one of those unconscious egoists who can only see things in relation as to how it affects them. That's rather frightening, sometimes, you know. And there's Clemency, Uncle Roger's wife. She's a scientist—she's doing some kind of very important research—she's ruthless too, in a kind of coldblooded impersonal way. Uncle Roger's the exact opposite—he's the kindest and most lovable person in the world, but he's got a really terrific temper. Things make his blood boil and then he hardly knows what he's doing. And there's father—"

She made a long pause.

"Father," she said slowly, "is almost too well controlled. You never know what he's thinking. He never shows any emotion at all. It's probably a kind of unconscious self defence against mother's absolute orgies of emotion, but sometimes—it worries me a little."

"My dear child," I said, "you're working yourself up unnecessarily. What it comes to in the end is that everybody, perhaps, is capable of murder."

"I suppose that's true. Even me."

"Not you!"

"Oh yes, Charles, you can't make me an exception. I suppose I could murder someone . . ." She was silent a moment or two, then added, "But if so, it would have to be for something really worth while!"

I laughed then. I couldn't help it. And Sophia smiled.

"Perhaps I'm a fool," she said, "but we've got to find out the truth about grandfather's death. We've got to. If only it was Brenda . . ."

I felt suddenly rather sorry for Brenda Leonides.

5

Along the path towards us came a tall figure walking briskly. It had on a battered old felt hat, a shapeless skirt, and a rather cumbersome jersey.

"Aunt Edith," said Sophia.

The figure paused once or twice, stooping to the flower borders, then it advanced upon us. I rose to my feet.

"This is Charles Hayward, Aunt Edith. My aunt, Miss de Haviland."

Edith de Haviland was a woman of about seventy. She had a mass of untidy grey hair, a weatherbeaten face and a shrewd and piercing glance.

"How d'ye do?" she said. "I've heard about you. Back from the East. How's your father?"

Rather surprised, I said he was very well.

"Knew him when he was a boy," said Miss de Haviland. "Knew his mother very well. You look rather like her. Have you come to help us—or the other thing?"

"I hope to help," I said rather uncomfortably.

She nodded.

"We could do with some help. Place swarming with policemen. Pop out at you all over the place. Don't like some of the types. A boy who's been to a decent school oughtn't to go into the police. Saw Moyra Kinoul's boy the other day holding up the traffic at Marble Arch. Makes you feel you don't know where you are!"

She turned to Sophia:

"Nannie's asking for you, Sophia. Fish."

"Bother," said Sophia. "I'll go and telephone about it."

She walked briskly towards the house. Miss de Haviland turned and walked slowly in the same direction. I fell into step beside her.

"Don't know what we'd all do without Nannies," said Miss de Haviland. "Nearly everybody's got an old Nannie. They come back and wash and iron and cook and do housework. Faithful. Chose this one myself—years ago."

She stooped and pulled viciously at an entangling twining bit of green.

"Hateful stuff—bindweed! Worst weed there is! Choking, entangling—and you can't get at it properly, runs along underground."

With her heel she ground the handful of greenstuff viciously underfoot.

"This is a bad business, Charles Hayward," she said. She was looking towards the house. "What do the police think about it? Suppose I mustn't ask you that. Seems odd to think of Aristide being poisoned. For that matter it seems odd to think of him being dead. I never liked him—never! But I can't get used to the idea of his being dead . . . Makes the house seem so—empty."

I said nothing. For all her curt way of speech, Edith de Haviland seemed in a reminiscent mood.

"Was thinking this morning—I've lived here a long time. Over forty years. Came here when my sister died. He asked me to. Seven children—and the youngest only a year old . . . Couldn't leave 'em to be brought up by a dago, could I? An impossible marriage, of course. I always felt Marcia must have been—well—bewitched. Ugly common little foreigner! He gave me a free hand—I will say that. Nurses, governesses, schools. And proper wholesome nursery food—not those queer spiced rice dishes he used to eat."

"And you've been here ever since?" I murmured.

"Yes. Queer in a way . . . I could have left, I suppose, when the children grew up and married . . . I suppose, really, I'd got interested in the garden. And then there was Philip. If a man marries an actress he can't expect to have any home life. Don't know why actresses have children. As soon as a baby's born they rush off and play in Repertory in Edinburgh or somewhere as remote as possible. Philip did the sensible thing—moved in here with his books."

"What does Philip Leonides do?"

"Writes books. Can't think why. Nobody wants to read them. All about obscure historical details. You've never even heard of them, have you?"

I admitted it.

"Too much money, that's what he's had," said Miss de Haviland. "Most people have to stop being cranks and earn a living."

"Don't his books pay?"

"Of course not. He's supposed to be a great authority on certain periods and all that. But he doesn't have to make his books pay—Aristide settled something like a hundred thousand pounds—something quite fantastic—on him! To avoid death duties! Aristide made them all financially independent. Roger runs Associated Catering—Sophia has a very handsome allowance. The children's money is in trust for them."

"So no one gains particularly by his death?"

She threw a me a strange glance.

"Yes, they do. They all get more money. But they could probably have had it, if they asked for it, anyway."

"Have you any idea who poisoned him, Miss de Haviland?"

She replied characteristically:

"No, indeed I haven't. It's upset me very much! Not nice to think one has a Borgia sort of person loose about the house. I suppose the police will fasten on poor Brenda."

"You don't think they'll be right in doing so?"

"I simply can't tell. She's always seemed to me a singularly stupid and commonplace young woman—rather conventional. Not my idea of a poisoner. Still, after all, if a young woman of twenty four marries a man close on eighty, it's fairly obvious that she's marrying him for his money. In the normal course of events she could have expected to become a rich widow fairly soon. But Aristide was a singularly tough old man. His diabetes wasn't getting any worse. He really looked like living to be a hundred. I suppose she got tired of waiting . . ."

"In that case," I said, and stopped.

"In that case," said Miss de Haviland briskly, "it will be more or less all right. Annoying publicity, of course. But after all, she isn't one of the family."

"You've no other ideas?" I asked.

"What other ideas should I have?"

I wondered. I had a suspicion that there might be more going on under the battered felt hat than I knew.

Behind the jerky, almost disconnected utterance, there was, I thought, a very shrewd brain at work. Just for a moment I even wondered whether Miss de Haviland had poisoned Aristide Leonides herself. . . .

It did not seem an impossible idea. At the back of my mind was the way she had ground the bindweed into the soil with her heel with a kind of vindictive thoroughness.

I remembered the word Sophia had used. Ruthlessness.

I stole a sideways glance at Edith de Haviland.

Given good and sufficient reason. . . . But what exactly would seem to Edith de Haviland good and sufficient reason?

To answer that, I should have to know her better.

6

The front door was open. We passed through it into a rather surprisingly spacious hall. It was furnished with restraint—well-polished dark oak and gleaming brass. At the back, where the staircase would normally appear, was a white panelled wall with a door in it.

"My brother-in-law's part of the house," said Miss de Haviland. "The ground floor is Philip and Magda's."

We went through a doorway on the left into a large drawing room. It had pale blue panelled walls, furniture covered in heavy brocade, and on every available table and on the walls were hung photographs and pictures of actors, dancers and stage scenes and designs. A Degas of ballet dancers hung over the mantelpiece. There were masses of flowers, enormous brown chrysanthemums and great vases of carnations.

"I suppose," said Miss de Haviland, "that you want to see Philip?"

Did I want to see Philip? I had no idea. All I had wanted to do was to see Sophia. That I had done. She had given emphatic encouragement to the Old Man's plan—but she had now receded from the scene and was presumably somewhere telephoning about fish, having given me no indication of how to proceed. Was I to approach Philip Leonides as a young man anxious to marry his daughter, or as a casual friend who had dropped in (surely not at such a moment!) or as an associate of the police?

Miss de Haviland gave me no time to consider her question. It was, indeed, not a question at all, but more an assertion. Miss de Haviland, I judged, was more inclined to assert than to question.

"We'll go to the library," she said.

She led me out of the drawing room, along a corridor and in through another door.

It was a big room, full of books. The books did not confine themselves to the bookcases that reached up to the ceiling. They were on chairs and tables and even on the floor. And yet there was no sense of disarray about them.

The room was cold. There was some smell absent in it that I was conscious of having expected. It smelt of the mustiness of old books and just a little of beeswax. In a second or two I realised what I missed. It was the scent of tobacco. Philip Leonides was not a smoker.

He got up from behind his table as we entered—a tall man aged somewhere around fifty, an extraordinarily handsome man. Everyone had laid so much emphasis on the ugliness of Aristide Leonides, that for some reason I expected his son to be ugly too. Certainly I was not prepared for this perfection of feature—the straight nose, the flawless line of jaw, the fair hair touched with grey that swept back from a well shaped forehead.

"This is Charles Hayward, Philip," said Edith de Haviland.

"Ah, how do you do?"

I could not tell if he had ever heard of me. The hand he gave me was cold. His face was quite incurious. It made me rather nervous. He stood there, patient and uninterested.

"Where are those awful policemen?" demanded Miss de Haviland. "Have they been in here?"

"I believe Chief Inspector—" (he glanced down at a card on the desk) "er—Taverner is coming to talk to me presently."

"Where is he now?"

"I've no idea, Aunt Edith. Upstairs, I suppose."

"With Brenda?"

"I really don't know."

Looking at Philip Leonides, it seemed quite impossible that a murder could have been committed anywhere in his vicinity.

"Is Magda up yet?"

"I don't know. She's not usually up before eleven."

"That sounds like her," said Edith de Haviland.

What sounded like Mrs. Philip Leonides was a high voice talking very rapidly and approaching very fast. The door behind me burst open and a woman came in. I don't know how she managed to give the impression of its being three women rather than one who entered.

She was smoking a cigarette in a long holder and was wearing a peach satin négligée which she was holding up with one hand. A cascade of Titian hair rippled down her back. Her face had that almost shocking air of nudity that a woman's has nowadays when it is not made up at all. Her eyes were blue and enormous and she was talking very rapidly in a husky rather attractive voice with a very clear enunciation.

"Darling, I can't stand it—I simply can't stand it—just think of the notices—it isn't in the papers yet, but of course it will be—and I simply can't make up my mind what I ought to wear at the inquest—very very subdued?—not black though, perhaps dark purple—and I simply haven't got a coupon left—I've lost the address of that dreadful man who sells them to me—you know, the garage somewhere near Shaftesbury Avenue—and if I went up there in the car the police would follow me, and they might ask the most awkward questions, mightn't they? I mean, what could one say? How calm you are, Philip! How can you be so calm? Don't you realise we can leave this awful house now. Freedom—freedom! Oh, how unkind—the poor old Sweetie—of course we'd never have left him while he was alive. He really did dote on us, didn't he—in spite of all the trouble that woman upstairs tried to make between us. I'm quite sure that if we had gone away and left him to her, he'd have cut us right out of everything. Horrible creature! After all, poor old Sweetie Pie was just on ninety—all the family feeling in the world couldn't have stood up against a dreadful woman who was on the spot. You know, Philip, I really believe that this would be a wonderful opportunity to put on the Edith Thompson play. This murder would give us a lot of advance publicity. Bildenstein said he could get the Thespian—that dreary play in verse about miners is coming off any minute—It's a wonderful part—wonderful. I know they say I must always play comedy because of my nose—but you know there's quite a lot of comedy to be got out of Edith Thompson—I don't think the author realised that—comedy heightens the suspense. I know just how I'd play it—commonplace, silly, make-believe up to the last minute and then—"

She cast out an arm—the cigarette fell out of the holder onto the polished mahogany of Philip's desk and began to burn it. Impassively he reached for it and dropped it into the waste paper basket.

"And then," whispered Magda Leonides, her eyes suddenly widening, her face stiffening, "just terror. . . ."

The stark fear stayed on her face for about twenty seconds, then her face relaxed, crumpled, a bewildered child was about to burst into tears.

Suddenly all emotion was wiped away as though by a sponge and turning to me, she asked in a businesslike tone:

"Don't you think that would be the way to play Edith Thompson?"

I said I thought that would be exactly the way to play Edith Thompson. At the moment I could only remember very vaguely who Edith Thompson was, but I was anxious to start off well with Sophia's mother.

"Rather like Brenda, really, wasn't she?" said Magda. "D'you know, I never thought of that. It's very interesting. Shall I point that out to the Inspector?"

The man behind the desk frowned very slightly.

"There's really no need, Magda," he said, "for you to see him at all. I can tell him anything he wants to know."

"Not see him?" Her voice went up. "But of course I must see him! Darling, darling, you're so terribly unimaginative! You don't realise the importance of details. He'll want to know exactly how and when everything happened, all the little things one noticed and wondered about at the time—"

"Mother," said Sophia, coming through the open door, "you're not to tell the Inspector a lot of lies."

"Sophia—darling . . ."

"I know, precious, that you've got it all set and that you're ready to give a most beautiful performance. But you've got it wrong. Quite wrong."

"Nonsense. You don't know—"

"I do know. You've got to play it quite differently, darling. Subdued—saying very little—holding it all back—on your guard—protecting the family."

Magda Leonides's face showed the naive perplexity of a child.

"Darling," she said, "do you really think—"

"Yes, I do. Throw it away. That's the idea."

Sophia added, as a little pleased smile began to show on her mother's face:

"I've made you some chocolate. It's in the drawing room."

"Oh—good—I'm starving—"

She paused in the doorway.

"You don't know," she said, and the words appeared to be addressed either to me or to the bookshelf behind my head, "how lovely it is to have a daughter!"

On this exit line she went out.

"God knows," said Miss de Haviland, "what she will say to the police!"

"She'll be all right," said Sophia.

"She might say anything."

"Don't worry," said Sophia. "She'll play it the way the producer says. I'm the producer!"

She went out after her mother, then wheeled back to say:

"Here's Chief Inspector Taverner to see you, father. You don't mind if Charles stays, do you?"

I thought that a very faint air of bewilderment showed on Philip Leonides's face. It well might! But his incurious habit served me in good stead. He murmured:

"Oh certainly—certainly," in a rather vague voice.

Chief Inspector Taverner came in, solid, dependable, and with an air of businesslike promptitude that was somehow soothing.

"Just a little unpleasantness," his manner seemed to say, "and then we shall be out of the house for good—and nobody will be more pleased than I shall. We don't want to hang about, I can assure you . . ."

I don't know how he managed, without any words at all, but merely by drawing up a chair to the desk, to convey what he did, but it worked. I sat down unobtrusively a little way off.

"Yes, Chief Inspector?" said Philip.

Miss de Haviland said abruptly:

"You don't want me, Chief Inspector?"

"Not just at the moment, Miss de Haviland. Later, if I might have a few words with you—"

"Of course. I shall be upstairs."

She went out, shutting the door behind her.

"Well, Chief Inspector?" Philip repeated.

"I know you're a very busy gentleman and I don't want to disturb you for long. But I may mention to you in confidence that our suspicions are confirmed. Your father did not die a natural death. His death was the result of an overdose of physostigmine—more usually known as eserine."

Philip bowed his head. He showed no particular emotion.

"I don't know whether that suggests anything to you?" Taverner went on.

"What should it suggest? My own view is that my father must have taken the poison by accident."

"You really think so, Mr. Leonides?"

"Yes, it seems to me perfectly possible. He was close on ninety, remember, and with very imperfect eyesight."

"So he emptied the contents of his eyedrop bottle into an insulin bottle. Does that really seem to you a credible suggestion, Mr. Leonides?"

Philip did not reply. His face became even more impassive.

Taverner went on:

"We have found the eyedrop bottle, empty—in the dustbin, with no fingerprints on it. That in itself is curious. In the normal way there should have been fingerprints. Certainly your father's, possibly his wife's or the valet's . . ."

Philip Leonides looked up.

"What about the valet?" he said. "What about Johnson?"

"You are suggesting Johnson as the possible criminal? He certainly had opportunity. But when we come to motive it is different. It was your father's custom to pay him a bonus every year—each year the bonus was increased. Your father made it clear to him that this was in lieu of any sum that he might otherwise have left him in his will. The bonus now, after seven years' service, has reached a very considerable sum every year and is still rising. It was obviously to Johnson's interest that your father should live as long as possible. Moreover they were on excellent terms, and Johnson's record of past service is unimpeachable—he is a thoroughly skilled and faithful valet attendant." He paused. "We do not suspect Johnson."

Philip replied tonelessly: "I see."

"Now, Mr. Leonides, perhaps you will give me a detailed account of your own movements on the day of your father's death?"

"Certainly, Chief Inspector. I was here, in this room, all that day—with the exception of meals, of course."

"Did you see your father at all?"

"I said good morning to him after breakfast as was my custom."

"Were you alone with him then?"

"My—er—stepmother was in the room."

"Did he seem quite as usual?"

With a slight hint of irony, Philip replied:

"He showed no foreknowledge that he was to be murdered that day."

"Is your father's portion of the house entirely separate from this?"

"Yes, the only access to it is through the door in the hall."

"Is that door kept locked?"

"No."

"Never?"

"I have never known it to be so."

"Anyone could go freely between that part of the house and this?"

"Certainly. It was only separate from the point of view of domestic convenience."

"How did you first hear of your father's death?"

"My brother Roger, who occupies the west wing of the floor above, came rushing down to tell me that my father had had a sudden seizure. He had difficulty in breathing and seemed very ill."

"What did you do?"

"I telephoned through to the doctor, which nobody seemed to have thought of doing. The doctor was out—but I left a message for him to come as soon as possible. I then went upstairs."

"And then?"

"My father was clearly very ill. He died before the doctor came."

There was no emotion in Philip's voice. It was a simple statement of fact.

"Where was the rest of your family?"

"My wife was in London. She returned shortly afterwards. Sophia was also absent, I believe. The two younger ones, Eustace and Josephine, were at home."

"I hope you won't misunderstand me, Mr. Leonides, if I ask you exactly how your father's death will affect your financial position."

"I quite appreciate that you want to know all the facts. My father made us financially independent a great many years ago. My brother he made Chairman and principal shareholder of Associated Catering—his largest

Company, and put the management of it entirely in his hands. He made over to me what he considered an equivalent sum—actually I think it was a hundred and fifty thousand pounds in various bonds and securities—so that I could use the capital as I chose. He also settled very generous amounts on my two sisters who have since died."

"But he left himself still a very rich man?"

"No, actually he only retained for himself a comparatively modest income. He said it would give him an interest in life. Since that time," for the first time a faint smile creased Philip's lips, "he has become, as a result of various undertakings, an even richer man than he was before."

"Your brother and yourself came here to live. That was not the result of any financial—difficulties?"

"Certainly not. It was a mere matter of convenience. My father always told us that we were welcome to make a home with him. For various domestic reasons this was a convenient thing for me to do.

"I was also," added Philip deliberately, "extremely fond of my father. I came here with my family in 1937. I pay no rent, but I pay my proportion of the rates."

"And your brother?"

"My brother came here as a result of the Blitz when his house in London was bombed in 1943."

"Now, Mr. Leonides, have you any idea what your father's testamentary dispositions are?"

"A very clear idea. He re-made his will shortly after peace was declared in 1945. My father was not a secretive man. He had a great sense of family. He held a family conclave at which his solicitor was also present and who, at his request, made clear to us the terms of the will. These terms I expect you already know. Mr. Gaitskill will doubtless have informed you. Roughly, a sum of a hundred thousand pounds free of duty was left to my stepmother in addition to her already very generous marriage settlement. The residue of his property was divided into three portions, one to myself, one to my brother, and a third in trust for the three grandchildren. The estate is a large one, but the death duties, of course, will be very heavy."

"Any bequests to servants or to charity?"

"No bequests of any kind. The wages paid to servants were increased annually if they remained in his service."

"You are not—you will excuse my asking—in actual need of money, Mr. Leonides?"

"Income tax, as you know, is somewhat heavy, Chief Inspector—but my income amply suffices for my needs—and for my wife's. Moreover my father frequently made us all very generous gifts, and had any emergency arisen, he would have come to the rescue immediately."

Philip added coldly and clearly:

"I can assure you that I had no financial reason for desiring my father's death, Chief Inspector."

"I am very sorry, Mr. Leonides, if you think I suggested anything of the kind. But we have to get at all the facts. Now I'm afraid I must ask you some rather delicate questions. They refer to the relations between your father and his wife. Were they on happy terms together?"

"As far as I know, perfectly."

"No quarrels?"

"I do not think so."

"There was a—great disparity in age?"

"There was."

"Did you—excuse me—approve of your father's second marriage?"

"My approval was not asked."

"That is not an answer, Mr. Leonides."

"Since you press the point, I will say that I considered the marriage—unwise."

"Did you remonstrate with your father about it?"

"When I heard of it, it was an accomplished fact."

"Rather a shock to you—eh?"

Philip did not reply.

"Was there any bad feeling about the matter?"

"My father was at perfect liberty to do as he pleased."

"Your relations with Mrs. Leonides have been amicable?"

"Perfectly."

"You were on friendly terms with her?"

"We very seldom meet."

Chief Inspector Taverner shifted his ground.

"Can you tell me something about Mr. Laurence Brown?"

"I'm afraid I can't. He was engaged by my father."

"But he was engaged to teach your children, Mr. Leonides."

"True. My son was a sufferer from infantile paralysis—fortunately a light case—and it was considered not advisable to send him to a public school. My father suggested that he and my young daughter Josephine should have a private tutor—the choice at the time was rather limited—since the tutor in question must be ineligible for military service. This young man's credentials were satisfactory, my father and my aunt (who has always looked after the children's welfare) were satisfied, and I acquiesced. I may add that I have no fault to find with his teaching which has been conscientious and adequate."

"His living quarters are in your father's part of the house, not here?"

"There was more room up there."

"Have you ever noticed—I am sorry to ask this—any signs of intimacy between Laurence Brown and your stepmother?"

"I have had no opportunity of observing anything of the kind."

"Have you heard any gossip or tittle tattle on the subject?"

"I don't listen to gossip or tittle tattle, Chief Inspector."

"Very creditable," said Inspector Taverner. "So you've seen no evil, heard no evil, and aren't speaking any evil?"

"If you like to put it that way, Chief Inspector."

Inspector Taverner got up.

"Well," he said, "thank you very much, Mr. Leonides."

I followed him unobtrusively out of the room.

"Whew," said Taverner, "he's a cold fish!"

7

"And now," said Taverner, "we'll go and have a word with Mrs. Philip. Magda West, her stage name is."

"Is she any good?" I asked. "I know her name, and I believe I've seen her in various shows, but I can't remember when and where."

"She's one of those Near Successes," said Taverner. "She's starred once or twice in the West End, she's made quite a name for herself in Repertory—she plays a lot for the little highbrow theatres and the Sunday clubs. The truth is, I think, she's been handicapped by not having to earn her living at it. She's been able to pick and choose, and to go where she likes and occasionally to put up the money to finance a show where she's fancied a certain part—usually the last part in the world to suit her. Result is, she's receded a bit into the amateur class rather than the professional. She's good, mind you, especially in comedy—but managers don't like her much—they say she's too independent, and she's a trouble maker—foments rows and enjoys a bit of mischief making. I don't know how much of it is true—but she's not too popular amongst her fellow artists."

Sophia came out of the drawing room and said, "My mother is in here, Chief Inspector."

I followed Taverner into the big drawing room. For a moment I hardly recognised the woman who sat on the brocaded settee.

The Titian hair was piled high on her head in an Edwardian coiffure, and she was dressed in a well cut dark grey coat and skirt with a delicately pleated pale mauve shirt fastened at the neck by a small cameo brooch. For the first time I was aware of the charm of her delightfully tip tilted nose. I was faintly reminded of Athene Seyler—and it seemed quite impossible to believe that this was the tempestuous creature in the peach négligée.

"Inspector Taverner?" she said. "Do come in and sit down. Will you smoke? This is a most terrible business. I simply feel at the moment that I just can't take it in."

Her voice was low and emotionless, the voice of a person determined at all costs to display self control. She went on: "Please tell me if I can help you in any way."

"Thank you, Mrs. Leonides. Where were you at the time of the tragedy?"

"I suppose I must have been driving down from London. I'd lunched that day at the Ivy with a friend. Then we'd gone to a dress show. We had a drink with some other friends at the Berkeley. Then I started home. When I got here everything was in commotion. It seemed my father-in-law had had a sudden seizure. He was—dead." Her voice trembled just a little.

"You were fond of your father-in-law?"

"I was devoted—"

Her voice rose. Sophia adjusted, very slightly, the angle of the Degas picture. Magda's voice dropped to its former subdued tone.

"I was very fond of him," she said in a quiet voice. "We all were. He was—very good to us."

"Did you get on well with Mrs. Leonides?"

"We didn't see very much of Brenda."

"Why was that?"

"Well, we hadn't much in common. Poor dear Brenda. Life must have been hard for her sometimes."

Again Sophia fiddled with the Degas.

"Indeed? In what way?"

"Oh, I don't know." Magda shook her head, with a sad little smile.

"Was Mrs. Leonides happy with her husband?"

"Oh, I think so."

"No quarrels?"

Again the slight smiling shake of the head.

"I really don't know, Inspector. Their part of the house is quite separate."

"She and Mr. Laurence Brown were very friendly, were they not?"

Magda Leonides stiffened. Her eyes opened reproachfully at Taverner.

"I don't think," she said with dignity, "that you ought to ask me things like that. Brenda was quite friendly to everyone. She is really a very amiable sort of person."

"Do you like Mr. Laurence Brown?"

"He's very quiet. Quite nice, but you hardly know he's there. I haven't really seen very much of him."

"Is his teaching satisfactory?"

"I suppose so. I really wouldn't know. Philip seems quite satisfied."

Taverner essayed some shock tactics.

"I'm sorry to ask you this, but in your opinion was there anything in the nature of a love affair between Mr. Brown and Mrs. Brenda Leonides."

Magda got up. She was very much the grande dame.

"I have never seen any evidence of anything of that kind," she said. "I don't think really, Inspector, that that is a question you ought to ask me. She was my father-in-law's wife."

I almost applauded.

The Chief Inspector also rose.

"More a question for the servants?" he suggested.

Magda did not answer.

"Thank you, Mrs. Leonides," said the Inspector and went out.

"You did that beautifully, darling," said Sophia to her mother warmly.

Magda twisted up a curl reflectively behind her right ear and looked at herself in the glass.

"Ye-es," she said, "I think it was the right way to play it."

Sophia looked at me.

"Oughtn't you," she asked, "to go with the Inspector?"

"Look here, Sophia, what am I supposed—"

I stopped. I could not very well ask outright in front of Sophia's mother exactly what my rôle was supposed to be. Magda Leonides had so far evinced no interest in my presence at all, except as a useful recipient of an exit line on daughters. I might be a reporter, her daughter's fiancé, or an obscure hanger on of the police force, or even an undertaker—to Magda Leonides they would one and all come under the general heading of audience.

Looking down at her feet, Mrs. Leonides said with dissatisfaction:

"These shoes are wrong. Frivolous."

Obeying Sophia's imperious wave of the head I hurried after Taverner. I caught up with him in the outer hall just going through the door to the stairway.

"Just going up to see the older brother," he explained.

I put my problem to him without more ado.

"Look here, Taverner, who am I supposed to be?"

He looked surprised.

"Who are you supposed to be?"

"Yes, what am I doing here in this house? If anyone asks me, what do I say?"

"Oh I see." He considered a moment. Then he smiled. "Has anybody asked you?"

"Well—no."

"Then why not leave it at that. Never explain. That's a very good motto. Especially in a house upset like this house is. Everyone is far too full of their own private worries and fears to be in a questioning mood. They'll take you for granted so long as you just seem sure of yourself. It's a great mistake ever to say anything when you needn't. H'm, now we go through this door and up the stairs. Nothing locked. Of course you realise, I expect, that these questions I'm asking are all a lot of hooey! Doesn't matter a hoot who was in the house and who wasn't, or where they all were on that particular day—"

"Then why—"

He went on: "Because it at least gives me a chance to look at them all, and size them up, and hear what they've got to say, and to hope that, quite by chance, somebody might give me a useful pointer." He was silent a moment and then murmured: "I bet Mrs. Magda Leonides could spill a mouthful if she chose."

"Would it be reliable?" I asked.

"Oh, no," said Taverner, "it wouldn't be reliable. But it might start a possible line of enquiry. Everybody in the damned house had means and opportunity. What I want is a motive."

At the top of the stairs, a door barred off the right hand corridor. There was a brass knocker on it and Inspector Taverner duly knocked.

It was opened with startling suddenness by a man who must have been standing just inside. He was a clumsy giant of a man with powerful shoulders, dark rumpled hair, and an exceedingly ugly but at the same time rather pleasant face. His eyes looked at us and then quickly away in that furtive embarrassed manner which shy but honest people often adopt.

"Oh, I say," he said. "Come in. Yes, do. I was going—but it doesn't matter. Come into the sitting room. I'll get Clemency—oh, you're there, darling. It's Chief Inspector Taverner. He—are there any cigarettes? Just wait a minute. If you don't mind—" He collided with a screen, said "I beg your pardon" to it in a flustered manner, and went out of the room.

It was rather like the exit of a bumble bee and left a noticeable silence behind it.

Mrs. Roger Leonides was standing up by the window. I was intrigued at once by her personality and by the atmosphere of the room in which we stood.

It was quite definitely her room. I was sure of that.

The walls were painted white—really white, not an ivory or a pale cream which is what one usually means when one says "white" in house decoration. They had no pictures on them except one over the mantelpiece, a geometrical fantasia in triangles of dark grey and battleship blue. There was hardly any furniture—only mere utilitarian necessities, three or four chairs, a glass topped table, one small bookshelf. There were no ornaments. There was light and space and air. It was as different from the big brocaded and flowered drawing room on the floor below as chalk from cheese. And Mrs. Roger Leonides was as different from Mrs. Philip Leonides as one woman could be from another. Whilst one felt that Magda Leonides could be, and often was, at least half a dozen different women, Clemency Leonides, I was sure, could never be anyone but herself. She was a woman of very sharp and definite personality.

She was about fifty, I suppose, her hair was grey, cut very short in what was almost an Eton crop but which grew so beautifully on her small well shaped head that it had none of the ugliness I have always associated with that particular cut. She had an intelligent, sensitive face, with light grey eyes of a peculiar and searching intensity. She had on a simple dark red woollen frock that fitted her slenderness perfectly.

She was, I felt at once, rather an alarming woman . . . I think because I judged that the standards by which she lived might not be those of an ordinary woman. I understood at once why Sophia had used the word ruthlessness in connection with her. The room was cold and I shivered a little.

Clemency Leonides said in a quiet well bred voice:

"Do sit down, Chief Inspector. Is there any further news?"

"Death was due to eserine, Mrs. Leonides."

She said thoughtfully, "So that makes it murder. It couldn't have been an accident of any kind, could it?"

"No, Mrs. Leonides."

"Please be very gentle with my husband, Chief Inspector. This will affect him very much. He worshipped his father and he feels things very acutely. He is an emotional person."

"You were on good terms with your father-in-law, Mrs. Leonides?"

"Yes, on quite good terms." She added quietly, "I did not like him very much."

"Why was that?"

"I disliked his objectives in life—and his methods of attaining them."

"And Mrs. Brenda Leonides?"

"Brenda? I never saw very much of her."

"Do you think it is possible that there was anything between her and Mr. Laurence Brown?"

"You mean—some kind of a love affair? I shouldn't think so. But I really wouldn't know anything about it."

Her voice sounded completely uninterested.

Roger Leonides came back with a rush, and the same bumble bee effect.

"I got help up," he said. "Telephone. Well, Inspector? Well? Have you got any news? What caused my father's death?"

"Death was due to eserine poisoning."

"It was? My God! Then it was that woman! She couldn't wait! He took her more or less out of the gutter and this is his reward. She murdered him in cold blood! God, it makes my blood boil to think of it."

"Have you any particular reason for thinking that?" Taverner asked.

Roger was pacing up and down, tugging at his hair with both hands.

"Reason? Why, who else could it be? I've never trusted her—never liked her! We've none of us liked her. Philip and I were both appalled when Dad came home one day and told us what he had done! At his age! It was madness—madness. My father was an amazing man, Inspector. In intellect he was as young and fresh as a man of forty. Everything I have in the world I owe to him. He did everything for me—never failed me. It was I who failed him—when I think of it—"

He dropped heavily onto a chair. His wife came quietly to his side.

"Now, Roger, that's enough. Don't work yourself up."

"I know, dearest—I know," he took her hand. "But how can I keep calm—how can I help feeling—"

"But we must all keep calm, Roger. Chief Inspector Taverner wants our help."

"That is right, Mrs. Leonides."

Roger cried:

"Do you know what I'd like to do? I'd like to strangle that woman with my own hands. Grudging that dear old man a few extra years of life. If I had her here—" He sprang up. He was shaking with rage. He held out convulsive hands. "Yes, I'd wring her neck, wring her neck . . ."

"Roger!" said Clemency sharply.

He looked at her, abashed.

"Sorry, dearest." He turned to us. "I do apologise. My feelings get the better of me. I—excuse me—"

He went out of the room again. Clemency Leonides said with a very faint smile.

"Really, you know, he wouldn't hurt a fly."

Taverner accepted her remark politely.

Then he started on his so-called routine questions.

Clemency Leonides replied concisely and accurately.

Roger Leonides had been in London on the day of his father's death at Box House, the headquarters of the Associated Catering. He had returned early in the afternoon and had spent some time with his father as was his custom. She herself had been, as usual, at the Lambert Institute on Gower Street where she worked. She had returned to the house just before six o'clock.

"Did you see your father-in-law?"

"No. The last time I saw him was on the day before. We had coffee with him after dinner."

"But you did not see him on the day of his death?"

"No. I actually went over to his part of the house because Roger thought he had left his pipe there—a very precious pipe, but as it happened he had left it on the hall table there, so I did not need to disturb the old man. He often dozed off about six."

"When did you hear of his illness?"

"Brenda came rushing over. That was just a minute or two after half past six."

These questions, as I knew, were unimportant, but I was aware how keen was Inspector Taverner's scrutiny of the woman who answered them. He asked her a few questions about the nature of her work in London. She said that it had to do with the radiation effects of atomic disintegration.

"You work on the atom bomb, in fact?"

"The work has nothing destructive about it. The Institute is carrying out experiments on the therapeutic effects."

When Taverner got up, he expressed a wish to look around their part of the house. She seemed a little surprised, but showed him its extent readily enough. The bedroom with its twin beds and white coverlets and its simplified toilet appliances reminded me again of a hospital or some monastic cell. The bathroom, too, was severely plain with no special luxury fitting and no array of cosmetics. The kitchen was bare, spotlessly clean, and well equipped with labour saving devices of a practical kind. Then we came to a door which Clemency opened saying: "This is my husband's special room."

"Come in," said Roger. "Come in."

I drew a faint breath of relief. Something in the spotless austerity elsewhere had been getting me down. This was an intensely personal room. There was a large roll top desk untidily covered with papers, old pipes and tobacco ash. There were big shabby easy chairs. Persian rugs covered the floor. On the walls were groups, their photography somewhat faded. School groups, cricket groups, military groups. Water colour sketches of deserts and minarets, and of sailing boats and sea effects and sunsets. It was, somehow, a pleasant room, the room of a lovable friendly companionable man.

Roger, clumsily, was pouring out drinks from a tantalus, sweeping books and papers off one of the chairs.

"Place is in a mess. I was turning out. Clearing up old papers. Say when." The Inspector declined a drink. I accepted. "You must forgive me just now," went on Roger. He brought my drink over to me, turning his head to speak to Taverner as he did so. "My feelings ran away with me."

He looked round almost guiltily, but Clemency Leonides had not accompanied us into the room.

"She's so wonderful," he said. "My wife, I mean. All through this, she's been splendid—splendid! I can't tell you how I admire that woman. And she's had such a hard time—a terrible time. I'd like to tell you about it. Before we were married, I mean. Her first husband was a fine chap—fine mind, I mean—but terribly delicate—tubercular as a matter of fact. He was doing some very valuable research work on crystallography, I believe. Poorly paid and very exacting, but he wouldn't give up. She slaved for him, practically kept him, knowing all the time that he was dying. And never a complaint—never a murmur of weariness. She always said she was happy. Then he died, and she was terribly cut up. At last she agreed to marry me. I was glad to be able to give her some rest, some happiness. I wished she would stop working, but of course she felt it her duty in war time, and she still seems to feel she should go on. She's been a wonderful wife—the most wonderful wife a man ever had. Gosh, I've been lucky! I'd do anything for her."

Taverner made a suitable rejoinder. Then he embarked once more on the familiar routine questions. When had he first heard of his father's illness?

"Brenda had rushed over to call me. My father was ill—she said he had had a seizure of some sort.

"I'd been sitting with the dear old boy only about half an hour earlier. He'd been perfectly all right then. I rushed over. He was blue in the face, gasping. I dashed down to Philip. He rang up the doctor. I—we couldn't do anything. Of course I never dreamed for a moment then that there had been any funny business. Funny? Did I say funny? God, what a word to use."

With a little difficulty, Taverner and I disentangled ourselves from the emotional atmosphere of Roger Leonides's room and found ourselves outside the door, once more at the top of the stairs.

"Whew!" said Taverner. "What a contrast from the other brother." He added, rather inconsequently "Curious things, rooms. Tell you quite a lot about the people who live in them."

I agreed and he went on.

"Curious the people who marry each other, too, isn't it?"

I was not quite sure if he was referring to Clemency and Roger, or to Philip and Magda. His words applied equally well to either. Yet it seemed to me that both the marriages might be classed as happy ones. Roger's and Clemency's certainly was.

"I shouldn't say he was a poisoner, would you?" asked Taverner. "Not off hand, I wouldn't. Of course, you never know. Now she's more the type. Remorseless sort of woman. Might be a bit mad."

Again I agreed. "But I don't suppose," I said, "that she'd murder anyone just because she didn't approve of their aims and mode of life. Perhaps, if she really hated the old man—but are any murders committed just out of pure hate?"

"Precious few," said Taverner. "I've never come across one myself. No, I think we're a good deal safer to stick to Mrs. Brenda. But God knows if we'll ever get any evidence."

8

A parlourmaid opened the door of the opposite wing to us. She looked scared but slightly contemptuous when she saw Taverner.

"You want to see the mistress?"

"Yes, please."

She showed us into a big drawing room and went out.

Its proportions were the same as the drawing room on the ground floor below. There were coloured cretonnes, very gay in colour, and striped silk curtains. Over the mantelpiece was a portrait that held my gaze riveted—not only because of the master hand that had painted it, but also because of the arresting face of the subject.

It was the portrait of a little old man with dark piercing eyes. He wore a black velvet skull cap and his head was sunk down in his shoulders, but the vitality and power of the man radiated forth from the canvas. The twinkling eyes seemed to hold mine.

"That's him," said Chief Inspector Taverner ungrammatically. "Painted by Augustus John. Got a personality, hasn't he?"

"Yes," I said and felt the monosyllable was inadequate.

I understood now just what Edith de Haviland had meant when she said the house seemed so empty without him. This was the Original Crooked Little Man who had built the Crooked Little House—and without him the Crooked Little House had lost its meaning.

"That's his first wife over there, painted by Sargent," said Taverner.

I examined the picture on the wall between the windows. It had a certain cruelty like many of Sargent's portraits. The length of the face was exaggerated, I thought—so was the faint suggestion of horsiness—the indisputable correctness—It was a portrait of a typical English Lady—in Country (not Smart) Society. Handsome, but rather lifeless. A most unlikely wife for the grinning powerful little despot over the mantelpiece.

The door opened and Sergeant Lamb stepped in.

"I've done what I could with the servants, sir," he said. "Didn't get anything."

Taverner sighed.

Sergeant Lamb took out his notebook and retreated to the far end of the room where he seated himself unobtrusively.

The door opened again and Aristide Leonides's second wife came into the room.

She wore black—very expensive black and a good deal of it. It swathed her up to the neck and down to the wrists. She moved easily and indolently, and black certainly suited her. Her face was mildly pretty and she had rather nice brown hair arranged in somewhat too elaborate a style. Her face was well powdered and she had on lipstick and rouge, but she had clearly been crying. She was wearing a string of very large pearls and she had a big emerald ring on one hand and an enormous ruby on the other.

There was one other thing I noticed about her. She looked frightened.

"Good morning, Mrs. Leonides," said Taverner easily. "I'm sorry to have to trouble you again."

She said in a flat voice:

"I suppose it can't be helped."

"You understand, don't you, Mrs. Leonides, that if you wish your solicitor to be present, that is perfectly in order."

I wondered if she did understand the significance of those words. Apparently not. She merely said rather sulkily:

"I don't like Mr. Gaitskill. I don't want him."

"You could have your own solicitor, Mrs. Leonides."

"Must I? I don't like solicitors. They confuse me."

"It's entirely for you to decide," said Taverner, producing an automatic smile. "Shall we go on, then?"

Sergeant Lamb licked his pencil. Brenda Leonides sat down on a sofa facing Taverner.

"Have you found out anything?" she asked.

I noticed her fingers nervously twisting and untwisting a pleat of the chiffon of her dress.

"We can state definitely now that your husband died as a result of eserine poisoning."

"You mean those eyedrops killed him?"

"It seems quite certain that when you gave Mr. Leonides that last injection, it was eserine that you injected and not insulin."

"But I didn't know that. I didn't have anything to do with it. Really I didn't, Inspector."

"Then somebody must have deliberately replaced the insulin by the eyedrops."

"What a wicked thing to do!"

"Yes, Mrs. Leonides."

"Do you think—someone did it on purpose? Or by accident? It couldn't have been a—a joke, could it?"

Taverner said smoothly:

"We don't think it was a joke, Mrs. Leonides."

"It must have been one of the servants."

Taverner did not answer.

"It must. I don't see who else could have done it."

"Are you sure? Think, Mrs. Leonides. Haven't you any ideas at all? There's been no ill feeling anywhere? No quarrel? No grudge?"

She still stared at him with large defiant eyes.

"I've no idea at all," she said.

"You had been at the cinema that afternoon, you said?"

"Yes—I came in at half past six—it was time for the insulin—I—I—gave him the injection just the same as usual and then he—he went all queer. I was terrified—I rushed over to Roger—I've told you all this before. Have I got to go over it again and again?" Her voice rose hysterically.

"I'm so sorry, Mrs. Leonides. Now can I speak to Mr. Brown?"

"To Laurence? Why? He doesn't know anything about it."

"I'd like to speak to him all the same."

She stared at him suspiciously.

"Eustace is doing Latin with him in the schoolroom. Do you want him to come here?"

"No—we'll go to him."

Taverner went quickly out of the room. The Sergeant and I followed.

"You've put the wind up her, sir," said Sergeant Lamb.

Taverner grunted. He led the way up a short flight of steps and along a passage into a big room looking over the garden. There a fair haired young man of about thirty and a handsome dark boy of sixteen were sitting at a table.

They looked up at our entrance. Sophia's brother Eustace looked at me, Laurence Brown fixed an agonised gaze on Chief Inspector Taverner.

I have never seen a man look so completely paralysed with fright. He stood up, then sat down again. He said, and his voice was almost a squeak,

"Oh—er—good morning, Inspector."

"Good morning," Taverner was curt. "Can I have a word with you?"

"Yes, of course. Only too pleased. At least—"

Eustace got up.

"Do you want me to go away, Chief Inspector?" His voice was pleasant with a faintly arrogant note.

"We—we can continue our studies later," said the tutor.

Eustace strolled negligently towards the door. He walked rather stiffly. Just as he went through the door, he caught my eye, drew a forefinger across the front of his throat and grinned. Then he shut the door behind him.

"Well, Mr. Brown," said Taverner. "The analysis is quite definite. It was eserine that caused Mr. Leonides's death."

"I—you mean—Mr. Leonides was really poisoned? I have been hoping—"

"He was poisoned," said Taverner curtly. "Someone substituted eserine eyedrops for insulin."

"I can't believe it. . . . It's incredible."

"The question is, who had a motive?"

"Nobody. Nobody at all!" The young man's voice rose excitedly.

"You wouldn't like to have your solicitor present, would you?" inquired Taverner.

"I haven't got a solicitor. I don't want one. I have nothing to hide—nothing . . ."

"And you quite understand that what you say is about to be taken down."

"I'm innocent—I assure you, I'm innocent."

"I have not suggested anything else." Taverner paused. "Mrs. Leonides was a good deal younger than her husband, was she not?"

"I—I suppose so—I mean, well, yes."

"She must have felt lonely sometimes?"

Laurence Brown did not answer. He passed his tongue over his dry lips.

"To have a companion of more or less her own age living here must have been agreeable to her?"

"I—no, not at all—I mean—I don't know."

"It seems to me quite natural that an attachment should have sprung up between you."

The young man protested vehemently.

"It didn't! It wasn't! Nothing of the kind! I know what you're thinking, but it wasn't so! Mrs. Leonides was very kind to me always and I had the greatest—the greatest respect for her—but nothing more—nothing more, I do assure you. It's monstrous to suggest things of that kind! Monstrous! I wouldn't kill anybody—or tamper with bottles—or anything like that. I'm very sensitive and highly strung. I—the very idea of killing is a nightmare to me—they quite understood that at the tribunal—I have religious objections to killing. I did hospital work instead—stoking boilers—terribly heavy work—I couldn't go on with it—but they let me take up educational work. I have done my best here with Eustace and with Josephine—a very intelligent child, but difficult. And everybody has been most kind to me—Mr. Leonides and Mrs. Leonides and Miss de Haviland. And now this awful thing happens. . . . And you suspect me—me—of murder!"

Inspector Taverner looked at him with a slow appraising interest.

"I haven't said so," he remarked.

"But you think so! I know you think so! They all think so! They look at me. I—I can't go on talking to you. I'm not well."

He hurried out of the room. Taverner turned his head slowly to look at me.

"Well, what do you think of him?"

"He's scared stiff."

"Yes, I know, but is he a murderer?"

"If you ask me," said Sergeant Lamb, "he'd never have had the nerve."

"He'd never have bashed anyone on the head, or shot off a pistol," agreed the Chief Inspector, "but in this particular crime what is there to do? Just monkey about with a couple of bottles. . . . Just help a very old man out of the world in a comparatively painless manner."

"Practically euthanasia," said the Sergeant.

"And then, perhaps, after a decent interval, marriage with a woman who inherits a hundred thousand pounds free of legacy duty, who already has about the same amount settled upon her, and who has in addition pearls and rubies and emeralds the size of what's-its-name eggs!

"Ah well—" Taverner sighed. "It's all theory and conjecture! I managed to scare him all right, but that doesn't prove anything. He's just as likely to be scared if he's innocent. And anyway, I rather doubt if he was the one actually to do it. More likely to have been the woman—only why on earth didn't she throw away the insulin bottle, or rinse it out?" He turned to the Sergeant. "No evidence from the servants about any goings on?"

"The parlourmaid says they're sweet on each other."

"What grounds?"

"The way he looks at her when she pours out his coffee."

"Fat lot of good that would be in a court of law! Definitely no carryings on?"

"Not that anybody's seen."

"I bet they would have seen, too, if there had been anything to see. You know I'm beginning to believe there really is nothing between them." He looked at me. "Go back and talk to her. I'd like your impression of her."

I went half reluctantly, yet I was interested.

9

I found Brenda Leonides sitting exactly where I had left her. She looked up sharply as I entered.

"Where's Inspector Taverner. Is he coming back?"

"Not just yet."

"Who are you?"

At last I had been asked the question that I had been expecting all the morning.

I answered it with reasonable truth.

"I'm connected with the police, but I'm also a friend of the family."

"The family! Beasts! I hate them all."

She looked at me, her mouth working. She looked sullen and frightened and angry.

"They've been beastly to me always—always. From the very first. Why shouldn't I marry their precious father? What did it matter to them? They'd all got loads of money. He gave it to them. They wouldn't have had the brains to make any for themselves!"

She went on:

"Why shouldn't a man marry again—even if he is a bit old? And he wasn't really old at all—not in himself. I was very fond of him. I was fond of him." She looked at me defiantly.

"I see," I said. "I see."

"I suppose you don't believe that—but it's true. I was sick of men. I wanted to have a home—I wanted someone to make a fuss of me and say nice things to me. Aristide said lovely things to me—and he could make you laugh—and he was clever. He thought up all sorts of smart ways to get round all these silly regulations. He was very very clever. I'm not glad he's dead. I'm sorry."

She leaned back on the sofa. She had rather a wide mouth, it curled up sideways in a queer sleepy smile.

"I've been happy here. I've been safe. I went to all those posh dressmakers—the ones I'd read about. I was as good as anybody. And Aristide gave me lovely things." She stretched out a hand looking at the ruby on it.

Just for a moment I saw the hand and arm like an outstretched cat's claw, and heard her voice as a purr. She was still smiling to herself.

"What's wrong with that?" she demanded. "I was nice to him. I made him happy." She leaned forward. "Do you know how I met him?"

She went on without waiting for an answer.

"It was in the Gay Shamrock. He'd ordered scrambled eggs on toast and when I brought them to him I was crying. 'Sit down,' he said, 'and tell me what's the matter.' 'Oh, I couldn't,' I said. 'I'd get the sack if I did a thing like that.' 'No, you won't,' he said, 'I own this place.' I looked at him then. Such an odd little old man he was, I thought at first—but he'd got a sort of power. I told him all about it. . . . You'll have heard about it all from them, I expect—making out I was a regular bad lot—but I wasn't. I was brought up very carefully. We had a shop—a very high class shop—art needlework. I was never the sort of girl who had a lot of boy friends or made herself cheap. But Terry was different. He was Irish—and he was going overseas. . . . He never wrote or anything—I suppose I was a fool. So there it was, you see. I was in trouble—just like some dreadful little servant girl. . . ."

Her voice was disdainful in its snobbery.

"Aristide was wonderful. He said everything would be all right. He said he was lonely. We'd be married at once, he said. It was like a dream. And then I found out he was the great Mr. Leonides. He owned masses of shops and restaurants and night clubs. It was quite like a fairy tale, wasn't it?"

"One kind of a fairy tale," I said drily.

"We were married at a little church in the City—and then we went abroad."

"And the child?"

She looked at me with eyes that came back from a long distance.

"There wasn't a child after all. It was all a mistake."

She smiled, the curled up sideways crooked smile.

"I vowed to myself that I'd be a really good wife to him, and I was. I ordered all the kinds of food he liked, and wore the colours he fancied and I did all I could to please him. And he was happy. But we never got rid of that family of his. Always coming and sponging and living in his pocket. Old Miss de Haviland—I think she ought to have gone away when he got married. I said so. But Aristide said, 'She's been here so long. It's her home now.' The truth is he liked to have them all about and underfoot. They were beastly to me, but he never seemed to notice that or to mind about it. Roger hates me—have you seen Roger? He's always hated me. He's jealous. And Philip's so stuck up he never speaks to me. And now they're trying to pretend I murdered him—and I didn't—I didn't!" She leaned towards me. "Please believe I didn't?"

I found her very pathetic. The contemptuous way the Leonides family had spoken of her, their eagerness to believe that she had committed the crime—now, at this moment, it all seemed positively inhuman conduct. She was alone, defenceless, hunted down.

"And if it's not me, they think it's Laurence," she went on.

"What about Laurence?" I asked.

"I'm terribly sorry for Laurence. He's delicate and he couldn't go and fight. It's not because he was a coward. It's because he's sensitive. I've tried to cheer him up and to make him feel happy. He has to teach those horrible children. Eustace is always sneering at him, and Josephine—well, you've seen Josephine. You know what she's like."

I said I hadn't met Josephine yet.

"Sometimes I think that child isn't right in her head. She has horrible sneaky ways, and she looks queer . . . She gives me the shivers sometimes."

I didn't want to talk about Josephine. I harked back to Laurence Brown.

"Who is he?" I asked. "Where does he come from?"

I had phrased it clumsily. She flushed.

"He isn't anybody particular. He's just like me . . . What chance have we got against all of them?"

"Don't you think you're being a little hysterical?"

"No, I don't. They want to make out that Laurence did it—or that I did. They've got that policeman on their side. What chance have I got?"

"You mustn't work yourself up," I said.

"Why shouldn't it be one of them who killed him? Or someone from outside? Or one of the servants?"

"There's a certain lack of motive."

"Oh! motive. What motive had I got? Or Laurence?"

I felt rather uncomfortable as I said:

"They might think, I suppose, that you and—er—Laurence—are in love with each other—that you wanted to marry."

She sat bolt upright.

"That's a wicked thing to suggest! And it's not true! We've never said a word of that kind to each other. I've just been sorry for him and tried to cheer him up. We've been friends, that's all. You do believe me, don't you?"

I did believe her. That is, I believed that she and Laurence were, as she put it, only friends. But I also believed that, possibly unknown to herself, she was actually in love with the young man.

It was with that thought in my mind that I went downstairs in search of Sophia.

As I was about to go into the drawing room, Sophia poked her head out of a door further along the passage.

"Hullo," she said, "I'm helping Nannie with lunch."

I would have joined her, but she came out into the passage, shut the door behind her, and taking my arm led me into the drawing room which was empty.

"Well," she said, "did you see Brenda? What did you think of her?"

"Frankly," I said, "I was sorry for her."

Sophia looked amused.

"I see," she said. "So she got you."

I felt slightly irritated.

"The point is," I said, "that I can see her side of it. Apparently you can't."

"Her side of what?"

"Honestly, Sophia, have any of the family ever been nice to her, or even fairly decent to her, since she came here?"

"No, we haven't been nice to her. Why should we be?"

"Just ordinary Christian kindliness, if nothing else."

"What a very high moral tone you're taking, Charles. Brenda must have done her stuff pretty well."

"Really, Sophia, you seem—I don't know what's come over you."

"I'm just being honest and not pretending. You've seen Brenda's side of it, so you say. Now take a look at my side. I don't like the type of young woman who makes up a hard luck story and marries a very rich old man on the strength of it. I've a perfect right not to like that type of young woman, and there is no earthly reason why I should pretend I do. And if the facts were written down in cold blood on paper, you wouldn't like that young woman either."

"Was it a made up story?" I asked.

"About the child? I don't know. Personally, I think so."

"And you resent the fact that your grandfather was taken in by it?"

"Oh, grandfather wasn't taken in." Sophia laughed. "Grandfather was never taken in by anybody. He wanted Brenda. He wanted to play Cophetua to her beggarmaid. He knew just what he was doing and it worked out beautifully according to plan. From grandfather's point of view the marriage was a complete success—like all his other operations."

"Was engaging Laurence Brown as tutor another of your grandfather's successes?" I asked ironically.

Sophia frowned.

"Do you know, I'm not sure that it wasn't. He wanted to keep Brenda happy and amused. He may have thought that jewels and clothes weren't enough. He may have thought she wanted a mild romance in her life. He may have calculated that someone like Laurence Brown, somebody really tame, if you know what I mean, would just do the trick. A beautiful soulful friendship tinged with melancholy that would stop Brenda from having a real affair with someone outside. I wouldn't put it past grandfather to have worked out something on those lines. He was rather an old devil, you know."

"He must have been," I said.

"He couldn't, of course, have visualised that it would lead to murder. . . . And that," said Sophia, speaking with sudden vehemence, "is really why I don't, much as I would like to, really believe that she did it. If she'd planned to murder him—or if she and Laurence had planned it together—grandfather would have known about it. I daresay that seems a bit far-fetched to you—"

"I must confess it does," I said.

"But then you didn't know grandfather. He certainly wouldn't have connived at his own murder! So there you are! Up against a blank wall."

"She's frightened, Sophia," I said. "She's very frightened."

"Chief Inspector Taverner and his merry merry men? Yes, I daresay they are rather alarming. Laurence, I suppose, is in hysterics?"

"Practically. He made, I thought, a disgusting exhibition of himself. I don't understand what a woman can see in a man like that."

"Don't you, Charles? Actually Laurence has a lot of sex appeal."

"A weakling like that," I said incredulously.

"Why do men always think that a caveman must necessarily be the only type of person attractive to the opposite sex? Laurence has got sex appeal all right—but I wouldn't expect you to be aware of it." She looked at me. "Brenda got her hooks into you all right."

"Don't be absurd. She's not even really good looking. And she certainly didn't—"

"Display allure? No, she just made you sorry for her. She's not actually beautiful, she's not in the least clever—but she's got one very outstanding characteristic. She can make trouble. She's made trouble, already, between you and me."

"Sophia," I cried aghast.

Sophia went to the door.

"Forget it, Charles. I must get on with lunch."

"I'll come and help."

"No, you stay here. It will rattle Nannie to have 'a gentleman in the kitchen.'"

"Sophia," I called as she went out.

"Yes, what is it?"

"Just a servant problem. Why haven't you got any servants down here and upstairs something in an apron and a cap opened the door to us?"

"Grandfather had a cook, housemaid, parlourmaid and valet-attendant. He liked servants. He paid them the earth, of course, and he got them. Clemency and Roger just have a daily woman who comes in and cleans. They don't like servants—or rather Clemency doesn't. If Roger didn't get a square meal in the City every day, he'd starve. Clemency's idea of a meal is lettuce, tomatoes and raw carrot. We sometimes have servants, and then mother throws one of her temperaments and they leave, and we have dailies for a bit and then start again. We're in the daily period. Nannie is the permanency and copes in emergencies. Now you know."

Sophia went out. I sank down in one of the large brocaded chairs and gave myself up to speculation.

Upstairs I had seen Brenda's side of it. Here and now I had been shown Sophia's side of it. I realised completely the justice of Sophia's point of view—what might be called the Leonides family's point of view. They resented a stranger within the gates who had obtained admission by what they regarded as ignoble means. They were entirely within their rights. As Sophia had said: On paper it wouldn't look well . . .

But there was the human side of it—the side that I saw and that they didn't. They were, they always had been, rich and well established. They had no conception of the temptations of the underdog. Brenda Leonides had wanted wealth, and pretty things and safety—and a home. She had claimed that in exchange she had made her old husband happy. I had sympathy with her. Certainly, while I was talking with her, I had had sympathy for her. . . . Had I got as much sympathy now?

Two sides to the question—different angles of vision—which was the true angle . . . the true angle . . .

I had slept very little the night before. I had been up early to accompany Taverner. Now, in the warm flower-scented atmosphere of Magda Leonides's drawing room, my body relaxed in the cushioned embrace of the big chair and my eyelids dropped. . . .

Thinking of Brenda, of Sophia, of an old man's picture, my thoughts slid together into a pleasant haze.

I slept. . . .

10

I returned to consciousness so gradually that I didn't at first realise that I had been asleep. The scent of flowers was in my nose. In front of me a round white blob appeared to float in space. It was some few seconds before I realised that it was a human face I was looking at—a face suspended in the air about a foot or two away from me. As my faculties returned, my vision became more precise. The face still had its goblin suggestion—it was round with a bulging brow, combed back hair and small rather beady, black eyes. But it was definitely attached to a body—a small skinny body. It was regarding me very earnestly.

"Hullo," it said.

"Hullo," I replied, blinking.

"I'm Josephine."

I had already deduced that. Sophia's sister, Josephine, was, I judged, about eleven or twelve years of age. She was a fantastically ugly child with a very distinct likeness to her grandfather. It seemed to me possible that she also had his brains.

"You're Sophia's young man," said Josephine.

I acknowledged the correctness of this remark.

"But you came down here with Chief Inspector Taverner. Why did you come with Chief Inspector Taverner?"

"He's a friend of mine."

"Is he? I don't like him. I shan't tell him things."

"What sort of things?"

"The things that I know. I know a lot of things. I like knowing things."

She sat down on the arm of the chair and continued her searching scrutiny of my face. I began to feel quite uncomfortable.

"Grandfather's been murdered. Did you know?"

"Yes," I said. "I knew."

"He was poisoned. With es-er-ine." She pronounced the word very carefully. "It's interesting, isn't it?"

"I suppose it is."

"Eustace and I are very interested. We like detective stories. I've always wanted to be a detective. I'm being one now. I'm collecting clues."

She was, I felt, rather a ghoulish child.

She returned to the charge.

"The man who came with Chief Inspector Taverner is a detective too, isn't he? In books it says you can always know plain clothes detectives by their boots. But this detective was wearing suede shoes."

"The old order changeth," I said.

Josephine interpreted this remark according to her own ideas.

"Yes," she said, "there will be a lot of changes here now, I expect. We shall go and live in a house in London on the embankment. Mother has wanted to for a long time. She'll be very pleased. I don't expect father will mind if his books go, too. He couldn't afford it before. He lost an awful lot of money over Jezebel."

"Jezebel?" I queried.

"Yes, didn't you see it?"

"Oh, was it a play? No, I didn't. I've been abroad."

"It didn't run very long. Actually, it was the most awful flop. I don't think mother's really the type to play Jezebel, do you?"

I balanced my impressions of Magda. Neither in the peach-coloured négligée nor in the tailored suit had she conveyed any suggestion of Jezebel, but I was willing to believe that there were other Magdas that I had not yet seen.

"Perhaps not," I said cautiously.

"Grandfather always said it would be a flop. He said he wouldn't put up any money for one of these historical religious plays. He said it would never be a box office success. But mother was frightfully keen. I didn't like it much myself. It wasn't really a bit like the story in the Bible. I mean, Jezebel wasn't wicked like she is in the Bible. She was all patriotic and really quite nice. That made it dull. Still, the end was all right. They threw her out of the window. Only no dogs came and ate her. I think that was a pity, don't you? I like the part about the dogs eating her best. Mother says you can't have dogs on the stage but I don't see why. You could have performing dogs." She quoted with gusto: " 'And they ate her all but the palms of her hands.' Why didn't they eat the palms of her hands?"

"I've really no idea," I said.

"You wouldn't think, would you, that dogs were so particular. Our dogs aren't. They eat simply anything."

Josephine brooded on this Biblical mystery for some seconds.

"I'm sorry the play was a flop," I said.

"Yes. Mother was terribly upset. The notices were simply frightful. When she read them, she burst into tears and cried all day and she threw her breakfast tray at Gladys, and Gladys gave notice. It was rather fun."

"I perceive that you like drama, Josephine," I said.

"They did a post mortem on grandfather," said Josephine. "To find out what he had died of. A P.M., they call it, but I think that's rather confusing, don't you? Because P.M. stands for Prime Minister too. And for afternoon," she added, thoughtfully.

"Are you sorry your grandfather is dead?" I asked.

"Not particularly. I didn't like him much. He stopped me learning to be a ballet dancer."

"Did you want to learn ballet dancing?"

"Yes, and mother was willing for me to learn, and father didn't mind, but grandfather said I'd be no good."

She slipped off the arm of the chair, kicked off her shoes and endeavoured to get onto what are called technically, I believe, her points.

"You have to have the proper shoes, of course," she explained, "and even then you get frightful abscesses sometimes on the ends of your toes." She resumed her shoes and inquired casually:

"Do you like this house?"

"I'm not quite sure," I said.

"I suppose it will be sold now. Unless Brenda goes on living in it. And I suppose Uncle Roger and Aunt Clemency won't be going away now."

"Were they going away?" I asked with a faint stirring of interest.

"Yes. They were going on Tuesday. Abroad, somewhere. They were going by air. Aunt Clemency bought one of those new featherweight cases."

"I hadn't heard they were going abroad," I said.

"No," said Josephine. "Nobody knew. It was a secret. They weren't going to tell anyone until after they'd gone. They were going to leave a note behind for grandfather."

She added:

"Not pinned to the pincushion. That's only in very old-fashioned books and wives do it when they leave their husbands. But it would be silly now because nobody has pincushions any more."

"Of course they don't. Josephine, do you know why your Uncle Roger was—going away?"

She shot me a cunning sideways glance.

"I think I do. It was something to do with Uncle Roger's office in London. I rather think—but I'm not sure—that he'd embezzled something."

"What makes you think that?"

Josephine came nearer and breathed heavily in my face.

"The day that grandfather was poisoned Uncle Roger was shut up in his room with him ever so long. They were talking and talking. And Uncle Roger was saying that he'd never been any good, and that he'd let grandfather down—and that it wasn't the money so much—it was the feeling he'd been unworthy of trust. He was in an awful state."

I looked at Josephine with mixed feelings.

"Josephine," I said, "hasn't anybody ever told you that it's not nice to listen at doors?"

Josephine nodded her head vigorously.

"Of course they have. But if you want to find things out, you have to listen at doors. I bet Chief Inspector Taverner does, don't you?"

I considered the point. Josephine went on vehemently:

"And anyway if he doesn't, the other one does, the one with the suede shoes. And they look in people's desks and read all their letters, and find out all their secrets. Only they're stupid! They don't know where to look!"

Josephine spoke with cold superiority. I was stupid enough to let the inference escape me. The unpleasant child went on:

"Eustace and I know lots of things—but I know more than Eustace does. And I shan't tell him. He says women can't ever be great detectives. But I say they can. I'm going to write down everything in a notebook and then, when the police are completely baffled, I shall come forward and say, 'I can tell you who did it.'"

"Do you read a lot of detective stories, Josephine?"

"Masses."

"I suppose you think you know who killed your grandfather?"

"Well, I think so—but I shall have to find a few more clues." She paused and added, "Chief Inspector Taverner thinks that Brenda did it, doesn't he? Or Brenda and Laurence together because they're in love with each other."

"You shouldn't say things like that, Josephine."

"Why not? They are in love with each other."

"You can't possibly judge."

"Yes, I can. They write to each other. Love letters."

"Josephine! How do you know that?"

"Because I've read them. Awfully soppy letters. But Laurence is soppy. He was too frightened to fight in the war. He went into basements, and stoked boilers. When the flying bombs went over here, he used to turn green—really green. It made Eustace and me laugh a lot."

What I would have said next, I do not know, for at that moment a car drew up outside. In a flash Josephine was at the window, her snub nose pressed to the pane.

"Who is it?" I asked.

"It's Mr. Gaitskill, grandfather's lawyer. I expect he's come about the will."

Breathing excitedly, she hurried from the room, doubtless to resume her sleuthing activities.

Magda Leonides came in the room and to my surprise came across to me and took my hands in hers.

"My dear," she said, "thank goodness you're still here. One needs a man so badly."

She dropped my hands, crossed to a highbacked chair, altered its position a little, glanced at herself in a mirror, then picking up a small Battersea enamel box from a table she stood pensively opening and shutting it.

It was an attractive pose.

Sophia put her head in at the door and said in an admonitory whisper, "Gaitskill!"

"I know," said Magda.

A few moments later, Sophia entered the room accompanied by a small elderly man, and Magda put down her enamel box and came forward to meet him.

"Good morning, Mrs. Philip. I'm on my way upstairs. It seems there's some misunderstanding about the will. Your husband wrote to me with the impression that the will was in my keeping. I understood from Mr. Leonides himself that it was at his vault. You don't know anything about it, I suppose?"

"About poor Sweetie's will?" Magda opened astonished eyes. "No, of course not. Don't tell me that wicked woman upstairs has destroyed it?"

"Now, Mrs. Philip," he shook an admonitory finger at her. "No wild surmises. It's just a question of where your father-in-law kept it."

"But he sent it to you—surely he did—after signing it. He actually told us he had."

"The police, I understand, have been through Mr. Leonides's private papers," said Mr. Gaitskill. "I'll just have a word with Chief Inspector Taverner."

He left the room.

"Darling," cried Magda. "She has destroyed it. I know I'm right."

"Nonsense, mother, she wouldn't do a stupid thing like that."

"It wouldn't be stupid at all. If there's no will she'll get everything."

"Sh—here's Gaitskill back again."

The lawyer re-entered the room. Chief Inspector Taverner was with him and behind Taverner came Philip.

"I understood from Mr. Leonides," Gaitskill was saying, "that he had placed his will with the Bank for safe keeping."

Taverner shook his head.

"I've been in communication with the Bank. They have no private papers belonging to Mr. Leonides beyond certain securities which they held for him."

Philip said: "I wonder if Roger—or Aunt Edith—Perhaps, Sophia, you'd ask them to come down here."

But Roger Leonides, summoned with the others to the conclave, could give no assistance.

"But it's nonsense—absolute nonsense," he declared. "Father signed the will and said distinctly that he was posting it to Mr. Gaitskill on the following day."

"If my memory serves me," said Mr. Gaitskill, leaning back and half-closing his eyes, "it was on November 24th of last year that I forwarded a draft drawn up according to Mr. Leonides's instructions. He approved the draft, returned it to me, and in due course I sent him the will for signature. After a lapse of a week, I ventured to remind him that I had not yet received the will duly signed and attested, and asking him if there was anything he wished altered. He replied that he was perfectly satisfied and added that after signing the will he had sent it to his Bank."

"That's quite right," said Roger eagerly. "It was about the end of November last year—you remember, Philip?—Father had us all up one evening and read the will to us."

Taverner turned towards Philip Leonides.

"That agrees with your recollection, Mr. Leonides?"

"Yes," said Philip.

"It was rather like the Voysey Inheritance," said Magda. She sighed pleasurably. "I always think there's something so dramatic about a will."

"Miss Sophia?"

"Yes," said Sophia. "I remember perfectly."

"And the provisions of that will?" asked Taverner.

Mr. Gaitskill was about to reply in his precise fashion, but Roger Leonides got ahead of him.

"It was a perfectly simple will. Electra and Joyce had died and their share of the settlements had returned to father. Joyce's son, William, had been killed in action in Burma, and the money he left went to his father. Philip and I and the children were the only relatives left. Father explained that. He left fifty thousand pounds free of duty to Aunt Edith, a hundred thousand pounds free of duty to Brenda, this house to Brenda or else a suitable house in London to be purchased for her, whichever she preferred. The residue to be divided into three portions, one to myself, one to Philip, the third to be divided between Sophia, Eustace and Josephine, the portions of the last two to be held in trust until they should come of age. I think that's right, isn't it, Mr. Gaitskill?"

"Those are—roughly stated—the provisions of the document I drew up," agreed Mr. Gaitskill, displaying some slight acerbity at not having been allowed to speak for himself.

"Father read it out to us," said Roger. "He asked if there was any comment we might like to make. Of course there was none."

"Brenda made a comment," said Miss de Haviland.

"Yes," said Magda with zest. "She said she couldn't bear her darling old Aristide to talk about death. It 'gave her the creeps', she said. And after he was dead she didn't want any of the horrid money!"

"That," said Miss de Haviland, "was a conventional protest, typical of her class."

It was a cruel and biting little remark. I realised suddenly how much Edith de Haviland disliked Brenda.

"A very fair and reasonable disposal of his estate," said Mr. Gaitskill.

"And after reading it what happened?" asked Inspector Taverner.

"After reading it," said Roger, "he signed it."

Taverner leaned forward.

"Just how and when did he sign it?"

Roger looked round at his wife in an appealing way. Clemency spoke in answer to that look. The rest of the family seemed content for her to do so.

"You want to know exactly what took place?"

"If you please, Mrs. Roger."

"My father-in-law laid the will down on his desk and requested one of us—Roger, I think—to ring the bell. Roger did so. When Johnson came in answer to the bell, my father-in-law requested him to fetch Janet Woolmer, the parlourmaid. When they were both there, he signed the will and requested them to sign their own names beneath his signature."

"The correct procedure," said Gaitskill. "A will must be signed by the testator in the presence of two witnesses who must affix their own signatures at the same time and place."

"And after that?" asked Taverner.

"My father-in-law thanked them, and they went out. My father-in-law picked up the will, put it in a long envelope and mentioned that he would send it to Mr. Gaitskill on the following day."

"You all agree," said Inspector Taverner, looking round, "that that is an accurate account of what happened?"

There were murmurs of agreement.

"The will was on the desk, you said. How near were any of you to that desk?"

"Not very near. Five or six yards, perhaps, would be the nearest."

"When Mr. Leonides read you the will was he himself sitting at the desk?"

"Yes."

"Did he get up, or leave the desk, after reading the will and before signing it?"

"No."

"Could the servants read the document when they signed their names?"

"No," said Clemency. "My father-in-law placed a sheet of paper across the upper part of the document."

"Quite properly," said Philip. "The contents of the will were no business of the servants."

"I see," said Taverner. "At least—I don't see."

With a brisk movement he produced a long envelope and leaned forward to hand it to the lawyer.

"Have a look at that," he said. "And tell me what it is."

Mr. Gaitskill drew a folded document out of the envelope. He looked at it with lively astonishment, turning it round and round in his hands.

"This," he said, "is somewhat surprising. I do not understand it at all. Where was this, if I may ask?"

"In the safe, amongst Mr. Leonides's other papers."

"But what is it?" demanded Roger. "What's all the fuss about?"

"This is the will I prepared for your father's signature, Roger—but—I can't understand it after what you have all said—it is not signed."

"What? Well, I suppose it is just a draft."

"No," said the lawyer. "Mr. Leonides returned me the original draft. I then drew up the will—this will," he tapped it with his finger, "and sent it to him for signature. According to your evidence he signed the will in front of you all—and the two witnesses also appended their signatures—and yet this will is unsigned."

"But that's impossible," exclaimed Philip Leonides, speaking with more animation than I had yet heard from him.

Taverner asked: "How good was your father's eyesight?"

"He suffered from glaucoma. He used strong glasses, of course, for reading."

"He had those glasses on that evening?"

"Certainly. He didn't take his glasses off until after he had signed. I think I am right?"

"Quite right," said Clemency.

"And nobody—you are all sure of that—went near the desk before the signing of the will?"

"I wonder now," said Magda, screwing up her eyes. "If one could only visualise it all again."

"Nobody went near the desk," said Sophia. "And grandfather sat at it all the time."

"The desk was in the position it is now? It was not near a door, or a window, or any drapery?"

"It was where it is now."

"I am trying to see how a substitution of some kind could have been effected," said Taverner. "Some kind of substitution there must have been. Mr. Leonides was under the impression that he was signing the document he had just read aloud."

"Couldn't the signatures have been erased?" Roger demanded.

"No, Mr. Leonides. Not without leaving signs of erasion. There is one other possibility. That this is not the document sent to Mr. Leonides by Gaitskill and which he signed in your presence."

"On the contrary," said Mr. Gaitskill. "I could swear to this being the original document. There is a small flaw in the paper—at the top left hand corner—it resembles, by a stretch of fancy, an aeroplane. I noticed it at the time."

The family looked blankly at one another.

"A most curious set of circumstances," said Mr. Gaitskill. "Quite without precedent in my experience."

"The whole thing's impossible," said Roger. "We were all there. It simply couldn't have happened."

Miss de Haviland gave a dry cough.

"Never any good wasting breath saying something that has happened couldn't have happened," she remarked. "What's the position now? That's what I'd like to know?"

Gaitskill immediately became the cautious lawyer.

"The position will have to be examined very carefully," he said. "The document, of course, revokes all former wills and testaments. There are a large number of witnesses who saw Mr. Leonides sign what he certainly believed to be this will in perfectly good faith. Hum. Very interesting. Quite a little legal problem."

Taverner glanced at his watch.

"I'm afraid," he said, "I've been keeping you from your lunch."

"Won't you stay and lunch with us, Chief Inspector?" asked Philip.

"Thank you, Mr. Leonides, but I am meeting Dr. Cray in Swinly Dean."

Philip turned to the lawyer.

"You'll lunch with us, Gaitskill?"

"Thank you, Philip."

Everybody stood up. I edged unobtrusively towards Sophia.

"Do I go or stay?" I murmured. It sounded ridiculously like the title of a Victorian song.

"Go, I think," said Sophia.

I slipped quietly out of the room in pursuit of Taverner. Josephine was swinging to and fro on a baize door leading to the back quarters. She appeared to be highly amused about something.

"The police are stupid," she observed.

Sophia came out of the drawing room.

"What have you been doing, Josephine?"

"Helping Nannie."

"I believe you've been listening outside the door."

Josephine made a face at her and retreated.

"That child," said Sophia, "is a bit of a problem."

11

I came into the A.C.'s room at the Yard to find Taverner finishing the recital of what had apparently been a tale of woe.

"And there you are," he was saying. "I've turned a lot of them inside out—and what do I get—nothing at all! No motives. None of them hard up. And all that we've got against the wife and her young man is that he made sheep's eyes at her when she poured him out his coffee!"

"Come, come, Taverner," I said. "I can do a little better than that for you."

"You can, can you? Well, Mr. Charles, what did you get?"

I sat down, lit a cigarette, leaned back and let them have it.

"Roger Leonides and his wife were planning a getaway abroad next Tuesday. Roger and his father had a stormy interview on the day of the old man's death. Old Leonides had found out something was wrong, and Roger was admitting culpability."

Taverner went purple in the face.

"Where the hell did you get all that from?" he demanded. "If you got it from the servants—"

"I didn't get it from the servants. I got it," I said, "from a private inquiry agent."

"What do you mean?"

"And I must say that in accordance with the canons of the best detective stories, he, or rather she—or perhaps I'd better say it—has licked the police hollow!

"I also think," I went on, "that my private detective has a few more things up his, her or its sleeve."

Taverner opened his mouth and shut it again. He wanted to ask so many questions at once that he found it hard to begin.

"Roger!" he said. "So Roger's a wrong'un, is he?"

I felt a slight reluctance as I unburdened myself. I had liked Roger Leonides. Remembering his comfortable friendly room, and the man's own friendly charm, I disliked setting the hounds of justice on his track. It was possible, of course, that all Josephine's information would be unreliable, but I did not really think so.

"So the kid told you?" said Taverner. "She seems to be wise to everything that goes on in that house."

"Children usually are," said my father drily.

This information, if true, altered the whole position. If Roger had been, as Josephine had confidently suggested, "embezzling" the funds of Associated Catering and if the old man had found it out, it might have been vital to silence old Leonides and to leave England before the truth came out. Possibly Roger had rendered himself liable to criminal prosecution.

It was agreed that inquiries should be made without delay into the affairs of Associated Catering.

"It will be an almighty crash, if that goes," my father remarked. "It's a huge concern. There are millions involved."

"If it's really in Queer Street, it gives us what we want," said Taverner. "Father summons Roger. Roger breaks down and confesses. Brenda Leonides was out at a cinema. Roger has only got to leave his father's room, walk into the bathroom, empty out an insulin phial and replace it with the strong solution of eserine and there you are. Or his wife may have done it. She went over to the other wing after she came home that day—says she went over to fetch a pipe Roger had left there. But she could have gone over to switch the stuff before Brenda came home and gave him his injection. She'd be quite cool and capable about it."

I nodded. "Yes, I fancy her as the actual doer of the deed. She's cool enough for anything! And I don't think that Roger Leonides would think of poison as a means—that trick with the insulin has something feminine about it."

"Plenty of men poisoners," said my father drily.

"Oh, I know, sir," said Taverner. "Don't I know!" he added with feeling. "All the same I shouldn't have said Roger was the type."

"Pritchard," the Old Man reminded him, "was a good mixer."

"Let's say they were in it together."

"With the accent on Lady Macbeth," said my father, as Taverner departed. "Is that how she strikes you, Charles?"

I visualised the slight graceful figure standing by the window in that austere room.

"Not quite," I said. "Lady Macbeth was essentially a greedy woman. I don't think Clemency Leonides is. I don't think she wants or cares for possessions."

"But she might care, desperately, about her husband's safety?"

"That, yes. And she could certainly be—well, ruthless."

"Different kinds of ruthlessness. . . ." That was what Sophia had said.

I looked up to see the Old Man watching me.

"What's on your mind, Charles?"

But I didn't tell him then.

I was summoned on the following day and found Taverner and my father together.

Taverner was looking pleased with himself and slightly excited.

"Associated Catering is on the rocks," said my father.

"Due to crash at any minute," said Taverner.

"I saw there had been a sharp fall in the shares last night," I said. "But they seem to have recovered this morning."

"We've had to go about it very cautiously," said Taverner. "No direct inquiries. Nothing to cause a panic—or to put the wind up our absconding gentleman. But we've got certain private sources of information and the information there is fairly definite. Associated Catering is on the verge of a crash. It can't possibly meet its commitments. The truth seems to be that it's been grossly mismanaged for years."

"By Roger Leonides?"

"Yes. He's had supreme power, you know."

"And he's helped himself to money—"

"No," said Taverner. "We don't think he has. To put it bluntly, he may be a murderer, but we don't think he's a swindler. Quite frankly he's just been—a fool. He doesn't seem to have had any kind of judgement. He's launched out where he should have held in—he's hesitated and retreated where he ought to have launched out. He's delegated power to the last sort of people he ought to have delegated it to. He's a trustful sort of chap, and he's trusted the wrong people. At every time, and on every occasion, he's done the wrong thing."

"There are people like that," said my father. "And they're not really stupid either. They're bad judges of men, that's all. And they're enthusiastic at the wrong time."

"A man like that oughtn't to be in business at all," said Taverner.

"He probably wouldn't be," said my father, "except for the accident of being Aristide Leonides's son."

"That show was absolutely booming when the old man handed it over to him. It ought to have been a gold mine! You'd think he could have just sat back and let the show run itself."

"No," my father shook his head. "No show runs itself. There are always decisions to be made—a man sacked here—a man appointed there—small questions of policy. And with Roger Leonides the answer seems to have been always wrong."

"That's right," said Taverner. "He's a loyal sort of chap, for one thing. He kept on the most frightful duds—just because he had an affection for them—or because they'd been there a long time. And then he sometimes had wild impractical ideas and insisted on trying them out in spite of the enormous outlay involved."

"But nothing criminal?" my father insisted.

"No, nothing criminal."

"Then why murder?" I asked.

"He may have been a fool and not a knave," said Taverner. "But the result was the same—or nearly the same. The only thing that could save Associated Catering from the smash was a really colossal sum of money by next" (he consulted a notebook) "by next Wednesday at the latest."

"Such a sum as he would inherit, or thought he would have inherited, under his father's will?"

"Exactly."

"But he wouldn't be able to have got that sum in cash."

"No. But he'd have got credit. It's the same thing."

The Old Man nodded.

"Wouldn't it have been simpler to go to old Leonides and ask for help?" he suggested.

"I think he did," said Taverner. "I think that's what the kid overheard. The old boy refused point blank, I should imagine, to throw good money after bad. He would, you know."

I thought that Taverner was right there. Aristide Leonides had refused the backing for Magda's play—he had said that it would not be a Box Office success. Events had proved him correct. He was a generous man to his family, but he was not a man to waste money in unprofitable enterprises. And Associated Catering ran to thousands, or probably hundreds of thousands. He had refused point blank, and the only way for Roger to avoid financial ruin was for his father to die.

Yes, there was certainly a motive there all right.

My father looked at his watch.

"I've asked him to come here," he said. "He'll be here any minute now."

"Roger?"

"Yes."

"Will you walk into my parlour said the spider to the fly?" I murmured.

Taverner looked at me in a shocked way.

"We shall give him all the proper cautions," he said severely.

The stage was set, the shorthand writer established. Presently the buzzer sounded, and a few minutes later Roger Leonides entered the room.

He came in eagerly—and rather clumsily—he stumbled over a chair. I was reminded as before of a large friendly dog. At the same time I decided quite definitely that it was not he who had carried out the actual process of transferring eserine to an insulin bottle. He would have broken it, spilled it, or muffed the operation in some way or other. No, Clemency's, I decided, had been the actual hand, though Roger had been privy to the deed.

Words rushed from him:

"You wanted to see me? You've found out something? Hullo, Charles, I didn't see you. Nice of you to come along. But please tell me, Sir Arthur—"

Such a nice fellow—really such a nice fellow. But lots of murderers had been nice fellows—so their astonished friends had said afterwards. Feeling rather like Judas, I smiled a greeting.

My father was deliberate, coldly official. The glib phrases were uttered. Statement . . . taken down . . . no compulsion . . . solicitor . . .

Roger Leonides brushed them all aside with the same characteristic eager impatience.

I saw the faint sardonic smile on Chief Inspector Taverner's face, and read from it the thought in his mind.

"Always sure of themselves, these chaps. They can't make a mistake. They're far too clever!"

I sat down unobtrusively in a corner and listened.

"I have asked you to come here, Mr. Leonides," my father said, "not to give you fresh information, but to ask for some information from you—information that you have previously withheld."

Roger Leonides looked bewildered.

"Withheld? But I've told you everything—absolutely everything!"

"I think not. You had a conversation with the deceased on the afternoon of his death?"

"Yes, yes, I had tea with him. I told you so."

"You told us that, yes, but you did not tell us about your conversation."

"We—just—talked."

"What about?"

"Daily happenings, the house, Sophia—"

"What about Associated Catering? Was that mentioned?"

I think I had hoped up to then that Josephine had been inventing the whole story—but if so, that hope was quickly quenched.

Roger's face changed. It changed in a moment from eagerness to something that was recognisably close to despair.

"Oh my God," he said. He dropped into a chair and buried his face in his hands.

Taverner smiled like a contented cat.

"You admit, Mr. Leonides, that you have not been frank with us?"

"How did you get to know about that? I thought nobody knew—I don't see how anybody could know."

"We have means of finding out these things, Mr. Leonides." There was a majestic pause. "I think you will see now that you had better tell us the truth."

"Yes, yes, of course. I'll tell you. What do you want to know?"

"Is it true that Associated Catering is on the verge of collapse?"

"Yes. It can't be staved off now. The crash is bound to come. If only my father could have died without ever knowing. I feel so ashamed—so disgraced—"

"There is a possibility of criminal prosecution?"

Roger sat up sharply.

"No, indeed. It will be bankruptcy—but an honourable bankruptcy. Creditors will be paid twenty shillings in the pound if I throw in my personal assets which I shall do. No, the disgrace I feel is to have failed my father. He trusted me. He made over to me this, his largest concern—and his pet concern. He never interfered, he never asked what I was doing. He just—trusted me. . . . And I let him down."

My father said drily:

"You say there was no likelihood of criminal prosecution? Why then, had you and your wife planned to go abroad without telling anybody of your intention?"

"You know that, too?"

"Yes, Mr. Leonides."

"But don't you see?" He leaned forward eagerly. "I couldn't face him with the truth. It would have looked, you see, as if I was asking for money? As though I wanted him to set me on my feet again. He—he was very fond of me. He would have wanted to help. But I couldn't—I couldn't go on—it would have meant making a mess of things all over again—I'm no good. I haven't got the ability. I'm not the man my father was. I've always known it. I've tried. But it's no good. I've been so miserable—God! you don't know how miserable I've been! Trying to get out of the muddle, hoping I'd just get square, hoping the dear old man would never need hear about it. And then it came—no more hope of avoiding the crash. Clemency—my wife—she understood, she agreed with me. We thought out this plan. Say nothing to anyone. Go away. And then let the storm break. I'd leave a letter for my father, telling him all about it—telling him how ashamed I was and begging him to forgive me. He's been so good to me always—you don't know! But it would be too late then for him to do anything. That's what I wanted. Not to ask him—or even to seem to ask him for help. Start again on my own somewhere. Live simply and humbly. Grow things. Coffee—fruit. Just have the bare necessities of life—hard on Clemency, but she swore she didn't mind. She's wonderful—absolutely wonderful."

"I see." My father's voice was dry. "And what made you change your mind?"

"Change my mind?"

"Yes. What made you decide to go to your father and ask for financial help after all?"

Roger stared at him.

"But I didn't!"

"Come now, Mr. Leonides."

"You've got it all wrong. I didn't go to him. He sent for me. He'd heard, somehow, in the City. A rumour, I suppose. But he always knew things. Someone had told him. He tackled me with it. Then, of course, I broke down . . . I told him everything. I said it wasn't so much the money—it was the feeling I'd let him down after he'd trusted me."

Roger swallowed convulsively.

"The dear old man," he said. "You can't imagine how good he was to me. No reproaches. Just kindness. I told him I didn't want help, that I preferred not to have it—that I'd rather go away as I'd planned to do. But he wouldn't listen. He insisted on coming to the rescue—on putting Associated Catering on its legs again."

Taverner said sharply: "You are asking us to believe that your father intended to come to your assistance financially?"

"Certainly he did. He wrote to his brokers then and there, giving them instructions."

I suppose he saw the incredulity on the two men's faces. He flushed.

"Look here," he said, "I've still got the letter. I was to post it. But of course later—with—with the shock and confusion, I forgot. I've probably got it in my pocket now."

He drew out his wallet and started hunting through it. Finally he found what he wanted. It was a creased envelope with a stamp on it. It was addressed, as I saw by leaning forward, to Messrs. Greatorex and Hanbury.

"Read it for yourselves," he said. "If you don't believe me."

My father tore open the letter. Taverner went round behind him. I did not see the letter then, but I saw it later. It instructed Messrs. Greatorex and Hanbury to realise certain investments and asked for a member of the firm to be sent down on the following day to take certain instructions re the affairs of Associated Catering. Some of it was unintelligible to me but its purport was clear enough. Aristide Leonides was preparing to put Associated Catering on its feet again.

Taverner said: "We will give you a receipt for this, Mr. Leonides."

Roger took the receipt. He got up and said:

"Is that all? You do see how it all was, don't you?"

Taverner said: "Mr. Leonides gave you this letter and you then left him? What did you do next?"

"I rushed back to my own part of the house. My wife had just come in. I told her what my father proposed to do. How wonderful he had been! I—really, I hardly knew what I was doing."

"And your father was taken ill—how long after that?"

"Let me see—half an hour, perhaps, or an hour. Brenda came rushing in. She was frightened. She said he looked queer. I—I rushed over with her. But I've told you this before."

"During your former visit, did you go into the bathroom adjoining your father's room at all?"

"I don't think so. No—no, I am sure I didn't. Why, you can't possibly think that I—"

My father quelled the sudden indignation. He got up and shook hands.

"Thank you, Mr. Leonides," he said. "You have been very helpful. But you should have told us all this before."

The door closed behind Roger. I got up and came to look at the letter lying on my father's table.

"It could be forgery," said Taverner hopefully.

"It could be," said my father, "but I don't think it is. I think we'll have to accept it as it stands. Old Leonides was prepared to get his son out of this mess. It could have been done more efficiently by him alive than it could by Roger after his death—especially as it now transpires that no will is to be found and that in consequence Roger's actual amount of inheritance is open to question. That means delays—and difficulties. As things now stand, the crash is bound to come. No, Taverner, Roger Leonides and his wife had no motive for getting the old man out of the way. On the contrary—"

He stopped and repeated thoughtfully as though a sudden thought had occurred to him, "On the contrary . . ."

"What's on your mind, sir?" Taverner asked.

The Old Man said slowly:

"If Aristide Leonides had lived only another twenty-four hours, Roger would have been all right. But he didn't live twenty-four hours. He died suddenly and dramatically within little more than an hour."

"Hm," said Taverner. "Do you think somebody in the house wanted Roger to go broke? Someone who had an opposing financial interest? Doesn't seem likely."

"What's the position as regards the will?" my father asked. "Who actually gets old Leonides's money?"

"You know what lawyers are. Can't get a straight answer out of them.

There's a former will. Made when he married the second Mrs. Leonides. That leaves the same sum to her, rather less to Miss de Haviland, and the remainder between Philip and Roger. I should have thought that if this will isn't signed, then the old one would operate, but it seems it isn't so simple as that. First the making of the new will revoked the former one and there are witnesses to the signing of it, and the 'testator's intention.' It seems to be a toss up if it turns out that he died intestate. Then the widow apparently gets the lot—or a life interest at any rate."

"So if the will's disappeared Brenda Leonides is the most likely person to profit by it?"

"Yes. If there's been any hocus pocus, it seems probable that she's at the bottom of it. And there obviously has been hocus pocus, but I'm dashed if I see how it was done."

I didn't see, either. I suppose we were really incredibly stupid. But we were looking at it, of course, from the wrong angle.

12

There was a short silence after Taverner had gone out.

Then I said:

"Dad, what are murderers like?"

The Old Man looked up at me thoughtfully. We understand each other so well that he knew exactly what was in my mind when I put that question. And he answered it very seriously.

"Yes," he said. "That's important now—very important, for you. . . . Murder's come close to you. You can't go on looking at it from the outside."

I had always been interested, in an amateurish kind of way, in some of the more spectacular "cases" with which the CID had dealt, but, as my father said, I had been interested from the outside—looking in, as it were, through the shop window. But now, as Sophia had seen much more quickly than I did, murder had become a dominant factor in my life.

The Old Man went on: "I don't know if I'm the right person to ask. I could put you on to a couple of the tame psychiatrists who do jobs for us. They've got it all cut and dried. Or Taverner could give you all the inside dope. But you want, I take it, to hear what I, personally, as the result of my experience of criminals, think about it?"

"That's what I want," I said gratefully.

My father traced a little circle with his finger on the desk top.

"What are murderers like? Some of them," a faint rather melancholy smile showed on his face, "have been thoroughly nice chaps."

I think I looked a little startled.

"Oh yes, they have," he said. "Nice ordinary fellows like you and me—or like that chap who went out just now—Roger Leonides. Murder, you see, is an amateur crime. I'm speaking of course of the kind of murder you have in mind—not gangster stuff. One feels, very often, as though these nice ordinary chaps, had been overtaken, as it were, by murder, almost accidentally. They've been in a tight place, or they've wanted something very badly, money or a woman—and they've killed to get it. The brake that operates with most of us doesn't operate with them. A child, you know, translates desire into action without compunction. A child is angry with its kitten, says 'I'll kill you,' and hits it on the head with a hammer—and then breaks its heart because the kitten doesn't come alive again! Lots of kids try to take a baby out of a pram and 'drown it,' because it usurps attention—or interferes with their pleasures. They get—very early—to a stage when they know that that is 'wrong'—that is, that it will be punished. Later, they get to feel that it is wrong. But some people, I suspect, remain morally immature. They continue to be aware that murder is wrong, but they do not feel it. I don't think, in my experience, that any murderer has really felt remorse. . . . And that, perhaps, is the mark of Cain. Murderers are set apart, they are 'different'—murder is wrong—but not for them—for them it is necessary—the victim has 'asked for it,' it was 'the only way.' "

"Do you think," I asked, "that if someone hated old Leonides, had hated him, say, for a very long time, that that would be a reason?"

"Pure hate? Very unlikely, I should say." My father looked at me curiously. "When you say hate, I presume you mean dislike carried to excess. A jealous hate is different—that rises out of affection and frustration. Constance Kent, everybody said, was very fond of the baby brother she killed. But she wanted, one supposes, the attention and the love that was bestowed on him. I think people more often kill those they love, than those they hate. Possibly because only the people you love can really make life unendurable to you.

"But all this doesn't help you much, does it?" he went on. "What you want, if I read you correctly, is some token, some universal sign that will help you to pick out a murderer from a household of apparently normal and pleasant people?"

"Yes, that's it."

"Is there a common denominator? I wonder. You know," he paused in thought, "if there is, I should be inclined to say it is vanity."

"Vanity?"

"Yes, I've never met a murderer who wasn't vain. . . . It's their vanity that leads to their undoing, nine times out of ten. They may be frightened of being caught, but they can't help strutting and boasting and usually they're sure they've been far too clever to be caught." He added: "And here's another thing, a murderer wants to talk."

"To talk?"

"Yes, you see, having committed a murder puts you in a position of great loneliness. You'd like to tell somebody all about it—and you never can. And that makes you want to all the more. And so—if you can't talk about how you did it, you can at least talk about the murder itself—discuss it, advance theories—go over it.

"If I were you, Charles, I should look out for that. Go down there again, mix with them all, get them to talk. Of course it won't be plain sailing. Guilty or innocent, they'll be glad of the chance to talk to a stranger, because they can say things to you that they couldn't say to each other. But it's possible, I think, that you might spot a difference. A person who has something to hide can't really afford to talk at all. The blokes knew that in Intelligence during the war. If you were captured, your name, rank and unit but nothing more. People who attempt to give false information nearly always slip up. Get that household talking, Charles, and watch out for a slip or for some flash of self revelation."

I told him then about what Sophia had said about the ruthlessness in the family—the different kinds of ruthlessness. He was interested.

"Yes," he said. "Your young woman has got something there. Most families have got a defect, a chink in the armour. Most people can deal with one weakness—but they mightn't be able to deal with two weaknesses of a different kind. Interesting thing, heredity. Take the de Haviland ruthlessness, and what we might call the Leonides's unscrupulousness—the de Havilands are all right because they're not unscrupulous, and the Leonides are all right because, though unscrupulous, they are kindly—but get a descendant who inherited both of those traits—see what I mean?"

I had not thought of it quite in those terms. My father said:

"But I shouldn't worry your head about heredity. It's much too tricky and complicated a subject. No, my boy, go down there and let them talk to you. Your Sophia is quite right about one thing. Nothing but the truth is going to be any good to her or to you. You've got to know."

He added as I went out of the room: "And be careful of the child."

"Josephine? You mean don't let on to her what I'm up to."

"No, I didn't mean that. I meant—look after her. We don't want anything to happen to her."

I stared at him.

"Come, come, Charles. There's a cold blooded killer somewhere in that household. The child Josephine appears to know most of what goes on."

"She certainly knew all about Roger—even if she did leap to the conclusion that he was a swindler. Her account of what she overheard seems to have been quite accurate."

"Yes, yes. Child's evidence is always the best evidence there is. I'd rely on it every time. No good in court, of course. Children can't stand being asked direct questions. They mumble or else look idiotic and say they don't know. They're at their best when they're showing off. That's what the child was doing to you. Showing off. You'll get more out of her in the same way. Don't go asking her questions. Pretend you think she doesn't know anything. That'll fetch her."

He added:

"But take care of her. She may know a little too much for somebody's safety."

13

I went down to the Crooked House (as I called it in my own mind) with a slightly guilty feeling. Though I had repeated to Taverner Josephine's confidences about Roger, I had said nothing about her statement that Brenda and Laurence Brown wrote love letters to each other.

I excused myself by pretending that it was mere romancing, and that there was no reason to believe that it was true. But actually I had felt a strange reluctance to pile up additional evidence against Brenda Leonides. I had been affected by the pathos of her position in the house—surrounded by a hostile family united solidly against her. If such letters existed doubtless Taverner and his myrmidons would find them. I disliked to be the means of bringing fresh suspicion on a woman in a difficult position. Moreover, she had assured me solemnly that there was nothing of that kind between her and Laurence and I felt more inclined to believe her than to believe that malicious gnome Josephine. Had not Brenda said herself that Josephine was "Not all there."

I stifled an uneasy certainty that Josephine was very much all there. I remembered the intelligence of her beady black eyes.

I had rung up Sophia and asked if I might come down again.

"Please do, Charles."

"How are things going?"

"I don't know. All right. They keep on searching the house. What are they looking for?"

"I've no idea."

"We're all getting very nervy. Come as soon as you can. I shall go crazy if I can't talk to someone."

I said I would come down straightaway.

There was no one in sight as I drove up to the front door. I paid the taxi and it drove away. I felt uncertain whether to ring the bell or to walk in. The front door was open.

As I stood there, hesitating, I heard a slight sound behind me. I turned my head sharply. Josephine, her face partially obscured by a very large apple, was standing in the opening of the yew hedge looking at me.

As I turned my head, she turned away.

"Hullo, Josephine."

She did not answer, but disappeared behind the hedge. I crossed the drive and followed her. She was seated on the uncomfortable rustic bench by the goldfish pond swinging her legs to and fro and biting into her apple. Above its rosy circumference her eyes regarded me sombrely and with what I could not but feel was hostility.

"I've come down again, Josephine," I said.

It was a feeble opening, but I found Josephine's silence, and her unblinking gaze, rather unnerving.

With excellent strategic sense, she still did not reply.

"Is that a good apple?" I asked.

This time Josephine did condescend to reply. Her reply consisted of one word.

"Woolly."

"A pity," I said. "I don't like woolly apples."

Josephine replied scornfully: "Nobody does."

"Why wouldn't you speak to me when I said Hullo?"

"I didn't want to."

"Why not?"

Josephine removed the apple from her face to assist in the clearness of her denunciation.

"You went and sneaked to the police," she said.

"Oh," I was rather taken aback. "You mean—about—"

"About Uncle Roger."

"But it's all right, Josephine," I assured her. "Quite all right. They know he didn't do anything wrong—I mean, he hadn't embezzled any money or anything of that kind."

Josephine threw me an exasperated glance.

"How stupid you are."

"I'm sorry."

"I wasn't worrying about Uncle Roger. It's simply that that's not the way to do detective work. Don't you know that you never tell the police until the very end?"

"Oh I see," I said. "I'm sorry, Josephine. I'm really very sorry."

"So you should be." She added reproachfully, "I trusted you."

I said I was sorry for the third time. Josephine appeared a little mollified. She took another couple of bites of apple.

"But the police would have been bound to find out about all this," I said. "You—I—we couldn't have kept it a secret."

"You mean because he's going bankrupt?"

As usual Josephine was well informed.

"I suppose it will come to that."

"They're going to talk about it tonight," said Josephine. "Father and Mother and Uncle Roger and Aunt Edith. Aunt Edith would give him her money—only she hasn't got it yet—but I don't think father will. He says if Roger has got in a jam he's only got himself to blame and what's the good of throwing good money after bad, and mother won't hear of giving him any because she wants father to put up the money for Edith Thompson. Do you know Edith Thompson? She was married, but she didn't like her husband. She was in love with a young man called Bywaters who came off a ship and he went down a different street after the theatre and stabbed him in the back."

I marvelled once more at the range and completeness of Josephine's knowledge; and also at the dramatic sense which, only slightly obscured by hazy pronouns, had presented all the salient facts in a nutshell.

"It sounds all right," said Josephine, "but I don't suppose the play will be like that at all. It will be like Jezebel again." She sighed. "I wish I knew why the dogs wouldn't eat the palms of her hands."

"Josephine," I said. "You told me that you were almost sure who the murderer was?"

"Well?"

"Who is it?"

She gave me a look of scorn.

"I see," I said. "Not till the last chapter? Not even if I promise not to tell Inspector Taverner?"

"I want just a few more clues," said Josephine.

"Anyway," she added, throwing the core of the apple into the goldfish pool, "I wouldn't tell you. If you're anyone, you're Watson."

I stomached this insult.

"O.K." I said. "I'm Watson. But even Watson was given the data."

"The what?"

"The facts. And then he made the wrong deductions from them. Wouldn't it be a lot of fun for you to see me making the wrong deductions?"

For a moment Josephine was tempted. Then she shook her head.

"No," she said, and added: "Anyway, I'm not very keen on Sherlock Holmes. It's awfully old fashioned. They drive about in dog carts."

"What about those letters?" I asked.

"What letters?"

"The letters you said Laurence Brown and Brenda wrote to each other."

"I made that up," said Josephine.

"I don't believe you."

"Yes, I did. I often make things up. It amuses me."

I stared at her. She stared back.

"Look here, Josephine. I know a man at the British Museum who knows a lot about the Bible. If I find out from him why the dogs didn't eat the palms of Jezebel's hands, will you tell me about those letters?"

This time Josephine really hesitated.

Somewhere, not very far away, a twig snapped with a sharp cracking noise. Josephine said flatly:

"No, I won't."

I accepted defeat. Rather late in the day, I remembered my father's advice.

"Oh well," I said, "it's only a game. Of course you don't really know anything."

Josephine's eyes snapped, but she resisted the bait.

I got up. "I must go in now," I said, "and find Sophia. Come along."

"I shall stop here," said Josephine.

"No, you won't," I said. "You're coming in with me."

Unceremoniously I yanked her to her feet. She seemed surprised and inclined to protest, but yielded with a fairly good grace—partly, no doubt, because she wished to observe the reactions of the household to my presence.

Why I was so anxious for her to accompany me I could not at the moment have said. It only came to me as we were passing through the front door.

It was because of the sudden snapping of a twig.

14

There was a murmur of voices from the big drawing room. I hesitated but did not go in. I wandered on down the passage and, led by some impulse, I pushed open a baize door. The passage beyond was dark but suddenly a door opened showing a big lighted kitchen. In the doorway stood an old woman—a rather bulky old woman. She had a very clean white apron tied round her ample waist and the moment I saw her I knew that everything was all right. It is the feeling that a good Nannie can always give you. I am thirty-five, but I felt just like a reassured little boy of four.

As far as I knew, Nannie had never seen me, but she said at once:

"It's Mr. Charles, isn't it? Come into the kitchen and let me give you a cup of tea."

It was a big happy feeling kitchen. I sat down by the centre table and Nannie brought me a cup of tea and two sweet biscuits on a plate. I felt more than ever that I was in the nursery again. Everything was all right—and the terrors of the dark room and the unknown were no more with me.

"Miss Sophia will be glad you've come," said Nannie. "She's been getting rather overexcited." She added disapprovingly: "They're all overexcited."

I looked over my shoulder.

"Where's Josephine? She came in with me."

Nannie made a disapproving clacking noise with her tongue.

"Listening at doors and writing down things in that silly little book she carries about with her," she said. "She ought to have gone to school and had children of her own age to play with. I've said so to Miss Edith and she agrees—but the master would have it that she was best here in her home."

"I suppose he's very fond of her," I said.

"He was, sir. He was fond of them all."

I looked slightly astonished, wondering why Philip's affection for his offspring was put so definitely in the past. Nannie saw my expression and flushing slightly, she said:

"When I said the master, it was old Mr. Leonides I meant."

Before I could respond to that, the door opened with a rush and Sophia came in.

"Oh Charles," she said, and then quickly: "Oh Nannie, I'm so glad he's come."

"I know you are, love."

Nannie gathered up a lot of pots and pans and went off into a scullery with them. She shut the door behind her.

I got up from the table and went over to Sophia. I put my arms round her and held her to me.

"Dearest," I said. "You're trembling. What is it?"

Sophia said: "I'm frightened, Charles. I'm frightened."

"I love you," I said. "If I could take you away—"

She drew apart and shook her head.

"No, that's impossible. We've got to see this through. But you know, Charles, I don't like it. I don't like the feeling that someone—someone in this house—someone I see and speak to every day is a cold blooded calculating poisoner . . ."

And I didn't know how to answer that. To someone like Sophia one can give no easy meaningless reassurances.

She said: "If only one knew—"

"That must be the worst of it," I agreed.

"You know what really frightens me?" she whispered. "It's that we may never know. . . ."

I could visualise easily what a nightmare that would be. . . . And it seemed to me highly probable that it never might be known who had killed old Leonides.

But it also reminded me of a question I had meant to put to Sophia on a point that had interested me.

"Tell me, Sophia," I said. "How many people in this house knew about the eserine eyedrops—I mean (a) that your grandfather had them, and (b) that they were poisonous and what would be a fatal dose?"

"I see what you're getting at, Charles. But it won't work. You see, we all knew."

"Well, yes, vaguely, I suppose, but specifically—"

"We knew specifically. We were all up with grandfather one day for coffee after lunch. He liked all the family round him, you know. And his eyes had been giving him a lot of trouble. And Brenda got the eserine to put a drop in each eye and Josephine who always asks questions about everything, said 'Why does it say: *"Eyedrops—not to be taken"* on the bottle? What would happen if you drank all the bottle?' And grandfather smiled and said: 'If Brenda were to make a mistake and inject eyedrops into me one day instead of insulin—I suspect I should give a big gasp, and go rather blue in the face and then die, because, you see, my heart isn't very strong.' And Josephine said: 'Oo,' and grandfather went on 'So we must be careful that Brenda does not give me an injection of eserine instead of insulin, mustn't we?'" Sophia paused and then said: "We were all there listening. You see? We all heard!"

I did see. I had had some faint idea in my mind that just a little specialized knowledge would have been needed. But now it was borne in upon me that old Leonides had actually supplied the blue print for his own murder. The murderer had not had to think out a scheme, or to plan or devise anything. A simple easy method of causing death had been supplied by the victim himself.

I drew a deep breath. Sophia, catching my thought, said: "Yes, it's rather horrible, isn't it?"

"You know, Sophia," I said slowly. "There's just one thing does strike me."

"Yes?"

"That you're right, and that it couldn't have been Brenda. She couldn't do it exactly that way—when you'd all listened—when you'd all remember."

"I don't know about that. She is rather dumb in some ways, you know."

"Not as dumb as all that," I said. "No, it couldn't have been Brenda."

Sophia moved away from me.

"You don't want it to be Brenda, do you?" she asked.

And what could I say? I couldn't—no, I couldn't—say flatly: "Yes, I hope it is Brenda."

Why couldn't I? Just the feeling that Brenda was all alone on one side, and the concentrated animosity of the powerful Leonides family was arrayed against her on the other side? Chivalry? A feeling for the weaker? For the defenceless? I remembered her sitting on the sofa in her expensive rich mourning, the hopelessness in her voice—the fear in her eyes.

Nannie came back rather opportunely from the scullery. I don't know whether she sensed a certain strain between myself and Sophia.

She said disapprovingly:

"Talking murders and such like. Forget about it, that's what I say. Leave it to the police. It's their nasty business, not yours."

"Oh Nannie—don't you realize that someone in this house is a murderer."

"Nonsense, Miss Sophia, I've no patience with you. Isn't the front door open all the time—all the doors open, nothing locked—asking for thieves and burglars."

"But it couldn't have been a burglar, nothing was stolen. Besides why should a burglar come in and poison somebody?"

"I didn't say it was a burglar, Miss Sophia. I only said all the doors were open. Anyone could have got in. If you ask me it was the Communists."

Nannie nodded her head in a satisfied way.

"Why on earth should Communists want to murder poor grandfather?"

"Well, everyone says that they're at the bottom of everything that goes on. But if it wasn't the Communists, mark my word, it was the Catholics. The Scarlet Woman of Babylon, that's what they are."

With the air of one saying the last word, Nannie disappeared again into the scullery.

Sophia and I laughed.

"A good old Black Protestant," I said.

"Yes, isn't she? Come on, Charles, come into the drawing room. There's a kind of family conclave going on. It was scheduled for this evening—but it's started prematurely."

"I'd better not butt in, Sophia."

"If you're ever going to marry into the family, you'd better see just what it's like when it has the gloves off."

"What's it all about?"

"Roger's affairs. You seem to have been mixed up in them already. But you're crazy to think that Roger would ever have killed grandfather. Why, Roger adored him."

"I didn't really think Roger had. I thought Clemency might have."

"Only because I put it into your head. But you're wrong there too. I don't think Clemency will mind a bit if Roger loses all his money. I think she'll actually be rather pleased. She's got a queer kind of passion for not having things. Come on."

When Sophia and I entered the drawing room, the voices that were speaking stopped abruptly. Everybody looked at us.

They were all there. Philip sitting in a big crimson brocaded armchair between the windows, his beautiful face set in a cold stern mask. He looked like a judge about to pronounce sentence. Roger was astride a big pouf by the fireplace. He had ruffled up his hair between his fingers until it stood up all over his head. His left trouser leg was rucked up and his tie was askew. He looked flushed and argumentative. Clemency sat beyond him; her slight form seemed too slender for the big stuffed chair. She was looking away from the others and seemed to be studying the wall panels with a dispassionate gaze. Edith sat in a grandfather chair, bolt upright. She was knitting with incredible energy, her lips pressed tightly together. The most beautiful thing in the room to look at was Magda and Eustace. They looked like a portrait by Gainsborough. They sat together on the sofa—the dark handsome boy with a sullen expression on his face, and beside him, one arm thrust out along the back of the sofa, sat Magda, the

Duchess of Three Gables in a picture gown of taffeta with one small foot in a brocaded slipper thrust out in front of her.

Philip frowned.

"Sophia," he said, "I'm sorry, but we are discussing family matters which are of a private nature."

Miss de Haviland's needles clicked. I prepared to apologise and retreat. Sophia forestalled me. Her voice was clear and determined.

"Charles and I," she said, "hope to get married. I want Charles to be here."

"And why on earth not?" cried Roger, springing up from his pouf with explosive energy. "I keep telling you, Philip, there's nothing private about this! The whole world is going to know tomorrow or the day after. Anyway, my dear boy," he came and put a friendly hand on my shoulder, "you know all about it. You were there this morning."

"Do tell me," cried Magda, leaning forward. "What is it like at Scotland Yard. One always wonders. A table. A desk? Chairs? What kind of curtains? No flowers, I suppose? A dictaphone?"

"Put a sock in it, mother," said Sophia. "And anyway, you told Vavasour Jones to cut that Scotland Yard scene. You said it was an anticlimax."

"It makes it too like a detective play," said Magda. "Edith Thompson is definitely a psychological drama—or psychological thriller—which do you think sounds best?"

"You were there this morning?" Philip asked me sharply. "Why? Oh, of course—your father—"

He frowned. I realised more clearly than ever that my presence was unwelcome, but Sophia's hand was clenched on my arm.

Clemency moved a chair forward.

"Do sit down," she said.

I gave her a grateful glance and accepted.

"You may say what you like," said Miss de Haviland apparently going on from where they had all left off, "but I do think we ought to respect Aristide's wishes. When this will business is straightened out, as far as I am concerned, my legacy is entirely at your disposal, Roger."

Roger tugged his hair in a frenzy.

"No, Aunt Edith. No!" he cried.

"I wish I could say the same," said Philip, "but one has to take every factor into consideration—"

"Dear old Phil, don't you understand? I'm not going to take a penny from anyone."

"Of course he can't!" snapped Clemency.

"Anyway, Edith," said Magda. "If the will is straightened out, he'll have his own legacy."

"But it can't possibly be straightened out in time, can it?" asked Eustace.

"You don't know anything about it, Eustace," said Philip.

"The boy's absolutely right," cried Roger. "He's put his finger on the spot. Nothing can avert the crash. Nothing."

He spoke with a kind of relish.

"There is really nothing to discuss," said Clemency.

"Anyway," said Roger, "what does it matter?"

"I should have thought it mattered a good deal," said Philip, pressing his lips together.

"No," said Roger. "No! Does anything matter compared with the fact that father is dead? Father is dead! And we sit here discussing mere money matters!"

A faint colour rose in Philip's pale cheeks.

"We are only trying to help," he said stiffly.

"I know, Phil, old boy, I know. But there's nothing anyone can do. So let's call it a day."

"I suppose," said Philip, "that I could raise a certain amount of money. Securities have gone down a good deal and some of my capital is tied up in such a way that I can't touch it: Magda's settlement and so on—but—"

Magda said quickly:

"Of course you can't raise the money, darling. It would be absurd to try—and not very fair on the children."

"I tell you I'm not asking anyone for anything!" shouted Roger. "I'm hoarse with telling you so. I'm quite content that things should take their course."

"It's a question of prestige," said Philip. "Father's. Ours."

"It wasn't a family business. It was solely my concern."

"Yes," said Philip, looking at him. "It was entirely your concern."

Edith de Haviland got up and said: "I think we've discussed this enough."

There was in her voice that authentic note of authority that never fails to produce its effect.

Philip and Magda got up. Eustace lounged out of the room and I noticed the stiffness of his gait. He was not exactly lame but his walk was a halting one.

Roger linked his arm in Philip's and said:

"You've been a brick, Phil, even to think of such a thing!" The brothers went out together.

Magda murmured, "Such a fuss!" as she followed them, and Sophia said that she must see about my room.

Edith de Haviland stood rolling up her knitting. She looked towards me and I thought she was going to speak to me. There was something almost like appeal in her glance. However, she changed her mind, sighed and went out after the others.

Clemency had moved over to the window and stood looking out into the garden. I went over and stood beside her. She turned her head slightly towards me.

"Thank goodness that's over," she said—and added with distaste: "What a preposterous room this is!"

"Don't you like it?"

"I can't breathe in it. There's always a smell of half dead flowers and dust."

I thought she was unjust to the room. But I knew what she meant. It was very definitely an interior.

It was a woman's room, exotic, soft, shut away from the rude blasts of outside weather. It was not a room that a man would be happy in for long. It was not a room where you could relax and read the newspaper and smoke a pipe and put up your feet. Nevertheless I preferred it to Clemency's own abstract expression of herself upstairs. On the whole I prefer a boudoir to an operating theatre.

She said, looking round: "It's just a stage set. A background for Magda to play her scenes against." She looked at me. "You realise, don't you, what we've just been doing? Act II—the family conclave. Magda arranged it. It didn't mean a thing. There was nothing to talk about, nothing to discuss. It's all settled—finished."

There was no sadness in her voice. Rather there was satisfaction. She caught my glance.

"Oh, don't you understand?" she said impatiently. "We're free—at last! Don't you understand that Roger's been miserable—absolutely miserable—for years? He never had any aptitude for business. He likes things like horses and cows and pottering round in the country. But he adored his father—they all did. That's what's wrong with this house—too much family. I don't mean that the old man was a tyrant, or preyed upon them, or bullied them. He didn't. He gave them money and freedom. He was devoted to them. And they kept on being devoted to him."

"Is there anything wrong in that?"

"I think there is. I think, when your children have grown up, that you should cut away from them, efface yourself, slink away, force them to forget you."

"Force them? That's rather drastic, isn't it? Isn't coercion as bad one way as another?"

"If he hadn't made himself such a personality—"

"You can't make yourself a personality," I said. "He was a personality."

"He was too much of a personality for Roger. Roger worshipped him. He wanted to do everything his father wanted him to do, he wanted to be the kind of son his father wanted. And he couldn't. His father made over Associated Catering to him—it was the old man's particular joy and pride, and Roger tried hard to carry on in his father's footsteps. But he hadn't got that kind of ability. In business matters Roger is—yes, I'll say it plainly—a fool. And it nearly broke his heart. He's been miserable for years, struggling, seeing the whole thing go down the hill, having sudden wonderful 'ideas' and 'schemes' which always went wrong and made it worse than ever. It's a terrible thing to feel you're a failure year after year. You don't know how unhappy he's been. I do."

Again she turned and faced me.

"You thought, you actually suggested to the police, that Roger would have killed his father—for money! You don't know how—how absolutely ridiculous that is!"

"I do know it now," I said humbly.

"When Roger knew he couldn't stave it off any more—that the crash was bound to come, he was actually relieved. Yes, he was. He worried about his father's knowing—but not about anything else. He was looking forward to the new life we were going to live."

Her face quivered a little and her voice softened.

"Where were you going?" I asked.

"To Barbadoes. A distant cousin of mine died a short time ago and left me a tiny estate out there—oh, nothing much. But it was somewhere to go. We'd have been desperately poor, but we'd have scratched a living—it costs very little just to live. We'd have been together—unworried, away from them all."

She sighed.

"Roger is a ridiculous person. He would worry about me—about my being poor. I suppose he's got the Leonides attitude to money too firmly in his mind. When my first husband was alive, we were terribly poor—and Roger thinks it was so brave and wonderful of me! He doesn't realise that I was happy—really happy! I've never been so happy since. And yet—I never loved Richard as I love Roger."

Her eyes half-closed. I was aware of the intensity of her feeling.

She opened her eyes, looked at me and said:

"So you see, I would never have killed anyone for money. I don't like money."

I was quite sure that she meant exactly what she said. Clemency Leonides was one of those rare people to whom money does not appeal. They dislike luxury, prefer austerity, and are suspicious of possessions.

Still, there are many to whom money has no personal appeal, but who can be tempted by the power it confers.

I said, "You mightn't want money for yourself—but wisely directed, money may do a lot of interesting things. It can endow research, for example."

I had suspected that Clemency might be a fanatic about her work, but she merely said:

"I doubt if endowments ever do much good. They're usually spent in the wrong way. The things that are worth while are usually accomplished by someone with enthusiasm and drive—and with natural vision. Expensive equipment and training and experiment never does what you'd imagine it might do. The spending of it usually gets into the wrong hands."

"Will you mind giving up your work when you go to Barbadoes?" I asked. "You're still going, I presume?"

"Oh yes, as soon as the police will let us. No, I shan't mind giving up my work at all. Why should I? I wouldn't like to be idle, but I shan't be idle in Barbadoes."

She added impatiently: "Oh, if only this could all be cleared up quickly and we could get away."

"Clemency," I said, "have you any idea at all who did do this? Granting that you and Roger had no hand in it (and really I can't see any reason to think you had), surely, with your intelligence, you must have some idea of who did?"

She gave me a rather peculiar look, a darting sideways glance. When she spoke her voice had lost its spontaneity. It was awkward, rather embarrassed.

"One can't make guesses, it's unscientific," she said. "One can only say that Brenda and Laurence are the obvious suspects."

"So you think they did it?"

Clemency shrugged her shoulders.

She stood for a moment as though listening, then she went out of the room, passing Edith de Haviland in the doorway.

Edith came straight over to me.

"I want to talk to you," she said.

My father's words leapt into my mind. Was this—

But Edith de Haviland was going on:

"I hope you didn't get the wrong impression," she said. "About Philip, I mean. Philip is rather difficult to understand. He may seem to you reserved and cold, but that is not so at all. It's just a manner. He can't help it."

"I really hadn't thought—" I began.

But she swept on.

"Just now—about Roger. It isn't really that he's grudging. He's never been mean about money. And he's really a dear—he's always been a dear—but he needs understanding."

I looked at her with the air, I hope, of one who was willing to understand. She went on:

"It's partly, I think, from having been the second of the family. There's often something about a second child—they start handicapped. He adored his father, you see. Of course, all the children adored Aristide and he adored them. But Roger was his especial pride and joy. Being the eldest—the first. And I think Philip felt it. He drew back right into himself. He began to like books and the past and things that were well divorced from everyday life. I think he suffered—children do suffer. . . ."

She paused and went on:

"What I really mean, I suppose, is that he's always been jealous of Roger. I think perhaps he doesn't know it himself. But I think the fact that Roger has come a cropper—oh, it seems an odious thing to say and really I'm sure he doesn't realise it himself—but I think perhaps Philip isn't as sorry about it as he ought to be."

"You mean really that he's rather pleased Roger has made a fool of himself."

"Yes," said Miss de Haviland. "I mean just exactly that."

She added, frowning a little:

"It distressed me, you know, that he didn't at once offer help to his brother."

"Why should he?" I said. "After all, Roger has made a muck of things. He's a grown man. There are no children to consider. If he were ill or in real want, of course his family would help—but I've no doubt Roger would really much prefer to start afresh entirely on his own."

"Oh! he would. It's only Clemency he minds about. And Clemency is an extraordinary creature. She really likes being uncomfortable and having only one utility teacup to drink out of. Modern, I suppose. She's no sense of the past, no sense of beauty."

I felt her shrewd eyes looking me up and down.

"This is a dreadful ordeal for Sophia," she said. "I am so sorry her youth should be dimmed by it. I love them all, you know. Roger and Philip, and now Sophia and Eustace and Josephine. All the dear children. Marcia's children. Yes, I love them dearly." She paused and then added sharply: "But, mind you, this side idolatry."

She turned abruptly and went. I had the feeling that she had meant something by her last remark that I did not quite understand.

15

"Your room's ready," said Sophia.

She stood by my side looking out at the garden. It looked bleak and grey now with the half denuded trees swaying in the wind.

Sophia echoed my thought as she said:

"How desolate it looks. . . ."

As we watched, a figure, and then presently another came through the yew hedge from the rock garden. They both looked grey and unsubstantial in the fading light.

Brenda Leonides was the first. She was wrapped in a grey chinchilla coat and there was something catlike and stealthy in the way she moved. She slipped through the twilight with a kind of eerie grace.

I saw her face as she passed the window. There was a half smile on it, the curving crooked smile I had noticed upstairs. A few minutes later Laurence Brown, looking slender and shrunken, also slipped through the twilight. I can only put it that way. They did not seem like two people walking, two people who had been out for a stroll. There was something furtive and unsubstantial about them like two ghosts.

I wondered if it was under Brenda's or Laurence's foot that a twig had snapped.

By a natural association of ideas, I asked:

"Where's Josephine?"

"Probably with Eustace up in the schoolroom." She frowned. "I'm worried about Eustace, Charles."

"Why?"

"He's so moody and odd. He's been so different ever since that wretched paralysis. I can't make out what's going on in his mind. Sometimes he seems to hate us all."

"He'll probably grow out of all that. It's just a phase."

"Yes, I suppose so. But I do get worried, Charles."

"Why, dear heart?"

"Really, I suppose, because mother and father never worry. They're not like a mother and father."

"That may be all for the best. More children suffer from interference than from non-interference."

"That's true. You know, I never thought about it until I came back from abroad, but they really are a queer couple. Father living determinedly in a world of obscure historical bypaths and mother having a lovely time creating scenes. That tomfoolery this evening was all mother. There was no need for it. She just wanted to play a family conclave scene. She gets bored, you know, down here and has to try and work up a drama."

For the moment I had a fantastic vision of Sophia's mother poisoning her elderly father-in-law in a light-hearted manner in order to observe a murder drama at first hand with herself in the leading rôle.

An amusing thought! I dismissed it as such—but it left me a little uneasy.

"Mother," said Sophia, "has to be looked after the whole time. You never know what she's up to!"

"Forget your family, Sophia," I said firmly.

"I shall be only too delighted to, but it's a little difficult at the present moment. But I was happy out in Cairo when I had forgotten them all."

I remembered how Sophia had never mentioned her home or her people.

"Is that why you never talked about them?" I asked. "Because you wanted to forget them?"

"I think so. We've always, all of us, lived too much in each other's pockets. We're—we're all too fond of each other. We're not like some families where they all hate each other like poison. That must be pretty bad, but it's almost worse to live all tangled up in conflicting affections."

She added: "I think that's what I meant when I said we all lived together in a little crooked house. I didn't mean that it was crooked in the dishonest sense. I think what I meant was that we hadn't been able to grow up independent, standing by ourselves, upright. We're all a bit twisted and twining."

I saw Edith de Haviland's heel grinding a weed into the path as Sophia added:

"Like bindweed . . ."

And then suddenly Magda was with us—flinging open the door—crying out:

"Darlings, why don't you have the lights on? It's almost dark."

And she pressed the switches and the lights sprang up on the walls and on the tables, and she and Sophia and I pulled the heavy rose curtains, and there we were in the flower-scented interior, and Magda, flinging herself on the sofa, cried:

"What an incredible scene it was, wasn't it? How cross Eustace was!

He told me he thought it was all positively indecent. How funny boys are!"

She sighed.

"Roger's rather a pet. I love him when he rumples his hair and starts knocking things over. Wasn't it sweet of Edith to offer her legacy to him? She really meant it, you know, it wasn't just a gesture. But it was terribly stupid—it might have made Philip think he ought to do it, too! Of course Edith would do anything for the family! There's something very pathetic in the love of a spinster for her sister's children. Someday I shall play one of those devoted spinster aunts. Inquisitive, and obstinate and devoted."

"It must have been hard for her after her sister died," I said, refusing to be sidetracked into discussion of another of Magda's rôles. "I mean if she disliked old Leonides so much."

Magda interrupted me.

"Disliked him? Who told you that? Nonsense. She was in love with him."

"Mother!" said Sophia.

"Now don't try and contradict me, Sophia. Naturally at your age, you think love is all two good looking young people in the moonlight."

"She told me," I said, "that she had always disliked him."

"Probably she did when she first came. She'd been angry with her sister for marrying him. I daresay there was always some antagonism—but she was in love with him all right! Darlings, I do know what I'm talking about! Of course, with deceased wife's sister and all that, he couldn't have married her, and I daresay he never thought of it—and quite probably she didn't either. She was quite happy mothering the children, and having fights with him. But she didn't like it when he married Brenda. She didn't like it a bit!"

"No more did you and father," said Sophia.

"No, of course we hated it! Naturally! But Edith hated it most. Darling, the way I've seen her look at Brenda!"

"Now, mother," said Sophia.

Magda threw her an affectionate and half guilty glance the glance of a mischievous spoilt child.

She went on, with no apparent realization of any lack of continuity. "I've decided Josephine really must go to school."

"Josephine? To school."

"Yes. To Switzerland. I'm going to see about it tomorrow. I really think we might get her off at once. It's so bad for her to be mixed up in a horrid business like this. She's getting quite morbid about it. What she needs is other children of her own age. School life. I've always thought so."

"Grandfather didn't want her to go to school," said Sophia slowly. "He was very much against it."

"Darling old Sweetie Pie liked us all here under his eye. Very old people are often selfish in that way. A child ought to be amongst other children. And Switzerland is so healthy—all the winter sports, and the air, and such much, much better food than we get here!"

"It will be difficult to arrange for Switzerland now with all the currency regulations, won't it?" I asked.

"Nonsense, Charles. There's some kind of educational racket—or you exchange with a Swiss child—there are all sorts of ways. Rudolf Alstir's in Lausanne. I shall wire him tomorrow to arrange everything. We can get her off by the end of the week!"

Magda punched a cushion, smiled at us, went to the door, stood a moment looking back at us in a quite enchanting fashion.

"It's only the young who count," she said. As she said it, it was a lovely line. "They must always come first. And, darlings—think of the flowers—the blue gentians, the narcissus. . . ."

"In November?" asked Sophia, but Magda had gone.

Sophia heaved an exasperated sigh.

"Really," she said, "Mother is too trying! She gets these sudden ideas, and she sends thousands of telegrams and everything has to be arranged at a moment's notice. Why should Josephine be hustled off to Switzerland all in a flurry?"

"There's probably something in the idea of school. I think children of her own age would be a good thing for Josephine."

"Grandfather didn't think so," said Sophia obstinately.

I felt slightly irritated.

"My dear Sophia, do you really think an old gentleman of over eighty is the best judge of a child's welfare?"

"He was about the best judge of anybody in this house," said Sophia.

"Better than your Aunt Edith?"

"No, perhaps not. She did rather favour school. I admit Josephine's got into rather difficult ways—she's got a horrible habit of snooping. But I really think it's just because she's playing detectives."

Was it only the concern for Josephine's welfare which had occasioned Magda's sudden decision? I wondered. Josephine was remarkably well informed about all sorts of things that had happened prior to the murder and which had been certainly no business of hers. A healthy school life with plenty of games would probably do her a world of good. But I did rather wonder at the suddenness and urgency of Magda's decision—Switzerland was a long way off.

16

The Old Man had said: "Let them talk to you."

As I shaved the following morning, I considered just how far that had taken me.

Edith de Haviland had talked to me—she had sought me out for that especial purpose. Clemency had talked to me (or had I talked to her?). Magda had talked to me in a sense—that is I had formed part of the audience to one of her broadcasts. Sophia naturally had talked to me. Even Nannie had talked to me. Was I any the wiser for what I had learned from them all? Was there any significant word or phrase? More, was there any evidence of that abnormal vanity on which my father had laid stress? I couldn't see that there was.

The only person who had shown absolutely no desire to talk to me in any way, or on any subject, was Philip. Was not that, in a way, rather abnormal? He must know by now that I wanted to marry his daughter. Yet he continued to act as though I was not in the house at all. Presumably he resented my presence there. Edith de Haviland had apologised for him. She had said it was just "manner." She had shown herself concerned about Philip. Why?

I considered Sophia's father. He was in every sense a repressed individual. He had been an unhappy jealous child. He had been forced back into himself. He had taken refuge in the world of books—in the historical past. That studied coldness and reserve of his might conceal a good deal of passionate feeling. The inadequate motive of financial gain by his father's death was unconvincing—I did not think for a moment that Philip Leonides would kill his father because he himself had not quite as much money as he would like to have. But there might have been some deep psychological reason for his desiring his father's death. Philip had come back to his father's house to live, and later, as a result of the Blitz Roger had come—and Philip had been obliged to see day by day that Roger was his father's favourite. . . . Might things have come to such a pass in his tortured mind that the only relief possible was his father's death? And supposing that that death should incriminate his elder brother? Roger was short of money—on the verge of a crash. Knowing nothing of that last interview between Roger and his father and the latter's offer of assistance, might not Philip have believed that the motive would seem so powerful that Roger would be at once suspected? Was Philip's mental balance sufficiently disturbed to lead him to do murder?

I cut my chin with the razor and swore.

What the hell was I trying to do? Fasten murder on Sophia's father? That was a nice thing to try and do! That wasn't what Sophia had wanted me to come down here for.

Or—was it? There was something, had been something all along, behind Sophia's appeal. If there was any lingering suspicion in her mind that her father was the killer, then she would never consent to marry me—in case that suspicion might be true. And since she was Sophia, clear-eyed and brave, she wanted the truth, since uncertainty would be an eternal and perpetual barrier between us. Hadn't she been in effect saying to me, "Prove that this dreadful thing I am imagining is not true—but if it is true, then prove its truth to me—so that I can know the worst and face it!"

Did Edith de Haviland know, or suspect, that Philip was guilty? What had she meant by "this side idolatry?"

And what had Clemency meant by that peculiar look she had thrown at me when I asked her who she suspected and she had answered: "Laurence and Brenda are the obvious suspects, aren't they?"

The whole family wanted it to be Brenda and Laurence, hoped it might be Brenda and Laurence, but didn't really believe it was Brenda and Laurence. . . .

And of course, the whole family might be wrong, and it might really be Laurence and Brenda after all.

Or, it might be Laurence, and not Brenda. . . .

That would be a much better solution.

I finished dabbing at my cut chin and went down to breakfast filled with the determination to have an interview with Laurence Brown as soon as possible.

It was only as I drank my second cup of coffee that it occurred to me that the Crooked House was having its effect on me also. I, too, wanted to find, not the true solution, but the solution that suited me best.

After breakfast I went out through the hall and up the stairs. Sophia had told me that I should find Laurence giving instruction to Eustace and Josephine in the schoolroom.

I hesitated on the landing outside Brenda's front door. Did I ring and knock, or did I walk right in? I decided to treat the house as an integral Leonides home and not as Brenda's private residence.

I opened the door and passed inside. Everything was quiet, there seemed to be no one about. On my left the door into the big drawing room was closed. On my right two open doors showed a bedroom and adjoining bathroom. This I knew was the bathroom adjoining Aristide Leonides's bedroom where the eserine and the insulin had been kept. The police had finished with it now. I pushed the door open and slipped inside. I realised then how easy it would have been for anyone in the house (or from outside the house for the matter of that!) to come up here and into the bathroom unseen.

I stood in the bathroom looking round. It was sumptuously appointed with gleaming tiles and a sunk bath. At one side were various electric appliances; a hot plate and grill under, an electric kettle—a small electric saucepan, a toaster—everything that a valet attendant to an old gentleman might need. On the wall was a white enamelled cupboard. I opened it. Inside were medical appliances, two medicine glasses, eyebath, eye dropper and a few labelled bottles. Aspirin, Boracic powder, iodine. Elastoplast bandages, etc. On a separate shelf were the stacked supply of insulin, two hypodermic needles, and a bottle of surgical spirit. On a third shelf was a bottle marked The Tablets—one or two to be taken at night as ordered. On this shelf, no doubt, had stood the bottle of eyedrops. It was all clear, well arranged, easy for anyone to get at if needed, and equally easy to get at for murder.

I could do what I liked with the bottles and then go softly out and downstairs again and nobody would ever know I had been there. All this was, of course, nothing new, but it brought home to me how difficult the task of the police was.

Only from the guilty party or parties could one find out what one needed.

"Rattle 'em," Taverner had said to me. "Get 'em on the run. Make 'em think we're on to something. Keep ourselves well in the limelight. Sooner or later, if we do, our criminal will stop leaving well alone and try to be smarter still—and then—we've got him."

Well, the criminal hadn't reacted to this treatment so far.

I came out of the bathroom. Still no one about. I went on along the corridor. I passed the dining room on the left, and Brenda's bedroom and bathroom on the right. In the latter, one of the maids was moving about. The dining room door was closed. From a room beyond that, I heard Edith de Haviland's voice telephoning to the inevitable fishmonger. A spiral flight of stairs led to the floor above. I went up them. Edith's bedroom and sitting room was here, I knew, and two more bathrooms and Laurence Brown's room. Beyond that again the short flight of steps down to the big room built out over the servant's quarters at the back which was used as a schoolroom.

Outside the door I paused. Laurence Brown's voice could be heard, slightly raised, from inside.

I think Josephine's habit of snooping must have been catching. Quite unashamedly I leaned against the door jamb and listened.

It was a history lesson that was in progress, and the period in question was the French *directoire*.

As I listened astonishment opened my eyes. It was a considerable surprise to me to discover that Laurence Brown was a magnificent teacher.

I don't know why it should have surprised me so much. After all, Aristide Leonides had always been a good picker of men. For all his mouselike exterior, Laurence had that supreme gift of being able to arouse enthusiasm and imagination in his pupils. The drama of Thermidor, the decree of Outlawry against the Robespierrists, the magnificence of Barras, the cunning of Fouché—Napoleon, the half starved young gunner lieutenant—all these were real and living.

Suddenly Laurence stopped, he asked Eustace and Josephine a question, he made them put themselves in the places of first one and then another figure in the drama. Though he did not get much result from Josephine whose voice sounded as though she had a cold in the head, Eustace sounded quite different from his usual moody self. He showed brains and intelligence and the keen historical sense which he had doubtless inherited from his father.

Then I heard the chairs being pushed back and scraped across the floor. I retreated up the steps and was apparently just coming down them when the door opened.

Eustace and Josephine came out.

"Hullo," I said.

Eustace looked surprised to see me.

"Do you want anything?" he asked politely.

Josephine, taking no interest in my presence, slipped past me.

"I just wanted to see the schoolroom," I said rather feebly.

"You saw it the other day, didn't you? It's just a kid's place really. Used to be the nursery. It's still got a lot of toys in it."

He held the door open for me and I went in.

Laurence Brown stood by the table. He looked up, flushed, murmured something in answer to my good morning and went hurriedly out.

"You've scared him," said Eustace. "He's very easily scared."

"Do you like him, Eustace?"

"Oh! he's all right. An awful ass, of course."

"But not a bad teacher?"

"No, as a matter of fact he's quite interesting. He knows an awful lot. He makes you see things from a different angle. I never knew that Henry the Eighth wrote poetry—to Anne Boleyn, of course—jolly decent poetry."

We talked for a few moments on such subjects as The Ancient Mariner, Chaucer, the political implications behind the Crusades, the Mediaeval approach to life, and the, to Eustace, surprising fact that Oliver Cromwell had prohibited the celebration of Christmas Day. Behind Eustace's scornful and rather ill-tempered manner there was, I perceived, an inquiring and able mind.

Very soon I began to realise the source of his ill humour. His illness had not only been a frightening ordeal, it had also been a frustration and a setback, just at a moment when he had been enjoying life.

"I was to have been in the eleven next term—and I'd got my house colours. It's pretty thick to have to stop at home and do lessons with a rotten kid like Josephine. Why, she's only twelve."

"Yes, but you don't have the same studies, do you?"

"No, of course she doesn't do advanced maths—or Latin. But you don't want to have to share a tutor with a girl."

I tried to soothe his injured male pride by remarking that Josephine was quite an intelligent girl for her age.

"D'you think so? I think she's awfully wet. She's mad keen on this detecting stuff—goes round poking her nose in everywhere and writing things down in a little black book and pretending that she's finding out a lot. Just a silly kid, that's all she is," said Eustace loftily.

"Anyway," he added, "girls can't be detectives. I told her so. I think mother's quite right and the sooner Jo's packed off to Switzerland the better."

"Wouldn't you miss her?"

"Miss a kid of that age?" said Eustace haughtily. "Of course not. My goodness, this house is the absolute limit! Mother always haring up and down to London and bullying tame dramatists to rewrite plays for her, and making frightful fusses about nothing at all. And father shut up with his books and sometimes not hearing you if you speak to him. I don't see why I should have to be burdened with such peculiar parents. Then there's Uncle Roger—always so hearty that it makes you shudder. Aunt Clemency's all right, she doesn't bother you, but I sometimes think she's a bit batty. Aunt Edith's not too bad, but she's old. Things have been a bit more cheerful since Sophia came back—though she can be pretty sharp sometimes. But it is a queer household, don't you think so? Having a stepgrandmother young enough to be your aunt or your older sister. I mean, it makes you feel an awful ass!"

I had some comprehension of his feelings. I remembered (very dimly) my own supersensitiveness at Eustace's age. My horror of appearing in any way unusual or of my near relatives departing from the normal.

"What about your grandfather?" I said. "Were you fond of him?"

A curious expression flitted across Eustace's face.

"Grandfather," he said, "was definitely antisocial!"

"In what way?"

"He thought of nothing but the profit motive. Laurence says that's completely wrong. And he was a great individualist. All that sort of thing has got to go, don't you think so?"

"Well," I said, rather brutally, "he has gone."

"A good thing, really," said Eustace. "I don't want to be callous, but you can't really enjoy life at that age!"

"Didn't he?"

"He couldn't have. Anyway, it was time he went. He—" Eustace broke off as Laurence Brown came back into the schoolroom.

Laurence began fussing about with some books, but I thought that he was watching me out of the corner of his eye.

He looked at his wrist-watch and said:

"Please be back here sharp at eleven, Eustace. We've wasted too much time the last few days."

"O.K., sir."

Eustace lounged towards the door and went out whistling.

Laurence Brown darted another sharp glance at me. He moistened his lips once or twice. I was convinced that he had come back into the schoolroom solely in order to talk to me.

Presently, after a little aimless stacking and unstacking of books and a pretence of looking for a book that was missing, he spoke:

"Er—How are they getting on?" he said.

"They?"

"The police."

His nose twitched. A mouse in a trap, I thought, a mouse in a trap.

"They don't take me into their confidence," I said.

"Oh. I thought your father was the Assistant Commissioner."

"He is," I said. "But naturally he would not betray official secrets."

I made my voice purposely pompous.

"Then you don't know how—what—if . . ." His voice trailed off. "They're not going to make an arrest, are they?"

"Not so far as I know. But then, as I say, I mightn't know."

Get 'em on the run, Inspector Taverner had said. Get 'em rattled. Well, Laurence Brown was rattled all right. He began talking quickly and nervously.

"You don't know what it's like. . . . The strain. . . . Not knowing what—I mean, they just come and go—Asking questions. . . . Questions that don't seem to have anything to do with the case. . . ."

He broke off. I waited. He wanted to talk—well, then, let him talk.

"You were there when the Chief Inspector made that monstrous suggestion the other day? About Mrs. Leonides and myself. . . . It was monstrous. It makes one feel so helpless. One is powerless to prevent people thinking things! And it is all so wickedly untrue. Just because she is—was—so many years younger than her husband. People have dreadful minds—dreadful minds. . . . I feel—I can't help feeling, that it is all a plot."

"A plot? That's interesting."

It was interesting, though not quite in the way he took it.

"The family, you know; Mr. Leonides's family, have never been sympathetic to me. They were always aloof. I always felt that they despised me."

His hands began to shake.

"Just because they have always been rich—and powerful. They looked down on me. What was I to them? Only the tutor. Only a wretched conscientious objector. And my objections were conscientious. They were indeed!"

I said nothing.

"All right then," he burst out. "What if I was—afraid? Afraid I'd make a mess of it. Afraid that when I had to pull a trigger—I mightn't be able to bring myself to do it. How can you be sure it's a Nazi you're going to kill? It might be some decent lad—some village boy—with no political leanings, just called up for his country's service. I believe war is wrong, do you understand? I believe it is wrong."

I was still silent. I believed that my silence was achieving more than any arguments or agreements could do. Laurence Brown was arguing with himself, and in so doing was revealing a good deal of himself.

"Everyone's always laughed at me." His voice shook. "I seem to have a knack of making myself ridiculous. It isn't that I really lack courage—but I always do the thing wrong. I went into a burning house to rescue a woman they said was trapped there. But I lost the way at once, and the smoke made me unconscious, and it gave a lot of trouble to the firemen finding me. I heard them say, 'Why couldn't the silly chump leave it to us?' It's no good my trying, everyone's against me. Whoever killed Mr. Leonides arranged it so that I would be suspected. Someone killed him so as to ruin me."

"What about Mrs. Leonides?" I asked.

He flushed. He became less of a mouse and more like a man.

"Mrs. Leonides is an angel," he said, "an angel. Her sweetness, her kindness to her elderly husband were wonderful. To think of her in connection with poison is laughable—laughable! And that thick-headed Inspector can't see it!"

"He's prejudiced," I said, "by the number of cases on his files where elderly husbands have been poisoned by sweet young wives."

"The insufferable dolt," said Laurence Brown angrily.

He went over to a bookcase in the corner and began rummaging the books in it. I didn't think I should get anything more out of him. I went slowly out of the room.

As I was going along the passage, a door on my left opened and Josephine almost fell on top of me. Her appearance had the suddenness of a demon in an old-fashioned pantomime.

Her face and hands were filthy and a large cobweb floated from one ear.

"Where have you been, Josephine?"

I peered through the half open door. A couple of steps led up into the attic-like rectangular space in the gloom of which several large tanks could be seen.

"In the cistern room."

"Why in the cistern room?"

Josephine replied in a brief businesslike way:

"Detecting."

"What on earth is there to detect among the cisterns?"

To this, Josephine merely replied:

"I must wash."

"I should say most decidedly."

Josephine disappeared through the nearest bathroom door. She looked back to say:

"I should say it's about time for the next murder, wouldn't you?"

"What do you mean—the next murder?"

"Well, in books there's always a second murder about now. Someone who knows something is bumped off before they can tell what they know."

"You read too many detective stories, Josephine. Real life isn't like that. And if anybody in this house knows something the last thing they seem to want to do is to talk about it."

Josephine's reply came to me rather obscured by the gushing of water from a tap.

"Sometimes it's something that they don't know that they do know."

I blinked as I tried to think this out. Then, leaving Josephine to her ablutions, I went down to the floor below.

Just as I was going out through the front door to the staircase, Brenda came with a soft rush through the drawing room door.

She came close to me and laid her hand on my arm, looking up in my face.

"Well?" she asked.

It was the same demand for information that Laurence had made, only it was phrased differently. And her one word far more effective.

I shook my head.

"Nothing," I said.

She gave a long sigh.

"I'm so frightened," she said. "Charles, I'm so frightened. . . ."

Her fear was very real. It communicated itself to me there in that narrow space. I wanted to reassure her, to help her. I had once more that poignant sense of her as terribly alone in hostile surroundings.

She might well have cried out: "Who is on my side?"

And what would the answer have been? Laurence Brown? And what, after all, was Laurence Brown? No tower of strength in a time of trouble. One of the weaker vessels. I remembered the two of them drifting in from the garden the night before.

I wanted to help her. I badly wanted to help her. But there was nothing much I could say or do. And I had at the bottom of my mind an embarrassed guilty feeling, as though Sophia's scornful eyes were watching me. I remembered Sophia's voice saying: "So she got you."

And Sophia did not see, did not want to see, Brenda's side of it. Alone, suspected of murder, with no one to stand by her.

"The inquest's tomorrow," Brenda said. "What—what will happen?"

There I could reassure her.

"Nothing," I said. "You needn't worry about that. It will be adjourned for the police to make enquiries. It will probably set the Press loose, though. So far, there's been no indication in the papers that it wasn't a natural death. The Leonides have got a good deal of influence. But with an adjourned inquest—well, the fun will start."

(What extraordinary things one said! The fun! Why must I choose that particular word?)

"Will—will they be very dreadful?"

"I shouldn't give any interviews if I were you. You know, Brenda, you ought to have a lawyer—" She recoiled with a terrific gasp of dismay. "No—no—not the way you mean. But someone to look after your interests and advise you as to procedure, and what to say and do, and what not to say and do.

"You see," I added, "you're very much alone."

Her hand pressed my arm more closely.

"Yes," she said. "You do understand that. You've helped, Charles, you have helped. . . ."

I went down the stairs with a feeling of warmth, of satisfaction. . . . Then I saw Sophia standing by the front door. Her voice was cold and rather dry.

"What a long time you've been," she said. "They rang up for you from London. Your father wants you."

"At the Yard?"

"Yes."

"I wonder what they want me for. They didn't say?"

Sophia shook her head. Her eyes were anxious. I drew her to me.

"Don't worry, darling," I said, "I'll soon be back."

17

There was something strained in the atmosphere of my father's room. The Old Man sat behind his table, Chief Inspector Taverner leaned against the window frame. In the visitor's chair, sat Mr. Gaitskill, looking ruffled.

"—extraordinary want of confidence," he was saying acidly.

"Of course, of course." My father spoke soothingly. "Ah hullo, Charles, you've made good time. Rather a surprising development has occurred."

"Unprecedented," Mr. Gaitskill said.

Something had clearly ruffled the little lawyer to the core. Behind him, Chief Inspector Taverner grinned at me.

"If I may recapitulate?" my father said. "Mr. Gaitskill received a somewhat surprising communication this morning, Charles. It was from a Mr. Agrodopolous, proprietor of the Delphos Restaurant. He is a very old man, a Greek by birth, and when he was a young man he was helped and befriended by Aristide Leonides. He has always remained deeply grateful to his friend and benefactor and it seems that Leonides placed great reliance and trust in him."

"I would never have believed Leonides was of such a suspicious and secretive nature," said Mr. Gaitskill. "Of course, he was of advanced years—practically in his dotage, one might say."

"Nationality tells," said my father gently. "You see, Gaitskill, when you are very old your mind dwells a good deal on the days of your youth and the friends of your youth."

"But Leonides's affairs had been in my hands for well over forty years," said Mr. Gaitskill. "Forty-three years and six months to be precise."

Taverner grinned again.

"What happened?" I asked.

Mr. Gaitskill opened his mouth, but my father forestalled him.

"Mr. Agrodopolous stated in his communication that he was obeying certain instructions given him by his friend Aristide Leonides. Briefly, about a year ago he had been entrusted by Mr. Leonides with a sealed envelope which Mr. Agrodopolous was to forward to Mr. Gaitskill immediately after Mr. Leonides's death. In the event of Mr. Agrodopolous dying first, his son, a godson of Mr. Leonides, was to carry out the same instructions. Mr. Agrodopolous apologises for the delay, but explains that he has been ill with pneumonia and only learned of his old friend's death yesterday afternoon."

"The whole business is most unprofessional," said Mr. Gaitskill.

"When Mr. Gaitskill had opened the sealed envelope and made himself acquainted with its contents, he decided that it was his duty—"

"Under the circumstances," said Mr. Gaitskill.

"To let us see the enclosures. They consist of a will, duly signed and attested, and a covering letter."

"So the will has turned up at last?" I said.

Mr. Gaitskill turned a bright purple.

"It is not the same will," he barked. "This is not the document I drew up at Mr. Leonides's request. This has been written out in his own hand, a most dangerous thing for any layman to do. It seems to have been Mr. Leonides's intention to make me look a complete fool."

Chief Inspector Taverner endeavoured to inject a little balm into the prevailing bitterness.

"He was a very old gentleman, Mr. Gaitskill," he said. "They're inclined to be cranky when they get old, you know—not balmy, of course, but just a little eccentric."

Mr. Gaitskill sniffed.

"Mr. Gaitskill rang us up," my father said, "and apprised us of the main contents of the will and I asked him to come round and bring the two documents with him. I also rang you up, Charles."

I did not see why I had been rung up. It seemed to me singularly unorthodox procedure on both my father's and Taverner's part. I should have learnt about the will in due course, and it was really not my business at all how old Leonides had left his money.

"Is it a different will?" I asked. "I mean, does it dispose of his estate in a different way?"

"It does indeed," said Mr. Gaitskill.

My father was looking at me. Chief Inspector Taverner was very carefully not looking at me. In some way, I felt vaguely uneasy. . . .

Something was going on in both their minds—and it was a something to which I had no clue.

I looked enquiringly at Gaitskill.

"It's none of my business," I said. "But—"

He responded.

"Mr. Leonides's testamentary dispositions are not, of course, a secret," he said. "I conceived it to be my duty to lay the facts before the police authorities first, and to be guided by them in my subsequent procedure. I understand," he paused, "that there is an—understanding, shall we say—between you and Miss Sophia Leonides?"

"I hope to marry her," I said, "but she will not consent to an engagement at the present time."

"Very proper," said Mr. Gaitskill.

I disagreed with him. But this was no time for argument.

"By this will," said Mr. Gaitskill, "dated November the 29th of last year Mr. Leonides, after a bequest to his wife of one hundred and fifty thousand pounds, leaves his entire estate, real and personal, to his granddaughter, Sophia Katherine Leonides absolutely."

I gasped. Whatever I had expected, it was not this.

"He left the whole caboodle to Sophia," I said. "What an extraordinary thing. Any reason?"

"He set out his reasons very clearly in the covering letter," said my father. He picked up a sheet of paper from the desk in front of him. "You have no objection to Charles reading this, Mr. Gaitskill?"

"I am in your hands," said Mr. Gaitskill coldly. "The letter does at least offer an explanation—and possibly (though I am doubtful as to this), an excuse for Mr. Leonides's extraordinary conduct."

The Old Man handed me the letter. It was written in a small crabbed handwriting in very black ink. The handwriting showed character and individuality. It was not at all like the handwriting of an old man—except perhaps for the careful forming of the letters, more characteristic of a bygone period, when literacy was something painstakingly acquired and correspondingly valued.

"Dear Gaitskill (it ran)

You will be astonished to get this, and probably offended. But I have my own reasons for behaving in what may seem to you an unnecessarily secretive manner. I have long been a believer in the individual. In a family (this I have observed in my boyhood and never forgotten) there is always one strong character and it usually falls to this one person to care for, and bear the burden, of the rest of the family. In my family I was that person. I came to London, established myself there, supported my mother and my aged grandparents in Smyrna, extricated one of my brothers from the grip of the law, secured the freedom of my sister from an unhappy marriage and so on. God has been pleased to grant me a long life, and I have been able to watch over and care for my children and their children. Many have been taken from me by death; the rest, I am happy to say, are under my roof. When I die, the burden I have carried must descend on someone else. I have debated whether to divide my fortune as equally as possible amongst my dear ones—but to do so would not eventually result in a proper equality. Men are not born equal—to off-set the natural inequality of Nature one must redress the balance. In other words, someone must be my successor, must take upon him or herself the burden of responsibility for the rest of the family. After close observation I do not consider either of my sons fit for this responsibility. My dearly loved son Roger has no business sense, and though of a lovable nature is too impulsive to have good judgement. My son Philip is too unsure of himself to do anything but retreat from life. Eustace, my grandson, is very young and I do not think he has the qualities of sense and judgement necessary. He is indolent and very easily influenced by the ideas of anyone whom he meets. Only my granddaughter Sophia seems to me to have the positive qualities required. She has brains, judgement, courage, a fair and unbiased mind and, I think, generosity of spirit. To her I commit the family welfare—and the welfare of my kind sister-in-law Edith de Haviland for whose life-long devotion to the family I am deeply grateful.

This explains the enclosed document. What will be harder to explain—or rather to explain to you, my old friend—is the deception that I have employed. I thought it wise not to raise speculation about the disposal of my money, and I have no intention of letting my family know that Sophia is to be my heir. Since my two sons have already had considerable fortunes settled upon them, I do not feel that my testamentary dispositions will place them in a humiliating position.

To stifle curiosity and surmise, I asked you to draw me up a will. This will I read aloud to my assembled family. I laid it on my desk, placed a sheet of blotting paper over it and asked for two servants to be summoned. When they came I slid the blotting paper up a little, exposing the bottom of a document, signed my name and caused them to sign theirs. I need hardly say that what I and they signed was the will which I now enclose and not the one drafted by you which I had read aloud.

I cannot hope that you will understand what prompted me to execute this trick. I will merely ask you to forgive me for keeping you in the dark. A very old man likes to keep his little secrets.

Thank you, my dear friend, for the assiduity with which you have always attended to my affairs. Give Sophia my dear love. Ask her to watch over the family well and shield them from harm.

Yours very sincerely,
Aristide Leonides."

I read this very remarkable document with intense interest.

"Extraordinary," I said.

"Most extraordinary," said Mr. Gaitskill, rising. "I repeat, I think my old friend Mr. Leonides might have trusted me."

"No, Gaitskill," said my father. "He was a natural twister. He liked, if I may put it so, doing things the crooked way."

"That's right, sir," said Chief Inspector Taverner. "He was a twister if there ever was one!"

He spoke with feeling.

Gaitskill stalked out unmollified. He had been wounded to the depths of his professional nature.

"It's hit him hard," said Taverner. "Very respectable firm, Gaitskill, Callum & Gaitskill. No hanky panky with them. When old Leonides put through a doubtful deal, he never put it through with Gaitskill, Callum & Gaitskill. He had half a dozen different firms of solicitors who acted for him. Oh, he was a twister!"

"And never more so than when making his will," said my father.

"We were fools," said Taverner. "When you come to think of it, the only person who could have played tricks with that will was the old boy himself. It just never occurred to us that he could want to!"

I remembered Josephine's superior smile as she had said: "Aren't the police stupid?"

But Josephine had not been present on the occasion of the will. And even if she had been listening outside the door (which I was fully prepared to believe!) she could hardly have guessed what her grandfather was doing. Why, then, the superior air? What did she know that made her say the police were stupid? Or was it, again, just showing off?

Struck by the silence in the room I looked up sharply—both my father and Taverner were watching me. I don't know what there was in their manner that compelled me to blurt out defiantly:

"Sophia knew nothing about this! Nothing at all."

"No?" said my father.

I didn't quite know whether it was an agreement or a question.

"She'll be absolutely astounded!"

"Yes?"

"Astounded!"

There was a pause. Then, with what seemed sudden harshness the telephone on my father's desk rang.

"Yes?" He lifted the receiver—listened and then said, "Put her through."

He looked at me.

"It's your young woman," he said. "She wants to speak to us. It's urgent."

I took the receiver from him.

"Sophia?"

"Charles? Is that you? It's—Josephine!" Her voice broke slightly.

"What about Josephine?"

"She's been hit on the head. Concussion. She's—she's pretty bad. . . . They say she may not recover. . . ."

I turned to the other two.

"Josephine's been knocked out," I said.

My father took the receiver from me. He said sharply as he did so:

"I told you to keep an eye on that child. . . ."

18

In next to no time Taverner and I were racing in a fast police car in the direction of Swinly Dean.

I remembered Josephine emerging, from among the cisterns, and her airy remark that it was "about time for the second murder." The poor child had had no idea that she herself was likely to be the victim of the "second murder."

I accepted fully the blame that my father had tacitly ascribed to me. Of course I ought to have kept an eye on Josephine. Though neither Taverner nor I had any real clue to the poisoner of old Leonides, it was highly possible that Josephine had. What I had taken for childish nonsense and "showing off" might very well have been something quite different. Josephine, in her favourite sports of snooping and prying, might have become aware of some piece of information that she herself could not assess at its proper value.

I remembered the twig that had cracked in the garden.

I had had an inkling then that danger was about. I had acted upon it at the moment, and afterwards it had seemed to me that my suspicions had been melodramatic and unreal. On the contrary. I should have realised that this was murder, that whoever committed murder had endangered their neck, and that consequently that same person would not hesitate to repeat the crime if by the way safety could be assured.

Perhaps Magda, by some obscure maternal instinct, had recognised that Josephine was in peril, and that may have been what occasioned her sudden feverish haste to get the child sent to Switzerland.

Sophia came out to meet us as we arrived. Josephine, she said, had been taken by ambulance to Market Basing General Hospital. Dr. Gray would let them know as soon as possible the result of the X-ray.

"How did it happen?" asked Taverner.

Sophia led the way round to the back of the house and through a door into a small disused yard. In one corner a door stood ajar.

"It's a kind of wash house," Sophia explained. "There's a cat hole cut in the bottom of the door, and Josephine used to stand on it and swing to and fro."

I remembered swinging on doors in my own youth.

The wash house was small and rather dark. There were wooden boxes in it, some old hose pipe, a few derelict garden implements and some broken furniture. Just inside the door was a marble lion door stop.

"It's the door stop from the front door," Sophia explained. "It must have been balanced on the top of the door."

Taverner reached up a hand to the top of the door. It was a low door, the top of it only about a foot above his head.

"A booby trap," he said.

He swung the door experimentally to and fro. Then he stooped to the block of marble but he did not touch it.

"Has anyone handled this?"

"No," said Sophia. "I wouldn't let any one touch it."

"Quite right. Who found her?"

"I did. She didn't come in for her dinner at one o'clock. Nannie was calling her. She'd passed through the kitchen and out into the stable yard about a quarter of an hour before. Nannie said, 'She'll be bouncing her ball or swinging on that door again.' I said I'd fetch her in."

Sophia paused.

"She had a habit of playing in that way, you said? Who knew about that?"

Sophia shrugged her shoulders.

"Pretty well everybody in the house, I should think."

"Who else used the wash house? Gardeners?"

Sophia shook her head.

"Hardly anyone ever goes into it."

"And this little yard isn't overlooked from the house?" Taverner summed it up. "Anyone could have slipped out from the house or round the front and fixed up that trap ready. But it would be chancy . . ."

He broke off, looking at the door, and swinging it gently to and fro.

"Nothing certain about it. Hit or miss. And likelier miss than hit. But she was unlucky. With her it was hit."

Sophia shivered.

He peered at the floor. There were various dents on it.

"Looks as though someone experimented first . . . to see just how it would fall. . . . The sound wouldn't carry to the house."

"No, we didn't hear anything. We'd no idea anything was wrong until I came out and found her lying face down—all sprawled out." Sophia's voice broke a little. "There was blood on her hair."

"That her scarf?" Taverner pointed to a checked woollen muffler lying on the floor.

"Yes."

Using the scarf he picked up the block of marble carefully.

"There may be fingerprints," he said, but he spoke without much hope. "But I rather think whoever did it was—careful." He said to me: "What are you looking at?"

I was looking at a broken backed wooden kitchen chair which was among the derelicts. On the seat of it were a few fragments of earth.

"Curious," said Taverner. "Someone stood on that chair with muddy feet. Now why was that?"

He shook his head.

"What time was it when you found her, Miss Leonides?"

"It must have been five minutes past one."

"And your Nannie saw her going out about twenty minutes earlier. Who was the last person before that known to have been in the wash house?"

"I've no idea. Probably Josephine herself. Josephine was swinging on the door this morning after breakfast, I know."

Taverner nodded.

"So between then and a quarter to one someone set the trap. You say that bit of marble is the door stop you use for the front door? Any idea when that was missing?"

Sophia shook her head.

"The door hasn't been propped open at all today. It's been too cold."

"Any idea where everyone was all the morning?"

"I went out for a walk. Eustace and Josephine did lessons until half past twelve—with a break at half past ten. Father, I think, has been in the library all the morning."

"Your mother?"

"She was just coming out of her bedroom when I came in from my walk—that was about a quarter past twelve. She doesn't get up very early."

We re-entered the house. I followed Sophia to the library. Philip, looking white and haggard, sat in his usual chair. Magda crouched against his knees, crying quietly. Sophia asked:

"Have they telephoned yet from the hospital?"

Philip shook his head.

Magda sobbed:

"Why wouldn't they let me go with her? My baby—my funny ugly baby. And I used to call her a changeling and make her so angry. How could I be so cruel? And now she'll die. I know she'll die."

"Hush, my dear," said Philip. "Hush."

I felt that I had no place in this family scene of anxiety and grief. I withdrew quietly and went to find Nannie. She was sitting in the kitchen crying quietly.

"It's a judgement on me, Mr. Charles, for the hard things I've been thinking. A judgement, that's what it is."

I did not try and fathom her meaning.

"There's wickedness in this house. That's what there is. I didn't wish to see it or believe it. But seeing's believing. Somebody killed the master and the same somebody must have tried to kill Josephine."

"Why should they try and kill Josephine?"

Nannie removed a corner of her handkerchief from her eye and gave me a shrewd glance.

"You know well enough what she was like, Mr. Charles. She liked to know things. She was always like that, even as a tiny thing. Used to hide under the dinner table and listen to the maids talking and then she'd hold it over them. Made her feel important. You see, she was passed over, as it were, by the mistress. She wasn't a handsome child, like the other two. She was always a plain little thing. A changeling, the mistress used to call her. I blame the mistress for that, for it's my belief it turned the child sour. But in a funny sort of way she got her own back by finding out things about people and letting them know she knew them. But it isn't safe to do that when there's a poisoner about!"

No, it hadn't been safe. And that brought something else to my mind. I asked Nannie: "Do you know where she kept a little black book—a notebook of some kind where she used to write down things?"

"I know what you mean, Mr. Charles. Very sly about it, she was. I've seen her sucking her pencil and writing in the book and sucking her pencil again. And 'don't do that,' I'd say, 'you'll get lead poisoning' and 'oh no, I shan't,' she said, 'because it isn't really lead in a pencil. It's carbon,' though I don't see how that could be so, for if you call a thing a lead pencil it stands to reason that that's because there's lead in it."

"You'd think so," I agreed. "But as a matter of fact she was right." (Josephine was always right!) "What about this notebook? Do you know where she kept it?"

"I've no idea at all, sir. It was one of the things she was sly about."

"She hadn't got it with her when she was found?"

"Oh no, Mr. Charles, there was no notebook."

Had someone taken the notebook? Or had she hidden it in her own room? The idea came to me to look and see. I was not sure which Josephine's room was, but as I stood hesitating in the passage Taverner's voice called me:

"Come in here," he said. "I'm in the kid's room. Did you ever see such a sight?"

I stepped over the threshold and stopped dead.

The small room looked as though it had been visited by a tornado. The drawers of the chest of drawers were pulled out and their contents scattered on the floor. The mattress and bedding had been pulled from the small bed. The rugs were tossed into heaps. The chairs had been turned upside down, the pictures taken down from the wall, the photographs wrenched out of their frames.

"Good Lord," I exclaimed. "What was the big idea?"

"What do you think?"

"Someone was looking for something."

"Exactly."

I looked round and whistled.

"But who on earth—Surely nobody could come in here and do all this and not be heard—or seen?"

"Why not? Mrs. Leonides spends the morning in her bedroom doing her nails and ringing up her friends on the telephone and playing with her clothes. Philip sits in the library browsing over books. The nurse woman is in the kitchen peeling potatoes and stringing beans. In a family that knows each other's habits it would be easy enough. And I'll tell you this. Anyone in the house could have done our little job—could have set the trap for the child and wrecked her room. But it was someone in a hurry, someone who hadn't the time to search quietly."

"Anyone in the house, you say?"

"Yes, I've checked up. Everyone has some time or other unaccounted for. Philip, Magda, the nurse, your girl. The same upstairs. Brenda spent most of the morning alone. Laurence and Eustace had a half hour break—from ten thirty to eleven—you were with them part of that time—but not all of it. Miss de Haviland was in the garden alone. Roger was in his study."

"Only Clemency was in London at her job."

"No, even she isn't out of it. She stayed at home today with a headache—she was alone in her room having that headache. Any of them—any blinking one of them! And I don't know which! I've no idea. If I knew what they were looking for in here—"

His eyes went round the wrecked room.

"And if I knew whether they'd found it . . ."

Something stirred in my brain—a memory . . .

Taverner clinched it by asking me:

"What was the kid doing when you last saw her?"

"Wait," I said.

I dashed out of the room and up the stairs. I passed through the left hand door and went up to the top floor. I pushed open the door of the cistern room, mounted the two steps and bending my head, since the ceiling was low and sloping, I looked round me.

Josephine had said when I asked her what she was doing there that she was "detecting."

I didn't see what there could be to detect in a cobwebby attic full of water tanks. But such an attic would make a good hiding place. I considered it probable that Josephine had been hiding something there, something that she knew quite well she had no business to have. If so, it oughtn't to take long to find it.

It took me just three minutes. Tucked away behind the largest tank, from the interior of which a sibilant hissing added an eerie note to the atmosphere, I found a packet of letters wrapped in a torn piece of brown paper.

I read the first letter.

> Oh Laurence—my darling, my own dear love . . . It was wonderful last night when you quoted that verse of poetry. I knew it was meant for me, though you didn't look at me. Aristide said, "You read verse well." He didn't guess what we were both feeling. My darling, I feel convinced that soon everything will come right. We shall be glad that he never knew, that he died happy. He's been good to me. I don't want him to suffer. But I don't really think that it can be any pleasure to live after you're eighty. I shouldn't want to! Soon we shall be together for always. How wonderful it will be when I can say to you: My dear dear husband. . . . Dearest, we were made for each other. I love you, love you, love you—I can see no end to our love, I—

There was a good deal more, but I had no wish to go on.

Grimly I went downstairs and thrust my parcel into Taverner's hands.

"It's possible," I said, "that that's what our unknown friend was looking for."

Taverner read a few passages, whistled and shuffled through the various letters.

Then he looked at me with the expression of a cat who has been fed with the best cream.

"Well," he said softly. "This pretty well cooks Mrs. Brenda Leonides's goose. And Mr. Laurence Brown's. So it was them, all the time . . ."

19

It seems odd to me, looking back, how suddenly and completely my pity and sympathy for Brenda Leonides vanished with the discovery of her letters, the letters she had written to Laurence Brown. Was my vanity unable to stand up to the revelation that she loved Laurence Brown with a doting and sugarly infatuation and had deliberately lied to me? I don't know. I'm not a psychologist. I prefer to believe that it was the thought of the child Josephine, struck down in ruthless self preservation, that dried up the springs of my sympathy.

"Brown fixed that booby trap, if you ask me," said Taverner, "and it explains what puzzled me about it."

"What did puzzle you?"

"Well, it was such a sappy thing to do. Look here, say the kid's got hold of these letters—letters that are absolutely damning! The first thing to do is to try and get them back—(after all, if the kid talks about them, but has got nothing to show, it can be put down as mere romancing) but you can't get them back because you can't find them. Then the only thing to do is to put the kid out of action for good. You've done one murder and you're not squeamish about doing another. You know she's fond of swinging on a door in a disused yard. The ideal thing to do is wait behind the door and lay her out as she comes through with a poker, or an iron bar, or a nice bit of hose-pipe. They're all there ready to hand. Why fiddle about with a marble lion perched on top of a door which is as likely as not to miss her altogether and which even if it does fall on her may not do the job properly (which actually is how it turns out)? I ask you—why?"

"Well," I said, "what's the answer?"

"The only idea I got to begin with was that it was intended to tie in with someone's alibi. Somebody would have a nice fat alibi for the time when Josephine was being slugged. But that doesn't wash because, to begin with, nobody seems to have any kind of alibi, and secondly someone's bound to look for the child at lunch time, and they'll find the booby trap and the marble block, the whole modus operandi will be quite plain to see. Of course, if the murderer had removed the block before the child was found, then we might have been puzzled. But as it is the whole thing just doesn't make sense."

He stretched out his hands.

"And what's your present explanation?"

"The personal element. Personal idiosyncrasy. Laurence Brown's idiosyncrasy. He doesn't like violence—he can't force himself to do physical violence. He literally couldn't have stood behind the door and socked the kid on the head. He could rig up a booby trap and go away and not see it happen."

"Yes, I see," I said slowly. "It's the eserine in the insulin bottle all over again?"

"Exactly."

"Do you think he did that without Brenda's knowing?"

"It would explain why she didn't throw away the insulin bottle. Of course, they may have fixed it up between them—or she may have thought up the poison trick all by herself—a nice easy death for her tired old husband and all for the best in the best of possible worlds! But I bet she didn't fix the booby trap. Women never have any faith in mechanical things working properly. And are they right. I think myself the eserine was her idea, but that she made her besotted slave do the switch. She's the kind that usually manages to avoid doing anything equivocable themselves. Then they keep a nice happy conscience."

He paused then went on:

"With these letters I think the D.P.P. will say we have a case. They'll take a bit of explaining away! Then, if the kid gets through all right everything in the garden will be lovely." He gave me a sideways glance. "How does it feel to be engaged to about a million pounds sterling?"

I winced. In the excitement of the last few hours, I had forgotten the developments about the will.

"Sophia doesn't know yet," I said. "Do you want me to tell her?"

"I understand Gaitskill is going to break the sad (or glad) news after the inquest tomorrow." Taverner paused and looked at me thoughtfully.

"I wonder," he said, "what the reactions will be from the family?"

20

The inquest went off much as I had prophesied. It was adjourned at the request of the police.

We were in good spirits for news had come through the night before from the hospital that Josephine's injuries were much less serious than had been feared and that her recovery would be rapid. For the moment, Dr. Gray said, she was to be allowed no visitors—not even her mother.

"Particularly not her mother," Sophia murmured to me. "I made that quite clear to Dr. Gray. Anyway, he knows Mother."

I must have looked rather doubtful for Sophia said sharply:

"Why the disapproving look?"

"Well—surely a mother—"

"I'm glad you've got a few nice old fashioned ideas, Charles. But you don't quite know what my mother is capable of yet. The darling can't help it, but there would simply have to be a grand dramatic scene. And dramatic scenes aren't the best things for anyone recovering from head injuries."

"You do think of everything, don't you, my sweet."

"Well, somebody's got to do the thinking now that grandfather's gone."

I looked at her speculatively. I saw that old Leonides's acumen had not deserted him. The mantle of his responsibilities was already on Sophia's shoulders.

After the inquest, Gaitskill accompanied us back to Three Gables. He cleared his throat and said pontifically:

"There is an announcement it is my duty to make to you all."

For this purpose the family assembled in Magda's drawing room. I had on this occasion the rather pleasurable sensations of the man behind the scenes. I knew in advance what Gaitskill had to say.

I prepared myself to observe the reactions of everyone.

Gaitskill was brief and dry. Any signs of personal feeling and annoyance were well held in check. He read first Aristide Leonides's letter and then the will itself.

It was very interesting to watch. I only wished my eyes could be everywhere at once.

I did not pay much attention to Brenda and Laurence. The provision for Brenda in this will was the same. I watched primarily Roger and Philip, and after them Magda and Clemency.

My first impression was that they all behaved very well.

Philip's lips were pressed closely together, his handsome head was thrown back against the tall chair in which he was sitting. He did not speak.

Magda, on the contrary, burst into speech as soon as Mr. Gaitskill finished, her rich voice surging over his thin tones like an incoming tide drowning a rivulet.

"Darling Sophia—how extraordinary. . . . How romantic. . . . Fancy old Sweetie Pie being so cunning and deceitful—just like a dear old baby. Didn't he trust us? Did he think we'd be cross? He never seemed to be fonder of Sophia than of the rest of us. But really, it's most dramatic."

Suddenly Magda jumped lightly to her feet, danced over to Sophia and swept her a very grand court curtsey.

"Madame Sophia, your penniless and broken down old mother begs you for alms." Her voice took on a cockney whine. "Spare us a copper, old dear. Your Ma wants to go to the pictures."

Her hand, crooked into a claw, twitched urgently at Sophia.

Philip, without moving, said through stiff lips:

"Please Magda, there's no call for any unnecessary clowning."

"Oh, but, Roger," cried Magda, suddenly turning to Roger. "Poor darling Roger. Sweetie was going to come to the rescue and then, before he could do it, he died. And now Roger doesn't get anything. Sophia," she turned imperiously, "you simply must do something about Roger."

"No," said Clemency. She had moved forward a step. Her face was defiant. "Nothing. Nothing at all."

Roger came shambling over to Sophia like a large amiable bear.

He took her hands affectionately.

"I don't want a penny, my dear girl. As soon as this business is cleared up—or has died down, which is more what it looks like—then Clemency and I are off to the West Indies and the simple life. If I'm ever in extremis I'll apply to the head of the family—" he grinned at her engagingly—"but until then I don't want a penny. I'm a very simple person really, my dear—you ask Clemency if I'm not."

An unexpected voice broke in. It was Edith de Haviland's.

"That's all very well," she said. "But you've to pay some attention to the look of the thing. If you go bankrupt, Roger, and then slink off to the ends of the earth without Sophia's holding out a helping hand, there will be a good deal of ill natured talk that will not be pleasant for Sophia."

"What does public opinion matter?" asked Clemency scornfully.

"We know it doesn't to you, Clemency," said Edith de Haviland sharply, "but Sophia lives in this world. She's a girl with good brains and a good heart, and I've no doubt that Aristide was quite right in his selection of her to hold the family fortunes—though to pass over your two sons in their lifetime seems odd to our English ideas—but I think it would be very unfortunate if it got about that she behaved greedily over this—and had let Roger crash without trying to help him."

Roger went over to his aunt. He put his arms round her and hugged her.

"Aunt Edith," he said. "You are a darling—and a stubborn fighter, but you don't begin to understand. Clemency and I know what we want—and what we don't want!"

Clemency, a sudden spot of colour showing in each thin cheek, stood defiantly facing them.

"None of you," she said, "understand Roger. You never have! I don't suppose you ever will! Come on, Roger."

They left the room as Mr. Gaitskill began clearing his throat and arranging his papers. His countenance was one of deep disapprobation. He disliked the foregoing scenes very much. That was clear.

My eyes came at last to Sophia herself. She stood straight and handsome by the fireplace, her chin up, her eyes steady. She had just been left an immense fortune, but my principle thought was how alone she had suddenly become. Between her and her family a barrier had been erected. Henceforth she was divided from them, and I fancied that she already knew and faced that fact. Old Leonides had laid a burden upon her shoulders—he had been aware of that and she knew it herself. He had believed that her shoulders were strong enough to bear it, but just at this moment I felt unutterably sorry for her.

So far she had not spoken—indeed she had been given no chance, but very soon now speech would be forced from her. Already, beneath the affection of her family, I could sense latent hostility. Even in Magda's graceful playacting there had been, I fancied, a subtle malice. And there were other darker undercurrents that had not yet come to the surface.

Mr. Gaitskill's throat clearings gave way to precise and measured speech.

"Allow me to congratulate you, Sophia," he said. "You are a very wealthy woman. I should not advise any—er—precipitate action. I can advance you what ready money is needed for current expenses. If you wish to discuss future arrangements I shall be happy to give you the best advice in my power. Make an appointment with me at Lincoln's Inn when you have had plenty of time to think things over."

"Roger," began Edith de Haviland obstinately.

Mr. Gaitskill snapped in quickly.

"Roger," he said, "must fend for himself. He's a grown man—er, fifty four, I believe. And Aristide Leonides was quite right, you know. He isn't a businessman. Never will be." He looked at Sophia. "If you put Associated Catering on its legs again, don't be under any illusions that Roger can run it successfully."

"I shouldn't dream of putting Associated Catering on its legs again," said Sophia.

It was the first time she had spoken. Her voice was crisp and businesslike.

"It would be an idiotic thing to do," she added.

Gaitskill shot a glance at her from under his brows, and smiled to himself. Then he wished everyone goodbye and went out.

There were a few moments of silence, a realisation that the family circle was alone with itself.

Then Philip got up stiffly.

"I must get back to the library," he said. "I have lost a lot of time."

"Father—" Sophia spoke uncertainly, almost pleadingly.

I felt her quiver and draw back as Philip turned cold hostile eyes on her.

"You must forgive me for not congratulating you," he said. "But this has been rather a shock to me. I would not have believed that my father would so have humiliated me—that he would have disregarded my lifetime's devotion—yes—devotion."

For the first time, the natural man broke through the crust of icy restraint.

"My God," he cried. "How could he do this to me? He was always unfair to me—always."

"Oh no, Philip, no, you mustn't think that," cried Edith de Haviland. "Don't regard this as another slight. It isn't. When people get old, they turn naturally to a younger generation. . . . I assure you it's only that. . . . And besides, Aristide had a very keen business sense. I've often heard him say that two lots of death duties—"

"He never cared for me," said Philip. His voice was low and hoarse. "It was always Roger—Roger. Well, at least—" an extraordinary expression of spite suddenly marred his handsome features, "father realised that Roger was a fool and a failure. He cut Roger out, too."

"What about me?" said Eustace.

I had hardly noticed Eustace until now, but I perceived that he was trembling with some violent emotion. His face was crimson; there were, I thought, tears in his eyes. His voice shook as it rose hysterically.

"It's a shame!" said Eustace. "It's a damned shame! How dare Grandfather do this to me? How dare he? I was his only grandson. How dare he pass me over for Sophia? It's not fair. I hate him. I hate him. I'll never forgive him as long as I live. Beastly tyrannical old man. I wanted him to die. I wanted to get out of this house. I wanted to be my own master. And now I've got to be bullied and messed around by Sophia, and made to look a fool. I wish I was dead. . . ."

His voice broke and he rushed out of the room.

Edith de Haviland gave a sharp click of her tongue.

"No self control," she murmured.

"I know just how he feels," cried Magda.

"I'm sure you do," said Edith with acidity in her tone.

"The poor sweet! I must go after him."

"Now, Magda—" Edith hurried after her.

Their voices died away. Sophia remained looking at Philip. There was, I think, a certain pleading in her glance. If so, it got no response. He looked at her coldly, quite in control of himself once more.

"You played your cards very well, Sophia," he said and went out of the room.

"That was a cruel thing to say," I cried. "Sophia—"

She stretched out her hands to me. I took her in my arms.

"This is too much for you, my sweet."

"I know just how they feel," said Sophia.

"That old devil, your grandfather, shouldn't have let you in for this."

She straightened her shoulders.

"He believed I could take it. And so I can. I wish—I wish Eustace didn't mind so much."

"He'll get over it."

"Will he? I wonder. He's the kind that broods terribly. And I hate father being hurt."

"Your mother's all right."

"She minds a bit. It goes against the grain to have to come and ask your daughter for money to put on plays. She'll be after me to put on the Edith Thompson one before you can turn round."

"And what will you say? If it keeps her happy . . ."

Sophia pulled herself right out of my arms, her head went back.

"I shall say No! It's a rotten play and mother couldn't play the part. It would be throwing the money away."

I laughed softly. I couldn't help it.

"What is it?" Sophia demanded suspiciously.

"I'm beginning to understand why your grandfather left you his money. You're a chip off the old block, Sophia."

21

My one feeling of regret at this time was that Josephine was out of it all. She would have enjoyed it all so much.

Her recovery was rapid and she was expected to be back any day now, but nevertheless she missed another event of importance.

I was in the rock garden one morning with Sophia and Brenda when a car drew up to the front door. Taverner and Sergeant Lamb got out of it. They went up the steps and into the house.

Brenda stood still, staring at the car.

"It's those men," she said. "They've come back, and I thought they'd given up—I thought it was all over."

I saw her shiver.

She had joined us about ten minutes before. Wrapped in her chinchilla coat, she had said "If I don't get some air and exercise, I shall go mad. If I go outside the gate there's always a reporter waiting to pounce on me. It's like being besieged. Will it go on for ever?"

Sophia said that she supposed the reporters would soon get tired of it.

"You can go out in the car," she added.

"I tell you I want to get some exercise."

Then she said abruptly:

"You've given Laurence the sack, Sophia. Why?"

Sophia answered quietly:

"We're making other arrangements for Eustace. And Josephine is going to Switzerland."

"Well, you've upset Laurence very much. He feels you don't trust him."

Sophia did not reply and it was at that moment that Taverner's car had arrived.

Standing there, shivering in the moist autumn air, Brenda muttered, "What do they want? Why have they come?"

I thought I knew why they had come. I had said nothing to Sophia of the letters I had found by the cistern, but I knew that they had gone to the Director of Public Prosecutions.

Taverner came out of the house again. He walked across the drive and the lawn towards us. Brenda shivered more violently.

"What does he want?" she repeated nervously. "What does he want?"

Then Taverner was with us. He spoke curtly in his official voice using the official phrases.

"I have a warrant here for your arrest—you are charged with administering eserine to Aristide Leonides on September 19th last. I must warn you that anything you say may be used in evidence at your trial."

And then Brenda went to pieces. She screamed. She clung to me. She cried out, "No, no, no, it isn't true! Charles, tell them it isn't true! I didn't do it. I didn't know anything about it. It's all a plot. Don't let them take me away. It isn't true, I tell you. . . . It isn't true. . . . I haven't done anything. . . ."

It was horrible—unbelievably horrible. I tried to soothe her, I unfastened her fingers from my arm. I told her that I would arrange for a lawyer for her—that she was to keep calm—that a lawyer would arrange everything. . . .

Taverner took her gently under the elbow.

"Come along, Mrs. Leonides," he said. "You don't want a hat, do you? No? Then we'll go off right away."

She pulled back, staring at him with enormous cat's eyes.

"Laurence," she said. "What have you done to Laurence?"

"Mr. Laurence Brown is also under arrest," said Taverner.

She wilted then. Her body seemed to collapse and shrink. The tears poured down her face. She went away quietly with Taverner across the lawn to the car. I saw Laurence Brown and Sergeant Lamb come out of the house. They all got into the car. . . . The car drove away.

I drew a deep breath and turned to Sophia. She was very pale and there was a look of distress on her face.

"It's horrible, Charles," she said. "It's quite horrible."

"I know."

"You must get her a really first class solicitor—the best there is. She—she must have all the help possible."

"One doesn't realise," I said, "what these things are like. I've never seen anyone arrested before."

"I know. One has no idea."

We were both silent. I was thinking of the desperate terror on Brenda's face. It had seemed familiar to me and suddenly I realised why. It was the same expression that I had seen on Magda Leonides's face the first day I had come to the Crooked House when she had been talking about the Edith Thompson play.

"And then," she had said, "sheer terror, don't you think so?"

Sheer terror—that was what had been on Brenda's face. Brenda was not a fighter. I wondered that she had ever had the nerve to do murder. But possibly she had not. Possibly it had been Laurence Brown, with his persecution mania, his unstable personality who had put the contents of one little bottle into another little bottle—a simple easy act—to free the woman he loved.

"So it's over," said Sophia.

She sighed deeply, then asked:

"But why arrest them now? I thought there wasn't enough evidence."

"A certain amount of evidence has come to light. Letters."

"You mean love letters between them?"

"Yes."

"What fools people are to keep these things!"

Yes, indeed. Fools. The kind of folly which never seemed to profit by the experience of others. You couldn't open a daily newspaper without coming across some instance of that folly—the passion to keep the written word, the written assurance of love.

"It's quite beastly, Sophia," I said. "But it's no good minding about it. After all, it's what we've been hoping all along, isn't it? It's what you said that first night at Mario's. You said it would be all right if the right person had killed your grandfather. Brenda was the right person, wasn't she? Brenda or Laurence?"

"Don't, Charles, you make me feel awful."

"But we must be sensible. We can marry now, Sophia. You can't hold me off any longer. The Leonides family are out of it."

She stared at me. I had never realised before the vivid blue of her eyes.

"Yes," she said. "I suppose we're out of it now. We are out of it, aren't we? You're sure?"

"My dear girl, none of you really had a shadow of motive."

Her face went suddenly white.

"Except me, Charles. I had a motive."

"Yes, of course—" I was taken aback. "But not really. You didn't know, you see, about the will."

"But I did, Charles," she whispered.

"What?" I stared at her. I felt suddenly cold.

"I knew all the time that grandfather had left his money to me."

"But how?"

"He told me. About a fortnight before he was killed. He said to me quite suddenly, 'I've left all my money to you, Sophia. You must look after the family when I'm gone.'"

I stared.

"You never told me."

"No. You see, when they all explained about the will and his signing it,

I thought perhaps he had made a mistake—that he was just imagining that he had left it to me. Or that if he had made a will leaving it to me, then it had got lost and would never turn up. I didn't want it to turn up—I was afraid."

"Afraid? Why?"

"I suppose—because of murder."

I remembered the look of terror on Brenda's face—the wild unreasoning panic. I remembered the sheer panic that Magda had conjured up at will when she considered playing the part of a murderess. There would be no panic in Sophia's mind, but she was a realist, and she could see clearly enough that Leonides's will made her a suspect. I understood better now (or thought I did) her refusal to become engaged to me and her insistence that I should find out the truth. Nothing but the truth, she had said, was any good to her. I remembered the passion, the earnestness with which she had said it.

We had turned to walk towards the house and suddenly, at a certain spot, I remembered something else she had said.

She had said that she supposed she could murder someone, but if so, she had added, it must be for something really worth while.

22

Round a turn of the rock garden Roger and Clemency came walking briskly towards us. Roger's flapping tweeds suited him better than his City clothes. He looked eager and excited. Clemency was frowning.

"Hullo, you two," said Roger. "At last! I thought they were never going to arrest that foul woman. What they've been waiting for, I don't know. Well, they've pinched her now, and her miserable boy friend—and I hope they hang them both."

Clemency's frown increased. She said:

"Don't be so uncivilised, Roger."

"Uncivilised? Bosh! Deliberate cold-blooded poisoning of a helpless trusting old man—and when I'm glad the murderers are caught and will pay the penalty you say I'm uncivilised! I tell you I'd willingly strangle that woman myself."

He added:

"She was with you, wasn't she, when the police came for her? How did she take it?"

"It was horrible," said Sophia in a low voice. "She was scared out of her wits."

"Serves her right."

"Don't be vindictive," said Clemency.

"Oh I know, dearest, but you can't understand. It wasn't your father. I loved my father. Don't you understand? I loved him!"

"I should understand by now," said Clemency.

Roger said to her, half jokingly:

"You've no imagination, Clemency. Suppose it had been I who had been poisoned—?"

I saw the quick droop of her lids, her half-clenched hands. She said sharply: "Don't say things like that even in fun."

"Never mind, darling, we'll soon be away from all this."

We moved towards the house. Roger and Sophia walked ahead and Clemency and I brought up the rear. She said:

"I suppose now—they'll let us go?"

"Are you so anxious to get off?" I asked.

"It's wearing me out."

I looked at her in surprise. She met my glance with a faint desperate smile and a nod of the head.

"Haven't you seen, Charles, that I'm fighting all the time? Fighting for my happiness. For Roger's. I've been so afraid the family would persuade him to stop in England. That we'd go on tangled up in the midst of them, stifled with family ties. I was afraid Sophia would offer him an income and that he'd stay in England because it would mean greater comfort and amenities for me. The trouble with Roger is that he will not listen. He gets ideas in his head—and they're never the right ideas. He doesn't know anything. And he's enough of a Leonides to think that happiness for a woman is bound up with comfort and money. But I will fight for my happiness—I will. I will get Roger away and give him the life that suits him where he won't feel a failure. I want him to myself—away from them all—right away. . . ."

She had spoken in a low hurried voice with a kind of desperation that startled me. I had not realised how much on edge she was. I had not realised, either, quite how desperate and possessive was her feeling for Roger.

It brought back to my mind that odd quotation of Edith de Haviland's. She had quoted the line "this side of idolatry" with a peculiar intonation. I wondered if she had been thinking of Clemency.

Roger, I thought, had loved his father better than he would ever love anyone else, better even than his wife, devoted though he was to her. I realised for the first time how urgent was Clemency's desire to get her husband to herself. Love for Roger, I saw, made up her entire existence. He was her child, as well as her husband and her lover.

A car drove up to the front door.

"Hullo," I said. "Here's Josephine back."

Josephine and Magda got out of the car. Josephine had a bandage round her head but otherwise looked remarkably well.

She said at once:

"I want to see my goldfish," and started towards us and the pond.

"Darling," cried Magda, "you'd better come in first and lie down a little, and perhaps have a little nourishing soup."

"Don't fuss, mother," said Josephine. "I'm quite all right, and I hate nourishing soup."

Magda looked irresolute. I knew that Josephine had really been fit to depart from the hospital for some days, and that it was only a hint from Taverner that had kept her there. He was taking no chances on Josephine's safety until his suspects were safe under lock and key.

I said to Magda:

"I daresay fresh air will do her good. I'll go and keep an eye on her."

I caught Josephine up before she got to the pond.

"All sorts of things have been happening while you've been away," I said.

Josephine did not reply. She peered with her shortsighted eyes into the pond.

"I don't see Ferdinand," she said.

"Which is Ferdinand?"

"The one with four tails."

"That kind is rather amusing. I like that bright gold one."

"It's quite a common one."

"I don't much care for that motheaten white one."

Josephine cast me a scornful glance.

"That's a shebunkin. They cost a lot—far more than goldfish."

"Don't you want to hear what's been happening, Josephine?"

"I expect I know about it."

"Did you know that another will has been found and that your grandfather left all his money to Sophia?"

Josephine nodded in a bored kind of way.

"Mother told me. Anyway, I knew it already."

"Do you mean you heard it in the hospital?"

"No, I mean I knew that grandfather had left his money to Sophia. I heard him tell her so."

"Were you listening again?"

"Yes. I like listening."

"It's a disgraceful thing to do, and remember this, listeners hear no good of themselves."

Josephine gave me a peculiar glance.

"I heard what he said about me to her, if that's what you mean."

She added: "Nannie gets wild if she catches me listening at doors. She says it's not the sort of thing a little lady does."

"She's quite right."

"Pooh," said Josephine. "Nobody's a lady nowadays. They say so on the Brains Trust. They said it was—ob-so-lete." She pronounced the word carefully.

I changed the subject.

"You've got home a bit late for the big event," I said. "Chief Inspector Taverner has arrested Brenda and Laurence."

I expected that Josephine, in her character of young detective, would be thrilled by this information, but she merely repeated in her maddening bored fashion:

"Yes, I know."

"You can't know. It's only just happened."

"The car passed us on the road. Inspector Taverner and the detective with the suede shoes were inside with Brenda and Laurence, so of course I knew they must have been arrested. I hope he gave them the proper caution. You have to, you know."

I assured her that Taverner had acted strictly according to etiquette.

"I had to tell him about the letters," I said apologetically. "I found them behind the cistern. I'd have let you tell him only you were knocked out."

Josephine's hand went gingerly to her head.

"I ought to have been killed," she said with complacency. "I told you it was about the time for the second murder. The cistern was a rotten place to hide those letters. I guessed at once when I saw Laurence coming out of there one day. I mean he's not a useful kind of man who does things with ball taps, or pipes or fuses, so I knew he must have been hiding something."

"But I thought—" I broke off as Edith de Haviland's voice called authoritatively:

"Josephine. Josephine, come here at once."

Josephine sighed.

"More fuss," she said. "But I'd better go. You have to, if it's Aunt Edith."

She ran across the lawn. I followed more slowly.

After a brief interchange of words Josephine went into the house. I joined Edith de Haviland on the terrace.

This morning she looked fully her age. I was startled by the lines of weariness and suffering on her face. She looked exhausted and defeated. She saw the concern in my face and tried to smile.

"That child seems none the worse for her adventure," she said. "We must look after her better in future. Still—I suppose now it won't be necessary?"

She sighed and said: "I'm glad it's over. But what an exhibition. If you are arrested for murder, you might at least have some dignity. I've no patience with people like Brenda who go to pieces and squeal. No guts, these people. Laurence Brown looked like a cornered rabbit."

An obscure instinct of pity rose in me.

"Poor devils," I said.

"Yes—poor devils. She'll have the sense to look after herself, I suppose? I mean the right lawyers—all that sort of thing."

It was queer, I thought, the dislike they all had for Brenda, and their scrupulous care for her to have all the advantages for defence.

Edith de Haviland went on:

"How long will it be? How long will the whole thing take?"

I said I didn't know exactly. They would be charged at the police court and presumably sent for trial. Three or four months, I estimated—and if convicted, there would be the appeal.

"Do you think they will be convicted?" she asked.

"I don't know. I don't know exactly how much evidence the police have. There are letters."

"Love letters? They were lovers then?"

"They were in love with each other."

Her face grew grimmer.

"I'm not happy about this, Charles. I don't like Brenda. In the past, I've disliked her very much. I've said sharp things about her. But now—I do feel that I want her to have every chance—every possible chance. Aristide would have wished that. I feel it's up to me to see that—that Brenda gets a square deal."

"And Laurence?"

"Oh Laurence!" she shrugged her shoulders impatiently. "Men must look after themselves. But Aristide would never forgive us if—" She left the sentence unfinished.

Then she said:

"It must be almost lunch time. We'd better go in."

I explained that I was going up to London.

"In your car?"

"Yes."

"H'm. I wonder if you'd take me with you. I gather we're allowed off the lead now."

"Of course I will, but I believe Magda and Sophia are going up after lunch. You'll be more comfortable with them than in my two seater."

"I don't want to go with them. Take me with you, and don't say much about it."

I was surprised, but I did as she asked. We did not speak much on the way to town. I asked her where I should put her down.

"Harley Street."

I felt some faint apprehension, but I didn't like to say anything. She continued:

"No, it's too early. Drop me at Debenhams. I can have some lunch there and go to Harley Street afterwards."

"I hope—" I began and stopped.

"That's why I didn't want to go up with Magda. She dramatizes things. Lot of fuss."

"I'm very sorry," I said.

"You needn't be. I've had a good life. A very good life." She gave a sudden grin. "And it's not over yet."

23

I had not seen my father for some days. I found him busy with things other than the Leonides case, and I went in search of Taverner.

Taverner was enjoying a short spell of leisure and was willing to come out and have a drink with me. I congratulated him on having cleared up the case and he accepted my congratulations, but his manner remained far from jubilant.

"Well, that's over," he said. "We've got a case. Nobody can deny that we've got a case."

"Do you think you'll get a conviction?"

"Impossible to say. The evidence is circumstantial—it nearly always is in a murder case—bound to be. A lot depends on the impression they make on the jury."

"How far do the letters go?"

"At first sight, Charles, they're pretty damning. There are references to their life together when her husband's dead. Phrases like—'it won't be long now.' Mind you, defence counsel will try and twist it the other way—the husband was so old that of course they could reasonably expect him to die. There's no actual mention of poisoning—not down in black or white—but there are some passages that could mean that. It depends what judge we get. If it's old Carberry he'll be down on them all through. He's always very righteous about illicit love. I suppose they'll have Eagles or Humphrey Kerr for the defence—Humphrey is magnificent in these cases—but he likes a gallant war record or something of that kind to help him do his stuff. A conscientious objector is going to cramp his style. The question is going to be will the jury like them? You can never tell with juries. You know, Charles, those two are not really sympathetic characters. She's a good looking woman who married a very old man for his money, and Brown is a neurotic conscientious objector. The crime is so familiar—so according to pattern that you can't really believe they didn't do it. Of course, they may decide that he did it and she knew nothing about it—or alternatively that she did it, and he didn't know about it—or they may decide that they were both in it together."

"And what do you yourself think?" I asked.

He looked at me with a wooden expressionless face.

"I don't think anything. I've turned in the facts and they went to the D.P.P. and it was decided that there was a case. That's all. I've done my duty and I'm out of it. So now you know, Charles."

But I didn't know. I saw that for some reason Taverner was unhappy.

It was not until three days later that I unburdened myself to my father. He himself had never mentioned the case to me. There had been a kind of restraint between us—and I thought I knew the reason for it. But I had to break down that barrier.

"We've got to have this out," I said. "Taverner's not satisfied that those two did it—and you're not satisfied either."

My father shook his head. He said what Taverner had said:

"It's out of our hands. There is a case to answer. No question about that."

"But you don't—Taverner doesn't—think that they're guilty?"

"That's for a jury to decide."

"For God's sake," I said, "don't put me off with technical terms. What do you think—both of you—personally?"

"My personal opinion is no better than yours, Charles."

"Yes, it is. You've more experience."

"Then I'll be honest with you. I just—don't know!"

"They could be guilty?"

"Oh yes."

"But you don't feel sure that they are?"

My father shrugged his shoulders.

"How can one be sure?"

"Don't fence with me, dad. You've been sure other times, haven't you? Dead sure? No doubt in your mind at all?"

"Sometimes, yes. Not always."

"I wish to God you were sure this time."

"So do I."

We were silent. I was thinking of those two figures drifting in from the garden in the dusk. Lonely and haunted and afraid. They had been afraid from the start. Didn't that show a guilty conscience?

But I answered myself: "Not necessarily." Both Brenda and Laurence were afraid of life—they had no confidence in themselves, in their ability to avoid danger and defeat, and they could see, only too clearly, the pattern of illicit love leading to murder which might involve them at any moment.

My father spoke, and his voice was grave and kind: "Come, Charles," he said, "let's face it. You've still got it in your mind, haven't you, that one of the Leonides family is the real culprit?"

"Not really. I only wonder—"

"You do think so. You may be wrong, but you do think so."

"Yes," I said.

"Why?"

"Because—" I thought about it, trying to see clearly—to bring my wits to bear—"because" (yes, that was it) "because they think so themselves."

"They think so themselves? That's interesting. That's very interesting. Do you mean that they all suspect each other, or that they know, actually, who did do it."

"I'm not sure," I said. "It's all very nebulous and confused. I think—on the whole—that they try to cover up the knowledge from themselves."

My father nodded.

"Not Roger," I said. "Roger wholeheartedly believes it was Brenda and he wholeheartedly wants her hanged. It's—it's a relief to be with Roger because he's simple and positive, and hasn't any reservations in the back of his mind.

"But the others are apologetic, they're uneasy—they urge me to be sure that Brenda has the best defence—that every possible advantage is given her—why?"

My father answered: "Because they don't really, in their hearts, believe she is guilty. . . . Yes, that's sound."

Then he asked quietly: "Who could have done it? You've talked to them all? Who's the best bet?"

"I don't know," I said. "And it's driving me frantic. None of them fits your 'sketch of a murderer' and yet I feel—I do feel—that one of them is a murderer."

"Sophia?"

"No. Good God, no!"

"The possibility's in your mind, Charles—yes, it is, don't deny it. All the more potently because you won't acknowledge it. What about the others? Philip?"

"Only for the most fantastic motive."

"Motives can be fantastic—or they can be absurdly slight. What's his motive?"

"He is bitterly jealous of Roger—always has been all his life. His father's preference for Roger drove Philip in upon himself. Roger was about to crash, then the old man heard of it. He promised to put Roger on his feet again. Supposing Philip learnt that. If the old man died that night there would be no assistance for Roger. Roger would be down and out. Oh! I know it's absurd—"

"Oh, no, it isn't. It's abnormal, but it happens. It's human. What about Magda?"

"She's rather childish. She—gets things out of proportion. But I would never have thought twice about her being involved if it hadn't been for the sudden way she wanted to pack Josephine off to Switzerland. I couldn't help feeling she was afraid of something that Josephine knew or might say . . ."

"And then Josephine was conked on the head?"

"Well, that couldn't be her mother!"

"Why not?"

"But, dad, a mother wouldn't—"

"Charles, Charles, don't you ever read the police news. Again and again a mother takes a dislike to one of her children. Only one—she may be devoted to the others. There's some association, some reason, but it's often hard to get at. But when it exists, it's an unreasoning aversion, and it's very strong."

"She called Josephine a changeling," I admitted unwillingly.

"Did the child mind?"

"I don't think so."

"Who else is there? Roger?"

"Roger didn't kill his father. I'm quite sure of that."

"Wash out Roger then. His wife—what's her name—Clemency?"

"Yes," I said. "If she killed old Leonides it was for a very odd reason."

I told him of my conversations with Clemency. I said I thought it possible that in her passion to get Roger away from England she might have deliberately poisoned the old man.

"She'd persuaded Roger to go without telling his father. Then the old man found out. He was going to back up Associated Catering. All Clemency's hopes and plans were frustrated. And she really does care desperately for Roger—beyond idolatry."

"You're repeating what Edith de Haviland said!"

"Yes. And Edith's another who I think—might have done it. But I don't know why. I can only believe that for what she considered good and sufficient reason she might take the law into her own hand. She's that kind of a person."

"And she also was very anxious that Brenda should be adequately defended?"

"Yes. That, I suppose, might be conscience. I don't think for a moment that if she did do it, she intended them to be accused of the crime."

"Probably not. But would she knock out the child Josephine?"

"No," I said slowly, "I can't believe that. Which reminds me that there's something that Josephine said to me that keeps nagging at my mind, and I can't remember what it is. It's slipped my memory. But it's something that doesn't fit in where it should. If only I could remember—"

"Never mind. It will come back. Anything or anyone else on your mind?"

"Yes," I said. "Very much so. How much do you know about infantile paralysis. Its after effects on character, I mean?"

"Eustace?"

"Yes. The more I think about it, the more it seems to me that Eustace might fit the bill. His dislikes and resentment against his grandfather. His queerness and moodiness. He's not normal.

"He's the only one of the family who I can see knocking out Josephine quite callously if she knew something about him—and she's quite likely to know. That child knows everything. She writes it down in a little book—"

I stopped.

"Good Lord," I said. "What a fool I am."

"What's the matter?"

"I know now what was wrong. We assumed, Taverner and I, that the wrecking of Josephine's room, the frantic search, was for those letters. I thought that she'd got hold of them and that she'd hidden them up in the cistern room. But when she was talking to me the other day she made it quite clear that it was Laurence who had hidden them there. She saw him coming out of the cistern room and went snooping around and found the letters. Then, of course she read them. She would! But she left them where they were."

"Well?"

"Don't you see? It couldn't have been the letters someone was looking for in Josephine's room. It must have been something else."

"And that something—"

"Was the little black book she writes down her 'detection' in. That's what someone was looking for! I think, too, that whoever it was didn't find it. I think Josephine has it. But if so—"

I half rose.

"If so," said my father, "she still isn't safe. Is that what you were going to say?"

"Yes. She won't be out of danger until she's actually started for Switzerland. They're planning to send her there, you know."

"Does she want to go?"

I considered.

"I don't think she does."

"Then she probably hasn't gone," said my father drily. "But I think you're right about the danger. You'd better go down there."

"Eustace?" I cried desperately. "Clemency?"

My father said gently:

"To my mind the facts point clearly in one direction. . . . I wonder you don't see it yourself. I . . ."

Glover opened the door.

"Beg pardon, Mr. Charles, the telephone. Miss Leonides speaking from Swinly. It's urgent."

It seemed like a horrible repetition. Had Josephine again fallen a victim. And had the murderer this time made no mistake? . . .

I hurried to the telephone.

"Sophia? It's Charles here."

Sophia's voice came with a kind of hard desperation in it.

"Charles, it isn't all over. The murderer is still here."

"What on earth do you mean? What's wrong? Is it Josephine?"

"It's not Josephine. It's Nannie."

"Nannie?"

"Yes, there was some cocoa—Josephine's cocoa, she didn't drink it. She left it on the table. Nannie thought it was a pity to waste it. So she drank it."

"Poor Nannie. Is she very bad?"

Sophia's voice broke.

"Oh, Charles, she's dead."

24

We were back again in the nightmare.

That is what I thought as Taverner and I drove out of London. It was a repetition of our former journey.

At intervals, Taverner swore.

As for me, I repeated from time to time, stupidly, unprofitably:

"So it wasn't Brenda and Laurence. It wasn't Brenda and Laurence."

Had I ever really thought it was? I had been so glad to think it. So glad to escape from other, more sinister, possibilities . . .

They had fallen in love with each other. They had written silly sentimental romantic letters to each other. They had indulged in hopes that Brenda's old husband might soon die peacefully and happily—but I wondered really if they had even acutely desired his death. I had a feeling that the despairs and longings of an unhappy love affair suited them as well or better than commonplace married life together. I didn't think Brenda was really passionate. She was too anaemic, too apathetic. It was romance she craved for. And I thought Laurence, too, was the type to enjoy frustration and vague future dreams of bliss rather than the concrete satisfactions of the flesh.

They had been caught in a trap and, terrified, they had not had the wit to find their way out. Laurence, with incredible stupidity, had not even destroyed Brenda's letters. Presumably Brenda had destroyed his, since they had not been found. And it was not Laurence who had balanced the marble door stop on the wash house door. It was someone else whose face was still hidden behind a mask.

We drove up to the door. Taverner got out and I followed him. There was a plain clothes man in the hall whom I didn't know. He saluted Taverner and Taverner drew him aside.

My attention was taken by a pile of luggage in the hall. It was labelled and ready for departure. As I looked at it Clemency came down the stairs and through the open door at the bottom. She was dressed in her same red dress with a tweed coat over it and a red felt hat.

"You're in time to say goodbye, Charles," she said.

"You're leaving?"

"We go to London tonight. Our plane goes early tomorrow morning."

She was quiet and smiling, but I thought her eyes were watchful.

"But surely you can't go now?"

"Why not?" Her voice was hard.

"With this death—"

"Nannie's death has nothing to do with us."

"Perhaps not. But all the same—"

"Why do you say 'perhaps not'? It has nothing to do with us. Roger and I have been upstairs, finishing packing up. We did not come down at all during the time that the cocoa was left on the hall table."

"Can you prove that?"

"I can answer for Roger. And Roger can answer for me."

"No more than that . . . You're man and wife, remember."

Her anger flamed out.

"You're impossible, Charles! Roger and I are going away—to lead our own life. Why on earth should we want to poison a nice stupid old woman who had never done us any harm?"

"It mightn't have been her you meant to poison."

"Still less are we likely to poison a child."

"It depends rather on the child, doesn't it?"

"What do you mean?"

"Josephine isn't quite the ordinary child. She knows a good deal about people. She—"

I broke off. Josephine had emerged from the door leading to the drawing room. She was eating the inevitable apple, and over its round rosiness her eyes sparkled with a kind of ghoulish enjoyment.

"Nannie's been poisoned," she said. "Just like grandfather. It's awfully exciting, isn't it?"

"Aren't you at all upset about it?" I demanded severely. "You were fond of her, weren't you?"

"Not particularly. She was always scolding me about something or other. She fussed."

"Are you fond of anybody, Josephine?" asked Clemency.

Josephine turned her ghoulish eyes towards Clemency.

"I love Aunt Edith," she said. "I love Aunt Edith very much. And I could love Eustace, only he's always such a beast to me and won't be interested in finding out who did all this."

"You'd better stop finding things out, Josephine," I said. "It isn't very safe."

"I don't need to find out any more," said Josephine. "I know."

There was a moment's silence. Josephine's eyes, solemn and unwinking, were fixed on Clemency. A sound like a long sigh, reached my ears. I swung sharply round. Edith de Haviland stood half way down the staircase—but I did not think it was she who had sighed. The sound had come from behind the door through which Josephine had just come.

I stepped sharply across to it and yanked it open. There was no one to be seen.

Nevertheless I was seriously disturbed. Someone had stood just within that door and had heard those words of Josephine's. I went back and took Josephine by the arm. She was eating her apple and staring stolidly at Clemency. Behind the solemnity there was, I thought, a certain malignant satisfaction.

"Come on, Josephine," I said. "We're going to have a little talk."

I think Josephine might have protested, but I was not standing any nonsense. I ran her along forcibly into her own part of the house. There was a small unused morning room where we could be reasonably sure of being undisturbed. I took her in there, closed the door firmly, and made her sit on a chair. I took another chair and drew it forward so that I faced her.

"Now, Josephine," I said, "we're going to have a show down. What exactly do you know?"

"Lots of things."

"That I have no doubt about. That noddle of yours is probably crammed to overflowing with relevant and irrelevant information. But you know perfectly what I mean. Don't you?"

"Of course I do. I'm not stupid."

I didn't know whether the disparagement was for me or the police, but I paid no attention to it and went on:

"You know who put something in your cocoa?"

Josephine nodded.

"You know who poisoned your grandfather?"

Josephine nodded again.

"And who knocked you on the head?"

Again Josephine nodded.

"Then you're going to come across with what you know. You're going to tell me all about it—now."

"Shan't."

"You've got to. Every bit of information you've got or ferret out has got to be given to the police."

"I won't tell the police anything. They're stupid. They thought Brenda had done it—or Laurence. I wasn't stupid like that. I knew jolly well they hadn't done it. I've had an idea who it was all along, and then I made a kind of test—and now I know I'm right."

She finished on a triumphant note.

I prayed to Heaven for patience and started again.

"Listen, Josephine, I daresay you're extremely clever—" Josephine looked gratified. "But it won't be much good to you to be clever if you're not alive to enjoy the fact. Don't you see, you little fool, that as long as you keep your secrets in this silly way you're in imminent danger?"

Josephine nodded approvingly.

"Of course I am."

"Already you've had two very narrow escapes. One attempt nearly did for you. The other has cost somebody else their life. Don't you see if you go on strutting about the house and proclaiming at the top of your voice you know who the killer is, there will be more attempts made—and that either you'll die or somebody else will?"

"In some books person after person is killed," Josephine informed me with gusto. "You end by spotting the murderer because he or she is practically the only person left."

"This isn't a detective story. This is Three Gables, Swinly Dean, and you're a silly little girl who's read more than is good for her. I'll make you tell me what you know if I have to shake you till your teeth rattle."

"I could always tell you something that wasn't true."

"You could, but you won't. What are you waiting for, anyway?"

"You don't understand," said Josephine. "Perhaps I may never tell. You see, I might be—fond of the person."

She paused as though to let this sink in.

"And if I do tell," she went on, "I shall do it properly. I shall have everybody sitting round, and then I'll go over it all—with the clues, and then I shall say, quite suddenly:

"And it was you . . ."

She thrust out a dramatic forefinger just as Edith de Haviland entered the room.

"Put that core in the waste paper basket, Josephine," said Edith. "Have you got a handkerchief? Your fingers are sticky. I'm taking you out in the car." Her eyes met mine with significance as she said: "She'll be safer out of here for the next hour or so." As Josephine looked mutinous, Edith added: "We'll go into Longbridge and have an ice cream soda."

Josephine's eyes brightened and she said: "Two."

"Perhaps," said Edith. "Now go and get your hat and coat on and your dark blue scarf. It's cold out today. Charles, you had better go with her while she gets them. Don't leave her. I have just a couple of notes to write."

She sat down at the desk, and I escorted Josephine out of the room. Even without Edith's warning, I would have stuck to Josephine like a leech.

I was convinced that there was danger to the child very near at hand.

As I finished superintending Josephine's toilet, Sophia came into the room. She seemed astonished to see me.

"Why, Charles, have you turned nursemaid? I didn't know you were here."

"I'm going into Longbridge with Aunt Edith," said Josephine importantly. "We're going to have ice creams."

"Brrrr, on a day like this?"

"Ice cream sodas are always lovely," said Josephine. "When you're cold inside, it makes you feel hotter outside."

Sophia frowned. She looked worried, and I was shocked by her pallor and the circles under her eyes.

We went back to the morning room. Edith was just blotting a couple of envelopes. She got up briskly.

"We'll start now," she said. "I told Evans to bring round the Ford."

She swept out to the hall. We followed her.

My eye was again caught by the suitcases and their blue labels. For some reason they aroused in me a vague disquietude.

"It's quite a nice day," said Edith de Haviland, pulling on her gloves and glancing up at the sky. The Ford 10 was waiting in front of the house. "Cold—but bracing. A real English autumn day. How beautiful trees look with their bare branches against the sky—and just a golden leaf or two still hanging . . ."

She was silent a moment or two, then she turned and kissed Sophia.

"Goodbye, dear," she said. "Don't worry too much. Certain things have to be faced and endured."

Then she said, "Come, Josephine," and got into the car. Josephine climbed in beside her.

They both waved as the car drove off.

"I suppose she's right, and it's better to keep Josephine out of this for a while. But we've got to make that child tell what she knows, Sophia."

"She probably doesn't know anything. She's just showing off. Josephine likes to make herself look important, you know."

"It's more than that. Do they know what poison it was in the cocoa?"

"They think it's digitalin. Aunt Edith takes digitalin for her heart. She has a whole bottle full of little tablets up in her room. Now the bottle's empty."

"She ought to keep things like that locked up."

"She did. I suppose it wouldn't be difficult for someone to find out where she hid the key."

"Someone? Who?" I looked again at the pile of luggage. I said suddenly and loudly:

"They can't go away. They mustn't be allowed to."

Sophia looked surprised.

"Roger and Clemency? Charles, you don't think—"

"Well, what do you think?"

Sophia stretched out her hands in a helpless gesture.

"I don't know, Charles," she whispered. "I only know that I'm back—back in the nightmare—"

"I know. Those were the very words I used to myself as I drove down with Taverner."

"Because this is just what a nightmare is. Walking about among people you know, looking in their faces—and suddenly the faces change—and it's not someone you know any longer—it's a stranger—a cruel stranger. . . ."

She cried: "Come outside, Charles—come outside. It's safer outside . . . I'm afraid to stay in this house. . . ."

25

We stayed in the garden a long time. By a kind of tacit consent, we did not discuss the horror that was weighing upon us. Instead Sophia talked affectionately of the dead woman, of things they had done, and games they had played as children with Nannie—and tales that the old woman used to tell them about Roger and their father and the other brothers and sisters.

"They were her real children, you see. She only came back to us to help during the war when Josephine was a baby and Eustace was a funny little boy."

There was a certain balm for Sophia in these memories and I encouraged her to talk.

I wondered what Taverner was doing. Questioning the household, I suppose. A car drove away with the police photographer and two other men, and presently an ambulance drove up.

Sophia shivered a little. Presently the ambulance left and we knew that Nannie's body had been taken away in preparation for an autopsy.

And still we sat or walked in the garden and talked—our words becoming more and more of a cloak for our real thoughts.

Finally, with a shiver, Sophia said:

"It must be very late—it's almost dark. We've got to go in. Aunt Edith and Josephine haven't come back . . . Surely they ought to be back by now?"

A vague uneasiness woke in me. What had happened? Was Edith deliberately keeping the child away from the Crooked House?

We went in. Sophia drew all the curtains. The fire was lit and the big drawing room looked harmonious with an unreal air of bygone luxury. Great bowls of bronze chrysanthemums stood on the tables.

Sophia rang and a maid who I recognised as having been formerly upstairs brought in tea. She had red eyes and sniffed continuously. Also I noticed that she had a frightened way of glancing quickly over her shoulder.

Magda joined us, but Philip's tea was sent in to him in the library.

Magda's role was a stiff frozen image of grief. She spoke little or not at all. She said once:

"Where are Edith and Josephine? They're out very late."

But she said it in a preoccupied kind of way.

But I myself was becoming increasingly uneasy. I asked if Taverner were still in the house and Magda replied that she thought so. I went in search of him. I told him that I was worried about Miss de Haviland and the child.

He went immediately to the telephone and gave certain instructions.

"I'll let you know when I have news," he said.

I thanked him and went back to the drawing room. Sophia was there with Eustace. Magda had gone.

"He'll let us know if he hears anything," I said to Sophia.

She said in a low voice:

"Something's happened, Charles, something must have happened."

"My dear Sophia, it's not really late yet."

"What are you bothering about?" said Eustace. "They've probably gone to the cinema."

He lounged out of the room. I said to Sophia: "She may have taken Josephine to a hotel—or up to London. I think she fully realised that the child was in danger—perhaps she realised it better than we did."

Sophia replied with a sombre look that I could not quite fathom.

"She kissed me goodbye. . . ."

I did not see quite what she meant by that disconnected remark, or what it was supposed to show. I asked if Magda was worried.

"Mother? No, she's all right. She's no sense of time. She's reading a new play of Vavasour Jones called 'The Woman Disposes'. It's a funny play about murder—a female Bluebeard—cribbed from 'Arsenic and Old Lace' if you ask me, but it's got a good woman's part, a woman who's got a mania for being a widow."

I said no more. We sat, pretending to read.

It was half past six when Taverner opened the door and came in. His face prepared us for what he had to say.

Sophia got up.

"Yes?" she said.

"I'm sorry. I've got bad news for you. I sent out a general alarm for the car. A motorist reported having seen a Ford car with a number something like that turning off the main road at Flackspur Heath—through the woods."

"Not—the track to the Flackspur Quarry?"

"Yes, Miss Leonides." He paused and went on: "The car's been found in the quarry. Both the occupants were dead. You'll be glad to know they were killed outright."

"Josephine!" It was Magda standing in the doorway. Her voice rose in a wail. "Josephine . . . My baby."

Sophia went to her and put her arms round her. I said: "Wait a minute."

I had remembered something! Edith de Haviland writing a couple of letters at the desk, going out into the hall with them in her hand.

But they had not been in her hand when she got into the car.

I dashed out into the hall and went to the long oak chest. I found the letters—pushed inconspicuously to the back behind a brass tea urn.

The uppermost was addressed to Chief Inspector Taverner.

Taverner had followed me. I handed the letter to him and he tore it open. Standing beside him I read its brief contents.

> My expectation is that this will be opened after my death. I wish to enter into no details, but I accept full responsibility for the deaths of my brother-in-law Aristide Leonides and Janet Rowe (Nannie). I hereby solemnly declare that Brenda Leonides and Laurence Brown are innocent of the murder of Aristide Leonides. Enquiry of Dr Michael Chavasse, 783 Harley Street will confirm that my life could only have been prolonged for a few months. I prefer to take this way out and to spare two innocent people the ordeal of being charged with a murder they did not commit. I am of sound mind and fully conscious of what I write.
>
> Edith Elfrida de Haviland.

As I finished the letter I was aware that Sophia, too, had read it—whether with Taverner's concurrence or not, I don't know.

"Aunt Edith . . ." murmured Sophia.

I remembered Edith de Haviland's ruthless foot grinding bindweed into the earth. I remembered my early, almost fanciful, suspicions of her. But why—

Sophia spoke the thought in my mind before I came to it.

"But why Josephine? Why did she take Josephine with her?"

"Why did she do it at all?" I demanded. "What was her motive?"

But even as I said that, I knew the truth. I saw the whole thing clearly. I realised that I was still holding her second letter in my hand. I looked down and saw my own name on it.

It was thicker and harder than the other one. I think I knew what was in it before I opened it. I tore the envelope along and Josephine's little black notebook fell out. I picked it up off the floor—it came open in my hand and I saw the entry on the first page . . .

Sounding from a long way away, I heard Sophia's voice, clear and self controlled.

"We've got it all wrong," she said. "Edith didn't do it."

"No," I said.

Sophia came closer to me—she whispered:

"It was—Josephine—wasn't it? That was it, Josephine."

Together we looked down on the first entry in the little black book, written in an unformed childish hand.

"Today I killed grandfather."

26

I was to wonder afterwards that I could have been so blind. The truth had stuck out so clearly all along. Josephine and only Josephine fitted in with all the necessary qualifications. Her vanity, her persistent self importance, her delight in talking, her reiteration on how clever she was, and how stupid the police were.

I had never considered her because she was a child. But children have committed murders, and this particular murder had been well within a child's compass. Her grandfather himself had indicated the precise method—he had practically handed her a blue print. All she had to do was to avoid leaving fingerprints and the slightest knowledge of detective fiction would teach her that. And everything else had been a mere hotch potch, culled at random from stock mystery stories. The notebook—the sleuthing—her pretended suspicions, her insistence that she was not going to tell till she was sure. . . .

And finally the attack on herself. An almost incredible performance considering that she might easily have killed herself. But then, childlike, she never considered such a possibility. She was the heroine. The heroine isn't killed. Yet there had been a clue there—the traces of earth on the seat of the old chair in the wash house. Josephine was the only person who would have had to climb up on a chair to balance the block of marble on the top of the door. Obviously it had missed her more than once (the dints in the floor), and patiently she had climbed up again and replaced it, handling it with her scarf to avoid fingerprints. And then it had fallen—and she had had a near escape from death.

It had been the perfect set up—the impression she was aiming for! She was in danger, she "knew something," she had been attacked!

I saw how that had deliberately drawn my attention to her presence in the cylinder room. And she had completed the artistic disorder of her room before going out to the wash house.

But when she had returned from hospital, when she had found Brenda and Laurence arrested, she must have become dissatisfied. The case was over—and she—Josephine, was out of the lime light.

So she stole the digitalin from Edith's room and put it in her own cup of cocoa and left the cup untouched on the hall table.

Did she know that Nannie would drink it? Possibly. From her words that morning, she had resented Nannie's criticisms of her. Did Nannie, perhaps, wise from a lifetime of experience with children, suspect? I think that Nannie knew, had always known, that Josephine was not normal. With her precocious mental development had gone a retarded moral sense. Perhaps, too, the various factors of heredity—what Sophia had called the "ruthlessness" of the family—had met together.

She had had an authoritarian ruthlessness of her grandmother's family, and the ruthless egoism of Magda, seeing only her own point of view. She had also presumably suffered, sensitive like Philip, from the stigma of being the unattractive—the changeling child—of the family. Finally, in her very marrow, had run the essential crooked strain of old Leonides. She had been Leonides's grandchild, she had resembled him in brain and in cunning—but his love had gone outwards to family and friends, hers had turned to herself.

I thought that old Leonides had realised what none of the rest of the family had realised, that Josephine might be a source of danger to others and to herself. He had kept her from school life because he was afraid of what she might do. He had shielded her, and guarded her in the home, and I understood now his urgency to Sophia to look after Josephine.

Magda's sudden decision to send Josephine abroad—had that, too, been due to a fear for the child? Not, perhaps, a conscious fear, but some vague maternal instinct.

And Edith de Haviland? Had she first suspected, then feared—and finally known?

I looked down at the letter in my hand.

> Dear Charles.
>
> This is in confidence for you—and for Sophia if you so decide. It is imperative that someone should know the truth. I found the enclosed in the disused dog kennel outside the back door. She kept it there. It confirms what I already suspected. The action I am about to take may be right or wrong—I do not know. But my life, in any case, is close to its end, and I do not want the child to suffer as I believe she would suffer if called to earthly account for what she has done.
>
> There is often one of the litter who is "not quite right."
>
> If I do wrong, God forgive me—but I do it out of love. God bless you both.
>
> Edith de Haviland.

I hesitated for only a moment, then I handed the letter to Sophia. Together we again opened Josephine's little black book.

> Today I killed grandfather.

We turned the pages. It was an amazing production. Interesting, I should imagine, to a psychologist. It set out, with such terrible clarity, the fury of thwarted egoism. The motive for the crime was set down, pitifully childish and inadequate.

> Grandfather wouldn't let me do bally dancing so I made up my mind I would kill him. Then we would go to London and live and mother wouldn't mind me doing bally.

I give only a few entries. They are all significant.

> I don't want to go to Switzerland—I won't go. If mother makes me I will kill her too—only I can't get any poison. Perhaps I could make it with youberries. They are poisonous, the book says so.
>
> Eustace has made me very cross to day. He says I am only a girl and no use and that its silly my detecting. He wouldn't think me silly if he knew it was me did the murder.
>
> I like Charles—but he is rather stupid. I have not decided yet who I shall make have done the crime. Perhaps Brenda and Laurence—Brenda is nasty to me—she says I am not all there but I like Laurence—he told me about Charlot Korday—she killed someone in his bath. She was not very clever about it.

The last entry was revealing.

> I hate Nannie . . . I hate her . . . I hate her . . . She says I am only a little girl. She says I show off. She's making mother send me abroad . . . I'm going to kill her too—I think Aunt Edith's medicine would do it. If there is another murder, then the police will come back and it will all be exciting again.
>
> Nannie's dead. I am glad. I haven't decided yet where I'll hide the bottle with the little pill things. Perhaps in Aunt Clemency's room—or else Eustace. When I am dead as an old woman I shall leave this behind me addressed to the Chief of the Police and they will see what a really great criminal I was.

I closed the book. Sophia's tears were flowing fast.

"Oh Charles—oh Charles—it's so dreadful. She's such a little monster—and yet—and yet it's so terribly pathetic."

I had felt the same.

I had liked Josephine . . . I still felt a fondness for her . . . You do not like anyone less because they have tuberculosis or some other fatal disease. Josephine was, as Sophia had said, a little monster, but she was a pathetic little monster. She had been born with a kink—the crooked child of the little crooked house.

Sophia asked:

"If—she had lived—what would have happened?"

"I suppose she would have been sent to a reformatory or a special school. Later she would have been released—or possibly certified, I don't know."

Sophia shuddered.

"It's better the way it is. But Aunt Edith—I don't like to think of her taking the blame."

"She chose to do so. I don't suppose it will be made public. I imagine that when Brenda and Laurence come to trial, no case will be brought against them and they will be discharged.

"And you, Sophia," I said, this time on a different note and taking both her hands in mine, "will marry me. I've just heard I'm appointed to Persia. We will go out there together, and you will forget the little Crooked House. Your mother can put on plays and your father can buy more books and Eustace will soon go to a university. Don't worry about them any more. Think of me."

Sophia looked at me straight in the eyes.

"Aren't you afraid, Charles, to marry me?"

"Why should I be? In poor little Josephine all the worst of the family came together. In you, Sophia, I fully believe that all that is bravest and best in the Leonides family has been handed down to you. Your grandfather thought highly of you and he seems to have been a man who was usually right. Hold up your head, my darling. The future is ours."

"I will, Charles. I love you and I'll marry you and make you happy." She looked down at the notebook. "Poor Josephine."

"Poor Josephine," I said.

"What's the truth of it, Charles?" said my father.

I never lie to the Old Man.

"It wasn't Edith de Haviland, sir," I said. "It was Josephine."

My father nodded his head gently.

"Yes," he said. "I've thought so for some time. Poor child . . ."

Ordeal by Innocence

I

It was dusk when he came to the ferry.

He could have been there much earlier. The truth was, he had put it off as long as he could.

First his luncheon with friends in Redquay; the light desultory conversation, the interchange of gossip about mutual friends—all that had meant only that he was inwardly shrinking from what he had to do. His friends had invited him to stay on for tea and he had accepted. But at last the time had come when he knew that he could put things off no longer.

The car he had hired was waiting. He said good-bye and left to drive the seven miles along the crowded coast road and then inland down the wooded lane that ended at the little stone quay on the river.

There was a large bell there which his driver rang vigorously to summon the ferry from the far side.

"You won't be wanting me to wait, sir?"

"No," said Arthur Calgary. "I've ordered a car to meet me over there in an hour's time—to take me to Drymouth."

The man received his fare and tip. He said, peering across the river in the gloom:

"Ferry's coming now, sir."

With a soft-spoken good night he reversed the car and drove away up the hill. Arthur Calgary was left alone waiting on the quayside. Alone with his thoughts and his apprehension of what was in front of him. How wild the scenery was here, he thought. One could fancy oneself on a Scottish loch, far from anywhere. And yet, only a few miles away, were the hotels, the shops, the cocktail bars and the crowds of Redquay. He reflected, not for the first time, on the extraordinary contrasts of the English landscape.

He heard the soft plash of the oars as the ferry boat drew in to the side of the little quay. Arthur Calgary walked down the sloping ramp and got into the boat as the ferryman steadied it with a boathook. He was an old man and gave Calgary the fanciful impression that he and his boat belonged together, were one and indivisible.

A little cold wind came rustling up from the sea as they pushed off.

"'Tis chilly this evening," said the ferryman.

Calgary replied suitably. He further agreed that it was colder than yesterday.

He was conscious, or thought he was conscious, of a veiled curiosity in the ferryman's eyes. Here was a stranger. And a stranger after the close of the tourist season proper. Moreover, this stranger was crossing at an unusual hour—too late for tea at the café by the pier. He had no luggage so he could not be coming to stay. (Why, Calgary wondered, *had* he come so late in the day? Was it really because, subconsciously, he had been putting this moment off? Leaving as late as possible, the thing that had to be done?) Crossing the Rubicon—the river . . . The river . . . his mind went back to that other river—the Thames.

He had stared at it unseeingly (was it only yesterday?) then turned to look again at the man facing him across the table. Those thoughtful eyes with something in them that he had not quite been able to understand. A reserve, something that was being thought but not expressed. . . .

"I suppose," he thought, "they learn never to show what they are thinking."

The whole thing was pretty frightful when one came right down to it. He must do what had to be done—and after that—*forget!*

He frowned as he remembered the conversation yesterday. That pleasant, quiet, noncommittal voice, saying:

"You're quite determined on your course of action, Dr. Calgary?"

He had answered, hotly:

"What else *can* I do? Surely you see that? You must agree? It's a thing I can't possibly shirk."

But he hadn't understood the look in those withdrawn grey eyes, and had been faintly perplexed by the answer.

"One has to look all around a subject—consider it from all aspects."

"Surely there can be only one aspect from the point of view of justice?"

He had spoken hotly, thinking for a moment that this was an ignoble suggestion of "hushing up" the matter.

"In a way, yes. But there's more to it than that, you know. More than—shall we say—justice?"

"I don't agree. There's the family to consider."

And the other had said quickly: "Quite—oh, yes—quite. I *was* thinking of them."

Which seemed to Calgary nonsense! Because if one were thinking of *them*—

But immediately the other man had said, his pleasant voice unchanged:

"It's entirely up to you, Dr. Calgary. You must, of course, do exactly as you feel you have to do."

The boat grounded on the beach. He had crossed the Rubicon.

The ferryman's soft West Country voice said:

"That will be fourpence, sir, or do you want a return?"

"No," Calgary said. "There will be no return." (How fateful the words sounded!)

He paid. Then he asked:

"Do you know a house called Sunny Point?"

Immediately the curiosity ceased to be veiled. The interest in the old man's eyes leaped up avidly.

"Why, surely. 'Tis there, up along to your right—you can just see it through them trees. You go up the hill and along the road to the right, and then take the new road through the building estate. 'Tis the last house—at the very end."

"Thank you."

"You did say Sunny Point, sir? Where Mrs. Argyle—"

"Yes, yes—" Calgary cut him short. He didn't want to discuss the matter. "Sunny Point."

A slow and rather peculiar smile twisted the ferryman's lips. He looked suddenly like an ancient sly faun.

"It was *her* called the house that—in the war. It were a new house, of course, only just been built—hadn't got a name. But the ground 'tis built on—that wooded spit—Viper's Point, that is! But Viper's Point wouldn't do for *her*—not for the name of her house. Called it Sunny Point, she did. But Viper's Point's what *we* allus call it."

Calgary thanked him brusquely, said good evening, and started up the hill. Everyone seemed to be inside their houses, but he had the fancy that unseen eyes were peering through the windows of the cottages; all watching him with the knowledge of where he was going. Saying to each other, "He's going to Viper's Point . . ."

Viper's Point. What a horribly apposite name that must have seemed . . .

For sharper than a serpent's tooth . . .

He checked his thoughts brusquely. He must pull himself together and make up his mind exactly what he was going to say. . . .

II

Calgary came to the end of the nice new road with the nice new houses on either side of it, each with its eighth of an acre of garden; rock plants, chrysanthemums, roses, salvias, geraniums, each owner displaying his or her individual garden taste.

At the end of the road was a gate with SUNNY POINT in Gothic letters on it. He opened the gate, passed through, and went along a short drive. The house was there ahead of him, a well-built, characterless modern house, gabled and porched. It might have stood on any good-class suburban site, or a new development anywhere. It was unworthy, in Calgary's opinion, of its view. For the view was magnificent. The river here curved sharply round the point almost turning back on itself. Wooded hills rose opposite; up-stream to the left was a further bend of the river with meadows and orchards in the distance.

Calgary looked for a moment up and down the river. One should have built a castle here, he thought, an impossible, ridiculous fairy tale, castle! The sort of castle that might be made of gingerbread or of frosted sugar. Instead there was good taste, restraint, moderation, plenty of money and absolutely no imagination.

For that, naturally, one did not blame the Argyles. They had only bought the house, not built it. Still, they, or one of them (Mrs. Argyle?) had chosen it. . . .

He said to himself: "*You can't put it off any longer . . .*" and pressed the electric bell beside the door.

He stood there, waiting. After a decent interval he pressed the bell again.

He heard no footsteps inside but, without warning, the door swung suddenly open.

He moved back a step, startled. To his already overstimulated imagination, it seemed as though Tragedy herself stood there barring his way. It was a young face; indeed it was in the poignancy of its youth that tragedy had its very essence. The Tragic Mask, he thought, should always be a mask of youth. . . . Helpless, foreordained, with doom approaching . . . from the future. . . .

Rallying himself, he thought, rationalising: "Irish type." The deep blue of the eyes, the dark shadow round them, the up-springing black hair, the mournful beauty of the bones of the skull and cheekbones—

The girl stood there, young, watchful and hostile.

She said:

"Yes? What do you want?"

He replied conventionally.

"Is Mr. Argyle in?"

"Yes. But he doesn't see people. I mean, people he doesn't know. He doesn't know you, does he?"

"No. He doesn't know me, but—"

She began to close the door.

"Then you'd better write . . ."

"I'm sorry, but I particularly want to see him. Are you—Miss Argyle?"

She admitted it grudgingly.

"I'm Hester Argyle, yes. But my father doesn't see people—not without an appointment. You'd better write."

"I've come a long way . . ." She was unmoved.

"They all say that. But I thought this kind of thing had stopped at last." She went on accusingly, "You're a reporter, I suppose?"

"No, no, nothing of the sort."

She eyed him suspiciously as though she did not believe him.

"Well, what do you want then?"

Behind her, some way back in the hall, he saw another face. A flat homely face. Describing it, he would have called it a face like a pancake, the face of a middle-aged woman, with frizzy yellowish grey hair plastered on top of her head. She seemed to hover, waiting, like a watchful dragon.

"It concerns your brother, Miss Argyle."

Hester Argyle drew in her breath sharply. She said, without belief, "Michael?"

"No, your brother Jack."

She burst out: "I knew it! I *knew* you'd come about Jacko! Why can't you leave us in peace? It's all over and finished with. Why go on about it?"

"You can never really say that anything is finished."

"But this *is* finished! Jacko is dead. Why can't you let him be? All that's *over*. If you're not a journalist, I suppose you're a doctor, or a psychologist, or something. Please *go* away. My father can't be disturbed. He's busy."

She began to close the door. In a hurry, Calgary did what he ought to have done at first, pulled out the letter from his pocket and thrust it towards her.

"I have a letter here—from Mr. Marshall."

She was taken aback. Her fingers closed doubtfully on the envelope. She said uncertainly:

"From Mr. Marshall—in London?"

She was joined now suddenly by the middle-aged woman who had been lurking in the recesses of the hall. She peered at Calgary suspiciously and he was reminded of foreign convents. Of course, this should have been a nun's face! It demanded the crisp white coif or whatever you called it, framed tightly round the face, and the black habit and veil. It was the face, not of a contemplative, but of the lay sister who peers at you suspiciously through the little opening in the thick door, before grudgingly admitting you and taking you to the visiting parlour, or to Reverend Mother.

She said: "You come from Mr. Marshall?"

She made it almost an accusation.

Hester was staring down at the envelope in her hand. Then, without a word, she turned and ran up the stairs.

Calgary remained on the doorstep, sustaining the accusing and suspicious glance of the dragon-cum-lay-sister.

He cast about for something to say, but he could not think of anything. Prudently, therefore, he remained silent.

Presently Hester's voice, cool and aloof, floated down to them.

"Father says he's to come up."

Somewhat unwillingly, his watchdog moved aside. Her expression of suspicion did not alter. He passed her, laid his hat on a chair, and mounted the stairs to where Hester stood waiting for him.

The inside of the house struck him as vaguely hygienic. It could almost, he thought, have been an expensive nursing home.

Hester led him along a passage and down three steps. Then she threw open a door and gestured to him to pass through it. She came in behind him, closing the door after her.

The room was a library, and Calgary raised his head with a sense of pleasure. The atmosphere of this room was quite different from the rest of the house. This was a room where a man *lived*, where he both worked and took his ease. The walls were lined with books, the chairs were large, rather shabby, but easeful. There was a pleasant disorder of papers on the desk, of books lying about on tables. He had a momentary glimpse of a young woman who was leaving the room by a door at the far end, rather an attractive young woman. Then his attention was taken by the man who rose and came to greet him, the open letter in his hand.

Calgary's first impression of Leo Argyle was that he was so attenuated, so transparent, as hardly to be there at all. A wraith of a man! His voice when he spoke was pleasant, though lacking in resonance.

"Dr. Calgary?" he said. "Do sit down."

Calgary sat. He accepted a cigarette. His host sat down opposite him. All was done without hurry, as though in a world where time meant very little. There was a faint gentle smile on Leo Argyle's face as he spoke, tapping the letter gently with a bloodless finger as he did so.

"Mr. Marshall writes that you have an important communication to make to us, though he doesn't specify its nature." His smile deepened as he added: "Lawyers are always so careful not to commit themselves, aren't they?"

It occurred to Calgary with a faint shock of surprise, that this man confronting him was a happy man. Not buoyantly or zestfully happy, as is the normal way of happiness—but happy in some shadowy but satisfactory retreat of his own. This was a man on whom the outer world did not impinge and who was contented that this should be so. He did not know why he should be surprised by this—but he was.

Calgary said:

"It is very kind of you to see me." The words were a mere mechanical introduction. "I thought it better to come in person than to write." He paused—then said in a sudden rush of agitation, "It is difficult—very difficult . . ."

"Do take your time."

Leo Argyle was still polite and remote.

He leaned forward; in his gentle way he was obviously trying to help.

"Since you bring this letter from Marshall, I presume that your visit has to do with my unfortunate son Jacko—Jack, I mean—Jacko was our own name for him."

All Calgary's carefully prepared words and phrases had deserted him. He sat here, faced with the appalling reality of what he had to tell. He stammered again.

"It's so terribly difficult . . ."

There was a moment's silence, and then Leo said cautiously:

"If it helps you—we're quite aware that Jacko was—hardly a normal personality. Nothing that you have to tell us will be likely to surprise us. Terrible as the tragedy was, I have been fully convinced all along that Jack was not really responsible for his actions."

"Of course he wasn't." It was Hester, and Calgary started at the sound of her voice. He had momentarily forgotten about her. She had sat down on the arm of a chair just behind his left shoulder. As he turned his head, she leaned forward eagerly towards him.

"Jacko was always awful," she said confidentially. "He was just the same as a little boy—when he lost his temper, I mean. Just caught up anything he could find and—and went for you . . ."

"Hester—Hester—my dear." Argyle's voice was distressed.

Startled, the girl's hand flew to her lips. She flushed and spoke with the sudden awkwardness of youth.

"I'm sorry," she said. "I didn't mean—I forgot—I—I oughtn't to have said a thing like that—not now that he's—I mean, now that it's all over and . . . and . . ."

"Over and done with," said Argyle. "All of this is in the past. I try—we all try—to feel that the boy must be regarded as an invalid. One of Nature's misfits. That, I think, expresses it best." He looked at Calgary. "You agree?"

"No," said Calgary.

There was a moment's silence. The sharp negative had taken both his listeners aback. It had come out with almost explosive force. Trying to mitigate its effect, he said awkwardly:

"I—I'm sorry. You see, you don't understand yet."

"Oh!" Argyle seemed to consider. Then he turned his head towards his daughter. "Hester, I think perhaps you'd better leave us—"

"I'm not going away! I've got to hear—to know what it's all about."

"It may be unpleasant—"

Hester cried out impatiently:

"What does it matter what other awful things Jacko may have done? That's all *over*."

Calgary spoke quickly.

"Please believe me—there is no question of anything that your brother has done—quite the opposite."

"I don't see—"

The door at the far end of the room opened and the young woman whom Calgary had just glimpsed earlier came back into the room. She wore an outdoor coat now, and carried a small attaché-case.

She spoke to Argyle.

"I'm going now. Is there anything else—?"

There was a momentary hesitation on Argyle's part (he would always hesitate, Calgary thought) and then he laid a hand on her arm and drew her forward.

"Sit down, Gwenda," he said. "This is—er—Dr. Calgary. This is Miss Vaughan, who is—who is—" Again he paused as though in doubt. "Who has been my secretary for some years now." He added: "Dr. Calgary has come to tell us something—or—ask us something—about Jacko—"

"To tell you something," Calgary interrupted. "And although you don't realise it, every moment you are making it more difficult for me."

They all looked at him in some surprise, but in Gwenda Vaughan's eyes he saw a flicker of something that looked like comprehension. It was as though he and she were momentarily in alliance, as though she had said: "Yes—I know how difficult the Argyles can be."

She *was* an attractive young woman, he thought, though not so very young—perhaps thirty-seven or eight. A well rounded figure, dark hair and eyes, a general air of vitality and good health. She gave the impression of being both competent and intelligent.

Argyle said with a frosty touch in his manner: "I am not at all aware of making things difficult for you, Dr. Calgary. Such was certainly not my intention. If you will come to the point—"

"Yes, I know. Forgive me for saying what I did. But it is the persistence with which you—and your daughter—are continually underlining that things are *over—done with—finished*. They are *not* over. Who is it who said: '*Nothing is ever settled until—*' "

" '*Until it is settled right,*' " Miss Vaughan finished for him. "Kipling."

She nodded at him encouragingly. He felt grateful to her.

"But I'll come to the point," Calgary went on. "When you've heard what I have to say, you'll understand my—my reluctance. More, my distress. To begin with, I must mention a few things about myself. I am a geophysicist, and have recently formed part of an Antarctic expedition. I only returned to England a few weeks ago."

"The Hayes Bentley Expedition?" asked Gwenda.

He turned towards her gratefully.

"Yes. It was the Hayes Bentley Expedition. I tell you this to explain my background, and also to explain that I have been out of touch for about two years with—with current events."

She went on helping him:

"You mean—with such things as murder trials?"

"Yes, Miss Vaughan, that is exactly what I mean."

He turned to Argyle.

"Please forgive me if this is painful, but I must just check over with you certain times and dates. On November 9th, the year before last, at about six o'clock in the evening, your son, Jack Argyle (Jacko to you), called here and had an interview with his mother, Mrs. Argyle."

"My wife, yes."

"He told her that he was in trouble and demanded money. This had happened before—"

"Many times," said Leo with a sigh.

"Mrs. Argyle refused. He became abusive, threatening. Finally he flung away and left, shouting out that he was coming back and that she had 'jolly well *got* to stump up.' He said, 'You don't want me to go to prison, do you?' and she replied, 'I am beginning to believe that it may be the best thing for you.' "

Leo Argyle moved uneasily.

"My wife and I had talked it over together. We were—very unhappy about the boy. Again and again we had come to his rescue, tried to give him a fresh start. It had seemed to us that perhaps the shock of a prison sentence—the training—" His voice died away. "But please go on."

Calgary went on:

"Later that evening, your wife was killed. Attacked with a poker and struck down. Your son's fingerprints were on the poker, and a large sum of money was gone from the bureau drawer where your wife had placed it earlier. The police picked up your son in Drymouth. The money was found on him, most of it was in five-pound notes, one of which had a name and address written on it which enabled it to be identified by the bank as one that had been paid out to Mrs. Argyle that morning. He was charged and stood his trial." Calgary paused. "The verdict was wilful murder."

It was out—the fateful word. *Murder* . . . Not an echoing word; a stifled word, a word that got absorbed into the hangings, the books, the pile carpet . . . The word could be stifled—but not the act. . . .

"I have been given to understand by Mr. Marshall, the solicitor for the defence, that your son protested his innocence when arrested, in a cheery, not to say cocksure manner. He insisted that he had a perfect alibi for the time of the murder which was placed by the police at between seven and seven-thirty. At that time, Jack Argyle said, he was hitch-hiking into Drymouth, having been picked up by a car on the main road from Redmyn to Drymouth about a mile from here just before seven. He didn't know the make of the car (it was dark by then) but it was a black or dark blue saloon driven by a middle-aged man. Every effort was made to trace this car and the man who drove it, but no confirmation of his statement could be obtained, and the lawyers themselves were quite convinced that it was a story hastily fabricated by the boy and not very cleverly fabricated at that. . . .

"At the trial the main line of defence was the evidence of psychologists who sought to prove that Jack Argyle had always been mentally unstable. The judge was somewhat scathing in his comments on this evidence and summed up dead against the prisoner. Jack Argyle was sentenced to imprisonment for life. He died of pneumonia in prison six months after he began to serve his sentence."

Calgary stopped. Three pairs of eyes were fastened on him. Interest and close attention in Gwenda Vaughan's, suspicion still in Hester's. Leo Argyle's seemed blank.

Calgary said, "You will confirm that I have stated the facts correctly?"

"You are perfectly correct," said Leo, "though I do not yet see why it has been necessary to go over painful facts which we are all trying to forget."

"Forgive me. I had to do so. You do not, I gather, dissent from the verdict?"

"I admit that the *facts* were as stated—that is, if you do not go behind the facts, it was, crudely, murder. But if you *do* go behind the facts, there is much to be said in mitigation. The boy was mentally unstable, though unfortunately not in the legal sense of the term. The McNaughton rules are narrow and unsatisfactory. I assure you, Dr. Calgary, that Rachel herself—my late wife, I mean—would have been the first to forgive and excuse that unfortunate boy for his rash act. She was a most advanced and humane thinker and had a profound knowledge of psychological factors. *She* would not have condemned."

"She knew just how awful Jacko could be," said Hester. "He always was—he just didn't seem able to help it."

"So you all," said Calgary slowly, "had no doubts? No doubts of his guilt, I mean."

Hester stared.

"How could we? Of course he was guilty."

"Not really *guilty*," Leo dissented. "I don't like that word."

"It isn't a true word, either." Calgary took a deep breath. "Jack Argyle was—innocent!"

2

It should have been a sensational announcement. Instead, it fell flat. Calgary had expected bewilderment, incredulous gladness struggling with incomprehension, eager questions. . . . There was none of that. There seemed only wariness and suspicion. Gwenda Vaughan was frowning. Hester stared at him with dilated eyes. Well, perhaps it was natural—such an announcement was hard to take in all at once.

Leo Argyle said hesitantly:

"You mean, Dr. Calgary, that you agree with my attitude? You don't feel he was responsible for his actions?"

"I mean he *didn't do it!* Can't you take it in, man? *He didn't do it*. He *couldn't* have done it. But for the most extraordinary and unfortunate combination of circumstances he could have *proved* that he was innocent. *I* could have proved that he was innocent."

"You?"

"I was the man in the car."

He said it so simply that for the moment they did not take it in. Before they could recover themselves, there was an interruption. The door opened and the woman with the homely face marched in. She spoke directly and to the point.

"I hear as I am passing the door outside. This man is saying that Jacko did not kill Mrs. Argyle. Why does he say this? How does he know?"

Her face, which had been militant and fierce, suddenly seemed to pucker.

"I must hear too," she said piteously. "I cannot stay outside and not know."

"Of course not, Kirsty. You're one of the family." Leo Argyle introduced her. "Miss Lindstrom, Dr. Calgary. Dr. Calgary is saying the most incredible things."

Calgary was puzzled by the Scottish name of Kirsty. Her English was excellent but a faint foreign intonation remained.

She spoke accusingly to him.

"You should not come here and say things like that—upsetting people.

They have accepted tribulation. Now you upset them by what you tell. What happened was the will of God."

He was repelled by the glib complacence of her statement. Possibly, he thought, she was one of those ghoulish people who positively welcome disaster. Well, she was going to be deprived of all that.

He spoke in a quick, dry voice.

"At five minutes to seven on that evening, I picked up a young man on the main Redmyn to Drymouth road who was thumbing for a lift. I drove him into Drymouth. We talked. He was, I thought, an engaging and likeable young man."

"Jacko had great charm," said Gwenda. "Everyone found him attractive. It was his temper let him down. And he was crooked, of course," she added thoughtfully. "But people didn't find that out for some time."

Miss Lindstrom turned on her.

"You should not speak so when he is dead."

Leo Argyle said with a faint asperity:

"Please go on, Dr. Calgary. Why didn't you come forward at the time?"

"Yes." Hester's voice sounded breathless. "Why did you skulk away from it all? There were appeals in the paper—advertisements. How could you be so selfish, so wicked—"

"Hester—Hester—" her father checked her. "Dr. Calgary is still telling us his story."

Calgary addressed the girl direct.

"I know only too well how you feel. I know what I feel myself—what I shall always feel . . ." He pulled himself together and went on:

"To continue with my story: There was a lot of traffic on the roads that evening. It was well after half past seven when I dropped the young man, whose name I did not know, in the middle of Drymouth. That, I understand, clears him completely, since the police are quite definite that the crime was committed between seven and half past."

"Yes," said Hester. "But you—"

"Please be patient. To make you understand, I must go back a little. I had been staying in Drymouth for a couple of days in a friend's flat. This friend, a naval man, was at sea. He had also lent me his car which he kept in a private lock-up. On this particular day, November the 9th, I was due to return to London. I decided to go up by the evening train and to spend the afternoon seeing an old nurse of whom our family were very fond and who lived in a little cottage at Polgarth about forty miles west of Drymouth. I carried out my programme. Though very old and inclined to wander in her mind, she recognised me and was very pleased to see me, and quite excited because she had read in the papers about my 'going to the Pole,' as she put it. I stayed only a short time, so as not to tire her, and on leaving decided not to return direct to Drymouth along the coast road as I had come, but instead to go north to Redmyn and see old Canon Peasmarsh, who has some very rare books in his library, including an early treatise on navigation from which I was anxious to copy a passage. The old gentleman refuses to have the telephone which he regards as a device of the devil, and on a par with radio, television, cinema organs and jet planes, so I had to take a chance of finding him at home. I was unlucky. His house was shuttered and he was evidently away. I spent a little time in the Cathedral, and then started back to Drymouth by the main road, thus completing the third side of a triangle. I had left myself comfortable time to pick up my bag from the flat, return the car to its lock-up, and catch my train.

"On the way, as I have told you, I picked up an unknown hitch-hiker, and after dropping him in the town, I carried out my own programme. After arrival at the station, I still had time in hand, and I went outside the station into the main street to get some cigarettes. As I crossed the road a lorry came round a corner at high speed and knocked me down.

"According to the accounts of passers-by, I got up, apparently uninjured and behaving quite normally. I said I was quite all right and that I had a train to catch and hurried back to the station. When the train arrived at Paddington I was unconscious and taken by ambulance to hospital, where I was found to be suffering from concussion—apparently this delayed effect is not uncommon.

"When I regained consciousness, some days later, I remembered nothing of the accident, or of coming to London. The last thing I could remember was starting out to visit my old nurse at Polgarth. After that, a complete blank. I was reassured by being told that such an occurrence is quite common. There seemed no reason to believe that the missing hours in my life were of any importance. Neither I myself, nor anyone else, had the faintest idea that I had driven along the Redmyn-Drymouth road that evening.

"There was only a very narrow margin of time before I was due to leave England. I was kept in hospital, in absolute quiet, with no newspapers. On leaving I drove straight to the airport to fly to Australia and to join up with the Expedition. There was some doubt as to whether I was fit to go, but this I overruled. I was far too busy with my preparations and anxieties to take any interest in reports of murders, and in any case excitement died down after the arrest, and by the time the case came to trial and was fully reported, I was on my way to the Antarctic."

He paused. They were listening to him with close attention.

"It was about a month ago, just after my return to England, that I made the discovery. I wanted some old newspapers for packing specimens. My landlady brought me up a pile of old papers out of her stokehold. Spreading one out on the table I saw the reproduced photograph of a young man whose face seemed very familiar to me. I tried to remember where I had met him and who he was. I could not do so and yet, very strangely, I remembered holding a conversation with him—it had been about eels. He had been intrigued and fascinated by hearing the saga of an eel's life. But when? Where? I read the paragraph, read that this young man was Jack Argyle, accused of murder, read that he had told the police that he had been given a lift by a man in a black saloon car.

"And then, quite suddenly, that lost bit of my life came back. *I* had picked up this self-same young man, and driven him into Drymouth, parting from him there, going back to the flat—crossing the street on foot to buy my cigarettes. I remembered just a glimpse of the lorry as it hit me—after that, nothing until hospital. I still had no memory of going to the station and taking the train to London. I read and re-read the paragraph. The trial was over a year ago, the case almost forgotten. 'A young fellow what did his mother in,' my landlady remembered vaguely. 'Don't know what happened—think they hanged him.' I read up the files of the newspapers for the appropriate dates, then I went to Marshall, Marshall & Marshall, who had been the lawyers for the defence. I learned that I was too late to free the unfortunate boy. He had died of pneumonia in prison. Though justice could no longer be done to him, justice *could* be done to his memory. I went with Mr. Marshall to the police. The case is being laid before the Public Prosecutor. Marshall has little doubt that he will refer it to the Home Secretary.

"You will, of course, receive a full report from him. He has only delayed it because I was anxious to be the one who first acquainted you with the truth. I felt that that was an ordeal it was my duty to go through. You understand, I am sure, that I shall always feel a deep load of guilt. If I had been more careful crossing the street—" He broke off. "I understand that your feelings towards me can never be kindly—though I am, technically, blameless—you, all of you, *must* blame me."

Gwenda Vaughan said quickly, her voice warm and kindly:

"Of course we don't blame you. It's just—one of those things. Tragic—incredible—but there it is."

Hester said:

"Did they believe you?"

He looked at her in surprise.

"The police—did they believe you? Why shouldn't you be making it all up?"

He smiled a little in spite of himself.

"I'm a very reputable witness," he said gently. "I have no axe to grind, and they have gone into my story very closely; medical evidence, various corroborating details from Drymouth. Oh yes. Marshall was cautious, of course, like all lawyers. He didn't want to raise your hopes until he was pretty certain of success."

Leo Argyle stirred in his chair and spoke for the first time.

"What exactly do you mean by *success?*"

"I apologise," said Calgary quickly. "That is not a word that can rightly be used. Your son was accused of a crime he did not commit, was tried for it, condemned—and died in prison. Justice has come too late for him. But such justice as can be done, almost certainly will be done, and will be seen to be done. The Home Secretary will probably advise the Queen that a free pardon should be granted."

Hester laughed.

"A free pardon—for something he didn't do?"

"I know. The terminology always seems unrealistic. But I understand that the custom is for a question to be asked in the House, the reply to which will make it clear that Jack Argyle did not commit the crime for which he was sentenced, and the newspapers will report that fact freely."

He stopped. Nobody spoke. It had been, he supposed, a great shock to them. But after all, a happy one.

He rose to his feet.

"I'm afraid," he said uncertainly, "that there is nothing more that I can say . . . To repeat how sorry I am, how unhappy about it all, to ask your forgiveness—all that you must already know only too well. The tragedy that ended his life, has darkened my own. But at least"—he spoke with pleading—"surely it means *something*—to know that he didn't do this awful thing—that his name—your name—will be cleared in the eyes of the world . . . ?"

If he hoped for a reply he did not get one.

Leo Argyle sat slumped in his chair. Gwenda's eyes were on Leo's face. Hester sat staring ahead of her, her eyes wide and tragic. Miss Lindstrom grunted something under her breath and shook her head.

Calgary stood helplessly by the door, looking back at them.

It was Gwenda Vaughan who took charge of the situation. She came up to him and laid a hand on his arm, saying in a low voice:

"You'd better go now, Dr. Calgary. It's been too much of a shock. They must have time to take it in."

He nodded and went out. On the landing Miss Lindstrom joined him.

"I will let you out," she said.

He was conscious, looking back before the door closed behind him, of Gwenda Vaughan slipping to her knees by Leo Argyle's chair. It surprised him a little.

Facing him, on the landing, Miss Lindstrom stood like a Guardsman and spoke harshly.

"You cannot bring him back to life. So why bring it all back into their minds? Till now, they were resigned. Now they will suffer. It is better, always, to leave well alone."

She spoke with displeasure.

"His memory must be cleared," said Arthur Calgary.

"Fine sentiments! They are all very well. But you do not really think of what it all means. Men, they never think." She stamped her foot. "I love them all. I came here, to help Mrs. Argyle, in 1940—when she started here a war nursery—for children whose homes had been bombed. Nothing was too good for those children. Everything was done for them. That is nearly eighteen years ago. And still, even after she is dead, I stay here—to look after them—to keep the house clean and comfortable, to see they get good food. I love them all—yes, I love them . . . and Jacko—he was no good! Oh yes, I loved him too. But—he was no good!"

She turned abruptly away. It seemed she had forgotten her offer to show him out. Calgary descended the stairs slowly. As he was fumbling with the front door which had a safety lock he did not understand, he heard light footsteps on the stairs. Hester came flying down them.

She unlatched the door and opened it. They stood looking at each other. He understood less than ever why she faced him with that tragic reproachful stare.

She said, only just breathing the words:

"Why did you come? Oh, why ever did you come?"

He looked at her helplessly.

"I don't understand you. Don't you want your brother's name cleared? Don't you want him to have justice?"

"Oh, justice!" She threw the word at him.

He repeated: "I don't understand . . ."

"Going on so about justice! What does it matter to Jacko now? He's dead. It's not Jacko who matters. It's *us!*"

"What do you mean?"

"It's not the guilty who matter. It's the innocent."

She caught his arm, digging her fingers into it.

"It's *we* who matter. Don't you see what you've done to us all?"

He stared at her.

Out of the darkness outside, a man's figure loomed up.

"Dr. Calgary?" he said. "Your taxi's here, sir. To drive you to Drymouth."

"Oh—er—thank you."

Calgary turned once more to Hester, but she had withdrawn into the house.

The front door banged.

3

Hester went slowly up the stairs pushing back the dark hair from her high forehead. Kirsten Lindstrom met her at the top of the stairs.

"Has he gone?"

"Yes, he's gone."

"You have had a shock, Hester." Kirsten Lindstrom laid a gentle hand on her shoulder. "Come with me. I will give you a little brandy. All this, it has been too much."

"I don't think I want any brandy, Kirsty."

"Perhaps you do not want it, but it will be good for you."

Unresisting, the young girl allowed herself to be steered along the passage and into Kirsten Lindstrom's own small sitting-room. She took the brandy that was offered her and sipped it slowly. Kirsten Lindstrom said in an exasperated voice:

"It has all been too sudden. There should have been warning. Why did not Mr. Marshall write first?"

"I suppose Dr. Calgary wouldn't let him. He wanted to come and tell us himself."

"Come and tell us himself, indeed! What does he think the news will do to us?"

"I suppose," said Hester, in an odd, toneless voice, "he thought we should be pleased."

"Pleased or not pleased, it was bound to be a shock. He should not have done it."

"But it was brave of him, in a way," said Hester. The colour came up in her face. "I mean, it can't have been an *easy* thing to do. To come and tell a family of people that a member of it who was condemned for murder and died in prison was really innocent. Yes, I think it was brave of him—but I wish he hadn't all the same," she added.

"That—we all wish that," said Miss Lindstrom briskly.

Hester looked at her with her interest suddenly aroused from her own preoccupation.

"So you feel that too, Kirsty? I thought perhaps it was only me."

"I am not a fool," said Miss Lindstrom sharply. "I can envisage certain possibilities that your Dr. Calgary does not seem to have thought about."

Hester rose. "I must go to Father," she said.

Kirsten Lindstrom agreed.

"Yes. He will have had time now to think what is best to be done."

As Hester went into the library Gwenda Vaughan was busy with the telephone. Her father beckoned to her and Hester went over and sat on the arm of his chair.

"We're trying to get through to Mary and to Micky," he said. "They ought to be told at once of this."

"Hallo," said Gwenda Vaughan. "Is that Mrs. Durrant? Mary? Gwenda Vaughan here. Your father wants to speak to you."

Leo went over and took up the receiver.

"Mary? How are you? How is Philip? . . . Good. Something rather extraordinary has happened . . . I thought you ought to be told of it at once. A Dr. Calgary has just been to see us. He brought a letter from Andrew Marshall with him. It's about Jacko. It seems—really a very extraordinary thing altogether—it seems that that story Jacko told at the trial, of having been given a lift into Drymouth in somebody's car, is perfectly true. This Dr. Calgary was the man who gave him the lift . . ." He broke off, as he listened to what his daughter was saying at the other end. "Yes, well, Mary, I won't go into all the details now as to why he didn't come forward at the time. He had an accident—concussion. The whole thing seems to be perfectly well authenticated. I rang up to say that I think we should all have a meeting here together as soon as possible. Perhaps we could get Marshall to come down and talk the matter over with us. We ought, I think, to have the best legal advice. Could you and Philip? . . . Yes . . . Yes, I know. But I really think, my dear, that it's *important* . . . Yes . . . well ring me up later, if you like. I must try and get hold of Micky." He replaced the receiver.

Gwenda Vaughan came towards the telephone.

"Shall I try and get Micky now?"

Hester said:

"If this is going to take a little time, could I ring up first, please, Gwenda? I want to ring up Donald."

"Of course," said Leo. "You are going out with him this evening, aren't you?"

"I *was*," said Hester.

Her father gave her a sharp glance.

"Has this upset you very much, darling?"

"I don't know," said Hester. "I don't know quite what I feel."

Gwenda made way for her at the telephone and Hester dialled a number.

"Could I speak to Dr. Craig, please. Yes. Yes. Hester Argyle speaking."

There was a moment or two of delay and then she said:

"Is that you, Donald? . . . I rang up to say that I don't think I can come with you to the lecture to-night. . . . No, I'm not ill—it's not that, it's just—well, just that we've—we've had some rather queer news."

Again Dr. Craig spoke.

Hester turned her head towards her father. She laid her hand over the receiver and said to him:

"It isn't a secret, is it?"

"No," said Leo slowly. "No, it isn't exactly a secret but—well, I should just ask Donald to keep it to himself for the present, perhaps. You know how rumours get around, get magnified."

"Yes, I know." She spoke again into the receiver. "In a way I suppose it's what you'd call good news, Donald, but—it's rather upsetting. I'd rather not talk about it over the telephone. . . . No, no, *don't* come here. . . . Please—*not*. Not this evening. To-morrow some time. It's about—Jacko. Yes—yes—my brother—it's just that we've found out that he didn't kill my mother after all. . . . But please don't say anything, Donald, or talk to *anyone*. I'll tell you all about it to-morrow. . . . No, Donald, *no* . . . I just can't see *anyone* this evening—not even you. Please. And don't say anything." She put down the receiver, and motioned to Gwenda to take over.

Gwenda asked for a Drymouth number. Leo said gently:

"Why don't you go to the lecture with Donald, Hester? It will take your mind off things."

"I don't want to, Father. I couldn't."

Leo said:

"You spoke—you gave him the impression that it wasn't good news. But you know, Hester, that's not so. We were startled. But we're all very happy about it—very glad . . . What else could we be?"

"That's what we're going to say, is it?" said Hester.

Leo said warningly:

"My dear child—"

"But it's not true, is it?" said Hester. "It's not good news. It's just terribly upsetting."

Gwenda said:

"Micky's on the line."

Again Leo came and took the receiver from her. He spoke to his son very much as he had spoken to his daughter. But his news was received rather differently from the way it had been received by Mary Durrant. Here there was no protest, surprise or disbelief. Instead there was quick acceptance.

"What the hell!" said Micky's voice. "After all this time? The missing witness! Well, well, Jacko's luck was out that night."

Leo spoke again. Micky listened.

"Yes," he said, "I agree with you. We'd better get together as quickly as possible, and get Marshall to advise us, too." He gave a sudden quick laugh, the laugh that Leo remembered so well from the small boy who had played in the garden outside the window. "What's the betting?" he said. *"Which of us did it?"*

Leo dropped the receiver down and left the telephone abruptly.

"What did he say?" Gwenda said.

Leo told her.

"It seems to me a silly sort of joke to make," said Gwenda.

Leo shot a quick glance at her. "Perhaps," he said gently, "it wasn't altogether a joke."

II

Mary Durrant crossed the room and picked up some fallen petals from a vase of chrysanthemums. She put them carefully into the waste-paper basket. She was a tall, serene-looking young woman of twenty-seven who, although her face was unlined, yet looked older than her years, probably from a sedate maturity that seemed part of her make-up. She had good looks, without a trace of glamour. Regular features, a good skin, eyes of a vivid blue, and fair hair combed off her face and arranged in a large bun at the back of her neck; a style which at the moment happened to be fashionable although that was not her reason for wearing it so. She was a woman who always kept to her own style. Her appearance was like her house; neat, well kept. Any kind of dust or disorder worried her.

The man in the invalid chair watching her as she put the fallen petals carefully away, smiled a slightly twisted smile.

"Same tidy creature," he said. "A place for everything and everything in its place." He laughed, with a faint malicious note in the laugh. But Mary Durrant was quite undisturbed.

"I do like things to be tidy," she agreed. "You know, Phil, you wouldn't like it yourself if the house was like a shambles."

Her husband said with a faint trace of bitterness:

"Well, at any rate I haven't got the chance of making it into one."

Soon after their marriage, Philip Durrant had fallen a victim to polio of the paralytic type. To Mary, who adored him, he had become her child as well as her husband. He himself felt at times slightly embarrassed by her possessive love. His wife had not got the imagination to understand that her pleasure in his dependence upon her sometimes irked him.

He went on now rather quickly, as though fearing some word of commiseration or sympathy from her.

"I must say your father's news beggars description! After all this time! How can you be so calm about it?"

"I suppose I can hardly take it in. . . . It's so extraordinary. At first I simply couldn't believe what father was saying. If it had been Hester, now, I should have thought she'd imagined the whole thing. You know what Hester's like."

Philip Durrant's face lost a little of its bitterness. He said softly:

"A vehement passionate creature, setting out in life to look for trouble and certain to find it."

Mary waved away the analysis. Other people's characters did not interest her.

She said doubtfully: "I suppose it's *true?* You don't think this man may have imagined it all?"

"The absent-minded scientist? It would be nice to think so," said Philip, "but it seems that Andrew Marshall has taken the matter seriously. And Marshall, Marshall & Marshall are a very hard-headed legal proposition, let me tell you."

Mary Durrant said, frowning: "What will it actually *mean*, Phil?"

Philip said: "It means that Jacko will be completely exonerated. That is, if the authorities are satisfied—and I gather that there is going to be no question of anything else."

"Oh, well," said Mary, with a slight sigh, "I suppose it's all very *nice*."

Philip Durrant laughed again, the same twisted, rather bitter laughter.

"Polly!" he said, "you'll be the death of me."

Only her husband had ever called Mary Durrant Polly. It was a name ludicrously inappropriate to her statuesque appearance. She looked at Philip in faint surprise.

"I don't see what I've said to amuse you so much."

"You were so gracious about it!" said Philip. "Like Lady Somebody at the Sale of Work praising the Village Institute's handiwork."

Mary said, puzzled: "But it *is* very nice! You can't pretend it's been satisfactory to have had a murderer in the family."

"Not really *in* the family."

"Well, it's practically the same thing. I mean, it was all very worrying, and made one most uncomfortable. Everybody was so agog and curious. I hated it all."

"You took it very well," said Philip. "Froze them with that icy blue gaze of yours. Made them pipe down and look ashamed of themselves. It's wonderful the way you manage never to show emotion."

"I disliked it all very much. It was all most unpleasant," said Mary Durrant, "but at any rate he died and it was over. And now—now, I suppose, it will all be raked up again. So tiresome."

"Yes," said Philip Durrant thoughtfully. He shifted his shoulders slightly, a faint expression of pain on his face. His wife came to him quickly.

"Are you cramped? Wait. Let me just move this cushion. There. That better?"

"You ought to have been a hospital nurse," said Philip.

"I've not the least wish to nurse a lot of people. Only you."

It was said very simply but there was a depth of feeling behind the bare words.

The telephone rang and Mary went to it.

"Hallo . . . yes . . . speaking . . . Oh, it's you . . ."

She said aside to Philip: "It's Micky."

"Yes . . . yes, we have heard. Father telephoned. . . . Well, of course . . . Yes . . . Yes . . . Philip says if the lawyers are satisfied it must be all right. . . . Really, Micky, I don't see why you're so upset. . . . I'm not aware of being particularly dense. . . . Really, Micky, I do think you—Hallo? . . . Hallo? . . ." She frowned angrily. "He's rung off." She replaced the receiver. "Really, Philip, I can't understand Micky."

"What did he say exactly?"

"Well, he seems in such a state. He said that I was dense, that I didn't realise the—the repercussions. Hell to pay! That's the way he put it. But why? I don't understand."

"Got the wind up, has he?" said Philip thoughtfully.

"But why?"

"Well, he's right, you know. There will be repercussions."

Mary looked a little bewildered.

"You mean that there will be a revival of interest in the case? Of course I'm glad Jacko is cleared, but it will be rather unpleasant if people begin talking about it again."

"It's not just what the neighbours say. There's more to it than that."

She looked at him enquiringly.

"The police are going to be interested, too!"

"The *police?*" Mary spoke sharply. "What's it got to do with them?"

"My dear girl," said Philip. *"Think."*

Mary came back slowly to sit by him.

"It's an unsolved crime again now, you see," said Philip.

"But surely they won't bother—after all this time?"

"A very nice bit of wishful thinking," said Philip, "but fundamentally unsound, I fear."

"Surely," said Mary, "after they've been so stupid—making such a bad mistake over Jacko—they won't want to rake it all up again?"

"They mayn't want to—but they'll probably have to! Duty is duty."

"Oh, Philip, I'm sure you're wrong. There will just be a bit of talk and then it will all die down."

"And then our lives will go on happily ever afterwards," said Philip in his mocking voice.

"Why not?"

He shook his head. "It's not as simple as that. . . . Your father's right. We must all get together and have a consultation. Get Marshall down as he said."

"You mean—go over to Sunny Point?"

"Yes."

"Oh, we can't do that."

"Why not?"

"It's not practicable. You're an invalid and—"

"I'm not an invalid." Philip spoke with irritation. "I'm quite strong and well. I just happen to have lost the use of my legs. I could go to Timbuctoo with the proper transport laid on."

"I'm sure it would be very bad for you to go to Sunny Point. Having all this unpleasant business raked up—"

"It's not my mind that's affected."

"—And I don't see how we can leave the house. There have been so many burglaries lately."

"Get someone to sleep in."

"It's all very well to say that—as though it was the easiest thing in the world."

"Old Mrs. Whatshername can come in every day. Do stop making housewifely objections, Polly. It's you, really, who doesn't want to go."

"No, I don't."

"We won't be there long," said Philip reassuringly. "But I think we've got to go. This is a time when the family's got to present a united front to the world. We've got to find out exactly how we stand."

III

At the Hotel in Drymouth, Calgary dined early and went up to his room. He felt profoundly affected by what he had passed through at Sunny Point. He had expected to find his mission painful and it had taken him all his resolution to go through with it. But the whole thing had been painful and upsetting in an entirely different way from the one he had expected. He flung himself down on his bed and lit a cigarette as he went over and over it in his mind.

The clearest picture that came to him was of Hester's face at that parting moment. Her scornful rejection of his plea for justice! What was it that she had said? "It's not the guilty who matter, it's the innocent." And then: "Don't you see what you've done to us all?" But what had he done? He didn't understand.

And the others. The woman they called Kirsty (why Kirsty? That was a Scottish name. She wasn't Scottish—Danish, perhaps, or Norwegian?). Why had she spoken so sternly—so accusingly?

There had been something odd, too, about Leo Argyle—a withdrawal, a watchfulness. No suggestion of the "Thank God my son was innocent!" which surely would have been the natural reaction!

And that girl—the girl who was Leo's secretary. She had been helpful to him, kindly. But she, too, had reacted in an odd way. He remembered the way she had knelt there by Argyle's chair. As though—as though—she were sympathising with him, consoling him. Consoling him for what? That his son was not guilty of murder? And surely—yes, surely—there was more there than a secretary's feelings—even a secretary of some years' standing. . . . What was it all *about?* Why did they—

The telephone on the table by the bed rang. He picked up the receiver.

"Hallo?"

"Dr. Calgary? There is someone asking for you."

"For me?"

He was surprised. As far as he was aware, nobody knew that he was spending the night in Drymouth.

"Who is it?"

There was a pause. Then the clerk said:

"It's a Mr. Argyle."

"Oh. Tell him—" Arthur Calgary checked himself on the point of saying that he would come down. If for some reason Leo Argyle had followed him to Drymouth and managed to find out where he was staying, then presumably the matter would be embarrassing to discuss in the crowded lounge downstairs.

He said instead:

"Ask him to come up to my room, will you?"

He rose from where he had been lying and paced up and down until the knock came on the door.

He went across and opened it.

"Come in, Mr. Argyle, I—"

He stopped, taken aback. It was not Leo Argyle. It was a young man in his early twenties, a young man whose dark, handsome face was marred by its expression of bitterness. A reckless, angry, unhappy face.

"Didn't expect me," said the young man. "Expected my—father. I'm Michael Argyle."

"Come in." Calgary closed the door after his visitor had entered. "How did you find out I was here?" he asked as he offered the boy his cigarette case.

Michael Argyle took one and gave a short unpleasant laugh.

"That one's easy! Rang up the principal hotels on the chance you might be staying the night. Hit it the second try."

"And why did you want to see me?"

Michael Argyle said slowly:

"Wanted to see what sort of a chap you were . . ." His eyes ran appraisingly over Calgary, noting the slightly stooped shoulders, the greying hair, the thin sensitive face. "So you're one of the chaps who went on the 'Hayes Bentley' to the Pole. You don't look very tough."

Arthur Calgary smiled faintly.

"Appearances are sometimes deceptive," he said: "I was tough enough. It's not entirely muscular force that's needed. There are other important qualifications; endurance, patience, technical knowledge."

"How old are you, forty-five?"

"Thirty—eight."

"You look more."

"Yes—yes, I suppose I do." For a moment a feeling of poignant sadness came over him as he confronted the virile youth of the boy facing him.

He asked rather abruptly:

"Why did you want to see me?"

The other scowled.

"It's natural, isn't it? When I heard about the news you'd brought. The news about my dear brother."

Calgary did not answer.

Michael Argyle went on:

"It's come a bit late for him, hasn't it?"

"Yes," said Calgary in a low voice. "It is too late for him."

"What did you bottle it up for? What's all this about concussion?"

Patiently Calgary told him. Strangely enough, he felt heartened by the boy's roughness and rudeness. Here, at any rate, was someone who felt strongly on his brother's behalf.

"Gives Jacko an alibi, that's the point, is it? How do you know the times were as you say they were?"

"I am quite sure about the times." Calgary spoke with firmness.

"You may have made a mistake. You scientific blokes are apt to be absentminded sometimes about little things like times and places."

Calgary showed slight amusement.

"You have made a picture for yourself of the absentminded professor of fiction—wearing odd socks, not quite sure what day it is or where he happens to be? My dear young man, technical work needs great precision; exact amounts, times, calculations. I assure you there is no possibility of my having made a mistake. I picked up your brother just before seven and put him down in Drymouth at five minutes after the half hour."

"Your watch could have been wrong. Or you went by the clock in your car."

"My watch and the clock in the car were exactly synchronised."

"Jacko could have led you up the garden path some way. He was full of tricks."

"There were no tricks. Why are you so anxious to prove me wrong?" With some heat, Calgary went on: "I expected it might be difficult to convince the authorities that they had convicted a man unjustly. I did not expect to find his own family so hard to convince!"

"So you've found all of us a little difficult to convince?"

"The reaction seemed a little—unusual."

Micky eyed him keenly.

"They didn't want to believe you?"

"It—almost seemed like that . . ."

"Not only seemed like it. It was. Natural enough, too, if you only think about it."

"But why? Why should it be natural? Your mother is killed. Your brother is accused and convicted of the crime. Now it turns out that he was innocent. You should be pleased—thankful. Your own brother."

Micky said:

"He wasn't my brother. And she wasn't my mother."

"What?"

"Hasn't anyone told you? We were all adopted. The lot of us. Mary, my eldest 'sister,' in New York. The rest of us during the war. My 'mother,' as you call her, couldn't have any children of her own. So she got herself a nice little family by adoption. Mary, myself, Tina, Hester, Jacko. Comfortable, luxurious home and plenty of mother love thrown in! I'd say she forgot we weren't her own children in the end. But she was out of luck when she picked Jacko to be one of her darling little boys."

"I had no idea," said Calgary.

"So don't pull out the 'own mother,' 'own brother' stop on me! Jacko was a louse!"

"But not a murderer," said Calgary.

His voice was emphatic. Micky looked at him and nodded.

"All right. It's your say so—and you're sticking to it. Jacko didn't kill her. Very well then—*who did kill her?* You haven't thought about that one, have you? Think about it now. Think about it—and then you'll begin to see what you're doing to us all. . . ."

He wheeled round and went abruptly out of the room.

4

Calgary said apologetically, "It's very good of you to see me again, Mr. Marshall."

"Not at all," said the lawyer.

"As you know, I went down to Sunny Point and saw Jack Argyle's family."

"Quite so."

"You will have heard by now, I expect, about my visit?"

"Yes, Dr. Calgary, that is correct."

"What you may find it difficult to understand is why I have come back here to you again. . . . You see, things didn't turn out exactly as I thought they would."

"No," said the lawyer, "no, perhaps not." His voice was as usual dry and unemotional, yet something in it encouraged Arthur Calgary to continue.

"I thought, you see," went on Calgary, "that that would be the end of it. I was prepared for a certain amount of—what shall I say—natural resentment on their part. Although concussion may be termed, I suppose, an Act of God, yet from their viewpoint they could be forgiven for harbouring resentment against me. I was prepared for that, as I say. But at the same time I hoped it would be offset by the thankfulness they would feel over the fact that Jack Argyle's name was cleared. But things didn't turn out as I anticipated. Not at all."

"I see."

"Perhaps, Mr. Marshall, you anticipated something of what would happen? Your manner, I remember, puzzled me when I was here before. *Did* you foresee the attitude of mind that I was going to encounter?"

"You haven't told me yet, Dr. Calgary, what that attitude was."

Arthur Calgary drew his chair forward. "I thought that I was *end*ing something, giving—shall we say—a different end to a chapter already written. But I was made to feel, I was made to *see*, that instead of *end*ing something I was *start*ing something. Something altogether new. Is that a true statement, do you think, of the position?"

Mr. Marshall nodded his head slowly. "Yes," he said, "it could be put that way. I did think—I admit it—that you were not realising all the implications. You could not be expected to do so because, naturally, you knew nothing of the background or the facts except as they were given in the law reports."

"No. No, I see that now. Only too clearly." His voice rose as he went on excitedly, "It wasn't really relief they felt, it wasn't thankfulness. It was apprehension. A dread of what might be coming next. Am I right?"

Marshall said cautiously: "I should think probably that you are quite right. Mind you, I do not speak of my own knowledge."

"And if so," went on Calgary, "then I no longer feel that I can go back to my work satisfied with having made the only amends that I can make. I'm still involved. I'm responsible for bringing a new factor into various people's lives. I *can't* just wash my hands of it."

The lawyer cleared his throat. "That, perhaps, is a rather fanciful point of view, Dr. Calgary."

"I don't think it is—not really. One must take responsibility for one's actions and not only one's *actions* but for the *result* of one's actions. Just on two years ago I gave a lift to a young hitch-hiker on the road. When I did that I set in train a certain course of events. I don't feel that I can disassociate myself from them."

The lawyer still shook his head.

"Very well, then," said Arthur Calgary impatiently. "Call it fanciful if you like. But my feelings, my conscience, are still involved. My only wish was to make amends for something it had been outside my power to prevent. I have not made amends. In some curious way I have made things worse for people who have already suffered. But I still don't understand clearly *why*."

"No," said Marshall slowly, "no, you would not see why. For the past eighteen months or so you've been out of touch with civilisation. You did not read the daily papers, the account of the criminal proceedings and the background account of this family that was given in the newspapers. Possibly you would not have read them anyway, but you could not have escaped, I think, *hearing* about them. The facts are very simple, Dr. Calgary. They are not confidential. They were made public at the time. It resolves itself very simply into this. If Jack Argyle did not (and by your account he cannot have committed the crime), *then who did?* That brings us back to the circumstances in which the crime was committed. It was committed between the hours of seven and seven-thirty on a November evening in a house where the deceased woman was surrounded by the members of her own family and household. The house was securely locked and shuttered and if anyone entered from outside, then the outsider must have been admitted by Mrs. Argyle herself or have entered with their own key. In other words, it must have been someone she knew. It resembles in some ways the conditions of the Borden case in America where Mr. Borden and his wife were struck down by blows of an axe on a Sunday morning. Nobody in the house heard anything, nobody was known or seen to approach the house. You can see, Dr. Calgary, why the members of the family were, as you put it, disturbed rather than relieved by the news you brought them?"

Calgary said slowly: "They'd rather, you mean, that Jack Argyle was guilty?"

"Oh yes," said Marshall. "Oh yes, very decidedly so. If I may put it in a somewhat cynical way, Jack Argyle was the perfect answer to the unpleasant fact of murder in the family. He had been a problem child, a delinquent boy, a man of violent temper. Excuses could be and were made for him within the family circle. They could mourn for him, have sympathy with him, declare to themselves, to each other, and to the world that it was not *really* his fault, that psychologists could explain it all! Yes, very, very convenient."

"And now—" Calgary stopped.

"And now," said Mr. Marshall, "it is different, of course. Quite different. Almost alarming perhaps."

Calgary said shrewdly, "The news I brought was unwelcome to you, too, wasn't it?"

"I must admit that. Yes. Yes, I must admit that I was—upset. A case which was closed satisfactorily—yes, I shall continue to use the word *satisfactorily*—is now reopened."

"Is that official?" Calgary asked. "I mean—from the police point of view, will the case be reopened?"

"Oh, undoubtedly," said Marshall. "When Jack Argyle was found guilty on overwhelming evidence—(the jury was only out a quarter of an hour)—that was an end of the matter as far as the police were concerned. But now, with the grant of a free pardon posthumously awarded, the case is opened again."

"And the police will make fresh investigations?"

"Almost certainly I should say. Of course," added Marshall, rubbing his chin thoughtfully, "it is doubtful after this lapse of time, owing to the peculiar features of the case, whether they will be able to achieve any result. . . . For myself, I should doubt it. They may know that someone in the house is guilty. They may get so far as to have a very shrewd idea of who that someone is. But to get definite evidence will not be easy."

"I see," said Calgary. "I see. . . . Yes, that's what she meant."

The lawyer said sharply: "Of whom are you speaking?"

"The girl," said Calgary. "Hester Argyle."

"Ah, yes. Young Hester." He asked curiously: "What did she say to you?"

"She spoke of the innocent," said Calgary. "She said it wasn't the guilty who mattered but the innocent. I understand now what she meant. . . ."

Marshall cast a sharp glance at him. "I think possibly you do."

"She meant just what you are saying," said Arthur Calgary. "She meant that once more the family would be under suspicion—"

Marshall interrupted. "Hardly once more," he said. "There was never *time* for the family to come under suspicion before. Jack Argyle was clearly indicated from the first."

Calgary waved the interruption aside.

"The family would come under suspicion," he said, "and it might remain under suspicion for a long time—perhaps for ever. If one of the family was guilty it is possible that they themselves would not know which one. They would look at each other and—wonder. . . . Yes, that's what would be the worst of all. They themselves would not know *which*. . . ."

There was silence. Marshall watched Calgary with a quiet, appraising glance, but he said nothing.

"That's terrible, you know . . ." said Calgary.

His thin, sensitive face showed the play of emotion on it.

"Yes, that's terrible. . . . To go on year after year not knowing, looking at one another, perhaps the suspicion affecting one's relationships with people. Destroying love, destroying trust . . ."

Marshall cleared his throat.

"Aren't you—er—putting it rather too vividly?"

"No," said Calgary, "I don't think I am. I think, perhaps, if you'll excuse me, Mr. Marshall, I see this more clearly than you do. I can imagine, you see, what it might mean."

Again there was silence.

"It means," said Calgary, "that it is the innocent who are going to suffer. . . . And the innocent should not suffer. Only the guilty. That's why—that's why I can't wash my hands of it. I *can't* go away and say 'I've done the right thing, I've made what amends I can—I've served the cause of justice.' Because you see what I have done has *not* served the cause of justice. It has not brought conviction to the guilty, it has not delivered the innocent from the shadow of guilt."

"I think you're working yourself up a little, Dr. Calgary. What you say has some foundation of truth, no doubt, but I don't see exactly what—well, what you can do about it."

"No. Nor do I," said Calgary frankly. "But it means that I've got to try. That's really why I've come to you, Mr. Marshall. I want—I think I've a right to know—the background."

"Oh, well," said Mr. Marshall, his tone slightly brisker. "There's no secret about all *that*. I can give you any *facts* you want to know. More than facts I am not in a position to give you. I've never been on intimate terms with the household. Our firm has acted for Mrs. Argyle over a number of years. We have co-operated with her over establishing various trusts and seeing to legal business. Mrs. Argyle herself I knew reasonably well and I also knew her husband. Of the atmosphere at Sunny Point, of the temperaments and characters of the various people living there, I only know as you might say, at second-hand through Mrs. Argyle herself."

"I quite understand all that," said Calgary, "but I've got to make a start somewhere. I understand that the children were not her own. That they were adopted?"

"That is so. Mrs. Argyle was born Rachel Konstam, the only daughter of Rudolph Konstam, a very rich man. Her mother was American and also a very rich woman in her own right. Rudolph Konstam had many philantrophic interests and brought his daughter up to take an interest in these benevolent schemes. He and his wife died in an aeroplane crash and Rachel then devoted the large fortune she inherited from her father and mother to what we may term, loosely, philanthropical enterprises. She took a personal interest in these benefactions and did a certain amount of settlement work herself. It was in doing the latter that she met Leo Argyle, who was an Oxford Don, with a great interest in economics and social reform. To understand Mrs. Argyle you have to realise that the great tragedy of her life was that she was unable to have children. As in the case with many women, this disability gradually overshadowed the whole of her life. When after visits to all kinds of specialists, it seemed clear that she could never hope to be a mother, she had to find what alleviation she could. She adopted first a child from a slum tenement in New York—that is the present Mrs. Durrant. Mrs. Argyle devoted herself almost entirely to charities connected with children. On the outbreak of war in 1939 she established under the auspices of the Ministry of Health a kind of war nursery for children, purchasing the house you visited, Sunny Point."

"Then called Viper's Point," said Calgary.

"Yes. Yes, I believe that was the original name. Ah, yes, perhaps in the end a more suitable name than the name she chose for it—Sunny Point. In 1940 she had about twelve to sixteen children, mostly those who had unsatisfactory guardians or who could not be evacuated with their own families. Everything was done for these children. They were given a luxurious home. I remonstrated with her, pointing out to her it was going to be difficult for the children after several years of war, to return from these luxurious surroundings to their own homes. She paid no attention to me. She was deeply attached to the children and finally she formed the project of adding some of them, those from particularly unsatisfactory homes or who were orphans, to her own family. This resulted in a family of five. Mary—now married to Philip Durrant—Michael, who works in Drymouth, Tina, a half-caste child, Hester, and of course, Jacko. They grew up regarding the Argyles as their father and mother. They were given the best education money could buy. If environment counts for anything they should have gone far. They certainly had every advantage. Jack—or Jacko, as they called him—was always unsatisfactory. He stole money at school and had to be taken away. He got into trouble in his first year at the university. Twice he avoided a jail sentence only by a very narrow margin. He always had an ungovernable temper. All this, however, you probably have already gathered. Twice embezzlement on his part was made good by the Argyles. Twice money was spent in setting him up in business. Twice these business enterprises failed. After his death an allowance was paid, and indeed is still paid, to his widow."

Calgary leant forward in astonishment.

"His *widow*? Nobody has ever told me that he was married."

"Dear, dear." The lawyer clicked his thumb irritably. "I have been remiss. I had forgotten, of course, that you had not read the newspaper reports. I may say that none of the Argyle family had any idea that he was married. Immediately after his arrest his wife appeared at Sunny Point in great distress. Mr. Argyle was very good to her. She was a young woman who had worked as a dance hostess in the Drymouth Palais de Danse. I probably forgot to tell you about her because she re-married a few weeks after Jack's death. Her present husband is an electrician, I believe, in Drymouth."

"I must go and see her," said Calgary. He added, reproachfully, "She is the first person I should have gone to see."

"Certainly, certainly. I will give you the address. I really cannot think *why* I did not mention it to you when you first came to me."

Calgary was silent.

"She was such a—well—negligible factor," said the lawyer apologetically. "Even the newspapers did not play her up much—she never visited her husband in prison—or took any further interest in him—"

Calgary had been deep in thought. He said now:

"Can you tell me exactly who was in that house on the night Mrs. Argyle was killed?"

Marshall gave him a sharp glance.

"Leo Argyle, of course, and the youngest daughter, Hester. Mary Durrant and her invalid husband were there on a visit. He had just come out of hospital. Then there was Kirsten Lindstrom—whom you probably met—she is a Swedish trained nurse and masseuse who originally came to help

Mrs. Argyle with her war nursery and has remained on ever since. Michael and Tina were not there—Michael works as a car salesman in Drymouth and Tina has a job in the County Library at Redmyn and lives in a flat there."

Marshall paused before going on.

"There was also Miss Vaughan, Mr. Argyle's secretary. She had left the house before the body was discovered."

"I met her also," said Calgary. "She seems very—attached to Mr. Argyle."

"Yes—yes. I believe there may shortly be an engagement announced."

"Ah!"

"He has been very lonely since his wife died," said the lawyer, with a faint note of reproof in his voice.

"Quite so," said Calgary.

Then he said:

"What about motive, Mr. Marshall?"

"My dear Dr. Calgary, I really cannot speculate as to that!"

"I think you can. As you have said yourself the facts are ascertainable."

"There was no direct monetary benefit to *anyone*. Mrs. Argyle had entered into a series of discretionary Trusts, a formula which as you know is much adopted nowadays. These Trusts were in favour of all the children. They are administered by three Trustees, of whom I am one, Leo Argyle is one and the third is an American lawyer, a distant cousin of Mrs. Argyle's. The very large sum of money involved is administered by these three Trustees and can be adjusted so as to benefit those beneficiaries of the Trust who need it most."

"What about Mr. Argyle? Did he profit in a monetary sense by his wife's death?"

"Not to any great extent. Most of her fortune, as I have told you, had gone into Trusts. She left him the residue of her estate, but that did not amount to a large sum."

"And Miss Lindstrom?"

"Mrs. Argyle had bought a very handsome annuity for Miss Lindstrom some years previously." Marshall added irritably, "Motive? There doesn't seem to me a ha'porth of motive about. Certainly not financial motive."

"And in the emotional field? Was there any special—friction?"

"There, I'm afraid, I can't help you." Marshall spoke with finality. "I wasn't an observer of the family life."

"Is there anyone who could?"

Marshall considered for a moment or two. Then he said, almost reluctantly:

"You might go and see the local doctor. Dr.—er—MacMaster, I think his name is. He's retired now, but still lives in the neighbourhood. He was medical attendant to the war nursery. He must have known and seen a good deal of the life at Sunny Point. Whether you can persuade him to tell you anything is up to you. But I think that if he chose, he might be helpful, though—pardon me for saying this—do you think it likely that you can accomplish anything that the police cannot accomplish much more easily?"

"I don't know," said Calgary. "Probably not. But I do know this. I've got to try. Yes, I've got to try."

5

The Chief Constable's eyebrows climbed slowly up his forehead in a vain attempt to reach the receding line of his grey hair. He cast his eyes up to the ceiling and then down again to the papers on his desk.

"It beggars description!" he said.

The young man whose business it was to make the right responses to the Chief Constable, said:

"Yes, sir."

"A pretty kettle of fish," muttered Major Finney. He tapped with his fingers on the table. "Is Huish here?" he asked.

"Yes, sir. Superintendent Huish came about five minutes ago."

"Right," said the Chief Constable. "Send him in, will you?"

Superintendent Huish was a tall, sad-looking man. His air of melancholy was so profound that no one would have believed that he could be the life and soul of a children's party, cracking jokes and bringing pennies out of little boys' ears, much to their delight. The Chief Constable said:

"Morning, Huish, this is a pretty kettle of fish we've got here. What d'you think of it?"

Superintendent Huish breathed heavily and sat down in the chair indicated.

"It seems as though we made a mistake two years ago," he said. "This fellow—what's-his-name—"

The Chief Constable rustled his papers. "Calory—no, Calgary. Some sort of a professor. Absentminded bloke, maybe? People like that often vague about times and all that sort of thing?" There was perhaps a hint of appeal in his voice, but Huish did not respond. He said:

"He's a kind of scientist, I understand."

"So that you think we've got to accept what he says?"

"Well," said Huish, "Sir Reginald seems to have accepted it, and I don't suppose there's anything would get past *him*." This was a tribute to the Director of Public Prosecutions.

"No," said Major Finney, rather unwillingly. "If the D.P.P.'s convinced, well I suppose we've just got to take it. That means opening up the case again. You've brought the relevant data with you, have you, as I asked?"

"Yes, sir, I've got it here."

The superintendent spread out various documents on the table.

"Been over it?" the Chief Constable asked.

"Yes, sir, I went all over it last night. My memory of it was fairly fresh. After all, it's not so long ago."

"Well, let's have it, Huish. Where are we?"

"Back at the beginning, sir," said Superintendent Huish. "The trouble is, you see, there really wasn't any doubt *at the time*."

"No," said the Chief Constable. "It seemed a perfectly clear case. Don't think I'm blaming you, Huish. I was behind you a hundred percent."

"There wasn't anything else really that we could think," said Huish thoughtfully. "A call came in that she'd been killed. The information that the boy had been there threatening her, the fingerprint evidence—his fingerprints on the poker, and the money. We picked him up almost at once and there the money was, in his possession."

"What sort of impression did he make on you at the time?"

Huish considered. "Bad," he said. "Far too cocky and plausible. Came reeling out with his times and his alibis. Cocky. You know the type. Murderers are usually cocky. Think they're so clever. Think whatever *they've* done is sure to be all right, no matter how things go for other people. He was a wrong 'un all right."

"Yes," Finney agreed, "he was a wrong 'un. All his record goes to prove that. But were you convinced at once that he was a killer?"

The superintendent considered. "It's not a thing you can be sure about. He was the type, I'd say, that very often ends up as a killer. Like Harmon in 1938. Long record behind *him* of pinched bicycles, swindled money, frauds on elderly women, and finally he does one woman in, pickles her in acid, gets pleased with himself and starts making a habit of it. I'd have taken Jacko Argyle for one of that type."

"But it seems," said the Chief Constable slowly, "that we were wrong."

"Yes," said Huish, "yes, we were wrong. And the chap's dead. It's a bad business. Mind you," he added, with sudden animation, "he was a wrong 'un all right. He may not have been a murderer—in fact he wasn't a murderer, so we find now—but he was a wrong 'un."

"Well, come on, man," Finney snapped at him, "who *did* kill her? You've been over the case, you say, last night. Somebody killed her. The woman didn't hit herself on the back of her head with the poker. Somebody else did. Who was it?"

Superintendent Huish sighed and leaned back in his chair.

"I'm wondering if we'll ever know," he said.

"Difficult as all that, eh?"

"Yes, because the scent's cold and because there'll be very little evidence to find and I should rather imagine that there never was very much evidence."

"The point being that it was someone in the house, someone close to her?"

"Don't see who else it could have been," said the superintendent. "It was someone there in the house or it was someone that she herself opened the door to and let in. The Argyles were the locking-up type. Burglar bolts on the windows, chains, extra locks on the front door. They'd had one burglary a couple of years before and it had made them burglar conscious." He paused and went on, "The trouble is, sir, that we didn't look elsewhere at the time. The case against Jacko Argyle was complete. Of course, one can see now, the murderer took advantage of that."

"Took advantage of the fact that the boy had been there, that he'd quarrelled with her and that he'd threatened her?"

"Yes. All that person had to do was to step in the room, pick up the poker in a gloved hand, from where Jacko had thrown it down, walk up to the table where Mrs. Argyle was writing and biff her one on the head."

Major Finney said one simple word:

"Why?"

Superintendent Huish nodded slowly.

"Yes, sir, that's what we've got to find out. It's going to be one of the difficulties. Absence of motive."

"There didn't seem at the time," said the Chief Constable, "to be any obvious motive knocking about, as you might say. Like most other women who have property and a considerable fortune of their own, she'd entered into such various schemes as are legally permitted to avoid death duties. A beneficiary trust was already in existence, the children were all provided for in advance of her death. They'd get nothing further when she did die. And it wasn't as though she was an unpleasant woman, nagging or bullying or mean. She'd lavished money on them all their lives. Good education, capital sums to start them in jobs, handsome allowances to them all. Affection, kindness, benevolence."

"That's so, sir," agreed Superintendent Huish. "On the face of it there's no reason for anyone to want her out of the way. Of course—" He paused.

"Yes, Huish?"

"Mr. Argyle, I understand, is thinking of remarrying. He's marrying Miss Gwenda Vaughan, who's acted as his secretary over a good number of years."

"Yes," said Major Finney thoughtfully. "I suppose there's a motive there. One that we didn't know about at the time. She's been working for him for some years, you say. Think there was anything between them at the time of the murder?"

"I should rather doubt it, sir," said Superintendent Huish. "That sort of thing soon gets talked about in a village. I mean, I don't think there were any goings-on, as you might say. Nothing for Mrs. Argyle to find out about or cut up rough about."

"No," said the Chief Constable, "but he might have wanted to marry Gwenda Vaughan quite badly."

"She's an attractive young woman," said Superintendent Huish. "Not glamorous, I wouldn't say that, but good-looking and attractive in a nice kind of way."

"Probably been devoted to him for years," said Major Finney. "These women secretaries always seem to be in love with their boss."

"Well, we've got a motive of a kind for those two," said Huish. "Then there's the lady help, the Swedish woman. She mightn't really have been as fond of Mrs. Argyle as she appeared to be. There might have been slights or imagined slights; things she resented. She didn't benefit financially by the death because Mrs. Argyle had already bought her a very handsome annuity. She *seems* a nice, sensible kind of woman and not the sort you can imagine hitting anyone on the head with a poker! But you never know, do you? Look at the Lizzie Borden case."

"No," said the Chief Constable, "you never know. There's no question of an outsider of any kind?"

"No trace of one," said the superintendent. "The drawer where the money was was pulled out. A sort of attempt had been made to make the room look as though a burglar had been there, but it was a very amateurish effort. Sort of thing that fitted in perfectly with young Jacko having tried to create that particular effect."

"The odd thing to me," said the Chief Constable, "is the money."

"Yes," said Huish. "That's very difficult to understand. One of the fivers Jack Argyle had on him was definitely one that had been given to Mrs. Argyle at the bank that morning. Mrs. Bottleberry was the name written on the back of it. *He* said his mother had given the money to him, but both Mr. Argyle and Gwenda Vaughan are quite definite that Mrs. Argyle came into the library at a quarter to seven and told them about Jacko's demands for money and categorically said she'd refused to give him any."

"It's possible, of course," the Chief Constable pointed out, "with what we know now, that Argyle and the Vaughan girl might have been lying."

"Yes, that's possibility—or perhaps—" the superintendent broke off.

"Yes, Huish?" Finney encouraged him.

"Say someone—we'll call him or her X for the moment—overheard the quarrel and the threats that Jacko was making. Suppose someone saw an opportunity there. Got the money, ran after the boy, said that his mother after all wanted him to have it, thus paving the way to one of the prettiest little frame-ups ever. Careful to use the poker that he'd picked up to threaten her with, without smearing his fingerprints."

"Dammit all," said the Chief Constable angrily. "None of it seems to fit with what I know of the family. Who else was in the house that evening besides Argyle and Gwenda Vaughan, Hester Argyle and this Lindstrom woman?"

"The eldest married daughter, Mary Durrant, and her husband were staying there."

"He's a cripple, isn't he? That lets him out. What about Mary Durrant?"

"She's a very calm piece of goods, sir. You can't imagine her getting excited or—well, or killing anyone."

"The servants?" demanded the Chief Constable.

"All dailies, sir, and they'd gone home by six o'clock."

"Let me have a look at the times."

The Superintendent passed the paper to him.

"H'm . . . yes, I see. Quarter to seven Mrs. Argyle was in the library talking to her husband about Jacko's threats. Gwenda Vaughan was present during part of the conversation. Gwenda Vaughan went home just after seven. Hester Argyle saw her mother alive at about two or three minutes to seven. After that, Mrs. Argyle was not seen till half past seven, when her dead body was discovered by Miss Lindstrom. Between seven and half past there was plenty of opportunity. Hester could have killed her, Gwenda Vaughan could have killed her after she left the library and before she left the house. Miss Lindstrom could have killed her when she 'discovered the body,' Leo Argyle was alone in his library from ten past seven until Miss Lindstrom sounded the alarm. He could have gone to his wife's sitting-room and killed her any time during that twenty minutes. Mary Durrant, who was upstairs, could have come down during the half hour and killed her mother. And"—said Finney thoughtfully—"Mrs. Argyle herself could have let anyone in by the front door as we thought she let Jack Argyle in. Leo Argyle said, if you remember, that he *thought* he did hear a ring at the bell, and the sound of the front door opening and closing, but he was very vague about the time. We assumed that that was when Jacko returned and killed her."

"He needn't have rung the bell," said Huish. "He had a key of his own. They all had."

"There's another brother, isn't there?"

"Yes, Michael. Works as a car salesman in Drymouth."

"You'd better find out, I suppose," said the Chief Constable, "what he was doing that evening."

"After two years?" said Superintendent Huish. "Not likely anyone will remember, is it?"

"Was he asked at the time?"

"Out testing a customer's car, I understand. No reason for suspecting him then, but he had a key and he *could* have come over and killed her."

The Chief Constable sighed.

"I don't know how you're going to set about it, Huish. I don't know whether we're ever going to get anywhere."

"I'd like to know myself who killed her," said Huish. "From all I can make out, she was a fine type of woman. She'd done a lot for people. For unlucky children, for all sorts of charities. She's the sort of person that oughtn't to have been killed. Yes. I'd like to know. Even if we can never get enough evidence to satisfy the D.P.P. I'd still like to *know*."

"Well, I wish you the best of luck, Huish," said the Chief Constable. "Fortunately we've nothing very much on just now, but don't be discouraged if you can't get anywhere. It's a very cold trail. Yes, it's a very cold trail."

6

The lights went up in the cinema. Advertisements flashed on to the screen. The cinema usherettes walked round with cartons of lemonade and of ice-cream. Arthur Calgary scrutinised them. A plump girl with brown hair, a tall dark one and a small, fair-haired one. That was the one he had come to see. Jacko's wife. Jacko's widow, now the wife of a man called Joe Clegg. It was a pretty, rather vapid little face, plastered with make-up, eyebrows plucked, hair hideous and stiff in a cheap perm. Arthur Calgary bought an ice-cream carton from her. He had her home address and he meant to call there, but he had wanted to see her first while she was unaware of him. Well, that was that. Not the sort of daughter-in-law, he thought, that Mrs. Argyle, from all accounts, would have cared about very much. That, no doubt, was why Jacko had kept her dark.

He sighed, concealed the ice-cream carton carefully under his chair, and leaned back as the lights went out and a new picture began to flash on the screen. Presently he got up and left the cinema.

At eleven o'clock the next morning he called at the address he had been given. A sixteen-year-old boy opened the door, and in answer to Calgary's enquiry, said:

"Cleggs? Top floor."

Calgary climbed the stairs. He knocked at a door and Maureen Clegg opened it. Without her smart uniform and her make-up, she looked a different girl. It was a silly little face, good-natured but with nothing particularly interesting about it. She looked at him doubtfully, frowned suspiciously.

"My name is Calgary. I believe you have had a letter from Mr. Marshall about me."

Her face cleared.

"Oh, so you're the one! Come in, do." She moved back to let him enter. "Sorry the place is in such a mess. I haven't had time to get around to things yet." She swept some untidy clothes off a chair and pushed aside the remains of a breakfast consumed some time ago. "Do sit down. I'm sure it's ever so good of you to come."

"I felt it was the least I could do," said Calgary.

She gave a little embarrassed laugh, as though not really taking in what he meant.

"Mr. Marshall wrote me about it," she said. "About that story that Jackie made up—how it was all true after all. That someone *did* give him a lift back that night to Drymouth. So it was you, was it?"

"Yes," said Calgary. "It was I."

"I really can't get over it," said Maureen. "Talked about it half the night, Joe and I did. Really, I said, it might be something on the pictures. Two years ago, isn't it, or nearly?"

"About that, yes."

"Just the sort of thing you do see on the pictures, and of course you say to yourself that sort of thing's all nonsense, it wouldn't happen in real life. And now there it is! It does happen! It's really quite exciting in a way, isn't it?"

"I suppose," said Calgary, "that it might be thought of like that." He was watching her with a vague kind of pain.

She chattered on quite happily.

"There's poor old Jackie dead and not able to know about it. He got pneumonia, you know, in prison. I expect it was the damp or something, don't you?"

She had, Calgary realised, a definite romantic image of prison in her mind's eye. Damp underground cells with rats gnawing one's toes.

"At the time, I must say," she went on, "him dying seemed all for the best."

"Yes, I suppose so. . . . Yes, I suppose it must have done."

"Well, I mean, there he was, shut up for years and years and years. Joe said I'd better get a divorce and I was just setting about it."

"You wanted to divorce him?"

"Well, it's no good being tied to a man who's going to be in prison for years, is it? Besides, you know, although I was fond of Jackie and all that, he wasn't what you call the steady type. I never did think really that our marriage would last."

"Had you actually started proceedings for divorce when he died?"

"Well, I had in a kind of way. I mean, I'd been to a lawyer. Joe got me to go. Of course, Joe never could stand Jackie."

"Joe is your husband?"

"Yes. He works in the electricity. Got a very good job and they think a lot of him. He always told me Jackie was no good, but of course I was just a kid and silly then. Jackie had a great way with him, you know."

"So it seems from all I've heard about him."

"He was wonderful at getting round women—I don't know why, really. He wasn't good-looking or anything like that. Monkey-face, I used to call him. But all the same, he'd got a way with him. You'd find you were doing anything he wanted you to do. Mind you, it came in useful once or twice. Just after we were married he got into trouble at the garage where he was working over some work done on a customer's car. I never understood the rights of it. Anyway, the boss was ever so angry. But Jackie got round the boss's wife. Quite old, she was. Must have been near on fifty, but Jackie flattered her up, played her off this way and that until she didn't know whether she was on her head or her heels. She'd have done anything for him in the end. Got round her husband, she did, and got him to say as he wouldn't prosecute if Jackie paid the money back. But he never knew where the money came from! It was his own wife what provided it. That really gave us a laugh, Jackie and me!"

Calgary looked at her with faint repulsion. "Was it—so very funny?"

"Oh, I think so, don't you? Really, it was a scream. An old woman like that crazy about Jackie and raking out her savings for him."

Calgary sighed. Things were never, he thought, the way you imagined them to be. Every day he found himself less attracted to the man whose name he had taken such trouble to vindicate. He was almost coming to understand and share the point of view which had so astounded him at Sunny Point.

"I only came here, Mrs. Clegg," he said, "to see if there was anything I could—well, do for you to make up for what had happened."

Maureen Clegg looked faintly puzzled.

"Very nice of you, I'm sure," she said. "But why should you? We're all right. Joe is making good money and I've got my own job. I'm an usherette, you know, at the Picture-drome."

"Yes, I know."

"We're going to get a telly next month," the girl went on proudly.

"I'm very glad," said Arthur Calgary, "more glad than I can say that this—this unfortunate business hasn't left any—well, permanent shadow."

He was finding it more and more difficult to choose the right words when talking to this girl who had been married to Jacko. Everything he said sounded pompous, artificial. Why couldn't he talk naturally to her?

"I was afraid it might have been a terrible grief to you."

She stared at him, her wide, blue eyes not understanding in the least what he meant.

"It was horrid at the time," she said. "All the neighbours talking and the worry of it all, though I must say the police were very kind, all things considered. Talked to me very politely and spoke very nice about everything."

He wondered if she had had any feeling for the dead man. He asked her a question abruptly.

"Did you think he'd done it?" he said.

"Do you mean, do I think he'd done his mother in?"

"Yes. Just that."

"Well, of course—well—well—yes, I suppose I did in a way. Of course, he *said* he hadn't, but I mean you never could believe anything Jackie said, and it did seem as though he must have done. You see, he could get very nasty, Jackie could, if you stood up against him. I knew he was in a hole of some kind. He wouldn't say much to me, just swore at me when I asked him about it. But he went off that day and he said that it was going to be all right. His mother, he said, would stump up. She'd have to. So of course I believed him."

"He had never told his family about your marriage, I understand. You hadn't met them?"

"No. You see, they were classy people, had a big house and all that. I wouldn't have gone down very well. Jackie thought it best to keep me dark. Besides, he said if he took me along his mother'd want to run my life as well as his. She couldn't help running people, he said, and he'd had enough of it—we did very well as we were, he said."

She appeared to display no resentment, but to think, indeed, that her husband's behaviour had been natural.

"I suppose it was a great shock to you when he was arrested?"

"Well, naturally. However *could* he do such a thing? I said to myself, but then, you can't get away from things. He always had a very nasty temper when anything upset him."

Calgary leaned forward.

"Let's put it like this. It really seemed to you not at all a surprising thing that your husband should have hit his mother on the head with a poker and stolen a large quantity of money from her?"

"Well, Mr.—er—Calgary, if you'll excuse me, that's putting it in rather a nasty way. I don't suppose he meant to hit her so hard. Don't suppose he meant to do her in. She just refused to give him some money, he caught up the poker and he threatened her, and when she stuck it out he lost control of himself and gave her a swipe. I don't suppose he meant to kill her. That was just his bad luck. You see, he needed the money very badly. He'd have gone to prison if he hadn't got it."

"So—you don't blame him?"

"Well, of course I blamed him. . . . I don't like all that nasty violent behaviour. And your own mother, too! No, I don't think it was a nice thing to do at all. I began to think as Joe was right in telling me I oughtn't to have had anything to do with Jackie. But, you know how it is. It's ever so difficult for a girl to make up her mind. Joe, you see, was always the steady kind. I've known him a long time. Jackie was different. He'd got education and all that. He seemed very well off, too, always splashing his money about. And of course he had a way with him, as I've been telling you. He could get round anybody. He got round me all right. 'You'll regret it, my girl,' that's what Joe said. I thought that was just sour grapes and the green-eyed monster, if you understand what I mean. But Joe turned out to be quite right in the end."

Calgary looked at her. He wondered if she still failed to understand the full implications of his story.

"Right in exactly what way?" he asked.

"Well, landing me up in the proper mess he did. I mean, we've always been respectable. Mother brought us up very careful. We've always had things nice and no talk. And there was the police arresting my husband! And all the neighbours knowing. In all the papers it was. *News of the World* and all the rest of them. And ever so many reporters coming round and asking questions. It put me in a very nasty position."

"But, my dear child," said Arthur Calgary, "you do realise now that he didn't do it?"

For a moment the fair, pretty face looked bewildered.

"Of course! I was forgetting. But all the same—well, I mean, he did go there and kick up a fuss and threaten her and all that. If he hadn't done that he wouldn't have been arrested at all, would he?"

"No," said Calgary, "no. That is quite true."

Possibly, he thought, this pretty, silly child was more of a realist than he was.

"Oo, it was awful," went on Maureen. "I didn't know *what* to do. And then Mum said better go over right away and see his people. They'd have to do something for me, she said. After all, she said, you've got your rights and you'd best show them as you know how to look after them. So off I went. It was that foreign lady help what opened the door to me and at first I couldn't make her understand. Seemed as if she couldn't believe it. 'It's impossible,' she kept saying. 'It's quite impossible that Jacko should be married to *you*.' Hurt my feelings a bit that did. 'Well married we are,' I said, 'and not in a registry office neither. In a church.' It was the way my Mum wanted! And she said, 'It's not true. I don't believe it.' And then Mr. Argyle came and *he* was ever so kind. Told me not to worry more than I could help, and that everything possible would be done to defend Jackie. Asked me how I was off for money—and sent me a regular allowance every week. He keeps it up, too, even now. Joe doesn't like me taking it, but I say to him, 'Don't be silly. They can spare it, can't they?' Sent me a very nice cheque for a wedding present as well, he did, when Joe and I got married. And he said he was very glad and that he hoped this marriage would be happier than the last one. Yes, he's ever so nice, Mr. Argyle is."

She turned her head as the door opened.

"Oh. Here's Joe now."

Joe was a thin-lipped, fair-haired young man. He received Maureen's explanations and introduction with a slight frown.

"Hoped we'd done with all that," he said disapprovingly. "Excusing me for saying so, sir. But it does no good to go raking up the past. That's what I feel. Maureen was unlucky, that's all there is to say about it—"

"Yes," said Calgary. "I quite see your point of view."

"Of course," said Joe Clegg, "she ought never to have taken up with a chap like that. *I* knew he was no good. There'd been stories about him already. He'd been under a Probation Officer twice. Once they begin like that, they go on. First it's embezzling, or swindling women out of their savings and in the end it's murder."

"But this," said Calgary, "wasn't murder."

"So you say, sir," said Joe Clegg. He sounded himself completely unconvinced.

"Jack Argyle has a perfect alibi for the time the crime was committed. He was in my car being given a lift to Drymouth. So you see, Mr. Clegg, he could not possibly have committed this crime."

"Possibly not, sir," said Clegg. "But all the same it's a pity raking it all up, if you'll excuse me. After all, he's dead now, and it can't matter to him. And it starts the neighbours talking again and making them think things."

Calgary rose. "Well, perhaps from your point of view that is one way of looking at it. But there is such a thing as justice, you know, Mr. Clegg."

"I've always understood," said Clegg, "that an English trial was as fair a thing as can be."

"The finest system in the world can make a mistake," said Calgary. "Justice, is, after all, in the hands of men, and men are fallible."

After he had left them and was walking down the street he felt more disturbed in his own mind than he could have thought possible. Would it really have been better, he said to himself, if my memory of that day had never come back to me? After all, as that smug, tight-lipped fellow has just said, the boy is dead. He's gone before a judge who makes no mistake. Whether he's remembered as a murderer or merely as a petty thief, it can make no difference to him now.

Then a sudden wave of anger rose in him. "But it ought to make a difference to someone!" he thought. "*Someone* ought to be glad. Why aren't they? This girl, well, I can understand it well enough. She may have had an infatuation for Jacko, but she never loved him. Probably isn't capable of loving anybody. But the others. His father. His sister, his nurse . . . They should have been glad. They should have spared a thought for him before they began to fear for themselves. . . . Yes—someone should have cared."

II

"Miss Argyle? At the second desk there."

Calgary stood for a moment watching her.

Neat, small, very quiet and efficient. She was wearing a dark blue dress, with white collar and cuffs. Her blue-black hair was coiled neatly on her neck. Her skin was dark, darker than an English skin could ever be. Her bones, too, were smaller. This was the half caste child that Mrs. Argyle had taken as a daughter into the family.

The eyes that looked up and met his were dark, quite opaque. They were eyes that told you nothing.

Her voice was low and sympathetic.

"Can I help you?"

"You are Miss Argyle? Miss Christina Argyle?"

"Yes."

"My name is Calgary, Arthur Calgary. You may have heard—"

"Yes. I have heard about you. My father wrote to me."

"I would like very much to talk to you."

She glanced up at the clock.

"The library closes in half an hour. If you could wait until then?"

"Certainly. Perhaps you would come and have a cup of tea with me somewhere?"

"Thank you." She turned from him to a man who had come up behind him. "Yes. Can I help you?"

Arthur Calgary moved away. He wandered round, examining the contents of the shelves, observant all the time of Tina Argyle. She remained the same, calm, competent, unperturbed. The half hour passed slowly for him, but at last a bell rang and she nodded to him.

"I will meet you outside in a few minutes' time."

She did not keep him waiting. She wore no hat, merely a thick dark coat. He asked her where they should go.

"I do not know Redmyn very well," he explained.

"There is a tea place near the Cathedral. It is not good, but for that reason it is less full than the others."

Presently they were established at a small table, and a desiccated bored waitress had taken their order with a complete lack of enthusiasm.

"It will not be a good tea," said Tina apologetically, "but I thought that perhaps you would like to be reasonably private."

"That is so. I must explain my reasons for seeking you out. You see, I have met the other members of your family, including, I may say, your brother Jacko's wife—widow. You were the only member of the family I had not met. Oh yes, and there is your married sister, of course."

"You feel it necessary to meet us all?"

It was said quite politely—but there was a certain detachment about her voice which made Calgary a little uncomfortable.

"Hardly as a social necessity," he agreed dryly. "And it is not mere curiosity." (But wasn't it?) "It is just that I wanted to express, personally, to all of you, my very deep regret that I failed to establish your brother's innocence at the time of the trial."

"I see . . ."

"If you were fond of him—Were you fond of him?"

She considered a moment; then said:

"No. I was not fond of Jacko."

"Yet I hear from all sides that he had—great charm."

She said clearly, but without passion:

"I distrusted and disliked him."

"You never had—forgive me—any doubts that he had killed your mother?"

"It never occurred to me that there could be any other solution."

The waitress brought their tea. The bread and butter was stale, the jam a curious jellified substance, the cakes garish and unappetising. The tea was weak.

He sipped his and then said:

"It seems—I have been made to understand—that this information I have brought, which clears your brother of the charge of murder, may have repercussions that will not be so agreeable. It may bring fresh—anxieties to you all."

"Because the case will have to be reopened?"

"Yes. You have already thought about that?"

"My father seems to think it is inevitable."

"I am sorry. I am really sorry."

"Why are you sorry, Dr. Calgary?"

"I hate to be the cause of bringing fresh trouble upon you."

"But would you have been satisfied to remain silent?"

"You are thinking in terms of justice?"

"Yes. Weren't you?"

"Of course. Justice seemed to me to be very important. Now—I am beginning to wonder whether there are things that are more important."

"Such as?"

His thoughts flew to Hester.

"Such as—innocence, perhaps."

The opaqueness of her eyes increased.

"What do you feel, Miss Argyle?"

She was silent for a moment or two, then she said:

"I am thinking of those words in Magna Carta. *'To no man will we refuse justice.'* "

"I see," he said. "That is your answer. . . ."

7

Dr. MacMaster was an old man with bushy eyebrows, shrewd grey eyes and a pugnacious chin. He leaned back in his shabby arm-chair and studied his visitor carefully. He found that he liked what he saw.

On Calgary's side also there was a feeling of liking. For the first time almost, since he had come back to England, he felt that he was talking to someone who appreciated his own feelings and point of view.

"It's very good of you to see me, Dr. MacMaster," he said.

"Not at all," said the doctor. "I'm bored to death since I retired from practice. Young men of my own profession tell me I must sit here like a dummy taking care of my groggy heart, but don't think it comes natural to me. It doesn't. I listen to the wireless, blah—blah—blah—and occasionally my housekeeper persuades me to look at television, flick, flick, flick. I've been a busy man, run off my feet all my life. I don't take kindly to sitting still. Reading tires my eyes. So don't apologise for taking up my time."

"The first thing I've got to make you understand," said Calgary, "is why I'm still concerning myself over all this. Logically speaking, I suppose, I've done what I came to do—told the unpalatable fact of my concussion and loss of memory, vindicated the boy's character. After that, the only sane and logical thing to do would be to go away and try to forget about it all. Eh? Isn't that right?"

"Depends," said Dr. MacMaster. "Something worrying you?" he asked in the ensuing pause.

"Yes," said Calgary. "Everything worries me. You see, my news was not received as I thought it would be."

"Oh well," said Dr. MacMaster, "nothing odd in that. Happens every day. We rehearse a thing beforehand in our own minds, it doesn't matter what it is, consultation with another practitioner, proposal of marriage to a young lady, talk with your boy before going back to school—when the thing comes off, it never goes as you thought it would. You've thought it out, you see; all the things that *you* are going to say and you've usually made up your mind what the answers are going to be. And, of course, that's what throws you off every time. The answers never are what you think they will be. That's what's upset you, I suppose?"

"Yes," said Calgary.

"What did you expect? Expected them to be all over you?"

"I expected"—he considered a moment—"blame? Perhaps. Resentment? Very likely. But also thankfulness."

MacMaster grunted. "And there's no thankfulness, and not as much resentment as you think there ought to be?"

"Something like that," Calgary confessed.

"That's because you didn't know the circumstances until you got there. Why have you come to me, exactly?"

Calgary said slowly:

"Because I want to understand more about the family. I only know the acknowledged facts. A very fine and unselfish woman doing her best for her adopted children, a public-spirited woman, a fine character. Set against that, what's called, I believe, a problem child—a child that goes wrong. The young delinquent. That's all I know. I don't know anything else. I don't know anything about Mrs. Argyle herself."

"You're quite right," said MacMaster. "You're putting your finger on the thing that matters. If you think it over, you know, that's always the interesting part of any murder. What the person was like who was murdered. Everybody's always so busy enquiring into the mind of the murderer. You've been thinking, probably, that Mrs. Argyle was the sort of woman who shouldn't have been murdered."

"I should imagine that everyone felt that."

"Ethically," said MacMaster, "you're quite right. But you know"—he rubbed his nose—"isn't it the Chinese who held that beneficence is to be accounted a sin rather than a virtue? They've got something there, you know. Beneficence does things to people. Ties 'em up in knots. We all know what human nature's like. Do a chap a good turn and you feel kindly towards him. You like him. But the chap who's had the good turn done to him, does he feel so kindly to you? Does he really like you? He ought to, of course, but does he?

"Well," said the doctor, after a moment's pause. "There you are. Mrs. Argyle was what you might call a wonderful mother. But she overdid the beneficence. No doubt of that. Or wanted to. Or definitely tried to do so."

"They weren't her own children," Calgary pointed out.

"No," said MacMaster. "That's just where the trouble came in, I imagine. You've only got to look at any normal mother cat. She has her kittens, she's passionately protective of them, she'll scratch anyone who goes near them. And then, in a week or so, she starts resuming her own life. She goes out, hunts a bit, takes a rest from her young. She'll still protect them if anyone attacks them, but she is no longer obsessed by them, all the time. She'll play with them a bit; then when they're a bit too rough, she'll turn on them and give them a spank and tell them she wants to be let alone for a bit. She's reverting, you see, to nature. And as they grow up she cares less and less about them, and her thoughts go more and more to the attractive Toms in the neighbourhood. That's what you might call the normal pattern of female life. I've seen many girls and women, with strong maternal instincts, keen on getting married but mainly, though they mayn't quite know it themselves—because of their urge to motherhood. And the babies come; they're happy and satisfied. Life goes back into proportion for them. They can take an interest in their husbands and in the local affairs and in the gossip that's going round, and of course in their children. But it's all in proportion. The maternal instinct, in a purely physical sense, is satisfied, you see.

"Well, with Mrs. Argyle the maternal instinct was very strong, but the physical satisfaction of bearing a child or children, never came. And so her maternal obsession never really slackened. She wanted children, lots of children. She couldn't have enough of them. Her whole mind, night and day, was on those children. Her husband didn't count any more. He was just a pleasant abstraction in the background. No, everything was the children. Their feeding, their clothing, their playing, everything to do with them. Far too much was done for them. The thing she didn't give them and that they needed, was a little plain, honest-to-goodness neglect. They weren't just turned out into the garden to play like ordinary children in the country. No, they had to have every kind of gadget, artificial climbing things and stepping stones, a house built in the trees, sand brought and a little beach made on the river. Their food wasn't plain, ordinary food. Why, those kids even had their vegetables sieved, up to nearly five years old, *and* their milk sterilised and the water tested and their calories weighed and their vitamins computed! Mind you, I'm not being unprofessional in talking to you like this. Mrs. Argyle was never my patient. If she needed a doctor she went to one in Harley Street. Not that she often went. She was a very robust and healthy woman.

"But I was the local doctor who was called in to see the children, though she was inclined to think I was a bit casual over them. I told her to let 'em eat a few blackberries from the hedges. I told her it wouldn't hurt them to get their feet wet and have an occasional cold in the head, and that there's nothing much wrong with a child who's got a temperature of 99. No need to fuss till it's over 101. Those children were pampered and spoon-fed and fussed over and loved and in many ways it didn't do them any good."

"You mean," said Calgary, "it didn't do Jacko any good?"

"Well, I wasn't really only thinking of Jacko. Jacko to my mind was a liability from the start. The modern label for him is 'a crazy mixed-up kid.' It's just as good as any other label. The Argyles did their best for him; they did everything that could have been done. I've seen a good many Jackos in my lifetime. Later in life, when the boy has gone hopelessly wrong, the parents say, 'If only I'd been stricter with him when he was young,' or else they say, 'I was too harsh, if only I'd been kinder.' I don't think myself it amounts to a penn'orth of difference. There are those who go wrong because they've had an unhappy home and essentially feel unloved. And again there are those who go wrong because at the least stress they're going to go wrong anyway. I put Jacko down as one of the latter."

"So you weren't surprised," said Calgary, "when he was arrested for murder?"

"Frankly, yes, I was surprised. Not because the idea of murder would have been particularly repugnant to Jacko. He was the sort of young man who is conscienceless. But the *kind* of murder he'd done did surprise me. Oh, I know he had a violent temper and all that. As a child he often hurled himself on another child or hit him with some heavy toy or bit of wood. But it was usually a child smaller than himself, and it was usually not so much blind rage as the wish to hurt or get hold of something that he himself wanted. The kind of murder I'd have expected Jacko to do, if he did one, was the type where a couple of boys go out on a raid; then, when the police come after them, the Jackos say 'Biff him on the head, bud. Let him have it. Shoot him down.' They're willing for murder, ready to incite to murder, but they've not got the nerve to do murder themselves with their own hands. That's what I should have said. Now it seems," added the doctor, "I would have been right."

Calgary stared down at the carpet, a worn carpet with hardly any of its pattern remaining.

"I didn't know," he said, "what I was up against. I didn't realise what it was going to mean to the others. I didn't see that it might—that it must—"

The doctor was nodding gently.

"Yes," he said. "It looks that way, doesn't it? It looks as though you've got to put it right there amongst them."

"I think," said Calgary, "that that's really what I came to talk to you about. There doesn't seem, on the face of it, any real motive for any of them to have killed her."

"Not on the face of it," agreed the doctor. "But if you go a little behind the face of it—oh, yes, I think there's plenty of reason why someone might have wanted to kill her."

"Why?" asked Calgary.

"You feel it's really your business, do you?"

"I think so. I can't help feeling so."

"Perhaps I should feel the same in your place . . . I don't know. Well, what I'd say is that none of them really belonged to themselves. Not so long as their mother—I'll call her that for convenience—was alive. She had a good hold of them still, you know, all of them."

"In what way?"

"Financially she'd provided for them. Provided for them handsomely. There was a large income. It was divided between them in such proportions as the Trustees thought fit. But although Mrs. Argyle herself was not one of the Trustees, nevertheless her wishes, so long as she was alive, were operative." He paused a minute and then went on.

"It's interesting in a way, how they all tried to escape. How they fought not to conform to the pattern that she'd arranged for them. Because she did arrange a pattern, and a very good pattern. She wanted to give them a good home, a good education, a good allowance and a good start in the professions that she chose for them. She wanted to treat them exactly as though they were hers and Leo Argyle's own children. Only of course they weren't hers and Leo Argyle's own children. They had entirely different instincts, feelings, aptitudes and demands. Young Micky now works as a car salesman. Hester more or less ran away from home to go on the stage. She fell in love with a very undesirable type and was absolutely no good as an actress. She had to come home. She had to admit—and she didn't like admitting—that her mother had been right. Mary Durrant insisted on marrying a man during the war whom her mother warned her not to marry. He was a brave and intelligent young man but an absolute fool when it came to business matters. Then he got polio. He was brought as a convalescent to Sunny Point. Mrs. Argyle was putting pressure on them to live there permanently. The husband was quite willing. Mary Durrant was holding out desperately against it. She wanted her home and her husband to herself. But she'd have given in, no doubt, if her mother hadn't died.

"Micky, the other boy, has always been a young man with a chip on his shoulder; he resented bitterly being abandoned by his own mother. He resented it as a child and he never got over it. I think, at heart, he always hated his adopted mother.

"Then there's the Swedish masseuse woman. She didn't like Mrs. Argyle. She was fond of the children and she's fond of Leo. She accepted many benefits from Mrs. Argyle and probably tried to be grateful but couldn't manage it. Still, I hardly think that her feelings of dislike could cause her to hit her benefactor on the head with a poker. After all, *she* could leave at any moment she liked. As for Leo Argyle—"

"Yes. What about him?"

"He's going to marry again," said Dr. MacMaster, "and good luck to him. A very nice young woman. Warmhearted, kind, good company and very much in love with him. Has been for a long time. What did *she* feel about Mrs. Argyle? You can probably guess just as well as I can. Naturally, Mrs. Argyle's death simplified things a good deal. Leo Argyle's not the type of man to have an affair with his secretary with his wife in the same house. I don't really think he'd have left his wife, either."

Calgary said slowly:

"I saw them both; I talked to them. I can't really believe that either of them—"

"I know," said MacMaster. "One can't believe, can one? And yet—one of that household did it, you know."

"You really think so?"

"I don't see what else there is to think. The police are fairly sure that it wasn't the work of an outsider, and the police are probably right."

"But which of them?" said Calgary.

MacMasters shrugged his shoulders. "One simply doesn't know."

"You've no idea yourself from your knowledge of them all?"

"Shouldn't tell you if I had," said MacMaster. "After all, what have I got to go on? Unless there's some factor that I've missed none of them seems a likely murderer to me. And yet—I can't rule any one of them out as a possibility. No," he added slowly, "my view is that we shall never know. The police will make enquiries and all that sort of thing. They'll do their best, but to get evidence after this time and with so little to go upon—" He shook his head. "No, I don't think that the truth will ever be known. There are cases like that, you know. One reads about them. Fifty—a hundred years ago, cases where one of three or four or five people must have done it but there wasn't enough evidence and no one's ever been able to say."

"Do you think it's going to be like that here?"

"We-ll," said Dr. MacMaster, "yes, I do. . . ." Again he cast a shrewd look at Calgary. "And that's what's so terrible, isn't it?" he said.

"Terrible," said Calgary, "because of the innocent. That's what she said to me."

"Who? Who said what to you?"

"The girl—Hester. She said I didn't understand that it was the innocent who mattered. It's what you've just been saying to me. That we shall never know—"

"—who is innocent?" The doctor finished for him. "Yes, if we could only know the truth. Even if it doesn't come to an arrest or trial or conviction. Just to *know*. Because otherwise—" He paused.

"Yes?" said Calgary.

"Work it out for yourself," said Dr. MacMaster. "No—I don't need to say that—you already have."

He went on:

"It reminds me, you know, of the Bravo Case—nearly a hundred years ago now, I suppose, but books are still being written about it; making out a perfectly good case for his wife having done it, or Mrs. Cox having done it, or Dr. Gully—or even for Charles Bravo having taken the poison in spite of the Coroner's verdict. All quite plausible theories—but no one now can ever know the truth. And so Florence Bravo, abandoned by her family, died alone of drink, and Mrs. Cox, ostracised, and with three little boys, lived to be an old woman with most of the people she knew believing her to be a murderess, and Dr. Gully was ruined professionally and socially—

"Someone was guilty—and got away with it. But the others were innocent—and didn't get away with anything.

"That mustn't happen here," said Calgary. "It mustn't!"

8

Hester Argyle was looking at herself in the glass. There was little vanity in her gaze. It was more an anxious questioning with behind it the humility of one who has never really been sure of herself. She pushed up her hair from her forehead, pulled it to one side and frowned at the result. Then, as a face appeared behind hers in the mirror, she started, flinched and swung round apprehensively.

"Ah," said Kirsten Lindstrom, "you are afraid!"

"What do you mean, afraid, Kirsty?"

"You are afraid of me. You think that I come up behind you quietly and that perhaps I shall strike you down."

"Oh, Kirsty, don't be so foolish. Of course I wouldn't think anything like that."

"But you did think it," said the other. "And you are right, too, to think such things. To look at the shadows, to start when you see something that you do not quite understand. Because there is something here in this house to be afraid of. We know that now."

"At any rate, Kirsty darling," said Hester, "I needn't be afraid of *you*."

"How do you know?" said Kirsten Lindstrom. "Did I not read in the paper a short while back of a woman who had lived with another woman for years, and then one day suddenly she kills her. Suffocates her. Tries to scratch her eyes out. And why? Because, she tells the police very gently, for some time she has seen that the devil is inhabiting the woman. She has seen the devil looking out of the other woman's eyes and she knows that she must be strong and brave and kill the devil!"

"Oh, well, I remember *that*," said Hester. "But that woman was mad."

"Ah," said Kirsten. "But she did not know herself that she was mad. And she did not seem mad to those round her, because no one knew what was going on in her poor, twisted mind. And so I say to you, you do not know what is going on in *my* mind. Perhaps *I* am mad. Perhaps I looked one day at your mother and thought that she was Anti-Christ and that I would kill her."

"But, Kirsty, that's nonsense! Absolute nonsense."

Kirsten Lindstrom sighed and sat down.

"Yes," she admitted, "it is nonsense. I was very fond of your mother. She was good to me, always. But what I am trying to say to you, Hester, and what you have got to understand and believe, is that you cannot say 'nonsense' to anything or anyone. You cannot trust me or anybody else."

Hester turned round and looked at the other woman.

"I really believe you're serious," she said.

"I am very serious," said Kirsten. "We must all be serious and we must bring things out into the open. It is no good pretending that nothing has happened. That man who came here—I wish he had not come, but he did, and now he has made it, I understand, quite plain that Jacko was not a murderer. Very well then, someone else is a murderer, and that someone else must be one of us."

"No, Kirsty, no. It could have been someone who—"

"Who what?"

"Well, who wanted to steal something, or who had a grudge against Mother for some reason in the past."

"You think your mother would let that someone in?"

"She might," said Hester. "You know what she was like. If somebody came with a hard luck story, if someone came to tell her about some child that was being neglected or ill-treated. Don't you think Mother would have let that person in and taken them to her room and listened to what they had to say?"

"It seems to me very unlikely," said Kirsten. "At least it seems to me unlikely that your mother would sit down at a table and let that person pick up a poker and hit her on the back of the head. No, she was at her ease, confident, with someone she knew in the room."

"I wish you wouldn't, Kirsty," cried Hester. "Oh, I wish you wouldn't. You're bringing it so near, so close."

"Because it *is* near, it *is* close. No, I will not say any more now, but I have warned you that though you think you know someone well, though you may think you trust them, you cannot be sure. So be on your guard. Be on your guard against me and against Mary and against your father and against Gwenda Vaughan."

"How can I go on living here and suspecting everybody?"

"If you will take my advice it will be better for you to leave this house."

"I can't just now."

"Why not? Because of the young doctor?"

"I don't know what you mean, Kirsty." Colour flamed up in Hester's cheeks.

"I mean Dr. Craig. He is a very nice young man. A sufficiently good doctor, amiable, conscientious. You could do worse. But all the same I think it would be better if you left here and went away."

"The whole thing's nonsense," Hester cried angrily, "nonsense, nonsense, nonsense. Oh, how I wish Dr. Calgary had never come here."

"So do I," said Kirsten, "with all my heart."

II

Leo Argyle signed the last of the letters which Gwenda Vaughan placed in front of him.

"Is that the last?" he asked.

"Yes."

"We've not done too badly today."

After a minute or two when Gwenda had stamped and stacked the letters, she asked:

"Isn't it about time that you—took that trip abroad?"

"Trip abroad?"

Leo Argyle sounded very vague. Gwenda said:

"Yes. Don't you remember you were going to Rome and to Sienna."

"Oh, yes, yes, so I was."

"You were going to see those documents from the archives that Cardinal Massilini wrote to you about."

"Yes, I remember."

"Would you like me to make the reservations by air, or would you rather go by train?"

As though coming back from a long way away, Leo looked at her and smiled faintly.

"You seem very anxious to get rid of me, Gwenda," he said.

"Oh no, darling, oh no."

She came quickly across and knelt down by his side.

"I never want you to leave me, never. But—but I think—oh, I think it would be better if you went away from here after—after . . ."

"After last week?" said Leo. "After Dr. Calgary's visit?"

"I wish he hadn't come here," said Gwenda. "I wish things could have been left as they were."

"With Jacko unjustly condemned for something he didn't do?"

"He might have done it," said Gwenda. "He might have done it any time, and it's a pure accident, I think, that he didn't do it."

"It's odd," said Leo, thoughtfully. "I never really could believe he did do it. I mean, of course, I had to give in to the evidence—but it seemed to me so unlikely."

"Why? He always had a terrible temper, didn't he?"

"Yes. Oh, yes. He attacked other children. Usually children rather smaller than himself. I never really felt that he would have attacked Rachel."

"Why not?"

"Because he was afraid of her," said Leo. "She had great authority, you know. Jacko felt it just like everybody else."

"But don't you think," said Gwenda, "that that was just why—I mean—" She paused.

Leo looked at her questioningly. Something in his glance made the colour come up into her cheeks. She turned away, went over to the fire and knelt down in front of it with her hands to the blaze. "Yes," she thought to herself, "Rachel had authority all right. So pleased with herself, so sure of herself, so much the queen bee bossing us all. Isn't that enough to make one want to take a poker, to make one want to strike her down, to silence her once and for all? Rachel was always right, Rachel always knew best, Rachel always got her own way."

She got up abruptly.

"Leo," she said. "Couldn't we—couldn't we be married quite soon instead of waiting until March?"

Leo looked at her. He was silent for a moment, and then he said:

"No, Gwenda, no. I don't think that would be a good plan."

"Why not?"

"I think," said Leo, "it would be a pity to rush into anything."

"What do you mean?"

She came across to him. She knelt down again beside him.

"Leo, what *do* you mean? You must tell me."

He said:

"My dear, I just think that we mustn't, as I said, rush into anything."

"But we *will* be married in March, as we planned?"

"I hope so . . . Yes, I hope so."

"You don't speak as though you were sure. . . . Leo, don't you care any more?"

"Oh, my dear," his hands rested on her shoulders, "of course I care. You mean everything in the world to me."

"Well, then," said Gwenda impatiently.

"No." He got up. "No. Not yet. We must wait. We must be sure."

"Sure of what?"

He did not answer. She said:

"You don't think—you can't think—"

Leo said: "I—I don't think anything."

The door opened and Kirsten Lindstrom came in with a tray which she put down on the desk.

"Here is your tea, Mr. Argyle. Shall I bring another cup for you, Gwenda, or will you join the others downstairs?"

Gwenda said:

"I will come down to the dining-room. I'll take these letters. They ought to go off."

With slightly unsteady hands she picked up the letters Leo had just signed and went out of the room carrying them. Kirsten Lindstrom looked after her, then she looked back at Leo.

"What have you said to her?" she demanded. "What have you done to upset her?"

"Nothing," said Leo. His voice was tired. "Nothing at all."

Kirsten Lindstrom shrugged her shoulders. Then, without another word, she went out of the room. Her unseen, unspoken criticism, however, could be felt. Leo sighed, leaning back in his chair. He felt very tired. He poured out his tea but he did not drink it. Instead, he sat there in his chair staring unseeingly across the room, his mind busy in the past.

The social club he had been interested in in the East End of London. . . . It was there that he had first met Rachel Konstam. He could see her now clearly in his mind's eye. A girl of medium height, stocky in build, wearing what he had not appreciated at the time were very expensive clothes, but wearing them with a dowdy air. A round-faced girl, serious, warm-hearted, with an eagerness and a naïveté which had appealed to him. So much that needed doing, so much that was worth doing! She had poured out words eagerly, rather incoherently, and his heart had warmed to her. For he, too, had felt that there was much that needed doing, much that was worth doing; though he himself had a gift of natural irony that made him doubtful whether work worth doing was always as successful as it ought to be. But Rachel had had no doubts. If you did this, if you did that, if such and such an institution were endowed, the beneficial results would follow automatically.

She had never allowed, he saw now, for human nature. She had seen people always as cases, as problems to be dealt with. She had never seen that each human being was different, would react differently, had its own peculiar idiosyncrasies. He had said to her then, he remembered, not to expect too much. But she had always expected too much, although she had immediately disclaimed his accusation. She had always expected too much, and so always she had been disappointed. He had fallen in love with her quite quickly, and had been agreeably surprised to find out that she was the daughter of wealthy parents.

They had planned their life together on a basis of high thinking and not precisely plain living. But he could see now clearly what it was that had principally attracted him to her. It was her warmth of heart. Only, and there was the tragedy, that warmth of heart had not really been for him. She had been in love with him, yes. But what she had really wanted from him and from life was children. And the children had not come.

They had visited doctors, reputable doctors, disreputable doctors, even quacks, and the verdict in the end had been one she was forced to accept. She would never have children of her own. He had been sorry for her, very sorry, and he had acquiesced quite willingly in her suggestion that they should adopt a child. They were already in touch with adoption societies when on the occasion of a visit to New York their car had knocked down a child running out from a tenement in the poorer quarter of the city.

Rachel had jumped out and knelt down in the street by the child who was only bruised, not hurt; a beautiful child, golden-haired and blue-eyed. Rachel had insisted on taking her to hospital to make sure there was no injury. She'd interviewed the child's relations; a slatternly aunt and the aunt's husband who obviously drank. It was clear that they had no feeling for the child they had taken in to live with them since her own parents were dead. Rachel had suggested that the child should come and stay with them for a few days, and the woman had agreed with alacrity.

"Can't look after her properly here," she'd said.

So Mary had been taken back to their suite at the hotel. The child had obviously enjoyed the soft bed and the luxurious bathroom. Rachel had bought her new clothes. Then the moment had come when the child had said:

"I don't want to go home. I want to stay here with you."

Rachel had looked at him, looked at him with a sudden passion of longing and delight. She had said to him as soon as they were alone:

"Let's keep her. It'll easily be arranged. We'll adopt her. She'll be our own child. That woman'll be only too pleased to be rid of her."

He had agreed easily enough. The child seemed quiet, well-behaved, docile. She'd obviously no feeling for the aunt and uncle with whom she lived. If this would make Rachel happy, they'd go ahead. Lawyers were consulted, papers were signed and henceforth Mary O'Shaughnessy was known as Mary Argyle, and sailed with them for Europe. He had thought that at last poor Rachel would be happy. And she had been happy. Happy in an excited, almost feverish kind of way, doting on Mary, giving her every kind of expensive toy. And Mary had accepted placidly, sweetly. And yet, Leo thought, there had always been something that disturbed him a little. The child's easy acquiescence. Her lack of any kind of home-sickness for her own place and people. True affection, he hoped, would come later. He could see no real signs of it now. Acceptance of benefits, complacence, enjoyment of all that was provided. But of love for her new adopted mother? No, he had not seen that.

It was from that time onwards, Leo thought, that he had somehow managed to slip to the background of Rachel Argyle's life. She was a woman who was by nature a mother, not a wife. Now with the acquiring of Mary, it was as though her maternal longings were not so much fulfilled as stimulated. One child was not enough for her.

All her enterprises from now on were connected with children. Her interest lay in orphanages, in endowments for crippled children, in cases of backward children, spastics, orthopaedics—always children. It was admirable. He felt all along that it was very admirable, but it had become the centre of her life. Little by little he began to indulge in his own activities. He began to go more deeply into the historical background of economics, which had always interested him. He withdrew more and more into his library. He engaged in research, in the writing of short, well-phrased monographs. His wife, busy, earnest, happy, ran the house and increased her activities. He was courteous and acquiescent. He encouraged her. "That is a very fine project, my dear." "Yes, yes, I should certainly go ahead with that." Occasionally a word of caution was slipped in. "You want, I think, to examine the position very thoroughly before you commit yourself. You mustn't be carried away."

She continued to consult him, but sometimes now it was almost perfunctory. As time went on she was more and more an authoritarian. She knew what was right, she knew what was best. Courteously he withdrew his criticism and his occasional admonitions.

Rachel, he thought, needed no help from him, needed no love from him. She was busy, happy, terrifically energetic.

Behind the hurt that he could not help feeling, there was also, queerly enough, a sense of pity for her. It was as though he knew that the path she was pursuing might be a perilous one.

On the outbreak of war in 1939, Mrs. Argyle's activities were immediately redoubled. Once she had the idea of opening a war nursery for children from the London slums, she was in touch with many influential people in London. The Ministry of Health was quite willing to co-operate and she had looked for and found a suitable house for her purpose. A newly built, up-to-date, house in a remote part of England likely to be free from bombing. There she could accommodate up to eighteen children between the ages of two and seven. The children came not only from poor homes but also from unfortunate ones. They were orphans, or illegitimate children whose mothers had no intention of being evacuated with them and who were bored with looking after them. Children from homes where they had been ill-treated and neglected. Three or four of the children were cripples. For orthopaedic treatment she engaged as well as a staff of domestic workers, a Swedish masseuse and two fully trained hospital nurses. The whole thing was done not only on a comfortable but on a luxurious basis. Once he remonstrated with her.

"You mustn't forget, Rachel, these children will have to go back to the background from which we took them. You mustn't make it too difficult for them."

She had replied warmly:

"Nothing's too good for these poor mites. Nothing!"

He had urged, "Yes, but they've got to go *back*, remember."

But she had waved that aside. "It mayn't be necessary. It may—we'll have to see in the future."

The exigencies of war had soon brought changes. The hospital nurses, restive at looking after perfectly healthy children when there was real nursing to be done, had frequently to be replaced. In the end one elderly hospital nurse and Kirsten Lindstrom were the only two left. The domestic help failed and Kirsten Lindstrom had come to the rescue there also. She had worked with great devotion and selflessness.

And Rachel Argyle had been busy and happy. There had been, Leo remembered, moments of occasional bewilderment. The day when Rachel, puzzled at the way one small boy, Micky, was slowly losing weight, his appetite failing, had called in the doctor. The doctor could find nothing wrong but had suggested to Mrs. Argyle that the child might be homesick. Quickly she'd rebuffed the idea.

"That's impossible! You don't know the home he has come from. He was knocked about, ill-treated. It must have been hell for him."

"All the same," Dr. MacMaster had said, "all the same, I shouldn't be surprised. The thing is to get him to talk."

And one day Micky had talked. Sobbing in his bed, he cried out, pushing Rachel away with his fists:

"I want to go home. I want to go home to our Mom and our Ernie."

Rachel was upset, almost incredulous.

"He *can't* want his mother. She didn't care tuppence for him. She knocked him about whenever she was drunk."

And he had said gently: "But you're up against nature, Rachel. She is his mother and he loves her."

"She was no kind of a mother!"

"He is her own flesh and blood. That's what he feels. That's what nothing can replace."

And she had answered: "But by now, surely he ought to look on *me* as his mother."

Poor Rachel, thought Leo. Poor Rachel, who could buy so many things.

. . . Not selfish things, not things for herself; who could give to unwanted children love, care, a home. All these things she could buy for them, but not their love for her.

Then the war had ended. The children had begun to drift back to London, claimed by parents or relatives. But not all of them. Some of them had remained unwanted and it was then that Rachel had said:

"You know, Leo, they're like our own children now. This is the moment when we can have a real family of our own. Four—five of these children can stay with us. We'll adopt them, provide for them and they'll really *be* our children."

He had felt a vague uneasiness, why he did not quite know. It was not that he objected to the children, but he had felt instinctively the falseness of it. The assumption that it was easy to make a family of one's own by artificial means.

"Don't you think," he had said, "that it's rather a risk?"

But she had replied:

"A risk? What does it matter if it is a risk? It's worth doing."

Yes, he supposed it was worth doing, only he was not quite as sure as she was. By now he had grown so far away, so aloof in some cold misty region of his own, that it was not in him to object. He said as he had said so many times:

"You must do as you please, Rachel."

She had been full of triumph, full of happiness, making her plans, consulting solicitors, going about things in her usual business-like way. And so she had acquired her family. Mary, that eldest child brought from New York; Micky, the homesick boy who had cried himself to sleep for so many nights, longing for his slum home and his negligent, bad-tempered mother; Tina, the graceful dark half-caste child whose mother was a prostitute and whose father had been a Lascar seaman. Hester, whose young Irish mother had borne an illegitimate child and who wanted to start life again. And Jacko, the engaging, monkey-faced little boy whose antics made them all laugh, who could always talk himself out of punishment, and charm extra sweets even from that disciplinarian, Miss Lindstrom. Jacko, whose father was serving a prison sentence and whose mother had gone off with some other man.

Yes, Leo thought, surely it was a worth-while job to take these children, to give them the benefits of a home and love and a father and mother. Rachel, he thought, had had a right to be triumphant. Only it hadn't worked out quite the way it was supposed to do. . . . For these children were not the children that he and Rachel would have had. Within them ran none of the blood of Rachel's hard-working thrifty forebears, none of the drive and ambition by which the less reputable members of her family had gained their assured place in society, none of the vague kindliness and integrity of mind that he remembered in his own father and grandfather and grandmother. None of the intellectual brilliance of his grandparents on the other side.

Everything that environment could do was done for them. It could do a great deal, but it could not do everything. There had been those seeds of weakness which had brought them to the nursery in the first place, and under stress those seeds might bear flower. That was exemplified very fully in Jacko. Jacko, the charming, agile Jacko, with his merry quips, his charm, his easy habit of twisting everyone round his finger, was essentially of a delinquent type. It showed very early in childish thieving, in lies; all things that were put down to his original bad upbringing. Things that could be, Rachel said, easily ironed out. But they never did get ironed out.

His record at school was bad. He was sent down from the university and from then it was a long series of painful incidents where he and Rachel, doing the best they could, tried to give the boy assurance of their love and their confidence, tried to find work that would be congenial to him where he could hope for success if he applied himself. Perhaps, Leo thought, they had been too soft with him. But no. Soft or hard, in Jacko's case, he thought the end would have been the same. What he wanted he must have. If he could not get it by any legitimate means he was quite willing to get it by any other means. He was not clever enough to be successful in crime, even petty crime. And so it had come to that last day when he had arrived broke, in fear of prison, angrily demanding money as his right, threatening. He had gone away, shouting out that he was coming back and that she had better have the money ready for him—*Or else!*

And so—Rachel had died. How remote all the past seemed to him. All those long years of the war with the boys and girls growing up. And he himself? Also remote, colourless. It was as though that robust energy and zest for life that was Rachel had eaten into him, leaving him limp and exhausted, needing, oh so badly, warmth and love.

Even now he could hardly remember when he had first become aware how close these things were to him. Close at hand . . . Not proffered to him, but there.

Gwenda. . . . The perfect, helpful secretary, working for him, always at hand, kind, helpful. There was something about her that had reminded him of what Rachel had been when he first met her. The same warmth, the same enthusiasm, the same warm-heartedness. Only in Gwenda's case, that warmth, that warm-heartedness, that enthusiasm were all for *him*. Not for the hypothetical children that she might one day have, just for him. It had been like warming one's hands at a fire. . . . Hands that were cold and stiff with disuse. When had he first realized that she cared for him? It was difficult to say. It had not been any sudden revelation.

But suddenly—one day—he had known that he loved her.

And that as long as Rachel lived they could never marry.

Leo sighed, sat up in his chair and drank his stone-cold tea.

9

Calgary had only been gone a few minutes when Dr. MacMaster received a second visitor. This one was well known to him and he greeted him with affection.

"Ah, Don, glad to see you. Come in and tell me what's on your mind. There is something on your mind. I always know when your forehead wrinkles in that peculiar way."

Dr. Donald Craig smiled at him ruefully. He was a good-looking serious young man who took himself and his work in a serious manner. The old retired doctor was very fond of his young successor though there were times when he wished that it was easier for Donald Craig to see a joke.

Craig refused the offer of a drink and came straight to the point.

"I'm badly worried, Mac."

"Not more vitamin deficiencies, I hope," said Dr. MacMaster. From his point of view vitamin deficiency had been a good joke. It had once taken a veterinary surgeon to point out to young Craig that the cat belonging to a certain child patient was suffering with an advanced case of ring-worm.

"It's nothing to do with the patients," said Donald Craig. "It's my own private affairs."

MacMaster's face changed immediately.

"I'm sorry, my boy. Very sorry. Have you had bad news?"

The young man shook his head.

"It's not that. It's—look here, Mac, I've got to talk to someone about it and you know them all, you've been here for years, you know all about them. And I've got to know too. I've got to know where I stand, what I'm up against."

MacMaster's bushy eyebrows rose slowly up his forehead.

"Let's hear the trouble," he said.

"It's the Argyles. You know—I suppose everyone knows—that Hester Argyle and I—"

The old doctor nodded his head.

"A nice little understanding," he said approvingly. "That's the old-fashioned term they used to use, and it was a very good one."

"I'm terribly in love with her," Donald said simply, "and I think—oh, I'm sure—that she cares too. And now all this happens."

A look of enlightenment came into the older doctor's face.

"Ah yes! Free pardon for Jacko Argyle," he said. "A free pardon that's come too late for him."

"Yes. That's just what makes me feel—I know it's an entirely wrong thing to feel, but I can't help it—that it would have been better if—if this new evidence hadn't come to light."

"Oh, you're not the only one who seems to feel that," said MacMaster. "It's felt, as far as I can find out, from the Chief Constable through the Argyle family down to the man who came back from the Antarctic and supplied the evidence." He added: "He's been here this afternoon."

Donald Craig looked startled.

"Has he? Did he say anything?"

"What did you expect him to say?"

"Did he have any idea of who—"

Slowly Dr. MacMaster shook his head.

"No," he said. "He's no idea. How could he have—coming out of the blue and seeing them all for the first time? It seems," he went on, "that nobody has any idea."

"No. No, I suppose not."

"What's upset you so much, Don?"

Donald Craig drew a deep breath.

"Hester rang me up that evening when this fellow Calgary had been there. She and I were going in to Drymouth after the surgery to hear a lecture on criminal types in Shakespeare."

"Sounds particularly suitable," said MacMaster.

"And then she rang me up. Said she wouldn't be coming. Said there had been news of a peculiar upsetting type."

"Ah. Dr. Calgary's news."

"Yes. Yes, although she didn't mention him at the time. But she was very upset. She sounded—I can't explain to you how she sounded."

"Irish blood," said MacMaster.

"She sounded altogether stricken, terrified. Oh, I can't explain it."

"Well, what do you expect?" the doctor asked. "She's not yet twenty, is she?"

"But *why* is she so upset? I tell you, Mac, she's scared stiff of something."

"M'm, yes, well—yes, that might be so, I suppose," said MacMaster.

"Do you think—what do you think?"

"It's more to the point," MacMaster pointed out, "what you are thinking."

The young man said bitterly:

"I suppose, if I wasn't a doctor, I shouldn't even begin to think of such things. She'd be my girl and my girl could do no wrong. But as it is—"

"Yes—come on. You'd better get it off your chest."

"You see, I know something of what goes on in Hester's mind. She—she's a victim of early insecurity."

"Quite so," said MacMaster. "That's the way we put it nowadays."

"She hasn't had time yet to get properly integrated. She was suffering, at the time of the murder, from a perfectly natural feeling of an adolescent young woman—resentment of authority—an attempt to escape from smother-love which is responsible for so much harm nowadays. She wanted to rebel, to get away. She's told me all this herself. She ran away and joined a fourth-class touring theatrical company. Under the circumstances I think her mother behaved very reasonably. She suggested that Hester should go to London and go to RADA and study acting properly if she wanted to do so. But that wasn't what Hester wanted to do. This running away to act was just a gesture really. She didn't really want to train for the stage, or to take up the profession seriously. She just wanted to show she could be on her own. Anyway, the Argyles didn't try to coerce her. They gave her a quite handsome allowance."

"Which was very clever of them," said MacMaster.

"And then she had this silly love affair with a middle-aged member of the company. In the end she realised for herself that he was no good. Mrs. Argyle came along and dealt with him and Hester came home."

"Having learnt her lesson, as they used to say in my young days," said MacMaster. "But of course one never liked learning one's lesson. Hester didn't."

Donald Craig went on anxiously:

"She was full, still, of pent-up resentment; all the worse because she had to acknowledge secretly, if not openly, that her mother had been perfectly right; that she was no good as an actress and that the man she had lavished her affections on wasn't worth it. And that, anyway, she didn't really care for him. 'Mother knows best.' It's always galling to the young."

"Yes," said MacMaster. "That was one of poor Mrs. Argyle's troubles, though she'd never have thought of it like that. The fact was she *was* nearly always right, that she *did* know best. If she'd been one of those women who run into debt, lose their keys, miss trains, and do foolish actions that other people have to help them out of, her entire family would have been much fonder of her. Sad and cruel, but there's life for you. And she wasn't a clever enough woman to get her own way by guile. She was complacent, you know. Pleased with her own power and judgment and quite, quite sure of herself. That's a very difficult thing to come up against when you're young."

"Oh, I know," said Donald Craig. "I realise all that. It's because I realise it so well that I feel—that I wonder—" He stopped.

MacMaster said gently:

"I'd better say it for you, hadn't I, Don? You're afraid that it was your Hester who heard the quarrel between her mother and Jacko, who got worked up by hearing it, perhaps, and who, in a fit of rebellion against authority, and against her mother's superior assumption of omniscience, went into that room, picked up the poker and killed her. That's what you're afraid of, isn't it?"

The young man nodded miserably.

"Not really. I don't really believe it, but—but I feel—I feel that it *could* have happened. I don't feel Hester has got the poise, the balance to—I feel she's young for her age, uncertain of herself, liable to have brain-storms. I look at that household and I don't feel that any of them are likely to have done such a thing until I come to Hester. And then—then I'm not sure."

"I see," said Dr. MacMaster. "Yes, I see."

"I don't really blame her," said Don Craig quickly. "I don't think the poor child really knew what she was doing. I can't call it murder. It was just an act of emotional defiance, of rebellion, of a longing to be free, of the conviction that she would never be free until—until her mother wasn't there any longer."

"And that last is probably true enough," said MacMaster. "It's the only kind of motive there is, and it's rather a peculiar one. Not the kind that looks strong in the eyes of the law. Wishing to be free. Free from the impact of a stronger personality. Just because none of them inherits a large sum of money on the death of Mrs. Argyle the law won't consider that they had a motive. But even the financial control, I should imagine, was very largely in Mrs. Argyle's hands through her influence with the Trustees. Oh yes, her death set them free all right. Not only Hester, my boy. It set Leo free to marry another woman. It set Mary free to look after her husband in the way she liked, it set Micky free to live his own life in the way he cared about living it. Even little dark horse Tina sitting in her library may have wanted freedom."

"I had to come and talk to you," said Donald. "I had to know what you thought, whether you thought that—that it could be true."

"About Hester?"

"Yes."

"I think it *could* be true," said MacMaster slowly. "I don't know that it is."

"You think it could have happened just as I say?"

"Yes. I think what you've imagined is not far-fetched and has an element of probability about it. But it's by no means certain, Donald."

The young man gave a shuddering sigh.

"But it's *got* to be certain, Mac. That's the one thing I do feel is necessary. I've got to *know*. If Hester tells me, if she tells me herself, then—then it will be all right. We'll get married as soon as possible. I'll look after her."

"It's as well Superintendent Huish can't hear you," said MacMaster dryly.

"I'm a law-abiding citizen as a rule," said Donald, "but you know very well yourself, Mac, how they treat psychological evidence in the law courts. In my view it was a bad accident, not a case of cold-blooded murder, or even hot-blooded murder for that matter."

"You're in love with the girl," said MacMaster.

"I'm talking to you in confidence, mind."

"I understand that," said MacMaster.

"All I'm saying is that if Hester tells me, and I know, we'll live it down together. But she must tell me. I can't go through life not knowing."

"You mean, you're not prepared to marry her with this probability overshadowing things?"

"Would you want to in my place?"

"I don't know. In my day, if it happened to me, and I was in love with the girl, I should probably be convinced she was innocent."

"It's not so much the guilt or innocence that matters, as that I've got to *know*."

"And if she did kill her mother, you're quite prepared to marry her and live happily ever afterwards, as they say?"

"Yes."

"Don't you believe it!" said MacMaster. "You'll be wondering if the bitter taste in your coffee is only coffee and thinking that the poker in the grate is a bit too hefty a size. And she'll see you thinking it. It won't do . . ."

IO

"I'm sure, Marshall, that you'll appreciate my reasons for asking you to come here and have this conference."

"Yes, certainly," said Mr. Marshall. "The fact is that if you had not proposed it, Mr. Argyle, I should myself have suggested coming down. The announcement was in all the morning papers this morning and there is no doubt at all that it will lead to a revival of interest in the case on the part of the press."

"We've already had a few of them ringing up and asking for interviews," said Mary Durrant.

"Quite so, it was only to be expected, I feel. I should advise that you take up the position that you have no comment to make. Naturally you are delighted and thankful, but you prefer not to discuss the matter."

"Superintendent Huish, who was in charge of the case at the time, has asked to come and have an interview with us to-morrow morning," said Leo.

"Yes. Yes, I'm afraid there will have to be a certain amount of reopening of the case, though I really cannot think that the police can have much hope of arriving at any tangible result. After all, two years have passed and anything that people might have remembered at the time—people in the village, I mean—will by now have been forgotten. A pity, of course, in some ways, but it can't be helped."

"The whole thing seems quite clear," said Mary Durrant. "The house was securely locked up against burglars but if anyone had come appealing to my mother over some special case or pretending to be a friend or friends of hers I have no doubt that person would have been admitted. That, I think, is what must have happened. My father here thought he heard a ring at the bell just after seven o'clock."

Marshall turned his head enquiringly to Leo.

"Yes, I think I did say so," said Leo. "Of course, I can't remember very clearly now, but at the time I was under the impression that I heard the bell. I was ready to go down and then I thought I heard the door open and close. There was no sound of voices or any question of anyone forcing an entry or behaving abusively. That I think I should have heard."

"Quite so, quite so," said Mr. Marshall. "Yes, I think there's no doubt that that is what must have happened. Alas, we know only too well the large number of unprincipled persons gaining admission to a house by a plausible tale of distress, and who having gained admission are willing to cosh the householder and make off with what money they can find. Yes, I think that we must assume now that that is what did happen."

He spoke in too persuasive a voice. He looked round the little assembly as he spoke, noting them carefully, and labelling them in his meticulous mind. Mary Durrant, good-looking, unimaginative, untroubled, even slightly aloof, apparently quite sure of herself. Behind her in his wheel-chair, her husband. An intelligent fellow, Philip Durrant, Marshall thought to himself. A man who might have done a good deal and gone far had it not been for his unreliable judgment in all matters of business. He was not, Marshall thought, taking all this as calmly as his wife was. His eyes were alert and thoughtful. He realised, none better, the implications of the whole matter. Of course, though, Mary Durrant might not be as calm as she appeared to be. Both as a girl and a woman, she had always been able to conceal her feelings.

As Philip Durrant moved slightly in his chair, his bright, intelligent eyes watching the lawyer with a faint mockery in them, Mary turned her head sharply. The complete adoration of the look she gave her husband almost startled the lawyer. He had known, of course, that Mary Durrant was a devoted wife, but he had so long considered her as a calm, rather passionless creature without strong affections or dislikes that he was surprised at this sudden revelation. So that was how she felt about the fellow, was it? As for Philip Durrant, he seemed uneasy. Apprehensive, Marshall thought, about the future. As well he might be!

Opposite the lawyer sat Micky. Young, handsome, bitter. Why had he got to be so bitter, Marshall thought parenthetically? Hadn't everything been done for him always? Why did he have to have this look of one who was perpetually against the world? Beside him sat Tina looking rather like a small elegant black cat. Very dark, soft-voiced, big dark eyes and a rather sinuous grace of movement. Quiet, yet perhaps emotional behind the quietness. Marshall really knew very little about Tina. She had taken up the work suggested to her by Mrs. Argyle, as a librarian in the County library. She had a flat in Redmyn and came home at week-ends. Apparently a docile and contented member of the family. But who knew? Anyway, she was out of it or ought to be. She had not been here that evening. Though, for all that, Redmyn was only twenty-five miles away. Still presumably Tina and Micky had been out of it.

Marshall swept a quick glance over Kirsten Lindstrom, who was watching him with a touch of belligerence in her manner. Supposing, he thought, it was *she* who had gone berserk and attacked her employer? It wouldn't really surprise him. Nothing really surprised you when you'd been in the law a number of years. They'd have a word for it in the modern jargon. Repressed spinster. Envious, jealous, nursing grievances real or fancied. Oh yes, they had a word for it. And how very convenient it would be, thought Mr. Marshall rather improperly. Yes, very convenient. A foreigner. Not one of the family. But would Kirsten Lindstrom have deliberately framed Jacko; have heard the quarrel and taken advantage of it? That was a great deal more difficult to believe. For Kirsten Lindstrom adored Jacko. She had always been devoted to all the children. No, he could not believe that of her. A pity because—but really he must not let his thoughts go along that line.

His glance went on to Leo Argyle and Gwenda Vaughan. Their engagement had not been announced, which was just as well. A wise decision. He had actually written and hinted as much. Of course it was probably an open secret locally and no doubt the police were on to it. From the point of view of the police it was the right kind of answer. Innumerable precedents. Husband, wife, and the other woman. Only, somehow or other, Marshall could not believe that Leo Argyle had attacked his wife. No, he really couldn't believe it. After all, he had known Leo Argyle for a number of years and he had the highest opinion of him. An intellectual. A man of warm sympathies, deep reading and an aloof philosophical outlook upon life. Not the sort of man to murder his wife with a poker. Of course, at a certain age, when a man fell in love—but no! That was newspaper stuff. Pleasant reading, apparently, for Sundays, all over the British Isles! But really, one could not imagine Leo . . .

What about the woman? He didn't know so much about Gwenda Vaughan. He observed the full lips and the ripe figure. She was in love with Leo all right. Oh yes, probably been in love with him for a long time. What about a divorce, he wondered. What would Mrs. Argyle have felt about divorce? Really he had no idea, but he didn't think the idea would appeal to Leo Argyle, who was one of the old-fashioned type. He didn't think that Gwenda Vaughan was Leo Argyle's mistress, which made it all the more probable that if Gwenda Vaughan had seen a chance to eliminate Mrs. Argyle with the certainty that no suspicion would attach to her—he paused before continuing the thought. Would she have sacrificed Jacko without a qualm? He didn't really think she had ever been very fond of Jacko. Jacko's charm had not appealed to her. And women—Mr. Marshall knew only too well—were ruthless. So one couldn't rule out Gwenda Vaughan. It was very doubtful after this time if the police would ever get any evidence. He didn't see what evidence there could be against her. She had been in the house that day, she had been with Leo in his library, she had said good night to him and left him and gone down the stairs. There was no one who could say whether or not she had gone aside into Mrs. Argyle's sitting-room, picked up that poker and walked up behind the unsuspecting woman as she bent over papers on the desk. And then afterwards, Mrs. Argyle having been struck down without a cry, all Gwenda Vaughan had to do was to throw down the poker and let herself out of the front door and go home, just as she always did. He couldn't see any possibility of the police or anyone else finding out if that was what she had done.

His eyes went on to Hester. A pretty child. No, not pretty, beautiful really. Beautiful in a rather strange and uncomfortable way. He'd like to know who her parents had been. Something lawless and wild about her. Yes, one could almost use the word desperate in connection with her. What had she had to be desperate about? She'd run away in a silly way to go on the stage and had had a silly affair with an undesirable man; then she had seen reason, come home with Mrs. Argyle and settled down again. All the same, you couldn't really rule out Hester, because you didn't know how her mind worked. You didn't know what a strange moment of desperation might do to her. But the police wouldn't know either.

In fact, thought Mr. Marshall, it seemed very unlikely that the police, even if they made up their own minds as to who was responsible, could really do anything about it. So that on the whole the position was satisfactory. Satisfactory? He gave a little start as he considered the word. But was it? Was stalemate really a satisfactory outcome to the whole thing? Did the Argyles know the truth themselves, he wondered. He decided against that. They didn't know. Apart, of course, from one person amongst them who presumably knew only too well. . . . No, they didn't know, but did they suspect? Well, if they didn't suspect now, they soon would, because if you didn't know you couldn't help wondering, trying to remember things. . . . Uncomfortable. Yes, yes, a very uncomfortable position.

All these thoughts had not taken very much time. Mr. Marshall came out of his little reverie to see Micky's eyes fixed on him with a mocking gleam in them.

"So that's your verdict, is it, Mr. Marshall?" Micky said. "The outsider, the unknown intruder, the bad character who murders, robs and gets away with it?"

"It seems," said Mr. Marshall, "as though that is what we will have to accept."

Micky threw himself back in his chair and laughed.

"That's our story, and we're going to stick to it, eh?"

"Well, yes, Michael, that is what I should advise." There was a distinct note of warning in Mr. Marshall's voice.

Micky nodded his head.

"I see," he said. "That's what you advise. Yes. Yes, I dare say you're quite right. But you don't believe it, do you?"

Mr. Marshall gave him a very cold look. That was the trouble with people who had no legal sense of discretion. They insisted on saying things which were much better not said.

"For what it is worth," he said, "that is my opinion."

The finality of his tone held a world of reproof. Micky looked round the table.

"What do we all think?" he asked generally. "Eh, Tina, my love, looking down your nose in your quiet way, haven't you any ideas? Any unauthorised versions, so to speak? And you, Mary? You haven't said much."

"Of course I agree with Mr. Marshall," said Mary rather sharply. "What other solution can there be?"

"Philip doesn't agree with you," said Micky.

Mary turned her head sharply to look at her husband. Philip Durrant said quietly:

"You'd better hold your tongue, Micky. No good ever came of talking too much when you're in a tight place. And we are in a tight place."

"So nobody's going to have any opinions, are they?" said Micky. "All right. So be it. But let's all think about it a bit when we go up to bed tonight. It might be advisable, you know. After all, one wants to know where one is, so to speak. Don't you know a thing or two, Kirsty? You usually do. As far as I remember, you always knew what was going on, though I will say for you, you never told."

Kirsten Lindstrom said, not without dignity:

"I think, Micky, that you should hold your tongue. Mr. Marshall is right. Too much talking is unwise."

"We might put it to the vote," said Micky. "Or write a name on a piece of paper and throw it into a hat. That would be interesting, wouldn't it; to see who got the votes?"

This time Kirsten Lindstrom's voice was louder.

"Be quiet," she said. "Do not be a silly, reckless little boy as you used to be. You are grown up now."

"I only said let's think about it," said Micky, taken aback.

"We shall think about it," said Kirsten Lindstrom.

And her voice was bitter.

II

Night settled down on Sunny Point.

Sheltered by its walls seven people retired to rest, but none of them slept well. . . .

Philip Durrant, since his illness and his loss of bodily activity, had found more and more solace in mental activity. Always a highly intelligent man, he now became conscious of the resources opening out to him through the medium of intelligence. He amused himself sometimes by forecasting the reactions of those around him to suitable stimuli. What he said and did was often not a natural outpouring, but a calculated one, motivated simply and solely to observe the response to it. It was a kind of game that he played; when he got the anticipated response, he chalked up, as it were, a mark to himself.

As a result of this pastime he found himself, for perhaps the first time in his life, keenly observant of the differences and realities of human personality.

Human personalities as such had not previously interested him very much. He liked or disliked, was amused or bored by, the people who surrounded him or whom he met. He had always been a man of action, and not a man of thought. His imagination, which was considerable, had been exercised in devising various schemes for making money. All these schemes had a sound core; but a complete lack of business ability always resulted in their coming to nothing. People, as such, had up till now only been considered by him as pawns in the game. Now, since his illness, cut off from his former active life, he was forced to take account of what people themselves were like.

It had started in the hospital when the love lives of the nurses, the secret warfare and the petty grievances of hospital life had been forced on his attention since there was nothing else to occupy it. And now it was fast becoming a habit with him. People—really that was all that life held for him now. Just people. People to study, to find out about, to sum up. Decide for himself what made them tick and find out if he was right. Really, it could all be very interesting. . . .

Only this very evening, sitting in the library, he had realised how little he really knew about his wife's family. What were they really like? What were they like inside, that is, not their outer appearance which he knew well enough.

Odd, how little you knew about people. Even your own wife?

He had looked thoughtfully over at Mary. How much did he really know about Mary?

He had fallen in love with her because he liked her good looks and her calm serious ways. Also, she had had money and that had mattered to him too. He would have thought twice about marrying a penniless girl. It had all been most suitable and he had married her and teased her and called her Polly and had enjoyed the doubtful look she gave him when he made jokes she could not see. But what, really, did he *know* about her? Of what she thought and felt? He knew, certainly, that she loved him with a deep and passionate devotion. And at the thought of that devotion he stirred a little uneasily, twisting his shoulders as though to ease them of a burden. Devotion was all very well when you could get away from it for nine or ten hours of the day. It was a nice thing to come home to. But now he was lapped round with it; watched over, cared for, cherished. It made one yearn for a little wholesome neglect. . . . One had, in fact, to find ways of escape. Mental ways—since none other were possible. One had to escape to realms of fancy or speculation.

Speculation. As to who was responsible for his mother-in-law's death, for instance. He had disliked his mother-in-law, and she had disliked him. She had not wanted Mary to marry him (would she have wanted Mary to marry anybody? he wondered), but she had not been able to prevent it. He and Mary had started life happy and independent—and then things had begun to go wrong. First that South American company—and then the Bicycle Accessories Ltd.—good ideas both of them—but the financing of them had been badly judged—and then there had been the Argentine railway strike which had completed the disasters. All purely bad luck, but in some way he felt that somehow Mrs. Argyle was responsible. She hadn't wished him to succeed. Then had come his illness. It had looked as though their only solution was to come and live at Sunny Point where a welcome was assured to them. He wouldn't have minded particularly. A man who was a cripple, only half a man, what did it matter where he was?—but Mary would have minded.

Oh well, it hadn't been necessary to live permanently at Sunny Point. Mrs. Argyle had been killed. The trustees had raised the allowance made to Mary under the trust and they had set up on their own again.

He hadn't felt any particular grief over Mrs. Argyle's death. Pleasanter, of course, if she had died of pneumonia or something like that, in her bed. Murder was a nasty business with its notoriety and its screaming headlines. Still, as murders go, it had been quite a satisfactory murder—the perpetrator obviously having a screw loose in a way that could be served up decently in a lot of psychological jargon. Not Mary's own brother. One of those "adopted children" with a bad heredity who so often go wrong. But things weren't quite so good now. To-morrow Superintendent Huish was coming to ask questions in his gentle West Country voice. One ought, perhaps, to think about the answers. . . .

Mary was brushing her long fair hair in front of the mirror. Something about her calm remoteness irritated him.

He said: "Got your story pat for to-morrow, Polly?"

She turned astonished eyes upon him.

"Superintendent Huish is coming. He'll ask you all over again just what your movements were on the evening of November 9th."

"Oh, I see. It's so long ago now. One can hardly remember."

"But *he* can, Polly. That's the point. *He* can. It's all written down somewhere in a nice little police notebook."

"Is it? Do they keep these things?"

"Probably keep everything in triplicate for ten years! Well, your movements are very simple, Polly. There weren't any. You were here with me in this room. And if I were you I shouldn't mention that you left it between seven and seven-thirty."

"But that was only to go to the bathroom. After all," said Mary reasonably, "everyone has to go to the bathroom."

"You didn't mention the fact to him at the time. I do remember that."

"I suppose I forgot about it."

"I thought it might have been an instinct of self-preservation. . . . Anyway, I remember backing you up. We were together here, playing picquet from six-thirty until Kirsty gave the alarm. That's our story and we're sticking to it."

"Very well, darling." Her agreement was placid—uninterested.

He thought: "Has she no imagination? Can't she foresee that we're in for a sticky time?"

He leaned forward.

"It's interesting, you know. . . . Aren't *you* interested in who killed her? We all know—Micky was quite right there—that it's one of us. Aren't you interested to know which?"

"It wasn't you or I," said Mary.

"And that's all that interests you? Polly, you're wonderful!"

She flushed slightly.

"I don't see what's so odd about that?"

"No, I can see you don't. . . . Well, I'm different. I'm curious."

"I don't suppose we ever shall know. I don't suppose the police will ever know."

"Perhaps not. They'll certainly have precious little to go upon. But we're in rather a different position to the police."

"What do you mean, Philip?"

"Well, we've got a few bits of inside knowledge. We know our little lot from inside—have a fairly good idea of what makes them tick. You should have, anyway. You've grown up with them all. Let's hear your views. Who do *you* think it was?"

"I've no idea, Philip."

"Then just make a guess."

Mary said sharply:

"I'd rather not know who did it. I'd rather not even think about it."

"Ostrich," said her husband.

"Honestly, I don't see the point of—guessing. It's much better not to know. Then we can all go on as usual."

"Oh no, we can't," said Philip. "That's where you're wrong, my girl. The rot's set in already."

"What do you mean?"

"Well, take Hester and her young man—earnest young Doctor Donald. Nice chap, serious, worried. He doesn't really think she did it—but he's not really sure she didn't do it! And so he looks at her, anxiously, when he thinks she isn't noticing. But she notices all right. So there you are! Perhaps she *did* do it—you'd know better than I would—but if she didn't, what the hell can she do about her young man? Keep on saying: 'Please, it wasn't me?' But that's what she'd say anyway."

"Really, Philip, I think you're imagining things."

"*You* can't imagine at all, Polly. Then take poor old Leo. Marriage bells with Gwenda are receding into the distance. The girl's horribly upset about it. Haven't you noticed?"

"I really don't see what Father wants to marry again for at his age."

"He sees all right! But he also sees that any hint of a love affair with Gwenda gives both of them a first-class motive for murder. Awkward!"

"It's fantastic to think for a moment that Father murdered Mother!" said Mary. "Such things don't happen."

"Yes, they do. Read the papers."

"Not our sort of people."

"Murder is no snob, Polly. Then there's Micky. Something's eating him all right. He's a queer, bitter lad. Tina seems in the clear, unworried, unaffected. But she's a little poker face if ever there was one. Then there's poor old Kirsty—"

A faint animation came into Mary's face.

"Now that *might* be a solution!"

"Kirsty?"

"Yes. After all, she's a foreigner. And I believe she's had very bad headaches the last year or two. . . . It seems much more likely that she should have done it than any of us."

"Poor devil," said Philip. "Don't you see that that's just what she is saying to herself? That we'll all agree together that she's the one? For convenience. Because she's not a member of the family. Didn't you see to-night that she was worried stiff? And she's in the same position as Hester. What can she say or do? Say to us all: 'I did *not* kill my friend and employer'? What weight can that statement carry? It's worse hell for her, perhaps, than for anyone else. . . . Because she's alone. She'll be going over in her mind every word she's ever said, every angry look she ever gave your mother—thinking that it will be remembered against her. Helpless to prove her innocence."

"I wish you'd calm down, Phil. After all, what can *we* do about it?"

"Only try to find out the truth."

"But how is that possible?"

"There might be ways. I'd rather like to try."

Mary looked uneasy.

"What sort of ways?"

"Oh, saying things—watching how people react—one could think up things"—he paused, his mind working—"things that would mean something to a guilty person, but not to an innocent one. . . ." Again he was silent, turning ideas over in his mind. He looked up and said: "Don't you want to help the innocent, Mary?"

"No." The word came out explosively. She came over to him and knelt by his chair. "I don't want you to mix yourself up in all this, Phil. Don't start saying things and laying traps. Leave it all alone. Oh, for God's sake, leave it *alone!*"

Philip's eyebrows rose.

"We-ell," he said. And he laid a hand on the smooth golden head.

II

Michael Argyle lay sleepless, staring into darkness.

His mind went round and round like a squirrel in a cage, going over the past. Why couldn't he leave it behind him? Why did he have to drag the past with him all through his life? What did it all matter anyway? Why did he have to remember so clearly the frowsty, cheerful room in the London slum, and he "our Micky." The casual exciting atmosphere! Fun in the streets! Ganging up on other boys! His mother with her bright golden head (cheap rinse, he thought, in his adult wisdom), her sudden furies when she would turn and lambaste him (gin, of course!) and the wild gaiety she had when she was in a good mood. Lovely suppers of fish and chips, and she'd sing songs—sentimental ballads. Sometimes they'd go to the pictures. There were always the Uncles, of course—that's what he always had to call them. His own dad had walked out before he could remember him. . . . But his mother wouldn't stand for the Uncle of the day laying a hand on him. "You leave our Micky alone," she'd say.

And then there had come the excitement of the war. Expecting Hitler's bombers—abortive sirens. Moaning Minnies. Going down into the Tubes and spending the nights there. The fun of it! The whole street was there with their sandwiches and their bottles of pop. And trains rushing through practically all night. That had been life, that had! In the thick of things!

And then he'd come down here—to the country. A dead and alive place where nothing ever happened!

"You'll come back, love, when it's all over," his mother had said, but lightly as though it wasn't really true. She hadn't seemed to care about his going. And why didn't she come too? Lots of the kids in the street had been evacuated with their Mums. But his mother hadn't wanted to go. She was going to the North (with the current Uncle, Uncle Harry!) to work in munitions.

He must have known then, in spite of her affectionate farewell. She didn't really care. . . . Gin, he thought, that was all she cared for, gin and the Uncles. . . .

And he'd been here, captured, a prisoner, eating tasteless, unfamiliar meals; going to bed, incredibly, at six o'clock, after a silly supper of milk and biscuits (milk and biscuits!), lying awake, crying, his head pushed down under the blankets, crying for Mom and home.

It was that woman! She'd got him and she wouldn't let him go. A lot of sloppy talk. Always making him play silly games. Wanting something from him. Something that he was determined not to give. Never mind. He'd wait. He'd be patient! And one day—one glorious day, he'd go *home*. Home to the streets, and the boys, and the glorious red buses and the Tube, and fish and chips, and the traffic and the area cats—his mind went longingly over the catalogue of delights. He must wait. The war couldn't go on forever. Here he was stuck in this silly place with bombs falling all over London and half London on fire—too! What a blaze it must make, and people being killed and houses crashing down.

He saw it in his mind all in glorious technicolour.

Never mind. When the war was over he'd go back to Mom. She'd be surprised to see how he'd grown.

In the darkness Micky Argyle expelled his breath in a long hiss.

The war *was* over. They'd licked Hitler and Musso. . . . Some of the children were going back. Soon, now. . . . And then *She* had come back from London and had said that he was going to stay at Sunny Point and be her own little boy. . . .

He had said: "Where's my Mom? Did a bomb get her?"

If she had been killed by a bomb—well, that would be not too bad. It happened to boys' mothers.

But Mrs. Argyle said "No," she hadn't been killed. But she had some rather difficult work to do and couldn't look after a child very well—that sort of thing, anyway; soft soap, meaning nothing. . . . His Mom didn't love him, didn't want him back—he'd got to stay here, for ever. . . .

He'd sneaked round after that, trying to overhear conversations, and at last he did hear something, just a fragment between Mrs. Argyle and her husband. "Only too pleased to get rid of him—absolutely indifferent"—and something about a hundred pounds. So then he knew—his mother had sold him for a hundred pounds. . . .

The humiliation—the pain—he'd never got over it. . . . And *She* had bought him! He saw her, vaguely, as embodied Power, someone against whom he, in his puny strength, was helpless. But he'd grow up, he'd be strong one day, a man. And then he'd kill her. . . .

He felt better once he'd made that resolution.

Later, when he went away to school, things were not so bad. But he hated the holidays—because of Her. Arranging everything, planning, giving him all sorts of presents. Looking puzzled, because he was so undemonstrative. He hated being kissed by her. . . . And later still, he'd taken a pleasure in thwarting her silly plans for him. Going into a bank! An oil company. Not he. He'd go and find work for himself.

It was when he was at the university that he'd tried to trace his mother. She'd been dead for some years, he discovered—in a car crash with a man who'd been driving roaring drunk . . .

So why not forget it all? Why not just have a good time and get on with life? He didn't know why not.

And now—what was going to happen now? *She* was dead, wasn't she? Thinking she'd bought him for a miserable hundred pounds. Thinking she could buy anything—houses and cars—and children since she hadn't any of her own. Thinking she was God Almighty!

Well, she wasn't. Just a crack on the head with a poker and she was a corpse like any other corpse! (Like the golden haired corpse in a car smash on the Great North Road. . . .)

She was dead, wasn't she? Why worry?

What was the matter with him? Was it—that he couldn't hate her any more because she was dead?

So that was Death . . .

He felt lost without his hatred—lost and afraid.

12

In her spotlessly kept bedroom, Kirsten Lindstrom plaited her grizzled blonde hair into two unbecoming plaits and prepared for bed.

She was worried and afraid.

The police didn't like foreigners. She had been in England so long that she herself did not feel foreign. But the police could not know that.

That Dr. Calgary—why did he have to come and do this to her?

Justice had been done. She thought of Jacko—and repeated to herself that justice had been done.

She thought of him as she had known him from a small boy.

Always, yes, always, a liar and a cheat! But so charming, so engaging. Always one forgave him. Always one tried to shield him from punishment.

He lied so well. That was the horrible truth. He lied so well that one believed him—that one couldn't help believing him. Wicked, cruel Jacko.

Dr. Calgary might think he knew what he was talking about! But Dr. Calgary was wrong. Places and times and alibis indeed! Jacko could arrange things of that kind easily enough. Nobody really knew Jacko as *she* had known him.

Would anybody believe her if she told them just exactly what Jacko was like? And now—to-morrow, what was going to happen? The police would come. And everyone so unhappy, so suspicious. Looking at each other. . . . Not sure what to believe.

And she loved them all so much . . . so much. She knew more about them all than anyone else could know. Far more than Mrs. Argyle had ever known. For Mrs. Argyle had been blinded by her intense maternal possessiveness. They were her children—she saw them always as belonging to her. But Kirsten had seen them as individuals—as themselves—with all their faults and virtues. If she had had children of her own, she might have felt possessive about them, she supposed. But she was not pre-eminently a maternal woman. Her principal love would have been for the husband she had never had.

Women like Mrs. Argyle were difficult for her to understand. Crazy about a lot of children who were not her own, and treating her husband as though he were not there! A good man, too, a fine man, none better. Neglected, pushed aside. And Mrs. Argyle too self-absorbed to notice what was happening under her nose. That secretary—a good-looking girl and every inch a woman. Well, it was not too late for Leo—or was it too late now? Now with murder raising its head from the grave in which it had been laid? Would those two ever dare to come together?

Kirsten sighed unhappily. What was going to happen to them all? To Micky, who had borne that deep, almost pathological grudge against his adopted mother. To Hester, so unsure of herself, so wild. Hester, who had been on the point of finding peace and security with that nice stolid young doctor. To Leo and Gwenda, who had had motive and, yes, it had to be faced, opportunity, as they both must realise. To Tina, that sleek little cat-like creature. To selfish, cold-hearted Mary, who until she had married had never shown affection for anybody.

Once, Kirsten thought, she herself had been full of affection for her employer, full of admiration. She couldn't remember exactly when she had begun to dislike her, when she had begun to judge her and find her wanting. So sure of herself, benevolent, tyrannical—a kind of living walking embodiment of MOTHER KNOWS BEST. And not really even a mother! If she *had* ever borne a child, it might have kept her humble.

But why go on thinking of Rachel Argyle? Rachel Argyle was dead.

She had to think of herself—and the others.

And of what might happen to-morrow.

II

Mary Durrant woke with a start.

She had been dreaming—dreaming that she was a child, back again in New York.

How odd. She hadn't thought of those days for years.

It was really surprising that she could remember anything at all. How old had she been? Five? Six?

She had dreamed that she was being taken home to the tenement from the hotel. The Argyles were sailing for England and not taking her with them after all. Anger and rage filled her heart for a moment or two until the realisation came that it had only been a dream.

How wonderful it had been. Taken into the car, going up in the elevator of the hotel to the eighteenth floor. The big suite, that wonderful bathroom; the revelation of what things there were in the world—if you were rich! If she could stay here, if she could keep all this—for ever . . .

Actually, there had been no difficulty at all. All that was needed was a show of affection; never easy for her, for she was not affectionate by disposition, but she had managed it. And there she was, established for life! A rich father and mother, clothes, cars, ships, aeroplanes, servants to wait on her, expensive dolls and toys. A fairy tale come true. . . .

A pity that all those other children had had to be there, too. That was the war, of course. Or would it have happened anyway? That insatiable mother love! Really something unnatural in it. So *animal*.

She had always felt a faint contempt for her adopted mother. Stupid in any case to choose the children she had chosen. The under-privileged! Criminal tendencies like Jacko's. Unbalanced like Hester. A savage like Micky. And Tina, a half-caste! No wonder they had all turned out badly. Though she couldn't really blame them for rebelling. She, herself, had rebelled. She remembered her meeting with Philip, a dashing young pilot. Her mother's disapproval. "These hurried marriages. Wait until the war is over." But she hadn't wanted to wait. She had as strong a will as her mother's, and her father had backed her up. They had married, and the war had ended soon afterwards.

She had wanted to have Philip all to herself—to get away out of her mother's shadow. It was Fate that had defeated her, not her mother. First the failure of Philip's financial schemes and then that horrifying blow—polio of the paralytic type. As soon as Philip was able to leave hospital they had come to Sunny Point. It had seemed inevitable that they would have to make their home there. Philip himself had seemed to think it inevitable. He had gone through all his money and her allowance from the Trust was not so very big. She had asked for a larger one, but the answer had been that perhaps for a while it would be wise to live at Sunny Point. But she wanted Philip to herself, all to herself, she didn't want him to be the last of Rachel Argyle's "children." She had not wanted a child of her own—she wanted only Philip.

But Philip himself had seemed quite agreeable to the idea of coming to Sunny Point.

"Easier for you," he said. "And people always coming and going there makes a distraction. Besides, I always find your father very good company."

Why didn't he want only to be with her as she wanted only to be with him? Why did he crave for other company—her father's, Hester's?

And Mary had felt a wave of futile rage sweep over her. Her mother, as usual, would get her own way.

But she hadn't got her own way . . . she had died.

And now it was going to be all raked up again. Why, oh, why?

And why was Philip being so trying about it all? Questioning, trying to find out, mixing himself up in what was none of his business?

Laying traps . . .

What *kind* of traps?

III

Leo Argyle watched the morning light fill the room slowly with dim grey light.

He had thought out everything very carefully.

It was quite clear to him—exactly what they were up against, he and Gwenda.

He lay looking at the whole thing as Superintendent Huish would look at it. Rachel coming in and telling them about Jacko—his wildness and his threats. Gwenda had tactfully gone into the next room, and he had tried to comfort Rachel, had told her she was quite right to have been firm, that helping Jacko in the past had done no good—that for better or worse he must take what was coming to him. And she had gone away easier in her mind.

And then Gwenda had come back into the room, and gathered up the letters for the post and had asked if there was anything that she could do, her voice saying more than the actual words. And he had thanked her and said no. And she had said good night and gone out of the room. Along the passage and down the stairs and past the room where Rachel was sitting at her desk and so out of the house with no one to watch her go. . . .

And he himself had sat on alone in the library, and there had been nobody to check whether he left it and went down to Rachel's room.

It was like that—opportunity for either of them.

And motive, because already by then he loved Gwenda and she loved him.

And there was nobody, ever, who could prove the guilt or innocence of either of them.

IV

A quarter of a mile away, Gwenda lay dry-eyed and sleepless.

Her hands clenched, she was thinking how much she had hated Rachel Argyle.

And now in the darkness, Rachel Argyle was saying: *"You thought you could have my husband once I was dead. But you can't—you can't. You will never have my husband."*

V

Hester was dreaming. She dreamt that she was with Donald Craig and that he had left her suddenly at the edge of an abyss. She had cried out in fear and then, on the other side of it, she saw that Arthur Calgary was standing holding out his hands to her.

She cried out to him reproachfully.

"Why have you done this to me?" and he answered:

"But I've come to *help* you . . ."

She woke up.

VI

Lying quietly in the small spare-room bed, Tina breathed gently and regularly, but sleep did not come.

She thought of Mrs. Argyle, without gratitude and without resentment—simply with love. Because of Mrs. Argyle she had had food and drink and warmth and toys and comfort. She had loved Mrs. Argyle. She was sorry she was dead. . . .

But it wasn't quite as simple as that.

It hadn't mattered when it was Jacko. . . .

But now?

13

Superintendent Huish looked round on them all, gently and politely. His tone when he spoke was persuasive and apologetic.

"I know it must be very painful to you all," he said, "to have to go over the whole thing again. But really, we've no choice in the matter. You saw the notice, I expect? It was in all the morning papers."

"A free pardon," said Leo.

"The phraseology always grates on people," said Huish. "An anachronism, like so much of legal terminology. But its meaning is quite clear."

"It means that you made a mistake," said Leo.

"Yes," Huish acknowledged it simply. "We made a mistake." He added, after a minute, "Of course, without Dr. Calgary's evidence it was really inevitable."

Leo said coldly:

"My son told you, when you arrested him, that he had been given a lift that night."

"Oh, yes. He told us. And we did our best to check—but we couldn't find any confirmation of the story. I quite realise, Mr. Argyle, that you must feel exceedingly bitter about the whole business. I'm not making excuses and apologies. All we police officers have to do is to collect the evidence. The evidence goes to the Public Prosecutor and he decides if there is a case. In this case he decided there was. If it's possible, I'd ask you to put as much bitterness as you can out of your mind and just run over the facts and times again."

"What's the use now?" Hester spoke up sharply. "Whoever did it is miles away and you'll never find him."

Superintendent Huish turned to look at her.

"That may be—and it may not," he said mildly. "You'd be surprised at the times we do get our man—sometimes after several years. It's patience does it—patience and never letting up."

Hester turned her head away, and Gwenda gave a quick shiver as though a cold wind had passed over her. Her lively imagination felt the menace behind the quiet words.

"Now if you please," said Huish. He looked expectantly at Leo. "We'll start with you, Mr. Argyle."

"What do you want to know exactly? You must have my original statement? I shall probably be less accurate now. Exact times are apt to slip one's memory."

"Oh, we realise that. But there's always the chance that some little fact may come to light, something overlooked at the time."

"Isn't it even possible," asked Philip, "that one might see things in better proportion looking back after the lapse of years?"

"It's a possibility, yes," said Huish, turning his head to look at Philip with some interest.

"Intelligent chap," he thought. "I wonder if he's got any ideas of his own about this. . . ."

"Now, Mr. Argyle, if you'll just run through the sequence of events. You'd had tea?"

"Yes. Tea had been in the dining-room at five o'clock as usual. We were all there for it with the exception of Mr. and Mrs. Durrant. Mrs. Durrant took tea for herself and her husband up to their own sitting-room."

"I was even more of a cripple then than I am now," said Philip. "I'd only just got out of hospital."

"Quite so." Huish turned back to Leo. "All of you—being—?"

"My wife and myself, my daughter Hester, Miss Vaughan and Miss Lindstrom."

"And then? Just tell me in your own words."

"After tea I came back in here with Miss Vaughan. We were at work upon a chapter of my book on Medieval Economics which I was revising. My wife went to her sitting-room and office, which is on the ground floor. She was, as you know, a very busy woman. She was looking over some plans for a new children's playground which she was intending to present to the Council here."

"Did you hear your son Jack's arrival?"

"No. That is, I did not know that it was he. I heard, we both heard, the front-door bell. We did not know who it was."

"Who did you think it was, Mr. Argyle?"

Leo looked faintly amused.

"I was in the fifteenth century at the time, not the twentieth. I didn't think at all. It could have been anybody or anything. My wife and Miss Lindstrom and Hester and possibly one of our daily helps would all be downstairs. Nobody," said Leo simply, "ever expected *me* to answer a bell."

"After that?"

"Nothing. Until my wife came in a good deal later."

"How much later?"

Leo frowned.

"By now I really couldn't tell you. I must have given you my estimate at the time. Half an hour—no, more—perhaps three-quarters."

"We finished tea just after half past five," said Gwenda. "I think it was about twenty minutes to seven when Mrs. Argyle came into the library."

"And she said?"

Leo sighed. He spoke distastefully.

"We have had all this so many times. She said Jacko had been with her, that he was in trouble, that he had been violent and abusive, demanding money and saying that unless he had some money at once it would be a matter of prison. That she had refused definitely to give him a penny. She was worried as to whether she had done right or not."

"Mr. Argyle, may I ask you a question. Why, when the boy made these demands for money, did your wife not call you? Why only tell you afterwards? Did that not seem odd to you?"

"No, it did not."

"It seems to me that that would have been the natural thing to do. You were not—on bad terms?"

"Oh no. It was simply that my wife was accustomed to dealing with all practical decisions single-handed. She would often consult me beforehand as to what I thought and she usually discussed the decisions she had taken with me afterwards. In this particular matter she and I had talked very seriously together about the problem of Jacko—what to do for the best. So far, we had been singularly unfortunate in our handling of the boy. She had paid out very considerable sums of money several times to protect him from the consequences of his actions. We had decided that if there was a next time, it would be best for Jacko to learn the hard way."

"Nevertheless, she was upset?"

"Yes. She was upset. If he had been less violent and threatening, I think she might have been broken down and helped him once more, but his attitude only stiffened her resolution."

"Had Jacko left the house by then?"

"Oh, yes."

"Do you know that of your own knowledge, or did Mrs. Argyle tell you?"

"She told me. She said he had gone away swearing, and threatening to come back, and that he'd said she'd better have some cash ready for him then."

"Were you—this is important—were you alarmed at the thought of the boy's return?"

"Of course not. We were quite used to what I can only call Jacko's bluster."

"It never entered your head that he would return and attack her."

"No. I told you so at the time. I was dumbfounded."

"And it seems you were quite right," said Huish softly. "It *wasn't* he who attacked her. Mrs. Argyle left you—when exactly?"

"That I do remember. We've been over it so often. Just before seven—about seven minutes to."

Huish turned to Gwenda Vaughan.

"You confirm that?"

"Yes."

"And the conversation went as Mr. Argyle has just said? You can't add to it? There is nothing he has forgotten?"

"I didn't hear all of it. After Mrs. Argyle had told us about Jacko's demands I thought I'd better remove myself in case they felt it embarrassing to talk freely before me. I went in there"—she pointed to the door at the back of the library—"to the small room where I type. When I heard Mrs. Argyle leave I came back."

"And that was at seven minutes to seven?"

"Just before five to seven, yes."

"And after that, Miss Vaughan?"

"I asked Mr. Argyle if he wanted to continue work, but he said his chain of thought was interrupted. I asked if there was any more I could do, but he said no. So I cleared up my things and went."

"The time?"

"Five minutes past seven."

"You went downstairs and through the front door?"

"Yes."

"Mrs. Argyle's sitting-room was immediately to the left of the front door?"

"Yes."

"Was the door open?"

"It was not closed—it was about a foot ajar."

"You didn't go inside or say good night to her?"

"No."

"Didn't you usually do so?"

"No. It would have been silly to disturb her at what she was doing, just to say good night."

"If you had gone in—you might have discovered her body lying there dead."

Gwenda shrugged her shoulders.

"I suppose so. . . . But I imagine—I mean we all imagined at the time, that she was killed later. Jacko would hardly have been able to—"

She stopped.

"You are still thinking on the lines of Jacko having killed her. But that is not so now. So she *might* have been there then, dead?"

"I suppose—yes."

"You left the house and went straight home?"

"Yes. My landlady spoke to me when I came in."

"Just so. And you didn't meet anyone on the way—near the house?"

"I don't think so . . . no." Gwenda frowned. "I can't really remember now. . . . It was cold and dark and this road is a cul-de-sac. I don't think I passed anyone until I came to the Red Lion. There were several people about there."

"Any cars pass you?"

Gwenda looked startled.

"Oh, yes, I do remember a car. It splashed my skirt. I had to wash the mud off when I got home."

"What kind of a car?"

"I don't remember. I didn't notice. It passed me just at the entrance to our road. It might have been going to any of the houses."

Huish turned back to Leo.

"You say you heard a ring at the bell some time after your wife left the room?"

"Well—I think I did. I've never been quite sure."

"What time was that?"

"I've no idea. I didn't look."

"Didn't you think it might be your son Jacko come back?"

"I didn't think. I was—at work again."

"One more point, Mr. Argyle. Did you have any idea that your son was married?"

"No idea at all."

"His mother didn't know, either? You don't think she knew but had not told you?"

"I'm quite sure she had no idea of such a thing. She would have come to me about it at once. It was the greatest shock to me when the wife turned up the next day. I could hardly believe it when Miss Lindstrom came into this room and said 'There is a young woman downstairs—a girl—who says she is Jacko's wife. It can't be *true*.' She was terribly upset, weren't you, Kirsty?"

"I could not believe it," said Kirsten. "I made her say it twice and then I came up to Mr. Argyle. It seemed incredible."

"You were very kind to her, I understand," said Huish to Leo.

"I did what I could. She's married again, you know. I'm very glad. Her husband seems a nice steady sort of chap."

Huish nodded. Then he turned to Hester.

"Now, Miss Argyle, just tell me again what you did after tea that day."

"I don't remember now," said Hester sulkily. "How can I? It's two years ago. I might have done anything."

"Actually I believe you helped Miss Lindstrom to wash up tea."

"That is quite right," said Kirsten. "And then," she added, "you went upstairs to your bedroom. You were going out later, you remember. You were going to see an amateur performance of *Waiting for Godot* at the Drymouth Playhouse."

Hester was still looking sullen and unco-operative.

"You've got it all written down," she said to Huish. "Why go on about it?"

"Because you never know what might be helpful. Now then, Miss Argyle, what time did *you* leave the house?"

"Seven o'clock—or thereabouts."

"Had you heard the altercation between your mother and your brother Jack?"

"No, I didn't hear anything. I was upstairs."

"But you saw Mrs. Argyle before you left the house?"

"Yes. I wanted some money. I was right out. And I remembered the petrol in my car was nearly down to empty. I'd have to fill up on the way to Drymouth. So when I was ready to start I went in to Mother and asked her for some money—just a couple of pounds—that's all I needed."

"And she gave them to you?"

"Kirsty gave them to me."

Huish looked slightly surprised.

"I don't remember that in the original statement."

"Well, that's what happened," said Hester defiantly. "I went in and said could I have some cash, and Kirsten heard me from the hall and called out that she'd got some and would give it to me. She was just going out herself. And Mother said, 'Yes, get it from Kirsty.'"

"I was just going down to the Women's Institute with some books on Flower Arrangement," said Kirsten. "I knew Mrs. Argyle was busy and didn't want to be disturbed."

Hester said in an aggrieved voice:

"What does it matter who gave me the money? You wanted to know when I last saw Mother alive. That was when. She was sitting at the table poring over a lot of plans. And I said I wanted cash, and then Kirsten called out that she'd give it to me. I took it from her and then went into Mother's room again and said good night to Mother and she said she hoped I'd enjoy the play, and to be careful driving. She always said that. And then I went out to the garage and got the car out."

"And Miss Lindstrom."

"Oh, she went off as soon as she'd given me the money."

Kirsten Lindstrom said quickly: "Hester passed me in the car just as I got to the end of our road. She must have started almost immediately after me. She went on up the hill to the main road whilst I turned left to the village."

Hester opened her mouth as though to speak, then quickly shut it again.

Huish wondered. Was Kirsten Lindstrom trying to establish that Hester would not have had time to commit the crime? Wasn't it possible that instead of Hester's saying a quiet good night to Mrs. Argyle, there had been an argument—a quarrel, and that Hester had struck her down?

Smoothly he turned to Kirsten and said:

"Now, Miss Lindstrom, let's have your account of what you remember."

She was nervous. Her hands twisted uncomfortably.

"We had tea. It was cleared away. Hester helped me. Then she went upstairs. Then Jacko came."

"You heard him?"

"Yes. I let him in. He said he had lost his key. He went straight in to his mother. He said at once, 'I'm in a jam. You've got to get me out of it.' I did not hear any more. I went back into the kitchen. There were things to prepare for supper."

"Did you hear him leave?"

"Yes, indeed. He was shouting. I came from the kitchen. He was standing there in the front hall—very angry—shouting out that he'd come back, that his mother had better have the money ready for him. Or else! That is what he said: 'Or else!' It was a threat."

"And then?"

"He went off banging the door. Mrs. Argyle came out in the hall. She was very pale and upset. She said to me, 'You heard?'

"I said: 'He is in trouble?'

"She nodded. Then she went upstairs to the library to Mr. Argyle. I laid the table for supper, and then I went up to put my outdoor things on. The Women's Institute were having a Flower Arrangement Competition next day. There were some Flower Arrangement books we had promised them."

"You took the books to the Institute—what time did you return to the house?"

"It must have been about half past seven. I let myself in with my key. I went in at once to Mrs. Argyle's room—to give her a message of thanks and a note—she was at the desk, her head forward on her hands. And there was the poker, flung down—and drawers of the bureau pulled out. There had been a burglar, I thought. She had been attacked. And I was right. *Now* you know that I was right! It *was* a burglar—someone from outside!"

"Someone whom Mrs. Argyle herself let in?"

"Why not?" said Kirsten defiantly. "She was kind—always very kind. And she was not afraid—of people or things. Besides it is not as though she were alone in the house. There were others—her husband, Gwenda, Mary. She had only to call out."

"But she didn't call out," Huish pointed out.

"No. Because whoever it was must have told her some very plausible story. She would always listen. And so, she sat down again at the desk—perhaps to look for her cheque-book—because she was unsuspicious—so he had the chance to snatch up the poker and hit her. Perhaps, even, he did not mean to kill her. He just wanted to stun her and look for money and jewellery and go."

"He didn't look very far—just turned out a few drawers."

"Perhaps he heard sounds in the house—or lost his nerve. Or found, perhaps, that he had killed her. And so, quickly, in panic, he goes."

She leaned forward.

Her eyes were both frightened and pleading.

"It *must* have been like that—it must!"

He was interested in her insistence. Was it fear for herself? She *could* have killed her employer there and then, pulling out the drawers to lend verisimilitude to the idea of a burglar. Medical evidence could not put the time of death closer than between seven and seven thirty.

"It seems as though it must be so," he acquiesced pleasantly. A faint sigh of relief escaped her. She sat back. He turned to the Durrants.

"You didn't hear anything, either of you?"

"Not a thing."

"I took a tray with tea up to our room," said Mary. "It's rather shut off from the rest of the house. We were there until we heard someone screaming. It was Kirsten. She'd just found Mother dead."

"You didn't leave the room at all until then?"

"No." Her limpid gaze met his. "We were playing picquet."

Philip wondered why he felt slightly discomposed. Polly was doing what he had told her to do. Perhaps it was the perfection of her manner, calm, unhurried, carrying complete conviction.

"Polly, love, you're a wonderful liar!" he thought.

"And I, Superintendent," he said, "was then, and am still, quite incapable of any comings and goings."

"But you're a good deal better, aren't you, Mr. Durrant," said the superintendent cheerfully. "One of these days we'll have you walking again."

"It's a long job."

Huish turned towards the other two members of the family who up to now had sat without making a sound. Micky had sat with his arms folded and a faint sneer on his face. Tina, small and graceful, leaned back in her chair, her eyes moving occasionally from face to face.

"Neither of you two were in the house, I know," he said. "But perhaps you'll just refresh my memory as to what you were doing that evening?"

"Does your memory really need refreshing?" asked Micky with his sneer even more pronounced. "I can still say my piece. I was out testing a car. Clutch trouble. I gave it a good long test. From Drymouth up Minchin Hill, along the Moor Road and back through Ipsley. Unfortunately cars are dumb, they can't testify."

Tina had turned her head at last. She was staring straight at Micky. Her face was still expressionless.

"And you, Miss Argyle? You work at the library at Redmyn?"

"Yes. It closes at half past five. I did a little shopping in the High Street. Then I went home. I have a flat—flatlet really—in Morecombe Mansions. I cooked my own supper and enjoyed a quiet evening playing gramophone records."

"You didn't go out at all?"

There was a slight pause before she said:

"No, I didn't go out."

"Quite sure about that, Miss Argyle?"

"Yes. I am sure."

"You have a car, haven't you?"

"Yes."

"She has a bubble," said Micky. "Bubble, bubble, toil and trouble."

"I have a bubble, yes," said Tina, grave and composed.

"Where do you keep it?"

"In the street. I have no garage. There is a side street near the flats. There are cars parked all along it."

"And you've—nothing helpful you can tell us?"

Huish hardly knew himself why he was so insistent.

"I do not think there is anything I could possibly tell you."

Micky threw her a quick glance.

Huish sighed.

"I'm afraid this hasn't helped you much, Superintendent," said Leo.

"You never know, Mr. Argyle. You realise, I suppose, one of the oddest things about the whole business?"

"I—? I'm not quite sure that I follow you."

"The money," said Huish. "The money Mrs. Argyle drew from the bank including that fiver with Mrs. Bottleberry, 17 Bangor Road written on the back of it. A strong part of the case was that that fiver and others were found on Jack Argyle when he was arrested. He swore he got the money from Mrs. Argyle, but Mrs. Argyle definitely told you and Miss Vaughan that she didn't give Jacko any money—so how did he get that fifty pounds? He couldn't have come back here—Dr. Calgary's evidence makes that quite clear. So he must have had it with him when he left here. Who gave it to him? Did you?"

He turned squarely on Kirsten Lindstrom, who flushed indignantly.

"Me? No, of course not. How could I?"

"Where was the money kept that Mrs. Argyle had drawn from the bank?"

"She usually kept it in a drawer of her bureau," said Kirsten.

"Locked?"

Kirsten considered.

"She would probably lock the drawer before she went up to bed."

Huish looked at Hester.

"Did you take the money from the drawer and give it to your brother?"

"I didn't even know he was there. And how could I take it without Mother knowing?"

"You could have taken it quite easily when your mother went up to the library to consult your father," Huish suggested.

He wondered whether she would see and avoid the trap.

She fell straight into it.

"But Jacko had already left by then. I—" She stopped, dismayed.

"I see you *do* know when your brother left," said Huish.

Hester said quickly and vehemently,

"I—I—know now—I didn't then. I was up in my room, I tell you. I didn't hear anything at all. And anyway I wouldn't have wanted to give Jacko any money."

"And I tell you this," said Kirsten. Her face was red and indignant. "If I had given Jacko money—it would have been my own money! I would not have stolen it!"

"I'm sure you wouldn't," said Huish. "But you see where that leads us. Mrs. Argyle, in spite of what she told *you*," he looked at Leo, "must have given him that money *herself*."

"I can't believe it. Why not tell me if she had done so?"

"She wouldn't be the first mother to be softer about her son than she wanted to admit."

"You're wrong, Huish. My wife never indulged in evasion."

"I think she did this time," said Gwenda Vaughan. "In fact she must have done . . . as the superintendent says, it's the only answer."

"After all," said Huish softly. "We've got to look at the whole thing from a different point of view now. At the time of the arrest we thought Jack Argyle was lying. But now we find he spoke the truth about the hitch-hike he had from Calgary, so presumably he was speaking the truth about the money too. He said that his mother gave it to him. Therefore presumably she did."

There was silence—an uncomfortable silence.

Huish got up. "Well, thank you. I'm afraid the trail is pretty cold by now, but you never know."

Leo escorted him to the door. When he came back he said with a sigh, "Well, that's over. For the present."

"For always," said Kirsten. "They will never know."

"What's the good of that to us?" cried Hester.

"My dear." Her father went over to her. "Calm down, child. Don't be so strung up. Time heals everything."

"Not some things. What shall we do? Oh! What shall we *do?*"

"Hester, come with me." Kirsten put a hand on her shoulder.

"I don't want anybody." Hester ran out of the room. A moment later they heard the front door bang.

Kirsten said:

"All this! It is not good for her."

"I don't think it's really true, either," said Philip Durrant thoughtfully.

"What isn't true?" asked Gwenda.

"That we shall never know the truth. . . . I feel a kind of pricking in my thumbs."

His face, faun-like and almost mischievous, lit up with a queer smile.

"Please, Philip, be careful," said Tina.

He looked at her in surprise.

"Little Tina. And what do you know about it all?"

"I hope," said Tina very clearly and distinctly, "that I do not know anything."

14

"Don't suppose you got anything?" said the Chief Constable.

"Nothing definite, sir," said Huish. "And yet—the time wasn't altogether wasted."

"Let's hear about it all."

"Well, our main times and premises are the same. Mrs. Argyle was alive just before seven, talked with her husband and Gwenda Vaughan, was seen afterwards downstairs by Hester Argyle. Three people can't be in cahoots. Jacko Argyle is now accounted for, so it means that she could have been killed by her husband, any time between five past seven and half past, by Gwenda Vaughan at five minutes past seven on her way out, by Hester just before that, by Kirsten Lindstrom when she came in later—just before half past seven, say. Durrant's paralysis gives him an alibi, but his wife's alibi depends on his word. She could have gone down and killed her mother if she wanted to between seven and half past if her husband was prepared to back her up. Don't see why she should, though. In fact, as far as I can see, only two people have got a real motive for the crime. Leo Argyle and Gwenda Vaughan."

"You think it's one of them—or both of them together?"

"I don't think they were in it together. As I see it, it was an impulsive crime—not a premeditated one. Mrs. Argyle comes into the library, tells them both about Jacko's threats and demands for money. Put it that, later, Leo Argyle goes down to speak to her about Jacko, or about something else. The house is quiet, nobody about. He goes into her sitting-room. There she is, her back to him, sitting at the desk. And there's the poker, still perhaps where Jacko threw it down after threatening her with it. Those quiet, repressed men do break out sometimes. A handkerchief over his hand so as not to leave prints, up with the poker, down with it on her head and it's done. Pull out a drawer or two to suggest a search for money. Then upstairs again till someone finds her. Or put it that Gwenda Vaughan on her way out looks into the room, and the urge comes over her. Jacko will be the perfect scapegoat, and the way to marriage with Leo Argyle is open."

Major Finney nodded thoughtfully.

"Yes. Could be. And of course they were careful not to announce an engagement too soon. Not till that poor little devil Jacko was safely convicted of murder. Yes, that seems fair enough. Crimes are very monotonous. Husband and third party, or wife and third party—always the same old pattern. But what can *we* do about it, Huish, eh? What can we do about it?"

"I don't see, sir," said Huish slowly, "what we can do about it. *We* may be sure—but where's the evidence? Nothing to stand up in court."

"No—no. But you are sure, Huish? Sure in your own mind?"

"Not as sure as I'd like to be," said Superintendent Huish, sadly.

"Ah! Why not?"

"The kind of man he is—Mr. Argyle, I mean."

"Not the kind to do murder?"

"It's not that so much—not the murder part of it. It's the boy. I don't see him deliberately framing the boy."

"It wasn't his own son, remember. He may not have cared much for the boy—he may even have been resentful—of the affection his wife lavished on him."

"That may be so. Yet he seems to have been fond of all the children. He looks fond of them."

"Of course," said Finney, thoughtfully. "He knew the boy wouldn't be hanged. . . . That might make a difference."

"Ah, you may have something there, sir. He may have thought that ten years in prison which is what a life sentence amounts to, might have done the boy no harm."

"What about the young woman—Gwenda Vaughan?"

"If she did it," said Huish, "I don't suppose she'd have any qualms about Jacko. Women are ruthless."

"Anyway, you're reasonably satisfied it's between those two?"

"Reasonably satisfied, yes."

"But no more?" the Chief Constable pressed him.

"No. There's *something* going on. Undercurrents, as you might say."

"Explain yourself, Huish."

"What I'd really like to know is what they think themselves. About each other."

"Oh, I see, I get you now. You're wondering if they themselves know who it was?"

"Yes. I can't make up my mind about it. Do they *all* know? And are they all agreed to keep it dark? I don't think so. I think it's even possible that they may all have different ideas. There's the Swedish woman—she's a mass of nerves. Right on edge. That may be because she did it herself. She's the age when women go slightly off their rocker in one way or another. She may be frightened for herself or for somebody else. I've the impression, I may be wrong, it's for somebody else."

"Leo?"

"No, I don't think it's Leo she's upset about. I think it's the young one—Hester."

"Hester, h'm? Any chance that it might have been Hester?"

"No ostensible motive. But she's a passionate, perhaps slightly unbalanced type."

"And Lindstrom probably knows a good deal more about the girl than we do."

"Yes. Then there's the little dark one who works in the County library."

"She wasn't in the house that night, was she?"

"No. But I think she knows something. Knows who did it, maybe."

"Guesses? Or knows?"

"She's worried. I don't think it's only guessing."

He went on: "And there's the other boy. Micky. He wasn't there, either, *but* he was out in a car, nobody with him. He *says* he was testing the car up towards the moor and Minchin Hill. We've only his word for it. He could have driven over, gone into the house, killed her and driven away again. Gwenda Vaughan said something that wasn't in her original statement. She said a car passed her, just at the entrance to the private road. There are fourteen houses in the road, so it might have been going to any one of them and nobody will remember after two years—but it means there's just a possibility that the car was Micky's."

"Why should he want to kill his adopted mother?"

"No reason that we know about—but there might be one."

"Who would know?"

"They'd all know," said Huish. "But they wouldn't tell us. Not if they knew they were telling us, that is."

"I perceive your devilish intention," said Major Finney. "Who are you going to work on?"

"Lindstrom, I think. If I can break down her defences. I also hope to find out if she herself had a grudge against Mrs. Argyle.

"And there's the paralysed chap," he added. "Philip Durrant."

"What about him?"

"Well, I think he's beginning to have a few ideas about it all. I don't suppose he'll want to share them with me, but I may be able to get an inkling of the way his mind is working. He's an intelligent fellow, and I should say pretty observant. He may have noticed one or two rather interesting things."

II

"Come out, Tina, and let's get some air."

"Air?" Tina looked up at Micky doubtfully. "But it's so cold, Micky." She shivered a little.

"I believe you hate fresh air, Tina. That's why you're able to stand being cooped up in that library all day long."

Tina smiled.

"I do not mind being cooped up in winter. It is very nice and warm in the library."

Micky looked down on her.

"And there you sit, all cuddled up like a cosy little kitten in front of the fire. But it'll do you good to get out, all the same. Come on, Tina. I want to talk to you. I want to—oh, to get some air into my lungs, forget all this bloody police business."

Tina got up from her chair with a lazy, graceful movement not unlike that of the kitten to which Micky had just compared her.

In the hall she wrapped a fur-collared tweed coat round her and they went out together.

"Aren't you even going to put a coat on, Micky?"

"No. I never feel the cold."

"Brrr," said Tina gently. "How I hate this country in the winter. I would like to go abroad. I would like to be somewhere where the sun was always shining and the air was moist and soft and warm."

"I've just been offered a job out in the Persian Gulf," said Micky, "with one of the oil companies. The job's looking after motor transport."

"Are you going?"

"No, I don't think so. . . . What's the good?"

They walked round to the back of the house and started down a zig-zag path through trees which led finally to the beach on the river below. Halfway down there was a small summer-house sheltered from the wind. They did not at once sit down but stood in front of it, gazing out over the river.

"It's beautiful here, isn't it?" said Micky.

Tina looked at the view with incurious eyes.

"Yes," she said, "yes, perhaps it is."

"But you don't really know, do you?" said Micky, looking at her affectionately, "you don't realise the beauty, Tina, you never have."

"I do not remember," said Tina, "in all the years we lived here that you ever enjoyed the beauty of this place. You were always fretting, longing to go back to London."

"That was different," said Micky shortly. "I didn't belong here."

"That is what is the matter, isn't it?" said Tina. "You do not belong anywhere."

"I don't belong anywhere," said Micky in a dazed voice. "Perhaps that's true. My goodness, Tina, what a frightening thought. Do you remember that old song? Kirsten used to sing it to us, I believe. Something about a dove. *O fair dove, O fond dove, O dove with the white, white breast*. Do you remember?"

Tina shook her head.

"Perhaps she sang it to you, but—no, I do not remember."

Micky went on, half speaking, half humming.

"O maid most dear, I am not here. I have no place, no part, No dwelling more by sea nor shore, But only in thy heart." He looked at Tina. "I suppose that could be true."

Tina put a small hand on his arm.

"Come, Micky, sit down here. It is out of the wind. It is not so cold."

As he obeyed her she went on:

"Must you be so unhappy always?"

"My dear girl, you don't begin to understand the first thing about it."

"I understand a good deal," said Tina. "Why can't you forget about her, Micky?"

"Forget about her? Who are you talking about?"

"Your mother," said Tina.

"Forget about her!" said Micky bitterly. "Is there much chance of forgetting after this morning—after the questions! If anyone's been murdered, they don't let you 'forget about her'!"

"I did not mean that," said Tina. "I meant your real mother."

"Why should I think about her? I never saw her after I was six years old."

"But, Micky, you did think about her. All the time."

"Did I ever tell you so?"

"Sometimes one knows about these things," said Tina.

Micky turned and looked at her.

"You're such a quiet, soft little creature, Tina. Like a little black cat. I want to stroke your fur the right way. Nice pussy! Pretty little pussy!" His hand stroked the sleeve of her coat.

Tina, sitting still, smiled at him as he did so. Micky said:

"You didn't hate her, did you, Tina? All the rest of us did."

"That was very unkind," said Tina. She shook her head at him and went on with some energy: "Look what she gave you, all of you. A home, warmth, kindness, good food, toys to play with, people to look after you and keep you safe—"

"Yes, yes," said Micky, impatiently. "Saucers of cream and lots of fur-stroking. That was all you wanted, was it, little pussy cat?"

"I was grateful for it," said Tina. "None of you were grateful."

"Don't you understand, Tina, that one can't be grateful when one ought to be? In some ways it makes it worse, feeling the obligation of gratitude. I didn't *want* to be brought here. I didn't *want* to be given luxurious surroundings. I didn't *want* to be taken away from my own home."

"You might have been bombed," Tina pointed out. "You might have been killed."

"What would it matter? I wouldn't mind being killed. I'd have been killed in my own place, with my own people about me. Where I belonged. There you are, you see. We're back to it again. There's nothing so bad as not belonging. But you, little pussy cat, you only care for material things."

"Perhaps that is true in a way," said Tina. "Perhaps that is why I do not feel like the rest of you. I do not feel that odd resentment that you all seem to feel—you most of all, Micky. It is easy for me to be grateful because, you see, I did *not* want to be *myself*. I did *not* want to be where I was. I wanted to escape from myself. I wanted to be someone else. And she made me into someone else. She made me into Christina Argyle with a home and with affection. Secure. Safe. I loved Mother because she gave me all those things."

"What about your own mother? Don't you ever think of her?"

"Why should I? I hardly remember her. I was only three years old, remember, when I came here. I was always frightened—terrified—with her. All those noisy quarrels with seamen, and she herself—I suppose, now that I am old enough to remember properly, that she must have been drunk most of the time." Tina spoke in a detached, wondering voice. "No, I do not think about her, or remember her. Mrs. Argyle was my mother. This is my home."

"It's so easy for you, Tina," said Micky.

"And why is it hard for you? Because you make it so! It was not Mrs. Argyle you hated, Micky, it was your own mother. Yes, I know that what I am saying is true. And if you killed Mrs. Argyle, as you may have done, then it was your own mother you wanted to kill."

"Tina! What the hell are you talking about?"

"And now," went on Tina, talking calmly, "you have nobody to hate any longer. And that makes you quite lonely, doesn't it? But you've got to learn to live without hate, Micky. It may be difficult, but it can be done."

"I don't know what you're talking about. What did you mean by saying that I may have killed her? You know perfectly well I was nowhere near here that day. I was testing out a customer's car up on the Moor Road, by Minchin Hill."

"Were you?" said Tina.

She got up and stepped forward till she stood at the Lookout Point from where you could look down to the river below.

"What are you getting at?" Micky came up behind her.

Tina pointed down to the beach.

"Who are those two people down there?"

Micky gave a quick cursory glance.

"Hester and her doctor pal, I think," he said. "But Tina, what did you mean? For God's sake don't stand there right at the edge."

"Why—do you want to push me over? You could. I'm very small, you know."

Micky said hoarsely:

"Why do you say I may have been here that evening?"

Tina did not answer. She turned and began walking back up the path to the house.

"Tina!"

Tina said in her quiet, soft voice:

"I'm worried, Micky. I'm very worried about Hester and Don Craig."

"Never mind about Hester and her boy-friend."

"But I do mind about them. I am afraid that Hester is very unhappy."

"We're not talking about them."

"I am talking about them. They matter, you see."

"Have you believed all along, Tina, that I was here the night Mother was killed?"

Tina did not reply.

"You didn't say anything at the time."

"Why should I? There was no need. I mean, it was so obvious that Jacko had killed her."

"And now it's equally obvious that Jacko didn't kill her."

Again Tina nodded.

"And so?" Micky asked. "And so?"

She did not answer him, but continued to walk up the path to the house.

III

On the little beach by the point, Hester scuffled the sand with the point of her shoe.

"I don't see what there is to talk about," she said.

"You've got to talk about it," said Don Craig.

"I don't see why. . . . Talking about a thing never does any good—it never makes it any better."

"You might at least tell me what happened this morning."

"Nothing," said Hester.

"What do you mean—nothing? The police came along, didn't they?"

"Oh yes, they came along."

"Well, then, did they question you all?"

"Yes," said Hester, "they questioned us."

"What sort of questions?"

"All the usual ones," said Hester. "Really just the same as before. Where we were and what we did, and when we last saw Mother alive. Really, Don, I don't want to talk about it any more. It's over now."

"But it isn't over, dearest. That's just the point."

"I don't see why *you* need to fuss," said Hester. "*You're* not mixed up in this."

"Darling, I want to help you. Don't you understand?"

"Well, talking about it doesn't help me. I just want to forget. If you'd help me to forget, that would be different."

"Hester, dearest, it's no good running away from things. You must face them."

"I've been facing them, as you call it, all the morning."

"Hester, I love you. You know that, don't you?"

"I suppose so," said Hester.

"What do you mean, you suppose so?"

"Going on and on about it all."

"But I have to do that."

"I don't see why. *You're* not a policeman."

"Who was the last person to see your mother alive?"

"I was," said Hester.

"I know. That was just before seven, wasn't it, just before you came out to meet me."

"Just before I came out to go to Drymouth—to the Playhouse," said Hester.

"Well, I was at the Playhouse, wasn't I?"

"Yes, of course you were."

"You did know then, didn't you, Hester, that I loved you?"

"I wasn't sure," said Hester. "I wasn't even sure then that I was beginning to love you."

"You'd no reason, had you, no earthly reason for doing away with your mother?"

"No, not really," said Hester.

"What do you mean by not really?"

"I often thought about killing her," said Hester in a matter-of-fact voice. "I used to say 'I wish she was dead, I wish she was dead.' Sometimes," she added, "I used to dream that I killed her."

"In what way did you kill her in your dream?"

For a moment Don Craig was no longer the lover but the interested young doctor.

"Sometimes I shot her," said Hester cheerfully, "and sometimes I banged her on the head."

Dr. Craig groaned.

"That was just dreaming," said Hester. "I'm often *very* violent in dreams."

"Listen, Hester." The young man took her hand in his. "You've got to tell me the truth. You've got to trust me."

"I don't understand what you mean," said Hester.

"The truth, Hester. I want the *truth*. I love you—and I'll stand by you. If—if you killed her I—I think I can find out the reasons why. I don't think it will have been exactly your fault. Do you understand? Certainly I'd never go to the police about it. It will be between you and me only. Nobody else will suffer. The whole thing will die down for want of evidence. But I've got to *know*." He stressed the last word strongly.

Hester was looking at him. Her eyes were wide, almost unfocused.

"What do you want me to say to you?" she said.

"I want you to tell me the truth."

"You think you know the truth already, don't you? You think—I killed her."

"Hester, darling, don't look at me like that." He took her by the shoulders and shook her gently. "I'm a doctor. I know the reasons behind these things. I know that people can't always be held responsible for their actions. I know you for what you are—sweet and lovely and essentially all right. I'll help you. I'll look after you. We'll get married, then we'll be happy. You need never feel lost, unwanted, tyrannised over. The things we do often spring from reasons most people don't understand."

"That's very much what we all said about Jacko, isn't it?" said Hester.

"Never mind Jacko. It's you I'm thinking about. I love you so very much, Hester, but I've got to know the truth."

"The truth?" said Hester.

A very slow, mocking smile curved the corners of her mouth upwards.

"Please, darling."

Hester turned her head and looked up.

"There's Gwenda calling me. It must be lunch time."

"Hester!"

"Would you believe me if I told you I didn't kill her?"

"Of course I'd—I'd believe you."

"I don't think you would," said Hester.

She turned sharply away from him and began running up the path. He made a movement to follow her, then abandoned it.

"Oh, hell," said Donald Craig. "Oh, *hell!*"

15

"But I don't want to go home just yet," said Philip Durrant. He spoke with plaintive irritability.

"But, Philip, really, there's nothing to stay here for, any longer. I mean, we had to come to see Mr. Marshall to discuss the thing, and then wait for the police interviews. But now there's nothing to stop us going home right away."

"I think your father's quite happy for us to stop on for a bit," said Philip. "He likes having someone to play chess with in the evenings. My word, he's a wizard at chess. I thought I wasn't bad, but I never get the better of him."

"Father can find someone else to play chess with," said Mary shortly.

"What—whistle someone up from the Women's Institute?"

"And anyway, we ought to go home," said Mary. "Tomorrow is Mrs. Carden's day for doing the brasses."

"Polly, the perfect housewife!" said Philip laughing. "Anyway, Mrs. Whatsaname can do the brasses without you, can't she? Or if she can't, send her a telegram and tell her to let them moulder for another week."

"You don't understand, Philip, about household things, and how difficult they are."

"I don't see that any of them are difficult unless you make them difficult. Anyway, *I* want to stop on."

"Oh, Philip," Mary spoke with exasperation, "I do so hate it here."

"But why?"

"It's so gloomy, so miserable and—and all that's happened here. The murder and everything."

"Now, come, Polly, don't tell me you're a mass of nerves over things of that kind. I'm sure you could take murder without turning a hair. No, you want to go home because you want to see to the brasses and dust the place and make sure no moths have got into your fur coat—"

"Moths don't go into fur coats in winter," said Mary.

"Well, you know what I mean, Polly. The general idea. But you see, from my point of view, it's so much more interesting here."

"More interesting than being in our own home?" Mary sounded both shocked and hurt.

Philip looked at her quickly.

"I'm sorry, darling, I didn't put it very well. Nothing could be nicer than our own home, and you've made it really lovely. Comfortable, neat, attractive. You see, it'd be quite different if—if I were like I used to be. I mean, I'd have lots of things to do all day. I'd be up to my ears in schemes. And it would be perfect coming back to you and having our own home, talking about everything that had happened during the day. But you see, it's different now."

"Oh, I know it's different in *that* way," said Mary. "Don't think I ever forget that, Phil. I do mind. I mind most terribly."

"Yes," said Philip, and he spoke almost between his teeth. "Yes, you mind too much, Mary. You mind so much that sometimes it makes me mind more. All I want is distraction and—no"—he held up his hand—"don't tell me that I can get distraction from jigsaw puzzles and all the gadgets of occupational therapy and having people to come and give me treatment, and reading endless books. I want so badly some times to get my teeth into something! And here, in this house, there *is* something to get one's teeth into."

"Philip," Mary caught her breath, "you're not *still* harping on—on that idea of yours?"

"Playing at Murder Hunt?" said Philip. "Murder, murder, who did the murder? Yes, Polly, you're not far off. I want desperately to know who did it."

"But why? And how can you know? If somebody broke in or found the door open—"

"Still harping on the outsider theory?" asked Philip. "It won't wash, you know. Old Marshall put a good face upon it. But actually he was just helping *us* to keep face. Nobody believes in that beautiful theory. It just isn't true."

"Then you must see, if it isn't true," Mary interrupted him, "if it isn't true—if it was, as you put it, one of us—then I don't want to know. Why should we know? Aren't we—aren't we a hundred times better not knowing?"

Philip Durrant looked up at her questioningly.

"Putting your head in the sand, eh, Polly? Haven't you any natural curiosity?"

"I tell you I don't want to know! I think it's all horrible. I want to forget it and not think about it."

"Didn't you care enough for your mother to want to know who killed her?"

"What good would it do, knowing who killed her? For two years we've been quite satisfied that Jacko killed her."

"Yes," said Philip, "lovely the way we've all been satisfied."

His wife looked at him doubtfully.

"I don't—I really don't know what you mean, Philip."

"Can't you see, Polly, that in a way this is a challenge to me? A challenge to my intelligence? I don't mean that I've felt your mother's death particularly keenly or that I was particularly fond of her. I wasn't. She'd done her very best to stop you marrying me, but I bore her no grudge for that because I succeeded in carrying you off all right. Didn't I, my girl? No, it's not a wish for revenge, it's not even a passion for justice. I think it's—yes, mainly curiosity, though perhaps there's a better side to it than that."

"It's the sort of thing you oughtn't to meddle about with," said Mary. "No good can come of your meddling about with it. Oh, Philip, please, please *don't*. Let's go home and forget all about it."

"Well," said Philip, "you can pretty well cart me anywhere you like, can't you? But I want to stay here. Don't you sometimes want me to do what *I* want to do?"

"I want you to have everything in the world you want," said Mary.

"You don't really, darling. You just want to look after me like a baby in arms and know what's best for me every day and in every possible way." He laughed.

Mary said, looking at him doubtfully:

"I never know when you're serious or not."

"Apart from curiosity," said Philip Durrant, "somebody ought to find out the truth, you know."

"Why? What good can it do? Having someone else sent to prison. I think it's a horrible idea."

"You don't quite understand," said Philip. "I didn't say that I'd turn in whoever it was (if I discovered who it was) to the police. I don't think that I would. It depends, of course, on the circumstances. Probably it wouldn't be any use my turning them over to the police because I still think that there couldn't be any real evidence."

"Then if there isn't any real evidence," said Mary, "how are you going to find out anything?"

"Because," said Philip, "there are lots of ways of finding out things, of knowing them quite certainly once and for all. And I think, you know, that that's becoming rather necessary. Things aren't going very well in this house and very soon they'll be getting worse."

"What do you mean?"

"Haven't you noticed anything, Polly? What about your father and Gwenda Vaughan?"

"What about them? Why my father should want to marry again at his age—"

"I can understand that," said Philip. "After all, he had rather a raw deal in marriage. He's got a chance now of real happiness. Autumn happiness, if you like, but he's got it. Or, shall we say, he had it. Things aren't going too well between them now."

"I suppose, all this business—" said Mary vaguely.

"Exactly," said Philip. "All this business. It's shoving them farther apart every day. And there could be two reasons for that. Suspicion or guilt."

"Suspicion of whom?"

"Well, let's say of each other. Or suspicion on one side and consciousness of guilt on the other and vice versa and as you were and as you like it."

"Don't, Philip, you're confusing me." Suddenly a faint trace of animation came into Mary's manner. "So you think it was Gwenda?" she said. "Perhaps you're right. Oh, what a blessing it would be if it was Gwenda."

"Poor Gwenda. Because she's one removed from the family, you mean?"

"Yes," said Mary. "I mean then it wouldn't be one of *us*."

"That's all you feel about it, is it?" said Philip. "How it affects *us*."

"Of course," said Mary.

"Of course, of course," said Philip irritably. "The trouble with you is, Polly, you haven't got any imagination. You can't put yourself in anyone else's place."

"Why should one?" asked Mary.

"Yes, why should one?" said Philip. "I suppose if I'm honest I'd say to pass the time away. But I can put myself in your father's place, or in Gwenda's, and if they're innocent, what hell it must be. What hell for Gwenda to be held suddenly at arms' length. To know in her heart that she's not going to be able to marry the man she loves after all. And then put yourself in your father's place. He knows, he can't help knowing, that the woman he is in love with had an opportunity to do the murder and had a motive, too. He *hopes* she didn't do it, he *thinks* she didn't do it, but he isn't *sure*. And what's more he never will be sure."

"At his age—" began Mary.

"Oh, at his age, at his age," said Philip impatiently. "Don't you realise it's worse for a man of that age? It's the last love of his life. He's not likely to have another. It goes deep. And taking the other point of view," he went on, "suppose Leo came out of the mists and shadows of the self-contained world that he's managed to live in so long. Suppose it was he who struck down his wife? One can almost feel sorry for the poor devil, can't one? Not," he added meditatively, "that I really can imagine his doing anything of the sort for a moment. But I've no doubt the police can imagine it all right. Now, Polly, let's hear your views. Who do you think did it?"

"How can I possibly know?" said Mary.

"Well, perhaps you can't know," said Philip, "but you might have a very good idea—if you thought."

"I tell you I refuse to think about the thing at all."

"I wonder why. . . . Is that just distaste? Or is it—perhaps—because you *do* know? Perhaps in your own cool, calm mind you're quite sure. . . . So sure that you don't want to think about it, that you don't want to tell *me?* Is it Hester you've got in mind?"

"Why on earth should Hester want to kill Mother?"

"No real reason, is there?" said Philip meditatively. "But you know, you do read of those things. A son or a daughter fairly well looked after, indulged, and then one day some silly little thing happens. Fond parent refuses to stump up for the cinema or for buying a new pair of shoes or says when you're going out with the boy-friend you've got to be in at ten. It mayn't be anything very important but it seems to set a match to a train that's already laid, and suddenly the adolescent in question has a brainstorm and up with a hammer or an axe, or possibly a poker, and that's that. Always hard to explain, but it happens. It's the culmination of a long train of repressed rebellion. That's a pattern which would fit Hester. You see, with Hester the trouble is that one doesn't know what goes on in that rather lovely head of hers. She's weak, of course, and she resents being weak. And your mother was the sort of person who would make her feel conscious of her weakness. Yes," said Philip, leaning forward with some animation, "I think I could make out quite a good case for Hester."

"Oh, will you stop talking about it," cried Mary.

"Oh, I'll stop talking," said Philip. "Talking won't get me anywhere. Or will it? After all, one has to decide in one's own mind what the pattern of the murder might be, and apply that pattern to each of the different people concerned. And then when you've got it taped out the way it must have been, *then* you start laying your little pitfalls and see if they tumble into them."

"There were only four people in the house," said Mary. "You speak as though there were half a dozen or more. I agree with you that Father couldn't possibly have done it, and it's absurd to think that Hester could have any real reason for doing anything of that kind. That leaves Kirsty and Gwenda."

"Which of them do you prefer?" asked Philip, with faint mockery in his tone.

"I can't really imagine Kirsty doing such a thing," said Mary. "She's always been so patient and good-tempered. Really quite devoted to Mother. I suppose she *could* go queer suddenly. One does hear of such things, but she's never *seemed* at all queer."

"No," said Philip thoughtfully, "I'd say Kirsty is a very normal woman, the sort of woman who'd have liked a normal woman's life. In a way she's something of the same type as Gwenda, only Gwenda is good-looking and attractive and poor old Kirsty is plain as a currant bun. I don't suppose any man's ever looked at her twice. But she'd have liked them to. She'd have liked to have fallen in love and married. It must be pretty fair hell to be born a woman and to be born plain and unattractive, especially if that isn't compensated for by having any special talent or brain. The truth is she'd been here far too long. She ought to have left after the war, gone on with her profession as masseuse. She might have hooked some well off elderly patient."

"You're like all men," said Mary. "You think women think of nothing but getting married."

Philip grinned.

"I still think it's all women's first choice," he said. "Hasn't Tina any boy-friends, by the way?"

"Not that I know of," said Mary. "But she doesn't talk much about herself."

"No, she's a quiet little mouse, isn't she? Not exactly pretty, but very graceful. I wonder what she knows about this business?"

"I don't suppose she knows anything," said Mary.

"Don't you?" said Philip. "I do."

"Oh, you just imagine things," said Mary.

"I'm not imagining this. Do you know what the girl said? She said she hoped she didn't know anything. Rather a curious way of putting things. I bet she *does* know something."

"What sort of thing?"

"Perhaps there's something that ties in somewhere, but she herself doesn't quite realise where it does tie in. I hope to get it out of her."

"Philip!"

"It's no good, Polly. I've got a mission in life. I've persuaded myself that it's very much in the public interest that I should get down to it. Now where shall I start? I rather think I'll work on Kirsty first. In many ways she's a simple soul."

"I wish—oh, how I wish," said Mary, "that you'd give all this crazy idea up and come home. We were so happy. Everything was going along so well—" Her voice broke as she turned away.

"Polly!" Philip was concerned. "Do you really mind so much? I didn't realise you were quite so upset."

Mary wheeled round, a hopeful look in her eye.

"Then you will come home and forget about it all?"

"I couldn't forget about it all," said Philip. "I'd only go on worrying and puzzling and thinking. Let's stay here till the end of the week anyway, Mary, and then, well, we'll see."

16

"Do you mind if I stay on a bit, Dad?" asked Micky.

"No, of course not. I'm delighted. Is it all right with your firm?"

"Yes," said Micky. "I rang 'em up. I needn't be back until after the week-end. They've been very decent about it. Tina's staying over the week-end too," he said.

He went to the window, looked out, walked across the room with hands in his pockets, gazing up at the book-shelves. He spoke then in a jerky, awkward voice.

"You know, Dad, I do appreciate, really all you've done for me. Just lately I've seen—well, I've seen how ungrateful I've always been."

"There's never been any question of gratitude," said Leo Argyle. "You are my son, Micky. I have always regarded you as such."

"An odd way of treating a son," said Micky. "You never bossed me about."

Leo Argyle smiled, his remote, far-away smile.

"Do you really think that's the only function of a father?"

He said, "To boss his children about?"

"No," said Micky, "no. I suppose it isn't." He went on, speaking in a rush. "I've been a damned fool," he said. "Yes. A damned fool. It's comic in a way. Do you know what I'd like to do, what I'm thinking of doing? Taking a job with an oil company out in the Persian Gulf. That was what Mother wanted to put me into to begin with—an oil company. But I wasn't having any then! Flung off on my own."

"You were at the age," said Leo, "when you wanted to choose for yourself, and you hated the idea of anything being chosen for you. You've always been rather like that, Micky. If we wanted to buy you a red sweater, you insisted you wanted a blue one, but all the time it was probably a red one you wanted."

"True enough," said Micky, with a short laugh. "I've been an unsatisfactory sort of creature always."

"Just young," said Leo. "Just kicking up your heels. Apprehensive of the bridle, of the saddle, of control. We all feel like that at one time in our lives, but we have to come to it in the end."

"Yes, I suppose so," said Micky.

"I'm very glad," said Leo, "that you have got this idea for the future. I don't think, you know, that just working as a car salesman and demonstrator is quite good enough for you. It's all right, but it doesn't lead anywhere."

"I like cars," said Micky. "I like getting the best out of them. I can do a line of talk when I have to. Patter, patter, all the smarmy bits, but I don't enjoy the life, blast it. This is a job to do with motor transport, anyway. Controlling the servicing of cars. Quite an important job."

"You know," said Leo, "that at any time you might want to finance yourself, to buy yourself into any business you thought worth while, the money is there, available. You know about the Discretionary Trust. I am quite prepared to authorise any necessary sum provided always that the business details are passed and acceptable. We would get expert opinion on that. But the money is there, ready for you if you want it."

"Thanks, Dad, but I don't want to sponge on you."

"There's no question of sponging, Micky, it's *your* money. Definitely made over to you in common with the others. All I have is the power of appointment, the when and the how. But it's not my money and I'm not giving it to you. It's yours."

"It's Mother's money really," said Micky.

"The Trust was made several years ago," said Leo.

"I don't want any of it!" said Micky. "I don't want to touch it! I couldn't! As things are, I *couldn't*." He flushed suddenly as he met his father's eye. He said uncertainly: "I didn't—I didn't quite mean to say that."

"Why can't you touch it?" said Leo. "We adopted you. That is, we took full responsibility for you, financial and otherwise. It was a business arrangement that you should be brought up as our son and properly provided for in life."

"I want to stand on my own feet," Micky repeated.

"Yes. I see you do. . . . Very well, then, Micky, but if you change your mind, remember the money is there, waiting."

"Thanks, Dad. It's good of you to understand. Or at least, not to understand, to let me have my way. I wish I could explain better. You see, I don't want to profit by—I can't profit by—oh, dammit all, it's all too difficult to talk about."

There was a knock on the door which was almost more a bump.

"That's Philip, I expect," said Leo Argyle. "Will you open the door for him, Micky."

Micky went across to open the door, and Philip, working his invalid chair, propelled himself into the room. He greeted them both with a cheerful grin.

"Are you very busy, sir?" he asked Leo. "If so, say so. I'll keep quiet and not interrupt you and just browse along the book-shelves."

"No," said Leo, "I have nothing to do this morning."

"Gwenda not here?" asked Philip.

"She rang up to say she had a headache and couldn't come today," said Leo. His voice was expressionless.

"I see," said Philip.

Micky said:

"Well, I shall go and dig out Tina. Make her go for a walk. That girl hates fresh air."

He left the room, walking with a light, springy step.

"Am I wrong," asked Philip, "or is there a change in Micky lately? Not scowling at the world as much as usual, is he?"

"He's growing up," said Leo. "It's taken rather a long time for him to do so."

"Well, he's chosen a curious time to cheer up," said Philip. "Yesterday's session with the police wasn't exactly encouraging, did you think so?"

Leo said quietly:

"It's painful, of course, to have the whole case reopened."

"A chap like Micky now," said Philip, working his way along the book-shelves, pulling out a volume or two in a desultory manner, "would you say he had much of a conscience?"

"That's an odd question, Philip."

"No, not really. I was just wondering about him. It's like being tone deaf. Some people can't really feel any pangs of guilt or remorse, or even regret for their actions. Jacko didn't."

"No," said Leo, "Jacko certainly didn't."

"And I wondered about Micky," said Philip. He paused, and then went on in a detached voice. "Do you mind if I ask you a question, sir? How much really do you know about the background of all this adopted family of yours?"

"Why do you want to know, Philip?"

"Just curiosity, I suppose. One always wonders, you know, how much there is in heredity."

Leo did not answer. Philip observed him with bright-eyed interest.

"Perhaps," he said, "I'm bothering you asking these questions."

"Well," said Leo, rising, "after all, why shouldn't you ask them? You're one of the family. They are at the moment, one can't disguise it, very pertinent questions to ask. But our family, as you put it, were not adopted in the usual regular sense of the term. Mary, your wife, was formally and legally adopted, but the others came to us in a much more informal manner. Jacko was an orphan and was handed over to us by an old grandmother. She was killed in the blitz and he stayed with us. It was as simple as that. Micky was illegitimate. His mother was only interested in men. She wanted £100 down and got it. We've never known what happened to Tina's mother. She never wrote to the child, she never claimed her after the war, and it was quite impossible to trace her."

"And Hester?"

"Hester was illegitimate too. Her mother was a young Irish hospital nurse. She married an American G.I. shortly after Hester came to us. She begged us to keep the child. She did not propose to tell her husband anything about its birth. She went to the States with her husband at the end of the war and we've never heard any more from her."

"All tragic histories in a way," said Philip. "All poor unwanted little devils."

"Yes," said Leo. "That's what made Rachel feel so passionately about them all. She was determined to make them feel wanted, to give them a real home, be a real mother to them."

"It was a fine thing to do," said Philip.

"Only—only it can never work out exactly as she hoped it might," said Leo. "It was an article of faith with her that the blood tie didn't matter. But the blood tie *does* matter, you know. There is usually something in one's own children, some kink of temperament, some way of feeling that you recognise and can understand without having to put into words. You haven't got that tie with children you adopt. One has no *instinctive* knowledge of what goes on in their minds. You judge them, of course, by yourself, by your own thoughts and feelings, but it's wise to recognise that those thoughts and feelings may be very widely divergent from theirs."

"You understood that, I suppose, all along," said Philip.

"I warned Rachel about it," said Leo, "but of course she didn't believe it. Didn't want to believe it. She wanted them to be her own children."

"Tina's always the dark horse, to my mind," said Philip. "Perhaps it's the half of her that isn't white. Who was the father, do you know?"

"He was a seaman of some kind, I believe. Possibly a Lascar. The mother," added Leo dryly, "was unable to say."

"One doesn't know how she reacts to things, or what she thinks about. She says so little." Philip paused, and then shot out a question: "What does she know about this business that she isn't telling?"

He saw Leo Argyle's hand, that had been turning over papers, stop. There was a moment's pause, and then Leo said:

"Why should you think she isn't telling everything she knows?"

"Come now, sir, it's pretty obvious, isn't it?"

"It's not obvious to me," said Leo.

"She knows something," said Philip. "Something damaging, do you think, about some particular person?"

"I think, Philip, if you'll forgive me for saying so, that it is rather unwise to speculate about these things. One can easily imagine so much."

"Are you warning me off, sir?"

"Is it really your business, Philip?"

"Meaning I'm not a policeman?"

"Yes, that's what I meant. Police have to do their duty. They have to enquire into things."

"And you don't want to enquire into them?"

"Perhaps," said Leo, "I'm afraid of what I should find."

Philip's hand tightened excitedly in his chair. He said softly:

"Perhaps *you* know who did it. Do you, sir?"

"No."

The abruptness and vigour of Leo's reply startled Philip.

"No," said Leo, bringing his hand down on the desk. He was suddenly no longer the frail, attenuated, withdrawn personality that Philip knew so well. "I don't know who did it! D'you hear? I don't know. I haven't the least idea. I don't—I don't *want* to know."

17

"And what are *you* doing, Hester, my love?" asked Philip.

In his wheeled-chair he was propelling himself along the passage. Hester was leaning out of the window halfway along it. She started and drew her head in.

"Oh, it's you," she said.

"Are you observing the universe, or considering suicide?" asked Philip.

She looked at him defiantly.

"What makes you say a thing like that?"

"Obviously it was in your mind," said Philip. "But, frankly, Hester, if you are contemplating such a step, that window is no good. The drop's not deep enough. Think how unpleasant it would be for you with a broken arm and a broken leg, say, instead of the merciful oblivion you are craving?"

"Micky used to climb down the magnolia tree from this window. It was his secret way in and out. Mother never knew."

"The things parents never know! One could write a book about it. But if it's suicide you are contemplating, Hester, just by the summer-house would be a better place to jump from."

"Where it juts out over the river? Yes, one would be dashed on the rocks below!"

"The trouble with you, Hester, is that you're so melodramatic in your imaginings. Most people are quite satisfied with arranging themselves tidily in the gas oven or measuring themselves out an enormous number of sleeping pills."

"I'm glad you're here," said Hester unexpectedly. "You don't mind talking about things, do you?"

"Well, actually, I haven't much else to do nowadays," said Philip. "Come into my room and we'll do some more talking." As she hesitated, he went on: "Mary's downstairs, gone to prepare me some delicious little morning mess with her own fair hands."

"Mary wouldn't understand," said Hester.

"No," Philip agreed, "Mary wouldn't understand in the least."

Philip propelled himself along and Hester walked beside him. She opened the door of the sitting-room and he wheeled himself in. Hester followed.

"But you understand," said Hester. "Why?"

"Well, there's a time, you know, when one thinks about such things. . . . When this business first happened to me, for instance, and I knew that I might be a cripple for life. . . ."

"Yes," said Hester, "that must have been terrible. Terrible. And you were a pilot, too, weren't you? You flew."

"Up above the world so high, like a tea-tray in the sky," agreed Philip.

"I'm terribly sorry," said Hester. "I am really. I ought to have thought about it more, and been more sympathetic!"

"Thank God you weren't," said Philip. "But anyway, that phase is over now. One gets used to anything, you know. That's something, Hester, that you don't appreciate at the moment. But you'll come to it. Unless you do something very rash and very silly first. Now come on, tell me all about it. What's the trouble? I suppose you've had a row with your boy-friend, the solemn young doctor. Is that it?"

"It wasn't a row," said Hester. "It was much worse than a row."

"It will come right," said Philip.

"No, it won't," said Hester. "It can't—ever."

"You're so extravagant in your terms. Everything's black and white to you, isn't it, Hester? No half-tones."

"I can't help being like that," said Hester. "I've always been like it. Everything I thought I could do or wanted to do has always gone wrong. I wanted to have a life of my own, to be someone, to do something. It was all no good. I was no good at *anything*. I've often thought of killing myself. Ever since I was fourteen."

Philip watched her with interest. He said in a quiet, matter-of-fact voice:

"Of course people do kill themselves a good deal, between fourteen and nineteen. It's an age in life when things are very much out of proportion. Schoolboys kill themselves because they don't think they can pass examinations and girls kill themselves because their mothers won't let them go to the pictures with unsuitable boy-friends. It's a kind of period where everything appears to be in glorious technicolour. Joy or despair. Gloom or unparalleled happiness. One snaps out of it. The trouble with you is, Hester, it's taken you longer to snap out of it than most people."

"Mother was always right," said Hester. "All the things she wouldn't let me do and I wanted to do. She was right about them and I was wrong. I couldn't bear it, I simply couldn't bear it! So I thought I'd got to be brave. I'd got to go off on my own. I'd got to test myself. And it all went wrong. I wasn't any good at acting."

"Of course you weren't," said Philip. "You've got no discipline. You can't, as they say in theatrical circles, take production. You're too busy dramatising yourself, my girl. You're doing it now."

"And then I thought I'd have a proper love affair," said Hester. "Not a silly, girlish thing. An older man. He was married, and he'd had a very unhappy life."

"Stock situation," said Philip, "and he exploited it, no doubt."

"I thought it would be a—oh, a grand passion. You're not laughing at me?" She stopped, looking at Philip suspiciously.

"No, I'm not laughing at you, Hester," said Philip gently. "I can see quite well that it must have been hell for you."

"It wasn't a grand passion," said Hester bitterly. "It was just a silly, cheap little affair. None of the things he told me about his life, or his wife, were true. I—I'd just thrown myself at his head. I'd been a fool, a silly, cheap little fool."

"You've got to learn a thing, sometimes, by experience," said Philip. "None of that's done you any harm, you know, Hester. It's probably helped you to grow up. Or it would help you if you let it."

"Mother was so—so competent about it all," said Hester, in a tone of resentment. "She came along and settled everything and told me that if I really wanted to act I'd better go to the dramatic school and do it properly. But I didn't really want to act, and I knew by that time I was no good. So I came home. What else could I do?"

"Probably heaps of things," said Philip. "But that was the easiest."

"Oh, yes," said Hester with fervour. "How well you understand. I'm terribly weak, you see. I always do want to do the easy thing. And if I rebel against it, it's always in some silly way that doesn't really work."

"You're terribly unsure of yourself, aren't you?" said Philip gently.

"Perhaps that's because I'm only adopted," said Hester. "I didn't find out about that, you know, not till I was nearly sixteen. I knew the others were and then I asked one day, and—I found that I was adopted too. It made me feel so awful, as though I didn't belong *anywhere*."

"What a terrible girl you are for dramatising yourself," said Philip.

"She wasn't my mother," said Hester. "She never really understood a single thing I felt. Just looked at me indulgently and kindly and made plans for me. Oh! I hated her. It's awful of me, I know it's awful of me, but I hated her!"

"Actually, you know," said Philip, "most girls go through a short period of hating their own mothers. There wasn't really anything very unusual about that."

"I hated her because she was right," said Hester. "It's so awful when people are always right. It makes you feel more and more inadequate. Oh, Philip, everything's so terrible. What am I going to do? What can I do?"

"Marry that nice young man of yours," said Philip, "and settle down. Be a good little G. P.'s wife. Or isn't that magnificent enough for you?"

"He doesn't want to marry me now," said Hester mournfully.

"Are you sure? Did he tell you so? Or are you only imagining it?"

"He thinks I killed Mother."

"Oh," said Philip, and paused a minute. "Did you?" he asked.

She wheeled round at him.

"Why do you ask me that? Why?"

"I thought it would be interesting to know," said Philip. "All in the family, so to speak. Not for passing on to the authorities."

"If I did kill her, do you think I'd tell you?" said Hester.

"It would be much wiser not to," agreed Philip.

"He told me he knew I'd killed her," said Hester. "He told me that if I'd only admit it, if I'd confess it to him, that it would be all right, that we'd be married, that he'd look after me. That—that he wouldn't let it matter between us."

Philip whistled.

"Well, well, well," he said.

"What's the good?" asked Hester. "What's the good of telling him I didn't kill her? He wouldn't believe it, would he?"

"He ought to," said Philip, "if you tell him so."

"I didn't kill her," said Hester. "You understand? I didn't kill her. I didn't, I didn't, I didn't." She broke off. "That sounds unconvincing," she said.

"The truth often does sound unconvincing," Philip encouraged her.

"We don't know," said Hester. "Nobody knows. We all *look* at each other. Mary looks at me. And Kirsten. She's so kind to me, so protective. She thinks it's me, too. What chance have I? That's it, don't you see? What chance have I? It would be better, much better, to go down to the Point, throw myself over. . . ."

"For God's sake, don't be a fool, Hester. There are other things to do."

"What other things? How can there be? I've lost everything. How can I go on living day after day?" She looked at Philip. "You think I'm wild, unbalanced. Well, perhaps I did kill her. Perhaps it's remorse gnawing at me. Perhaps I can't forget—*here*." She put her hand dramatically to her heart.

"Don't be a little idiot," said Philip. He shot out an arm and pulled her to him.

Hester half fell across his chair. He kissed her.

"What you need is a husband, my girl," he said. "Not that solemn young ass, Donald Craig, with his head full of psychiatry and jargon. You're silly and idiotic and—completely lovely, Hester."

The door opened. Mary Durrant stood abruptly still in the doorway. Hester struggled to an upright position and Philip gave his wife a sheepish grin.

"I'm just cheering up Hester, Polly," he said.

"Oh," said Mary.

She came in carefully, placing the tray on a small table. Then she wheeled the table up beside him. She did not look at Hester. Hester looked uncertainly from husband to wife.

"Oh well," she said, "perhaps I'd better go and—go and—" She didn't finish.

She went out of the room, shutting the door behind her.

"Hester's in a bad way," said Philip. "Contemplating suicide. I was trying to dissuade her," he added.

Mary did not answer.

He stretched out a hand towards her. She moved away from him.

"Polly, have I made you angry? Very angry?"

She did not reply.

"Because I kissed her, I suppose? Come, Polly, don't grudge me one silly little kiss. She was so lovely and so silly—and I suddenly felt—well, I felt it would be fun to be a gay dog again and have a flirtation now and then. Come, Polly, kiss me. Kiss and make friends."

Mary Durrant said:

"Your soup will get cold if you don't drink it."

She went through the door to the bedroom and shut it behind her.

18

"There's a young lady down below wanting to see you, sir."

"A young lady?" Calgary looked surprised. He could not think who was likely to visit him. He looked at the work which littered his desk, and frowned. The voice of the hall porter spoke again, discreetly lowered.

"A real young lady, sir, a very nice young lady."

"Oh, well. Show her up then."

Calgary could not help smiling to himself slightly. The discreet undertones and the assurance tickled his sense of humour. He wondered who it could be who wanted to see him. He was completely astonished when his door bell buzzed and on going to open it he was confronted by Hester Argyle.

"You!" The exclamation came out with full surprise. Then, "Come in, come in," he said. He drew her inside and shut the door.

Strangely enough, his impression of her was almost the same as the first time he had seen her. She was dressed with no regard to the conventions of London. She was hatless, her dark hair hanging round her face in a kind of elf lock disarray. The heavy tweed coat showed a dark green skirt and sweater underneath. She looked as though she had just come in breathless from a walk on the moor.

"Please," said Hester, "please, you've got to help me."

"To help you?" He was startled. "In what way? Of course I'll help you if I can."

"I didn't know what to do," said Hester. "I didn't know who to come to. But someone's got to help me. I can't go on, and you're the person. You started it all."

"You're in trouble of some kind? Bad trouble?"

"We're all in trouble," said Hester. "But one's so selfish, isn't one? I mean, I only think of myself."

"Sit down, my dear," he said gently.

He cleared papers off an arm-chair and settled her there. Then he went over to his corner cupboard.

"You must have a glass of wine," he said. "A glass of dry sherry. Will that suit you?"

"If you like. It doesn't matter."

"It's very wet and cold out. You need something."

He turned, decanter and glass in hand. Hester was slumped down in the chair with a queer kind of angular grace that touched him by its complete abandonment.

"Don't worry," he said gently, as he put the glass by her side and filled it. "Things are never quite so bad as they seem, you know."

"People say that, but it's not true," said Hester. "Sometimes they're worse than they seem." She sipped the wine, then she said accusingly, "We were all right till you came. Quite all right. Then—then it all started."

"I won't pretend," said Arthur Calgary, "that I don't know what you mean. It took me completely aback when you first said that to me, but now I understand better what my—my information must have brought to you."

"So long as we thought it was Jacko—" Hester said and broke off.

"I know, Hester, I know. But you've got to go behind that, you know. What you were living in was a false security. It wasn't a real thing, it was only a thing of make-believe, of cardboard—a kind of stage scenery. Something that represented security but which was not really, and could never be, security."

"You're saying, aren't you," said Hester, "that one must have courage, that it's no good snatching at a thing because it's false and easy?" She paused a minute and then said: "*You* had courage! I realise that. To come and tell us yourself. Not knowing how we'd feel, how we'd react. It was brave of you. I admire bravery because, you see, I'm not really very brave myself."

"Tell me," said Calgary gently, "tell me just what the trouble is now. It's something special, isn't it?"

"I had a dream," said Hester. "There's someone—a young man—a doctor—"

"I see," said Calgary. "You are friends, or, perhaps, more than friends?"

"I thought," said Hester, "we were more than friends. . . . And he thought so too. But you see, now that all this has come up—"

"Yes?" said Calgary.

"He thinks I did it," said Hester. Her words came with a rush. "Or perhaps he doesn't think I did it but he's not sure. He can't be sure. He thinks—I can see he thinks—that I'm the most likely person. Perhaps I am. Perhaps we all think that about each other. And I thought, somebody has got to help us in the terrible mess we're in, and I thought of you because of the dream. You see, I was lost and I couldn't find Don. He'd left me and there was a great big sort of ravine thing—an abyss. Yes, that's the word. An abyss. It sounds so deep, doesn't it? So deep and so—so unbridgeable. And you were there on the other side and you held out your hands and said 'I want to help you.'" She drew a deep breath. "So I came to you. I ran away and I came here because you've got to help us. If you don't help us, I don't know what's going to happen. You *must* help us. You brought all this. You'll say, perhaps, that it's nothing to do with you. That having once told us—told us the truth about what happened—that it's no business of yours. You'll say—"

"No," said Calgary, interrupting her. "I shall not say anything of the kind. It is my business, Hester. I agree with you. When you start a thing you have to go on with it. I feel that every bit as much as you do."

"Oh!" Colour flamed up into Hester's face. Suddenly, as was the way with her, she looked beautiful. "So I'm not alone!" she said. "There *is* someone."

"Yes, my dear, there is someone—for what he's worth. So far I haven't been worth very much, but I'm trying and I've never stopped trying to help." He sat down and drew his chair nearer to her. "Now tell me all about it," he said. "Has it been very bad?"

"It's one of us, you see," said Hester. "We all know that. Mr. Marshall came and we pretended it must have been someone who got in, but he knew it wasn't. It's one of us."

"And your young man—what's-his-name?"

"Don. Donald Craig. He's a doctor."

"Don thinks it's you?"

"He's afraid it's me," said Hester. She twisted her hands in a dramatic gesture. She looked at him. "Perhaps you think it's me, too?"

"Oh, no," said Calgary. "Oh no, I know quite well that you're innocent."

"You say that as though you were really quite sure."

"I am quite sure," said Calgary.

"But why? How can you be so sure?"

"Because of what you said to me when I left the house after telling all of you. Do you remember? What you said to me about innocence. You couldn't have said that—you couldn't have felt that way—unless you were innocent."

"Oh," cried Hester. "Oh—the relief! To know there's someone who really feels like that!"

"So now," said Calgary, "we can discuss it calmly, can't we?"

"Yes," said Hester. "It feels—it feels quite different now."

"Just as a matter of interest," said Calgary, "and keeping firmly in mind that you know what I feel about it, why should anyone for one moment think that you would kill your adopted mother?"

"I might have done," said Hester. "I often felt like it. One does sometimes feel just mad with rage. One feels so futile, so—so helpless. Mother was always so calm and so superior and knew everything, and was right about everything. Sometimes I would think, 'Oh! I would like to kill her.'" She looked at him. "Do you understand? Didn't you ever feel like that when you were young?"

The last words gave Calgary a sudden pang, the same pang perhaps that he had felt when Micky in the hotel at Drymouth had said to him, "You look older!" "When he was young?" Did it seem so very long ago to Hester? He cast his mind back. He remembered himself at nine years old consulting with another small boy in the gardens of his prep school, wondering ingeniously what would be the best way to dispose of Mr. Warborough, their form master. He remembered the helplessness of rage that had consumed him when Mr. Warborough had been particularly sarcastic in his comments. That, he thought, was what Hester had felt too. But whatever he and young—what was his name now?—Porch, yes, Porch had been the boy's name—although he and young Porch had consulted and planned, they had never taken any active steps to bring about the demise of Mr. Warborough.

"You know," he said to Hester, "you ought to have got over those sort of feelings a good many years ago. I can understand them, of course."

"It was just that Mother had that effect upon me," said Hester. "I'm beginning to see now, you know, that it was my own fault. I feel that if only she'd lived a little longer, just lived till I was a little older, a little more settled, that—that we'd have been friends in a curious way. That I'd have been glad of her help and her advice. But—but as it was I couldn't bear it; because, you see, it made me feel so ineffectual, so stupid. Everything I did went wrong and I could see for myself that the things I did were foolish things. That I'd only done them because I wanted to rebel, wanted to prove that I was myself. And I wasn't *anybody*. I was fluid. Yes, that's the word," said Hester. "It's exactly the word. Fluid. Never taking a shape for long. Just trying on shapes—shapes—shapes of other people that I admired. I thought, you see, if I ran away and went on the stage and had an affair with someone, that—"

"That you would feel yourself, or at any rate, feel somebody?"

"Yes," said Hester. "Yes, that's just it. And of course really I see now that I was just behaving like a silly child. But you don't know how I wish, Dr. Calgary, that Mother was alive now. Because it's so unfair—unfair on her, I mean. She did so much for us and gave us so much. We didn't give her anything back. And now it's too late." She paused. "That's why," she said, with a sudden renewal of vigour, "I've determined to stop being silly and childish. And you'll help me, won't you?"

"I've already said I'll do anything in the world to help you."

She gave him a quick, rather lovely smile.

"Tell me," he said, "exactly what has been happening."

"Just what I thought would happen," said Hester. "We've all been looking at each other and wondering and we don't know. Father looks at Gwenda and thinks perhaps it was her. She looks at Father and isn't sure. I don't think they're going to get married now. It's spoilt everything. And Tina thinks Micky had something to do with it. I don't know why because he wasn't there that evening. And Kirsten thinks I did it and tries to protect me. And Mary—that's my older sister who you didn't meet—Mary thinks Kirsten did it."

"And who do you think did it, Hester?"

"Me?" Hester sounded startled.

"Yes, you," said Calgary. "I think, you know, it's rather important to know that."

Hester spread out her hands. "I don't know," she wailed. "I just don't know. I'm—it's an awful thing to say—but I'm frightened of everybody. It's as though behind each face there was another face. A—sinister sort of face that I don't know. I don't feel sure that Father's Father, and Kirsten keeps saying that I shouldn't trust anybody—not even her. And I look at Mary and I feel I don't know anything about her. And Gwenda—I've always liked Gwenda. I've been glad that Father was going to marry Gwenda. But now I'm not sure about Gwenda any more. I see her as somebody different, ruthless and—and revengeful. I don't know what anybody's like. There's an awful feeling of unhappiness."

"Yes," said Calgary, "I can well imagine that."

"There's so much unhappiness," said Hester, "that I can't help feeling perhaps there's the murderer's unhappiness too. And that might be the worst of all. . . . Do you think that's likely?"

"It's possible, I suppose," said Calgary, "and yet I doubt—of course I'm not an expert—I doubt if a murderer is ever really unhappy."

"But why not? I should think it would be the most terrible thing to be, to know you'd killed someone."

"Yes," said Calgary, "it is a terrible thing and therefore I think a murderer must be one of two kinds of people. Either a person to whom it has *not* been terrible to kill anyone, the kind of person who says to himself, 'Well, of course it was a pity to have to do that but it was necessary for my own well being. After all, it's not my fault. I just—well, just had to do it.' Or else—"

"Yes?" said Hester. "What's the other kind of murderer?"

"I'm only guessing, mind you, I don't know, but I think if you were what you call the other kind of murderer, you wouldn't be able to live with your unhappiness over what you'd done. You'd either have to confess it or else you'd have to rewrite the story for yourself, as it were. Putting the blame on someone else, saying 'I should never have done such a thing unless—' such and such a thing had happened. 'I'm not really a murderer because I didn't mean to do it. It just happened, and so really it was fate and not myself.' Do you understand a little what I am trying to say?"

"Yes," said Hester, "and I think it's very interesting." She half-closed her eyes. "I'm just trying to think—"

"Yes, Hester," said Calgary, "think. Think as hard as you can because if I'm ever going to be able to help you I've got to see things through your mind."

"Micky hated Mother," said Hester slowly. "He always did . . . I don't know why. Tina, I think, loved her. Gwenda didn't like her. Kirsten was always loyal to Mother though she didn't always think that Mother was right in all the things she did. Father—" She paused for a long time.

"Yes?" Calgary prompted her.

"Father's gone a long way away again," said Hester. "After Mother died, you know, he was quite different. Not so—what shall I call it—remote. He's been more human, more alive. But now he's gone back to some—some sort of shadowy place where you can't get at him. I don't know what he felt about Mother, really. I suppose he loved her when he married her. They never quarrelled, but I don't know what he felt about her. Oh"—her hands flew out again—"one doesn't know what anyone feels, does one, really? I mean, what goes on behind their faces, behind their nice everyday words? They may be ravaged with hate or love or despair, and one wouldn't *know*! It's frightening. . . . Oh, Dr. Calgary, it's frightening!"

He took both her hands in his.

"You're not a child any longer," he said. "Only children are frightened. You're grown-up, Hester. You're a woman." He released her hands and said in a matter-of-fact tone: "Is there anywhere you can stay in London?"

Hester looked slightly bewildered.

"I suppose so. I don't know. Mother usually stayed at Curtis's."

"Well, that's a very nice, quiet hotel. I should go there and book a room if I were you."

"I'll do anything you tell me to do," said Hester.

"Good girl," said Calgary. "What's the time?" He looked up at the clock. "Hallo, it's about seven o'clock already. Supposing you go and book yourself a room, and I'll come along about quarter to eight to take you out to dinner. How would that suit you?"

"It sounds wonderful," said Hester. "Do you really mean it?"

"Yes," said Calgary, "I really mean it."

"But after that? What's going to happen next? I can't go on staying, can I, at Curtis's for ever?"

"Your horizon always seems bounded by infinity," said Calgary.

"Are you laughing at me?" she asked him doubtfully.

"Just a little," he said, and smiled.

Her expression wavered and then she, too, smiled.

"I suppose really," she said confidentially, "I've been dramatising myself again."

"It's rather a habit of yours, I suspect," said Calgary.

"That's why I thought I should do well on the stage," said Hester. "But I didn't. I was no good at all. Oh, I was a lousy actress."

"You'll get all the drama you want out of ordinary life, I should say," said Calgary. "Now I'm going to put you in a taxi, my dear, and you go off to Curtis's. And wash your face and brush your hair," he went on. "Have you got any luggage with you?"

"Oh, yes. I've got a sort of overnight bag."

"Good." He smiled at her. "Don't worry, Hester," he said again. "We'll think of something."

19

"I want to talk to you, Kristy," said Philip.

"Yes, of course, Philip."

Kirsten Lindstrom paused in her task. She had just brought in some washing which she was putting away in the chest of drawers.

"I want to talk to you about all this business," said Philip. "You don't mind, do you?"

"There is too much talk already," said Kirsten. "That is my view."

"But it would be as well, wouldn't it," said Philip, "to come to some conclusion among ourselves. You know what's going on at present, don't you?"

"Things are going wrong everywhere," said Kirsten.

"Do you think Leo and Gwenda will ever get married now?"

"Why not?"

"Several reasons," said Philip. "First of all, perhaps, because Leo Argyle, being an intelligent man, realises that a marriage between him and Gwenda will give the police what they want. A perfectly good motive for the murder of his wife. Or, alternatively, because Leo suspects that Gwenda is the murderer. And being a sensitive man, he doesn't really like taking as a second wife the woman who killed his first wife. What do you say to that?" he added.

"Nothing," said Kirsten. "What should I say?"

"Playing it very close to your chest, aren't you, Kirsty?"

"I don't understand you."

"Who are you covering up for, Kirsten?"

"I am not 'covering up,' as you call it, for anyone. I think there should be less talk and I think people should not stay on in this house. It is not good for them. I think you, Philip, should go home with your wife to your own home."

"Oh, you do, do you? Why, in particular?"

"You are asking questions," said Kirsten. "You are trying to find out things. And your wife does not want you to do it. She is wiser than you are. You might find out something you did not want to find out, or that she did not want you to find out. You should go home, Philip. You should go soon."

"I don't want to go home," said Philip. He spoke rather like a petulant small boy.

"That is what children say," said Kirsten. "They say I don't want to do this and I don't want to do that, but those who know more of life, who see better what is happening, have to coax them to do what they do not want to do."

"So this is your idea of coaxing, is it?" said Philip. "Giving me orders."

"No, I do not give you orders. I only advise you." She sighed. "I would advise all of them the same way. Micky should go back to his work as Tina has gone back to her library. I am glad Hester has gone. She should be somewhere where she is not continually reminded of all this."

"Yes," said Philip. "I agree with you there. You're right about Hester. But what about you yourself, Kirsten? Oughtn't you to go away too?"

"Yes," said Kirsten with a sigh. "I ought to go away."

"Why don't you?"

"You would not understand. It is too late for me to go."

Philip looked at her thoughtfully. Then he said:

"There are so many variations, aren't there—variations on a single theme. Leo thinks Gwenda did it, Gwenda thinks Leo did it. Tina knows something that but makes her suspect who did it. Micky knows who did it but doesn't care. Mary thinks Hester did it." He paused and then went on, "But the truth is, Kirsty, that those are only variations on a theme as I said. We know who did it quite well, don't we, Kirsty. You and I?"

She shot a quick, horrified glance at him.

"I thought as much," said Philip exultantly.

"What do you mean?" said Kirsten. "What are you trying to say?"

"I *don't* really know who did it," said Philip. "*But you do*. You don't only think you know who did it, you actually *do know*. I'm right, aren't I?"

Kirsten marched to the door. She opened it, then turned back and spoke.

"It is not a polite thing to say, but I will say it. You are a fool, Philip. What you are trying to do is dangerous. You understand one kind of danger. You have been a pilot. You have faced death up there in the sky. Can you not see that if you get anywhere near the truth, you are in just as great danger as you ever were in the war?"

"And what about you, Kirsty? If you know the truth, aren't you in danger too?"

"I can take care of myself," said Kirsten grimly. "I can be on my guard. But you, Philip, are in an invalid-chair and helpless. Think of that! Besides," she added, "I do not air my views. I am content to let things be—because I honestly think that that is best for everyone. If everyone would go away and attend to their own business, then there would be no further trouble. If I am asked, I have my official view. I say still that it was Jacko."

"Jacko?" Philip stared.

"Why not? Jacko was clever. Jacko could plan a thing and be sure he would not suffer from the consequences. Often he did that as a child. After all, to fake an alibi. Is that not done every day?"

"He couldn't have faked this one. Dr. Calgary—"

"Dr. Calgary—Dr. Calgary," said Kirsten with impatience, "because he is well known, because he has a famous name, you say, 'Dr. Calgary' as though he were God! But let me tell you this. When you have had concussion as he had concussion, things may be quite different from the way you remember them. It may have been a different day—a different time—a different place!"

Philip looked at her, his head slightly on one side.

"So that's your story," he said. "*And* you're sticking to it. A very creditable attempt. But you don't believe it yourself, do you, Kirsty?"

"I've warned you," said Kirsten, "I can't do more."

She turned away, then popped her head in again to say in her usual matter-of-fact voice:

"Tell Mary I have put the clean washing away in the second drawer there."

Philip smiled a little at the anti-climax, then the smile died away . . .

His sense of inner excitement grew. He had a feeling he was getting very near indeed. His experiment with Kirsten had been highly satisfactory, but he doubted that he would get any more out of her. Her solicitude for him irritated him. Just because he was a cripple did not mean that he was as vulnerable as she made out. He, too, could be on his guard—and for heaven's sake, wasn't he watched over incessantly? Mary hardly ever left his side.

He drew a sheet of paper towards him and began to write. Brief notes, names, question marks. . . . A vulnerable spot to probe. . . .

Suddenly he nodded his head and wrote: *Tina* . . .

He thought about it. . . .

Then he drew another sheet of paper towards him.

When Mary came in, he hardly looked up.

"What are you doing, Philip?"

"Writing a letter."

"To Hester?"

"Hester? No. I don't even know where she's staying. Kirsty just had a postcard from her with London written at the top, that was all."

He grinned at her.

"I believe you're jealous, Polly. Are you?"

Her eyes, blue and cold, looked into his.

"Perhaps."

He felt a little uncomfortable.

"Who are you writing to?" She came a step nearer.

"The Public Prosecutor," said Philip cheerfully, though within him a cold anger stirred. Couldn't a fellow write a letter, even, without being questioned about it?

Then he saw her face and he relented.

"Only a joke, Polly. I'm writing to Tina."

"To Tina? Why?"

"Tina's my next line of attack. Where are you going, Polly?"

"To the bathroom," said Mary as she went out of the room.

Philip laughed. To the bathroom, as on the night of the murder. . . . He laughed again as he remembered their conversation about it.

II

"Come on, sonny," said Superintendent Huish encouragingly. "Let's hear all about it."

Master Cyril Green took a deep breath. Before he could speak, his mother interposed.

"As you might say, Mr. Huish, I didn't take much notice at the time. You know what these children are. Always talking and thinking about space ships and things. And he comes home to me and he says, 'Mum, I've seen a sputnik, it's come down.' Well, I mean, before that it was flying saucers. It's always something. It's these Russians that go putting things into their heads."

Superintendent Huish sighed and thought how much easier it would be if mothers would not insist on accompanying their sons and talking for them.

"Come on, Cyril," he said, "you went home and told your Mum—that's right, isn't it?—that you'd seen this Russian sputnik—whatever it was."

"Didn't know no better then," said Cyril. "I was only a kid then. That's two years ago. Course, I know better now."

"Them bubble cars," his mother put in, "was quite new at the time. There hadn't been one about locally, so naturally when he saw it—and bright red too—he didn't realise as it was just an ordinary car. And when we heard the next morning as Mrs. Argyle had been done in, Cyril he says to me, 'Mum,' he says, 'it's them Russians,' he says, 'they come down in that sputnik of theirs and they must have got in and killed her.' 'Don't talk such nonsense,' I said. And then of course later in the day we hear her own son has been arrested for having done it."

Superintendent Huish addressed himself patiently once more to Cyril.

"It was in the evening, I understand? What time, do you remember?"

"I'd had me tea," said Cyril, breathing hard in the effort of remembrance, "and Mum was out at the Institute, so I went out again a bit with the boys and we larked around a bit up that way down the new road."

"And what was you doing there, I'd like to know," his mother put in.

P. C. Good, who'd brought in this promising piece of evidence, interposed. He knew well enough what Cyril and the boys had been doing down the new road. The disappearance of chrysanthemums had been angrily reported from several householders there, and he knew well enough that the bad characters of the village surreptitiously encouraged the younger generation to supply them with flowers which they themselves took to market. This was not the moment, P. C. Good knew, to go into past cases of delinquency. He said heavily:

"Boys is boys, Mrs. Green, they gets larking around."

"Yes," said Cyril, "just having a game or two, we were. And that's where I saw it. 'Coo,' I said, 'what's this?' O' course I know now. I'm not a silly kid any longer. It was just one o' them bubble cars. Bright red, it was."

"And the time?" said Superintendent Huish patiently.

"Well, as I say, I'd had me tea an' we'd gone out there and larked around—must have been near on seven o'clock, because I heard the clock strike and 'Coo,' I thought, 'Mum'll be home and won't she create if I'm not there.' So I went home. I told her then that I thought I'd seen that Russian satellite come down. Mum said it were all lies, but it wasn't. Only o' course, I knows better now. I was just a kid then, see."

Superintendent Huish said that he saw. After a few more questions he dismissed Mrs. Green and her offspring. P. C. Good, remaining behind, put on the gratified expression of a junior member of the force who has shown intelligence and hopes that it will count in his favour.

"It just come to me," said P. C. Good, "what that boy'd been around saying about Russians doing Mrs. Argyle in. I thought to meself, 'Well, that may mean something.' "

"It does mean something," said the superintendent. "Miss Tina Argyle has a red bubble car, and it looks as though I'd have to ask her a few more questions."

III

"You were there that night, Miss Argyle?"

Tina looked at the superintendent. Her hands lay loosely in her lap, her eyes, dark, unwinking, told nothing.

"It is so long ago," she said, "really I cannot remember."

"Your car was seen there," said Huish.

"Was it?"

"Come now, Miss Argyle. When we asked you for an account of your movements on that night, you told us that you went home and didn't go out that evening. You made yourself supper and listened to the gramophone. Now, that isn't true. Just before seven o'clock your car was seen in the road quite near to Sunny Point. What were you doing there?"

She did not answer. Huish waited a few moments, then he spoke again.

"Did you go into the house, Miss Argyle?"

"No," said Tina.

"But you were there?"

"You say I was there."

"It's not just a question of my saying so. We've got evidence that you were there."

Tina sighed.

"Yes," she said. "I did drive out there that evening."

"But you say you didn't go into the house?"

"No, I didn't go into the house."

"What did you do?"

"I drove back again to Redmyn. Then, as I told you, I made myself some supper and put on the gramophone."

"Why did you drive out there if you didn't go into the house?"

"I changed my mind," said Tina.

"What made you change your mind, Miss Argyle?"

"When I got there I didn't want to go in."

"Because of something you saw or heard?"

She did not answer.

"Listen, Miss Argyle. That was the night that your mother was murdered. She was killed between seven and half past that evening. You were there, your car was there, at some time before seven. How long it was there we do not know. It is possible, you know, that it may have been there for some time. It may be that you went into the house—you have a key, I think—"

"Yes," said Tina, "I have a key."

"Perhaps you went into the house. Perhaps you went into your mother's sitting-room and found her there, dead. Or perhaps—"

Tina raised her head.

"Or perhaps I killed her? Is that what you want to say, Superintendent Huish?"

"It is one possibility," said Huish, "but I think it's more likely, Miss Argyle, someone else did the killing. If so, I think you know—or have a very strong suspicion—who the killer was."

"I did not go into the house," said Tina.

"Then you saw something or heard something. You saw someone go into the house or someone leave the house. Someone perhaps who was not known to be there. Was it your brother Michael, Miss Argyle?"

Tina said:

"I saw nobody."

"But you heard something," said Huish shrewdly. "What did you hear, Miss Argyle?"

"I tell you," said Tina, "I simply changed my mind."

"You'll forgive me, Miss Argyle, but I don't believe that. Why should you drive out from Redmyn to visit your family, and drive back again without seeing them? Something made you change your mind about that. Something you saw or heard." He leaned forward. "I think you know, Miss Argyle, who killed your mother."

Very slowly she shook her head.

"You know *something*," said Huish. "Something that you are determined not to tell. But think, Miss Argyle, think very carefully. Do you realise what you are condemning your entire family to go through? Do you want them all to remain under suspicion—for that's what's going to happen unless we get at the truth. Whoever killed your mother doesn't deserve to be shielded. For that's it, isn't it? You're shielding someone."

Again that dark, opaque look met his.

"I know nothing," said Tina. "I didn't hear anything and I didn't see anything. I just—changed my mind."

20

Calgary and Huish looked at each other. Calgary saw what seemed to him one of the most depressed and gloomy-looking men he had ever seen. So profoundly disillusioned did he appear that Calgary felt tempted to suppose that Superintendent Huish's career had been one long series of failures. He was surprised to discover on a later occasion that Superintendent Huish had been extremely successful professionally. Huish saw a lean, prematurely grey-haired man with slightly stooping shoulders, a sensitive face and a singularly attractive smile.

"You don't know who I am, I'm afraid," Calgary began.

"Oh, we know all about you, Dr. Calgary," said Huish. "You're the joker in the pack who queered the Argyle case." A rather unexpected smile lifted the corners of his sad-looking mouth.

"You can hardly regard me favourably then," said Calgary.

"It's all in the day's work," said Superintendent Huish. "It seemed a clear case and nobody can be blamed for thinking it so. But these things happen," he went on. "They're sent to try us, so my old mother used to say. We don't bear malice, Dr. Calgary. After all, we do stand for Justice, don't we?"

"So I've always believed, and shall continue to believe," said Calgary. "To no man will we deny justice," he murmured softly.

"Magna Carta," said Superintendent Huish.

"Yes," said Calgary, "quoted to me by Miss Tina Argyle."

Superintendent Huish's eyebrows rose.

"Indeed. You surprise me. That young lady, I should say, has not been particularly active in helping the wheels of justice to turn."

"Now why do you say that?" asked Calgary.

"Frankly," said Huish, "for withholding information. There's no doubt about that."

"Why?" asked Calgary.

"Well, it's a family business," said Huish. "Families stick together. But what was it you wanted to see me about?" he continued.

"I want information," said Calgary.

"About the Argyle case?"

"Yes. I realise that I must seem to you to be butting in in a matter that's not my concern—"

"Well, it is your concern in a way, isn't it?"

"Ah, you do appreciate that. Yes. I feel responsible. Responsible for bringing trouble."

"You can't make an omelette without breaking eggs, as the French say," said Huish.

"There are things I want to know," said Calgary.

"Such as?"

"I'd like a great deal more information about Jacko Argyle."

"About *Jacko* Argyle. Well, now, I didn't expect you to say that."

"He'd got a bad record, I know," said Calgary. "What I want is a few details from it."

"Well, that's simple enough," said Huish. "He'd been on probation twice. On another occasion, for embezzlement of funds, he was just saved by being able to put up the money in time."

"The budding young criminal, in fact?" asked Calgary.

"Quite right, sir," said Huish. "Not a murderer, as you've made clear to us, but a good many other things. Nothing, mind you, on a grand scale. He hadn't got the brains or the nerve to put up a big swindle. Just a small-time criminal. Pinching money out of tills, wheedling it out of women."

"And he was good at that," said Calgary. "Wheedling money out of women, I mean."

"And a very nice safe line it is," said Superintendent Huish. "Women fell for him very easily. Middle-aged or elderly were the ones he usually went for. You'd be surprised how gullible that type of woman can be. He put over a very pretty line. Got them to believe he was passionately in love with them. There's nothing a woman won't believe if she wants to."

"And then?" asked Calgary.

Huish shrugged his shoulders.

"Well, sooner or later they were disillusioned. But they don't prosecute, you know. They don't want to tell the world that they've been fooled. Yes, it's a pretty safe line."

"Was there ever blackmail?" Calgary asked.

"Not that we know of," said Huish. "Mind you, I wouldn't have put it past him. Not out and out blackmail, I'd say. Just a hint or two, perhaps. Letters. Foolish letters. Things their husbands wouldn't like to know about. He'd be able to keep a woman quiet that way."

"I see," said Calgary.

"Is that all you wanted to know?" asked Huish.

"There's one member of the Argyle family I haven't met yet," said Calgary. "The eldest daughter."

"Ah, Mrs. Durrant."

"I went to her house, but it was shut up. They told me she and her husband were away."

"They are at Sunny Point."

"Still there?"

"Yes. He wanted to stay on. Mr. Durrant," added Huish, "is doing a bit of detecting, I understand."

"He's a cripple, isn't he?"

"Yes, polio. Very sad. He hasn't much to do with his time, poor chap. That's why he's taken up this murder business so eagerly. Thinks he's on to something, too."

"And is he?" asked Calgary.

Huish shrugged his shoulders.

"He might be, at that," he said. "He's a better chance than we have, you know. He knows the family and he's a man with a good deal of intuition as well as intelligence."

"Do you think he'll get anywhere?"

"Possibly," said Huish, "but he won't tell *us* if he does. They'll keep it all in the family."

"Do you yourself know who's guilty, Superintendent?"

"You mustn't ask me things like that, Dr. Calgary."

"Meaning that you do know?"

"One can think one knows a thing," said Huish slowly, "but if you haven't got evidence there's not much you can do about it, is there?"

"And you're not likely to get the evidence you want?"

"Oh! we're very patient," Huish said. "We shall go on trying."

"What's going to happen to them all if you don't succeed?" said Calgary, leaning forward. "Have you thought of that?"

Huish looked at him.

"That's what's worrying you, is it, sir?"

"They've *got* to know," said Calgary. "Whatever else happens, they've got to *know*."

"Don't you think they do know?"

Calgary shook his head.

"No," he said slowly, "that's the tragedy."

II

"Oo," said Maureen Clegg, "it's you again!"

"I'm very, very sorry to bother you," said Calgary.

"Oh, but you're not bothering me a bit. Come in. It's my day off."

That fact Calgary had already found out, and was the reason for his being here.

"I'm expecting Joe back in a minute," said Maureen. "I haven't seen any more about Jacko in the papers. I mean not since it said how he got a free pardon and a bit about a question being asked in Parliament and then saying that it was quite clear he didn't do it. But there's nothing more about what the police are doing and who really did it. Can't they find out?"

"Have you still no idea yourself?"

"Well, I haven't really," said Maureen. "I shouldn't be surprised, though, if it was the other brother. Very queer and moody he is. Joe sees him sometimes driving people around. He works for the Bence Group, you know. He's rather good-looking but terribly moody, I should think. Joe heard a rumour he was going out to Persia or somewhere and that looks bad, I think, don't you?"

"I don't see why it should look bad, Mrs. Clegg."

"Well, it's one of those places the police can't get at you, isn't it?"

"You think that he is running away?"

"He may feel he's got to."

"I suppose that's the sort of thing people do say," Arthur Calgary said.

"Lots of rumours flying around," said Maureen. "They say the husband and the secretary were going on together, too. But if it was the husband I should think he would be more likely to poison her. That's what they usually do, isn't it?"

"Well, you see more films that I do, Mrs. Clegg."

"I don't really look at the screen," said Maureen. "If you work there, you know, you get terribly bored with films. Hallo, here's Joe."

Joe Clegg also looked surprised to see Calgary and possibly not too pleased. They talked together for a while and then Calgary came to the purpose of his visit.

"I wonder," he said, "if you'd mind giving me a name and address?"

He wrote it down carefully in his note-book.

III

She was about fifty, he thought, a heavy cumbrous woman who could never have been good-looking. She had nice eyes, though, brown and kindly.

"Well, really, Dr. Calgary—" She was doubtful, upset. "Well, really, I'm sure I don't know. . . ."

He leaned forward, trying his utmost to dispel her reluctance, to soothe her, to make her feel the full force of his sympathy.

"It's so long ago now," she said. "It's—I really don't want to be reminded of—of things."

"I do understand that," said Calgary, "and it's not as though there were any question of anything being made public. I do assure you of that."

"You say you want to write a book about it, though?"

"Just a book to illustrate a certain type of character," said Calgary. "Interesting, you know, from a medical or psychological standpoint. No names. Just Mr. A., Mrs. B. That sort of thing."

"You've been to the Antarctic, haven't you?" she said suddenly.

He was surprised at the abruptness with which she had changed the subject.

"Yes," he said, "yes, I was with the Hayes Bentley Expedition."

The colour came up in her face. She looked younger. Just for a moment he could see the girl she had once been. "I used to read about it . . . I've always been fascinated, you know, with anything to do with the Poles. That Norwegian, wasn't it, Amundsen, who got there first? I think the Poles are much more exciting than Everest or any of these satellites, or going to the Moon or anything like that."

He seized on his cue and began to talk to her about the Expedition. Odd that her romantic interest should lie there, in Polar Explorations. She said at last with a sigh:

"It's wonderful hearing about it all from someone who's actually been there." She went on: "You want to know all about—about Jackie?"

"Yes."

"You wouldn't use my name or anything like that?"

"Of course not. I've told you so. You know how these things are done. Mrs. M. Lady Y. That sort of thing."

"Yes. Yes, I've read that kind of book—and I suppose it was, as you said, path—patho—"

"Pathological," he said.

"Yes, Jackie was definitely a pathological case. He could be ever so sweet, you know," she said. "Wonderful, he was. He'd say things and you'd believe every word of it."

"He probably meant them," said Calgary.

" 'I'm old enough to be your mother,' I used to say to him, and he'd say he didn't care for girls. Crude, he used to say girls were. He used to say women who were experienced and mature were what attracted him."

"Was he very much in love with you?" said Calgary.

"He said he was. He seemed to be . . ." Her lips trembled. "And all the time, I suppose, he was just after the money."

"Not necessarily," said Calgary, straining the truth as far as he could. "He may have been genuinely attracted, you know, as well. Only—he just couldn't help being crooked."

The pathetic middle-aged face brightened a little.

"Yes," she said, "it's nice to think that. Well, there it was. We used to make plans; how we'd go away together to France, or Italy, if this scheme of his came off. It just needed a bit of capital, he said."

The usual approach, thought Calgary, and wondered how many pathetic women fell for it.

"I don't know what came over me," she said. "I'd have done anything for him—*anything*."

"I'm sure you would," said Calgary.

"I dare say," she said bitterly, "I wasn't the only one."

Calgary rose.

"It's been very good of you to tell me all this," he said.

"He's dead now. . . . But I shall never forget him. That monkey-face of his! The way he looked so sad and then laughed. Oh, he had a way with him. He wasn't all bad, I'm sure he wasn't *all* bad."

She looked at him wistfully.

But for that Calgary had no answer.

21

There had been nothing to tell Philip Durrant that this day was different from any other day.

He had no idea that to-day would decide his future once and for all.

He woke in good health and spirits. The sun, a pale autumnal sun, shone in at the window. Kirsten brought him a telephone message which increased his good spirits.

"Tina's coming over for tea," he told Mary when she came in with his breakfast.

"Is she? Oh, yes, of course, it's her afternoon off, isn't it?"

Mary sounded preoccupied.

"What's the matter, Polly?"

"Nothing."

She chipped off the top of his egg for him. At once, he felt irritated.

"I can still use my hands, Polly."

"Oh, I thought it would save you trouble."

"How old do you think I am? Six?"

She looked faintly surprised. Then she said abruptly:

"Hester's coming home to-day."

"Is she?" He spoke vaguely, because his mind was full of his plans for dealing with Tina. Then he caught sight of his wife's expression.

"For goodness' sake, Polly, do you think I've got a guilty passion for the girl?"

She turned her head aside.

"You're always saying she's so lovely."

"So she is. If you like beautiful bones and a quality of the unearthly." He added dryly: "But I'm hardly cut out to be a seducer, am I?"

"You might wish you were."

"Don't be ridiculous, Polly. I never knew you had this tendency to jealousy."

"You don't know anything about me."

He started to rebut that, but paused. It came to him, with something of a shock, that perhaps he didn't know very much about Mary.

She went on:

"I want you to myself—all to myself. I want there to be nobody in the world but you and me."

"We'd run out of conversation, Polly."

He had spoken lightly, but he felt uncomfortable. The brightness of the morning seemed suddenly dimmed.

She said: "Let's go home, Philip, please let's go home."

"Very soon we will, but not just yet. Things are coming along. As I told you, Tina's coming this afternoon." He went on, hoping to turn her thoughts into a new channel: "I've great hopes of Tina."

"In what way?"

"Tina knows something."

"You mean—about the murder?"

"Yes."

"But how can she? She wasn't even here that night."

"I wonder now. I think, you know, that she *was*. Funny how odd little things turn up to help. That daily, Mrs. Narracott—the tall one, she told me something."

"What did she tell you?"

"A bit of village gossip. Mrs. Somebody or other's Ernie—no—Cyril. He'd had to go with his mother to the police station. Something he'd seen on the night poor Mrs. Argyle was done in."

"What had he seen?"

"Well, there Mrs. Narracott was rather vague. She hadn't got it out of Mrs. Somebody yet. But one can guess, can't one, Polly? Cyril wasn't inside the house, so he must have seen something outside. That gives us two guesses. He saw Micky or he saw Tina. It's my guess that Tina came out here that night."

"She'd have said so."

"Not necessarily. It sticks out a mile that Tina knows something she isn't telling. Say she drove out that night. Perhaps she came into the house and found your mother dead."

"And went away again without saying anything? Nonsense."

"There may have been reasons. . . . She may have seen or heard something that made her think she knew who'd done it."

"She was never particularly fond of Jacko. I'm sure she wouldn't have wanted to shield him."

"Then perhaps it wasn't Jacko she suspected. . . . But later, when Jacko was arrested, she thought that what she had suspected was quite wrong. Having said she wasn't here, she had to stick to it. But now, of course, it's different."

Mary said impatiently:

"You just imagine things, Philip. You make up a lot of things that can't possibly be true."

"They're quite likely to be true. I'm going to try and make Tina tell me what she knows."

"I don't believe she knows anything. Do you really think she knows who did it?"

"I wouldn't go as far as that. I think she either saw—or heard—something. I want to find out what that something is."

"Tina won't tell if she doesn't want to."

"No, I agree. And she's a great one for keeping things to herself. Little poker face, too. Never shows anything. But she's not really a good liar—not nearly as good a liar as you are, for instance. . . . My method will be to guess. Put my guess to her as a question. To be answered yes or no. Do you know what will happen then? One of three things. She'll either say yes—and that will be that. Or she will say no—and since she isn't a good liar I shall know whether her no is genuine. Or she will refuse to answer and put on her poker face—and that, Polly, will be as good as yes. Come now you must admit that there are possibilities with this technique of mine."

"Oh, leave it all alone, Phil! Do leave it alone! It will all die down and be forgotten."

"No. This thing has got to be cleared up. Otherwise we'll have Hester throwing herself out of windows and Kirsty having a nervous breakdown. Leo's already freezing up into a kind of stalactite. As for poor old Gwenda, she's on the point of accepting a post in Rhodesia."

"What does it matter what happens to them?"

"Nobody matters but us—that's what you mean?"

His face was stern and angry. It startled Mary. She had never seen her husband look like that before.

She faced him defiantly.

"Why should I care about other people?" she asked.

"You never have, have you?"

"I don't know what you mean."

Philip gave a sharp exasperated sigh. He pushed his breakfast tray aside.

"Take this thing away. I don't want any more."

"But Philip—"

He made an impatient gesture. Mary picked up the tray and carried it out of the room. Philip wheeled himself over to the writing-table. Pen in hand, he stared out of the window. He felt a curious oppression of spirit. He had been so full of excitement a short while ago. Now he felt uneasy and restless.

But presently he rallied. He covered two sheets of paper rapidly. Then he sat back and considered.

It was plausible. It was possible. But he wasn't entirely satisfied. Was he really on the right tack? He couldn't be sure. Motive. Motive was what was so damnably lacking. There was some factor, somewhere, that had escaped him.

He sighed impatiently. He could hardly wait for Tina to arrive. If only this could be cleared up. Just among themselves. That was all that was necessary. Once they *knew*—then they would all be free. Free of this stifling atmosphere of suspicion and hopelessness. They could all, except one, get on with their own lives. He and Mary would go back home and—

His thoughts stopped. Excitement died down again. He faced his own problem. *He didn't want to go home.* . . . He thought of its orderly perfection, its shining chintzes, its gleaming brass. A clean, bright, well-tended cage! And he in the cage, tied to his invalid-chair, surrounded by the loving care of his wife.

His wife . . . When he thought of his wife, he seemed to see two people. One the girl he had married, fair-haired, blue-eyed, gentle, reserved. That was the girl he had loved, the girl he teased whilst she stared at him with a puzzled frown. That was his Polly. But there was another Mary—a Mary who was hard as steel, who was passionate, but incapable of affection—a Mary to whom nobody mattered but herself. Even he only mattered because he was hers.

A line of French verse passed through his mind—how did it go?

Venus toute entière à sa proie attaché . . .

And that Mary he did not love. Behind the cold blue eyes of that Mary was a stranger—a stranger he did not know. . . .

And then he laughed at himself. He was getting nervy and het up like everybody else in the house. He remembered his mother-in-law talking to him about his wife. About the sweet little fair-haired girl in New York. About the moment when the child had thrown her arms round Mrs. Argyle's neck and had cried out: "I want to stay with you. I don't want to leave you *ever*!"

That had been affection, hadn't it? And yet—how very unlike Mary. Could one change so much between child and woman? How difficult, almost impossible it was for Mary ever to voice affection, to be demonstrative?

Yet certainly on that occasion—His thoughts stopped dead. Or was it really quite simple? Not affection—just calculation. A means to an end. A show of affection deliberately produced. What was Mary capable of to get what she wanted?

Almost anything, he thought—and was shocked with himself for thinking it.

Angrily he dashed down his pen, and wheeled himself out of the sitting-room into the bedroom next door. He wheeled himself up to the dressing-table. He picked up his brushes and brushed back his hair from where it was hanging over his forehead. His own face looked strange to him.

Who am I, he thought, and where am I going? Thoughts that had never occurred to him before. . . . He wheeled his chair close to the window and looked out. Down below, one of the daily women stood outside the kitchen window and talked to someone inside. Their voices, softly accented in the local dialect, floated up to him. . . .

His eyes widening, he remained as though tranced.

A sound from the next room awakened him from his preoccupation. He wheeled himself to the connecting door.

Gwenda Vaughan was standing by the writing-table. She turned towards him and he was startled by the haggardness of her face in the morning sunshine.

"Hallo, Gwenda."

"Hallo, Philip. Leo thought you might like the *Illustrated London News*."

"Oh, thanks."

"This is a nice room," said Gwenda, looking round her. "I don't believe I've ever been in it before."

"Quite the Royal Suite, isn't it?" said Philip. "Away from everybody. Ideal for invalids and honeymoon couples."

Just too late he wished he had not used the last two words. Gwenda's face quivered.

"I must get on with things," she said vaguely.

"The perfect secretary."

"Not even that nowadays. I make mistakes."

"Don't we all?" He added deliberately: "When are you and Leo getting married?"

"We probably never shall."

"That would be a real mistake," said Philip.

"Leo thinks it might cause unfavourable comment—from the police!"

Her voice was bitter.

"Dash it all, Gwenda, one has to take some risks."

"I'm willing to take risks," said Gwenda. "I've never minded taking risks. I'm willing to gamble on happiness. But Leo—"

"Yes? Leo?"

"Leo," said Gwenda, "will probably die as he has lived, the husband of Rachel Argyle."

The anger and bitterness in her eyes startled him.

"She might just as well be alive," said Gwenda. "She's *here*—in the house—all the time. . . ."

22

Tina parked her car on the grass by the churchyard wall. She removed the paper carefully from the flowers she had brought, then she walked in through the cemetery gates and along the main path. She did not like the new cemetery. She wished it had been possible for Mrs. Argyle to have been buried in the old churchyard which surrounded the church. There seemed an old-world peace there. The yew tree and the moss-grown stones. In this cemetery, so new, so well arranged, with its main walk and the paths radiating off it, everything seemed as slick and mass-produced as the contents of a supermarket.

Mrs. Argyle's grave was well kept. It had a square marble surrounded filled with granite chips, a granite cross rising from the back of it.

Tina, holding her carnations, bent to read the inscription. "In loving memory of Rachel Louise Argyle, who departed this life on November 9th, 195 ." Below it was the text:

"Her children shall rise up and call her blessed."

There was a footstep behind her and Tina turned her head, startled.

"Micky!"

"I saw your car. I followed you. At least—I was coming here anyway."

"You were coming here? Why?"

"I don't know. Just to say good-bye, perhaps."

"Good-bye to—her?"

He nodded.

"Yes. I've taken that job with the oil company I told you about. I'm going off in about three weeks."

"And you came here to say good-bye to Mother first?"

"Yes. Perhaps to thank her and to say I'm sorry."

"What are you sorry for, Micky?"

"I'm not sorry that I killed her if that's what you're trying to imply. Have you been thinking I killed her, Tina?"

"I was not sure."

"You can't be sure now, either, can you? I mean it's no good my telling you that I didn't kill her."

"Why are you sorry?"

"She did a lot for me," said Micky slowly. "I was never the least bit grateful. I resented every single damn thing she did. I never gave her a kind word, or a loving look. I wish now that I had, that's all."

"When did you stop hating her? After she was dead?"

"Yes. Yes, I suppose so."

"It wasn't her you hated, was it?"

"No—no. You were right about that. It was my own mother. Because I loved her. Because I loved her and she didn't care a button for me."

"And now you're not even angry about that?"

"No. I don't suppose she could help it. After all, you're born what you are. She was a sunny, happy sort of creature. Too fond of men and too fond of the bottle, and she was nice to her kids when she felt like being nice. She wouldn't have let anyone else hurt them. All right, so she didn't care for me! All these years I refused to live with that idea. Now I've accepted it." He stretched out a hand. "Give me just one of your carnations, will you, Tina?" He took it from her and bending down, laid it on the grave below the inscription. "There you are, Mum," he said. "I was a rotten son to you, and I don't think you were a very wise Mother to me. But you meant well." He looked at Tina. "Is that a good enough apology?"

"I think it will do," said Tina.

She bent down and put her own bunch of carnations there.

"Do you often come here and put flowers?"

"I come here once a year," said Tina.

"Little Tina," said Micky.

They turned together and walked back down the cemetery path.

"I didn't kill her, Tina," said Micky. "I swear I didn't. I want you to believe me."

"I was there that night," said Tina.

He wheeled round.

"You were there? You mean at Sunny Point?"

"Yes. I was thinking of changing my job. I wanted to consult Father and Mother about it."

"Well," said Micky, "go on."

When she did not speak, he took her arm and shook her. "Go on, Tina," he said. "You've got to tell me."

"I haven't told anyone so far," said Tina.

"Go on," said Micky again.

"I drove there. I didn't take the car right up to the gate. You know there's a place half-way where it's easier to turn it?"

Micky nodded.

"I got out of the car there and I walked towards the house. I felt unsure of myself. You know how difficult it was in some ways to talk to Mother. I mean, she always had her own ideas. I wanted to put the case as clearly as I could. And so I walked to the house and then back towards the car, and then back again. Thinking things out."

"What time was this?" asked Micky.

"I don't know," said Tina. "I can't remember now. I—time doesn't mean very much to me."

"No, darling," said Micky. "You always have that air of infinite leisure."

"I was under the trees," said Tina, "and walking very softly—"

"Like the little cat you are," said Micky affectionately.

"—When I heard them."

"Heard what?"

"Two people whispering."

"Yes?" Micky's body had tensed. "What did they say?"

"They said—one of them said, 'Between seven and seven-thirty. That's the time. Now remember that and don't make a muck of it. Between seven and seven-thirty.' The other person whispered, 'You can trust me,' and then the first voice said, 'And after that, darling, everything will be wonderful.' "

There was a silence, then Micky said:

"Well—why have you held this up?"

"Because I didn't know," said Tina. "I didn't know who was speaking."

"But surely! Was it a man or a woman?"

"I don't know," said Tina. "Don't you see, when two people are whispering, you don't hear the *voice*. It's just—well, just a whisper. I think, of course I think, it was a man and a woman because—"

"Because of what they said?"

"Yes. But I didn't know who they were."

"You thought," said Micky, "that it might have been Father and Gwenda?"

"It's possible, isn't it?" said Tina. "It might have meant that Gwenda was to leave the house and come back between those times, or it might have been Gwenda telling Father to come down between seven and half past."

"If it was Father and Gwenda, you wouldn't want to turn them over to the police. Is that it?"

"If I were sure," said Tina. "But I'm not sure. It could have been someone else. It could have been—Hester and someone? It could even have been Mary, but not Philip. No, not Philip, of course."

"When you say Hester and someone, who do you mean?"

"I don't know."

"You didn't see him—the man, I mean?"

"No," said Tina. "I didn't see him."

"Tina, I think you're lying. It was a man, wasn't it?"

"I turned back," said Tina, "towards the car, and then someone came by on the other side of the road, walking very fast. He was just a shadow in the darkness. And then I thought—I thought I heard a car start up at the end of the road."

"You thought it was *me* . . ." said Micky.

"I didn't know," said Tina. "It *could* have been you. It was about your size and height."

They reached Tina's little car.

"Come on, Tina," said Micky, "get in. I'm coming with you. We'll drive down to Sunny Point."

"But, Micky—"

"It's no use my telling you it wasn't me, is it? What else should I say? Come on, drive to Sunny Point."

"What are you going to do, Micky?"

"Why should you think I'm going to do anything? Weren't you going to Sunny Point anyway?"

"Yes," said Tina, "I was. I had a letter from Philip." She started the little car. Micky, sitting beside her, held himself very taut and rigid.

"Heard from Philip, did you? What had he to say?"

"He asked me to come over. He wanted to see me. He knows this is my half-day."

"Oh. Did he say what he wanted to see you about?"

"He said he wanted to ask me a question and he hoped that I'd give him the answer to it. He said that I needn't tell him anything—he'd tell me. I would only have to say yes or no. He said that whatever I told him he'd hold in confidence."

"So he's up to something, is he?" said Micky. "Interesting."

It was a very short distance to Sunny Point. When they got there, Micky said:

"You go in, Tina. I'm going to walk up and down the garden a bit, thinking of things. Go on. Have your interview with Philip."

Tina said:

"You're not going to—you wouldn't—"

Micky gave a short laugh.

"Suicide from Lover's Leap? Come now, Tina, you know me better than that."

"Sometimes," said Tina, "I think one does not know anybody."

She turned away from him and walked slowly into the house. Micky looked after her, his head thrust forward, his hands in his pockets. He was scowling. Then he walked round the corner of the house looking up at it thoughtfully. All his boyhood memories came back to him. There was the old magnolia tree. He'd climbed up there many a time and through the landing window. There was the small plot of earth that had been supposed to be his own garden. Not that he'd ever taken very kindly to gardens. He'd always preferred taking any mechanical toys he had to pieces. "Destructive little devil," he thought with faint amusement.

Ah well, one didn't really change.

Inside the house, Tina met Mary in the hall. Mary looked startled at seeing her.

"Tina! Have you come over from Redmyn?"

"Yes," said Tina. "Didn't you know I was coming?"

"I'd forgotten," said Mary. "I believe Philip did mention it."

She turned away.

"I'm going into the kitchen," she said, "to see if the Ovaltine has come. Philip likes it last thing at night. Kirsten is just taking him up some coffee. He likes coffee better than tea. He says tea gives him indigestion."

"Why do you treat him like an invalid, Mary?" said Tina. "He's not really an invalid."

There was a touch of cold anger in Mary's eyes.

"When you've got a husband of your own, Tina," she said, "you'll know better how husbands like to be treated."

Tina said gently:

"I'm sorry."

"If only we could get out of this house," said Mary. "It's so *bad* for Philip being here. And Hester's coming back today," she added.

"Hester?" Tina sounded surprised. "Is she? Why?"

"How should I know? She rang up last night and said so. I don't know what train she's coming by. I suppose it'll be the express, as usual. Someone will have to go in to Drymouth to meet her."

Mary disappeared along the passage to the kitchen. Tina hesitated a moment, then she walked up the stairs. On the landing the first door to the right opened and Hester came through it. She looked startled at seeing Tina.

"Hester! I heard you were coming back but I'd no idea you'd arrived."

"Dr. Calgary drove me down," said Hester. "I came straight up to my room—I don't think anyone knows I've arrived."

"Is Dr. Calgary here now?"

"No. He just dropped me and went on into Drymouth. He wanted to see someone there."

"Mary didn't know you'd arrived."

"Mary never knows anything," said Hester. "She and Philip isolate themselves from everything that goes on. I suppose Father and Gwenda are in the library. Everything seems to be going on just the same as usual."

"Why shouldn't it?"

"I don't really know," said Hester vaguely. "I just suspected that it would all be different somehow."

She moved past Tina and down the stairs. Tina went on past the library and along the passage to the suite at the end which the Durrants occupied. Kirsten Lindstrom, standing just outside Philip's door with a tray in her hand, turned her head sharply.

"Why, Tina, you made me jump," she said. "I was just taking Philip some coffee and biscuits." She raised a hand to knock. Tina joined her.

After knocking, Kirsten opened the door and passed in. She was a little ahead of Tina and her tall angular frame blocked Tina's view, but Tina heard Kirsten's gasp. Her arms gave way and the tray crashed to the ground, cup and plates smashing against the fender.

"Oh, no," cried Kirsten, "oh *no*!"

Tina said:

"Philip?"

She passed the other woman and came forward to where Philip Durrant's chair had been brought up to the desk. He had, she supposed, been writing. There was a ball-point pen lying close to his right hand, but his head was dropped forward in a curious twisted attitude. And at the base of his skull she saw something that looked like a bright red lozenge staining the whiteness of his collar.

"He has been killed," said Kirsten. "He has been killed—stabbed. There, through the bottom of the brain. One little stab and it is fatal."

She added, her voice rising:

"I warned him. I did all I could. But he was like a child—enjoying himself playing with tools that were dangerous—not seeing where he was going."

It was like a bad dream, Tina thought. She stood there softly at Philip's elbow, looking down at him whilst Kirsten raised his limp hand and felt the wrist for the pulse that was not there. What had he wanted to ask her? Whatever he wanted, he would never ask it now. Without really thinking objectively, Tina's mind was taking in and registering various details. He had been writing, yes. The pen was there, but there was no paper in front of him. Nothing written. Whoever had killed him had taken away what he'd written. She said, speaking quietly and mechanically:

"We must tell the others."

"Yes, yes, we must go down to them. We must tell your father."

Side by side the two women went to the door, Kirsten's arm round Tina. Tina's eyes went to the dropped tray and the broken crockery.

"That does not matter," said Kirsten. "All that can be cleared up later."

Tina half stumbled and Kirsten's arm restrained her.

"Be careful. You will fall."

They went along the passage. The door of the library opened. Leo and Gwenda came out. Tina said in her clear, low voice:

"Philip has been killed. Stabbed."

It was like a dream, Tina thought. The shocked exclamations of her father and Gwenda flowing past her, going to Philip. . . . To Philip, who was dead. Kirsten left her and hurried down the stairs.

"I must tell Mary. It must be broken to her gently. Poor Mary. It will be a terrible shock."

Tina followed her slowly. More than ever she felt dazed and dreamlike, a strange pain catching at her heart. Where was she going? She did not know. Nothing was real. She came to the open front door and passed through it. It was then she saw Micky coming round the corner of the house. Automatically as though this was where her footsteps had been leading her all the time, she went straight to him.

"Micky," she said. "Oh, Micky!"

His arms were open. She went straight into them.

"It's all right," said Micky. "I've got you."

Tina crumpled slightly in his arms. She dropped to the ground, a small huddled heap, just as Hester came running from the house.

"She's fainted," Micky said helplessly. "I've never known Tina to faint before."

"It's the shock," said Hester.

"What do you mean—the shock?"

"Philip has been killed," said Hester. "Didn't you know?"

"How could I know? When? How?"

"Just now."

He stared at her. Then he picked up Tina in his arms. With Hester accompanying him, he took her into Mrs. Argyle's sitting-room and laid her on the sofa.

"Ring up Dr. Craig," he said.

"That's his car now," said Hester, looking out of the window. "Father was calling him on the telephone about Philip. I—" She looked round. "I don't want to meet him."

She ran out of the room and up the stairs.

Donald Craig got out of his car and came in through the open front door. Kirsten came from the kitchen to meet him.

"Good afternoon, Miss Lindstrom. What's this I hear? Mr. Argyle tells me that Philip Durrant has been *killed. Killed?*"

"It is quite true," said Kirsten.

"Has Mr. Argyle rung up the police?"

"I do not know."

"Any chance that he's just wounded?" said Don. He turned to take his medical bag out of the car.

"No," said Kirsten. Her voice was flat and tired. "He is dead. I am quite sure of that. He has been stabbed—here."

She put her hand to the back of her own head.

Micky came out into the hall.

"Hallo, Don, you had better have a look at Tina," he said. "She's fainted."

"Tina? Oh yes, that's the—the one from Redmyn, isn't it? Where is she?"

"She is in there."

"I'll just have a look at her before I go upstairs." As he went into the room he spoke over his shoulder to Kirsten. "Keep her warm," he said. "Get some hot tea or coffee for her as soon as she comes round. But you know the drill—"

Kirsten nodded.

"Kirsty!" Mary Durrant came slowly along the hall from the kitchen—Kirsten went to her—Micky stared at her helplessly.

"It's not true." Mary spoke in a loud harsh voice. "It's not *true*! It's a lie you've made up. He was all right when I left him just now. He was quite all right. He was writing. I told him not to write. I *told* him not to. What made him do it? Why should he be so pig-headed? Why wouldn't he leave this house when I wanted him to?"

Coaxing her, soothing her, Kirsten did her best to make her relax.

Donald Craig strode out of the sitting-room.

"Who said that girl had fainted?" he demanded.

Micky stared at him.

"But she did faint," he said.

"Where was she when she fainted?"

"She was with me . . . She came out of the house and walked to meet me. Then—she just collapsed."

"Collapsed, did she? Yes, she collapsed all right," said Donald Craig grimly. He moved quickly towards the telephone. "I must get hold of an ambulance," he said, "at once."

"An ambulance?" Both Kirsten and Micky stared at him. Mary did not seem to have heard.

"Yes." Donald was dialling angrily. "That girl didn't faint," he said. "She was stabbed. Do you hear? Stabbed in the back. We've got to get her to hospital at once."

23

In his hotel room, Arthur Calgary went over and over the notes he had made.

From time to time, he nodded his head.

Yes . . . he was on the right tack now. To begin with, he had made the mistake of concentrating on Mrs. Argyle. In nine cases out of ten that would have been the right procedure. But this was the tenth case.

All along he had felt the presence of an unknown factor. If he could once isolate and identify that factor, the case would be solved. In seeking it he had been obsessed by the dead woman. But the dead woman, he saw now, was not really important. *Any* victim, in a sense, would have done.

He had shifted his viewpoint—shifted it back to the moment when all this had begun. He had shifted it back to Jacko.

Not just Jacko as a young man unjustly sentenced for a crime he did not commit—but Jacko, the intrinsic human being. Was Jacko, in the words of the old Calvinistic doctrine, "a vessel appointed to destruction"? He'd been given every chance in life, hadn't he? Dr. MacMaster's opinion, at any rate, was that he was one of those who are born to go wrong. No environment could have helped him or saved him. Was that true? Leo Argyle had spoken of him with indulgence, with pity. How had he put it? "One of Nature's misfits." He had accepted the modern psychological approach. An invalid, not a criminal. What had Hester said? Bluntly, that Jacko was always awful!

A plain, childish statement. And what was it Kirsten Lindstrom had said? That Jacko was wicked! Yes, she had put it as strongly as that. Wicked! Tina had said: "I never liked him or trusted him." So they all agreed, didn't they, in general terms? It was only in the case of his widow that they'd come down from the general to the particular. Maureen Clegg had thought of Jacko entirely from her own point of view. She had wasted herself on Jacko. She had been carried away by his charm and she was resentful of the fact. Now, securely remarried, she echoed her husband's views. She had given Calgary a forthright account of some of Jacko's dubious dealings, and the methods by which he had obtained money. *Money* . . .

In Arthur Calgary's fatigued brain the word seemed to dance on the wall in gigantic letters. Money! Money! Money! Like a *motif* in an opera, he thought. Mrs. Argyle's money! Money put into trust! Money put into an annuity! Residual estate left to her husband! Money got from the bank! Money in the bureau drawer! Hester rushing out to her car with no money in her purse, getting two pounds from Kirsten Lindstrom. Money found on Jacko, money that he swore his mother had given him.

The whole thing made a pattern—a pattern woven out of irrelevant details about money.

And surely, in that pattern, the unknown factor was becoming clear.

He looked at his watch. He had promised to ring up Hester at an agreed time. He drew the telephone towards him and asked for the number.

Presently her voice came to him, clear, rather childish.

"Hester. Are you all right?"

"Oh, yes, *I'm* all right."

It took him a moment or two to grasp the implication of that accented word. Then he said sharply:

"What has happened?"

"Philip has been killed."

"Philip! Philip Durrant?"

Calgary sounded incredulous.

"Yes. And Tina, too—at least she isn't dead yet. She's in hospital."

"Tell me," he ordered.

She told him. He questioned and re-questioned her narrowly until he got all the facts.

Then he said grimly:

"Hold on, Hester, I'm coming. I'll be with you"—he looked at his watch—"in an hour's time. I've got to see Superintendent Huish first."

II

"What exactly do you want to know, Dr. Calgary?" asked Superintendent Huish, but before Calgary could speak the telephone rang on Huish's desk and the superintendent picked it up. "Yes. Yes, speaking. Just a moment." He drew a piece of paper towards him, picked up a pen and prepared to write. "Yes. Go ahead. Yes." He wrote. "What? How do you spell that last word? Oh, I see. Yes, doesn't seem to make much sense yet, does it? Right. Nothing else? Right. Thanks." He replaced the receiver. "That was the hospital," he said.

"Tina?" asked Calgary.

The superintendent nodded.

"She regained consciousness for a few minutes."

"Did she say anything?" asked Calgary.

"I don't really know just why I should tell you that, Dr. Calgary."

"I ask you to tell me," said Calgary, "because I think that I can help you over this business."

Huish looked at him consideringly.

"You've taken all this very much to heart, haven't you, Dr. Calgary?" he said.

"Yes, I have. You see, I felt responsible for reopening the case. I even feel responsible for these two tragedies. Will the girl live?"

"They think so," said Huish. "The blade of the knife missed the heart, but it may be touch and go." He shook his head. "That's always the trouble," he said. "People will *not* believe that a murderer is unsafe. Sounds a queer thing to say, but there it is. They all knew there was a murderer in their midst. They ought to have told what they knew. The only safe thing if a murderer is about is to tell the police anything you know *at once*. Well, they didn't. They held out on me. Philip Durrant was a nice fellow—an intelligent fellow; but he regarded this as a kind of game. He went poking about laying traps for people. And he got somewhere, or he thought he got somewhere. And somebody else thought he was getting somewhere. Result: I get a call to say he's dead, stabbed through the back of the neck. That's what comes of messing about with murder and not realising its dangers." He stopped and cleared his throat.

"And the girl?" asked Calgary.

"The girl knew something," said Huish. "Something she didn't want to tell. It's my opinion," he said, "she was in love with the fellow."

"You're talking about—Micky?"

Huish nodded. "Yes. I'd say, too, that Micky was fond of her, in a way. But being fond of anyone isn't enough if you're mad with fear. Whatever she knew was probably more deadly than she herself realised. That's why, after she found Durrant dead and she came rushing out straight into his arms, he took his chance and stabbed her."

"That's merely conjecture on your part, isn't it, Superintendent Huish?"

"Not entirely conjecture, Dr. Calgary. The knife was in his pocket."

"The actual knife?"

"Yes. It had blood on it. We're going to test it, but it'll be her blood all right. Her blood and the blood of Philip Durrant!"

"But—it couldn't have been."

"Who says it couldn't have been?"

"Hester. I rang her up and she told me all about it."

"She did, did she? Well, the facts are very simple. Mary Durrant went down to the kitchen, leaving her husband alive, at ten minutes to four—at that time there were in the house Leo Argyle and Gwenda Vaughan in the library, Hester Argyle in her bedroom on the first floor, and Kirsten Lindstrom in the kitchen. Just after four o'clock, Micky and Tina drove up. Micky went into the garden and Tina went upstairs, following close on Kirsten's footsteps, who had just gone up with coffee and biscuits for Philip. Tina stopped to speak to Hester, then went on to join Miss Lindstrom and together they found Philip dead."

"And all this time Micky was in the garden. Surely that's a perfect alibi?"

"What you don't know, Dr. Calgary, is that there's a big magnolia tree growing up by the side of the house. The kids used to climb it. Micky in particular. It was one of his ways in and out of the house. He could have shinned up that tree, gone into Durrant's room, stabbed him, back and out again. Oh, it needed split-second timing, but it's astonishing what audacity will do sometimes. And he was desperate. At all costs he had to prevent Tina and Durrant meeting. To be safe, he had to kill them both."

Calgary thought for a moment or two.

"You said just now, Superintendent, that Tina has recovered consciousness. Wasn't she able to say definitely who stabbed her?"

"She wasn't very coherent," said Huish slowly. "In fact I doubt if she was conscious in the proper sense of the term."

He gave a tired smile.

"All right, Dr. Calgary, I'll tell you exactly what she said. First of all she said a name. *Micky . . .*"

"She has accused him, then," said Calgary.

"That's what it looks like," said Huish, nodding his head. "The rest of what she said didn't make sense. It's a bit fantastic."

"What did she say?"

Huish looked down at the pad in front of him.

"'*Micky.*' Then a pause. Then, '*The cup was empty . . .*' then another pause, and then, '*The Dove on the mast.*' " He looked at Calgary. "Can you make any sense of that?"

"No," said Calgary. He shook his head and said wonderingly: "*The Dove on the mast . . .* That seems a very extraordinary thing to say."

"No masts and no doves as far as we know," said Huish.

"But it meant something to her, something in her own mind. But it mayn't, you know, have been anything to do with the murder. Goodness knows what realms of fancy she's floating in."

Calgary was silent for some moments. He sat thinking things over. He said: "You've arrested Micky?"

"We've detained him. He will be charged within twenty-four hours."

Huish looked curiously at Calgary.

"I gather that this lad, Micky, wasn't *your* answer to the problem?"

"No," said Calgary. "No, Micky wasn't my answer. Even now—I don't know." He got up. "I still think I'm right," he said, "but I quite see that I've not got enough to go on for you to believe me. I must go out there again. I must see them all."

"Well," said Huish, "be careful of yourself, Dr. Calgary. What *is* your idea, by the way?"

"Would it mean anything to you," said Calgary, "if I told you that it is my belief that this was a crime of passion?"

Huish's eyebrows rose.

"There are a lot of passions, Dr. Calgary," he said. "Hate, avarice, greed, fear, they're all passions."

"When I said a crime of passion," said Calgary, "I meant exactly what one usually means by that term."

"If you mean Gwenda Vaughan and Leo Argyle," said Huish, "that's what we've thought all along, you know, but it doesn't seem to fit."

"It's more complicated than that," said Arthur Calgary.

24

It was again dusk when Arthur Calgary came to Sunny Point on an evening very like the evening when he had first come there. Viper's Point, he thought to himself as he rang the bell.

Once again events seemed to repeat themselves. It was Hester who opened it. There was the same defiance in her face, the same air of desperate tragedy. Behind her in the hall he saw, as he had seen before, the watchful, suspicious figure of Kirsten Lindstrom. It was history repeating itself.

Then the pattern wavered and changed. The suspicion and the desperation went out of Hester's face. It broke up into a lovely, welcoming smile.

"You," she said. "Oh, I'm so glad you've come!"

He took her hands in his.

"I want to see your father, Hester. Is he upstairs in the library?"

"Yes. Yes, he's there with Gwenda."

Kirsten Lindstrom came forward towards them.

"Why do you come here again?" she said accusingly. "Look at the trouble you brought last time! See what has happened to us all. Hester's life ruined, Mr. Argyle's life ruined—and two deaths. Two! Philip Durrant and little Tina. And it is *your* doing—all your doing!"

"Tina is not dead yet," said Calgary, "and I have something here to do that I cannot leave undone."

"What have you got to do?" Kirsten still stood barring his way to the staircase.

"I've got to finish what I began," said Calgary.

Very gently he put a hand on her shoulder and moved her slightly aside. He walked up the stairs and Hester followed him. He turned back over his shoulder and said to Kirsten: "Come, too, Miss Lindstrom, I would like you all to be here."

In the library, Leo Argyle was sitting in a chair by the desk. Gwenda Vaughan was kneeling in front of the fire, staring into its embers. They looked up with some surprise.

"I'm sorry to burst in upon you," said Calgary, "but as I've just been saying to these two, I've come to finish what I began." He looked round. "Is Mrs. Durrant in the house still? I should like her to be here also."

"She's lying down, I think," said Leo. "She—she's taken things terribly hard."

"I should like her to be here all the same." He looked at Kirsten. "Perhaps you would go and fetch her."

"She may not want to come," said Kirsten sullenly.

"Tell her," said Calgary, "that there are things she may want to hear about her husband's death."

"Oh, go on, Kirsty," said Hester. "Don't be so suspicious and so protective of us all. I don't know what Dr. Calgary's going to say, but we ought all to be here."

"As you please," said Kirsten.

She went out of the room.

"Sit down," said Leo. He indicated a chair on the other side of the fireplace, and Calgary sat there.

"You must forgive me," said Leo, "if I say at this moment that I wish you'd never come here in the first place, Dr. Calgary."

"That's unfair," said Hester fiercely. "That's a terribly unfair thing to say."

"I know what you must feel," said Calgary, "I think in your place I should feel much the same. Perhaps I even shared your view for a short period, but on reflection I still cannot see that there was anything else that I could have done."

Kirsten re-entered the room. "Mary is coming," she said.

They sat in silence waiting and presently Mary Durrant entered the room. Calgary looked at her with interest, since it was the first time he had seen her. She looked calm and composed, neatly dressed, every hair in place. But her face was masklike in its lack of expression and there was an air about her as of a woman who walks in her sleep.

Leo made an introduction. She bowed her head slightly.

"It is good of you to come, Mrs. Durrant," said Calgary. "I thought you ought to hear what I have to say."

"As you please," said Mary. "But nothing that you can say or anyone can say will bring Philip back again."

She went a little way away from them and sat down in a chair by the window. Calgary looked round him.

"Let me first say this: When I came here the first time, when I told you that I was able to clear Jacko's name, your reception of my news puzzled me. I understand it now. But the thing that made the greatest impression upon me was what this child here"—he looked at Hester—"said to me as I left. She said that it was not justice that mattered, it was what happened to the innocent. There is a phrase in the latest translation of the Book of Job that describes it. *The calamity of the innocent*. As a result of my news that is what you have all been suffering. The innocent should not suffer, and must not suffer, and it is to end the suffering of the innocent that I am here now to say what I have to say."

He paused for a moment or two but no one spoke. In his quiet pedantic voice, Arthur Calgary went on:

"When I came here first, it was not, as I thought, to bring you what might be described as tidings of great joy. You had all accepted Jacko's guilt. You were all, if I may say so, *satisfied* with it. It was the best solution that there could be in the murder of Mrs. Argyle."

"Isn't that speaking a little harshly?" asked Leo.

"No," said Calgary, "it is the truth. Jacko was satisfactory to you all as the criminal since there could be no real question of an outsider having committed the crime, and because in the case of Jacko you could find the necessary excuses. He was unfortunate, a mental invalid, not responsible for his actions, a problem or delinquent boy! All the phrases that we can use nowadays so happily to excuse guilt. You said, Mr. Argyle, that you did not blame him. You said his mother, the victim, would not have blamed him. Only one person blamed him." He looked at Kirsten Lindstrom. "*You* blamed him. You said fairly and squarely that he was wicked. That is the term you used. 'Jacko was wicked,' you said."

"Perhaps," said Kirsten Lindstrom. "Perhaps—yes, perhaps I said that. It was true."

"Yes, it was true. He *was* wicked. If he had not been wicked none of this would have happened. Yet you know quite well," said Calgary, "that my evidence cleared him of the actual crime."

Kirsten said:

"One cannot always believe evidence. You had concussion. I know very well what concussion does to people. They remember things not clearly but in a kind of blur."

"So that is still your solution?" said Calgary. "You think that Jacko actually committed that crime and that in some way he managed to fake an alibi? Is that right?"

"I do not know the details. Yes, something of that sort. I still say he did it. All the suffering that has gone on here and the deaths—yes, these terrible deaths—they are all *his* doing. All Jacko's doing!"

Hester cried:

"But Kirsten, you were always devoted to Jacko."

"Perhaps," said Kirsten, "yes, perhaps. But I still say he was wicked."

"There I think you are right," said Calgary, "but in another way you are wrong. Concussion or no concussion, my memory is perfectly clear. On the night of Mrs. Argyle's death I gave Jacko a lift at the stated time. There is no possibility—and I repeat those words strongly—there is no possibility that Jacko Argyle killed his adopted mother that night. His alibi holds."

Leo moved with a trace of restlessness. Calgary went on:

"You think that I'm repeating the same thing over and over again? Not quite. There are other points to be considered. One of them is the statement that I got from Superintendent Huish that Jacko was very glib and assured when giving his alibi. He had it all pat and ready, the times, the place, *almost as though he knew he might need it*. That ties up with the conversation I had about him with Dr. MacMaster, who has had a very wide experience of borderline delinquent cases. He said he was not so surprised at Jacko having the seeds of murder in his heart, but he was surprised that he had actually carried one out. He said the type of murder he would have expected was one where Jacko egged on *someone else* to commit the crime. So I came to the point where I asked myself this: Did Jacko know that a crime was to be committed that night? Did he know that he would need an alibi and did he deliberately go about giving himself one? If so, *someone else* killed Mrs. Argyle, *but*—Jacko knew she was going to be killed and one may fairly say that he was the instigator of the crime."

He said to Kirsten Lindstrom:

"*You feel that, don't you? You still feel it, or you want to feel it?* You feel that it was Jacko who killed her, *not you* . . . You feel it was under his orders and under his influence you did it. Therefore you want all the blame to be *his!*"

"I?" said Kirsten Lindstrom. "I? What are you saying?"

"I'm saying," said Calgary, "that there was only one person in this house who could in any way fit into the role of Jacko Argyle's accomplice. And that is *you*, Miss Lindstrom. Jacko had a record behind him, a record of being able to inspire passion in middle-aged women. He employed that power deliberately. He had the gift of making himself believed." He leaned forward. "He made love to you, didn't he?" he said gently. "He made you believe that he cared for you, that he wanted to marry you, that after this was over and he'd got more control of his mother's money, you would be married and go away somewhere. That is right, isn't it?"

Kirsten stared at him. She did not speak. It was as though she were paralysed.

"It was done cruelly and heartlessly and deliberately," said Arthur Calgary. "He came here that night desperate for some money, with the shadow over him of arrest and a jail sentence. Mrs. Argyle refused to give him money. When he was refused by her he applied to you."

"Do you think," said Kirsten Lindstrom, "do you think that I would have taken Mrs. Argyle's money to give him instead of giving him my own?"

"No," said Calgary, "you would have given him your own if you'd had any. But I don't think you had. . . . You had a good income from the annuity which Mrs. Argyle had bought for you, but I think he'd already milked you dry of that. So he was desperate that evening and when Mrs. Argyle had gone up to her husband in the library, you went outside the house where he was waiting and he told you what you had to do. First you must give him the money and then, before the theft could be discovered, Mrs. Argyle had to be killed. Because she would not have covered up the theft. He said it would be easy. You had just to pull out the drawers to make it look as though a burglar had been there and to hit her on the back of the head. It would be painless, he said. She would not feel anything. He himself would establish an alibi, so that you must be careful to do this thing within the right time limits, between seven and seven-thirty."

"It's not true," said Kirsten. She had begun to tremble. "You are mad to say such things."

Yet there was no indignation in her voice. Strangely enough, it was mechanical and weary.

"Even if what you say is true," she said, "do you think I would let him be accused of the murder?"

"Oh yes," said Calgary. "After all, he had told you he would have an alibi. You expected him, perhaps, to be arrested and then to prove his innocence. That was all part of the plan."

"But when he couldn't prove his innocence," said Kirsten. "Would I not have saved him then?"

"Perhaps," said Calgary, "perhaps—but for one fact. The fact that on the morning after the murder *Jacko's wife turned up here*. You didn't know he was married. The girl had to repeat the statement two or three times before you would believe her. At that moment your world crashed round you. You saw Jacko for what he was—heartless, scheming, without a particle of affection for you. You realised what he had made you do."

Suddenly Kirsten Lindstrom was speaking. The words came rushing out incoherently.

"I loved him . . . I loved him with all my heart. I was a fool, a credulous middle-aged doting fool. He made me think it—he made me believe it. He said he had never cared for girls. He said—I cannot tell you all the things he said. I loved him. I tell you I loved him. And then that silly, simpering child came here, that common little thing. I saw it was all lies, all wickedness, wickedness. . . . *His* wickedness, not mine."

"The night I came here," said Calgary, "you were afraid, weren't you? You were afraid of what was going to happen. You were afraid for the others. Hester, whom you loved, Leo, whom you were fond of. You saw, perhaps, a little of what this might do to them. But principally you were afraid for *yourself*. And you see where fear has led you. . . . You have two more deaths on your hands now."

"You are saying I killed Tina and Philip?"

"Of course you killed them," said Calgary. "Tina has recovered consciousness."

Kirsten's shoulders dropped in the sagging of despair.

"So she has told that I stabbed her. I did not think she even knew. I was mad, of course. I was mad by then, mad with terror. It was coming so close—so close."

"Shall I tell you what Tina said when she regained consciousness?" said Calgary. "She said 'The cup was empty.' I knew what that meant. You pretended to be taking up a cup of coffee to Philip Durrant, but actually you had already stabbed him and were coming *out* of that room when you heard Tina coming. So you turned round and pretended you were taking the tray *in*. Later, although she was shocked almost into unconsciousness by his death, she noticed automatically that the cup that had dropped on the floor was an empty cup and there was no stain of coffee left by it."

Hester cried out:

"But Kirsten couldn't have stabbed her! Tina walked downstairs and out to Micky. She was quite all right."

"My dear child," said Calgary, "people who have been stabbed have walked the length of the street without even knowing what has happened to them! In the state of shock Tina was in she would hardly have felt anything. A pinprick, a slight pain perhaps." He looked again at Kirsten. "And later," he said, "you slipped that knife into Micky's pocket. That was the meanest thing of all."

Kirsten's hands flew out pleadingly.

"I couldn't help it—I could not help it. . . . It was coming so near. . . . They were all beginning to find out. Philip was finding out and Tina—I think Tina must have overheard Jacko talking to me outside the kitchen that evening. They were all beginning to know. . . . I wanted to be safe. I wanted—*one can never be safe!*" Her hands dropped. "I didn't want to kill Tina. As for Philip—"

Mary Durrant rose. She came across the room slowly but with increasing purpose.

"You killed Philip?" she said. "*You* killed Philip."

Suddenly, like a tigress she sprang at the other woman. It was Gwenda, quick-witted, who sprang to her feet and caught hold of her. Calgary joined her and together they held her back.

"You—you!" cried Mary Durrant.

Kirsten Lindstrom looked at her.

"What business was it of *his?*" she asked. "Why did he have to snoop round and ask questions? *He* was never threatened. It was never a matter of life or death for *him*. It was just—an amusement." She turned and walked slowly towards the door. Without looking at them she went out.

"Stop her," cried Hester. "Oh, we must stop her."

Leo Argyle said:

"Let her go, Hester."

"But—she'll kill herself."

"I rather doubt it," said Calgary.

"She has been our faithful friend for so long," said Leo. "Faithful, devoted—and now this!"

"Do you think she'll—give herself up?" said Gwenda.

"It's far more likely," said Calgary, "that she'll go to the nearest station and take a train for London. But she won't, of course, be able to get away with it. She'll be traced and found."

"Our dear Kirsten," said Leo again. His voice shook. "So faithful, so good to us all."

Gwenda caught him by the arm and shook it.

"How can you, Leo, how can you? Think what she did to us all—what she has made us suffer!"

"I know," said Leo, "but she suffered herself, you know, as well. I think it is *her* suffering we have felt in this house."

"We might have gone on suffering for ever," said Gwenda, "as far as she was concerned! If it hadn't been for Dr. Calgary here." She turned towards him gratefully.

"So at last," said Calgary, "I have done something to help, though rather late in the day."

"Too late," said Mary, bitterly. "Too late! Oh, why didn't we know—why didn't we *guess?*" She turned accusingly on Hester. "I thought it was *you*. I always thought it was *you*."

"*He* didn't," said Hester. She looked at Calgary.

Mary Durrant said quietly: "I wish I were dead."

"My dear child," said Leo, "how I wish I could help you."

"Nobody can help me," said Mary. "It's all Philip's own fault, wanting to stay on here, wanting to mess about with this business. Getting himself killed." She looked round at them. "None of you understand." She went out of the room.

Calgary and Hester followed her. As they went through the door, Calgary, looking back, saw Leo's arm pass round Gwenda's shoulders.

"She warned me, you know," said Hester. Her eyes were wide and scared. "She told me right at the beginning not to trust her, to be as afraid of her as I was of everyone else. . . ."

"Forget it, my dear," said Calgary. "That is the thing you have to do now. *Forget*. All of you are free now. The innocent are no longer in the shadow of guilt."

"And Tina? Will she get well? She is not going to die?"

"I don't think she will die," said Calgary. "She's in love with Micky, isn't she?"

"I suppose she might be," said Hester, in a surprised voice. "I never thought about it. They've always been brother and sister, of course. But they're not really brother and sister."

"By the way, Hester, would you have any idea what Tina meant when she said, 'The dove on the mast'?"

"Dove on the mast?" Hester frowned. "Wait a minute. It sounds terribly familiar. *The dove on the mast, as we sailed fast, Did mourn and mourn and mourn*. Is that it?"

"It might be," said Calgary.

"It's a song," said Hester. "A sort of lullaby song. Kirsten used to sing it to us. I can only remember bits of it. '*My love he stood at my right hand*,' and something something something. '*Oh, maid most dear, I am not here, I have no place, no part, No dwelling more by sea nor shore, But only in thy heart*.'"

"I see," said Calgary. "Yes, yes, I see . . ."

"Perhaps they'll get married," said Hester, "when Tina gets well, and then she can go out to Kuwait with him. Tina always wanted to be somewhere where it's warm. It's very warm in the Persian Gulf, isn't it?"

"Almost too warm, I should say," said Calgary.

"Nothing's too warm for Tina," Hester assured him.

"And you will be happy now, my dear," said Calgary, taking Hester's hands in his. He made an effort to smile. "You'll marry your young doctor and you'll settle down and you'll have no more of these wild imaginings and terrific despairs."

"Marry *Don?*" said Hester, in a surprised tone of voice. "Of course I'm not going to marry *Don*."

"But you love him."

"No, I don't think I do, really . . . I just thought I did. But he didn't believe in me. He didn't *know* I was innocent. He ought to have known." She looked at Calgary. "*You* knew! I think I'd like to marry you."

"But, Hester, I'm years older than you are. You can't really—"

"That is—if you want me," said Hester with sudden doubt.

"Oh, I want you!" said Arthur Calgary.